THE SISTERS

THE SISTERS

Robert Littell

Bantam Books
Toronto • New York • London • Sydney • Auckland

THE SISTERS
A Bantam Book / February 1986

Library of Congress Cataloging-in-Publication Data

Littell, Robert, 1935–
The sisters.

I. Title.
PS3562.I7827S5   1986   813'.54   85-47797
ISBN 0-553-05097-4

Published simultaneously in the United States and Canada

PRINTED IN THE UNITED STATES OF AMERICA

BP   0   9   8   7   6   5   4   3   2   1

For my father,
Leon Littell

BOOK I

Night

Outside it was night; inside too . . .

1

❦

"I'm just thinking out loud," Francis was saying. An angelic smile manned the usual fortifications of his face. "What if . . ." His voice trailed off uncertainly.

"What if *what*?" Carroll prompted. A muscle twitched impatiently in his cheek.

"What if—"

They were, by any standards, the Company's odd couple. Office scuttlebutt held that when one itched the other scratched, but that wasn't it; that wasn't it at all. It was more a matter of symbiosis; of constituting two sides of the same coin. Looking at any given skyline, Francis would see forest, Carroll trees; Francis wrote music, Carroll lyrics; Francis would leap with almost feminine intuition in the general direction of unlikely ends while Carroll, a pedestrian at heart, would trail after him lingering over means.

"What if," Francis was saying, "we were to put our man Friday onto someone with Mafia connections?"

"Mafia connections?"

Francis pulled thoughtfully at an earlobe that looked as if it had been pulled at before. "Exactly."

Francis wore an outrageous silk bow tie that he had picked up for a song at a rummage sale. His sixth-floor neighbors thought it was out of character, which only showed that they didn't really understand his character. It was the unexpected splash of color, the tiny touch of defiance, the unconventional link in an otherwise perfectly conformist chain that set him apart from everyone else.

Carroll, on the other hand, liked to look as if he *belonged*. He favored conventional three-piece suits and starched collars that left crimson welts clinging like leeches to his thin, pale neck. Laughing behind his back, the neighbors spoke about his penchant for hair shirts worn, so they assumed, to atone for unspecified sins.

They were half right. There *were* sins, though Carroll never felt the slightest urge to atone for them.

"The Mafia is out of the question," Carroll announced flatly, a crooked forefinger patrolling between his collar and his neck. He looked past Francis the way he stared over the shoulder of anyone he deigned to talk to. "They will want to be paid in the end. And not necessarily in money. Besides, there's no compartmentalization. If this thing is going to succeed, it has to be tightly compartmentalized. Like a submarine."

"Quite right," Francis remarked, blushing apologetically. "I can't imagine what I could have been thinking of." His face screwed up, his eyes narrowed into slits, a sure sign that his mind was leaping toward another unlikely end.

Francis and Carroll were minor legends in the Company. Somewhere along the line one of the CIA's army of PhD's who majored in African dialects and minored in Whitman had dubbed them "The sisters Death and Night." The name stuck. If you mentioned the Sisters in an intraoffice memo, and capitalized the S, almost everyone tucked away in the Company's cradle-to-grave complex knew whom you were talking about. But only the handful with "eyes-only" authorizations in their dossiers had an inkling of what they actually did for a living.

What they did was plot.

And what they were plotting on that perfect August day was a perfect crime.

"What we will need," Francis thought out loud, defining the problem, "is someone who can carry out an assignment without knowing it came from us."

"Someone who thinks he is being employed by others," Carroll ventured, lingering over means.

"Exactly," Francis agreed enthusiastically.

In an organization where people knew secrets, or made it their business to look as if they did, Francis stood out with his aura of absolute innocence. He invariably wore an expression that fell midway between curious and reluctant, and a Cheshire cat's pained smile that hinted at nothing more morally compromising than the death of an occasional rodent. It was common knowledge around the shop that he regularly lied about his name during the annual lie-detector tests—and always managed to fool the black box.

Compared to Francis, Carroll was an open book. When he felt frustrated, it appeared on his face like a flag. He had started out in the business with "Wild Bill" Donovan's Office of Strategic Services during the "Wrong War" (as he liked to call it; he felt that America had defeated the *wrong* enemy), and quickly made a name for himself by scribbling in the margin of one report: "The matter is of the highest possible importance and should accordingly be handled on the lowest possible level." What he meant, of course, was that *he* should handle it; at the tender age of twenty-nine, he had already been convinced of everyone's incompetence but his own. (Perhaps stunned by his audacity, his superiors gave him the brief. In due course Carroll engineered the defection of a German diplomat carrying a valise full of secret documents, and the betrayal to the Gestapo of the Soviet agent who had acted as their go-between. By 1945 Carroll was already focusing on the *right* enemy.)

Nowadays some of their Company colleagues whispered that the Sisters were past their prime, washed up, over the hill; old farts who amused the technocrats calling the tune; has-beens who gave the men in the Athenaeum (as the Sisters, classicists to the core, called the front office) something to talk about at in-house pours. ("The Sisters proposed that we . . ." "They weren't *serious*?" "I'm afraid they were." "What did you tell them?" "I told them they were *mad!*") There were even a few with regular access to the Sisters' product who recommended giving them medical discharges—and there was no suggestion that the problem was physical. They'd been around too long, it was said, they'd seen too much—as if being around too long and seeing too much inevitably led to deeper disorders. Still, several people in high places took them seriously enough to justify giving them space (which, with its Soviet magazines scattered around a shabby Formica coffee table, looked suspiciously like a dentist's office in Tashkent), a man Friday (whose real name, believe it or not, was Thursday) and a gorgeous secretary with an incredibly short skirt and incredibly long legs and a way of clutching files to her breasts that left the rare visitor noticeably short of breath. After all, it was said, the Sisters had had their share of triumphs. Not that long ago, with an almost Machiavellian leap of imagination, they had ferreted out a Russian sleeper in the CIA's ranks. While everyone else frantically searched the files for someone with a record of failed operations against the Russians, Francis thought the problem through from the Soviet point of view and decided that the merchants who ran the mole would have boosted his career with an occasional *success*. Working on that assumption, the Sisters combed the files looking for someone with one or two conspicuous successes and a string of failures. The suspect they uncovered was delivered to the tender mercies of the Company's most experienced interrogator, one G. Sprowls. After an intense interrogation that lasted seven months, G. Sprowls came up with the right questions and the suspect came up with the wrong answers. There was no trial. The suspect simply disappeared from the face of the earth, at which point the CIA awarded a medal and a pension to his widow rather than acknowledge that it had been infiltrated.

"Someone who thinks he is being employed by others," Carroll was saying thoughtfully—he appeared to be talking to the poster tacked to the back of the door that read "Fuck Communism!"—"can't very well point a finger at us if he is caught, can he?"

There was a single soft knock at the door. Without waiting for permission, the gorgeous secretary, who drew pay and broke hearts under her married name, Mrs. Cresswell, sailed into the dentist's office, wordlessly deposited a box of candies on the coffee table, and then, like a spider ducking soundlessly back into its hole, disappeared. Carroll tore off the lid and studied the contents. He detested nuts and cherries—one gave him hives, the other diarrhea—but could never for the life of him remember which ones didn't have them.

"Look at the code on the back of the lid," Francis said with an air of someone indulging his partner's idiosyncrasy.

"I don't understand codes," Carroll muttered. He snatched a candy at random, peeled off the tinfoil and, baring decaying yellowish teeth, gingerly bit into it. "Caramel," he announced with satisfaction, and he popped the rest of the candy into his mouth. He was working on his third caramel when he suddenly snapped his fingers. "I've got it!" he cried, though the caramel sticking to his teeth made his words difficult to understand. "What we need," he explained when he could finally articulate, "is someone who is highly skilled, intelligent, trained in fieldwork and willing to follow orders without inquiring into their source as long as they arrive in the correct form."

Francis said, "I don't quite follow—"

Carroll rocked back onto the rear legs of his chair. "What we need—" His lips twisted into an expression of grim satisfaction; another flag snapping on the halyard of his face.

"What we need," Francis repeated, his eyes watering in anticipation. Having come up with a perfect crime, he considered it in the nature of things that Carroll should come up with a perfect criminal.

"What we need—" Carroll whined, and because in his experience walls more often than not concealed *ears*, he plucked a pencil from a coffee table and finished the sentence on a sheet of scrap paper.

"—is a sleeper!"

"A sleeper, of course!" Francis wrote in turn.

Carroll retrieved the pencil. "But how on earth will we find one?" he wrote.

Francis grabbed the pencil out of Carroll's fingers. "We might get the Potter to give us the use of one," he wrote.

The Sisters melted back into their chairs, drained. Whistling softly through his teeth, Francis collected the scraps of paper they had written on; they had divided up office chores, and it was his job to shred all secret documents.

Carroll's cheek muscle twitched uncontrollably. "He might just do it," he said in a hollow voice, and in a gesture that had nothing, and everything, to do with ends and means, he waved vaguely, weakly toward the dirty window; toward the dirty city; toward the dirty world out there waiting to be *manipulated.*

2

❧

They made their way in lock step down a freshly painted corridor of power toward the Athenaeum. "You'd think our masters would get tired of battleship gray," Francis commented. His nose wrinkled up in disgust. "Imagine how different this place would look in pale green, or off-white even."

Carroll was too absorbed in his own schemes to worry about color schemes. "He's going to agree," he concluded, as if wishing could make it so. "I know him from the days when he ran errands for Dulles in Switzerland. He likes to keep several irons in several fires."

"Then we must make this seem like just another iron," Francis said under his breath, and flashing an ingratiating smile at one of the Pillars of Hercules, as the Deputy Director's two secretaries were known (one handled people, the other paper), he announced in a voice ideally suited to pulpits, "We are responding, like good dogs, to our master's whistle."

"Where *do* you get your ties?" the Pillar who handled people asked, waving them toward the appropriate door. She reached under her desk and dispatched a surge of electricity toward the appropriate lock. The door clicked open just as Francis reached it.

"What do you think of our halls?" demanded the Deputy Director, swiveling away from *his* man Friday to confront the Sisters.

"I would have made a case for pale green or off-white if someone had consulted me," Francis replied sulkily.

"Oh," said the Deputy Director, obviously disappointed. "I more or less liked the battleship atmosphere conveyed by the gray. Keep us all on our toes, don't you think, Harry?"

The Deputy Director's man Friday nodded in brisk agreement. He was immaculately dressed except for a discreet sprinkle of dandruff on his sloping Brooks Brothers shoulders.

"Yes, well," the Deputy Director said enthusiastically. He pasted back a stray strand of battleship-gray hair with several fingertips. "If you don't mind, I'd like to make this a quickie," he announced. "I'm supposed to be up on the Hill in forty-five minutes. There will be photographers. I still have to have my hair trimmed." He swiveled back toward his Harry in panic. "You're absolutely sure I'm scheduled for Matthew? That new man who handled me last week butchered my sideburns."

"I checked on it myself this morning," Harry said impassively. "Matthew has cleared his book for you."

Relieved of another nightmare, the Deputy Director returned to the Sisters. "About this Op Proposal of yours"—he pulled a lemon-colored file card from a lemon-colored folder and tapped it with the back of a manicured fingernail—"you really think he may be ripe?"

Carroll arched his neck to relieve the pressure of his collar. "He's lost three sleepers in six months," he explained to a point on the wall over the Deputy Director's head. "His name is mud."

"He's been put out to pasture," Francis added hopefully. "He is bound to be nursing bruises. And then there is the matter of that wife of his . . ."

"*I* didn't know he'd been put out to pasture," the Deputy Director whined in irritation. "How did *you* know?"

"We learned about it from the Germans," Carroll said reluctantly; he had a journalist's instinct for sources.

"*Our* Germans or *their* Germans?" the Deputy Director wanted to know.

"Ours. It was buried in one of their Y summaries about a month ago," Francis added. "I suspect no one picked up on it because they identified him by his real name, Feliks Arkantevich Turov, as opposed to his working name, and not too many people put the two together."

"But you put the two together," the Deputy Director's man commented dryly. He was one of those who favored terminating the Sisters with medical discharges.

9

"That's correct," Carroll shot back without looking at him. "We have a head for names."

Francis added, "And faces. And places." And he beamed a smile of pained innocence in Harry's general direction.

The Deputy Director closed the lemon-colored folder with an irritated snap—he didn't mind dissension as long as it took place behind his back—and slipped it into a file drawer labeled "Current." "How do you propose to get at him?" he asked.

Carroll treated himself to a deep breath; they were almost home. "We'll use the Germans as cutouts," he said. "They'll farm the contract out to some free-lancers. If he's not buying, he's not buying from the free-lancers."

"If he buys," Francis chimed in, "we will plant our man Friday on the receiving line when he comes over. He will skim off the cream while it is still fresh and leave the milk for the farmers to market."

"You'll have to give the Germans something for their trouble," the Deputy Director commented unhappily.

"Maybe money," suggested Carroll. "Maybe access to the cream."

"Maybe only brownie points," offered Francis. "They wag their tails every time we toss them a bone."

The Deputy Director glanced quickly at his wristwatch. "Work linear," he advised. "Limit this to you two. Me. My man Friday. Your man Friday. We can circulate the product later to our clients without saying where it came from."

"We always compartmentalize," Carroll said matter-of-factly. "It is our trademark."

The Deputy Director cleared his throat nervously. "Just so long as you don't compartmentalize *me* out of the picture."

Everyone smiled at the utter absurdity of the idea.

Carroll had one hand on the doorknob when the Deputy Director called after them. "By the way, what is it you expect to get from him if he buys?"

The Sisters exchanged looks. "Odds and ends," Francis said, smiling innocently.

"Ends and odds," Carroll agreed, and he brought a palm up to his cheek to still his wildly twitching muscle.

3

Under the angled beams of his attic workshop, in a cone of pale light cast by a naked bulb dangling overhead, the Potter, Feliks Arkantevich Turov, rinsed his small, powerful hands in a pan of lukewarm water, then kicked the wheel and leaned over the turntable. The fingers of his right hand curled around the outside of the damp clay. His left hand dipped delicately into the cylinder, the thumb hooked back over the lip so that it rested lightly on his right hand. The act of touching transformed the two hands into one perfectly coordinated pincerlike instrument. Wedging the clay cylinder between the tip of one finger and the joint of another, he brought up the wall.

The Potter had learned the art at the feet of a Japanese master who claimed that throwing a beautiful pot was as difficult as printing your shadow on the sidewalk. In the end, potting represented a classic case of mind over matter. Some days were better than others, but when the Potter was very good, he could overcome the natural tendency of the clay to become what *it* wanted to become; he could tame it, channel its power, control its pulse; he could force it to flower under his fingers into a form that already existed in his head.

If only he could control his life the way he controlled the clay! At fifty-six, the Potter already felt as if he were "tied up to the pier of old age" (Turgenev's phrase, first quoted to him by Piotr Borisovich, his last, his best sleeper). Turov's face resembled nothing so much as wax about to melt, giving him a distinctly blurred look; people who didn't know him well often had difficulty bringing him into focus. He was short to begin with—five feet, four inches. Since his obligatory retirement earlier in the year, his shoulders had gradually sagged, as if laboring under a great weight; his body had taken on a dwarfish appearance, underscoring its essential awkwardness. Only his forearms and his hands, conditioned by hundreds of hours of kneading clay, retained anything resembling youthfulness. To his own eye, he looked like one of those worn-out government functionaries visible in the streets at the start of any workday; they never seemed to hurry, eloquent evidence that they had precious little enthusiasm for getting where they were going. Like the bureaucrats, the Potter seemed to be living off emotional capital instead of income, the way a starving man lives off the protein already stored in his body.

The Potter fixed the lip of the cylinder, braked the wheel to a stop with a scuffed boot, then reached for the length of piano wire Piotr Borisovich had once fashioned for him and cut the vase off the wheel. He turned it upside down and tapped on the base, then set the vase on a shelf next to his electric kiln. When the spirit moved him, he would glaze it and fire it and offer it to some neighbors who always brought him a handful of mushrooms when they came back from their country *dacha*. Either that or he would smash it into a thousand pieces during another tantrum.

Outside, gusts of soot brushed past the grimy attic window. The Potter glanced at the sliver of Moscow River he could see off in the distance between two buildings. In the old days, when things were going well, when he had been the *novator*—the man in charge—of the sleeper school, he and Svetochka had occupied an apartment *overlooking* the river. There had been a bedroom, a living room, a study, a heated workroom for his potter's wheel, a kitchen, even a bathroom—an almost unheard-of eighty-eight square meters—and they had it all to themselves. Then, when Svetochka called him "my Jew," there had been affection in her voice. Nowadays they lived in a building with paper-thin walls and shared forty-five square meters with another family. And there was anger in her voice no matter what she called him. Or even worse, boredom. On more than one occasion he had caught her suppressing a yawn when they made love. If he didn't notice her suppressing yawns anymore, it was because he looked up less. With his head buried between her legs, he still managed to forget the unlaundered years (Piotr Borisovich's phrase; from the moment they met, the Potter had been struck by his way with words): the rats scurrying around the labyrinth in the late thirties, when he first joined what was then called the NKVD; the seventeen months spent behind German lines in the early forties; "sanitation" expeditions in the wake of the advancing Red Army in the middle forties; then the endless death watch of the late forties and early fifties as everyone wordlessly waited for the old buzzard in the Kremlin to give up the ghost.

The Potter could hear the telephone ringing under his feet. He could make out the sound of Svetochka's stiletto heels as she raced to answer it before the people who shared the flat could. In ten minutes the woman whom everyone invariably mistook for his daughter would slip into her imitation fur "soul warmer" and leave. Another rendezvous with another hairdresser, she would say. Another store selling imitation leather gloves that you can't tell from the real thing, she would say. Only when she came back later—much later—her hair wouldn't look any different, and there would be no imitation leather gloves in her pockets. They had run out just before her turn came, she would say.

It occurred to the Potter, not for the first time, that illusions don't die, they rot like fish in the sun. They torture you with *ifs:* what might have been if one of his sleepers hadn't refused to obey his "awakening" signal and disappeared; if a second, happier in America than in Russia, hadn't gone over to the other side; if a third, inside the CIA, hadn't been ferreted out by someone with an astonishing capacity to think the problem through from the Russian point of view. All within a six-month period. The Potter had trained the sleepers in question. He was accordingly rated on how well they performed. When the ax finally fell, there had been talk of exile in Central Asia, talk even of a prison sentence. But his record had been impeccable up to then. So they had put him out to what they thought of, all things considered, as generous pasture: a smaller apartment, a monthly stipend large enough to keep him in clay and vodka, even a self-winding Czechoslovak wristwatch delivered, without ceremony—with a certain amount of embarrassment—on his last day in harness. "For Feliks Arkantevich," the inscription read, "for twenty-seven years of service to the state." Service to the state! He might have been a street cleaner for all anyone could tell from the inscription.

Surprisingly, Svetochka had taken his fall in stride. Not to worry, she had said, Svetochka likes her Feliks even without access to the school's warehouse; Svetochka will always be Feliks' little girl. Eventually her last pair of American stockings had gone into the garbage, and her tone had begun to change. The Potter took to waiting on a side street near the warehouse; friends slipped him an occasional American lipstick or eyebrow pencil, and Svetochka would throw her arms around his thick neck and make love to him that night the way she had when he had been the *novator*. But neither the lipsticks nor her ardent moods lasted very long.

"Feliks!" Svetochka's high-pitched voice drifted up through the floorboards. "Can you hear me, Feliks? There's a phone call. Someone's asking for you. Feliks?"

"He's coming," Svetochka assured the caller, afraid that he was one of Feliks' friends from the warehouse and might get impatient and hang up. "Only a moment."

"So: I will wait," the voice said quietly.

"*Slouchouyou*," the Potter mumbled into the receiver. He had an instinctive distrust of telephones common to people who came to them relatively late in life. "What do you want?"

A voice with an accent the Potter couldn't quite place replied, "So: if you please, note the number I will give you, yes? If you need a private taxi, dial it and one will come to your corner."

The Potter's hand, suddenly damp with perspiration, gripped the phone. "I don't take taxis. They are too expensive. When I go somewhere, I use the metro or walk."

"Who is it?" Svetochka whispered.

"Please note the number," the voice on the other end of the line insisted. "You never know when you will need it. So: B, one-forty-one, twenty-one."

"What does he want?" Svetochka whispered.

"You have the number, yes?" the voice asked. "B, one-forty-one, twenty-one."

14

"I tell you that I do not use taxis," the Potter blurted out, suddenly frightened. "Go to hell with your number." And he slammed down the receiver.

"Who was that?"

"Nobody."

"How can you say it was nobody? Somebody phones you up and according to you it's nobody." Tears of frustration formed under Svetochka's heavily made-up lids. "Somebody is not nobody!" she cried in that tightly controlled voice that angry Muskovites use in communal apartments.

The Potter had a good idea of what the call was all about. He had made more than one like it during his four-year stint as KGB *rezident* in New York. It was a contact, an approach, an invitation to what the Merchants at Moscow Center called a *treff*—a secret meeting. Only it wasn't the Moscow Merchants who had initiated it; on that he would have wagered a great deal.

Svetochka began struggling into her soul warmer. "Where are you going now?" the Potter demanded.

"Nowhere," she sneered. "Nobody is who called. And nowhere is where I'm going."

The Potter sprang across the room and gripping the lapels of her coat in one fist, lifted her off the ground.

"You are hurting Svetochka, Feliks," she whispered. Seeing the look on his face, she pleaded, "Feliks is hurting his Svetochka."

The Potter set her down, slipped a hand inside her coat and clumsily tried to embrace her. "I only wanted to know where you were going," he remarked, as if it could account for the outburst, the months of tension that preceded it, the conversationless meals, the slow seeping away of intimacy.

"All you had to do was ask," Svetochka snapped, conveniently forgetting that he had. She fended him off deftly. "Svetochka is going to baby-sit for a girlfriend so she can go birthday shopping for her husband."

"Children are in school at this hour," the Potter said.

"Her child is too young for school."

"There are neighborhood nurseries for babies."

"This baby has a fever," Svetochka explained quickly. "He can't go out." With her teeth clenched, she spit out,

15

"Svetochka doesn't ask you where you are going every time you put on your coat."

"You are lying," the Potter said simply, tiredly. "There was no hairdresser. There were no imitation leather gloves. There is no sick baby."

"You have a nerve . . ." Svetochka was screaming now. Down the corridor, the people who shared the apartment discreetly closed the door to their bedroom. "You didn't never use to . . ." Her phrases came in gasps; they no longer seemed to be glued together by grammar or sense. ". . . not going to only always take this . . ."

"Enough," the Potter muttered under his breath.

". . . think maybe you are doing to Svetochka favors . . ."

"Enough, if you please."

"Well, it don't even work like you maybe think . . ."

The Potter's arm swept out in anger, brushing a glazed bowl, one of the best he had ever made, off a table. It struck the floor, shattering at Svetochka's feet.

"Enough!" shouted the Potter.

Svetochka, who fancied herself something of an actress, could change moods in a flash. Now she screwed up her face to indicate that she had been mortally offended. "It is not Svetochka who will clean this up," she observed icily. Pivoting on a spiked heel, leaving the door to the corridor gaping open behind her, she stalked from the apartment.

The Potter poured himself a stiff vodka. When he had been *novator*, he had drunk nothing but eighty-proof Polish Bison vodka. Now he had to make do with cheap Russian vodka, to which he added the skin in the interior of walnuts to give it color and taste. Svetochka would come back later than usual to punish him for his outburst. He would mumble vague apologies. They would both act as if everything had been his fault. The Potter would shave for the first time in days, hoping she would notice and take it as a sign that he wanted to make love. He would watch her undress and make a clumsy effort to fondle her breasts. She would put on plastic hair curlers and turn away in bed, complaining about a headache. He would make an awkward declaration of love. Because the Russian language was devoid of articles, it would have the staccato quality of a telegram.

It was Piotr Borisovich who, during one of his English-polishing sessions with the Potter, had commented on the difference between English and Russian. Where English dallied, meandered, embellished, Russian took the shortest path between two points; Russian political thinking could trace its roots to the Russian language, Piotr Borisovich had said. In what sense? the Potter had asked. In the sense that Communism was essentially a shortcut. Are you against shortcuts? the Potter had asked; it had been early in their relationship and he was on the alert for ideological faults. I am all for them, Piotr Borisovich had replied, his head cocked, his eyes smiling, on the condition that they get you there sooner.

Curious he should think of Piotr Borisovich now. Or shortcuts.

The Potter shrugged. In his heart of hearts, he understood they were all connected: the phone call, Svetochka, Piotr Borisovich, shortcuts. For the next two days he tried to put it out of his mind. And thought he had succeeded. Then, without premeditation—he wasn't sure whom he was calling until he dialed—he picked up the phone and composed the number. He heard the phone ring once. Then the voice with the accent he couldn't quite place said, "B, one-forty-one, twenty-one?" as if it were a question.

Almost as if he were following a script, the Potter supplied the answer.

4

❧

Carroll was spitting a cherry-flavored candy into the wastepaper basket when Mrs. Cresswell poked her head in the door. "Thursday said to tell you he's almost through with it."

Francis wrung his hands in anticipation. "Tell him to bring it straight in," he instructed her.

"As if he would do anything else with it," muttered Mrs. Cresswell.

"Secretarial help," noted Francis, staring directly at her knees, "is not what it used to be."

The message had arrived that morning on a direct scrambler channel from the BND, the West German Federal Intelligence Service, encoded in a one-time cipher that had been earmarked for the operation when the Sisters had sent the go-ahead. One-time pads represent the last word in compartmentalization. Their beauty, which is to say their security, lies in the fact that only two people on earth hold the key: the person who enciphers on the originating end, and—in this particular case—Thursday, sweating away in his windowless cubbyhole just down the hall from the Sisters' bailiwick.

"I take it as a bad sign that they're filing so quickly," Carroll mused. He scanned the box of candies for a promising shape.

"I don't know," Francis said. "If they had nothing positive to report they would have let the string run out a bit more before filing a no-show."

Carroll bit into another piece of candy, made a face and spit it into the wastepaper basket. "The Germans—*our* Germans—are like schoolchildren, on that tiny point we can agree, I would think," he said. "They will set up their approach with

18

meticulous care, make one pass at the target, then phone in with juicy details of their success or failure. It is part of their sense of insecurity that comes from having lost the wrong war."

Someone knocked at the door. Carroll sprang to open it, overturning his box of candies. Thursday stood on the threshold, vibrating with excitement. "He has bitten," he giggled. And he read the plain text from his yellow legal pad: " 'The fish is on the line.' "

Francis took possession of the page from Thursday's legal pad and the original coded message; at the close of the work-day he would make sure they wound up in the office shredder. "The trick now," he remarked as if he were dealing with nothing more important than that evening's meal, "is to play him in very slowly."

5

❧

For reasons of security, the Russians were keeping their distance. It was a Cuban cutout in New Orleans who contacted the Soviet agent known by his code name, Khanda. The cutout was a prostitute who worked a back street full of bars masquerading as nightclubs, so it was the most natural thing in the world for Khanda to saunter up to her and ask how much she charged. When she told him, he said he would be willing to pay twice what she asked if she, in turn, would be willing to accept American Express traveler's checks.

The cutout recognized this as the code identifying Khanda, and led him up to her room on the fourth floor.

Khanda had the instincts of a puritan; being with a whore made him uneasy. When the cutout invited him to take off his jacket and loosen his tie, he politely refused. He was in a hurry, he explained. What was it she had for him?

She rummaged through a sewing basket for her microdot reader, and handed it to him along with a picture postcard she had received from one of her regular clients in Mexico City. The message on it, and the address, had been typed on an old typewriter that had a new ribbon and no R. ". . . -eally g-eat time he-e . . ." it said. Khanda held the postcard under a lamp and examined it closely, but he couldn't see anything out of the ordinary. "It's the i in the word 'time,' " the cutout told him, and she handed him an eyebrow tweezers so he could pry the microdot from the dot over the i and insert it in the reader.

Khanda quickly copied the message onto the back of an envelope. When he had finished, the cutout casually asked him if he would like to make love. There would be no charge, she added, since they were, after all, colleagues. Khanda thanked her profusely but said he was expected somewhere.

Back in his own apartment, Khanda studied the message on the back of the envelope. His first reaction was to feel extremely flattered. They obviously had a great deal of esteem for him if they were assigning this mission to him. His second sensation was one of exhilaration. If he could pull it off, he would become what, in his wildest dreams, he had always wanted to`be: important; a hero, even, in certain circles. He closed his eyes and imagined the blind man fumbling with the Order of Lenin, trying to pin it onto his lapel. He wondered if he would have to put up with a kiss on each cheek, or whether, in deference to his being a foreigner, they would agree to skip that part.

Khanda didn't like being kissed by men.

6

❧

There were four people ahead of the Potter in the queue. Two empty taxis, their checkered doors splattered with dried mud, raced past in quick succession. Moscow was struggling under the heel of an unseasonal cold snap; temperatures had plunged during the night. The Potter pulled down the earflaps of his *oushanka* and stamped his feet, which were already beginning to feel numb inside his galoshes. A third taxi flashed by at breakneck speed.

"Bastards!" complained a heavyset man in front of the Potter. "They're warm as hell with their heaters going full blast. They don't give a damn for us stranded out here in the cold."

A fourth taxi wormed its way toward the corner along Zubovsky Boulevard, coming from the Krimsky Bridge. The skin on the back of the Potter's neck crawled; his *body* knew this one was it before he did. The cab pulled up before the queue. The driver, a squirrellike man with a worker's cap pulled low over his eyes and a scarf wrapped around his lower jaw, leaned across and rolled down the passenger window the width of a fist. The man in front of the Potter elbowed his way between the two women at the head of the queue and shouted out his destination. "The Exhibition of Economic Achievements, off Mistra Avenue, comrade." The exhibition was on the other side of the city, normally a profitable run for a taxi driver, because while the meter was running, he could pick up several passengers heading in the same direction and pocket their fares.

"*Nyet, nyet,*" barked the driver, waving his hand in irritation.

The women who had been shoved aside smiled smugly. Each offered an address; each was refused in turn.

"And what about you, comrade fur cap?" the driver called when the Potter failed to come forward with an address. "Where are you heading on this arctic day?"

"Anywhere," the Potter replied, a sardonic grimace deforming his chapped lips.

The driver appeared startled. The Potter jumped to the conclusion that he had guessed wrong. And suddenly a sense of relief—of having gotten off a hook—flooded through his nervous system. He started to turn away; he would rethink this whole business.

Just then, to everyone's astonishment, the driver jerked his head toward the back seat. "Get in," he ordered.

The Potter hesitated. The heavyset man, the two women, stared at him, straining to place his face. If the driver agreed to take him "anywhere," he must be someone important. A member of the Central Committee perhaps. Or a manager of one of those new hard-currency stores that carried Western products.

Sensing the Potter's indecision, the driver reached back and pushed open the rear door. The Potter shrugged—it suddenly seemed easier to go with the current—and ducked into the back seat.

"Where are you taking me?" the Potter asked as the driver spun his taxi through a maze of side streets behind the Church of St. Nicholas of the Weavers. Ignoring the question, the driver turned into Pirogovskaya Street, then pulled up abruptly. He studied the rearview mirror; the Potter glanced over his shoulder. No one came out of the side street after them. Satisfied, the driver slipped the taxi into gear and headed toward the Novodevichy Monastery. Ahead, the Potter could make out the five gilded bulb-shaped domes of the Virgin of Smolensk Church.

An image of Piotr Borisovich leapt to his mind. He had been standing next to an open hotel window staring out at Moscow his last night in the country. He had gotten roaring drunk on French champagne, and had started to sing snatches of Moussorgsky's *Khovanshchina*, an opera that recounted the story of Czar Peter's revolt against the Regent Sophia; Peter banished her to the Novodevichy Monastery, lynched three hundred of her *streltsy* under the windows of her cell and nailed the hand of Prince Khovansky, her principal ally, to her door. Piotr Borisovich's voice had been pitched low and surprisingly on-key. Then, suddenly sober, he had stopped singing and cocked his head and smiled the way he always smiled—with his eyes, not his mouth. Little wrinkles had formed at the corners of his eyes, making him appear older than he was. Violence is in our blood, he had said, looking out at Moscow but thinking of America. Violence and a passion for plotting. You and I, the Potter had agreed, are the last practitioners of a dying art.

The way he said the sentence had made it seem as if they were on a holy crusade.

"End of the line, comrade fur cap." The driver braked to a stop in front of the gate leading to the Novodevichy Cemetery.

The Potter noticed the meter wasn't running, so he nodded and let himself out of the taxi. It roared off. The Potter stood a moment on the sidewalk savoring the cold—the taxi had been overheated, but in Moscow no one ever complained of being subjected to too much heat—then turned and made his way into the heart of the cemetery, past rows of eroded tombstones. The paths, as far as he could tell, were deserted. In matters like this, the Potter knew from experience, no one hurried. When they were absolutely sure he wasn't being followed, they would come for him. He wandered past a stand of graves—Gogol's, Chekhov's, Mayakovsky's, Esenin's (the last two were suicides; the violence, the plotting had been too much for them). His feet were beginning to feel numb again; if the cold snap kept up he would have to start wearing his wool-lined slippers inside his galoshes, as he did at the height of winter. He paused before the glistening white marble bust of Stalin's beautiful young wife. She had stormed out of a Kremlin dinner party one night in 1932, gone home, put a pistol to her head and, as Piotr Borisovich once quipped, introduced a foreign object into her brain. Another suicide! More violence! "To Nadezhda Alliluyeva," the inscription on the bust read, "from a member of the Communist Party, J. Stalin."

"Psssssssst!"

The Potter turned to see a little man with shirred skin squinting at him from several meters away. He must have stepped from behind a tombstone, because he hadn't been there a moment before. The man beckoned with an emaciated finger. The Potter approached. The man removed his hat, an unexpected sign of deference considering who they were and what they were up to. "I have confirmed," he announced, nodding a very bald head, "that you are alone. Down that path, through that gate, you will discover another taxi waiting for you."

"Where will it take me?" the Potter asked, knowing the question would never be answered.

"Anywhere!" replied the little bald man with a mischievous wink, and planting his hat squarely on his head, he darted with unexpected sprightliness between two tombstones and disappeared.

7

❧

Atop the great baroque belfry in the center of the monastery grounds, two men dressed in ankle-length mink coats and mink hats stood with their backs to the wind. Because they were vaguely related (one's mother's brother had been the other's uncle by marriage), because they directed Department 13 of the First Chief Directorate, the sabotage and assassination unit of the Komitet Gosudarstvennoy Bezopasnosti, better known by its initials KGB, their subordinates referred to them as the Cousins. The younger of the two, in his early forties, stared down at the cemetery through binoculars. The other, who was blind, the result of being tortured by the Gestapo during the Great Patriotic War, asked, "Is the bald man one of ours or theirs?"

"Theirs. Oskar must have pulled him out of a hat for this operation," the younger man answered.

"We should remember to log him," the blind man said.

"Small fish, big pond," the man with the binoculars replied. "Oskar will make us a present of him if we ask. In any case, we must be careful not to frighten any of them off before this whole thing becomes history."

The man with the binoculars watched the Potter enter the second taxi. "I will tell you the truth," he admitted. "I didn't think he would go for it."

"Did you know him personally?" inquired the blind man. He used the past tense, as if he were speaking about someone dead and buried.

"I met him years ago just after he came back from New York," the younger man replied. "He was a great hero to us all then." He fitted his binoculars back into their leather case. "He had served Mother Russia well. We looked up to him."

Below, the driver gunned his motor and the taxi lurched away from the curb. The blind man bent an ear toward the sound, then tapped his long, thin white baton several times on the ground in satisfaction. "He is still serving Mother Russia," he said thoughtfully, and he pressed his lips into what, on his scarred features, passed for a smile.

8

❧

The *yafka* (Russian for "safe house") turned out to be on Volodarskaya Street, down the block from the Church of the Dormition of the Potters.

When he discovered Feliks' hobby was throwing pots, Piotr Borisovich, sporting an ancient fedora that had seen one too many rainstorms, had hauled him off, one sparkling Sunday before he graduated to the "field," to see the mosaics and decorative brickwork of the church. What do you think? Piotr Borisovich had demanded, delighted to have come up with something in Moscow that the *novator* didn't know about. What I think, the Potter had responded, is that religion is the opiate of the people. Piotr Borisovich had laughed like a schoolboy. But what do *you* think? he had persisted, trying as usual to get past the cliché. Speaking as an atheist, the Potter had observed, I think that no amount of mosaics can obscure the fact that a church is essentially a lie. Piotr Borisovich had shaken his head. You forget what Spinoza said, he had remarked, his voice unaccustomedly moody: there are no lies, only crippled truths.

Crippled truths, the Potter reflected now, making his way up a dark staircase, the stench of urine drifting past his nostrils at each landing, may be better than no truths at all. In what sense? he could imagine Piotr Borisovich inquiring encouragingly. In the sense, he could hear himself replying, that if something is worth doing, an argument can be made that it is worth doing badly.

The Potter struck a match and peered at the number on the door. It was missing, but the outline of where it had been was unmistakable. The Potter shook out the match and deposited it in a trouser cuff and knocked lightly on the door.

"Come."

The room had two windows with their shades drawn and an uncomfortably bright electric light and two folding metal chairs and a calendar on a wall set to the previous month.

"We are September, not August," the Potter observed. He walked over and tore off August and crumpled it into a ball and tossed it onto the floor. As an afterthought, he glanced behind the calendar. All he found was more wall.

"So," said the man sitting on one of the two folding metal chairs. He was of medium height, unshaven, with a silver-rimmed pince-nez wedged onto the bridge of a long, lean Roman nose. "I thank you for taking advantage of our taxi service."

"Your precautions were impeccably professional," the Potter said.

The man accepted this with a nod. "Coming from the *novator,* I take that as a compliment. I shall pass it on to my associates, yes? They too will take it as a compliment."

He was being buttered up, the Potter realized, by the man with the accent he couldn't quite place. There was a hint of German in it, a hint of Polish; a Ukrainian, perhaps, who had spent his formative years in a German concentration camp in Poland. Or a Pole who had been pressed into the Red Army. Or a bilingual German.

"So," the man began again, clearing his throat nervously, "for the purpose of this conversation, it may be useful for me to have a name, yes?"

"It would be useful," the Potter agreed.

"You will call me Oskar. So: my associates and I are prepared to get you out of the country—"

"I have a wife," the Potter said stiffly.

"When I speak of you, it goes without saying I mean you and your wife."

"Such details go *with* saying," the Potter corrected him grimly.

"I take your point," Oskar acknowledged affably.

"You talk of getting us out of the country. Out of the country where?"

"Initially, you will go to Vienna, yes? The debriefing will be conducted there. In pleasant surroundings, it goes without . . . it goes *with* saying. The representatives of several intelligence services will want to buy time with you. After all, it is not every day that we can come up with a *novator*, yes?"

"Yes," the Potter agreed. Buy time. That made Oskar a free-lancer. Though in all probability he was a free-lancer on a leash. But whose leash? "It is not every day."

"After Vienna," Oskar continued, "we will supply you with identities, with a legend, with bank accounts, with a modest business even. A pottery studio might be appropriate. You can live where you want."

"Could we go to Paris?"

Oskar smiled for the first time. "You have been to Paris, yes?"

"Yes." In fact the Potter had passed through Paris on the way back from his tour of duty in New York. "My wife dreams of it."

"Paris is entirely within the realm of possibility," Oskar said with the tone of someone who considered the matter settled.

"How do you plan to get us out of the country?" the Potter wanted to know.

Oskar permitted himself a gesture of impatience. The Potter politely retracted the question. Oskar said, "That brings us to the part of the conversation where you suggest what, specifically, you can offer to us to justify our efforts, not to speak of our risks."

The Potter suppressed a faint smile. " 'Justify' in the sense of provide financial profit?"

Oskar knew he had to choose his words carefully. "If we decide to get you out, we will want to be rewarded for our efforts. It is a fact of life that there are organizations in the West that will pay generously for your information. But you misjudge us if you think the money is for us. It will fund projects designed to undermine a regime, a system, a philosophy that we consider odious." Lowering his voice to a whisper, Oskar intoned Dostoevsky's famous phrase, "Where there is sorrow and pain, the soil is sacred, yes?"

"Yes," the Potter remarked dryly. Somehow he believed Oskar. He had the look of an idealist, which is to say the look of someone with a short life expectancy. "My having been a *novator*—doesn't that, in itself, justify your efforts, your risks?"

Oskar shrugged.

"There were circuits in New York," the Potter said softly. He had been trained to keep secrets; giving them away didn't come naturally. "There was an entire *rezidentura*. There was an *istochnik*—a source of information—in the United Nations Secretariat."

"So: that was all some time ago," Oskar noted. "And you have been out of circulation for six months now."

"Try it out on your principals," the Potter insisted. "In any case, it is all I have to offer."

"Of course I will try it out," Oskar said. "But I suspect that your *rezidentura*, your *istochnik*, are what the Americans call"—here he switched to English—"old hats." Speaking again in Russian, he added, "You are familiar with the expression, yes?"

"Yes," repeated the Potter, remembering Piotr Borisovich's ancient fedora, wondering what he had gotten himself into; wondering if in the end they would get out of him the thing he valued more than the pupil of his eye. "I am painfully familiar with old hats."

9

⚜

Oskar inserted a key and let himself in the service door. It was a little-used back entrance to a stuffy transit hotel on Sushchevsky Bank Street, behind the Riga Station. The narrow service stairs hadn't been swept in years, but then the few people who used it generally had other things on their minds beside cleanliness. The doors on all the floors except the fourth were bolted shut. Upstairs, Oskar felt his way along the pitch-dark corridor, one hand on the wall, the other raised protectively before his eyes. It occurred to him that the people who frequented the fourth floor could easily afford to supply light bulbs, but probably felt more comfortable in the dark. At the third door along the corridor wall, Oskar knocked and then entered without waiting for an invitation. He stuffed his scarf into the sleeve of his raincoat, and hung it on the clothes tree alongside the two mink coats. So: if the Cousins were wearing their mink coats now, when it was not even freezing out, God knows what they would do in January when the temperature could drop to minus thirty. Well, everyone had his threshold of pain, or cold, or corruptibility, yes? It remained to be seen what the Potter's was.

The blind man recognized Oskar's footfall. "You're early," he called, "which means things went badly."

"Things went quickly," Oskar corrected him. "It would have been very curious—suspicious even, yes?—if he had offered us precisely what we wanted the first time around."

"He needs to marinate," agreed the other man in the room.

The blind man tapped his baton against his shoe impatiently. "He should be pushed," he insisted. "You could play the tape recording of the meeting back to him. He has already done enough to merit a firing squad."

"With all respect," the younger Cousin said—he was, after all, dealing with someone who, on paper at least, was his superior—"he needs to be pulled, not pushed."

"He has a violent temper, yes?" Oskar noted. "If he crosses frontiers, whether physical or psychological, he must have the impression that he is controlling his own destiny."

"What will you do now?" the blind man asked, conceding to the others the question of pace.

"So," Oskar said, "I will report back to my German Merchants. Then I will sit by the phone and reflect on what the peasants say—that all things come to those who wait, yes?"

10

Carroll and Francis were confirmed bachelors. It wasn't that
they didn't like women; they just didn't trust them. And what
sex drive either came equipped with at birth had long since
been channeled into other pursuits. Carroll lived with an unmarried sister in a rented apartment in Georgetown. Francis
lived alone in a downtown residence hotel with a kitchenette
crawling with cockroaches. He sprayed once a week, ironed
his own shirts, darned his own socks and except on Tuesdays
and Fridays made his own dinners. On Tuesdays he grabbed a
bite in a delicatessen and went to a motion picture; to a spy
film whenever possible. On Fridays he dined out with Carroll.
They had been meeting Fridays more or less to review their
week's work since they began sharing an office, some twelve
years before. For eight of those years they had been faithful to
a particular Chinese restaurant. Then they discovered the chef
sprinkled monosodium glutamate on all his dishes. Now they
ate Chinese health food.

Francis lifted the metal lid on his dish from Column B and
sniffed suspiciously at the contents. The gesture annoyed Carroll. "I don't know how you can be so calm," he whispered
fiercely. His own face was a mask of frustration. "After what's
happened . . ."

"Nothing happened that wasn't expected," Francis said.

"What if he doesn't have what we want?" Carroll whined.

For a moment Francis thought his partner might actually
burst into tears. "The Potter was the *novator*," he reminded
Carroll. "He was in charge of the sleeper school. He has it."

"Imagine offering us a ten-year-old *rezidentura*, or an

istochnik at the United Nations! What does he take us for, amateurs?"

"You act as if he meant it as a personal insult," Francis reproached Carroll. "He's dealing with free-lancers, remember, not us. He was simply testing the temperature of the water."

"I hope to God you're right," Carroll said. The muscle in his cheek twitched several times, then stopped of its own accord. "Our whole scheme depends on him."

Francis' eyes narrowed; some music was forming in the back of his brain. "I'm just thinking out loud, but it might not do any harm to shake him up a bit. . . ."

Carroll snapped his fingers; lyrics had leapt into his head. "What if we sent *him* the names of the *rezidentura* and the *istochnik*!"

"I knew you'd come up with something," Francis remarked, and he tucked the corner of his napkin into his collar to protect his taxicab-yellow bow tie and attacked the plate of whole-wheat noodles, Chinese cabbage and steamed shrimp.

11

❧

"Svetochka," moaned Svetochka, kicking off her worn suede boots, collapsing into an easy chair that badly needed recovering, "is dead."

She had just come back from the store with two tins of salted fish, a kilo of onions, a box of rice. "Seven lines," she moaned, feeling very sorry for herself. "One for the fish, one for the onions, one for the rice. That's three. Then one to pay the cashier. That makes four. Then back to the first line to collect the fish, another to collect the onions, a third to collect the rice. That's seven. You know your Lenin, Feliks. Is there something in it about Communism needing *lines*?"

The Potter smiled for the first time in days. "There are lines because there are shortages," he explained.

"And why," Svetochka demanded, massaging the balls of her feet, "if everybody is working according to their ability, do we still have shortages?"

The Potter helped himself to some more vodka. "In the old days, before the revolution, they used to say that the shortage would be divided among the peasants. Now we are fairer—we divide the shortage among everyone. That's Communism."

"Well," she replied with a sigh, "Svetochka preferred it when you had your ration privileges at the food center. The people who work there are much more polite." A faraway look crept into her eyes; she might have been talking about heaven. "They even have someone who opens the door for you when your arms are loaded. They *recommended* things. The lettuce is especially fresh, they say." Tears spilled from her eyes. "Lettuce in *winter*! God knows where it came from. The

36

okra is from Central Asia, they say. The oranges from Cuba. Try—"

"Enough." The Potter cut her off with an impatient wave of his hand.

"You have one answer for everything, Feliks. Enough! *I've had enough of your enough!* When we first met you had a ration at the food center and a *dacha* and a chauffeured automobile when you phoned up for one. You came home from that warehouse of yours with something for Svetochka almost every day. I wore lipstick colors nobody in Moscow ever saw before."

"Enough," muttered the Potter. He felt as if he were being tuned too high.

"You said you would take your Svetochka to Paris one day," she taunted him. "You said we would take the elevator to the top of an enormous steel tower and look out over the world and laugh our heads off."

The Potter tilted his head onto the back of his chair and closed his eyes tiredly. "What if I told you I would still take you to Paris?" he asked quietly.

She flung herself at his feet, hugged his knees. "Oh, Feliks, if only you could! Svetochka doesn't want to grow old without making love in Paris. We'd make love *before* dinner, the way we used to. Do you remember what an appetite you had afterward?"

"I still have an appetite," the Potter commented bitterly. He opened his legs and felt her nestle between them. "I lost my job and my ration and my *dacha* and my chauffeured automobile, but I never lost my appetite."

12

The second meeting took place in the second taxi. Oskar was driving. "So: I passed your offer on to my potential clients," he announced, concentrating on the road, his voice drifting back over his shoulder. "Here is their response."

He handed a note back to his passenger as he accelerated past a long line of people waiting in a corner taxi queue. A young woman in a tattered fur coat and fur hat leapt after him, desperately waving a ten-ruble note. In the back seat, the Potter unfolded the piece of paper. There were two columns, one marked A, the other B. Nine names were listed under Column A—the entire New York *rezidentura*. One name, that of an African diplomat who had spent his formative years at Patrice Lumumba University in Moscow, was listed under Column B—the *istochnik* at the United Nations.

"In America, Chinese restaurants have a Column A and B on their menus," the Potter noted absently. "They certainly went to a lot of trouble to say no."

"I interpret it as a sign of personal respect for you, yes?" Oskar remarked.

They were passing the zoo, and the Potter thought he could make out the bleating of some frustrated animal coming from one of the buildings; then it occurred to him that the sound might have originated in his own imagination. He leaned forward so that his mouth was close to Oskar's ear. "I have given the matter a great deal of thought," he told him.

"So: I suspected you would."

Oskar was beginning to get on the Potter's nerves. "You are very sure of yourself," he noted.

Oskar shrugged. "You were the *novator*. If you really

38

want to get out of Russia, you will come up with something to pay your way, yes?"

Behind the taxi, a siren wailed. Oskar pulled the car over sharply to the right. A Zil limousine with lace curtains on its rear windows raced down the middle lane toward the Kremlin. Up ahead, a policeman held up cross traffic until the Zil had passed.

"That's probably—" Oskar named an alternate member of the Politburo, an expert on agriculture whose star was considered to be on the rise. "I hear he has a mistress stashed away in one of those new buildings behind the zoo. So: where were we?"

The Potter said, "I lost three sleepers in six months. One of them simply disappeared. He was a physicist by training. He was inserted into America so that he could eventually take over a network of subagents working at various atomic installations. With his background in physics, he would have been in a position to evaluate their information, direct them to fill in gaps in our knowledge, that sort of thing. Four of the subagents were eventually caught and put on trial in America. Two others were never identified. I don't know the names of the two, but I could supply enough information about them— where they worked during what years, their professional qualifications, a description of the family of one, the sexual preferences of the other, so that your clients can identify them."

Oskar pulled up at a red light. Just abreast of them, a man and a woman in a Czech Skoda were arguing bitterly. "I go over it again and again," the Potter could hear the man yell, "and I can't find the beginning."

"The beginning of what?" the woman cried.

"The beginning of where it went wrong," the man replied. "The beginning of—" The light changed and the Czech car raced off.

Oskar threw his taxi into first and started down the street after the Skoda. "So: it went wrong," he called over his shoulder, "right after the Bolshevik revolution when some comrades proposed opening a special restaurant for members of the Party. Those who were against it argued that Communists should starve along with the working classes. Those who were for it argued that they couldn't lead the working class to paradise if they didn't have the physical strength. The matter was brought to Lenin. You know the story, yes? Lenin ruled in favor of establishing a special restaurant. Things were never the same after that, yes? I will let you off in front of the Hotel Ukraina. So, enter the lobby and buy a newspaper from the kiosk, then go on about your business."

"What about my offer?" the Potter asked.

"I will call you when I get a response, yes?" Oskar said without noticeable enthusiasm.

13

The blind man's white baton came down like a whip against the legs of his chair. "So much for your *pulling*," he announced in a voice that left no room for discussion. "Now we will do some *pushing*!"

14

✤

The Deputy Assistant Procurator, a burnt-out middle-aged time-server with long clumps of hair pasted across his scalp like fingers, kept the Potter waiting ten minutes before he even looked up. There was a chair in front of the polished table that served as his desk, but he never offered him the use of it. "You have been summoned," the Deputy Assistant Procurator eventually said—it was at this point that he glanced at the Potter for the first time—"summoned, eh, in accordance with—" He named an article of the penal code. The Deputy Assistant Procurator shuffled through a sheaf of official-looking papers with seals and signatures on the bottom of each one. "You are informed . . ." He removed his eyeglasses and cleaned them with the tip of his tie, then carefully hooked them back over his ears. ". . . informed, eh, that criminal proceedings have been opened against you in connection with charges of, eh, pilfering state property from the warehouse annex of the state security institution that you were formerly in command of." He lost his place and peered at the paper he was reading. "Eh, in command of. You are advised to retain a lawyer. You are further advised that the penalty, if convicted of violating the particular article of the penal code with which you are charged, is ten years at a strict-regime labor camp, confiscation of all personal property, annulment of pension and, eh, voting rights." The Deputy Assistant Procurator looked up. "Do you have any comment to make?"

The Potter said in English, "I hear it was charged against me that I sought to destroy institutions."

"What does that mean?" snapped the Deputy Assistant Procurator in annoyance.

"It is a line written by the American poet Walter Whitman."

"It doesn't help your case to be quoting an *American* poet."

"He is considered to be very progressive," the Potter said sarcastically.

The Deputy Assistant Procurator pushed a paper across the table toward the Potter, and held out a ball-point pen. "Sign your full name at the bottom to indicate you are familiar with the contents."

The Potter accepted the pen and looked down at the paper. It was all a mistake, of course. He had served the state too long and too well to be accused now of swiping the odd bit of clothing or an occasional lipstick from the American warehouse. Compared to some of his colleagues or superiors, the Potter's acquisitions had been extremely modest; a senior section chief had once trucked out painters and carpenters and electricians employed by the Center and set them to work rebuilding his *dacha*, and nobody had uttered a word. The Potter forced himself to focus on the paper. Over "Name of accused" someone had typed in "Feliks Arkantevich Turov." So it wasn't a mistake after all. Over "Race" it said "Jew." In what sense is a Jew always, ever a Jew? Piotr Borisovich had once laughingly asked, and then, suddenly serious, he had answered his own question: In the sense that every ten or twenty years, the state will go out of its way to remind him. But why was the state, which in the Potter's experience never did anything haphazardly, choosing this particular moment to remind him of his racial roots? And why was the state suddenly concerned with his penny-ante pilfering?

"I haven't got, eh, all morning," said the burnt-out Deputy Assistant Procurator, who had precisely that.

The Potter reached down and scratched his signature across the bottom of the sheet, acknowledging that criminal proceedings had been opened against him; acknowledging also that his life, or what was left of it, was spiraling out of control.

15

Svetochka turned up the volume on the radio so that their neighbors couldn't eavesdrop. "What did he want?" she demanded, though she could tell by his face that she might be better off if she didn't know.

"They are looking into irregularities," the Potter said vaguely. He would never survive a strict-regime labor camp; if he were tied up to the pier of old age now, imagine what he'd be in ten years. And if, by some miracle, he lived through it, Svetochka certainly wouldn't be waiting for him when he got out.

"What kind of irregularities?"

The Potter gripped his glass of tea in both hands to warm his fingers. "There was some pilfering at the warehouse while I was the *novator*." Lipsticks, makeup, earrings, perfume, cigarettes, cigarette lighters, underwear, nylon stockings, records, cinema magazines, once a dress, once a pair of women's blue jeans, all manufactured in America, had disappeared.

"How can they prove it was you who took them?" Svetochka asked.

"When they are at the appropriate stage of the investigation," the Potter said numbly, "you will tell them."

Svetochka reacted as if she had been slapped across the face. "How can you bring yourself to say such a thing? Svetochka would never do anything to hurt her Feliks."

"You will be offered the opportunity to save yourself," the Potter explained with a calmness he didn't feel. "You will hesitate long enough to convince yourself of your loyalty to me, but in the end you will do what has to be done."

"Oh, Feliks," she cried. "You can't let them do this to Svetochka."

The words seemed to echo through the Potter's head. To Svetochka! He would lose his pension and wind up in a strict-regime labor camp for ten years, and they were doing this to *her*. Stirring a spoonful of jam into his tea, he smiled grimly.

"You must give them what they want, Feliks."

He shook his head. "I am in a difficult position," he said. "I am not yet sure who wants what."

Svetochka nervously uncrossed and recrossed her legs, giving the Potter a glimpse of garter belt, of thigh. Once, when she had drunk too much vodka, she had admitted that, as a young girl, she planted herself in front of a mirror and practiced crossing her legs in a way that would permit the men facing her to see up her skirt. Later, when he had reminded her of this, she had denied it indignantly. But the perfection of the gesture spoke for itself.

"There was a phone call for you while you were out," Svetochka announced absently. "Someone named Oskar . . ."

He stopped stirring his tea. If he could give Oskar what *he* wanted, there still might be a way out. "What did he say?" the Potter asked.

"It was a funny message. He said to tell you he is in possession of a piece of paper, that it is divided into two columns, one marked A, the other B. He said there was one name in each column."

"One name in each column?"

Svetochka nodded. "He said you would understand. Who is this Oskar?"

"He is a middleman," the Potter answered. "He brings buyers and sellers together."

Svetochka wasn't listening. "There must be a solution," she blurted out. "It is only a question of finding it."

"There is," the Potter said quietly.

"Then take it!"

"It would mean betraying a friend." The Potter had known all along it would come down to this. He tried to imagine what advice Piotr Borisovich would give him. We are in a ruthless business, he could hear Piotr Borisovich saying. We are not

humanists, so why pretend to be? Save yourself, he could hear
Piotr Borisovich saying. If I were in your shoes, I certainly
would.

On the radio, the Moscow Symphony Orchestra reached
the end of one movement and began tuning up before starting
another. In the audience, people coughed. Svetochka breathed
a name into the silence. "Piotr Borisovich?" The orchestra
launched into the new movement.

The Potter looked quickly away, confirming her guess.

"If you give them Piotr," she plunged on, thinking she
was talking about the Deputy Assistant Procurator and warehouse pilfering, "they will leave you and Svetochka alone?"

"If I give them Piotr Borisovich"—the Potter felt as if he
were finally getting the spiraling clay under some kind of
control—"we can go to live in Paris."

Svetochka's eyes widened. "Paris," she repeated. She didn't
hesitate. "He betrayed you," she spat out. "You can betray
him!"

The Potter's hand shook; tea spilled onto his trousers.
"What do you mean, betrayed me?"

She avoided his eye. "When you started bringing him
around, he was very polite, very respectful at first. Later,
when he didn't think you would notice, he would look up
Svetochka's skirt, brush the back of his hand against Svetochka's
breast. Svetochka knew what he was thinking. You went off
once, you said it was to Poland. Remember? You were away
for ten days." She appeared to run out of words; out of breath
too.

"Go on," the Potter ordered weakly.

"Ten days you were away. He dropped by. He said he
was looking for you, but we both understood that he knew
you were not in Moscow. We drank some vodka. Svetochka
was lonely without her Feliks. Before she knew what had
happened, we were in—" She burst out furiously, "Does
Svetochka have to draw you a picture?"

"I don't believe you," the Potter cried. "You are lying."

"If Svetochka is lying," she retorted, her voice barely
audible above the music, her eyes flashing, "how would she
know that Piotr Borisovich was circumcised?"

16

❧

"So: you got my message?"

"I got it."

Oskar seemed just as tense as the Potter. "You understood it, yes?"

"I understood it," the Potter acknowledged. He watched the trolley cars slide noiselessly past in the street below. What sound they made was dampened by the storm windows fitted over the regular windows. Someone had been very lazy. In summer such windows were usually taken off. Maybe it wasn't a question of cold, though. Maybe it was a question of security. Cotton had been stretched along the sill between the windows to absorb the condensation, and moss had been placed on the cotton—a touch that indicated that the regular resident of the apartment had peasant roots. "Your potential clients already knew the identities of the people in question," the Potter continued tonelessly. "They were not buying."

"So: I assume you have come up with another proposition," Oskar remarked casually, "or you wouldn't be here, yes?"

The Potter wondered if Oskar was as sure of himself as he sounded. "Another proposition, yes."

Svetochka had been right, of course, about Piotr Borisovich. On several occasions the Potter and his pupil had visited the Sandunovsky Bathhouse together. There, stark naked amid the smoke screen of steam and the stale smell of sweat and birch bark, they had nibbled on sticks of salted fish and talked in undertones about the idealism that somehow had gotten lost in the shuffle in Russia. Glancing down, the Potter had noticed that Piotr Borisovich was circumcised. "It is a rare thing in

47

Russia," Piotr Borisovich had commented, his eyes following the Potter's gaze. Indeed it was! Since the revolution, even Jews hesitated when it came to having their children circumcised. The Potter had been born before the revolution, but his parents had seen the handwriting on the wall. His father had decided that with all the anti-Semitism in Russia, the day might come when the boy's safety would depend on his *not* being circumcised. Piotr Borisovich's father, curiously, hadn't even been Jewish. But he once came across a pamphlet describing the medical advantages of circumcision. Practicing what the author-doctor preached, he had himself circumcised though he was already a grown man, and his son circumcised at birth. The circumcision had almost been the undoing of the father. Trapped behind German lines at one point during the war, he had been taken for a Jew. He had been awaiting execution in a cell when the Red Army counterattacked and liberated the town.

It struck the Potter, who had an inner ear permanently tuned to pick up such details, how ironic it would be if the circumcision turned out to be the undoing of the son.

The Potter turned to confront Oskar. "The last sleeper to pass through my school while I was the *novator*," he briskly informed him, "was named Piotr Borisovich Revkin." He could see interest burning, like a pilot light, in Oskar's normally masked eyes. "He was inserted into America two years ago. He lives in a section of New York under deep cover, waiting for the signal indicating his controllers have decided to give him a mission."

Oskar couldn't suppress the note of excitement that crept into his voice. "You know the name under which he operates, yes? You know *where* he is?"

The Potter nodded.

Oskar took a step in the Potter's direction. "You are familiar with the signal that can awaken this sleeper of yours, yes?"

"Yes."

"So: my clients will want to know how you came into possession of this information," Oskar said.

"His cover name is part of the legend we worked out

together at the sleeper school," the Potter explained. "The location I know because, for personal reasons that had to do with an affinity we shared for a certain poet, he sent me, in violation of standing rules, a picture postcard of the house he lives in."

"And the awakening signal?"

"When we selected an awakening signal, I always made it a point to choose a phrase that was already embedded in a sleeper's memory—a familiar motto, a line of a song or a poem he had known since childhood. There was a line of poetry that we both knew . . ." The Potter's voice choked for an instant. Did one betrayal inevitably lead to another? What level of Dante's hell was he sentencing himself to? He drew a deep breath. ". . . knew and appreciated. I wrote out the awakening signal in my own hand in his dossier."

"If my potential clients accept and you don't have the information you claim to have . . ." Oskar left the sentence hanging.

The Potter said softly, "I am not an idiot. I know the rules of the game." Against his will, a brittle laugh seeped from the back of his throat. "I helped write them."

17

❧

The younger Cousin helped the blind man off with his coat. Tapping his white baton before his feet, the blind man made his way into the hotel room. "Well, Oskar," he called out, uncertain where in the room Oskar was, "in the end pushing him didn't do any harm, did it?"

Oskar said, "So: it is my opinion he would have come around eventually."

The younger man waved Oskar off. He had once seen the blind man lash out with his baton at the legs of someone who crossed him.

Oskar shrugged. "The important thing," he told the blind man, "is that he has come through with what you wanted. It is true what he said about the awakening signal, yes?"

The blind man found the seat with his baton and settled into it. The younger man extracted a red file from a briefcase and opened it on the table. The blind man ran his fingertips over several pages as if they were written in braille. "Of course the awakening signal is in his handwriting," he said. "That's how we first discovered that he knew it."

"If he had typed in the signal," said the younger man, "it might never have occurred to us to use him. He'd still be bringing home American mascara to that bitch of a wife of his."

"What about the postcard?" Oskar asked. "It is conceivable that the Americans will administer truth drugs to him. Every detail must check out if they are to swallow the whole story."

"There was a postcard," the younger man confirmed. "Only the sleeper in question never sent it."

"We arranged for it to be sent," the blind man confessed smugly, "to fill in the single gap in the *novator*'s knowledge. Since he and this sleeper of his aren't going to meet again, he will never find that out."

"So: all that remains to be done now is to convince my clients to accept the deal, and then ship the *novator* and that whore of his out of the country, yes?"

"Your clients will agree to the deal," the blind man announced in a tone that left no room for doubt. And with a laugh that contained no trace of humor, he added, "I was never more sure of anything in my life."

18

❧

Francis had come down with a head cold. It was serious enough to make him skip his Tuesday-night film. Wednesday morning he telephoned Mrs. Cresswell to say he had a fever and would not be coming in. She put him on hold for a moment, which irritated Francis because it conveyed the impression that he required *permission* to stay away from the office. Then Carroll came on the line. "Mrs. Cresswell tells me you are under the weather," he said. Something in Carroll's voice made Francis suspect that his cheek muscle was atwitch.

"I have a hundred and one," Francis informed him as if it were an accomplishment.

"A hundred and one *what*?" Carroll's mind was on other things.

"A hundred and one degrees of fever!" Francis cried into the mouthpiece. "I can't see to drive."

"It's not enough," Carroll retorted. "Grab a cab." And lowering his voice to a hoarse whisper, he confided, "We are starting to haul in our fish."

Francis swallowed. *We are starting to haul in our fish!* It was the most original operation he had ever been involved in in his career. If it succeeded, history would be diverted as if it were nothing more than an inconvenient stream!

"Did you hear what I said?" Carroll hissed into the phone.

"I shall be right in," Francis said with great dignity. "I only need to put on an appropriate tie."

19

For eighteen excruciating days, the Potter didn't hear a word from Oskar. After the first week went by in sinister silence he broke down and dialed B one-forty-one, twenty-one, but almost had his eardrum shattered by the peculiar whining sound that in Moscow indicates the number is out of order. Had it all been a hoax? Someone's idea of indoor sport? Or even worse, a trap designed to test his loyalty? But if it were a trap, why would they wait to spring it?

In the state he was in, throwing pots was out of the question. They spiraled off into lopsided shapes that had nothing in common with the conception in his head. So the Potter paced: the attic, the bedroom, the corridor, the streets around the apartment building in which he lived. Nine days after his last session with Oskar, the Potter was prowling around the attic when he heard the phone ringing underfoot. He raced downstairs, but Svetochka beat him to it. "I understand," she was saying into the mouthpiece. Her posture was rigid, her face frozen in an expression of a sullen child. "We will both be there. You will be able to set your watch by our arrival."

The call turned out to be a summons from the Deputy Assistant Procurator's office for a groundbreaking session. Svetochka astonished the Potter by scrubbing every trace of makeup off her face, wearing her lowest heels and her drabbest clothes—until it dawned on him that it was her idea of how to impress Deputy Assistant Procurators with one's innocence. At the interview, Svetochka rose to the occasion and denied everything, starting with her age. "I happen, Comrade Procurator," she announced, baring teeth that looked as if they had been *sharpened*, "to be twenty-nine years of age, and not thirty-one."

The Deputy Assistant Procurator peered at a photocopy of her internal passport through a magnifying glass. "It says here in black and white that you were born in . . ." He read off a month and a year. "Subtract that from today"—he began counting on his fingers—"and you are left with thirty-one."

Svetochka's jaw angled up in displeasure. "The woman who issued me the passport wore thick eyeglasses. She made an error when she copied the date off my birth certificate."

"And where, if I may make so bold as to pose the question"—the Potter recognized this as a standard bureaucratic effort at irony—"is this, eh, birth certificate?"

"My mother had it."

"And where"—bureaucratic exasperation now—"is your mother?"

"In a coffin, underground, in row seven, aisle D of the municipal cemetery of Smolensk."

"I see," moaned the Deputy Assistant Procurator, though of course he didn't see at all. For thanks to Svetochka, he got so bogged down with inconsequential matters (height, weight, color of eyes, Party background, education, date of marriage, et cetera, et cetera) that he had to schedule a second session to attack the question of pilfering from the warehouse of a state institution. And by that time, Oskar had gotten back to them.

He called from a public phone one midnight. So: if the Potter would go down to the corner, a taxi would pick him up. Do you know what time it is? the Potter asked, relieved to have finally heard from Oskar but anxious, for tactical reasons, not to let him know it. Ignoring the question, Oskar said only that the Potter was to bring his wife with him, yes? Why bring my wife? the Potter was on the verge of demanding, but Oskar had clicked off the line.

Svetochka relished the envious stares of the others in the taxi queue when the first cab that came along refused everyone except them. The little man with shirred skin, the one who had popped up near Nadezhda Alliluyeva's tomb in the Novodevichy Cemetery, was planted behind the wheel. "Still going *anywhere*?" he asked, and he laughed a madman's laugh. He eventually deposited his passengers before a drab prefabricated apartment house on Krasnaya Street, a stone's throw from the planetarium.

Did every site in Moscow hold memories for the Potter? When Piotr Borisovich discovered that the Potter had never been to a planetarium, he had immediately arranged a visit. Revolutions had been the theme of the day. They had served up on the overhead dome, as if it were a meal, the sky as it looked over Petrograd the night the Bolsheviks stormed the Winter Palace in 1917. Then they projected the sky as it looked over Philadelphia after the signing of the Declaration of Independence, July 4, 1776. Walking back to the hotel afterward, Piotr Borisovich had started rambling on about American history. Did the Potter know, he had asked, that both Thomas Jefferson and John Adams died within hours of each other, on July 4, 1826, fifty years to the day after they signed the Declaration? James Monroe, another signer and the last President to have been forged by the American Revolution, died five years to the day later. In the decades before the Civil War, the veterans of Bunker Hill, Lexington, Valley Forge, gradually died off. In the end, Piotr Borisovich had said, the Americans and the Russians were confronted by the same problem: how to transmit the idealism of the founding revolutionists to the generations that came after them. The Americans, according to Piotr Borisovich, had never solved the problem. And we Russians, the Potter had asked, have we solved it? Piotr Borisovich had glanced sideways at the Potter, calculating how frank he dared get with the *novator* who controlled his life as surely as a puppeteer controls his marionette. It is my opinion, Piotr Borisovich had finally said—he appeared to be avoiding the question, but of course he wasn't—that revolutions don't so much change things as *rearrange* them. The Potter had accepted the statement for what it was: in the Soviet context, people consecrated friendships by uttering things which, if reported to the authorities, could get them fired or jailed or, occasionally, shot. And the Potter had responded in the same currency. I agree with you completely, he had said in a formal voice he normally reserved for oaths or rites. The people who made our revolution, theirs too, dreamed bigger dreams than we dare dream today.

The moment had contained something of the aura of an exchange of rings at a marriage ceremony. But then Piotr Borisovich, who had become the son the Potter could never father, had betrayed him. And now he, in turn, would betray Piotr Borisovich. It would end, the Potter could hear Piotr Borisovich saying with that bitter laugh of his that sounded like steam escaping from a partly open valve, in night, in death. And he remembered the line of Walter Whitman's that he had started to quote in reply and Piotr Borisovich, his head cocked quizzically, had completed.

" '. . . the hands of the sisters Death and Night,' " the Potter had recited.

Piotr Borisovich had picked up where he left off: " '. . . incessantly softly wash again, and ever again, this soil'd world.' "

"So," Oskar was saying—he had been waiting in the shadows of the first-floor landing—"we meet again." He reached for Svetochka's hand and bent his lips to the back of it, which made the Potter think that Oskar's accent was Polish after all. "Your husband, dear lady, calls me Oskar, and there is no reason under the sun why you should not do likewise, yes? Meeting you makes my day."

No one had ever kissed Svetochka's hand before, and it went to her head. "The pleasure," she chirped, adopting airs the Potter never knew she was equipped with, "is mutual."

Using a latchkey attached to a thin gold chain, Oskar let himself into an apartment on the fifth floor. The three of them groped their way along a darkened hallway toward a door. Light seeped from under it. A soft whirring sound came from beyond it. "Let me do the talking," Oskar cautioned as he ushered them into the room.

A Jew wearing an embroidered skullcap and peering through incredibly thick eyeglasses sat bent over a pedal-operated pre-war Singer sewing machine. Oskar muttered something in Yiddish, and the young man nodded shyly at the Potter and Svetochka. "You are the fortunate ones," he said in Russian. He stood up and came around in front of his Singer and squinting professionally through his thick lenses, sized them up. "They will look perfectly American when I am through with them," he promised.

"American!" Svetochka's eyes cocked open.

The Jew, who was in his early twenties, handed Oskar a pad and a pencil, then produced a measuring tape. "Arms up, if you please," he instructed the Potter, and he began calling out measurements—neck, shoulders, chest, waist, inseam, sleeve. "You wear your skirt too low on your hips," he commented to Svetochka as he moved around her taking measurements. To Oskar the Jew said, "What will you do for shoes?"

"Only give me the sizes, I will provide them."

Later, outside the building, the Potter took Oskar aside. "What was all that about?" he demanded.

"So: you will be leaving the country in five days' time under valid American passports," Oskar explained. "It is a crucial part of the operation that you pass in every detail for Americans, yes?" And he went on to explain when, and how, they would get out of Russia.

"It is that simple?" the Potter asked in amazement.

"You would be happier crossing the border in the Arctic Circle on snowshoes, with dogs barking in the distance, yes?" Oskar emitted the only laugh the Potter was ever to hear from him. "So: it is my opinion that you have read too many cheap spy novels."

The next afternoon Svetochka withdrew two hundred rubles from her bank account and spent every last kopeck of it at the ornately decorated Gastronom No. 1 on Gorky Street, popularly known as Yeliseyevsky's after the owner of the delicatessen before the revolution. Rubbing elbows with the Gastronom's regular clients, the wives and daughters of Central Committee members, leaving large tips on every counter that she came to, Svetochka managed to get out of the store with a supply of blinis, a package of salted crackers, a container of thick cream, a tin of Beluga caviar, several fresh Norwegian herrings and two bottles of Polish Bison vodka.

"What have you done?" the Potter groaned when he saw her purchases set out on the small table in their bedroom.

"We won't need rubles in Paris," Svetochka announced

innocently, "so Svetochka decided to spend as much as she could here before we leave."

"You idiot! The last thing we want to do is attract attention to ourselves." He collapsed into a wooden chair and stared at the display of luxury that any other time would have set his mouth to watering.

Crestfallen, Svetochka spread some caviar on a salted cracker, poured some vodka (which she had put outside a window to chill) into a glass and offered them to the Potter.

"I am not hungry," he grumbled.

Svetochka planted herself in a chair facing him. "What if we stimulate your appetite?" she asked suggestively, and she slowly, deliberately crossed, and then recrossed, her legs.

They made love with the light on, something they hadn't done in months. Working the Potter's dwarfish body as if she were preparing a field for planting, faking an orgasm (and when she finally had one, exaggerating its intensity), Svetochka caused him to forget, if only for a moment, Piotr Borisovich and Oskar and the pier of old age to which he felt moored. Later, munching on biscuits coated with caviar, washing them down with chilled vodka, Svetochka blew lightly into his ear and whispered, "That is only a sample of what Svetochka will do to her Feliks when we get to Paris."

20

Two days before they were scheduled to leave Russia, the
Potter decided the time had come to pay a last visit to Piotr
Borisovich's father. Not only did he want to see the old man
before he left; there was also the practical matter of recovering
the package he had carefully stashed away in a secret compartment under the floorboards of his house.

The day of the visit the Potter spent several hours doing
some elementary street work to make sure he wasn't being
followed. It had been quite a while since he had practiced
tradecraft, but the gestures he had learned as a young man, and
had perfected during his four years as *rezident* in New York,
came back fairly easily. He used reflecting surfaces—doors of
polished cars, buses—as mirrors to observe what was going on
around him in the street without appearing to. He made it a
point to be the last one to board a trolley, and the last to leap
off before it started again. He lingered in front of store windows on the Arbat and looked in them to see who else might
be lingering in front of other store windows. He ducked into
an underground tunnel that pedestrians used to cross October
Square, hurried halfway down it and then suddenly doubled
back on his tracks—and watched to see who else might double
back on his tracks. He entered GUM, the archaic bazaarlike
department store across Red Square from the Kremlin, through
one door, allowed himself to become caught up in a mob
stampeding for a counter that had just put East German um-
brellas on sale, and then made his way out of another door. He
ducked into a prewar apartment building near Pushkin Square,
climbed to the sixth floor, where the corridor connected with
an adjoining building, and emerged from an entrance of a

different building on a different street. It was midafternoon before he decided his wake was clean. He caught a taxi to the Central Depot and boarded a bus for Peredelkino, a village about forty kilometers from Moscow.

In the half year since his last trip to Peredelkino, Moscow had sprawled, like a lazy lady, farther into the countryside. Prefabricated concrete apartment buildings had sprouted on either side of the road; to the Potter's eye they had the aesthetic appeal of pillboxes. Streets that had been bulldozed into existence, but not yet paved, ran off like rivulets in every direction. Beyond the last building, in still-unleveled fields covered with corn stumps, the skeletons of giant cranes, some on their sides, some upright already, hinted at the further expansion of the city limits. "There are no limits to cities," Piotr Borisovich had once remarked as he and the Potter drove through what was then the suburb into the countryside. He had thought a moment and then revised his sentence: *There are no limits,* he had said, though at the time the Potter hadn't been sure what he was getting at.

Now he thought he understood. And he wondered, not for the first time, whether he had been Piotr Borisovich's teacher, or Piotr Borisovich had been his.

Outside of Moscow, the first peasant cottages, looking distinctly one-dimensional through the dirty window of the bus, appeared on either side of the Minsk highway. With their painted, carved wooden shutters and carefully tended vegetable gardens—in Russia, something like half the fresh vegetables came from these tiny peasant plots—they provided quite a contrast to those pillboxes that would eventually rise in their places.

In the old days, before the revolution, the peasants going off to the fields used to leave their doors unlocked and food set out on the table in case anyone happened by. But then the Bolshevik grain-confiscating squads had happened by, and the peasants had started locking their doors. Probably because of his peasant roots, Piotr Borisovich had talked a great deal about the subject during his stay at the Potter's school. The trouble, he would say, his voice reduced to the soft purr he used when he felt deeply about something, was that the Bolsheviks, being city-bred and city-oriented, never quite knew what to do with the eighty percent of the population that lived outside the cities. The peasants were the enemy, the Potter would explode. In their heart of hearts, they were all capitalists—they wanted to *own* the land they worked. What they wanted—Piotr Borisovich would shake his head in disagreement—was to *own* the *crop* they harvested, and not have it carted off without compensation to feed the workers in the cities.

They hadn't seen eye to eye on everything, the Potter and Piotr Borisovich, but their differences only seemed to bind them closer together—to reinforce the notion, foreign to Soviet Russia, that holding different opinions was perfectly normal.

Arriving at Peredelkino, the Potter walked the four kilometers along a rutted road from the depot to the peasant's cottage the old man had moved into. "I always wanted to water, and be watered," he had said then, but he had been exhibiting symptoms of senility already, or at least that's what they had claimed when the theoretical journal for which he worked decided it was time for him to retire. The Potter himself had never been convinced that the old man's wandering mind—he alighted on subjects like a butterfly, and left a butterfly's imprint on them—was worn thin. It might just as well have been his way of coping with a world glued together by a peculiar attitude toward power: confronted by hypocrisy, people simply shrugged.

The old man, whose name was Boris Alexandrovich Revkin, had had a good run for his money. He had worked his way up to become a division propagandist in the Red Army during the Great Patriotic War, and had gone to work after the war as an editor for a well-known theoretical journal. One of his early articles dealt with something called "left deviationism." In it, Revkin had used the expression "political narcissism" to describe the Chinese Communist leadership. When asked, at the weekly editorial meeting, where he got the expression, he had replied, "Why, where else, I invented it!" The chief editor, who had made his reputation by taking a single line from Marx and writing a four-hundred-page book on it, had laughed outright. "If all you want are lines out of Marx and Lenin,"

Revkin had cried indignantly, "get someone else to do it."
Assuming that his audacity indicated he had friends in high
places, the chief editor shipped the article over to the Central
Committee for a decision. When it came back, four months
later, it contained a handwritten notation in the upper-left-
hand corner. "Publish," it read, followed by an initial: "S."

Which is how Boris Alexandrovich Revkin became the
Soviet Union's resident expert on "left deviationism."

His spine curved into the shape of a parenthesis by his
years of harvesting cotton, the old man was on his hands and
knees weeding between the green peppers in his vegetable
garden when the Potter, his collar open, his suit jacket slung
over his shoulder, finally arrived. The sun, sinking through a
stand of white birches, dispatched slats of yellowish light across
the ground. Revkin looked up, squinting into the light, and
spotted the Potter mopping the perspiration off his neck with
his handkerchief. "Contrary to appearances," the old man
cackled, struggling to his feet, wiping his palms on his overalls,
masking behind a studied briskness his pleasure at seeing the
Potter, "sunsets don't grow on trees. What brings you all this
way, Feliks? You have news of Piotr, maybe?"

"No news," the Potter said quickly. "What brings me all
this way is you." He fished one of Svetochka's bottles of Bison
vodka from his jacket pocket and handed it to Revkin. "A
small present," he mumbled in embarrassment.

"Ha! Now I know you want something!" cried the old
man, hopping over a row of baby cabbages, snatching the
bottle from the Potter. He led the way to his cottage, lighted
the stove, put some water to boil on it. When it grew dark he
closed the shutters, served tea (which he himself drank, peasant-
style, through a lump of sugar wedged between his teeth),
eventually reheated some cooked cabbage with chunks of meat
in it, on the assumption, which the Potter never challenged,
that his visitor would stay the night. In time the vodka, served
with the meal, loosened the old man's tongue and he began to
reminisce, his words slurred, his voice hoarse, about what he
called the bad old days: the Big Mustache (Stalin) and the Little
Mustache (Hitler); the exhilarating struggle against the *Nemtsi*,
the tongueless ones, the Germans; the endless double lines of

beardless farmboys in gray caps with thick winter longcoats rolled and strapped on their backs making their way through ruined villages as delayed-action mines exploded in the distance; two teenagers with signs around their necks saying they had been collaborators, hanging by their twisted necks from tree limbs. The end of one story tugged at the beginning of another. His well of memories had no bottom.

Stretched out on a battered couch, the Potter nodded off, then woke with a start to hear the old man droning on. "I knew the Germans would lose the war," he was saying, "but not because of the reasons we used to give in our newspapers. They were going to lose the war—are you paying attention, Feliks?—because their ultimate goal wasn't to win it, but to fight it. Do you follow the distinction, Feliks? If they had wanted to win the war, you see, they would have mobilized everybody who could have helped, instead of eliminating them in death camps. To me it was always as evident as the nose on your face, Feliks. They wanted to lose the war and bring the world crashing down on their heads like dishes spilling from a shelf. They were acting out myths"—the old man poured the last of the vodka into his glass and tossed it off—"but then, in one way or another, all of us are acting out myths. You. Me." A distant look came into his ancient eyes. "Piotr even. Even Piotr." The old man cackled gleefully. "Especially Piotr. I always said he was meant to be a prince, or to kill a prince. I was never sure which. What do you think, Feliks? . . . Feliks?"

The old man gently drew a cover over the Potter, stoked the fire, carefully allotted two more logs to it, and shuffling off to his bed in the far corner of the room, drew the Army blanket that served as a curtain and went to sleep himself.

The Potter woke up in the pitch darkness and heard the old man snoring from behind the curtain. Moving quietly, he struck a match, lighted a candle and made his way into the unheated room that Revkin used to store his vegetables for the winter. He found the loose floorboard without any trouble, pried it up with a kitchen knife and retrieved the package wrapped in a woman's kerchief. He unfolded the cloth and examined the contents. It was all there. He had hidden it away years before, when he had returned from his tour in New

York. At the time he had been riding high, and the precaution had been a professional reflex; an act of tradecraft that wasn't spelled out in any of the textbooks; a hedge against difficult times that was second nature to people in his business. Later, when he had been obliged to retire as *novator* and move into a small apartment with another family, he removed the package from its original hiding place and stashed it away under the floorboards of the old man's cottage.

The Potter had started to slip the floorboard back into place when he noticed the second oval of flickering candlelight superimpose itself on the first. He turned to see the old man standing in the doorway, the hem of his nightdress brushing his bare feet.

"I knew it was there," he snapped, inclining his head toward the package. "And I know what brings you all this way."

"I would have come anyway—" the Potter started to protest, but the old man, smiling sadly, interrupted him.

"What brings you all this way, Feliks," he said, blinking away the film of moisture forming over his eyes, "is to say good-bye."

The Potter couldn't, didn't, deny it.

And then the old man astonished the Potter. "If you can get out the way Piotr got out," he whispered fiercely, "more power to you. My future is in my past. For you, for Piotr, there is still life before death."

The Potter was up and dressed at first light; he wanted to get back to Moscow as early as possible. He looked around for a scrap of paper on which he could jot a note. His eyes fell on the Army blanket that screened off the old man's bed from the rest of the room. It seemed incredibly still, as if there were no life beyond it. . . . The skin tightened on the Potter's face. He tiptoed to the curtain and peeled back an edge. The old man lay on his back, his mouth gaping open, his eyes, unblinking, fixed on the ceiling over his head. The Potter stepped up to the bed and placed a palm on Revkin's chest. He felt his rib cage under the quilt. It was deathly still.

Another myth acted out! And what timing. For the old

man had been the hostage that kept Piotr Borisovich on the straight and narrow. With him gone, the Potter would be free to betray his last, his best sleeper—and then, if he moved rapidly, save him from the results of that betrayal.

21

❦

Carroll's cheeks were swollen from having swallowed a candy with finely chopped walnuts in it, and Thursday had trouble making out what he said. Francis provided a running translation. "He says you are to touch base with the West Germans. He says it is a matter of protocol."

Carroll said, ". . . eason hem ang ound en u alk otter."

"He says there's no reason for them to hang around when you talk to the Potter."

"In other words," Thursday said, "I'm to skim off the cream, as we say in the trade, and leave the milk for them."

"Ite," Carroll mumbled.

"Right," Francis repeated.

"I'm to get three items from him," continued Thursday. He wanted to show that he had memorized his instructions. He ticked off the items.

". . . r ack eeee oes," said Carroll.

"Or back he goes," translated Francis.

"If he doesn't come across with the aforementioned items," repeated Thursday, "back he goes, on the next plane out, wife and all."

"Ite." Carroll nodded, touching an inflamed cheek with his fingertips to make contact with his twitching nerve.

"Right," Francis interpreted.

"Un ore ing," muttered Carroll.

"I got that," said Thursday, smiling brightly. "He said, 'One more thing.'"

Carroll glared at him over his half-empty box of candy. In the Company's early days, a good man Friday was seen and not heard. Still, they were lucky to have one as thick as

Thursday. If anyone could carry out instructions without really understanding what he was doing, it was him. "Ve eving," Carroll said, "u unicate ith *obody*, ot ven ector, out is."

Francis raised a pencil and tapped Thursday on the shoulder as if he were knighting him. "He says, above everything, you communicate with *nobody*, not even the Director, about this."

Thursday giggled excitedly. "Mum's the word," he said.

22

⚜

"You what?"

"Svetochka couldn't abandon them like that, Feliks," she pleaded. "They would die of dehydration."

The Potter strained to control himself. No matter how many times he went over it with her, she still didn't seem to grasp the situation. They had to walk out of the house as if they were coming back in two hours, and avoid at all costs making it appear that they were going away for a long time. Not to mention forever! "What exactly did you tell them?"

"Svetochka didn't tell them anything," she insisted, fighting back tears. "Svetochka only asked them to water the plants."

Above all, he must not make her nervous, he reminded himself. "It is not serious," he told her. "They may think we are going to visit the old man in Peredelkino for a day or so."

Svetochka breathed a sigh of relief. "About my sister," she started to say, but the Potter cut her off.

"Not a word," he ordered. "News travels fast. If you tell her, she will phone up her husband, and his brother works as a Merchant for the Center and will immediately suspect something if he hears I am leaving the country. You can always send her a picture postcard from Paris," he added.

"Paris," she repeated wistfully, her round face relaxing into a distant smile. "Will she be jealous!"

It wasn't the easiest thing in the world to turn your back and walk away from everything you had, you knew, you were. The Potter understood this more than most people. He had discussed it at great length with Piotr Borisovich before he had turned *his* back (albeit on assignment). They had come to the conclusion that you had to bring something with you from your past, no matter how insignificant it was, in order to get a hook into the future. It provided a transition. It helped you keep your sanity when you finally realized that none of what was happening to you was a dream—or a nightmare. When his time came to leave, Piotr Borisovich had taken with him a small, well-thumbed American paperback edition of Whitman poems, with the lines they both loved, the ones about the sisters Death and Night, underlined in pencil.

The Potter too had given in to the temptation of traveling with a security blanket. Locking up his attic workroom, he had treated himself to a last look around. It had meant a great deal to him, his workroom, especially since he didn't have an office to go to anymore. If he took something with him, he decided, it would come from here. He was sorry to leave his wheel behind—he had constructed it himself from a kit imported from Finland—but there was nothing to do about that. He would buy a new wheel in the West, an electric one maybe, whose speed was controlled with a pedal. His eye had fallen on the length of wire he used to cut his pots off the wheel. Piotr Borisovich had made it for him with a middle A string from an old piano, and a thick piece of bamboo at each end to grip it with. On the spur of the moment, the Potter had pocketed the wire, switched off the bulb and left.

"You are absolutely positive there is no danger?" Svetochka asked him for the hundredth time as they prepared to leave the apartment. She was wearing her highest spikes and her shortest skirt, which was her idea of how women looked in Europe.

"There is no danger as long as you do precisely what I told you," the Potter promised her. He wondered, even as he spoke, if it were true.

"Paris," Svetochka repeated under her breath, as if the mere mention of the word could still her doubts, calm her nerves, give her the nervous energy she needed to cross thresholds. And the Potter understood that what she carried with her from her past in order to get a hook into the future was her longing for something that, until now, she could never have.

The little man with the shirred skin was waiting behind the wheel of the taxi parked in front of their door. Seeing the Potter and his wife, he crooked his emaciated finger in their direction. When they had settled into the back seat, he tipped his hat to them in the rearview mirror. The last time the Potter had seen this gesture, the little man had accompanied it with a mischievous wink. Now he exhibited all the formality of an undertaker. "I am told," he said over his shoulder, throwing the taxi into gear, drifting out into traffic, "that you are going to the Holy Land."

Svetochka glanced quickly at the Potter, but he cut off her protest with a warning look.

"We are not paid for what we do," the little man continued intently, "we are volunteers. Getting Jews out of Russia is God's work. I take it as an honor to be part of Oskar's organization."

"How many have you gotten out?" the Potter asked politely.

The little man preened behind the wheel of the taxi. "I myself have been involved in fourteen confutations before you two." He laughed self-consciously. "For reasons I have never fathomed, that is what Oskar calls it when we smuggle someone out of the country. A confutation."

The little man's use of the word "confutation" had a calming effect on the Potter. It was a professional term, and reinforced the impression that Oskar was the professional he claimed to be. And getting out of Russia would very much depend on Oskar being a professional.

The little man maneuvered the taxi through afternoon traffic. He drove slowly, cautiously, observing every sign, signaling every turn until he came to a light turning red. Accelerating sharply, he shot across the intersection.

"Nicely done," the Potter observed, and he turned to look at their wake. Nobody was following them.

The Potter noticed that they were heading in the opposite direction from Moscow Airport, but he said nothing. "Listen carefully," the driver called back over his shoulder. "There is a pedestrian island ahead, where the peripheric becomes Valovaya." He glanced at the dashboard clock. "We are right on schedule," exclaimed the little man. "I will pull over. You will get out and jump across the island into the taxi you will find waiting on the opposite lane."

The pedestrian island came into view ahead. "I wish you both Godspeed," the little man cried in an excited, high-pitched voice as he braked to a stop next to the island. The traffic piled up behind the taxi. Drivers leaned on their horns in annoyance. The Potter jerked open the door on his side, pulled Svetochka from the back seat and practically dragged her across the island into the back seat of the taxi that was headed in the opposite direction. Without waiting for the door to close, the driver—it was the squirrellike man who had kept a scarf over his lower jaw the first time the Potter had set out to meet Oskar—floored the gas pedal and propelled the taxi into the traffic flowing through the peripheric.

The Potter twisted in his seat to look behind them. The tradecraft was fairly elementary, but extremely efficient. One instant you were going in one direction. The next instant you were off in the opposite direction. If someone were following you, he'd have to make a highly visible U-turn.

Nobody did.

"We are as clean as the freshly scrubbed ass of a baby," the driver, who had been studying his rearview mirror, said after a moment. He turned south at the next crossroad. The taxi passed under a sign that indicated the airport was dead ahead.

They crossed a circus caravan heading into the city, with several overweight lions lazing in cages in flat trucks, and the head of a giraffe projecting over the cab of a large van. Several dozen open trucks filled with cabbages and early apples from nearby collective farms were backed up behind the caravan. The highway widened as they got closer to the airport. It was six lanes, three in each direction, when they finally spotted the hangars and control tower and radars and turned off onto the flat approach road.

"The meter is running," the driver reminded them in a tight voice. He adjusted his scarf so that it covered the lower part of his face. "Be sure to pay me when I let you off—it looks more natural that way. And for God's sake don't forget the two valises in the trunk compartment."

"Svetochka is frightened," Svetochka suddenly whispered

in the Potter's ear. She looked as if she were ready to throw up.

"Think of yourself as an actress playing a role—two roles, actually," he whispered back. "You had the makings of a great star once. You can do it."

Svetochka swallowed. "Svetochka will try," she murmured.

The taxi slowed as it entered the circular driveway in front of the terminal and pulled up before the main doors. "Remember," the Potter instructed Svetochka, "you are a happy Russian wife off with her husband to the Black Sea for some sand and sun."

Svetochka drew a deep breath. Then, moistening her lips, flashing her most superior smile, she slipped into the role. "Do pay the man, Feliks," she ordered in a loud voice. "I don't want to miss a minute more of sun than I have to."

The Potter glanced at the meter and counted out some rubles. Then he went around to the trunk compartment and removed the two valises in it. The taxi roared away from the curb before the Potter could close the lid of the trunk compartment. A uniformed policeman farther along the curb called after the squirrellike driver, but he never looked back and he never slowed down.

Standing in the gutter, the Potter stared after the departing taxi, then started to carry the valises toward the door. From the curb Svetochka berated him. "Darling, there are porters who do that sort of thing."

The Potter dropped the valises and signaled with a forefinger. A porter strolled over and placed the two valises onto his dolly. "Domestic or foreign?" he asked in a sullen voice.

"Domestic," Svetochka told him. The porter nodded and wheeled his dolly off. The Potter and Svetochka fell in behind him.

Oskar's scheme was elegantly simple. Using their own internal passports and a set of genuine Aeroflot tickets for a flight about to leave for the Crimea, they would pass through the cursory checkpoint at the "Domestic" entrance. At some point two Americans (hired for the occasion by Oskar) with reservations and tickets for an Austian Airlines flight to Vienna would pass through the door marked "International" twenty meters farther down the driveway, where the control was more strict. There, frontier officers who spoke several languages not only checked passports and visas and currency forms, but cast an experienced eye over the traveler's valises and clothing; if there was any doubt, the passenger would be engaged in conversation.

Smiling broadly, chatting away as if she had nothing more on her mind than whether she had taken along enough bathing costumes, Svetochka presented their internal passports and their airline tickets to the guard at the door. He glanced at the photos on the internal passports and then looked up at the faces in front of him, lingered for a moment more than he had to on Svetochka, checked the date on the tickets, put a tick next to their names on a boarding list, and waved them through.

The Potter had the same relationship with airports that he had with telephones: he used them without enthusiasm. Once inside, he paid off the porter and retrieved their valises. Carrying one in each hand, he led Svetochka through the crowded hall toward the staircase that descended to the toilets. Downstairs, a janitor in overalls was backing toward them mopping the linoleum as he went along. Svetochka said, "Excuse me, can we pass?"

The janitor turned. It was Oskar. Svetochka gasped in surprise, then, recovering, started to bring her hand up so that Oskar could kiss the back of it, but abandoned the idea when she saw the frown of disapproval on his face.

The Potter had half-expected Oskar to turn up; he knew from personal experience that there was an irresistible urge to hover in the wings during any delicate operation. It was not so much a matter of making sure it went off without a hitch as of *taking pleasure* from its going off without a hitch. In Oskar's shoes, he would have done the same.

"So," Oskar said quietly, "you have only to follow me." He put aside his mop and led them to an unmarked, unlocked door. "Five minutes, yes?" he reminded them as they ducked into the small room in which the janitors stored cleaning products. "I will rap twice when the coast is clear." So saying, he let himself out the door on the other side of the storage room—which led to the toilets on the "International" side.

Svetochka and the Potter snapped open their valises. Inside each was a second, smaller valise, this one of American manufacture and plastered with old stickers in English. Inside the second valises were several sets of clothing with American labels sewn into them. They had been made to measure by the Jewish tailor that Oskar had taken them to. "Look at this underwear," Svetochka whispered as she stripped off her Russian garments. "It is genuine nylon!"

They quickly dressed in the new set of American clothes, fitted on their American shoes, pocketed their American passports and Austrian Airlines tickets to Vienna, and packed their old clothing away in the valises they would leave behind in the room. As a final touch, the Potter slung an American camera over his shoulder.

"How does Svetochka look?" Svetochka demanded, adjusting the pleats in her navy-blue skirt.

"You look, as they say in America, like a million dollars," the Potter told her. And he meant it. The Jewish tailor had dressed her better than she normally dressed herself. "Are you ready to play your second role?"

Svetochka nodded, and repeated the English phrases he had made her memorize. "What does he say? With his accent I can't understand a word." She smiled and asked in Russian, "How was that?"

"Excellent."

The Potter transferred the length of piano wire with the bamboo grips on each end to the pocket of his American suit jacket. While Svetochka put the finishing touches on her makeup, he checked to make sure the package he had recovered from the old man's cottage was securely wedged between several shirts at the bottom of his American valise.

There were two soft raps on the door leading to the "International" toilets. Oskar squeezed into the small storage room. "So: it is time to go," he said. He inspected them from head to toe. "You will easily pass for Americans. The plane for Vienna is boarding now. Surveillance is light. The two frontier specialists on duty are posted, as we knew they would be, at the front gate. The people at the Austrian Airlines desk will assume that if you got past the frontier specialists, you are the genuine article." To Svetochka he added, "If someone talks to you in English, just smile and repeat what Feliks taught you to say. Feliks will answer in English if he has to."

Oskar opened the door a crack to make sure that the hall outside the "International" toilets was empty. Then he motioned them out of the room. Carrying the smaller, American valises, the Potter and Svetochka climbed the stairs toward the main "International" hall. At the top step the Potter paused to look back. Oskar had turned away and was rinsing a mop out in a pail of water. There are no good-byes for people in our line of work, Piotr Borisovich had noted when the Potter accompanied him to the airport on the first leg of the voyage that would take him to his assignment in New York. The Potter had felt a lump mounting to his throat; he couldn't have said anything if he had wanted to. Piotr Borisovich had emitted a thin, brittle laugh and had stalked away. The Potter had stared after him for a long moment, wondering if they would ever meet again, then had turned back toward his limousine.

In the main "International" hall, the Potter led the way toward the Austrian Airlines boarding gate. From invisible loudspeakers a crisp voice announced in Russian, and then in German, that the flight to Vienna was now boarding. In the "Domestic" half of the terminal, Oskar's Americans, who had entered the airport through the guarded "International" door on one set of documents, would be boarding the plane to the Crimea using duplicates of the internal passports of the Turovs, Feliks and Svetlana, and a second set of tickets. When the boarding lists of the Crimea and Vienna flights were checked by the frontier police, everyone would be accounted for.

The Potter and Svetochka were passing the counter where babushka dolls of all sizes were being sold. The Vienna gate loomed ahead. Suddenly the Potter felt a hand on his shoulder. "Feliks?" a voice asked quietly.

The Potter turned and found himself looking into the unsmiling face of the dapper flaps-and-seals man from the sleeper school. He wore pointed Italian shoes and sported a hairline mustache on his upper lip. His real name was Grishka something or other, but everyone had called him Starets, or Holy Man, because he happened to have been born in the same village in the remote Tobolsk Guberniya of Siberia as the original Starets, Rasputin. It had been a standing joke at the sleeper school to cross yourself when you passed the Starets in a corridor. The last time the Potter had seen the flaps-and-seals man was during the sleeper school ceremony at which the Potter was handed an inscribed Czechoslovak wristwatch.

"Grishka," the Potter spluttered, mustering all the enthusiasm he could. He had never really liked the flaps-and-seals man; he was too obvious a Party hack, too ready to report snatches of idle conversation he may have overheard. "What on earth are you doing here?"

The Starets lowered his voice. "I am off to Vienna for a flaps-and-seals job." The Starets had been farmed out to local *rezidents* quite a few times during his years at the sleeper school. A local agent would want to get into a letter or a valise without the owner becoming aware of it. The Starets would be called into town for a one-shot assignment, opening and closing the flaps and seals so perfectly that nobody would know they had been broken into.

"And you?" the Starets asked. He nodded at Svetochka over the Potter's shoulder. They had met at various social functions held during the Potter's tenure as *novator*. To the Potter he said, "I thought you were on the Center's shit list."

"I am on assignment too," the Potter said quickly. The words just came out. He couldn't think of anything better to say.

By now the Starets was studying his clothing and his valise with its American stickers. His eyes narrowed. When he spoke, his tone of voice was guarded. "You are going to Vienna with *her*?"

The Potter had the sinking sensation experienced by cornered animals. He might have been able to convince the Starets that *he* was going to Vienna on assignment. But Russians in his position—Russians in *any* position!—were never allowed out of the country with their wives. The wives were kept back as hostages against their return.

"Last and final call for Austrian Airlines flight 407 to Vienna," the voice on the loudspeaker system announced.

"I am under orders to the Vienna *rezident*," the Potter

76

said quietly. "We are supposed to look like American tourists arriving from Moscow."

The Starets was openly suspicious now. "I don't believe you," he said flatly. "If what you say is true, I would have been instructed not to engage you in conversation and jeopardize your cover."

The Potter smiled thinly. "You are in the process of blowing an operation that has been in the works for a long time," he informed the Starets. "It was to make this operation credible that I was retired as *novator* of the sleeper school. If all this preparation is wasted, it will go hard on you."

The Starets insisted stubbornly, "I must check what you tell me with the Center."

The Potter came to a decision. "I will show you my orders," he said. "It will save you from looking like a fool." He turned to Svetochka. "Wait for me here," he instructed her. Motioning with his hand, he indicated that the Starets was to follow him. He led him down the stairs to the "International" toilets. Oskar, dressed in street clothing, was emerging from the janitor's storage room. "I need to use the room for a moment," the Potter told him. Oskar glanced sharply at the Starets. "It is all right," the Potter said, as if he were anticipating a question other than the one in Oskar's eyes. "I can vouch for him. He is the flaps-and-seals man from the sleeper school. I want to show him my Vienna orders."

Without a word, Oskar stepped aside and allowed the two men to enter the small room. The Potter went in first. The Starets followed. It never occurred to him to worry about his safety. He was a head taller than the Potter, and a good deal huskier; on top of everything, he was a member of the Moscow Center's amateur karate team. Inside, the Potter removed his ticket pouch from his breast pocket, took out the ticket, and handed it to the Starets. "Hold the next-to-last page up to the light," he ordered him. "There is a travel authorization, an unlimited-funds authorization, an access-to-codes authorization. You will recognize the signature."

The Potter said it all with such authority that the Starets began rehearsing what he could say to explain his interference in an ongoing operation. The *novator* had been fired from the sleeper school, not transferred to another directorate, he could argue. He was traveling with his wife, a point that would be in the Starets' favor; nobody traveled abroad with a wife. It wasn't his fault if someone at the Center had failed to alert him that they were booked onto the same flight. The Starets held the ticket to the light and squinted up at it. Just as it dawned on him that no secret writing was emerging, he felt the strand of piano wire slip over his head and settle around his neck. He started to reach for it as the incredibly strong hands of the Potter, straining against the bamboo grips at each end of the wire, tightened it across his Adam's apple. The Starets attempted to scream, but all that emerged from his throat was a strangled gasp. There were karate movements that might have saved him: an elbow to the solar plexus, a foot lock that could send an attacker plunging sideways. But these were things remembered during intraservice matches. With the wire vise tightening on his neck, every instinct screamed out to him to wedge a finger between the wire and the throat, to alleviate the horrible pressure that was building up in his lungs.

His sight went first; suddenly he was blind. Then he lost control of his bowels. Then his muscles went limp.

The Potter let the lifeless form settle slowly to the floor, where it lay in a heap like dirty laundry. He reached for a limp wrist and felt for a pulse. Finding none, he retrieved his plane ticket, stared for an instant at the corpse, then let himself out of the storage room.

Oskar had disappeared. The Potter didn't hold it against him. Oskar had counted on getting the Potter and his wife out of the country without leaving a trace. No matter how things turned out in the small janitor's room, it wouldn't be healthy for him to stick around. For the Potter, everything now depended on when they found the body. If the Vienna-bound plane was still in Soviet air space, the Chief Directorate of Border Guards, a KGB department, had the authority to order it back to interrogate the passengers. If that happened, the Potter was doomed.

"You look as if you've seen a ghost," Svetochka whispered when the Potter returned. "What happened to your friend?"

"I made up a story about us being authorized to leave the country."

"And he swallowed it?"

The Potter nodded grimly.

"Then why are your hands shaking?"

"Come on," the Potter snapped. He hefted the two valises, one in each hand. At the counter, Svetochka presented their American passports and tickets as the Potter deposited the valises onto the scale.

"You are traveling light," the woman behind the counter said pleasantly in English, which she spoke with a thick German accent.

Svetochka smiled nervously at the Potter and articulating carefully, said, "What does he say? With his accent I cannot understand a word."

The woman behind the counter was too busy tagging the valises to catch Svetochka's mistake. She pushed a foot pedal and the conveyor belt started up, carrying off the valises. "Have a good flight," said the woman, handing the tickets and passports, and a pair of boarding passes, back across the counter.

"We will try," the Potter replied.

They boarded the plane, found their seats, strapped on their seat belts—and waited. "What if he comes on the plane and speaks to you in Russian?" Svetochka whispered worriedly.

The Potter stared out of an oval window at the uniformed border guard at the foot of the ramp. A civilian walked up to the guard and together they double-checked the manifest. One of them tapped the paper with the point of a pencil. A passenger was missing. Would they allow the plane to take off without him?

Svetochka plucked at the Potter's sleeve. "What if?" she demanded. "What if? What if?"

"He will not board the plane," the Potter replied woodenly.

"How can you be sure?"

The Potter avoided her eye. "I *am* sure."

Outside, one of the uniformed frontier officers who had been stationed at the "International" entrance trotted up with a list of his own in his hands. The three men compared lists. The civilian shook his head in puzzlement. Why would someone check in through the main entrance and then not show up at the plane? The pilot of the Austrian Airlines plane descended the stairs. There was a hurried conversation among the four men. The pilot glanced at his wristwatch several times. The civilian hurried over to the terminal door and plucked a telephone off its hook. The pilot boarded the plane and said something to one of the stewardesses, who walked down the center aisle counting noses. She reported the results to the pilot, who descended the stairs again. The civilian returned to the ramp. Gesturing toward the control tower, the sky, his wristwatch, the pilot argued with the three Russians. They listened, exchanged looks, raised eyebrows in indecision. Finally the civilian shrugged and signed the manifest; allowing a plane to take off with one passenger too few was not as serious as allowing it to take off with one passenger too many. The pilot bolted up the stairs and tugged the plane door closed after himself. Workmen in green overalls pulled the stairs clear of the plane. A moment later one of the engines coughed into life. And then a second.

As the plane started to taxi toward the end of the runway, the Potter reached into his jacket pocket to grasp his hook into the future—his potter's wire. It wasn't there! He patted the other pocket. It too was empty. His body melted into the seat. In his hurry to board the plane he had left his signature on the Starets' body.

At the end of the runway, the engines revved up. The plane's vibrations reached the Potter's bones. He gripped the armrest until his knuckles turned white. Looking out of the window, he caught sight of a red-and-white-striped wind sleeve dancing in crosscurrents of air. It looked obscene, first inflating and then going limp, then inflating again. He wished he could make love to Svetochka, and then was struck by the fact that each time in his life he had killed someone, his mind had turned to—taken refuge in—the thought of lovemaking. Perhaps murder and copulation were related in the same way that death and night were related. Perhaps they were sisters!

The plane lurched down the runway, and the Potter had the terrible sensation that his presence on board would prevent it from taking off. Had the Russians invented the ultimate method of keeping people in the country? Their guilt at leaving made the plane *heavier* than air! Just as he convinced himself that it was scientifically possible (people who are very frightened, Piotr Borisovich once observed, usually experience a moment of madness), the Austrian plane groped its way off the runway, sank back again, then lifted off for good. Under his feet, the Potter felt the comforting crunch of the wheels folding into the fuselage.

Now there was nothing left to do but watch the minutes tick by—and wait.

23

✿

The blind man examined the corpse with the tip of his thin white baton. "Strangled, you say?"

"With a length of wire," the police officer said brightly. As the local Ministerstvo Vnutrennikh Del (MVD) man, he had been summoned by the janitor who discovered the body. Now he was more than a little awed to find himself in the presence of two directors of the KGB's Department 13.

"So: strangled with a length of potter's wire," Oskar added pointedly.

"How can you be sure it is potter's wire?" the blind Cousin inquired.

"Because of the bamboo on either end," the younger of the two Cousins explained. "Potters use such pieces of wire to slice their pots off the wheel."

The blind man tapped his cane against the MVD man's leg. "That should narrow the problem down considerably," he noted. "The killer is obviously a potter. Moreover, to strangle someone of this size, he would have to have incredibly strong hands."

The younger Cousin saw what the blind man was driving at. "Potters have strong hands from wedging clay," he told the MVD man.

The police officer said, "The airport doctor who examined the victim estimated that he had been dead about half an hour. We've had two planes take off during that time—one to the Crimea, one to Vienna. Our potter might be on one of them. The plane to Vienna is still in Soviet air space and subject to our orders. I suggest we recall both planes immediately."

The blind Cousin snapped, "Out of the question." He

82

offered no explanation. The MVD man knew better than to seek one.

The younger Cousin asked the MVD man, "How long before the Vienna plane is out of Soviet air space?"

"I would say"—he made a quick calculation—"another hour and a half."

"Here are your instructions," announced the blind man. "You are to lock up this room and forget about the corpse for another two hours. Then you will note in your call book that the janitor has just informed you of the presence, in his supply room, of a dead man. You will investigate immediately. You will issue a report saying that he was strangled with a length of potter's wire, and you suspect he was part of a ring of smugglers that had a falling-out. Only that."

The local MVD man saluted the blind man and left the room.

The stench was becoming overpowering. The blind man found the door with his baton and ducked through it. The younger Cousin and Oskar followed him out.

Oskar quietly told the Cousins, "The Potter identified the victim as the flaps-and-seals man from the sleeper school. He was apparently booked on the Vienna flight, recognized Turov and became suspicious."

"No matter how meticulously you plan an operation," the younger Cousin said philosophically, "you can't foresee everything."

"It is precisely our business to foresee everything," the blind man snapped in irritation. His baton beat out an angry rhythm against a radiator. One year of planning had almost been ruined by a coincidence. "Still, this may work for us in the end," he said. He turned toward the younger Cousin. "I want you to make sure word of the crime appears in *Pravda*. Bury it in the middle of a story on the airport police so it won't be too conspicuous—a passing reference to a body found strangled yesterday in a storage room. Mention the only clue—a length of potter's wire." The blind man turned away and stared off into space with his sightless eyes. Revenge, the peasants said, was a dish that tasted better cold. He had waited long enough, and plotted carefully enough, and he would have his meal. "The fact that the Potter murdered a man in order to get out of the country," the blind man mused out loud, "will be useful to us when the time comes to go public."

24

Under the silver wing, the high Carpathians gradually flattened into rolling foothills. The plane banked and then leveled out over a vast plain. A meandering river came into view. The Potter pressed his cheek to the inner window; there had been moments right after the takeoff when its coolness against his skin had been the only thing that had kept him sane. "That must be the Danube," he muttered.

Svetochka free-associated. "The waltz," she said in an awed voice.

"The river," the Potter corrected her.

The plane banked again, maneuvering into its landing pattern. Vienna tilted into the frame of the oval window like a lopsided photograph. Every time the plane banked, it slid back into view, nearer, more distinct: cathedral spires, university towers, Hapsburg palaces, the famous Rathaus; a potpourri of styles (neo-Gothic, Italian Renaissance, modern Gothic, Greek); and one or two prominent buildings that Piotr Borisovich, who always averted his eyes when he passed any of Moscow's seven grotesque Stalin Gothics, would have laughingly referred to as neoridiculous.

Svetochka drank it all in over the Potter's shoulder—the terminal, its roof garden with people waving happily, the planes with exotic markings parked along the tarmac—as they touched down, taxied and then braked to a stop. Her eyes were misty with emotion, and she blew her nose noisily into a handkerchief that she plucked from the Potter's jacket pocket. "What happens when we get off the plane?" she whispered.

"What happens when you go into the sea?" he replied cryptically. "You get wet."

Svetochka tossed her head in exasperation. "Will we be met is what Svetochka wants to know."

"We will be met," said the Potter, who knew the mechanics of things like this the way a watchmaker knows the inside of a timepiece, "by someone who will invite us to pay for our passage."

Sensing a storm building up in him, Svetochka nestled close and said very softly, "Svetochka is very glad to be here. Soon she will show you how glad she is."

The sun was sinking below the rim of the runway as they left the plane. The Potter spotted the welcoming committee the instant he stepped onto the top of the ramp. Any idiot could have. One was a little man who gripped a black umbrella by the middle and pinned his black homburg to his head with the curved handle so the hat wouldn't be carried off in the wind. The second, probably the junior of the two, judging by his position several steps behind and to the left of the little man, wore a long trench coat and black galoshes. The passengers filing off the plane were steered toward a waiting bus. When Svetochka and the Potter reached the tarmac, the little man with the homburg pinned to his head by the umbrella handle stepped forward. "Delighted you could come," he announced in an English thick with a guttural Bavarian drawl.

"What does he say?" Svetochka asked, dutifully pronouncing her memorized lines. "With his accent, I can't understand—"

"He wants us to follow him," the Potter whispered in Russian. Steering Svetochka by an elbow, he followed the little man toward a small pickup truck parked on the other side of the plane.

The procession passed under the plane. Water glistened on the silver belly; to the Potter, it looked as if the plane was sweating. Two other Germans in trench coats were waiting next to the open rear doors of the small pickup truck. The Potter and Svetochka climbed into the back and sat down on a low metal bench. Outside, the man wearing the homburg and the two others talked in undertones. Ten minutes went by. Eventually Galoshes arrived and hefted the two American valises plastered with labels into the pickup. Then he and Homburg took their places on the metal bench across from the

Potter. Nobody said a word. The rear doors were slammed closed and locked. The other two Germans climbed into the front seats. The motor turned over. The pickup was thrown into gear and began to crawl across the runway toward the other side of the airport.

They rolled along for several minutes. They must have passed close to the end of the runway, because they heard the stutter of propeller engines revving up for a takeoff, and saw, through the small scarred rear window, the flashing green of a starboard wing light. After a while the pickup came to a stop. The Potter could make out men talking quietly in German, then the sound of an entrance in a chain-link fence being pulled back.

Svetochka looked at him in bewilderment. "And Paris?" she asked plaintively. Inhibited by the silent stares of the two Germans, she shivered and drew closer to the Potter.

The pickup stopped before the giant doors of an enormous hangar. The driver came around and opened the back door. Svetochka started to slide out, but Galoshes put a restraining hand on her arm. "Only him," he said. Looking the Potter in the eye, Homburg nodded toward the open door.

"You will wait for me here," the Potter told Svetochka in Russian. He patted her knee on his way out of the pickup.

"What is happening?" she called after him in fright. "Why can't Svetochka come with you?"

Dusk was settling over the distant runway like soot. Some mechanics in overalls were working on the motor of an airplane nearby, but they didn't look up. The driver put his shoulder to the giant door and rolled it back enough for the Potter to slip into the hangar. Then he pulled the door closed with a resounding clang.

The hangar was empty; not a person, not a plane, not a vehicle of any kind was in sight. The Potter had a sudden urge to yell and hear his voice come back at him from a far corner. A narrow steel staircase climbed up one wall to a balcony with half a dozen small offices on it. The doors of the offices were made of frosted glass. A light burned in the second office. Mounting the steps, listening to his own footfalls echoing through the hangar, the Potter homed in on the light. He reached the door, pushed it open and entered.

Hunched behind a metal desk, a thin young man with protruding amphibian eyes peered up at the Potter through round steel-rimmed eyeglasses. He seemed to be on the verge of giggling, which made the Potter wonder if he had somehow missed the humor in the situation. Beware of people who laugh in the wrong places, Piotr Borisovich had once quipped; they are more dangerous than those who don't laugh in the right places.

"You will be the American," the Potter said in Russian.

The thin young man was in fact the Sisters' man Friday. "What makes you think I am American?" he asked. He spoke fluent Russian, but with a pronounced Brooklyn accent.

"There is always an American at the end of the line," the Potter said moodily. "Besides, Oskar spoke about his people collecting money for the information I would provide." The Potter lowered himself into a folding metal chair. "The only ones with money to spare these days are the Americans."

Thursday didn't find this comment to his taste. "You miss the point if you think of this in terms of money," he observed. "We are fighting atheistic international Communism—"

The Potter cut him off with a wave of his hand. "Spare me, if you please, your Sermon on the Mount."

The skin on Thursday's neck reddened. "Your kind could do with a little bit of Sermon on the Mount!" He burst out giggling. "Suppose," he suggested in English, a gleam in his protruding eyes, "we talk turkey."

"Suppose," the Potter agreed, though he was not quite sure what the expression meant. Reluctance welled up in him like bile. Betraying Piotr Borisovich into the hands of this giggling preacher who sat across the desk from him seemed . . . grotesque! If he could stall long enough, he still had the package he had recovered from the old man's cottage.

"As I understand it," Thursday continued, switching back to Russian, leaning across his desk, flicking his tongue over his lips in expectation, "you are to show your appreciation for your deliverance by giving me three items of information."

"That is not the order of things I had in mind," the Potter

said. "Before I pay my way, I will want some indication from your superiors"—his way of saying that he considered Thursday too junior to deal with—"concerning my and my wife's future." ("My future," Piotr Borisovich once exclaimed in a moment of intense depression—he had been quoting the poet Akhmatova at the time, and his words had made a deep impression on the Potter—"is in my past." Curiously, the old man had used the same expression the night he died.)

Thursday started to giggle again when a telephone hidden away in a desk drawer rang. He yanked open the drawer and placed the telephone on the desk. It was one of those old-fashioned European models, black, with a second earpiece that you could unhook and hold to your free ear. "Yes," Thursday said into the mouthpiece in English, staring all the time across the desk at the Potter with his goiter eyes. He listened to the voice on the other end of the line. "I see," he said slowly. "Really," he said. "With a length of potter's wire?" he said. He clucked his tongue. "I wonder who could have done such a naughty thing," he said. "I appreciate the call," he said. He dropped the receiver onto its cradle and hooked the earpiece back into place. "Well," Thursday observed, "that more or less changes everything, doesn't it?"

There was a commotion in the hangar below. Svetochka's stiletto heels beat out a panicky rhythm as she raced up the steel staircase. Homburg and Galoshes pounded up the steps after her. All three burst into the room. Svetochka lurched into the Potter's arms. Homburg, his face beet red from exertion, said, "She started to scream something about wanting to see him. There were workers around. I didn't want to attract attention, so I let her come in. She saw the light and ran up before we could stop her."

Thursday waved Svetochka to another of the folding metal chairs. She sat on the edge of it and crossed her legs. Thursday was distracted by the glimpse of thigh. "To pick up where we left off," he told the Potter, slipping into his Brooklyn-accented Russian, "you were on the verge of disclosing to me three items of information."

The Potter felt as if the four walls were pressing in on him. Voices suddenly reverberated. The bulb overhead seemed unbearably bright. These were things that happened in night-mares. If only this *were* taking place in a dream; in a nightmare even! "I am ready to cooperate," he replied carefully, feeling his way, "as soon as we have established the framework within which each increment of cooperation is compensated by an increment of . . ."

Thursday was giggling excitedly. "You sound like a law-yer playing for time, but that is the one thing you don't have. Time, friend, is what you've run out of. An Aeroflot flight for Moscow leaves here in"—he peered at his wristwatch—"twenty-seven minutes. You and the young lady will be placed on that plane by my associates here unless you supply me with the information I want."

It dawned on Svetochka that the young man leering at her through round lenses was proposing to send them back. "You know, Feliks, you must tell him," she whispered in the voice of a schoolteacher instructing a stubborn pupil.

"Our Russian friends," Thursday continued, "will be only too happy to get their hands on you. It seems that they are investigating a murder that took place in the airport just before the plane you were on departed. A man was strangled to death in a storage room near the toilets. The only clue was a length of potter's wire found next to the body. During the war, if I remember correctly, strangling was your trademark—"

"Feliks!" Svetochka breathed. She sat back on her folding metal chair and stared at the Potter. She was very frightened. "If you go back," she moaned, "they will say that I was your accomplice. They will put both of us up against walls and shoot us!"

Thursday sensed the moment had come to mix in a carrot or two. "As soon as you've given me the three items that were agreed upon," he told the Potter in what he thought was a soothing voice, "we will arrange for you to be taken to a small hotel in Vienna. You will be very comfortable. You will un-dergo the usual debriefing. At the same time, concrete arrange-ments will be made for your future. It is understood by everyone concerned that you will eventually want to settle in Paris." Thursday waved an arm at Homburg and Galoshes, and they backed out of the room, closing the door behind them. "Paris,"

Thursday added, as if it were the detail that could tip the scale, "is supposed to be beautiful in the fall."

"For God's sake," Svetochka cried, "for *Svetochka's sake*, tell him what he wants to know."

Thursday fought down an urge to giggle; his face contorted as if he were suppressing a yawn. He spread his hands awkwardly, palms up, as if to say: It is up to you, friend.

25

Carroll's cheek muscle had gone on another rampage. Francis felt giddy, as if he had flown too high without oxygen, or drunk too much champagne.

Carroll read what Francis had written on his yellow legal pad: "He is living under the assumed name of Peter Raven."

Francis reached for the pad and added, "The Potter would know the name because he was the one who worked out the legend with the sleeper."

Carroll brought a damp palm to his cheek to pacify the twitching muscle. "The awakening signal," he scribbled on his pad, "is a line from Walt Whitman: 'The hands of the sisters Death and Night incessantly softly wash again, and ever again, this soil'd world.' The i in 'Night' is to be dotted with a microdot containing the location of a dead-letter drop. The dead-letter drop will have in it an innocent-looking advertisement containing numbered microdots that give the details of the mission he is assigned."

Francis wrinkled up his face as if he had swallowed something bitter. "Thursday says the Potter selected as an awakening signal a line of poetry that both he and his sleeper admired," he wrote. Out loud he added, "Shows he had bad taste. Personally I never liked Whitman. All those unbuttoned shirts! All that hair on his chest! He was a poser. It follows that his poetry is a pose."

Carroll looked at the deciphered cable again. "The sleeper is living in a brownstone at number 145 Love Apple Lane in Brooklyn Heights," he wrote.

"Do we know exactly how the Potter knew that?" Francis asked.

Carroll carefully wrote out, "Thursday says the Potter received a picture postcard in the mail one day, with a photograph of the house on it, from his sleeper. Walt Whitman once lived in the brownstone. There's a bronze plaque next to the door. 'Here lived—' That sort of thing. The sleeper couldn't resist telling the Potter he was living in Whitman's house. So he sent him a picture postcard with some banal message on it."

Francis snickered. "Having a great time. Wish you were here," he said out loud.

Carroll did something he rarely did—he looked directly at the person he was speaking to. "We have gotten our hands on a perfect criminal," he said.

"I suppose we have," Francis agreed in a voice that held more than a trace of awe in it.

26

❧

Carroll was ignoring forests and lingering over trees: what form the awakening signal would take; how it would be delivered; where the first dead-letter drop would be (Francis was partial to country drops, which is to say places rarely frequented, while Carroll, who saw safety in numbers, favored city drops); how much money should initially be given to the sleeper (Carroll and Francis planned to finance the venture on a fifty-fifty basis); making arrangements at the inn in Pennsylvania (they had already procured the rifle; one of them would have to drive out and plant it there before the sleeper arrived). Nuts and bolts. Details. The kind of thing that bored Francis to death, but gave Carroll an orgasm.

As it was a Tuesday, Francis had stopped by his apartment long enough to change into more casual clothing, then had driven downtown to his favorite delicatessen for a hot roast-beef sandwich on rye with half sour pickles on the side. Later he walked over to the movie theater two blocks farther east and bought a ticket to see Elizabeth Taylor and Laurence Harvey in *Butterfield 8*. He had missed the film when it first came around, and was delighted to have a chance to see it. He got there early and had no trouble finding a good seat in the smoking section. The house filled up, the lights went out, the film flashed on. Not surprisingly, Francis had difficulty concentrating on the movie. Too many thoughts competed for attention in his head. Normal intelligence activities involved, at best, small triumphs—"taste treats" is what Carroll, thinking no doubt of his candies, called them—which gave the illusion of having some impact on current events. But only one in ten thousand—a Sorge, for instance, whose information from Tokyo permitted Stalin to thin out his defenses against the Japanese and concentrate on the Germans—really affected the course of history. Well, Francis too was going to affect history.

The music built to a crescendo. The image on the screen began to fade out. Francis extracted a cigarette from a pack and reached into his jacket pocket for a book of matches. He had given up smoking years before on medical advice, and only treated himself to a cigarette at the end of his regular Tuesday-night film. As always on these occasions, there was a single match left in the book. Francis used it to light his cigarette, inhaled, tossed the empty matchbook under his seat, and smiling as if he had nothing more weighty on his conscience than the death of a rodent, headed for the entrance and the warm, moist September air.

27

❧

The first people to arrive for the ad-hoc Damage Control Board meeting at the retired general's house were the Center's handymen. Wielding odd-looking devices that they plugged in and maneuvered like vacuum cleaners, they proceeded to "clean" house. What they were looking for were magnetic fields, the kind given off by hidden microphones. What they found was one earring, lost by the general's wife months before, and several coins that had slipped behind the cushions of a couch.

The general's study, on the second floor of a private house on Lenin Hills, had a splendid view of the city, and the guests who had never been up to the room before made appropriate noises of appreciation. A soccer match was in progress in the Lenin Stadium, across the river, and every once in a while a roar, not unlike the sound of surf pounding against a shore, wafted up.

"Does anyone happen to know the score?" the GRU man asked.

"One–zero in favor of Dynamo," announced the Central Committee representative, "but that was as of fifteen minutes ago."

"Did you catch the move the Bulgarian wingback put on the Dynamo goalie last week?" asked the lieutenant colonel representing the Party Control Commission. "His hips went one way and his body the other."

The KGB's Second Chief Directorate man offered around his pack of Chesterfields. "Will someone please tell me why is it we have a defection every time Spartacus has a home game? I'd like to know if there is a connection between the two."

"It's an American plot," quipped the GRU man, "to drive us crazy."

There was the sound of a thin baton tapping along the wooden floor. The people at the window exchanged glances. Department 13 of the First Chief Directorate usually sent someone over to these postmortem sessions in case of a decision to eliminate the defector. But for one of the Cousins to show up meant that they were dealing with no ordinary defection. "This could turn out to be more interesting than the soccer game," the representative from the Politburo whispered to the others.

The blind man found a seat at the long table with his baton and settled into it. The others in the room followed suit. The general, wearing well-tailored civilian clothes with an Order of Lenin conspicuous on his breast, limped into the room and took his place at the head of the table. "The score is one–one," he announced in a gruff voice. "Zhilov scored with a bullet from thirty meters. Anyone wants mineral water, help yourselves. Don't stint. I don't pay. The state does. What's on our plate today?"

The KGB's Second Chief Directorate man, the specialist on defectors, pulled a dossier from a plastic portfolio. "Turov," he read, "Feliks Arkantevich."

The general's eyebrows arched up. "The old *novator* from the sleeper school?"

"The same," acknowledged the KGB man. "He and his wife were booked onto a flight to the Crimea two days ago. Instead they wound up on a scheduled flight to Vienna. It all looks as if it was very well organized. It may have been the Israelis; Turov is a Jew. It may have been one of the émigré groups working on a German leash. Whoever it was supplied him with false papers, reservations, even two people to take their places on the Crimea flight."

"I assume you are looking into *how* he got out," the general interrupted. "The special area of interest of this board is what he took with him."

The KGB man shrugged. "Turov's been out of circulation for six months."

The lieutenant colonel from the Party Control Commission said, "He can tell them almost everything there is to know about our sleeper school—how we recruit candidates, how we train them, how we inject them into America—"

"It is unlikely he can tell them anything they don't already know," insisted the KGB man. "About twelve months ago one of Turov's sleepers went over to the Americans when he received his awakening signal. You chaired a damage-control session on him, General."

"If Turov has nothing of value to offer, why did someone go to all that trouble to get him out?" the blind man, sitting on the right hand of the general, inquired quietly.

"A pertinent question," acknowledged the general.

From across the river, a hollow roar drifted up from Lenin Stadium. A young aide in uniform dashed into the study and whispered something in the general's ear. "Two–one, Dynamo, on a penalty shot by Misha Tsipin," the general announced gleefully. He turned to the KGB man. "Why *did* they go to all that trouble to get him out?" he asked with exaggerated politeness. He had developed a theory when he received his first star that politeness, out of context, was appropriately menacing. "Surely he had something of value to offer them."

The KGB man turned a page in his dossier. "There is still one sleeper on the active list who was trained by Turov while he was *novator*. He is planted in America, awaiting the signal that will activate him."

"Does Turov know the identity under which the sleeper operates?" the General asked.

The KGB man nodded gloomily. "In the sleeper's dossier, the legend was typed. But the awakening signal was written in ink. We have ascertained that the handwriting is Turov's."

"To sum up," said the general, shifting uncomfortably in his chair because of his gout, "we must assume that the defector Turov is familiar with the identity under which the sleeper is operating, as well as the coded signal that will convince him he is being activated to perform a mission for Moscow Center."

There was dead silence around the table. The Central Committee representative poured a glass of mineral water and sipped it thoughtfully. The KGB man pulled his Chesterfields from his pocket. "Does the General object if I smoke?" he asked in a subdued voice.

"I most emphatically do," snapped the general. "Cigarette smoke stimulates bile, which poisons the blood and leads to attacks of gout. Ten minutes in a room with cigarette smoke and no amount of acupuncture can alleviate the pain."

The pack of cigarettes disappeared back into the KGB man's pocket.

The Party Control Commission representative remarked, "What good would all this information do Turov, or the Americans, assuming, as we must, that he conveys it to them, unless he knew *where* to find the sleeper? Before I was posted to the Party Control Commission, I was assigned to the KGB's Second Chief Directorate. I remember how these things worked. Once the sleeper passed out of the *novator*'s hands—once he graduated from the school to fieldwork—his dossier was taken over by the particular Merchant at Moscow Center who would run him. The sleeper's location in America would be known to the Merchant, but not to the *novator*—especially not to a *novator* who had been put out to pasture and no longer had access to dossiers of his graduates."

The KGB man nodded. "Our comrade from the Party Control Commission is quite correct. There is no way that Turov could be familiar with the sleeper's location in America. He could be anywhere, for all he knows."

The blind man tapped his baton against the leg of his chair. "Turov knows where the sleeper is," he stated flatly.

"That is simply not possible," the KGB man insisted in a nervous voice. "There is no way he could have had access to that piece of information."

The blind man reached into his breast pocket, extracted a brown envelope and offered it to the general. From beyond the window there was another roar, but nobody paid attention to it. The general pulled two pieces of paper from the envelope. "Photocopies," he said.

"Two sides of an American picture postcard," the blind man acknowledged. "These were picked up as part of a regular intercept program on foreign-source mail passing through the Central Post Office. The picture postcard in question was sent to Turov from Brooklyn, New York, several months after the sleeper was inserted into America. The awakening phrase in the sleeper's dossier, the one in Turov's own handwriting, happens to be a line taken from the works of the revisionist American poet Whitman."

"And the picture on the postcard," announced the general, examining it closely, "shows the facade of a house in Brooklyn Heights that Whitman once lived in."

"The message on the picture postcard," continued the blind man, "is not important. But the handwriting is—it's definitely that of the sleeper. He was informing his *novator,* despite express rules which forbid this kind of communication, that he had rented rooms in a building once occupied by Whitman."

"If Turov knows where the sleeper is in America," said the Party Control Commission representative, "this is very bad news indeed."

"It opens the possibility," said the blind man, staring sightlessly in the general's direction, "that the *novator* will convey to the American Central Intelligence Agency information that will permit its operatives to activate and control a Soviet agent in place. Once awakened by the proper coded signal, the sleeper will assume he is being run by his superiors in Moscow, and carry out his orders. Which means that the Americans have the potential of committing a crime—any crime—and then arranging for the blame to fall on us."

"The ideal solution to the problem," the general mused—he appeared to be talking to himself—"would be to eliminate the sleeper before the possibility you raise becomes a reality."

The blind man scraped his chair back from the table and crossed his legs. "We have two Canadians on tap in Toronto for an eventuality such as this. But the chances of their getting to the sleeper before the Central Intelligence Agency activates him are almost nonexistent. The CIA has had Turov for two days already. They will recognize the obvious advantage, the necessity even, of moving rapidly."

"Which leaves us with a potentially explosive problem on our hands," the general noted. His voice had turned polite again; he was extremely irritated.

"We are not without potential solutions," suggested the blind man.

The Politburo representative leaned forward. He was a classic case of someone whose importance derived from the fact that he reported back to important people. "Would the director of Department 13 care to be more specific?" he asked in a way that left the blind man little choice.

In his eagerness to know the answer, the general reiterated the question. "What are the potential solutions?"

"Like any good lawyer," explained the blind man, "we must construct our case proving that the CIA is responsible for the crime, always assuming one will be committed. To begin with, we have the defection of the *novator* of the sleeper school, the awakening signal, the legend, the copy of the picture postcard, all of which tend to support our story that the control of the sleeper was exercised by the CIA, and not Moscow Center."

"We will have a hard time convincing the world of that," the Politburo man said dryly.

"When the time comes to convince the world," the blind man said matter-of-factly, "we will arrange for someone inside the American intelligence community to testify on our behalf."

"This is within the realm of possibility?" the general asked, making no effort to mask his astonishment.

"It is within the realm of certainty," announced the blind man.

Later, while various participants were waiting in the foyer for their limousines to be summoned, the general hobbled over to the blind man and the KGB's Second Chief Directorate man. "I neglected to ask you whether there were any ongoing operations that were likely to be jeopardized by the defection of the *novator*. It is something I should include in my post-mortem report."

The KGB man shook his head. "We have no problems," he said.

The general directed his voice at the blind man. "How about Department 13?"

"Actually, we have one operation under way in America," he said. "We are running an agent, via a Cuban cutout. His principal mission is to neutralize some of the more outspoken anti-Castro people in the country."

"Wetwork?" asked the general, an eyebrow dancing up in interest.

"Wetwork," acknowledged the blind man, using the professional term for assassinations. "The agent is listed in your current operations portfolio under the code name Khanda, which is Hindu for 'double-edged sword.' As far as I can tell, the defection of the *novator* will have no effect on Khanda."

Another roar drifted up from Lenin Stadium across the Moscow River. The general's young aide came trotting into the foyer. "Dynamo scored again in the final seconds," he cried. "It's all over, with Dynamo on top three–one."

The general's face relaxed into one of those famous sour smiles he was noted for using when he appeared on television. "Let us hope," he remarked, "that all of our games end on a similar note."

28

Outside it was night; inside too—a "Ninth-month midnight," in the words of Whitman.

Mesmerized by the headlights, Svetochka had stared for the better part of an hour at the traffic on the Ringstrasse, the boulevard that circled the inner city. Suddenly she had drawn the thick curtains across the bay window with an angry jerk, cutting off the noise of traffic so abruptly it seemed as if a needle had been lifted off a phonograph record.

She had been pleased at first with the small hotel on the quiet side street off the Ringstrasse; with the subtle click of the desk clerk's heels; with the three-room top-floor suite; with the four-poster bed; with the cream-colored sheets and the enormous fluffy square pillows in lace cases. She had stripped to the skin in the white-tiled bathroom and soaked in the high tub for the better part of an hour, and then phoned down for tea and little cakes the size of fingernails. But when they arrived, lined up in rows on an oval silver tray, she discovered she was unable to swallow. Her throat had constricted, her stomach had knotted up.

"In fear," she burst out when the Potter insisted on knowing why. "Svetochka can't eat, Svetochka can't shit, Svetochka can't think straight because Svetochka is *afraid*!"

"Afraid of what?" the Potter pleaded with her. "We are safe here. The hotel is guarded. The top floor is sealed off. The Austrians, the Americans, they will not allow anything to happen to us."

It was at this point that Svetochka became mesmerized by the headlights on the Ringstrasse, and then jerked closed the thick curtains, creating a night inside the room to match the night outside.

"The Austrians, the Americans," she spat out, "can't protect Svetochka from *you!*"

"From me?" The Potter moved toward her, intending to take her in his arms, fumble for a breast, apologize profusely for existing.

Svetochka shrank back against a wall. She had always been aroused by the Potter's potential for violence; aroused even more by her ability to control it, tame him. But she had lost the thread of confidence. She stared across the room, imagining the Potter's hands molding themselves around her neck. Now that she knew they had been used to strangle someone, her skin crawled, her heart ached at the idea of being caressed by them. "Don't come near Svetochka," she whispered fiercely.

"What do you think I will do to you?" the Potter demanded.

Svetochka's breath came in short, desperate gasps. She fumbled for words. "I think maybe . . . you will . . . *hurt* . . . Svetochka."

The Potter's voice filtered out of the darkness as if it were a faint suggestion of light. "Are you afraid of night, Svetochka? Are you afraid of death?"

From the shadows along the wall, Svetochka moaned. "Aren't you?"

The Potter felt for the wall switch, found it, illuminated the filaments in the tiny flame-shaped bulbs in the overhead chandelier. In his official capacity as *novator*, he had once asked Piotr Borisovich the very same question. I live by Jung's dictum, his last, his best sleeper had replied without hesitation. Jung's dictum? (The Potter hadn't been familiar with it, Jung being *persona non grata* in the Soviet Union.) That the second part of life is ruined, Piotr Borisovich had explained, his head cocked, his eyes studying the *novator*, unless we are prepared to welcome death. "I welcome death," the Potter told Svetochka now, "as another in a long line of possible solutions to my problem."

After a while Svetochka calmed down, though she grew

tense when he got up to turn out the overhead bulbs; the filaments of light had become linked to the filaments of Svetochka's sanity. Seeing the expression on her face, the Potter left the light on.

Thursday rang up on the house phone to see how they were getting along. The Potter told him they were getting along nicely, thank you. Thursday asked if they lacked anything, anything at all. All they had to do was name it, he insisted, giggling nervously through the phone. You are too kind for words, the Potter responded in the tight voice that indicated he had taken an important decision. When Thursday hung up, the Potter announced he was going to shower, and beckoned Svetochka to follow him. In the bathroom he turned on the hot and cold taps full force to mask his voice from the microphones that were bound to be planted. He brought his lips close to Svetochka's ear. "I am leaving," he told her.

"Leaving?"

"Leaving you. Leaving here."

Relief swept through Svetochka's body at the thought of being rid of him. "Where will you go?" she whispered back.

The word emerged from the back of the Potter's consciousness. *"Anywhere,"* he said.

"You said the hotel was guarded," Svetochka said. She was desperate for him to be gone. The idea of being touched by him sent pulses of fear up her spine. "You think they'll let you simply walk out of here?"

"I have a plan," the Potter confided, and drawing her closer to the water gushing from the ornate taps, he told her what it was.

Her first screams, hollow shrieks that sounded as if they had originated in a tunnel, echoed through the corridor shortly after midnight. Thursday, barefoot, wearing a flowery silk ankle-length robe, scampered over from his room down the hall and pounded on the door. The Austrian squad leader and the four heavies on the night shift turned up moments later. All five had drawn their pistols. Svetochka, still screaming, threw open the door. She was stark naked. "We were making love," she gasped, flinging one hand modestly over her full breasts.

Thursday's eyes bulged even more than they usually did. "Calm yourself," he shouted excitedly in his Brooklyn-accented Russian.

Svetochka, the amateur actress, got a grip on herself. "I went into the bathroom to perform an act of feminine hygiene," she said with dignity. "When I returned to the bedroom—" She began sobbing, abandoning her breasts and covering her eyes with her hands to hide the lack of tears.

Thursday brushed past her into the bedroom. The Austrians crowded in after him. The bay window was wide open, the curtains billowing inward in the night air. "The son of a bitch jumped!" Thursday exclaimed. He gripped the sill and leaned over it. The gutter was illuminated by an old-fashioned curved lamp protruding from the wall of the hotel. Thursday stared at the street, trying to make out the spread-eagled body on the cobblestones. He wondered how the Sisters would take the news of the death of the Potter. The Austrian squad leader, leaning out of the window next to Thursday, muttered, "*Est niemand unten.*" He's right, Thursday realized. There was no body to be seen in the street below. He and the Austrian squad leader turned back to the room to question Svetochka.

Six floors below, the heavy front door of the small hotel on the quiet street opened, and a short, thick-set, dwarfish figure emerged. He was carrying a small American valise in his right hand. He appeared to hesitate for the barest fraction of a second, angling up his face to the night as if it were tangible, like rain; as if he intended to quench a thirst from it. Then he turned on his heel and strode off briskly up the incline toward the all-night taxi ramp at the edge of the Ringstrasse.

BOOK II

Death

Of course I can, Appleyard asserted. I can do anything. I can do snow falling. I can do smoke rising. I can do the sun setting. I can do someone dying. The last two are actually very similar. . . .

1

The American agent known to the Cousins by the code name Khanda picked up his visa from the Mexican consulate in New Orleans the last week in September, on the day the newspapers first ran the item about the forthcoming visit of the Prince of the Realm to a particular city. Traveling under the alias of Alek James Hidell, he set out by bus for Laredo, Texas, then strolled across to Nuevo Laredo and continued on in a Mexican bus.

Once in Mexico City, Khanda made contact with his Cuban cutout. Normally all contacts between Khanda and his Merchant were handled by the Cubans. But because the assignment was so sensitive, the rule was ignored and the Cuban set up a treff with the Russians. There were two of them. The first, named Vladimir Volkov, was the Department 13 man in Mexico. The other, the younger of the two Cousins who ran Department 13, had flown to Mexico especially for this meeting.

The first session took place in a seedy motel near the city's airport. The Cubans provided warm bodies to seal off the area. The Russians turned up with a bottle of decent Polish vodka and a five-hundred-gram tin of black beluga caviar. Khanda had grown particularly fond of caviar during the two years he had spent in Russia, so the meeting got off on the right foot.

Khanda was five feet, ten inches in height, lean, wiry even, with a look of grim determination etched into the thin lines of his mouth. He impressed people as being sulky, but the very few who knew him more than casually saw him as someone with a permanent chip on his shoulder, a score to settle.

Speaking Russian, the three chatted about Khanda's life in America. The Russians asked whether his wife had any idea of what he was up to. He assured them she didn't. She knew about the clip-fed rifle, fitted with the telescopic sight, that he had bought from a mail-order house in Chicago, but she believed his story that he used it for target practice. The Cousin broached the delicate subject of what had gone wrong the previous spring when Khanda tried to assassinate an outspoken anti-Castro military officer. "It was night," Khanda told them with a nervous shrug. "I couldn't see too well. I missed."

The Russians, both of whom were experienced in handling Department 13 field men, were careful not to bruise his ego. "It could happen to anyone," the Cousin said sympathetically.

Khanda produced the article he had clipped from the newspaper, and they talked at length about the Prince's forthcoming visit. Volkov flattened a detailed map of the city on a table, weighing down the corners with ashtrays. The three of them pored over it. Experts had studied the situation, the Cousin said. They had decided that there were two ways for the Prince to reach the luncheon site from the airport. He traced the routes with his thumb. The Prince could go down Main Street, turn onto the boulevard and proceed directly to the site. Or he could jog right off Main onto Elm Street, then head for the freeway and the site. "What you must do," the younger Cousin said, "is go there and study the two routes carefully."

Khanda, who had been trained at Department 13's secret espionage school outside of Minsk, squinted at the map as if it were a landscape and he was a gardener. "I have to find work in a building that will give me a clean shot at him no matter which of the two routes he chooses," he said.

They discussed, in very general terms, angles of fire, distances at which the Italian rifle fitted with the telescopic sight could be considered accurate, how many shots Khanda might reasonably expect to fire, escape routes from the scene of the crime and, eventually, from the country.

The room grew dark as the sun disappeared behind the airport hangars. Volkov drew the shades and switched on several lights. The younger Cousin handed Khanda an envelope filled with American money. "There's not too much in it because we don't want you to draw attention to yourself," he explained.

Khanda smiled faintly. "I don't need much," he said.

Volkov said, "You have two months to organize things."

Khanda said, "That should give me enough time."

The younger Cousin said, "We all know you're the best man for the job."

"If anybody can pull this off," Volkov chimed in, "it's you."

"I'll do my best to justify your confidence," Khanda said

The younger Cousin accepted this with an appreciative nod.

2

⚜

It had been a long time since the Potter's last, best sleeper had been called by his Russian name; so long, in fact, that to his own ear it didn't seem to refer to him anymore. His papers referred to him as Raven, a name that the Potter hadn't liked at all (even though it had the advantage of being close to his real name of Revkin) when they were working up his legend back in the sleeper school in Moscow. I would prefer something more common, the Potter had said, by which he meant a name that filled several columns, several pages even, in the local phone book, and he had come up with half a dozen suggestions: Carter, Jackson, Livingstone, Parker, Taylor, Turner. But Piotr Borisovich had insisted. It's me who has to live with the name, he had argued, so it's important I feel comfortable with it.

In the end the Potter had agreed reluctantly to "Raven," the name of the killer in Graham Greene's *This Gun for Hire*. To Piotr Borisovich, Greene's Raven had something of a fallen angel about him, which is roughly how he saw himself; like the Greene character, he fancied he came equipped with a sense of morality that belonged to another time, another place, which was a roundabout way of saying that he couldn't control what century he happened to have been born in, that it wasn't his fault if morally speaking he had to improvise.

For a long time Piotr Borisovich had been delighted with his new name, and the fallen-angel status that went with it. "Peter Raven," he would introduce himself boldly to women, doffing his hat, cocking his head, smiling with his eyes until little fanlike wrinkles formed at their corners. In recent weeks, though, for reasons he had not yet put his finger on, he had taken to whispering his old name to himself when he was alone, like some high priest murmuring the sacred name of God in the holy of holies so that the correct pronunciation would not be lost to posterity.

"Piotr Borisovich Revkin," the Sleeper whispered now, articulating each syllable.

"What was that?" Kaat called down. She was leaning over the banister at the top of the stairs, a forefinger nervously curled through the necklace of worry beads dangling from her neck. The blue point with the gray nose and gray paws sprawled at her feet, peering down, looking from one to the other as if she could follow the conversation.

"What are you doing here?" the Sleeper demanded. "You're supposed to be at work." He looked at her sharply. "Are you spying on me?"

"I thought I heard you say something," Kaat explained. She began to nibble on a fingernail.

"You're biting your nail again," the Sleeper told her.

"I'm hungry," Kaat said.

"You're nervous," the Sleeper corrected her.

"Have it your way," Kaat said. "What *were* you saying?"

"If it makes any difference, I said you were particularly imaginative last night," the Sleeper said. Again little wrinkles spread out from the corners of his eyes.

"Liar!" Kaat shot back. Then, "You think so?"

"I think so," the Sleeper acknowledged.

"How did you find Millie?" Kaat challenged.

"Millie I found . . . conventionally violent," the Sleeper replied thoughtfully.

"You like violence, don't you?" Kaat commented in a melancholy undertone.

"I like sex," the Sleeper corrected her, "and to the degree that violence is related to it, I *appreciate* violence."

The Potter, too, probably because of his own relationship with that bitch of a wife of his, had several times, in his conversations with the Sleeper, referred to the relationship between sex and violence. It turns you on, he had once suggested. (He had arranged for one of the Center's female stringers to come up to the Sleeper's apartment the night before, and was surveying the damage the morning after.) You mean violence turns me on to sex? the Sleeper had asked. I mean sex turns you on to violence, the Potter had said. The Sleeper had nodded moodily, acknowledging the insight. I'd give my right arm to know why you recruited me for the sleeper school, he had said suddenly; it was not something they had talked about before. I recruited you, the Potter had informed him, because you are a man of strengths. The Sleeper couldn't restrain a snicker. I see myself as a man of weaknesses, he had said, surveying the apartment in disgust. But the Potter had only shaken his head knowingly. Your principal strength, he had remarked, is that you are aware of your weaknesses.

"God knows why I go on living with you," Kaat called down from the banister.

The Sleeper shrugged. "Nobody's forcing you."

"Here's the thing," Kaat burst out. "I like the sense of mystery you convey. That's what drew me to you in the first place, the feeling that I could peel layers of you away, as if you were an onion, and never get to a center. But I admit it: sometimes you drive me straight up the wall." She started to bite a nail again, caught his look and stopped.

Wearing Indian sandals, a copper-colored miniskirt and a tie-dyed T-shirt with the word "Maybe" stenciled across the front, Kaat scooped up her cat (which she called Meow) and came tripping down the stairs. "I'm off to the mortuary," she announced, massaging her forehead with her thumb and third finger as if she were keeping a migraine at bay.

"Why don't you leave the cat home for once?" the Sleeper asked.

Kaat shook her head. "She doesn't like to be separated from me. You know that."

The Sleeper said, "I don't know how you do what you do."

"It's a job like any other," Kaat said. "Setting the hair of dead people pays better than setting the hair of the living. And it's a great comfort to the relatives to see their loved ones looking lifelike. Besides, I don't consider dead people dead. They're just in passage between two incarnations." Kaat turned back at the front door. The cat, nestled in the crook of an

elbow, purred with a dignified rolling of R's. "I almost forgot," Kaat said. "A letter came for you this morning. I left it
in the salad bowl in the kitchen on top of Millie's birth-control
pills." She smiled hesitantly in the Sleeper's direction. "I passed
my ring over your horoscope again," she told him.

"And?"

"It's pretty much what I told you last night. From the
twenty-seventh of this month until the thirteenth of October,
you are particularly vulnerable to anaxiphilia—"

"Another one of your A words," he moaned.

"Millie gave it to me last week. She found it in a movie-
magazine horoscope. It means the falling in love with a *schnook*
by someone who ought to know better."

"I don't see myself falling in love with anyone," said the
Sleeper.

You will never fall in love, the Potter had once told Piotr
Borisovich after they had had a bit too much vodka at a private
military restaurant. Falling in love is needing someone, and the
only person you need is yourself.

"I don't see you needing anyone either," Kaat told him
now. He glanced quickly at her, but she was already changing
the subject. "As for your physical safety, you should be particularly prudent on the ides. This month's are past, happily for
you. October's come on the fifteenth. November's are on the
thirteenth. Also, watch out for vicious circles."

"How can you tell a vicious circle from a normal circle?"
the Sleeper asked sarcastically.

"All circles," Kaat snapped with a flash of temper—how
could he be so thick as not to see it?—"are potentially vicious." Smiling vaguely at a fleeting thought, tucking the cat
firmly under her arm, she disappeared out of the door.

The Sleeper shook his head in frustration. She wasn't the
easiest person in the world to live with, this catlike Kaat
with her collection of words beginning in A and the sunken
eyes that stared out with an almost mystical intensity at the
world she could never quite get a handle on. She had been
violated once, the Sleeper knew; violated again when the man she
loved at the time refused to have anything to do with a violated
woman. More than once the Sleeper had seen her wince at

what he took to be the memory of pain. The thing she valued most in lovers these days—she made no bones about it—was kindness.

It was the thing the Sleeper gave her the least of.

The letter was where Kaat had tossed it. The address on the envelope had been typed out on a typewriter with a red ribbon. Peter Raven, 145 Love Apple Lane, Brooklyn, New York. The postmark indicated it had been mailed in New York two days before. There was no return address. The Sleeper held the envelope up to the light filtering through the kitchen window. He could see the outline of a folded piece of paper inside.

He didn't like the look of it. At all.

It flashed through his mind that maybe they had gotten wind of his living arrangements, that they were furious with him for drawing attention to himself when he should have been melting into the foliage of what people considered a more conventional sexual arrangement. Yet the Sleeper's *menage à trois* provided the ultimate cover, in the sense that it went against preconceived notions. Who would ever believe that a man living with two women was in reality a Soviet agent?

The Sleeper laughed out loud. He was jumping at shadows. It was ridiculous to think they could have learned about his roommates. Or that having learned of the situation they would risk communicating with him about it. The letter was probably nothing more than the announcement of the opening, on Pierrepont Street, of a new coffee shop where the local talent could read aloud poetry at night. Or another reminder from the Keep Brooklyn Heights Clean Committee to curb the dog he didn't own.

The Sleeper slit open the envelope with a kitchen knife, extracted the folded piece of paper and opened it. And the words, typed on the same red ribbon, leapt off the page at him.

. . . the hands of the sisters Death and Night incessantly softly wash again, and ever again, this soil'd world

So it had finally come! It was only now, reading and rereading the words, that he realized that in some distant reach of his brain he had nursed the faint hope that they might have forgotten about him; misplaced his file; restaffed the appropriate department with technocrats who preferred electronic gadgets to flesh-and-blood sleepers. Yet he was too rational a creature not to know that what had happened was inevitable. They hadn't brought him in from Frunze in Central Asia, educated him at Moscow University, trained him for nineteen solid months at the Potter's school, and then gone to all the expense and trouble of inserting him in America to forget about him.

Dazed to the point of dizziness, feeling as if he were groping his way across the vaguely familiar terrain of an unpleasant dream, the Sleeper took the letter upstairs to his attic workshop. He thought of the Potter kicking away at his Finnish wheel in *his* attic workshop. He wondered if he still used the piano wire the Sleeper had fashioned for him to cut his pots off the wheel. He wondered too if the Potter had managed to hold on to Svetochka; during the week they had made love together, she had told the Sleeper that she didn't plan to hang around forever with "the Jewish dwarf," as she called him.

Someone—probably Kaat, because she made a fetish of breathing fresh air—had left an attic window open, and the dozen or so mobiles that the Sleeper had in stock were all spinning wildly. It was strange, he was the first to admit, how he had been drawn to the business of finding fulcrums. The Potter had suggested it as one of many possible professions that would give him the independence he needed to function as a sleeper. The Potter had even offered to teach him how to throw pots, but from the moment the wild-eyed Uzbek had shown him what a fulcrum was, and taught him to weld, he had been hooked. Aside from its other advantages, being an artisan of some sort meant he wasn't on any payroll and attracted little attention from the government agencies that thrived on Social Security numbers, tax forms and the like.

He retrieved the flamethrower cigarette lighter from the cigar box full of old lighters, unscrewed the back and pulled out the thin cylindrical microdot reader. Working with an

Xacto blade and a tweezers, he carefully pried the microdot away from the dot over the i in the word "Night" and deposited it on the lens of the reader. Then he angled the cylinder up to the desk lamp. What emerged was a negative in which the printing appeared in white. "Piotr Borisovich," it said. (Had some sixth sense caused him to start pronouncing his Russian name out loud so that when he came across it in print he would know instantly that it referred to him?) The microdot went on to describe the location of a dead-letter drop in an alleyway around the corner from the old Brooklyn Eagle Building in Brooklyn Heights. (Whoever was getting in touch with the Sleeper obviously preferred country drops to city drops, a detail that the Sleeper took as a sign of high professionalism.) The message wound up with the words "much luck" and a postscript that read, "The Potter sends you his personal wishes for the success of your assignment."

So the Potter had a finger in the pie! It was a reassuring thought to the Sleeper, whose comfortable world of fulcrums had just been shattered. It meant that his father was still alive in Peredelkino. And it guaranteed that whatever it was they wanted him to do would be doable; the Potter would not have put his seal on the letter if it weren't. Spying, the Potter had drummed into the head of his last, best sleeper, was an exploration of the art of the possible.

The Sleeper went over to close the attic window, but instead found himself gazing out moodily over the carriage-house roofs on Love Apple Lane. He remembered staring out over Moscow from the open hotel window his last night in Russia. He had gotten roaring drunk on French champagne, and surprised himself by dredging up from some corner of his memory snatches of Moussorgsky's *Khovanshchina*. The opera had made him think of the three hundred *streltsy* lynched by Peter the Great on the monastery wall, and he had turned to the Potter and (suddenly emotional, though the Potter never sensed it, he was sure) had said: Violence is in our blood, violence and a passion for plotting. You and I, the Potter had agreed, are the last practitioners of a dying art. Funny how the dwarfish *novator* had gotten under his skin; funny also how he had made the filthy business of spying seem like a holy crusade.

It was curious he should think of the Potter now. Curious, too, that it should occur to him for the first time that the Potter had never held out the promise of a holy grail at the end of the holy crusade.

3

❧

For Piotr Borisovich Revkin, life had more or less begun with a holy crusade (the Great Patriotic War) and a holy grail at the end of it (to find himself, amid incredible slaughter, still alive). Revkin had been a strapping curly-haired fifteen-year-old who already shaved with his father's pearl-handled straight-edge when the local Party recruiters in Frunze, scraping the bottom of the manpower barrel, called up youngsters who *looked* seventeen. When the one-armed sergeant major who filled in the forms found out that Revkin spoke fluent English, there had been some talk of sending him to Moscow to translate the operating manuals that came with American Lend-Lease equipment. But then the sergeant major discovered why Revkin spoke English. His mother, it turned out, had been an American feminist in the mold of Emma Goldman who had emigrated to Russia in the early thirties to construct the future. She had been arrested and tried as a Trotskyite "wrecker" during one of the mid-thirties purges. Convicted of the specific charge of throwing sand into the gears of some factory equipment in order to sabotage Stalin's five-year plan, she had been dispatched to a Gulag camp, from which she had never returned. (Her last words to her son as she was being led from the courtroom had been an old Russian proverb: "To dine with the devil," she called in English over the heads of the guards, "use a long spoon!") Eventually a package of thick socks and lard that her Russian husband, Piotr Borisovich's father, sent her came back with "VMN," the Cyrillic letters for "Highest Degree of Punishment," stamped on it, indicating that the idealistic feminist had finished up in front of a firing squad.

To make sure that the same fate didn't befall the rest of the family—in those days, simply being related to a condemned person was *prima facie* evidence of anti-Soviet intentions—Piotr Borisovich's father had abandoned his job as a journalist, his apartment, his stamp collection, his hand-carved chess set (the last two were sold to raise cash), and had gone into hiding with his son on a cotton collective, where the work of harvesting was so backbreaking that the manager didn't ask too many questions of those willing to do it. In the course of four harvests the spine of the father took on a permanent curve. When Piotr Borisovich watched his father, bathed in sweat, bending under the weight of the bales of cotton, he swore to himself that one day he would make it all up to him.

In the end it was the war that "saved" them from the long arm of the vengeful Bolsheviks. The elder Revkin, making use of his journalistic credentials, went off to serve as a propagandist with a newly formed division. And the younger Revkin wound up as a front-line combat soldier.

About the war, Piotr Borisovich never said a word. Not one. To anybody.

After the fall of Germany, Piotr Borisovich, by then a war-weary veteran of seventeen, returned to Frunze, a sprawling city of low buildings and wide streets with narrow canals through which icy mountain water was circulated to bring temperatures down during the hot summer months. He was something of a local hero, which qualified him for a place in the reviewing stand during the May Day parade. On the breast of his worn Army tunic he wore the Order of the Red Banner, which made him, according to the Frunze Party newspaper, one of the youngest soldiers in the Red Army to possess the medal. He had earned it, the story explained, because of his exploits as a sniper; he had been officially credited with the deaths of one hundred and forty-four fascists, which didn't take into account the twenty-two for which he had no corroboration. The newspaper added the enticing detail that the young fascist-slayer always sighted on the jugular—and rarely missed.

For the next several years the Army sent Piotr Borisovich, by then a teenager with a ready, if somewhat sardonic, smile, around Central Asia giving marksmanship demonstrations to new recruits. He might have ended his days as a rifle instructor if it hadn't been for a sharp-eyed State Security talent scout who, one fine day, saw Piotr Borisovich place twenty-five bullets into a bull's-eye at a hundred meters and decided to take a look at the boy's dossier. When he discovered that Piotr Borisovich spoke fluent English, his interest turned to enthusiasm.

But in those days State Security did not simply approach a potential recruit and make a pitch. For reasons that had to do with the deep sense of insecurity of all successful revolutionaries (what would prevent others from following in their footsteps and toppling them?), the elders in the organization preferred to get a hook into a candidate first. The obvious hook in Piotr Borisovich's case was his father, who by that time was working for a well-known theoretical journal as its resident expert on left deviationism. The senior Revkin was suddenly arrested on the charge that he had failed to include in his dossier the pertinent detail that the enemy of the people to whom he had been married was American. It was at this point, with his father cooling his heels in Moscow's Lubyanka prison, that the younger Revkin was summoned to the local State Security headquarters for what he later laughingly referred to as a "friendly chat."

The three men and one woman who faced Piotr Borisovich across the table didn't mince words. With his war record, above all with his knowledge of English, the interviewers pointed out, Piotr Borisovich could eventually render considerable service to the Motherland. And the rewards, they made it very clear, would be generous: he would never have to worry about material things for the rest of his days. The young Revkin, anxious not to fall into the same trap as his father, said that there was no way he could accept an appointment with State Security, because he was the son of a convicted enemy of the people who had suffered the highest degree of punishment. One of the interviewers waved a hand. "We know all about that," he said. "Did you know that my mother was American?" Piotr Borisovich asked. "That too, that too," he was assured. "Did you know that my father is at this very moment in prison?" The interviewers exchanged looks. During the period of collectivization of agriculture in the early thirties, one of them said, his eyebrows arched to indicate he was conveying important information, all relatively well-off peasants were rounded up and shipped off to Siberia—their land, their animals, their houses, their equipment confiscated. The only exceptions were *kulaks* who had sons serving in the Red Army. The principle was established then: a son's service to the Motherland can mitigate a father's sin.

Piotr Borisovich signed on the dotted line, then raised his right hand and swore an oath of allegiance to the Motherland and the father figure who presided over it. Two days later he received a telephone call from *his* father. He had been released from jail, welcomed back to work at the theoretical journal, even given a small raise. And mystery of mysteries, a brand-new refrigerator that he had neither ordered nor paid for had been delivered to his tiny apartment. Was he going crazy? Or had Communism, in the form of a refrigerator for everyone, finally come to Russia?

Without even applying for one of the coveted places in the school, Piotr Borisovich received written notice that he had been accepted in Moscow University. He was assigned his own room in an apartment on Lenin Hills within walking distance of the university. Each month he found in his mailbox an envelope with one hundred rubles in it, an enormous sum by student standards. On the eve of school vacations, the amount was always doubled. Little was asked of Piotr Borisovich in return except to educate himself in the ways of the world. Every six months or so he was summoned to appear before a review board which met in an apartment in downtown Moscow (Piotr Borisovich never again set foot in a State Security building) to give an account of what he was doing. Why had this trimester's grade in the origins of Marxism-Leninism fallen below the previous trimester's grade? he was politely asked, as if his tutors had nothing more in mind than the sharpening of his intellect. What did he think of the three African students in his advanced English class? he was asked, as if his tutors were simply checking on the company he kept. Only once did Piotr Borisovich have reason to believe that the State Security organs were watching him more closely than he imagined. Did he ever hear anyone criticize the Soviet leadership? he was asked. No, he replied. Did the words "Russia is an intellectual wasteland" strike him as being familiar? He may have heard words to that effect, he admitted. Where? He didn't remember. Who uttered them? He didn't remember that either. Wasn't it the young professor of American poetry, the one who read Whitman aloud to his class all the time, who the previous week had said this to several students during a coffee break in the cafeteria? Now that they mentioned it, admitted Piotr Borisovich, it may have been. Then why hadn't he reported this anti-Soviet remark to the authorities? Because, Piotr Borisovich explained lamely, it had seemed inconsequential at the time. Don't let a lapse like that happen a second time, one of the tutors warned.

That night Piotr Borisovich got a phone call from his father. An odd thing had happened that day, he said. Two burly men had turned up at his door, flashed a paper he never got a chance to read, and removed his refrigerator. With all his food still in it!

Several days later, mumbling vaguely about how they had mistaken the number on the apartment door, the two moving men returned Revkin's refrigerator. The next time Piotr Borisovich heard an anti-Soviet remark, he reported it immediately to the authorities.

What with his hundred-ruble stipend and his apartment on Lenin Hills, Piotr Borisovich had no problem attracting a steady stream of women to his bed. No sooner had one affair ended than another was under way. At times, affairs overlapped; at times all three shared the same bed. During his last year at the university, Piotr Borisovich fell in love with an older woman whose husband, a doctor, had been arrested in what would turn out to be Stalin's last purge. Piotr Borisovich managed to talk her into going to bed with him, but when he phoned her to arrange a sequel, she refused. Furious, Piotr Borisovich began calling her up while he was making love with other girls and describing in precise detail what they were doing. He even passed the phone to his bed partners and had them describe events from their point of view. The doctor's wife wasn't turned on—but Piotr Borisovich was. Phoning up one lover while he was making love to another became his fetish.

If the tutors knew about it—and it was unthinkable that they didn't—they never brought up the subject at the semiannual review.

Why they had turned a blind eye to his fetish became clear after Piotr Borisovich was graduated from Moscow University. The Moscow Merchant who became his control obviously considered his sexual prowess to be a major part of his qualifications. Coached by his Merchant, Piotr Borisovich assumed the role of a young dissident writer living illegally (without a resident's permit) in a garret off Gorky Street in downtown Moscow. He would hang around the restaurants and hotel bars frequented by Western tourists, coming on as a frustrated literatus famished for any contact with the West, whether in the form of books, records, blue jeans or warm female bodies doused with French perfume. More often than not, within three days of meeting a single woman, Piotr Borisovich had an intense love affair going. The inevitable partings, with Piotr Borisovich vowing to smuggle love poems out of the country and the women promising to smuggle Western novels back to him, were arranged to give the female tourist the sense that she was running risks for love, not to mention puncturing holes in the infamous Iron Curtain. Weeks or months later, the unsuspecting women would receive a note, smuggled out of Russia by a "friend" of Piotr Borisovich's, saying that he had been arrested by the authorities because of his clandestine contact with the recipient of the letter; that they were now demanding that she cooperate with the Russians by providing relatively inconsequential scraps of information that she might stumble across at work; that he, Piotr Borisovich, preferred to suffer in a damp prison cell than have her run any risk for him; that his love for her would not be affected in the slightest when, as he thoroughly expected, she told the Russians to go to hell.

The ploy didn't always work, but it brought positive results often enough to provide Piotr Borisovich with a unique career in the KGB. When he wasn't operating out of his garret, with its mattress on the floor and its piles of well-thumbed American and English paperbacks strewn haphazardly about, he lived in a well-furnished three-room apartment across the Moscow River from the Kremlin, owned a secondhand Volkswagen, even had the use of a *dacha* set in a stand of white birches in a bend of the Moscow River an hour and a half down the Smolensk highway from the capital. He had girlfriends galore (who thought he worked as a courier for the diplomatic service, which accounted for the periods when he dropped from sight), more money than he could spend, access to the KGB's department store with its shelves full of Chivas Regal and Chanel No. 5 and Lucky Strike cigarettes (he ordered by phone; unmarked packages were hand-delivered to his door). The months, the years ticked pleasantly, painlessly by. It was difficult to see how life could have been better.

And yet in a remote corner of his consciousness, in a part of himself he had never dared expose, there was a hesitation; a shadow of a doubt; a vague feeling of having missed a boat. The uneasiness was especially strong when, on the rare occasions Piotr Borisovich found himself alone, he thumbed through an American paperback edition of Whitman poems and came again across the lines about the sisters Death and Night. Surely there had to be something more to it all before Death and Night rang down, like a fire curtain, on his life.

It was at this point in Piotr Borisovich's gloriously dull existence that he received the summons to report to a military hotel. It specified a date, an hour, and was signed with the word "novator," the one in charge. A sergeant in civilian clothes led him up to the third floor and opened what looked like a broom closet. It turned out to be the entrance to a secret staircase that led to a spacious apartment on the hotel's top floor. Finding himself alone in the apartment, Piotr Borisovich took a look around. In the middle of a coffee table was a bowl filled with American candy bars. An American record player, a Magnavox, stood on a shelf, along with an enormous collection of American records, everything from Nat King Cole to the latest Broadway musicals. Bookshelves were stacked with American magazines—*Newsweek, Time, Life, Esquire, Coronet, The Saturday Evening Post*—and copies of *The New York Times*, which (judging from the wrapper) were flown in daily from Helsinki.

Whoever lived in the apartment was obviously quite an Americanophile.

Piotr Borisovich was surveying the view from the apartment's windows—he could see the Kremlin towers, and Saint Basil's Cathedral rising above the Kremlin wall across the Moscow River—when he heard someone at the door. He turned. A man so short he appeared almost dwarflike threw the bolt on the inside of the door and then faced Piotr Borisovich. The man squinted at him for a moment, then said in English, "Could I trouble you to step away from the window. All I can see is your silhouette. It is not enough." When Piotr Borisovich hesitated, he added, "If you please."

Piotr Borisovich walked to the middle of the room. The newcomer made no move to shake hands. He motioned his guest to a chair, pulled up another one so that it was facing him and sat down. Their knees were almost touching. "I am not a devotee of Dostoevsky," the newcomer announced forthrightly. "But he has had a great influence on me. It happened this way: several hours after Nicholas I countermanded Dostoevsky's death sentence, Dostoevsky wrote a letter in which he said, 'Life is a gift.' With your combat record in the war, this is something that is surely embedded in the marrow of your bones. All life is a gift, and you are wasting yours."

"You think so?" Piotr Borisovich retorted belligerently. He was put off by the frankness of the approach.

"I know so," the visitor insisted passionately. "I know because I have been watching you—literally watching you! —for the better part of two years now. You are one of those people who thrive on tension; you are addicted to it, as if it were a drug and you needed a daily fix. I suspect that that is what got you through the war in one piece. You are uneasy unless you are living on a limb that could break at any moment. You are not too imaginative, not at all fanatical; you are a plodder who sees things through once he starts something." The Potter paused for breath. "Because of the execution of your mother, because of your experiences in the war, you tend to ignore the past and live in the present, though to keep your sanity you occasionally throw little hooks into the past—I am referring to your habit of phoning up a previous bed partner while you are making love to someone new." An apologetic grimace deformed the Potter's face. "You see, I have made it

my business to figure you out. I know everything there is to
know about you. I know about your father; I know how he
acquired his refrigerator, and how his spine got that curve in it.
And knowing all this, I am going to make you an offer. I am
going to propose to you a way of life in which you will do
what you do *well*, not for material rewards, not for the Motherland or the cause, not for the sex, not even for your father's
continued well-being, *but in order to earn my approval.*"

Piotr Borisovich stared with new interest at the speaker,
who was gripping the arms of his chair with hands that appeared to be incredibly strong. He was no youngster. But
there was a steadiness to his regard, a flame in his eyes that
commanded instant respect; instant allegiance even.

"I accept," Piotr Borisovich blurted out before he knew
he intended to respond.

The other man didn't smile. "This has been a wretched
century," he noted, and then he said something that made their
line of work seem like a crusade. "You and I are going to try
to make the next one better." He stood up and offered Piotr
Borisovich his hand. "My name is Feliks Arkantevich Turov,"
he said formally. "I am the *novator* of the sleeper school, in
which you are now enrolled."

For the next nineteen months, the period during which
Piotr Borisovich was under the Potter's wing, he lived in the
top-floor apartment of the military hotel. The workload was
unrelenting—six days a week, ten hours a day, which didn't
include the Sleeper's "free" time, during which he was expected to become acquainted with American popular music
(there was usually a disc playing in the background) or dip into
the library to familiarize himself with Steinbeck, Hemingway,
Dreiser, Jack London, Mark Twain and F. Scott Fitzgerald.
Formal classwork—courses given by the Potter himself or one
of his assistants—generally took up the mornings. These included the theory and practice of espionage, the philosophy of
Marx, Engels and Lenin as it applied to intelligence activities,
and an intensive study of every facet of the United States: its
history, geography, political development, military establishment, FBI organization and methods of law enforcement. There
were daily classes given by the Potter on spoken English,

which concentrated on polishing the Sleeper's knowledge of colloquialisms; he learned how to curse like a stevedore and to charm someone with slightly off-color jokes. He studied the intricacies of baseball and football from films until he knew what a balk was, and could predict with considerable accuracy whether a quarterback would run or pass.

The thread that ran through all the courses was to develop the Sleeper's professionalism. He memorized the standard operating procedures for sleepers until he could rattle them off in his sleep. Once awakened, for instance, a sleeper must ignore all communications that arrived out of prearranged channels and pretended to come from friends and relatives. The logic for the rule was obvious: informal messages from friends or relatives might actually have been sent by the enemy in an effort to confuse a sleeper or divert him from his mission. The Americans had succeeded in doing just this in the mid-fifties: an agent received a written message from his wife saying she had defected; when the agent went to meet her, he found the FBI (which had forged the letter) waiting for him. It was a point that the Potter put a great deal of emphasis on.

"What would you do if you were on a mission and got a message from your father?" the Potter asked.

"I'd ignore it."

"What if you got a message from, say, me?"

"I'd ignore that too."

"What if you heard a voice you knew on the phone? My voice, for instance, telling you a mission had been canceled?"

"I'd assume someone in the American intelligence establishment knew of the connection between us and was imitating your voice. I'd interpret it as a danger signal and take steps to make sure the person pretending to be you couldn't communicate with me again."

Afternoons at the sleeper school were usually devoted to technical subjects. Piotr Borisovich learned microphotography, regular photography, secret writing, how to communicate through dead-letter drops, how to surveille others, how to detect and evade the surveillance of others. Once a week he was driven out to a remote KGB rifle range to familiarize himself with pistols and rifles available in America, and perfect his marksmanship on these unfamiliar weapons.

For every hour of classwork, there was an hour of tradecraft in the streets. Under the watchful gaze of the Potter, who was something of an expert on the subject (he was something of an expert on *every* subject, Piotr Borisovich would say), the Sleeper, among other things, learned how to scout the route a dignitary would take in order to select the best site from which to assassinate him.

Evenings the Potter personally projected American movies— the sleeper school had an enormous library of Hollywood films that had been captured from the Germans during the war—for the Sleeper in the top-floor apartment of the military hotel. Everything that dealt with police or law-enforcement agencies was generally shown twice. One night they would watch Yul Brynner heading a ring of narcotics smugglers. The next, a police thriller starring Alan Ladd or Edward G. Robinson.

The last months at the school were spent working up the Sleeper's legend—the identity under which he would penetrate and live in the United States. (It was at this point that the wild-eyed Uzbek took the Sleeper in hand and taught him how to make mobiles.) Together the Potter and the Sleeper pored over source books compiled over the years by KGB agents in the United States, working out addresses where the Sleeper had lived as a child, places he had vacationed at, descriptions of his parents and the location of their tombstones, the names and descriptions of neighbors, of schools he had attended, of jobs he had worked at, of his bosses and coworkers, even of girls he had dated. No item was too small to include in the Sleeper's biography; it was the odd detail, the Potter stressed again and again, that would convince an interrogator that a suspect was telling the truth. The fact that someone lisped when he talked, that a girl wore padded brassieres, that a drugstore where the Sleeper had worked as a fountain clerk specialized in egg creams (which the Sleeper learned how to make in case anyone should ever ask him), were priceless pearls in the necklace of the Sleeper's new identity.

Through it all the two men developed a relationship that provided the Potter with the son he had never been able to father, and the Sleeper with a surrogate father. As the Potter had predicted, the Sleeper found himself attacking his studies with an ardor designed to impress his mentor and earn his approval. And the Potter discovered in his last, best sleeper the rarest of Soviet birds—a kindred spirit.

From the moment that they consecrated their budding friendship—when each, in turn, uttered something which, if reported to the authorities, could get him fired or jailed or even shot—there had been an unspoken complicity between them. For each of them, the part of their relationship that had to do with friendship outweighed the part of their relationship that had to do with work.

Eventually the Potter took the Sleeper to the American warehouse located in the basement of one of the KGB's safe houses, which is the point at which Piotr Borisovich understood that school was almost out. The Potter supplied him with American clothes, and instructed him to wear them so that when he was infiltrated into America they would no longer be new. Cracking open a bottle of Bison vodka that night, the Potter presented to his pupil a scroll announcing that he had been appointed a lieutenant colonel in the KGB. The Sleeper was touched, not so much by the rank, but by the fact that he owed the appointment to the *novator*.

When it came time to leave, the Potter accompanied the Sleeper to the airport in his chauffeured limousine. In the parking lot near the terminal, they both became tense. They started off toward the terminal together, not daring to look at one another, the Potter walking as if he were following a coffin. The Sleeper indicated with a gesture that it would be better if he went on alone. He could see that the Potter was at a loss for words; was fearful that if he found them, whatever he said would sound foolish. The Sleeper emitted a thin, brittle laugh and turned on his heel and stalked off. He could feel the Potter's eyes boring into him; could sense the depth of the affection in the Potter's regard. But when he gave in and glanced back, the Potter had already turned toward his limousine.

The Sleeper understood that both of them suspected their paths would never cross again.

4

❦

That there was a Man Friday network was due to a peculiar quirk of office egos. The young assistants had the security clearances of their masters, but the status of field mice, which meant that they didn't have the rank to take meals in the senior dining room, or the grace to eat with the groundlings. The result was a cozy Man Friday clubroom on the fourth floor, with a soft-drink vending machine in one corner and a pool table on which many a man Friday sharpened his eye.

"Eight ball in the side pocket," said the Deputy Director's man Friday, whose name was Harry. "What's this about your Potter skipping town before the farmers could milk him?"

Thursday watched with bulging eyes as Harry drew a bead on the eight ball. "How did you hear about it?" he asked.

Harry dispatched the cue ball into the eight ball, and the eight ball into the side pocket. "Four ball straight in," he said. "The Sisters' Op Proposal updater passed through the Deputy Director's in basket, which just happens to be on my desk." With a flick of his wrist, he sank the four ball.

"Yeah, well, the Austrians were about as amateur as they come," Thursday explained. He giggled at the thought of how amateur they had been.

"And the Potter, obviously, was an old pro," Harry added with more than a trace of arrogance as he surveyed the table for another shot.

"That was it exactly," Thursday agreed quickly. "The amateurs versus the old pro."

"Seven ball is dead in the corner," announced Harry.

Thursday squinted at the seven ball. "I've got five bucks says it's not."

"You're on." Leaning over the table, the Deputy Director's man Friday sent the cue ball into the one ball, and the seven, which was touching the one, was propelled straight into the corner pocket.

"Shit," said the Sisters' man Friday.

"You were in Vienna, weren't you?" Harry asked casually. "Fourteen in the side."

Thursday sensed that some of the blame for the loss of the Potter's warm body might rub off on him. "It was a German show," he said defensively. "I was only there to skim off the cream."

"Oh?" Harry seemed mildly surprised. "There was no mention of any cream in the Sisters' updater." He shot and missed.

Thursday shrugged. "I don't know what's in the updater," he said, "but I got what I was sent to get." He studied the table for a shot, but couldn't find one. "I'll play safe," he announced.

"And what is it you were sent to get?" Harry asked.

"Listen," Thursday said uneasily, "I work for the Sisters."

"Just between us," Harry coaxed, "I'm curious to know what the cream was."

Thursday tapped the cue ball lightly, burying it behind a group of balls next to the cushion. He giggled with pleasure at the shot. "If it'll get no further than this room," he said.

5

✤

Two old hags lugging enormous plastic shopping bags were systematically searching through garbage cans in the alley behind the Brooklyn Eagle Building, and the Sleeper had to wait until they finished their scavenging before he could approach the dead-letter drop. He counted down four garages from the corner, then slipped between the wooden fence that marked the limit of the garden behind the Eagle Building and the side of the garage, and began searching for the brick with the word "Mother" chalked on it. It will all boil down, the Potter had once told him with an embarrassed smile, to whether, when you search for your first set of instructions, you do so with a sense of urgency. The Sleeper had been struck by the Potter's choice of words at the time. Why urgency? he had asked curiously. Because urgency, the Potter had replied, is what modern war has lost. My principal task as *novator*, as I see it, is to instill in my sleepers the sense of urgency that was present when the person you were shooting at was also shooting at you.

The Sleeper found the brick, opened his pocketknife and began to pry it out with the blade. To his satisfaction, he discovered he *was* working with a sense of urgency; his pulse pounded, his skin tingled with urgency. For a fleeting moment he thought he might lose control of his bladder in his desire to get to the heart of the dead-letter drop. He worked the brick free and bent to peer into the hole. There was nothing in it; no instructions, no war to go to, shooting or otherwise. He reached in and searched the drop with his fingertips—and found the small, squat metallic capsule wedged into a crack at the back of the opening. The capsule had been dulled with black shoe polish so as not to attract attention. The Sleeper replaced the brick, unscrewed the capsule, removed the scrap of paper and threw the capsule into the space behind the garage full of bottle shards and rusted tins.

At first glance, the message looked like a printed advertisement for a Brooklyn firm specializing in cleaning coal furnaces. But the paper felt odd to the touch—probably because it had been coated with potassium permanganate, a normal precaution to make sure it would ignite when exposed to the slightest heat.

Back home in his workshop, the Sleeper examined the leaflet with a magnifying glass, spotted three i's with dots that looked suspiciously thick, and went to work. He carefully pried the dots off with an Xacto blade, then deposited them one at a time on the lens of his microdot reader.

Once again his skin tingled with a sense of urgency.

The microdots were numbered. The first instructed him to pack a bag and leave home within one hour of having read the order. It listed an interim destination, and told him what kind of transportation to use. It also told him what kind of weapon he would find at the interim destination.

The second microdot identified his ultimate destination, and specified his itinerary and the pace at which he should travel in order to arrive there on a specific day. It cautioned that he was not to arrive early.

The third microdot identified the target, listed the day and hour of his arrival in the city, traced the routes he could take to get from the airport to the luncheon site, discussed in very general terms angles of fire, distances at which the weapon could be considered accurate, how many shots the Sleeper might reasonably expect to fire, escape routes from the scene of the crime and, eventually, from the country. On completion of the mission, the microdot added, the Sleeper would be repatriated to the Motherland and sent into luxurious retirement. This was to be his first, and last, assignment.

The Sleeper read the name of the target again to make sure he had gotten it right. Any levelheaded person would panic at the idea; panic, it seemed to him, was the only sensible response to such an order. Did he really believe that he would go through with it? But if he didn't at least *try* to obey his orders, his father would suffer. So, too, would his surrogate father, the Potter; for it was a principle of the sleeper school that the Potter's career was tied to the success or failure of his students.

Overhead, one of the Sleeper's mobiles swayed gently in currents of air. The beak-shaped end of it dipped like a duck drinking from a puddle, until the fulcrum worked its magic and the beak lifted. The whole business of spying, the Sleeper realized, was a kind of mobile: the Potter, his wife, the Sleeper, his father, the Merchants in Moscow who thought up projects for him. But where in all this was the fulcrum to be found?

The Sleeper struck a match and brought the flame near the edge of the printed leaflet. The paper exploded into flame with a whooshing sound and he had to drop it in the sink to avoid being singed. A stinging odor filled the attic. The Sleeper opened a window to air it out.

"What's that smell?" Millie called from the upstairs bedroom. "Kaat, something's burning in the attic. Come quickly! Kaat!"

Kaat and Millie came racing up the stairs to the door of the attic workshop, Kaat with her soft sandal tread, Millie with her spiked heels stabbing the floorboards. "Peter?" Kaat called through the locked door.

"Open up," Millie chimed in. She banged a fist against the door.

"I'm coming," called the Sleeper. He quickly copied off his itinerary on the back of an envelope, put his microdot reader away, ran some water in the basin and washed the three microdots and the ashes down the drain. Then he opened the door for the two women.

"What's up?" Kaat said, sniffing away as if she were hunting truffles, relieved to see that the entire attic was not going up in flames.

"He's not up!" Millie joked, glancing lewdly at the Sleeper's crotch. "I suppose there has to be a first time for everything," she added with a sigh.

"Don't be vulgar," Kaat snapped at Millie.

Millie, who was four years younger and a head shorter than Kaat, pouted. "What's vulgar about an erection?" she demanded. Her nostrils, which were large to begin with, flared. "Vulgarity is in the ear of the be-listener. Anyway, that's what my math teacher always used to say."

"Your math teacher said that?" asked the Sleeper.

Millie shrugged innocently. "After class. In bed," she said.

Kaat had the impression that Millie knew just what effect she was creating. "I thought you suffered from aculculia," Kaat remarked.

"Another one of your A words," the Sleeper groaned in despair.

"I love her A words," Millie declared with passion.

"Aculculia is a mental block against arithmetic," explained Kaat.

"I did have a block against arithmetic," Millie said. "That's why I slept with the teacher."

Kaat had to laugh at that.

Millie laughed too. "Do you have any new A words?" she asked.

"Two," replied Kaat. "I found out that I'm an aelurophile, which means cat lover. And that I'm amphierotic, which means I can be aroused by members in good standing of either sex."

Millie said, "You're too much, Kaat. Don't you think she's too much, Peter?"

The Sleeper nodded dutifully. "I always thought Kaat was too much," he agreed.

"I'm not sure it sounds like a compliment when you say it like that," Kaat noted.

"Listen, it's only two-thirty," Millie pointed out. She slipped into what she thought of as her Katharine Hepburn voice. "What if we all moseyed on down to the master bedroom for a roll in the hay?"

"What does that mean, 'moseyed'?" asked the Sleeper.

"I'm only good at A words," Kaat observed maliciously.

"You don't know what 'mosey' means?" Millie asked incredulously.

The Sleeper shook his head.

"It means to sort of stroll, to meander, to make your way

slowly. It's a cowboy word. You do know what 'roll in the hay' means?"

The Sleeper laughed. "I know what it means. But I haven't got time. I have to go on a trip."

"Go where?" Kaat wanted to know.

"You never said anything about going on a trip," Millie muttered. She clearly had her heart set on a roll in the hay.

"I had a call this morning," the Sleeper improvised. "An old friend of mine, someone I knew in the Army, invited me down to his place in Pennsylvania."

"How long will you be gone?" Kaat asked quietly. She brought a fingernail to her mouth and began to nibble on it.

"Ten days. Two weeks maybe."

"Two weeks!" Millie exploded. "What are we going to do for sex?"

"You can always fall back on Kaat's amphieroticism," the Sleeper said.

"It's not the same without a man," Millie said sulkily.

Kaat asked, "Where exactly are you going?"

"I already told you," the Sleeper said vaguely. "Pennsylvania."

"Will you call us?" Millie asked. She batted her eyelashes suggestively. "You know. Like you did when you went to Denver to show your mobiles."

The fanlike wrinkles formed at the corners of the Sleeper's eyes. "You liked that?" he asked. "Hearing me describe what I was doing to another woman?"

"Personally," confessed Millie, "I liked hearing her describe what she was doing to you."

"How about you?" the Sleeper asked Kaat.

The cat named Meow nosed open the door to the attic and padded silently into the room to arch her back against the side of Kaat's calf. Kaat scooped up the cat and stroked her under the chin. "Here's the thing . . ." she began.

"Why do you always begin your important sentences with 'Here's the thing'?" the Sleeper asked.

"Always," Millie agreed.

"Here's the thing," Kaat said, ignoring them both. "In one of my previous incarnations I must have been a member of a harem, because I like sharing my lovers, which is to say that I'm mildly jealous but not possessive. If it turns you on to phone up while you're making love to someone else, that's just another way of sharing, as far as I'm concerned."

"I love you, Kaat," Millie said in a soft voice. "I mean it. I really do."

Kaat smiled at her, and kissed her lightly on the lips. Then they both set to packing the worn leather valise that Peter kept in the back of an upstairs hall closet. Passing the kitchen on her way down to the basement laundry room to collect his socks, Kaat heard Peter talking on the phone. "Where does it leave from?" he was asking. "Is that 'gray' as in the color gray?" He listened for a moment. "How long will I have to wait for the connection in Scranton?"

Half an hour later, Kaat and Millie zippered up Peter's valise and wrestled it downstairs, which was difficult because Millie was so unstable on her heels that she tottered from side to side. The Sleeper (having collected false driver's licenses and Social Security cards, along with a supply of cash, from a hiding place in his attic workshop) sauntered down after them. Kaat noticed that he was carrying his copy of Walt Whitman.

The Sleeper noticed her noticing it. "I'm taking it to read on the train," he explained.

"On the train," Kaat repeated.

"What's wrong with going by train?" the Sleeper asked.

"I love trains," Millie declared. "I love to pee while they're in stations."

"Well," said the Sleeper, at a loss for words.

"Well," Millie ventured. "I guess this is where someone says the thing about parting being such sweet sorrow, or whatever."

"I guess," Kaat agreed.

The Sleeper glanced at Kaat and saw her studying him from the depth of those sunken eyes that always made her look as if she knew more than she said. He would miss Millie's body, he decided, but he would miss Kaat; all of her. It suddenly occurred to him that he didn't even have a picture of Kaat. And he knew from experience that after a week or two he wouldn't be able to remember what she looked like. He never seemed to remember what the women in his life looked like once they were out of sight.

"See you," Millie said, and she reached out and rubbed his crotch playfully.

"Good-bye," Kaat said solemnly.

Millie laughed nervously. "Jesus, you'd think he was going forever."

"I'm sorry," Kaat blurted out, "but I'm only good at arrivals."

The Sleeper came up with the thin, brittle laugh that summed up his attitude toward the business of parting forever from people he liked. He grabbed his valise, and plunging past the plaque indicating that Whitman had once lived here, disappeared from view.

"Hey," Millie said to Kaat with as much enthusiasm as she could muster. "What about that roll in the hay?"

6

❧

The man bolted to a sitting position in the bed. Sweat drenched his undershirt. For a long, terrifying moment he didn't know who he was. Fighting back a pervasive panic, he tried to figure out *where* he was. He could hear the whine of a machine, and he remembered having to summon the night clerk to show him how to work the air conditioning. He was in a hotel, that was it. Slowly he began to reconstruct what he was doing there. He had been in Canada but he had left there. By train. Going south. To New York. Of course! To New York to save someone. Someone he had betrayed. To save his last, his best sleeper!

And then it all came flooding back, like a high tide, until he was awash in damp, chilly memories. He was trying to get to Piotr Borisovich before he could carry out the orders he was certain to receive; to tell him of his betrayal and the death of his father; to free him. The Potter permitted the air to seep from his lungs in relief. He finally knew who he was, and where he was, and what he was doing there.

None of the information was very comforting.

He got out of bed and stumbled through the half-light to the washbasin in the corner of the room. He turned on one tap. A gurgling sound, extraordinarily human, came from it. But no water. He tried the other tap. It coughed several times, then emitted a thin stream of rusty, lukewarm water. The Potter splashed some of it on his face. It tasted stale. He glanced at himself in the tarnished mirror over the basin. He thought of Svetochka, and tried to summon up her face, her voice, a particular mannerism; anything at all. But all he managed was her pubic hair, which was curly and wiry, like steel

141

wool, and the tiny mole on the inside of her right thigh, and the hair under her arms and on her legs. He had failed to memorize the rest of her.

The Potter went over to the window, which was almost opaque from decades of dirt and rain, and studied the street below. A garbage truck was making its slow way down the block. Two garbage men wearing overalls and thick gloves hefted metal garbage cans onto a churning mechanism in the rear of the truck, then sent the empty cans clattering back to the sidewalk like spent projectiles ejected from a cannon. The Potter had arrived in New York after midnight, and had decided to pass what was left of the night in a cheap hotel near the docks below Brooklyn Heights that he remembered from his days as *rezident* in the city. He had been tempted to go directly to the Whitman house, on the theory that the shortest distance between two points was a straight line. But the shortest route wasn't necessarily the safest. For the people who had gotten the Potter to betray the Sleeper, the people who had presumably awakened the Sleeper, might very likely be keeping tabs on him. Having crossed a continent and an ocean, having made his way to within a long stone's throw of the house on Love Apple Lane, the Potter had to tread now as if he were crossing a mine field. For that he needed daylight. He had been so impatient for it to come that he had imagined it, and the light in his mind's eye had kept him from falling asleep. When he finally drifted off, he had woken up without the slightest idea of who he was. Amnesia, of course, was an obvious, even convenient form of flight from reality. Looking out now at the street, the Potter was almost sorry he had reconstructed his identity.

Almost.

Prowling around the room impatiently, the Potter forced himself to wait until the streets of Brooklyn Heights were crowded with people rushing off to work. They seemed to have a reasonable amount of enthusiasm for getting where they were going, but the Potter attributed this to capitalism's ability to buy off the proletariat with the equivalent of an extra wet dream a week. Love Apple Lane, with its neat brownstones and miniature gardens, went off at right angles from Henry

Street. If number 145 (the Potter could see the brass plaque glinting near the front door) were staked out, it was not visible to the naked eye. But it wouldn't be. Someone (with a camera fitted with a telephoto lens to record comings and goings) could be watching from behind any one of a dozen curtained windows across the street. To know for sure, the Potter would have to stake out the block, observe the men, and even the women, who came and went, establish a pattern that might give away a change in shifts. But the Potter knew he didn't have a day or two to spare for that. There was an alley lined with private garages behind Love Apple Lane, and he decided it offered the best avenue of approach. Several men in business suits were backing their cars out of garages. Nearby, a teenage boy in blue jeans and a sweatshirt sat cross-legged on the ground pumping up the wheels of his bicycle.

"If you please, how can you tell which one of these houses is number 145?" the Potter asked.

The boy looked up, then went back to his pumping. "You can always go around the front where the numbers are," he said.

"I am allergic to streets," the Potter told him. "I am more comfortable in alleys."

This seemed to amuse the boy, because he smiled up at the Potter. His mouth was metallic with braces. "One-forty-five is the guy with the two girls," he said. "The guy that makes those floating mobiles."

"That is the one," the Potter agreed.

"It's down there," said the boy. He pointed with his chin toward the far end of the alley.

The Potter said, "If I wrote out a note, would you deliver it to the door for me? I would be willing to compensate you."

"Compensate?"

"Pay. Money."

"How much?"

"How would three dollars be?"

The boy stopped pumping abruptly. "Why not?" he said.

The Potter pulled a piece of paper from his pocket, and bracing it against a garage door, scribbled a note. He knew that the Sleeper wouldn't respond to a personal note; he had been trained not to. So he wrote out several lines that the Sleeper would think only the real Potter would know. He folded the note several times, counted out three dollars and handed it to the boy. "Take a good look at me so you can describe me to the man who makes the mobiles," he said. "Tell him the person who gave you this note is waiting for him in the coffee shop in the lobby of the St. George Hotel. You think you can remember all that?"

"The lobby of the St. George Hotel," the boy repeated brightly.

He packed away his pump, climbed on the bicycle and pedaled off toward the end of the alley. Leaning his bike against a fence, he looked back and waved, then disappeared into a garden. The Potter left the alley and headed in the opposite direction from the St. George for several blocks. When he was sure he wasn't being followed, he doubled back on his tracks.

He was working on his third cup of coffee in a corner booth of the coffee shop when the boy appeared outside the door. He was walking his bike because he was with someone—a woman in her thirties, the Potter quickly calculated, though it would have been impossible to say if it was her early thirties or her late thirties. The boy put his face to the window of the coffee shop and spotted the Potter. He turned his back toward him and said something to the woman, who stared over his head at the corner booth. She spoke to the boy, then came around the shop to the door and walked directly up to the booth in which the Potter sat. She opened the note that he had sent over with the boy and read what he had written aloud.

"The lines about the sisters Death and Night—they were favorites of his." She stared at the Potter intently, waiting for him to react. "He even has them underlined."

"In pencil," the Potter added, feeling his way. "We both like very much the poetry of Walter Whitman."

She felt awkward standing there, looking down at him. "Do you mind if I join you?" she asked.

"If you please," the Potter said, motioning her toward the bench. He signaled with his finger for another cup of coffee.

They surveyed each other across the gulf of the unwashed table as the waiter brought the coffee. It was served in a cheap, thick cup. Some of the coffee had spilled onto the cheap, thick saucer. The woman plucked a napkin from a metal dispenser and carefully fitted it into the saucer so that it would soak up the spilled coffee. "Funny," she observed absently, "how people always talk about how you shouldn't cry over spilled milk, but they never think about spilled coffee."

"You should always cry over spilled milk," the Potter told her. "Spilled coffee also, if it seems appropriate."

"Peter called him Walter too," she noted. She nibbled nervously at a fingernail.

"I beg your pardon."

She looked up quickly. "Peter always referred to Whitman as Walter, the way you did a moment ago."

"That was his name, Walter. Walter Whitman."

The woman shook her head. "Everyone calls him Walt. He called himself Walt."

The Potter lifted his shoulders in a vague shrug.

"He's left, you know," the woman said. Her body was just across the table, but her voice seemed to come from far away. "Forever. He's not coming back."

So he had arrived too late. "Did he tell you that?" the Potter asked, a note of desperation seeping into his tone.

She shook her head once, angrily. "He didn't have to. It was evident. He took his copy of Whitman with him. *Walt* Whitman. It's probably the only thing—the only material thing—he really gave a damn about." She studied the Potter from the depth of her sunken eyes.

"Here's the thing. He talked about a teacher he once had, someone who was tied up to the pier of old age. I never forgot that phrase. He talked about someone who made him think he was on a crusade. He said his teacher was an amateur potter with powerful forearms and hands." She reached across the table and ran the tips of two fingers along the Potter's forearm. Her touch was so light it made him shiver. "He talked once about showing the mosaics of a church to someone, and driving out to the countryside to visit his father with someone. If he told one story, he told a hundred. And I understood, although he never said so specifically, that these weren't different *someones*, but one *someone*. He even described, in great detail, making love to the wife of someone." Her eyes flashed up. "I was a fool to tell you that. Maybe you didn't know it."

The Potter couldn't bring himself to speak.

"My name is Kaat," she said to change the subject. She spelled it for him.

"What kind of name is Kaat?" he asked.

"It's my maiden name," she explained. "I was married once, when I was nineteen. I got divorced a year later. I didn't want to wear the name of a man I didn't live with, didn't love, so I went back to my own name. My first name I detest. So I call myself by my maiden name, Kaat. Everyone else does too." She smiled at a memory. "The first time I told Peter about Kaat being my maiden name, he said something that made me wonder who he really was."

"You wondered who he was?"

"My maiden name reminded him of someone else who went by her maiden name, a woman called Krupskaya. She was Lenin's wife. Nobody called her Nadezhda, which was her first name, or Mrs. Lenin. They called her Krupskaya. But you know all that, don't you?" She smiled across the table at him, and the Potter noticed, for the first time, that she had a way of smiling with her mouth and taking it back with her eyes. "Admit you know who Krupskaya was," she insisted. She pulled the coffee cup closer and tried to see her reflection in the muddy liquid. "There were things—little things—that gave him away."

All those months, those years, of creating a legend; of piling up details, as if they were bricks, until they constituted an impressive building; of training the Sleeper to fit inconspicuously into a society, the Potter thought. And this girl comes along out of nowhere and sees right through him. "What do you mean, gave him away?" he asked, and was astonished to recognize in his own voice a note of professional curiosity. He had thought he was through with all that.

"More coffee?" the waiter called over from the counter. The Potter waved a finger no.

"He never drank coffee," Kaat remembered. "He drank tea, and once, when he thought nobody was around, I caught him straining it through a sugar cube clutched between his teeth. Russians do that, don't they?" She tilted her head and angled up her chin, as if challenging him to contradict her. "Peter was Russian. I bet you are too."

The Potter could either deny it and lose her, or admit it and use her. She knew the Sleeper had left. She knew him well enough to sense that he had left for good. Maybe she knew where he had gone. The Potter drew a deep breath. "His name was Piotr Borisovich Revkin."

"And who are you?"

"I was the teacher. My name is Feliks. Feliks Turov."

Across the table, Kaat pressed her eyes shut, obviously relieved, then opened them and for lack of anything more original to say fell back on the standard formula for meetings, "How do you do?"

"How do you do," the Potter replied, inclining his head formally, and he remembered Piotr Borisovich exploding into laughter during one of their early sessions on the top floor of the military hotel and sputtering: What a curious thing to say when you meet someone—how *do* you *do*?

"Now that you've told me this much," Kaat ventured, "you might as well tell me everything." And she encouraged him with one of those smiles that she took back with her eyes.

And so the Potter, calculating that he had very little to lose, lowered his voice and told her what seemed safe to tell her: about the Sleeper working (as he discreetly put it) for the Soviet government; about how he had learned the Sleeper had been betrayed; about how he had used the false passport and the American money he had stashed away years before to cross Europe and the Atlantic to Canada, and then made his way to New York, to Brooklyn Heights, to Love Apple Lane—to warn the Sleeper, to tell him of the death of his father; to free him.

Kaat, in turn, described the departure of the Sleeper four days earlier. He had received a letter in the morning mail (no, she hadn't noticed the postmark) and announced, in midafternoon, that he was going to visit an old Army friend in Pennsylvania. On her way down to the basement laundry room she had overheard him on the kitchen phone inquiring where something left from, inquiring also how long he would have to wait for a connection in Scranton. "He asked the person on the other end if it was 'gray' as in the color 'gray,' " Kaat remembered. "Later he made a point of saying he was going by train, but I knew he was going by Greyhound." When the Potter looked confused, she added, "Greyhound is the name of a bus company."

"Of course! He went to Scranton by Greyhound. But where did he go after Scranton?"

"I can always ask him where he is when he calls up," Kaat said.

The Potter stared at her. "What makes you think he will call you up, if you please?"

"Here's the thing," Kaat began, flustered. "Peter—how can I explain this?—Peter's not exactly like other men. Sexually, I mean. He's anfractuous." She spotted the puzzled look in the Potter's eyes. "You won't know what 'anfractuous' means. It's one of my A words. It means full of windings and turnings."

"An—"

"—fractuous. When I first met Peter—I lived in an apartment farther down Love Apple Lane, and my cat, whose name is Meow, escaped into his backyard—he was living with Millie. We hit it off, the three of us, and they eventually invited me to join them."

"The boy with the bicycle said there were two women living with Piotr."

Kaat nodded. "Everybody on the block knows about us. We're something of a vicious triangle. She likes me, I like him and he likes—liked—her."

"You said something about him phoning."

"I was getting to that," insisted Kaat. "One of Peter's sexual windings and turnings is that when he's away from home, he makes love to other women. And he likes to phone us up and describe it while he's doing it. Sometimes he even puts the woman on and makes her describe it."

The Potter recalled the Sleeper's sexual habits from Moscow, remembered analyzing his fetish of phoning up previous bed partners while making love to someone else as his way of throwing little hooks into the past; remembered also concluding that the Sleeper's strength was that he knew his weaknesses. "You like this sort of thing?" he asked Kaat now.

Her eyebrows shot up. "Of course I do. Doesn't everyone?"

He avoided the issue. "You think he will call up from Pennsylvania while he is having sex with someone?"

"He has every time he went away before," Kaat pointed out. "He was in Denver last February to show his mobiles and called up three times."

Kaat studied the Potter with her deep-set eyes. "When he phones up," she explained to the Potter excitedly, "I can tell him that you're here, that you want to see him—"

The Potter shook his head. "He will not believe you," he said flatly. "He has been trained *not* to believe you. He has been trained to disregard all contact that appears to originate with friends. He will think the Americans put you up to it. He will suspect the call is being traced and hang up on you. He will never call back again."

"What can I tell him, then?" Kaat asked in despair, chewing again on a fingernail.

"You cannot tell him anything," the Potter instructed her. "You can only listen to what he says and try to figure out where he is. And then let me know."

The Potter glanced at the coffee-shop window and saw that the boy with the bicycle was still there, staring at them through the glass. "What does he want?" he asked Kaat.

"I wasn't sure what I'd find when I got here," she explained, "so I asked him to hang around just in case I needed someone to scream for help." She waved to the boy, who waved back and leaping onto his bicycle, pedaled off.

"Assuming we do find out where Peter is," Kaat concluded thoughtfully, "the trouble is, he may no longer be there by the time we arrive. Pennsylvania is a big state, you know," she added gloomily.

"What do you mean, 'when *we* arrive'?"

"I'm going with you," Kaat announced.

The Potter waved a hand in frustration. "That is out of the question," he declared.

Kaat squinted at him across the table. "Then when I find out where he is, I'll go without you!"

149

"Why do you want to go?" the Potter demanded in exasperation.

"I have nothing to stay here for now," Kaat fired back. For her the couple (or "triple," as Millie liked to call it) was essentially a conspiracy; an "us" against a "them"; something to help her survive endings, which were invariably unhappy. She sensed that she had lost Peter forever. What was more normal than to be drawn to a new mystery, a new conspiracy? She stared at the Potter for a long moment. Then he lowered his eyes. "So that's settled," Kaat said. Before he could argue, she added, "I've had an anacalypsis. That means 'revelation,' as in 'brilliant idea.' Peter's obviously somewhere around Scranton. Why don't we rent a car and drive to Scranton? Millie can hold the fort on Love Apple Lane and record the conversation if Peter phones up. Millie's a model, you see. She has one of those tape machines hooked up to the phone so she won't miss a booking. We can call her up from Scranton and get her to play the conversation back to us. That way, Feliks—you don't mind if I call you Feliks, do you?—there'll be less time between his phone call and our arrival; there'll be more of a chance of still finding him there." She noticed the expression on his face. "Don't worry," she whispered. "I'm not a political person—I have no ideological ax to grind." She raised her right hand as if she were taking an oath. "I promise to be a noiseless patient spider seeking spheres to connect." And she added, "That's another line from your *Walter* Whitman."

The Potter had to admit that Kaat's scheme was as good as any he could devise. And traveling with the girl, unorthodox as it seemed, offered certain advantages, from a professional point of view. For one thing, he would be less likely to stand out in a crowd. He could use her to rent cars and buy train tickets and reserve hotel rooms, thus exposing himself less. More important, she would be the one to call the Sleeper's number in Brooklyn Heights, a fact that would arouse less suspicion if, as he suspected, the phone were being tapped by the people who had awakened the Sleeper.

"I accept your proposition with pleasure," the Potter announced with irritating politeness.

"You are bowing to the inevitable," she noted, "but you

are bowing gracefully. And gracefulness, in my book, is next to cleanliness. And everyone knows what cleanliness is next to." She reached across the table for his hand. The Potter was familiar with the American habit of shaking hands to conclude a deal, and he offered his. But she didn't want to shake hands; she wanted to study his fingernails. She brought his hand across the table and leaned over it. "Do you believe in reincarnation?" she asked. She didn't wait for him to reply; somehow she knew what he would say. Like Peter, he had the look of someone rooted in reality. "I do," she insisted. "I've had four lives already that I remember. This is my fifth." She studied his fingernails, touched one as if she were testing its texture, then turned his hand over and peered at his palm. "You've had at least two previous incarnations," she said. "You were a victim in both—that much any idiot can see."

"That," the Potter told her with undisguised sarcasm, "should give me a certain amount of training for my present incarnation."

7

The Potter lingered in the shadows of the warehouse across the street from the pier waiting for Kaat to pass. She was driving one of those ridiculous American automobiles with shark's fins rising in the back and chrome everywhere. When she failed to find him, she followed his instructions and circled the block. He let her come around three more times to make sure she was not being followed—or hadn't betrayed him!—before he stepped out under the streetlight and flagged her down.

"I was beginning to think you'd never turn up," she groaned as the Potter tossed his valise into the back and slid into the passenger seat. She sounded winded, as if she had been running; tired, as if she hadn't had a good night's sleep for some time.

A cat, rolling its R's in a mixture of pain and frustration, howled in the back seat.

"What is that?" the Potter asked, startled.

"That," announced Kaat, throwing the car into gear, "is my cat. She is in heat—"

"What does that mean, in heat?"

Kaat looked quickly at the Potter. "It means she's having her period. She wants a male of the species, is what it means. She howls for days when she's in heat. Millie refused to keep her, but I don't hold it against her. Millie is basically a dog person. I don't mind dogs personally as long as they have the sense of independence of a cat. The female of the species is especially independent. Having a female cat has advantages and disadvantages, but males are impossible unless you fix them, and that's one thing I could never bring myself to do. I mean, can you imagine the *guilt* you must feel living with an anorchous cat—"

"That must be one of your A words," the Potter noted.

Kaat maneuvered the rented Chevrolet onto the ramp leading to the Brooklyn Bridge and Manhattan. "You catch on fast," she said. "It means without testicles."

"You are talking a great deal," the Potter said in a voice so utterly calm that Kaat found it irritating.

"That is because I am appropriately nervous," Kaat admitted. "My mouth is dry. My pulse is racing. I am suppressing the desire to scream. All that business about going to the other end of Brooklyn to rent a car, of circling the block until I found you. You will have to understand that this is the first genuine nonsexual adventure of my life, and I am taking it very seriously."

The Potter studied her out of the corner of his eye as she steered the car through evening traffic, across Manhattan toward the Holland Tunnel. She gripped the wheel with both hands, which he noticed now were long and exceptionally pale, with a ring on every finger except her thumb. Several of the nails were bitten down to the quick. It occurred to the Potter that she drove well, working the clutch and the gearshift effortlessly, weaving in and out of lanes, leaning on the horn in exasperation when the car in front went too slowly for her, all the while keeping up a steady stream of conversation. "I studied art," she was saying, "because I was convinced I'd been a painter of still lifes in one of my four previous incarnations. I actually went to Florence for a year to learn how to restore still lifes. Did you know that it's easier to restore very old paintings than relatively new ones? That's because it takes a hundred years before paint is really dry on a canvas." Kaat sighed. "There's a certain symmetry to my life, I have to admit it. I began with still lifes and wound up with still lives," she plunged on, casting an occasional sideways glance at the Potter to make sure he was paying attention. "I started restoring paintings for a living and wound up restoring corpses."

The Potter, who had had a good deal of experience with death in his day, asked how she felt in the presence of death.

"Here's the thing," she answered as the cat leapt with a

sour howl onto the back of the driver's seat and stretched out behind Kaat's neck. "Since I believe the spirit of the dead person is merely in a limbo between two incarnations," Kaat continued, arching her neck against the cat, "I guess I don't feel sad, if that's what you mean. How about you? How do you feel in the presence of death?"

The Potter turned away to stare out of the side window. "It has been my experience," he observed with a certain melancholy, "that being in the presence of night, of death, loosens one's bowels, dulls one's appetites, dampens one's enthusiasm, since it demonstrates in an unforgettable way how that fragile thing called life will inevitably end."

Kaat shook her head vigorously. "When all is said and done, we haven't got much in common, you and I," she told him. Ahead, the streets were crammed with cars and trucks approaching the Holland Tunnel tollbooths. She shrugged fatalistically. "I suppose we are antiscians. That refers to people who live on the same meridian, but on either side of the equator, which means that at high noon their shadows fall in opposite directions."

The Potter nodded in agreement. "We come from different planets," he said. "When you were in school, your mother gave you a sandwich and sent you off on a bus."

"Something like that," Kaat agreed.

"My mother gave me an ear of corn. A plowhorse came by to take us to school. There was nobody to help us climb up on him. So we would drop the ear of corn on the ground, and when he lowered his head we would grab his ears and shinny up his neck. I remember that there were seven of us crammed onto the back of the horse by the time he got to school. And we considered it luxurious not to have to walk, because the roads were a sea of mud."

Kaat rolled down her window, paid the toll and maneuvered the Chevrolet into the lane of traffic that seemed to be going through the tunnel the fastest. The Potter sank deeper into his seat. He disliked tunnels passionately; it wasn't so much that he felt trapped in them as physically squeezed by them. During the Great Patriotic War, he had spent several weeks hiding in an abandoned mine while Waffen SS squads combed the countryside, shooting partisans and Communists on sight. In the night, when the wind was right, he had been able to hear the shots reverberating through the valley.

From some backwater of his mind, he dredged up memories. "It was during the war," he said out loud, though he wasn't sure why he wanted to tell her this, "that one of my comrades, a university professor, took to referring to me as the ascian. How is that for an A word?"

"Ascian." Kaat tried it out. "It has a very soothing sound. What does it mean?"

"It refers," the Potter told her, "to someone who doesn't cast a shadow at all in sunlight."

Kaat looked at him curiously. "And you don't cast a shadow in sunlight?" she asked sharply.

"In those days I didn't. I don't know about now."

They talked about more down-to-earth matters after that. The Potter directed Kaat into a labyrinth of narrow back streets on the Jersey side of the river north of the tunnel. It was an area he had come to know during his tenure as *rezident* in New York.

If Kaat was curious how the Potter came by his experience—"Left at the next corner, left again, right at that warehouse"—she never let on. Following his instructions, she eventually brought the Chevrolet to a stop in a deserted alleyway down the block from an all-night bar with a broken neon sign sizzling over its door. When she cut the motor she could hear the faint sound of a tide lapping against pilings, and make out the outline of several freighters tied to piers beyond a chain-link fence at the end of the block.

"You will wait for me here," the Potter instructed her.

"You actually expect me *not* to go with you?" She shivered at the idea of remaining alone in the car.

She must have transmitted her alarm to the cat, because it began emitting that throaty howl again.

"Can't you keep the animal quiet?" the Potter demanded.

"No," Kaat said flatly. "What do I do if you don't come back?"

"If I am not back in, say, twenty minutes, go home and forget you ever met me."

The cat perked up behind Kaat's neck. Kaat seemed to perk up too. "Go home, he says," she told the cat. "What home? I have no home; I have only a former home. Even if I had a home to go home to, how in God's name would I find my way out of this maze? What are we doing here anyway, if you don't mind my asking?"

The Potter rummaged in his valise for something, found what he was looking for and slipped it into his jacket pocket. "I used up all the money I had getting myself to New York," he told her. "I need more. There used to be people here who bought things of value without asking questions."

"You could have asked me if you needed money."

"I need other things too."

"Like what?"

"I need bullets. Also a gun to put them in."

"Why do you need a gun?"

"I need a gun," the Potter explained patiently, "because I am beginning to be frightened. I will tell you something you will probably find amusing. If I had to do it all over again, I wouldn't." He opened the door. "Lock this after me. Keep the cat quiet if you can." He laughed under his breath. "If anything happens to me, perhaps we will meet in another incarnation."

Kaat grabbed his sleeve. "Here's the thing: you're frightened. Fear is contagious. I've caught it. Me also, if I had it to do over again, I wouldn't."

They exchanged gentle, conspiratorial smiles. "That," the Potter told her quietly, "may be the first sensible thing I have heard you say."

At the end of the alley the Potter turned, and for an instant Kaat thought he was going to wave, but he only shook his head in confusion and continued on toward the all-night bar.

The bartender was the only one who looked up when the Potter came through the door, though the dozen or so men scattered around the booths appeared to suspend all conversation. The Potter hefted himself onto a stool and eyed the collection of baseball bats in an umbrella stand near the cash register. The bartender, a heavyset, balding man in his forties who looked as if he might have once been a baseball player, eyed the Potter suspiciously.

"Why are you looking at me like that?" the Potter finally asked.

"Well, now, someone who didn't know better might say I was sizing you up," the bartender replied.

A sailor in one of the booths snickered.

"I would like a drink, if you please," the Potter ventured.

"You have definitely come to the right place," the bartender said. "Don't tell me what you want—let me guess." He squinted at the Potter, screwed up his beefy lips, rubbed a forefinger along the side of his bulbous nose. "Vodka!" he exploded. "Bison vodka when you can get it. Am I right or am I right?"

"How do you do it?" the Potter asked.

The bartender leaned across the counter toward the Potter until their faces were inches apart. "No offense intended, but you talk with some kind of foreign-type accent, so I figured you must be off the Polak ship three piers down. And any idiot knows that Polaks drink vodka. Good vodka when they can get their mitts on it. Any vodka when they can't." He laughed at his own joke.

"A glass of Bison vodka would certainly be welcome," the Potter acknowledged.

The bartender leaned back. "Don't have Bison vodka," he said. "But I can give you a shot of good old New Jersey vodka."

"I never heard of New Jersey vodka," the Potter admitted.

"That don't surprise me none," said the bartender. "New Jersey vodka is what's left over when they finish refining petroleum." Several of the sailors in the booths laughed out loud at that. Smiling maliciously, the bartender poured out a shot glass full and set it before the Potter.

The Potter raised the glass to his nose and sniffed the contents. It smelled vaguely like glue. Then he brought it to his lips and drank a small quantity. It seared the back of his throat. He gasped. The bartender slapped the bar in pleasure. "Moonshine," he explained when he stopped laughing. "Good old hundred-proof New Jersey moonshine."

At the booths the sailors resumed their conversations. Nodding toward the moonshine, the bartender said, "No harm intended."

"No harm done," the Potter said amiably. "Listen, I have been here before. To this bar. Years ago."

The bartender's attitude changed. His eyes appeared to cloud over. "You don't say," he muttered guardedly.

"I do say. There used to be a narrow staircase back there that smelled of urine. It led to a corridor that also smelled of urine. At the end of the corridor was a room in which men played cards for big stakes. They were usually Italians, though there was an occasional Jew. The Italians all wore diamond cufflinks, I remember."

"You have a very good memory," the bartender conceded grudgingly. "Be careful it don't get you in no trouble."

"I also remember that there was a button under the bar that you pushed when someone started up the back stairs."

"Say, you really are one smart cookie. What ship did you say you were off?"

"I didn't say," the Potter said. "Why don't you reach under the counter and ring the bell now." With that, he slipped off his stool and headed toward the back of the bar and the staircase. It still smelled of urine. Ahead, the Potter thought he could make out the distant sound of a buzzer. The upstairs corridor had been painted recently, and the smell of paint overpowered the smell of urine that had almost asphyxiated him the last time he had come through it; he had been in the market for a rifle equipped with a new U.S. Army night sight at the time. The door at the end of the corridor had been fitted with a peephole. The Potter knocked politely and then stared up into the peephole so that whoever was on the other side could get a good look at him.

Eventually a bolt was thrown, then a second one. The Potter tried the knob. The door clicked open. He entered the room. There were five men seated around a glass-covered table, with colored chips and cards scattered around it. All of them were in their shirtsleeves. Four of the five wore diamond cufflinks. Another man, with his jacket on, sat on a window-sill. Still another, wearing a raincoat, lounged with his back to a wall. The Potter closed the door and stepped boldly into the room. The man lounging against the wall shifted position so that his back was pressed to the door.

"Do you have a name?" This from the man without diamond cufflinks.

"I have an occupation," the Potter announced. "I am a seller."

"A traveling salesman has found his way to our door," quipped the man on the windowsill.

One of the Italians peered up at the Potter through thick eyeglasses with gold rims. "We have met maybe before," he suggested.

"It is possible," the Potter agreed, although he couldn't place the face.

"And what treasure is it you are selling?" the same Italian inquired with infinite politeness.

The Potter reached into his jacket pocket and took out a package wrapped in an old kerchief. He undid the rubber bands that bound it and removed the cloth. Then he stepped forward and deposited two engraved plates on the table.

The player without diamond cufflinks whistled through his front teeth. "Twenty-dollar plates!"

He passed the plates to one of the Italians, who held them up to the light and studied them. He must have been something of an expert, because the others seemed to be waiting for his verdict. "The engraving is first class," he finally announced. "Where did he get these?"

"Where," the Italian without diamond cufflinks repeated the question, "did you get these?"

"How I came by them does not concern you," the Potter replied evenly. (The man lounging against the door straightened up, but one of the Italians shook his head imperceptibly, and the man relaxed again.) "They are of German origin," the Potter went on. "They were made by the same artist who engraved the Third Reich's deutsche-mark plates. The original intention was to print up a supply of funds for German agents working out of Mexico during the war. But the Russians reached Berlin before the plates could be put to use."

"And wound up in your hands," said the Italian who

thought he recognized the Potter. "Which means that your accent must be Russian."

One of the players studying the plates whispered, "These are worth a fortune."

"What if we are not buyers?" another Italian said. "What if we are takers?"

"If you are takers," the Potter pointed out, "it follows that you will have to spend a certain amount of money to dispose of a body. The sum of money I want from you is so modest that it will be cheaper for you to pay me than to kill me."

The man lounging on the windowsill grunted. "Maybe we won't see the situation the way you see it," he warned.

"I am betting that you will."

"You are betting your life on it," suggested the Italian holding the plates. He looked up. "How much is modest in your book?"

The Potter took a deep breath. "I require five thousand dollars in small bills," he said. "I also require a handgun. Any one will do as long as it is in working condition."

"He needs five thousand dollars," the man without diamond cufflinks repeated with a laugh. "He needs a handgun. So what else does he need?"

The Potter remained silent.

"A guy with an accent waltzes in off the street—how do we know this is not a setup?" the man lounging against the door demanded.

"You will never in your life get another opportunity to come into possession of plates of this quality," the Potter said. "You are all gamblers, aren't you?"

The man without diamond cufflinks scraped back his chair, walked over to a buffet and picked up the telephone. "Charlie, do me a favor, huh," he said into the receiver. "Duck outside and take a good long look around. Then come back and let me know what you seen."

The Potter retreated to a wall. The men at the table passed the plates around and talked Italian in undertones. After a while the telephone sounded. The man lounging on the windowsill sauntered over and picked up the receiver. He listened for a long moment. "Okay," he said, and hung up. "There's a Chevy parked in the alleyway. There's a girl and a pussycat in it. The doors are locked. The girl refused to open. Nothing else is in sight."

The men around the table exchanged looks. "Well," said the man without cufflinks, "do we buy from him, or do we bury him?"

The man with the gold-rim glasses burst into guttural laughter. "For five thousand dollars, we can't go wrong." He gestured to the man on his right. "Pay him, Frankie. Eugene, remove the bullets from your gun and give it to him."

Eugene didn't like the idea of parting with his pistol; it was an Italian Beretta, .22-caliber, that he had won in a crap game the previous year, and he had become attached to it. "Why does it have to be my gun?" he whined.

The Italian who held the plates looked up sharply. Eugene puffed up his cheeks and let out the air in an annoyed burst. Then he removed the clip from his Beretta and thumbed the bullets out of it into his palm before reinserting the empty clip back into the pistol.

The Italian who thought he recognized the Potter was staring at him curiously. Suddenly his face brightened. "I know where I seen you before," he said. "It was here, in this room. Seven, maybe eight years ago. You were a buyer then, not a seller. How the mighty have fallen."

Pocketing the money and the pistol, the Potter turned toward the door. Eugene still blocked his way, and seemed in no mood to move.

"He is a Russian secret agent," the man who recognized the Potter announced to the others.

"Get out of my way," the Potter ordered Eugene in a low voice that he hoped was full of menace.

"Maybe you think you can make me," Eugene shot back, caressing the knuckles of one hand with the palm of the other.

"Leave him leave," the man who had identified the Potter ordered.

Eugene reluctantly stepped to one side. With a last look over his shoulder, the Potter left the room. He fled along the corridor, down the staircase through the bar—the bartender was nowhere in sight—into the street. The neon sizzled over his head like the rattle of a snake. The night air sent a chill through the Potter, and he realized he had been sweating profusely—from fear, probably, though he hadn't been aware of it at the time. Fear to him implied that there was hope. This was an illusion he didn't harbor.

He ducked into the alleyway and saw the Chevy and waved to Kaat. She waved back, though her waving had an agitated aspect to it, and then the Potter realized she wasn't waving, but pointing, and he turned back to see the hulking figure of the bartender advancing toward him in a shuffling step used by wrestlers when they stalk an opponent. He was gripping one of those American baseball bats in both hands, and thrashing it about in front of him with short snaps of his thick wrists. "What I am going to break first is your ankles," he called in an excited voice. "Then I am going to break your kneecaps. Then your rib cage. Then your wrists. Then your neck. Then your skull." He laughed hysterically, shuffling forward all the while. "You were wrong about how much it costs to bury someone. I work cut-rate. A package deal is what I offer. The body, buried, for twenty-five hundred dollars. Niggers, foreigners, I do for the fun of it."

The Potter backed away until he was up against the front grille of the Chevrolet. Swinging the baseball bat, grinning into the darkness, the bartender closed in on him. A loss of nerve hit the Potter—it manifested itself as a sudden weakness in his knees, a ringing in his ears. It was not only a question of the violence that would be done to him, but to the girl in the car behind him: having disposed of the Potter, the bartender would then feel obliged to attend to the eyewitness. The bartender was so close now that the Potter imagined that he could feel the rush of air that preceded the swishing bat. The Potter knew he had to move, to do *something*, but for the life of him he couldn't see what he could do. The bartender was too big, too methodical. And then Kaat, behind the wheel of the Chevrolet, switched on the car's high beams and leaned on the horn. Startled, blinded, the bartender jerked an arm up in front of his eyes. The Potter stepped forward and kicked him sharply in the crotch. The big man groaned and doubled over. The bat

162

clattered to the pavement. The Potter moved around behind the kneeling figure, took a grip on his thick neck and began to squeeze. Gasping, the bartender tried to pry the Potter's fingers loose, but the years of kneading clay had strengthened them into a vise. After a while the bartender went limp in the Potter's oustretched arms. He let the corpse slip to the ground. Kaat flicked off the high beams, and the Potter could see her peering out at him from the window of the Chevrolet. Violence is in my blood, he wanted to tell her, but the pale mask of a face that stared back at him seemed to say that that was something she knew already.

8

❧

Khanda arrived in the designated city at the end of the first week of October, and using the alias O. Lee settled into a one-story rooming house in a run-down section of town. One block away, past a yellow-brick self-service laundry and a pharmacy with a parking lot next to it full of pickup trucks, he could make out the center of the city rising from the flat like a wart. He had bought a street map of the city and had traced the two possible routes from the airport to the luncheon site, one in blue, one in red. In the days that followed, he went over the routes again and again, and eventually compiled a list of buildings from which he could get a shot at the target no matter which of the two routes was finally selected. Several of the possibilities he ruled out because of the nature of the business conducted in them; he stood precious little chance of getting a job in a bank, or an insurance company, for instance. Eventually he narrowed the possibilities down to two buildings. On the thirteenth, he put on a tie and jacket and presented himself at the employment office of a lumber company whose top floors dominated the route between the airport and the city proper. He was interviewed by a wispy woman with a harelip who became suspicious at his failure to produce references from previous jobs. His application was turned down.

On the fifteenth of the month he made an application for work in his second choice, a rust-colored brick warehouse on the corner of Houston and Elm that dominated a roughly diamond-shaped plaza through which the target would have to pass on his way to the luncheon. The building had been constructed at the turn of the century as railroad offices, had been turned into a branch office of a plow company, and only recently been con-

verted into a warehouse. Khanda, again wearing a tie and jacket, sensed that he was making a good impression on the woman who interviewed him this time. He explained away his lack of references by saying that he had attempted free-lance journalism since his discharge from the Marines. The interviewer asked when he could start, assuming his application for employment was accepted. Khanda flashed a boyish smile and replied eagerly, "First thing tomorrow morning." The interviewer smiled back. And Khanda knew he had the job.

9

❧

Thursday spotted the item in the New York *Daily News*, to which he subscribed at office expense so he could follow the comic strips. A minor-league left-fielder who had made it up to the majors for three months and four days almost two decades before had been found murdered near the New Jersey docks. "It's the *way* he was killed," Thursday told the Sisters when he showed them the item.

Francis, who was wearing a new orange polka-dot bow tie that seemed almost fluorescent, screwed up his nose in disgust. "I abhor physical violence," he observed. He handed the newspaper, with the item circled in red, across to Carroll, who was spitting a piece of caramel laced with pistachio into his palm. Carroll read the article casually. Then his brow furrowed, and he read the article a second time. "You don't think it's him?" he asked Thursday, staring at a point on the wall over his right shoulder.

"During the war," Thursday recounted in that smug way he had of offering up footnotes to history, "he left a trail of strangled German corpses. The British claimed there were eight. The Germans—our Germans—listed eleven in his dossier. Then there was the little matter"—here Thursday capped a giggle before it could leak to the surface—"of the man who was strangled in the airport just about the time our friend the Potter enplaned for the Free World."

Francis waved a hand vaguely, as if he were trying to discourage a fly from touching down near him. His wrist was limp, a sure sign that he was not convinced.

Thursday seemed offended. "I took the initiative of phoning a lieutenant in homicide whom I had some dealings with,

166

the one who was assisting us in our inquiries, as the British like to say, when we tried to make the suicide of the Bulgarian diplomat's wife look like murder in order to hook the diplomat. Anyway, my source says that the late left-fielder worked as a bartender in a watering hole frequented by members of the Mafia; that the man who killed him had been dealing with the very same mafiosi; that one of them, known to the imaginative New York City Police Department as Luigi the Lean, recognized him as a Russian who had been around years before trying to purchase a rifle with a U.S. Army night sight on it. Luigi also told my source that the Russian's car was parked in a nearby alleyway, exactly where the body of the late left-fielder was eventually discovered; that the car had two passengers, a young woman and a pussycat."

Carroll astonished everyone in the room by *whinnying*. "It's the Potter, all right," he concluded.

"How on earth did he get from that hotel room in Vienna to the docks of New Jersey?" Francis wanted to know.

"The Potter has always been a resourceful man," Carroll pointed out. He turned on Thursday with such ferocity that the poor man had the urge to duck. "Did you body-search him when he arrived in Vienna?" Carroll demanded. "Did you at least go through his belongings?"

Thursday grimaced. "I assumed our German friends would tend to routine matters like that," he replied lamely.

"You *assumed*," Carroll sneered.

Francis said stoically, "A man like the Potter would have squirreled away a supply of Western currency, spare passports, a kilo or two of cocaine even, for that proverbial rainy day."

"That's probably what he was doing down at the docks," Carroll concluded. "Trading in his cocaine for greenbacks."

"And the late left-fielder made the mistake of trying to increase his employers' profits," Francis guessed.

Thursday eyed Carroll's box of candies; considering that he had been the one to spot the crucial item in the newspaper, he thought that Carroll might break with tradition and offer him one. But Carroll had other things on his mind. "You can slink back to your cubbyhole," he instructed Thursday. "We'll whistle when we need you."

As soon as the door closed behind their man Friday, Francis said to Carroll, "What do you think?"

"What I think . . ." he began, and then, motioning with his head toward a wall, he reached for pencil and paper. "What I think," he scribbled on a legal pad, "is that he came to warn the Sleeper and found him gone."

"What if," Francis wrote, "he tracks the Sleeper down?"

"The only people in the world," Carroll wrote, "who know where the Sleeper is going, and what route he is taking, are in this room. How could he track him down?"

"How could he get from Vienna to New York?" Francis wrote in turn—and Carroll could almost *hear* his exasperation. "He is a resourceful man, you said it yourself," Francis wrote. "What if the Sleeper told someone where he was going? What if he left footprints?"

Carroll shook his head. "The Sleeper's not one of those who leaves traces everywhere he crawls—like a snail does when it crosses a leaf. You are jumping at shadows," Carroll concluded.

Francis took the pencil, hesitated, then bent his head and wrote, "You are sure?"

Carroll, staring at the wall over Francis' shoulder, nodded. "I'm sure," he said out loud.

Francis waved a hand vaguely. Once again his wrist was limp; once again he was not convinced. He began collecting the leaves of yellow paper with the intention of shredding them before he left the office.

Carroll turned his attention back to the box of candy. "Damned pistachios will be the death of me," he muttered under his breath as he fumbled with the tinfoil of another candy.

10

It was not Francis' usual night to take in a film, but a nagging doubt lurking like a migraine behind his forehead persuaded him he ought to. Francis liked neat packages. The Potter turning up in America represented a complication. People had to be notified. Contingency plans had to be drawn. Precautions had to be taken.

Later, Francis wouldn't even remember what film he had seen that night, so deep was his absorption with the problem at hand. He stared at the screen in the filtered darkness without registering the images. He listened to the dialogue without making any sense of the words. When the final freeze frame faded and the houselights came up, he had more or less put everything into perspective. He reached into his pocket for the cigarette he ritually smoked at the end of a film. He used the single match left in the book to light it and discarded the empty matchbook under his seat. The sweepers could clean up after him, he reassured himself. Taking a deep, distasteful drag (how he longed to give up smoking entirely), he casually sauntered (Francis prided himself on his ability to saunter; he thought of it as a dying art) up the center aisle toward the exit.

11

❧

Killers, the Potter liked to tell his student sleepers when he was initiating them into the theory and practice of espionage, almost always came in twos. Which was another way of saying that if someone was worth killing, he (or—why not?—she) was worth killing well. If one assassin failed, so the conventional wisdom went, the second might be able to profit from the confusion caused by the first attempt and carry out the assignment. The classical example of this, of course, was the assassination of Czar Alexander II in 1881. The first bomb thrower managed to wound some guards and horses. When Alexander made the mistake of stepping out of the carriage to survey the damage, the second bomber nailed him.

Both the Soviet and the American espionage services tended to have their killers work in tandem. Two of the best in the business, known in professional circles as the Canadians because of their nationality, were vacationing in Ottawa after successfully carrying out an assignment from the Romanian counterespionage service to "neutralize" a Romanian exile. The man in question had published details of the sexual dalliances of members of Bucharest's ruling circle. Marriages had broken up. Careers had been ruined. The Canadians had been contacted. They had gone to London, tracked their victim until they had become familiar with his routines, then dispatched him at high noon in Piccadilly Circus by jabbing him in the groin with the poisoned tip of an umbrella as he waited impatiently for a bus.

The Canadians had completed three assignments since the first of the year and complained openly of "metal fatigue," but their Merchant, thinking they were referring to the aluminum castings of their gyrojet pistols, promised to supply new ones. Left with no choice, the Canadians, posing as homosexuals, made their way to Niagara Falls, wandered arm in arm across the border as if they had nothing more on their minds than sightseeing, picked up the new gyrojet pistols, false identifications, a supply of cash and two valises full of clothing at a safe house in Buffalo, then rented a black Dodge and headed southeast toward Lancaster, Pennsylvania.

The Canadian who wore a tiny woman's watch on his wrist and traveled under the name of Ourcq did most of the driving. He was in his middle forties, balding, bloated, effeminate, with the beginnings of a paunch that no amount of Canadian Air Force exercises could get rid of. The other Canadian, a rail-thin man with wavy hair who was using the name Appleyard, passed the time working on a crossword-puzzle paperback. He had spent several years as a soundman on radio soap operas, and could imitate almost anything. Whenever he was stumped over a word, he would purse his lips, fill his cheeks with air, produce a scrap of tinfoil or sandwich wrap, bring a palm up to his lips, stare off at some middle distance— and come out with noises: horses' hooves, a door opening, a kettle boiling, the whine of a jet engine starting up, static on a radio, fire in a chimney. He claimed he could do snow falling, smoke rising, the sun setting, the sound of someone dying; the last two, he said, were indistinguishable from each other. He was imitating a train pulling into a station when Ourcq glanced at him and said, "What the fuck's the name of the fucking place in Lancaster again?"

Appleyard reached into the inside pocket of his jacket for the itinerary they had picked up at the Buffalo safe house. "It's called 'Seventh Heaven,'" he replied presently, and puckering his lips, he produced a perfect imitation of surf lapping against a shore.

After a while Ourcq shook his head in despair. "It's a shit assignment," he decided. His brow wrinkled up in disgust. "Asking us to be fucking sweepers! There are fucking professional sweepers for fucking sweeping."

"Maybe the professional sweepers were off killing, so they sent the professional killers to sweep."

Ourcq was not amused. "What if the fucker who is following the other fucker isn't following the other fucker after all?" he moaned. "Then we come all this fucking way for nothing."

"Maybe he's not as much of a dwarf as they say he is and we won't recognize him," Appleyard added. "Maybe he is not accompanied by a woman with a pussycat."

"Me, I don't see why they couldn't let the fucker who is the fucker who's being followed take care of the fucker who is doing the following," Ourcq insisted.

Appleyard, who sometimes had trouble following Ourcq's sentence structure, clucked his tongue to imitate the sound of tumblers falling in a combination lock. "Maybe," he offered, "they didn't want the follower and the followee to meet."

"It is no fucking way," Ourcq muttered, "to run a fucking cold war."

Appleyard nodded in vague agreement and went back to his crossword puzzle.

12

The walls, it seems, did have ears.

"I'm just thinking out loud," Francis' voice came from the tape. "What if . . ."

"You bastard," Carroll spat at the interrogator without ever looking him in the eye. He brought several fingers to his cheek to deal with his twitching muscle, and arched his neck to take the pressure off the welt under his starched collar.

"What if *what?*" Carroll's voice on the tape prompted impatiently.

"What if we were to put our man Friday onto someone with Mafia connections?" Francis said on the tape recording.

The interrogator, whose name tag identified him as G. Sprowls, depressed the Stop button on the tape recorder. He had a conspiratorial half-smile installed on his otherwise impassive face—a half-smile which looked as if it had been recently taken from a deep freeze and not yet defrosted. "Now, why," G. Sprowls inquired gently, trying as usual to imply that there was some sort of complicity between the questioner and the person he was questioning, "was Francis suggesting that your man Friday contact the Mafia?"

"In the course of any given day," Carroll replied loftily, "we throw around dozens of ideas. That's what we are paid to do, in case you don't know it. We think up angles, avenues of approach—"

"I am fully aware of what you are paid to do," G. Sprowls said. The half-smile glistened on his lips like dew on a petal. "But you haven't answered my question, have you? Why the Mafia?"

"I don't remember," Carroll maintained, a muscle twitching quietly in his cheek. He longed to plunge his hand into a box of candy, but decided the interrogator would interpret it as a sign of weakness if he asked for one. "We'd have to go over any jottings Francis or I made to see what we were onto at that moment."

"Francis shreds the notes at the end of each workday," the interrogator reminded Carroll. He smiled pleasantly. "You've already told me that." He depressed the Fast Forward button until the tape reached number one-forty-eight, then put it on Play again. "What we will need"—it was Francis' voice again—"is someone who can carry out an assignment without knowing it came from us."

G. Sprowls pushed the Stop button. "Exactly what assignment were you talking about?"

The interrogation of the Sisters was in its fourth day. It began at the end of the first week of November on the express order of a very nervous Director of the Central Intelligence Agency when Thursday's indiscretions on the Man Friday network filtered up to the Athenaeum. G. Sprowls, the Company's utility infielder who specialized in tying up loose ends, was summoned back from Mexico where he was finishing the interrogation of a junior code clerk who seemed to have an endless string of mistresses. (G. Sprowls's tentative conclusion was that the code clerk was nothing more sinister than an accomplished lover.) The first thing G. Sprowls did on arriving in Washington was to isolate the Sisters; they were installed in separate but equal apartments in a safe house in Wilmington, Delaware, and brought out, one at a time, into the Grill Room, as G. Sprowls liked to call it, for their daily four-hour sessions.

Another, less experienced interrogator might have started the ball rolling by hooking each of the Sisters up to a lie-detector machine and then confronting them with the discrepancies between their version of events, contained in the Sisters' formal Op Proposal updater, and Thursday's version, passed on to the Deputy Director's man Friday over a pool table. But G. Sprowls knew the discrepancies were too vague, too undefined, to get a handle on. Did Thursday really skim off some cream when the Potter came across in Vienna, for instance, or

174

did Thursday, in his eagerness to appear important, merely convince himself that he had? Did the Sisters set out to lure the Potter to the West in order to get access to someone who could carry out an assignment without knowing it came from them? If so, what assignment had they invented for him to carry out? Did they think they had authorization? Did they actually have the authorization they thought they had? If they had received orders, had they interpreted them correctly?

All of this, to G. Sprowls's jaundiced eye, represented the proverbial can of worms. What he needed to do was question the Sisters at great length in order to be able to compose the right questions. That was the process he had used to break the Soviet sleeper in the CIA ranks whom the Sisters themselves had unmasked not long before. The disadvantage of working this way was that it was slow. The advantage was that it was sure.

"What we need—" Carroll was saying on the tape.

"What we need," Francis's voice repeated eagerly on the tape.

"What we need—" Carroll, from the tape recorder, whined.

The tape continued to run through the playing head, but there was no sound for roughly three minutes. Then Carroll's voice, distant, hollow, could be heard saying, "He might just do it."

G. Sprowls stopped the tape recorder. "Who might do what?" he inquired.

Carroll shook his head. He didn't remember.

"What were you doing during the long silence?" G. Sprowls asked.

"Thinking."

"Not writing?"

"We may have been jotting notes to ourselves," Carroll conceded.

"If there were notes," G. Sprowls remarked, flashing his half-smile as if it were a storm warning, "Francis would have shredded them at the end of the workday?"

Carroll's cheek muscle twitched once. "That's correct," he said.

"What was it," G. Sprowls wondered out loud, "that was so important you couldn't say it—you had to write it?"

When his turn came, Francis took a slightly different tack. "Of course I understand you are going through the motions," he confided to G. Sprowls at one point. An angelic smile took up a defensive position on his face to deal with the conspiratorial half-smile confronting him. "The last thing in the world you really want is for me to tell you what we are up to."

To G. Sprowls, it seemed almost as if Francis were daring him, inviting him even, to discover it. "So you are up to something?" he inquired.

Francis spread his hands innocently. "Josef Stalin started out his professional life as a seminarian," he retorted, "which explains why he was obsessed with confessions. What is your excuse?"

"Assuming you are up to something," G. Sprowls persisted, ignoring the historical diversion, "do you have authorization?"

"As a general rule," Francis noted, "Carroll and I are pointed in the right direction by our betters."

"Then perhaps you can explain why the Director himself authorized this interrogation?"

"That is clearly a matter you will have to pursue with the Director."

G. Sprowls selected another tape from his collection and played it for Francis. His voice could be heard saying, "Shows he had bad taste. Personally I never liked Whitman. All those unbuttoned shirts! All that hair on his chest! He was a poser. It follows that his poetry is a pose." There was a moment of silence, after which Francis asked on the tape, "Do we know exactly how the Potter knew that?" Then there was a very long stretch of tape without anything. Finally Francis's voice was heard again. "Having a great time. Wish you were here," he snickered. Carroll's voice, faint, said, "We have gotten our hands on a perfect criminal." To which Francis, a bit awed judging from his tone, replied, "I suppose we have."

G. Sprowls glanced at his wristwatch. They had been at it for more than three hours. Francis showed not the faintest sign of fraying at the edges. "Why," G. Sprowls tried, "were you discussing Whitman?"

In all his life Francis had never smiled more innocently. "Don't tell me, let me guess. You are one of those Whitman hysterics who can't put up with the slightest criticism of the master."

If G. Sprowls came equipped with one thing for the business of interrogation, it was a thick skin. "What could Carroll have meant," he went on as if Francis's response had not registered, "when he said that you had gotten your hands on a perfect criminal?"

"I would have to refresh my memory from my notes to answer you," Francis said.

"And the notes—"

"—were shredded," Francis finished the thought for him, "at the close of every workday."

"By you."

"By me."

"I see."

"Do you?"

13

The Sleeper was tired: of spending his evenings alone in his room; of taking his breakfast while it was still dark outside; of trudging off into the fields every morning with the rifle slung over his shoulder and two sandwiches (the Hunter's Special, prepared by the inn's chef) in the pocket of his brand-new Sears, Roebuck bush jacket; of working the bolt until his fingers blistered; of waiting; most of all, of waiting. But he had a fixed schedule, and a fixed itinerary, and there was no question of deviating from it. An order, the Potter had drummed into his head at the sleeper school, is to an agent as commandments one through ten are to an Orthodox priest. It was a matter of the Sleeper's being patient one more day. Tomorrow he would be off and running again, and anything, including a cramped, smoke-filled Greyhound bus, would be better than being cooped up in the phony luxury of Seventh Heaven, an inn just outside Lancaster with its birds wheeling freely through the lobby and the corridors, the birdshit stains on the furniture, the traditional Pennsylvania Dutch meal with its seven sweet and seven sour courses at every dinner.

Again and again, the Sleeper's thoughts drifted, almost against his will, to the mission. If his father's well-being, and in a sense the Potter's too, didn't depend on his performing well, he doubted if he would go through with it. One prince more or less in the world wouldn't change anything as far as he could see. But he had been backed into a corner; the one luxury he no longer had was choice. He imagined the moment when he would reach his ultimate destination, and wondered what his chances were of succeeding; he guessed they were quite good, or he wouldn't have been sent out in the first place. He wondered too what would happen to him after the mission. He wouldn't be returning to his comfortable life in Brooklyn Heights, of that he was certain. If he managed to survive, his masters would surely repatriate him to some corner of the Soviet Union remarkable for its remoteness.

If he was suddenly lonely, if he ached above all for just one more night in the same bed as Kaat, he could take comfort from the fact that he had accomplished what he came for. On the first day, he had zeroed in the rifle, bracing it on the elbow of a dead maple tree, aiming through the four-power telescopic sight and firing at a homemade bull's-eye. The rifle had been firing low and to the left. Using a small screwdriver, the Sleeper gradually adjusted the sight. After that he went to work recapturing the talent he had had when he served as a sniper during the Great Patriotic War.

It came back fairly quickly. In the beginning, he had trouble concentrating and felt unsure of himself. He missed more things than he hit. By the third day, however, he was beginning to get his concentration—and his confidence—back. He started once again to think of the rifle as an extension of his arm, and aiming became just a matter of pointing. He had been told in his instructions that he would be firing at a slowly moving target, but the possibility existed that it might be moving rapidly. So the Sleeper fired mainly at moving targets— rabbits, birds, ducks skimming the surface of ponds. He had always had a sixth sense for leading a target; an almost Zen feeling that all he had to do was point at the place where the target would be when the bullet got there. By the afternoon of the fifth day, and all during the sixth, he was snapping off shots and hitting practically everything he aimed at.

"So how'd it go today?" the wife of the inn owner asked when the Sleeper showed up at the bar for the Seventh Heaven Happy Hour. She was a handsome woman in her late twenties, married to a grouchy man a good deal older than she was. Her name was Marjorie, but the waiters and several of the inn's regular customers called her Sergeant Major, as if it were a rank; one of the younger, more insolent waiters even saluted her when he delivered a check to the cash register. "What did you bag?" she wanted to know.

"Everything I aimed at," the Sleeper replied testily. A bird flew in from the lobby and plunked down on the bar nearby.

"You're that good?" Sergeant Major asked, smiling suggestively.

The Sleeper stared at her curiously. "Why don't you put me to the test?"

"Maybe I'll do just that," she shot back, and she dispatched a damp palm down her thigh to smooth out an imagined wrinkle in her tight skirt.

It was after eleven when she scratched her long fingernails on his door. He let her in and locked it after her. She had brought a bottle of cognac and two glasses, but the Sleeper made it clear he didn't go in for preliminaries. He asked her what she was wearing under her dress. Instead of answering, she bent and caught the hem and peeled it over her head. Underneath, she was naked, round, in places as soft as a sponge. She had hair under her arms and legs, which reminded the Sleeper of the women he had made love to in Russia; he liked hair on the female body. Somehow it seemed to make them less abstract, more real. Sergeant Major stretched out on the bed and parted her legs and raised one knee and moistened her thumb and forefinger and pinched her nipples to make them erect. "Now," she announced with a nervous laugh, "we'll see how good a shot you really are."

Some time passed. Neither of them had any idea of how much. Eventually Sergeant Major rolled off the Sleeper's body and laced her fingers through her hair. The Sleeper had the impression she was surfacing, like a deep sea diver. "I've read about that," she whispered hoarsely, "but I've never actually tried it—I wasn't sure I'd enjoy it."

"Did you? Enjoy it?"

Sergeant Major smiled a faraway smile; she was coming up, but she had not yet reached the surface. "Do you know any other tricks?" she asked.

The Sleeper nodded lazily. He reached for the phone. Sergeant Major was intrigued. "Who are you calling at this ungodly hour?"

The night clerk who doubled as a switchboard operator

came on. "I want a number in Brooklyn," the Sleeper told him. "After you get it for me, I want to hear the click you make when you get off the line."

The number rang a long time before anyone picked up the phone on the other end. "Yeah?" Millie finally said, suppressing a yawn. "Who the hell is it?"

"It's me," the Sleeper said.

Millie came awake instantly. "You know what time it is, for Christ's sake?"

"What are you wearing?" the Sleeper demanded.

Millie's tone changed. "A T-shirt."

"Take it off."

After a moment she said, "Okay, it's off."

"Take the phone over to the couch and curl up," the Sleeper instructed her. "You're going to hear a bedtime story."

Millie purred like a cat. "It's one of *those* phone calls," she said. "I can't wait!"

14

❧

At the foot of a bed, the cat angled a paw over its head to keep the light out. Kaat kicked off her shoes and stretched out on one of the twin beds. They had just come back, the three of them, from a diner across the street from the motel. The desk clerk had given them a mimeographed street map of Scranton. Kaat removed the antique gold ring, which she wore around her neck attached to a length of silk string, and dangled it over the map.

"If you please," the Potter asked, "what are you doing?"

"I'm trying to find out where he is in Scranton," she told him, her eyes concentrating on the ring.

"And the ring is going to tell you?"

"If it does tell me," she retorted, "you'll be an autologophagist."

"Which is?"

Kaat glanced up from her pendulum. "An autologophagist is someone who eats his words," she said.

The Potter settled onto the edge of the other bed. "What made you become interested in words beginning with A?" he wanted to know.

Kaat shrugged defensively. "Everybody who collects things specializes," she explained. "Stamp collectors collect art stamps or French stamps or whatever. Antique dealers collect porcelain. Kids collect matchbooks. I collect A words. I suppose you could say I'm basically an A person. It's no accident that Kaat has two lovely A's smack in the middle of it." She nibbled thoughtfully on a fingernail.

"Try phoning again," the Potter advised her. He busied himself loading the Beretta with the bullets she had bought for him that afternoon. Normally the clip held eight bullets, but the Potter squeezed ten in. Giving yourself an extra margin was what separated the professionals from the amateurs. He wondered how professional he really was in the end. The whole idea of going out on a limb with this odd girl who nourished herself mostly on her own fingernails and passed pendulums over maps seemed more ridiculous than ever. To begin with, the chances were that the Sleeper would never call Millie in Brooklyn Heights. Even if he did, there was only a remote possibility that he would tell her where he was. The Americans, he remembered from his days as *rezident*, had an expression that perfectly described what he was on: they called it a wild-goose chase.

The girl, moreover, was beginning to get on his nerves. She had carried on a running monologue during the ride down to Scranton, almost as if she dreaded silence, as if only a string of words could keep her phantoms at bay. (Silence, the Sleeper once laughingly told the Potter, was a gift two people could offer each other only after they were intimate.) The Potter had discovered a great deal about Kaat during those hours in the car. She shivered before it got cold, she admitted; according to her, the chills originated in her imagination. She liked making love and being made love to, she said; she relished the sensation of not knowing where her body ended and a lover's began. When the street (as she called real life) got too rough for her, she sought refuge in her mind's eye, which she sharpened, she said, as if it were a pencil.

"Call her up again, if you please," the Potter repeated now.

Kaat put aside the map and pendulum, picked up the phone and gave the number to the receptionist. A moment later she could hear the telephone in Brooklyn Heights ringing. Instead of Millie's recorded voice coming on as before, Millie herself snatched up the receiver. "Kaat, is that you?" she cried.

"Where have you been?" Kaat demanded.

"She is in?" the Potter asked. He came around to sit next to Kaat on the bed.

"Thank God it's you," Millie cried. "Peter phoned."

"He's called," Kaat whispered triumphantly to the Potter.

"Who are you talking to?" Millie asked.

"Nobody. What did he say?"

"Wait a sec. I'll play the tape for you."

"She's playing the tape for me," Kaat whispered. She and the Potter bent their heads so they could both listen to the voice coming from the earpiece.

The Sleeper's voice came over the line. "You're going to hear a bedtime story," he said.

"It's one of *those* phone calls," Millie's voice replied. "I can't wait!"

A woman's voice could be heard. She was breathing hard. Kaat and the Potter exchanged looks. "I don't have the vaguest idea what to say," the woman pleaded.

Fainter, the Sleeper's voice: "Tell her what we're doing. Describe it."

The woman laughed uneasily. "You want me to tell her everything?"

"Absolutely everything," Millie insisted on the tape.

"Well," the woman began, talking between gasps, "I'm lying on my stomach . . . on my stomach, see, with my ass more or less, eh, elevated"—the woman giggled hysterically here—"holy shit. 'Elevated' is the right word, and he's, eh, he's—" She stopped abruptly, almost as if she were too preoccupied to talk.

"He's *what*?" Millie prompted on the tape.

The real Millie came back on the line. "Are you catching all this, Kaat? Are you turned on?"

"I'm catching it," Kaat said. "I'm suffering from apodysophilla—that's a feverish desire to undress," she explained.

"He's"—it was the woman's voice on the tape again—"oh, Jesus." She expelled a lungful of air, and what began as a husky sigh wound up as a throaty scream.

The Potter turned his head away so that Kaat couldn't see his expression.

"He's inside me now," the woman continued, her voice weaker than before. "He's reaching under my stomach with a hand and rubbing my clit." She gasped as if she were in pain.

"Keep talking," the Sleeper's voice ordered in the background.

"He's . . . behind me . . . not moving . . . perfectly still," the woman said more calmly now. "It's me that's . . . doing . . . the moving. When I . . . when I back up I get . . . his dick going . . . deep. When I move forward . . . I get his finger." She giggled again. "I can pick my poison!"

On the tape, Millie could be heard moaning. The real Millie came back on the line. "That's me moaning," she laughed.

"As if I couldn't tell," Kaat retorted. She sounded annoyed. "Did you ask him where he was, for Christ's sake, or did you just beat off?"

"I asked him, I asked him," Millie assured Kaat.

"Say, where are you two?" Millie said on the tape.

"She wants to know where we are," the woman told the Sleeper.

"Don't tell her," the Sleeper could be heard saying.

"We're in a bed," the woman told Millie between gasps.

"Give me a little hint," Millie begged on the tape.

The woman giggled again. "We're in a . . . hotel in Holland," she told Millie. "We're in seventh heaven, with birds flying through the corridors—"

There was a click on the tape. Millie came back on the line. "He hung up before she could say any more," she said.

After Millie had hung up, Kaat and the Potter sat on the edge of the bed staring at the floor. Kaat chewed on a fingernail. Eventually the Potter said, "The phone call didn't tell us very much."

At the foot of the bed the cat stretched, then coiled again. Kaat said, "We know he's somewhere in Pennsylvania. What did the woman say? A hotel in Holland. Seventh heaven, with birds—"

"—flying through the corridors," the Potter remembered.

Kaat snapped her fingers. "My ex might be able to help us," she announced brightly.

"What is an ex?"

"My ex. My first husband."

"Did you marry again after you left him?" the Potter asked.

Kaat shook her head no.

"Then why do you call him your first husband?"

Kaat shrugged. "Even when I married him I thought of him as my first husband," she said, suddenly melancholy, suddenly distant. "He had the look, the smell, of a first husband. He was much older than me," she said as if it explained everything, which made the Potter wonder if Svetochka had referred to him, behind his back, as her first husband. "He was a country singer," Kaat plunged on. "Still is, I imagine, though his voice was beginning to go the last time I heard him. He spent twenty-three years wandering around the back roads of America, with his beat-up guitar in the trunk of a beat-up station wagon. That's how I met him. It was in Oklahoma. I was sixteen going on twenty-five, if you know what I mean. I heard him sing in a bar in Wetumka, Oklahoma. My ex, whose name is W. A. Henry Oaks, though everyone called him W.A., my ex claimed that every town was famous for a different position."

"Different position?"

"Different *sexual* position. Wetumka, according to W.A., was famous for the Wetumka. The next day we drove north to Weleetka, where W.A. was playing a bowling alley, and I discovered the Weleetka. After that there was the Okmulgee, which only thin people can do. Thank God we were thin! Later, when we wanted to use a certain position again, we referred to it as the Wetumka, or the Weleetka, or the Okmulgee." Kaat began chewing wistfully on a fingernail.

"What was the Okmulgee?" the Potter asked, not sure whether he believed the story—or whether he wanted to know.

"You're sure you want to know?"

"I take back the question."

She laughed and told him. "You're blushing," she said when she had finished.

The Potter went back to his own bed. "If you think your first husband can help us, phone him up," he said moodily. He didn't know how he got into these conversations with her. He seemed to follow her wherever she led. He would have to concentrate on the problem at hand; use her if there were ways she could help him; discard her when it became clear that she could serve no purpose. All this talk of sexual positions just blurred the picture. He would have to make a greater effort to keep things in focus.

Kaat eventually got her ex husband on the phone. "What time is it on the Coast?" she asked him. "Then I didn't wake you?" she asked him. "No, I'm not sorry I didn't wake you," she snapped. "Listen, W.A., don't start on me, all right?" She listened to the voice on the phone for a moment, shook her head and planted her eyeballs in the tops of their sockets. "Here's the thing, W.A.," she said when she could get a word in, and she went on to tell him why she had called. For reasons she couldn't explain just now, she and a friend were trying to track down another friend in a hotel somewhere in Pennsylvania. The only clues they had came from a woman who said that the hotel was in Holland, that they were in seventh heaven with birds flying through the corridors.

W.A. let out a howl at the other end of the phone. "Heck, I played that joint three, four years ago," he cried. "The owner is a certified maniac about birds. He has got dozens of them zooming around the halls. One of them even shat on my guitar while I was singing. Got me such a laugh I tried to incorporate it in my act, but I couldn't get the goddamned bird to shit twice in the same place."

"You actually know where this hotel is?" Kaat asked.

" 'Course I know. Holland is the nickname of a county outside of Lancaster, in the heart of Pennsylvania Dutch country. The hotel is called Seventh Heaven."

15

♣

"Can you do someone going to a refrigerator for a glass of milk?" asked Sergeant Major.

"He can fucking do anything," Ourcq, in a sour mood, muttered under his breath.

They had arrived at Seventh Heaven just as the Sleeper was checking out. Ourcq took one look at the birds perched around the lobby and the birdshit stains on the carpets and announced he was ready to follow the Sleeper. Appleyard had to remind him of the pertinent rule in the standard operating procedures for sweepers: when you are sweeping someone's wake, you have to linger twenty-four hours after he leaves to make sure he is clean.

Appleyard took a sip of his Scotch on the rocks to moisten his lips. Drumming the balls of his fingers on the top of the bar, he produced footsteps approaching the refrigerator. With a sharp cluck of his tongue he made the sound of the door being opened. He snapped his fingernail against the whiskey glass to duplicate the sound of the milk bottle being taken out. Blowing through puckered lips, he imitated milk being poured into a glass. Sucking in air, he produced the sound of drinking. And he capped it all with a genuine belch of pleasure.

Sergeant Major and a young couple at the bar applauded. "He's really good," the woman insisted to her husband. "He could be on television."

Ourcq looked at the time on the woman's watch on his wrist, then glanced through the arch into the lobby and spotted the girl at the front desk. She had a pussycat tucked under her right arm as if it were a rolled-up newspaper. "Imitate the sound of a fucking pistol with a fucking silencer attached going off," Ourcq instructed Appleyard, and he gestured with his eyes toward the lobby.

Appleyard peered over Ourcq's shoulder—and with a spitting sound produced the effect Ourcq had asked for.

In the lobby, the desk clerk brushed away a bird that had landed on the register and shook his head. Are you sure? the girl seemed to be saying. Even at this distance, it was evident that she was disappointed. The desk clerk shook his head again. He was probably telling her that the person in question hadn't left a forwarding address. Ourcq laughed to himself. Some people didn't like pussycats following them.

The cat, surveying the world from under the girl's arm, stared wide-eyed at a bird that planed past its head. The cat's tail spiraled up playfully. The girl snapped at the cat and turned back toward the front door.

"It is time for us to leave this fucking Seventh Heaven," Ourcq told Appleyard. He peeled off some bills and deposited them on the bar.

"Can you do a deep-sea diver surfacing?" the woman at the bar asked Appleyard.

"Can you do a bird pulling a worm from its hole?" asked Sergeant Major.

"Of course I can," Appleyard asserted. "I can do anything. I can do snow falling. I can do smoke rising. I can do the sun setting. I can do someone dying. The last two are actually very similar. Only I don't maybe have time right now." With that, he gulped down the rest of his Scotch, set the glass back on the bar and trailed after Ourcq toward the door.

16

❧

The Potter, not Kaat, happened to be driving, which is what saved their lives. He had been watching the headlights overtaking them in the rearview mirror. For some reason it made him think of Oskar's taxi worming its way along Zubovsky Boulevard from the Krimsky Bridge. When the car that was overtaking them pulled abreast on a straight stretch of road, and then stayed abreast, the skin on the back of the Potter's neck crawled; once again his body knew before he did. He glanced sideways and noticed it was a black Dodge with two men in the front seat. One of them was pointing at him, and then the Potter knew what his body knew. "Sweepers!" he muttered as his foot shot out and jammed down on the brake.

He never heard the shot. The only evidence that one had been fired was the neat hole that appeared in the window on the Potter's side of the car, and an instant later a second hole that turned up in the window on Kaat's side, inches in front of the Potter and Kaat. The Potter, behind the Dodge now, swerved to the left just as a second bullet drilled a small hole in the front window and buried itself in the rear seat above the head of the sleeping cat.

Kaat gasped and brought a fingernail to her lips. "What's—" (Later, when she recalled what had happened, she would comment on the Potter's ataraxia—utter calmness.)

The Potter accelerated and brought the Chevrolet hurtling up to the Dodge, and into it. The man twisting in the passenger seat trying to squeeze off a shot through his own rear window was flung sideways against the door. The driver spun his steering wheel to the right and braked in order to skid his car to a stop and block the road. He would have succeeded, except that he skidded half a yard too far. The Potter spotted a gap between the back of the Dodge and the nearest trees and drove his Chevrolet through it. The left wheels climbed up onto a shoulder, the car teetered, Kaat screamed. In the back seat the cat landed on all four feet on the side window. Then the Chevrolet sank back down on its four wheels and hurtled away from the Dodge behind them.

The Potter, leaning forward, peering into the night, gripping the wheel intently, tried desperately to sort things out. He had a short lead on the Dodge, but they would back and fill and start after him in a matter of seconds, and he had no doubt that the Dodge could outrun the Chevrolet. Ahead, on the farthest edge of his high beams, he caught a glimpse of a narrow bridge and a highway marker indicating that an intersection was coming up right after it. The next instant the Chevrolet was rolling over the bridge, and the intersection was looming ahead. In his rearview mirror the Potter caught sight of two dancing pinpoints of light. His hand shot out and pushed in a knob, cutting his own headlights. Night enveloped them, shrouded them, smothered them. Kaat whimpered some words, but the Potter didn't try to understand what she was saying. When he judged that they were almost up to the intersection, he braked and spun the wheel to the right and then speeded up again, expecting any instant that the Chevrolet would come crashing to a stop against the trunk of a tree. Through the front window he could make out a faint ribbon of grayness stretched ahead; under the wheels he could feel the smoothness of a road. He cut the engine and braked, more gently this time, and brought the car to a dead stop.

"Don't make a sound, don't move, if you please," the Potter whispered fiercely, and flinging open the door, he plunged from the car. He tugged his Beretta from his jacket pocket and pulled back the slide on the top of the barrel, chambering a round, and started back up the road toward the intersection. Thoughts, plots, plans, possibilities raced through his mind; his life, Kaat's also, would depend on his calculations being correct. Ahead, the Dodge squealed to a stop at the intersection. So far, so good. The two men in it would cut their engine and turn off their own headlights and get out of the car, each on his side, and peer in the three directions the Chevrolet could have gone for a glimpse of a taillight, the sound of a racing motor.

Suddenly a single powerful beam stabbed out into the night from the Dodge, and the Potter realized with a start that the car was equipped with a spotlight. It swept the road ahead, then swiveled past nearby tree trunks and bushes and leapt forward to illuminate the road to the left of the Dodge. The Potter knew he had only a few seconds left before the spot stabbed down the road he was on and pinned him in its beam. He lurched forward a few paces, then sank heavily to one knee, and gripping the Beretta with both hands, aimed. The spotlight began to swivel past trees in his direction. Squeeze, don't jerk the trigger, he shouted at himself in his head, and he willed his muscles to go through the motions *slowly*. Just as the light blinded him, he fired two quick shots. Glass shattered. Light ceased to exist. The Potter fired twice more at the part of the Dodge's silhouette where the front wheel would be, and heard a soft hissing sound. At the front door of the Dodge, several small sparks, as momentary and as bright as flashing fireflies, speckled the darkness, followed by spitting noises, and there was a scratching in the road just to the Potter's left, as if someone were trying to strike a safety match against it. The Potter leapt to one side and lumbered back along the soft shoulder away from the Dodge and its fireflies, toward the Chevrolet. Behind him doors slammed. Someone kicked a tire and cursed. The Potter could hear footfalls as two men started trotting down the road after him.

Winded, the Potter came up to the Chevrolet and dived into the driver's seat and hit the starter. The motor coughed into life. Grinding the Chevrolet into gear, the Potter let the car leap forward. Something punctured the car's trunk compartment with a whine. Then the Potter was in second gear and the car was rolling smoothly and the gap between the fireflies in his rearview mirror and them widened. The Potter sucked air into his bursting lungs and looked at Kaat to see if she were all right, but she was trembling and staring back over her shoulder with an infinitely sad look in her eyes. Following her glance, the Potter caught sight of the small bloodstained body of Kaat's Meow lying like a discarded fur mitten on the rear seat.

"I wonder," Kaat said in an almost inaudible voice, "what she will turn up as in her next incarnation."

17

❦

Khanda slid into the booth across from the portly man whose name was Rubenstein. They were about a mile and a half from the downtown wart, in a zone where an ordinance was in force banning liquor that was paid for by the drink. Hence the charade that this was a private club, and the people in it regular members. In fact, anyone could buy a membership at the door for an evening, and the price translated into a certain number of free drinks. The police gave the club a wide berth (except when they changed into civilian clothes and turned up for some drinks on the house) because Rubenstein had a reputation for being generous when it came to slipping small envelopes into jacket pockets at police headquarters.

Eyeing Khanda across the table, Rubenstein mumbled something about his not being at all what he expected.

"What did you expect," Khanda asked.

"Considering what you are going to do, someone a bit older, more worldly," Rubenstein admitted.

Khanda shrugged. Rubenstein asked how much progress he had made. Khanda told him about the job he had gotten in the warehouse. He had scouted the upper floors, he said, and he thought he had found the perfect sniper's nest, one that would give him at least three shots at the target as the limousine was moving almost directly away from him.

"What about the getaway?" Rubenstein inquired.

"What about the getaway?" Khanda shot back. "That's supposed to be your bailiwick."

"If you can get out of the building, I can get you out of the country," Rubenstein promised.

Khanda said he thought there would be enough confusion

after the shooting for him to make it down a back staircase to the street before the police could figure out where the shots had come from and seal off the building.

"Have you timed it?" Rubenstein asked.

"Not yet," Khanda admitted. "But I figure if I abandon the rifle instead of trying to hide it, I can be out of there in a matter of minutes."

"You have to walk out so you don't attract attention to yourself," Rubenstein cautioned.

"I'm not stupid," Khanda said.

Rubenstein asked what kind of rifle Khanda planned to use. He had been associated with the Chicago underworld before he was recruited by the Russians, and knew a thing or two about firearms.

Khanda told him about the rifle he had bought through a mail-order house. "At the distance I plan to shoot from," he said, "I'll have trouble missing."

Rubenstein nodded. "In the right hands the rifle should be deadly," he agreed. He pushed aside the Scotch glasses and unfolded a small map of the city on the table. "After the shooting, you board a bus here," he said, pointing to an intersection not far from the assassination site. "You get off here. Then you walk toward my apartment, which is here. I'll pick you up in my car and drive you to a private airport outside the city. Our mutual friends will have a small plane waiting to take us to Mexico. I've dealt drugs in Mexico. I know my way around there. From Mexico, our Cuban friends will get you by boat to Cuba, and from there, by an Aeroflot flight, to Moscow."

Khanda studied the map. "It looks good," he said, nodding. "It looks very good."

"It always looks good," Rubenstein said moodily, "until something unexpected happens. The main thing is for you not to panic. If you can make it to where I can find you, I can guarantee I'll get you to Moscow."

Khanda sipped his drink. Rubenstein asked Khanda if he had any other questions. "This is the moment to ask them," he said, "since it would be wiser if we never met again."

"When I was in that school of theirs in Minsk," Khanda ventured, "we learned that assassins always work in pairs.

Have you heard any talk about someone else having the same assignment as me?"

"As far as I know," Rubenstein assured Khanda, "you're all alone in this."

Khanda seemed relieved. "Well," he said, "I guess that covers just about everything," and he smiled boyishly and spread his hands.

To Rubenstein he looked like a traveling salesman who had wound up his pitch. "Good luck and all that sort of thing," he told him.

They shook hands. Khanda slid out of the seat, and hiking up his trousers, strode through the semidarkness of the club toward the street door. Rubenstein stared after him. He had to admit it, he didn't much like the look of him. There was an arrogance to his eyes, an iciness to the set of his lips that disturbed Rubenstein, left him with a bad taste in his mouth. Well, so much the better. It would only make carrying out his instructions that much easier.

If for some reason he couldn't organize Khanda's escape, he was under orders to organize his death.

18

⚜

G. Sprowls was not a happy man. Normally his superiors left him with a free hand when it came to conducting interrogations. He set the pace; he delivered the goodies. This time, however, they were putting pressure on him. Nobody came right out and told him to speed things up. Rather there were subtle hints—delivered almost daily—that speed was essential. Various highly placed people would phone to see if progress had been made. There would be pregnant pauses on the other end of the line when G. Sprowls hedged. The impression would then be conveyed that time was of the essence. If, as the superficial facts seemed to suggest, the Sisters had set in motion an operation on their own, the aristocrats in the Company's front office wanted to know about it, and fast. The point being that they could then exercise the option of either canceling it—or taking credit for it.

Which is why G. Sprowls decided, several days before he was as ready as he would have liked to be, that the time had come to hook Francis up to a lie detector.

"I thought you said you wouldn't get around to this until the end of the week," Francis remarked absently as the technician inflated the rubber tube around his chest that would measure his breathing rhythm. Francis might have been getting his annual electrocardiogram for all the attention he paid.

G. Sprowls disregarded the comment, as usual. "Is that too tight?" he asked, his half-smile frozen on his face.

"Not at all," Francis said politely.

The technician, a man in his early sixties, hovered over the black box so that he could read the trace produced by the three styluses. "Anytime you are, I am," he told G. Sprowls.

"For what it's worth," Francis said pleasantly, "I am ready too."

G. Sprowls turned to the first page in his loose-leaf book. He studied what he had written for several minutes, then nodded at the technician, who threw a switch setting the styluses in motion. "We'll begin with some control questions, if you don't mind," G. Sprowls said. "Would you be so kind as to state your full name as it appears on your birth certificate."

"Francis Augustus," Francis said, and he added his family name.

"State your marital status."

Francis adjusted the knot of his mauve bow tie. "Happily, blissfully, single," he replied.

"State your age, your home address, the model of the car you drive."

"I am, at last count, forty-four years of age. I live at—" He gave the address of his downtown residence hotel. "I am the proud owner of a rather beat-up but serviceable fifty-nine Ford."

The technician looked up from the trace and nodded.

"We will turn now," G. Sprowls said, "to the details surrounding the defection from Russia of Feliks Arkantevich Turov, known also as the Potter."

"By all means," Francis agreed heartily.

"Will you tell us where the idea that the Potter might want to defect originated?"

"Either Carroll or I, I forget who, noticed an item in one of the West German Y summaries that mentioned that Turov had been put out to pasture. We had more or less followed his career; we were, you might say, fans of his. We knew he had suffered a series of setbacks in recent months."

"Can you be more specific?" G. Sprowls ordered.

"I can try to be," Francis agreed, flashing an innocent smile. "Three of the sleepers that Turov had trained had bitten the dust, as they say in the wild west. Turov was bound to be blamed for their loss."

"You and Carroll contributed to the Potter's downfall when you ferreted out one of his sleepers, I remember."

"So did you," Francis shot back. "We exposed him, you broke him."

G. Sprowls ignored him. "Aside from the loss of the three sleepers, and the subsequent disgrace of the Potter, was there any other reason to think he might be ripe for defection?"

Francis swallowed a yawn. "We knew in a very general way that he was married to a woman much younger than he was who was likely to put a great deal of pressure on him."

"What kind of pressure?"

"The money that had been available, the apartment overlooking the Moscow River, the chauffeured limousine, the access to Western products, all of these would disappear. If he wanted to keep the woman, and we suspected he did, he would have to come up with the equivalent."

G. Sprowls glanced at the technician, who lifted his eyes to gaze through the upper part of his bifocals. "So far, so good," he said.

"Let's talk about authorization for a moment," G. Sprowls suggested.

"Let's," Francis repeated amiably.

"The effort to get the Potter to defect was authorized, according to my notes, by the Deputy Director for Operations. Is that your understanding?"

"We proposed, he disposed."

"When you proposed, as you put it, did you also tell the Deputy Director precisely what you expected to get from the Potter if he could be induced to defect?"

"Absolutely," Francis replied.

"His version is that you said you expected to get odds and ends."

"Odds and ends are what we thought we would get," Francis agreed. A smile of transparent innocence spread across his features. "You are not thinking this through," he chastised G. Sprowls. "If we had been operating behind the Deputy Director's back, why would we have sent our man Friday to Vienna to skim off the cream? Surely one of us would have gone in his place."

G. Sprowls leaned forward. It was precisely this point that baffled him. "The fact of the matter is that your man Friday did skim off the cream," he went on. "The fact of the matter is that he was acting on your specific instructions. The fact of the matter is that you wound up with more than odds and ends."

Francis shook his head in mild frustration. "The Potter trained sleepers. What could have been more logical than to ask him, at the moment he came across the frontier, if he would have the kindness to give us, as a token of his good faith, the names and addresses of any sleepers who might still be in circulation?"

"You acknowledge that that was the cream that your man Friday was sent to skim off?"

"We would have been idiots if we hadn't sent him to try," Francis insisted.

G. Sprowls flipped to the next page in his loose-leaf book and studied it for a long moment. "Your man Friday," he said without looking up, "has told us that the Potter gave him the name and address and awakening signal of a Soviet sleeper living in Brooklyn Heights, and that he passed this information on to you. Is his version of events correct?"

"Perfectly correct, yes."

"Yet your Op Proposal updater filed with the Deputy Director, a photocopy of which I have before me, contained no mention of the fact that you had come into possession of this information," G. Sprowls drawled.

It struck Francis that G. Sprowls tended to slip into a drawl when he thought he had a nibble and was starting to gently reel in the line. "No mention at all," he acknowledged cheerfully.

"Of course you can account for this discrepancy," G. Sprowls said in his slow drawl.

"Of course."

G. Sprowls looked up from his loose-leaf notebook and issued a formal invitation. "Feel free to do so," he said.

Francis actually sighed here. "We naturally attempted to verify the information when our man Friday—our *former* man Friday is probably more accurate—passed it on to us," he said. "There was a person by that name living at the address in Brooklyn Heights specified by the Potter. Except that he had decamped. Skedaddled. Flown the coop. A discreet phone call elicited the information that he was off somewhere on a business trip. Quite obviously, there were only two ways of confirming the Potter's information. We could have hooked the Potter up to one of these contraptions"—Francis cast a benign smile at the black box behind him—"over in Austria. Except the Potter had slipped through our man Friday's not very sticky fingers and was no longer available. Or we could wait for the alleged sleeper to return to his nest in Brooklyn Heights, then send him the awakening signal, along with an order or two— tell him to scratch his ass in front of the information booth at Grand Central station at high noon, for instance—and see if he responded. In any case, it would have been ridiculously premature for us to have put any of this into our Op Proposal updater—surely even you can understand that. People of our caliber only deal with confirmed information. Consider this: perhaps the Potter was not a defector, but someone planted on us in order to make us swallow false information. Perhaps he was a genuine defector who, once across, decided to give us bubbles that burst when you tried to get a grip on them. Perhaps our *former* man Friday was inventing the whole thing."

G. Sprowls looked Francis in the eye. "And you are willing to state categorically that neither you nor Carroll awakened the alleged sleeper and sent him on his merry way?"

"Categorically, yes."

The technician shrugged uncertainly. "Could he make a positive declaration? 'I state categorically that neither I nor to my knowledge Carroll'—that sort of thing."

G. Sprowls focused his half-smile on Francis.

Francis exhaled sharply through his nostrils and nodded. "I state categorically that neither I nor to my knowledge Carroll awakened the alleged sleeper residing in Brooklyn Heights and dispatched him on a mission. Does that do the trick?"

On the spur of the moment (the question was not in his loose-leaf book) G. Sprowls asked, "Have you had any contact with agents or representatives of another country?"

Francis' face glistened with innocence as he replied, "I have not had any contact with agents or representatives of another country."

G. Sprowls glanced at the technician, who bent over the styluses scratching away in the black box. Finally the technician looked up. "He's telling the truth," he concluded.

"All of it and nothing but," Francis added cheerfully, "so help me God." And he added mischievously, "You are barking up the wrong tree."

Carroll didn't fare as well as Francis when G. Sprowls put him through his paces that very same afternoon. "He's lying," the technician announced evenly, staring at the telltale traces through the bottom half of his bifocals.

G. Sprowls cleared his throat. Curiously, he seemed embarrassed for Carroll, almost as if he had stripped him of his clothing. "So you are up to something after all," he said.

A muscle twitched in Carroll's cheek. "We are not up to anything we should not be up to," he declared.

"Whatever you're doing," G. Sprowls filled in the gap, "you have authorization to do it?"

"We are good soldiers," Carroll insisted, his eyes staring vacantly at some point on the far wall. "We are patriots—the word is not used lightly. We serve the best interests of our country in ways that our superiors indicate to us." Unable to control himself any longer, Carroll burst out, "The first war I fought in was the wrong war. The next one will be the right war. We must at all costs be prepared for it."

"I see," G. Sprowls said, although he didn't see at all what Carroll was getting at. He decided to let the business of wrong wars and right wars go for the moment, and concentrate on the question of authorization. If he could discover who Carroll thought had given him authorization, perhaps he could uncover what Carroll felt authorized to do.

"It is fairly simple," Carroll replied in answer to another question. He seemed eager to justify himself. "Things were said by highly placed people in public places—at in-house pours, at a reception for a British colleague, at a medal-pinning ceremony honoring the fellow down the corridor from us who was retiring."

G. Sprowls appeared to sympathize completely with Carroll. "You read between the lines," he suggested in a slow drawl.

"The Director was obviously in no position to give an explicit order," Carroll said. "So he did the next best thing. It is out of the realm of possibility that he would have said what he did if he hadn't expected someone to take his words to heart; and if he hadn't expected someone to act on them." He arched his neck to relieve the pressure from his starched collar. "We are, Francis and I, old hands. We were, as Francis likes to say, pointed in the right direction. Where is the crime if we marched?"

"When you marched," G. Sprowls drawled softly, his half-smile inviting confession, offering absolution, "you mean that you organized the defection of the Potter in order to get access to the identity and awakening signal of a Soviet sleeper; that you then used this signal to awaken him and send him off on an assignment that you knew your superiors would approve of."

For an endless moment the styluses scraped noisily away in the black box. Again a muscle twitched in Carroll's cheek. "That's roughly it," he acknowledged wearily.

On a hunch, G. Sprowls slipped in a question. "Have you had any contact with agents or representatives of another country?"

Carroll closed his eyes in frustration. "You don't understand anything I've told you, in the end," he said.

"Would you like me to repeat the question?" G. Sprowls asked.

"No contact with agents or representatives of another country," Carroll said in a dull voice.

The technician looked up at G. Sprowls and nodded. Carroll was telling the truth.

"And Francis is involved in this with you?" G. Sprowls wanted to know.

"Francis speaks for Francis," Carroll snapped. "I speak for myself."

"About the assignment you gave to the Soviet sleeper," G. Sprowls said casually.

"When he carries it out," Carroll replied carefully, self-justification unfurling across his face like a flag, "you will know it instantly. Everyone will know it instantly. People we

203

don't even know will stop us in the corridor and shake our hands."

The technician tried to catch G. Sprowls's attention; to indicate to him, with a roll of his eyes, that Carroll was stark raving mad. But G. Sprowls was concentrating on making Carroll think he sympathized with him. Exaggerating his drawl, he started to pose another question.

Carroll cut him off. "I can't tell you any more than I've already told you," he said curtly. And he closed his mouth in a way that indicated he had no intention of opening it again in the immediate future.

19

G. Sprowls ate cold sandwiches in his office that evening, and worked late into the night. Seeing the light through his transom, the night security officer knocked on the door to make sure he had authorization. G. Sprowls, irritated at the interruption, showed him a chit signed by none other than the Director himself.

The thing that was baffling G. Sprowls as he pored over the printouts, notched with numbers to indicate what question was being asked at any given moment, was how Francis and Carroll, who worked together, could be telling completely different stories, with no trace that either one was lying. Had Carroll gone off on a tangent of his own? The routine tape recordings of their office chitchat made this seem unlikely. Whatever they were doing, they were obviously doing together. Yet Carroll had admitted they were up to something. And Francis had denied it.

And they were both telling the truth.

G. Sprowls removed his eyeglasses and massaged his eyes with a thumb and forefinger. His lids felt inflamed, his eyes more comfortable closed than open. He was tempted to lean his head on the desk, to doze off, dreaming, no doubt, of styluses scratching away on paper and a dwarflike figure pinned, like a gypsy moth, to a piece of cork in a collector's case. As usual, G. Sprowls resisted. With a determined gesture he fitted his eyeglasses back over his rather oversized ears and started where he always started when he couldn't put his finger on something he suspected was there: at the beginning. "We'll begin with some control questions, if you don't mind," the transcript read. "Would you be so kind as to state your full name as it appears on your birth certificate."

G. Sprowls glanced across at the stylus traces that corresponded to the answer. There wasn't a waver in them. "Francis Augustus," Francis had replied, adding his family name.

His name!

G. Sprowls's brow furrowed thoughtfully. A conversation in the lunchroom some four or five years before came back to him. Several middle-echelon ex-field hands responsible for funneling money to friendly trade-union people in Latin America had been talking about a wild scheme that had circulated in the form of a lemon-colored Op Proposal, only to be shot out of the sky by a prudent department head. The scheme called for bribing the captain of a supertanker to run his ship onto some rocks off Cuba, causing an enormous oil spill that would pollute the coastline, ruin Cuba's fishing and tourist industry, and in general divert economic resources away from Castro's military and industrial buildup. "Sounds like something the Sisters might have thought up," one of the ex-field hands had said, and when G. Sprowls, just back from an overseas tour and new to Washington, had asked who the Sisters were, he had gotten the full description. There was Carroll with his three-piece suits and red welts around his neck from the starched collars which, so it was said, he wore to atone for unspecified sins; and there was Francis, who sported outrageous bow ties, an expression on his face midway between curious and reluctant and a Cheshire cat's innocent smile—so innocent, in fact, that he regularly lied about his *name* during the annual lie-detector tests and managed to fool the black box.

G. Sprowls reached into a drawer and took out Francis's service file. He thumbed through the sheets in it until he came to the one he was looking for—a photocopy of Francis's birth certificate. The name listed on it was Francis Algernon. Not Francis Augustus.

So he had lied, while hooked up to the black box, about his name.

G. Sprowls gazed up from Francis' service file, the half-smile warped into a grimace of satisfaction. He had heard about people who could beat the black box, but he had never come across one before. The box registered stress that someone would feel when he didn't tell the truth—moisture on the palms, a slight change in pulse rate or respiration. But Francis was obviously one of those extremely rare individuals who didn't feel stress of any kind when he lied. And if Francis was able to lie about his name, he would have been able to lie about the Potter and the Sleeper.

20

Almost everything the Sleeper knew about tradecraft he had learned from the Potter. During the first months at the Moscow sleeper school, the Potter had concentrated on sharpening his student's powers of observation. Piotr Borisovich would be dispatched to spend an afternoon in the lobby of a large tourist hotel, with instructions to note everything that happened and report back to the Potter. "You omitted the arrival of the fat American woman carrying a shopping bag from a Paris department store," the Potter would say after debriefing the Sleeper. "Also the Intourist woman who had a dispute with someone on the phone and burst into tears when she hung up. Also the man in the wheelchair who asked you for a match. The man in the wheelchair, in case you are curious, works for me. He was there to watch you."

So it went. One day Piotr Borisovich would be assigned to follow a junior diplomat from a junior country—but always from in front, since people seldom suspected anyone in front of following them. Another time the Sleeper would be sent across the city and back, and then asked if anyone had been following him. At the beginning, there might be no one, but his imagination would get the best of him and he would think there had been someone. On still another occasion there might be someone, but the Sleeper would not spot him and would report back that his wake had been clean. Slowly, however, he began to get the hang of it. He had a natural instinct for the streets, a good memory for faces, sharp eyes and a knack for improvisation, which in the end is the hallmark of a good agent. As the Potter drummed into his head: there were no rules. He himself, he explained by way of giving an example, had once hobbled after an Israeli agent in New York for the better part of an afternoon, on the theory that the agent would never suspect a crippled man of following him.

In time the Sleeper's tradecraft became as good as the Potter's. He too learned how to take advantage of the reflecting surfaces in the street to keep track of everything that was going on around him; not just store windows, but doors of cars, windows of buses, distant mirrors on the walls of department stores. It was a rare event when he couldn't pick out of a crowd the man or woman, and once, a teenager on roller skates, whom the Potter had put on his tail. (One tip the Sleeper never forgot: if you spot someone following you and don't want him to know he's been spotted, pick your nose.) It became a standing joke between them that once the Sleeper had identified the tail, he bought him a vodka if he was a man, and seduced her if it turned out to be a woman.

Now, whiling away two and a half days between buses in a small town in Ohio, the Sleeper, without consciously thinking about it, found himself scanning the rush-hour crowd for that telltale jerk of a head that turned away when he looked at it; for the glimpse of someone who didn't move through the streets at the rhythm of the crowd around him, but seemed to linger at store windows studying objects that, judging from appearances, he seemed unlikely to buy. The last thing the Sleeper expected was to spot anyone—which is why he felt shaken when he spotted two shadows. The first one, in his middle forties, balding, bloated, effeminate, was in a telephone booth, dialing as if his life depended on it. What gave him away was that the Sleeper remembered seeing him twice before earlier in the afternoon, both times in telephone booths dialing like mad. The second man, rail-thin, with wavy hair and lips that seemed to be pursed and producing sounds, the Sleeper noticed because every time he saw him he was gazing up at street signs as if he were lost.

The Sleeper immediately dismissed the possibility that they were two local hoodlums who had spotted a stranger in town and were planning to roll him. If they had followed him for any length of time, they would be aware that he had arrived by Greyhound bus and was staying in a not very luxurious hotel near the station—hardly the mark of someone who might be carrying a good deal of cash on him. (Ironically, the Sleeper did have more than six thousand dollars in small bills, most of which he had stuffed into the top half of the viola-da-gamba case in which the rifle, broken down into component parts, fitted.) Which narrowed it down to people who were in the same business he was in.

But on which side was the irritating question.

Forcing himself to act as if nothing unusual had happened, the Sleeper caught his bus early the next morning and, following his itinerary to the letter, headed farther west. The two men—he had nicknamed the one with the pursed lips Whistler, and the effeminate one Whistler's Mother—weren't in the bus with him, nor did he spot them trailing after him in automobiles, nor were they around when he touched down that night in a motel on the outskirts of Indianapolis. Walking through the city the next morning, the Sleeper used every reflecting surface he could find, but the two men were nowhere to be seen. He was beginning to think he might have imagined the whole thing when, thirty-six hours after he had left the small town in Ohio, he saw them again. When he turned to look over his shoulder, he spotted Whistler gazing up at a street sign at an intersection. Half an hour later he saw Whistler's Mother squeezed into a phone booth in a drugstore, dialing away as if he were reporting a fire.

The Sleeper thought he could perceive a time pattern in the movements of Whistler and Whistler's Mother. Like him, they would have taken roughly twelve hours to get from the small town in Ohio to Indianapolis. Yet he hadn't spotted them for thirty-six hours. Which meant that they had not bothered to tail him for twenty-four hours. And that little detail told the Sleeper two things: they were most likely professional sweepers who lingered for a day after he moved on to ensure that nobody else was following him; and they obviously had a duplicate of his itinerary.

The theory was easy enough to verify. The next day the Sleeper boarded a bus that would take him across Illinois to St. Louis. Two blocks from the Greyhound terminal he let out a cry of panic and went racing up the aisle to the driver with a story about having forgotten the valise that had all his music in it. The driver shrugged a pair of fat shoulders, swung the bus over to the curb, opened the doors with a rush of air and let the Sleeper off. "You can catch another bus around noon," the driver shouted down, "but you'll have to buy another ticket 'cause this one's been punched, and there ain't no way in the world I can unpunch it."

Doubling back on his tracks, the Sleeper returned to the motel on the outskirts of Indianapolis. He made his way down a long, narrow alley past several overflowing garbage cans to the kitchen door. The only person in the kitchen was a black dishwasher wearing pink rubber gloves that reached to his elbows. He was finishing up the breakfast dishes. Depositing his viola-da-gamba case and his worn leather valise under a table, the Sleeper walked over to the swinging doors and looked through the small porthole into the dining room. An elderly waiter was setting the tables for lunch. Beyond the dining room was the bar. Two men sat on stools in front of it, sipping drinks, glancing occasionally at the check-in desk, which they could see in the mirror behind the bar.

The two men were Whistler and Whistler's Mother.

Which meant that they were sweepers: *nash*, literally *ours*, sent by the people who had drawn up his itinerary, his masters in Moscow.

But why did his masters in Moscow feel he needed sweepers trailing after him? What did they know that he didn't know? Had there been a leak that could compromise his mission, not to mention his life? Were they afraid that he would lose his nerve? Had they sent the sweepers after him to make sure he went through with it? He was tempted to stop them on the street, invite them—in Russian; would they be embarrassed!—to a bar for a glass of vodka, the way he did in Moscow when he spotted the man whom the Potter had put on his tail.

But this wasn't Moscow, and he wasn't a neophyte sleeper learning the fundamentals of tradecraft. This was America. And he was on a mission that would end, if he was successful, in someone else's death; in his own death if he was not.

Mulling over the various possibilities, the Sleeper retraced his steps and caught the noon bus to St. Louis. There was a half-hour holdover at Terre Haute. When he got back to the bus, he found a woman sitting in his seat. She was wearing blue jeans and white ankle-length socks and high heels. She was chewing gum and reading an old issue of *Vogue* and shaking her head in despair, activating long pendulum earrings that the Sleeper expected to chime the hour. "Hey, you don't mind none if I take the window?" she asked, looking up with a faint smile. "Buses give me claustro-whatever."

Depositing his viola-da-gamba case in the rack overhead, the Sleeper slid wordlessly into the aisle seat next to her. "That's very gentlemanly of you," the woman said. "There are not many gentlemen around these days. Say, what did you say your name was?"

"I didn't say what my name was," the Sleeper answered. "But I will be glad to tell you." He gave her the name he was traveling under.

"My name is Orr," she said, "with two R's. Geraldine Orr. My friends call me Jerry."

"I am extremely happy to make your acquaintance," the Sleeper told her, his appetite whetted by the curve of her breasts inside her black turtleneck sweater.

"Likewise, I'm sure," said Jerry Orr.

It came out in conversation that she had been offered a job checking hats and selling cigarettes in a nightclub in St. Louis. She had worked there several years before, but had left to live with a garage mechanic in Terre Haute. That had ended badly when he went off with his childhood sweetheart, a Wave stationed in Norfolk. "Couples are basically collisions," Jerry Orr said with a sigh, and the Sleeper agreed heartily. Couples, in his experience, were unnatural combinations, something people created for economic or logistical reasons. But when you came right down to it, after the newness wore off, living as a couple was like condemning yourself to permanent house arrest; you limited your possibilities, and hence your potential. Even Millie's "triple," which at least had the saving grace of offering variety, had begun to feel like a prison of sorts. The Sleeper thought of Kaat. There had been something unusual about her, he had to admit it. If you had to be trapped in a couple, it was better to be trapped with someone like Kaat in the end.

"I don't ever want to get involved again," Jerry Orr was saying, "because it takes too much out of me. Emotionally, I mean. I like people who are just passing through, if you see what I mean."

The Greyhound picked up speed as it crossed the high plateau on which Terre Haute was planted. Long fields stretched off like religious wafers to the horizon. It occurred to the Sleeper that if the world were really flat, the horizon he could see from the window of the bus might be the bitter end of it. Soon after, the Wabash was behind them and the bus was heading down Route 70 into Illinois. The Sleeper thought about the man he was traveling across the country to kill. He had seen a photograph of him in a copy of *Newsweek* discarded on a bench at the bus terminal. He seemed like a decent enough man, fiddling with the button of his suit jacket, eyeing the camera with sardonic detachment. The Sleeper shrugged away the image of the man he would see, if all went according to plan, through the telescopic sight on his rifle. He felt devoid of energy; of hope. He remembered another snatch of Walter Whitman. "The past and present wilt . . . I have drained them." Which left the future. To get his mind off it, he reached across and brushed the back of Jerry Orr's wrist with his fingertips. "I'll be in St. Louis for two days and two nights," he told her. And he added pointedly, "I'm just passing through, if you see what I mean."

The faint smile on Jerry Orr's face brightened. She saw what he meant.

21

✣

Kaat had gone into mourning for her dead cat. "Why would they want to kill her?" she cried, biting furiously on a fingernail. The Potter's answer—that they hadn't wanted to kill her cat; they had wanted to kill *them*!—didn't diminish her sense of loss. The fact that the cat was dead and buried (in a trench by the side of a back road, covered with gravel and dead leaves) and they were alive seemed to impress her more than anything the Potter could offer her in the way of comfort. Then, almost six hours to the minute after the bullet pierced the back of the car and lodged by pure chance in the cat's body, she shook herself the way a dog does when it comes in out of the rain. "Here's the thing," she said in a serious voice, and it was evident to the Potter that she had stopped thinking about the cat and started thinking about herself. "I want out. I'm not made for this kind of adventure. I have butterflies in my stomach just thinking about what happened."

She saw the confusion on the Potter's face as he tried to figure out how someone could have butterflies in the stomach. "It means I'm nervous," she explained in exasperation. "It means I have gas. It means I fart all the time."

The Potter had seen people crack before, and with less cause; had been surprised that she had not cracked sooner. "A night's rest, perhaps," he muttered, as if sleep could solve her problem, could dissipate the gas, could restore her sense of her own dignity, could give her the courage to go on.

"Park me somewhere," she pleaded, and her voice had the unmistakable vibrations of fear in it. "Park me anywhere."

"And Piotr Borisovich?"

She avoided his eye and concentrated on a fingernail.

"Look," he said finally—the Chevrolet's headlights had just picked up a sign indicating they were crossing the border into Indiana—"if I can catch up with Piotr and talk to him, maybe I can save his life."

"Why is someone trying to kill him?" Kaat asked in a voice so devoid of inquisitiveness it was obvious she would have been just as happy if he didn't answer.

"Piotr Borisovich is an espionage agent," the Potter said in a whisper, as if he were afraid of being overheard. "He has been sent on a mission, that much is obvious. This is what I think: whoever sent him on this mission wants Piotr to be caught, so that the blame for the mission will fall on the Russians."

"What am I doing here?" Kaat mumbled, staring out of her side of the car.

"It was your idea to come," the Potter blurted out. "I need you. Believe me, if you please. If you please?"

The Potter was squinting into the headlights of an oncoming car. When it passed, he glanced quickly at her. "It is important for me," he said suddenly. "I must save him." And he repeated, "If you please? He is the son I never had."

Kaat looked straight into his eyes as if she could see through them to some dark center, some remote corner where he would not give any more of himself away.

The moment passed. He turned back to the highway. "Stay, please, at least until he makes one more phone call to your friend in Brooklyn, New York," he said in a flat voice.

"Why not?" she replied, moved by his physical ugliness; by his need for her; above all by the difficulty he had expressing it.

After she agreed, the Potter broached the subject of the car. "You want me to steal an automobile that belongs to someone else?" Kaat exploded when he first raised the possibility.

"We cannot keep driving around in this one," the Potter insisted, and he explained some of the facts of life to Kaat. There were two men behind them who would presumably mount a spare tire in place of the flat tire with the bullet hole in it, and start out after them. If they managed to catch up with them they would kill the Potter, and then feel obliged to deal with any witnesses in a similar way.

Kaat asked how the two men in the Dodge could possibly find them, given the twists and turns the Potter had taken in the hour after the incident at the crossroad. "We don't have any idea where we are going," she pointed out with irreproachable logic, "so how can they know where we're going?"

It was a reasonable question, to which the Potter offered a reasonable explanation. They had run into the two men in the Dodge right after they had almost caught up with the Sleeper; they had most likely been spotted making inquiries at the inn with the curious name of Seventh Heaven. Which meant that whoever had awakened the Sleeper and dispatched him on his mission had been covering his tracks with what the professionals called sweepers. And that, in turn, meant that every time they managed to get close to the Sleeper, they risked a new run-in with the men in the Dodge. Driving around in the Chevrolet would only make matters easier for the sweepers.

Kaat still wasn't convinced about the need for a new car until the Potter told her *how* she would steal it—at which point she made a hundred-and-eighty-degree turn and waxed enthusiastic about the idea and began peering eagerly through the front window looking for a suitable location. On the outskirts of a small town in southern Indiana they found what they were looking for: a low, modern circular structure with pulsating neon arrows pointing the way from the main road, and raucous rock music filling the night around it.

The parking lot in back of the nightclub already held more than three dozen cars. The Potter drew up on the far edge of the lot, near a line of trees, and cut the motor. He rummaged around in the trunk for the tool kit that came with the tire iron, found a screwdriver in it and began to remove the Chevrolet's license plates. Once he had them off he told Kaat he was ready if she was. She took a deep breath to calm her nerves, unbuttoned, at the Potter's suggestion—he had a mania for details like this—another button of her shirt, and went around to plant herself on the curb near the front door of the nightclub.

Within minutes a red two-door Ford pulled up and two

girls spilled from its doors. The Potter, watching from the corner of the nightclub, waved Kaat off; he wanted a newer, heavier car, also one that was more subdued and less likely to attract attention. The boy who was driving the Ford honked his horn at the girls as they disappeared through the door of the nightclub, and gunning his engine, raced off to park in the lot.

The Potter let four more cars go by before he found one that appealed to him. Eventually a blue four-door Chrysler eased to a stop in front of the entrance. A girl and a boy emerged from the back seat, a second girl from the front seat. They were well dressed, slightly older than the other clients of the nightclub; they gave the impression of college kids who had borrowed a car from one of their parents for a night of slumming.

The Potter pointed at the car and nodded vigorously. Kaat mustered a toothy smile and trotted around to the driver's side. "There's a new service starting tonight," she informed the driver. "We park your car for you, and bring it around when you're ready to leave." And she added, "There's no charge, but if you'd like to give me something for my trouble, I won't say no."

The boy behind the wheel hesitated, then caught sight of his girl observing him. Not wanting to appear unsophisticated, he climbed out of the car, fished a dollar bill from his shirt pocket, handed it to Kaat with a nod and went off to join his friends. Kaat slid in behind the wheel and drove the Chrysler over to where the Chevrolet was parked. The Potter appeared a moment later and began attaching the license plates from the Chevrolet.

"I don't believe it!" Kaat exclaimed as they sped away from the nightclub in the Chrysler. "I actually did it. Me! I stole a car!" She pressed her hands to her ears in exhilaration. "In my next incarnation," she abruptly announced, her eyes pressed shut as if she were visualizing it, "I want to do that kind of thing more often. I want to *not* suppress farts and *not* set the hair of dead people and *not* obey the law all the goddamned time." She slid down in the seat so that her head rested on the back of it, kicked off her shoes and propped her feet up on the dashboard. "Do people steal cars in Russia?" she asked after a while.

"There aren't that many cars in Russia to steal," the Potter replied with a laugh. "There is very little crime in the ordinary sense of the word—muggings, bank robberies, burglaries. On the other hand, everyone steals from the state whenever they can. People work less and accept their full salary. They take bribes for doing what they are supposed to do anyway. You might say that we have no crime, but more than our share of corruption."

The way he said it made her turn her head toward him. "Why do you serve the state if there is so much corruption?" she asked softly.

The Potter waved a hand in irritation; she didn't understand at all. He was a Chekist from the old school; he had made his commitment to Leninism early in life, and stuck to it even when the excesses of the cult of the personality became apparent. If there had been a viable alternative, he had never been aware of it. Western democracies were decadent; they weighed competing philosophies rather than deciding where the rights of the matter lay. Stalinism, moreover, was not the inevitable result of Leninism, but an aberration. Mankind's best—for the Potter, its only—hope rested in the idealistic seeds buried within Leninism. But how could he explain all this to her? He decided to try; it suddenly seemed important to tell her *who* he was.

"The roots of the Russian state are idealistic," he said. "Because things have taken a bad turn is no reason for someone to abandon the original dream. All dreams turn sour at some point. Only the faint of heart, or those whose original commitment was self-serving, lose faith. That is something you, being American, should understand better than most people. Your country started out with idealistic roots too, but your 'All men are created equal' didn't include Negroes. It took a civil war to bring them into the mainstream of the country's idealism. You still haven't solved the problem completely. But the important thing is that you are evolving. My country will evolve too. It will move closer to a situation in which its actions match the idealism of its founders."

"You believe that? You believe Russia will rediscover its idealistic roots?"

The Potter said quietly, "I am obliged to believe it."

"What about Peter?" she asked after a moment's reflection. She appeared to wince at the memory of a pain when she pronounced his name. "Does he believe in Russia? Does he think what he is doing will help it evolve?"

"We both of us thought that what we were doing would help it survive," the Potter replied, thinking of the unlaundered years, "and as long as it survived, it would evolve."

Kaat reached over to rest her hand on the Potter's, but he jerked it away. It wasn't that he was afraid of physical contact with her; it was more a matter of wanting it too much.

They continued on in a westerly direction, one of them driving, the other dozing in the passenger seat. They stopped at an all-night diner next to a drive-in movie, and Kaat phoned Millie back in Brooklyn, but she hadn't heard anything more from Peter. The Potter was afraid they had lost him forever, but Kaat remained hopeful. She found a road map and spread it across her knees and dangled her grandmother's ring over it, and announced that they should continue west. They stopped in a cheap motel, slept four hours, ate breakfast at a truckers' watering hole, then continued on west. By noon they had made it as far as Indianapolis. Kaat disappeared into a telephone booth while the Potter downed a cheeseburger, and emerged a few moments later shaking her head in disappointment.

They slept outside Indianapolis that night in a motel with a sign that said "No dogs" and had yellowish powder sprinkled on the sides of the cabins to discourage the strays that did show up. As soon as they settled into their room, Kaat phoned Millie, but all she got was the tape-recording machine. "It's me again," she said into it. "I'll call back." She wandered into the bathroom and the Potter heard her drawing a bath, heard also (his ear was fine-tuned to such things) that she didn't throw the lock on the door. Could he—dared he—take it as an invitation? In their cheap motel the night before, he had dreamed that his bed was a raft tossing about on a turbulent sea, surrounded by a circular horizon as sharp and as menacing as a razor blade. His mouth had felt parched, and it was only when he looked over, still in his dream, at the next raft and saw the naked woman clinging to it that he identified his thirst. What he wanted, he had realized with surprise, was to take her in his mouth as if she were a wet sponge, to suck the last drop of moisture from her. Now, listening to her in the bathroom— the toilet flushed, the water stopped running in the tub, a body settled gingerly into it—he permitted himself the luxury of imagining Kaat's body; of composing it the way a police artist puts together a composite portrait of a criminal: pointed breasts with insolent nipples, a visible rib cage, lean thighs, a soft bed of pubic hair, a flat backside that arched smoothly up to thin, bony shoulders. He felt the stirring of an erection—but only the stirring! He was, he reminded himself with a tired shrug, tied up irrevocably to that pier of old age.

He slipped off his jacket and loosened his tie, wedged the back of a chair under the doorknob as a precaution, removed the clip from his Beretta and then reinserted it, savoring the metallic sound of its being wedged home, and put the pistol under his pillow. He walked over to the bathroom door, listened for a long moment, then rapped lightly on it with his knuckles. "Did you say something?" he called, hoping she had; hoping she would.

"No," she answered. He could hear her splash in the water. He put his hand on the knob and silently turned it and felt it give way. And he realized that there was nothing to stop him from opening the door except his own view of himself as someone Kaat would not voluntarily choose to make love with.

It was enough. He let the knob ease back. It closed with an audible click.

"Are you still there?" Kaat, suddenly alert, asked from the bathroom.

The Potter listened to his own breathing until it was regular again. "No," he replied, and he went over to the bed and pulled off his shoes and stretched out on it.

She emerged from the bathroom a quarter of an hour later dressed in an ankle-length printed woolen nightdress that she must have owned since she was a teenager. She peeled back the blanket of the other bed and slipped between the coarse sheets. "You wanted to ask me something?" she said, looking across the room at him from the other raft. When he didn't answer, she said, "Before, when you were at the door of the bathroom. What did you want to ask me?"

"I wanted to ask you what it was like . . ." he began, and he left the rest of the question hanging.

She regarded him for a moment with her deep-set eyes. "Here's the thing," she said matter-of-factly. "With two, it is very often heavy, pompous, weighed down with appropriate sentiments, impossibly serious. But with three it has the saving grace of at least being humorous. Something funny is always happening. All the ridiculous things we do to each other, the way we attack each other's bodies, the awkward angles our limbs make as we flail away at each other—it's all very comic really. Have you ever looked at dogs copulating and not laughed? Watching humans make love is pretty much the same. Being watched too." She smiled across at the Potter, adrift on his raft. "Does that answer your question?"

He nodded in a distracted way. "Excuse me, if you please. I didn't mean to . . ."

"It's all right," she said, and he glanced sharply at her and realized it was.

Kaat tried Millie once more before they went to sleep. She answered on the second ring. "He called," she cried in an agitated voice. "Half an hour ago. You want to hear the tape?"

Kaat motioned to the Potter and held the earpiece so they could both listen to it. "Of course I want to hear the tape," she told Millie.

The Sleeper's voice could be heard on the line. "Are you in the mood for a bedtime story?" he asked Millie. He must have been in a public place, because from the background came the sound of people talking, of dishes being rattled.

"Am I ever," Millie said gleefully on the tape.

A woman's voice asked, "Why are you giving me that?"

"So you can say hello," the Sleeper told her.

"Hello," the woman said into the phone without much enthusiasm.

"Hello," Millie answered on the tape.

"All those hellos!" the real Millie complained to Kaat.

"You want *what?*" the woman could be heard asking the Sleeper. She laughed uneasily. "You have got to be kidding." The woman said to Millie, "Are you still there?" Then she gasped.

"Am I ever," Millie told her. "Where are you?"

"I remembered to ask her right off where she was," Millie told Kaat.

"Well," said the woman, and then she gasped again and was silent for a time.

"Old Peter must be shoving it right in," Millie whispered to Kaat. She spoke quickly, as if she were afraid of interrupting the tape recording.

"This is crazy," the woman could be heard saying. She must have brought the telephone close to her mouth then, because her voice became very distinct. "We're in this restaurant on top of the hotel. The view's terrific, though to tell you the honest-to-God truth, I haven't paid much attention to it. He doesn't want me to tell you the name of the hotel, or the name of the city we're in. We're over the river now, but we—" She gasped, then laughed weakly.

"Go on," the Sleeper could be heard encouraging her.

"—we won't be over the river for long. We made love in the hotel before we came up here to eat." Her voice became muted; she was holding a hand over the mouthpiece. "Do you want me to tell her about that part?" She came back on the line to Millie. "Okay. What he wants me to tell you is what we're doing now. Here's what we're doing now," she began in a singsong voice, as if she were starting a composition on how she spent her summer vacation. "The restaurant is kind of dark, see, and the tablecloth comes down low over the edge, and we're sitting on a banquette-type bench with our backs to the river, only the river isn't there anymore, see, the river has moved on and the city is there now, and I'm not wearing any underwear, right—" She stopped talking for a long moment. "Oh God." Another pause. "Yeah, well, like I was saying, I'm not wearing any underwear, see, and your friend here has disappeared under the table because nobody's looking our way, and even if they were looking our way it is much too dark for them to see anything, and me, I am just sitting here with my back against this banquette-type bench with my legs apart talking to you on this phone they plugged in, looking as if nothing . . . nothing out of the ordinary is going on, only it is. If you ask me, something very out of the ordinary is going on." Suddenly the woman hissed in panic, "The waiter's heading this—"

And then the phone went dead on the tape recording.

Millie giggled and told Kaat, "I'll say something out of the ordinary is going on. Jesus! You got to hand it to him, does he have his nerve!"

This time Kaat woke W.A. up when she phoned him on the Coast. "What are ex-husbands for if you can't ring them any hour of the day or night," she told him.

"You exaggerate," W.A. reproached her. "You always did. Maybe that's what was wrong between us."

"What was wrong between us," Kaat fired back, "is that there was nothing but sex between us."

"You used to think the sex was pretty damn good," W.A. muttered unhappily.

Kaat's voice softened. "It was more than pretty damn good," she said. "I just wanted more than sex, W.A."

"Have you found the more with somebody else?"

"Not yet, W.A. But I'm still looking."

"Break your heart," W.A. said gruffly. "What's it to me? Why'd you call?"

Kaat told him. The friend they were trying to catch up with was in a restaurant on top of a hotel. Apparently it had a great view. It seemed to be situated over a river, too, except the river moved on, whatever that meant, and the city took its place.

"Whatever game you're playing sure sounds like fun," W.A. said. "Call me back in fifteen minutes." And he hung up.

"What did he say?" the Potter asked.

"He said for me to call him back in a quarter of an hour."

"Why?"

"He probably wants to look something up in his diary," Kaat said.

A feeling of frustration consumed the Potter. Here they

were waiting for Kaat's ex, as she called him, to look up something in his diary! It was the kind of thing that happened in spy stories, but not in real life. It went against every instinct in his body, against every experience he had ever had, against everything he had taught the sleepers who passed through his school in Moscow. Yet what choice did he have? And he had always said there were no rules.

"You're sure she said the river moved on and the city took its place?" W.A. asked Kaat when she called back.

"That's what she said," Kaat insisted. "Does it make any sense to you, W.A.?"

"The river has got to be the Mississippi," W.A. said. "The city has got to be St. Louis. The restaurant has got to be the revolving restaurant over a hotel named the Riverview. They wanted me to play there right after they built it, but I got seasick because of the motion and vomited and couldn't perform."

"W.A., if I were in L.A. right now, you know what I'd do?"

"Heck, let me guess," W.A. said, shifting his voice into what he considered to be his seductive register.

"You've got one dirty mind," Kaat chastised him. "That's not what I'd do. What I'd do is give you a kiss on the lips."

"I'll take whatever I can get," W.A. said.

Kaat hung up the receiver and regarded the Potter, who was already shoving the few things he had into his small overnight bag. He straightened, his eyes closed of their own accord and he found, to his astonishment, that he could *remember* Kaat, remember what she looked like, and with his eyes still closed he said in a hollow voice, "I am still needing you."

Kaat spoke slowly, discovering herself in every word, in the spaces between the words. "I still need to be needed."

Within twenty minutes they had woken up the night clerk to pay their hotel bill, loaded the little they had in the Chrysler and started west on Route 70 toward St. Louis. The road was still wet from a late-night cloudburst, and the occasional car or truck passing in the opposite direction sent pinpricks of light spitting up at them from the rain-soaked highway; the effect,

Kaat said, was like watching fireworks burst under them. First light, seeping over the brim of dark clouds stretched along the horizon, caught up with them as they crossed the Wabash. By the time sun popped up behind the brim of clouds, almost like a target in a shooting gallery, they had taken a good bite out of southern Illinois. They stopped at a service station for gas and paper cups filled with muddy coffee dispensed from a bright red vending machine. The Potter went around back and urinated at the edge of a clearing rather than use the rest room, which smelled as if it hadn't been hosed out in years. On their way out of the service station, they passed a hand-lettered sign that wished them "Happy Motoring," "an example," the Potter noted in annoyance, "of the curious American idea that motoring involved something more than getting from one place to another."

Gazing out at farmers already perched on their tractors, at the furrowed fields that looked as if giant fingernails had been scratched across the surface of the earth, Kaat remarked that getting from one place to the other, for her at least, had never been accompanied by a feeling of pleasure. "I suppose you have to want not to get where you're going in order to really enjoy the trip," she said thoughtfully.

They passed through a series of villages masquerading as towns, and towns with all the trappings of cities except size, and the Potter commented that every town and village in Russia had its Communist Party headquarters, whereas in America the thing they all had in common seemed to be the funeral home, usually Colonial or at least neo, always sober, with a gleaming black hearse with lace curtains on its windows stationed in the driveway, nose outward, as if ready for a fast getaway. "From a business point of view," Kaat noted absently— she had had a certain amount of experience with funeral homes— "you can always rely on people dying."

They spoke in undertones about the institution of death; of how some people avoided the notion of its being an end by visualizing it as a beginning; of how others, tired of beginnings, took comfort in anticipating the closing of the curtain, the end of the act. At one point the Potter said he thought it was a phenomenon peculiar to America that the approaches to its great cities were more often than not lined with used-car lots and cemeteries. In the chaos of the inner cities there was barely room for automobiles or the living, and the Potter considered there was a certain logic to the used and the dead setting up camp on the periphery. It was where they belonged, he said; it left the center of the cities reserved for the living, he said, and he thought to himself: for the killing also.

St. Louis turned out to be no exception—though the cemetery that filled the fields on either side of the road was a graveyard not for people but for cars. They were piled on top of each other, silent, solemn leaning towers of rust, monuments, the Potter said, to the two unpardonable transgressions of people and machines: growing old and growing obsolete.

The Potter pressed his foot down on the accelerator and sped past the gateway of the city toward the rendezvous with the living, the killing at its center.

22

Ourcq was stretched out on the bed, his scuffed black oxfords still on his feet, inflating and deflating his stomach in one of the Canadian Air Force exercises designed to strengthen abdominal muscles. Appleyard stood gazing out of the window, listening to the rain beat against the panes, memorizing the sound. Moistening his lips, pursing them, he began to imitate the rain, and when he had gotten it just right he slowly turned up the volume until it sounded as if it were raining *inside* the room. Ourcq's head snapped around in Appleyard's direction. "Can't you imitate the fucking sun shining for a change?" he flared.

With a shrug, Appleyard cut off the sound of rain. "I can do the sun setting, but not shining," he said.

Ourcq sat up in bed. "How much fucking longer we got to stay cooped up in this fucking pigeonhole?"

Appleyard glanced at his wristwatch. "He checked out four hours ago. We should hang around for another twenty hours if we go by the book."

"Twenty fucking hours!" Ourcq groaned. "Fucking sweeping is fucking impossible."

"You want me maybe to get some magazines up here?" Appleyard offered.

"Something with a lot of fucking ass in it," Ourcq agreed. "Get a receipt and we'll put it on the fucking expense account."

Appleyard started to slip into his suit jacket. Just then the phone next to the bed purred. Appleyard, struck by the sound, imitated it.

Ourcq said, "Who the fuck would be calling us?" as he reached for the receiver. He listened for a moment, then muttered to the person on the other end, "You don't fucking say," and hung up.

"It's the fucking girl," Ourcq told Appleyard. He looked around for his suit jacket. "She doesn't have the fucking pussycat under her fucking arm, but he's sure it's her."

Two minutes later Ourcq and Appleyard arrived in the lobby. Separately. Ourcq, who hated stairs, had taken the elevator; Appleyard, who suffered from nosebleeds in elevators, had taken the staircase. Ourcq nodded toward the desk clerk who had tipped them off. The desk clerk nodded toward a door behind the newspaper stand. Ourcq and Appleyard wandered casually across to the door and stood with their backs to it for a moment, surveying the lobby. Ourcq said, "The fucking dwarf's still unaccounted for. You stay here and keep a fucking eye peeled for him. I'll go find the fucking girl."

"Why don't I maybe go find the girl for once?" Appleyard complained.

"Because it is me who gives the fucking orders," Ourcq whined. "Besides, I am a better fucking shot than you are."

"I missed," Appleyard explained, obviously not for the first time, a pained expression clinging to his face, "because he jerked the car when I pulled the trigger. It could happen to anyone."

"But it fucking happened to you," Ourcq insisted without a shred of sympathy. He opened the door a crack, saw that the long corridor on the other side of it was empty, and ducked through, closing the door behind him. He kept his right hand on the butt of his pistol in its shoulder holster as he moved along the corridor, trying doorknobs on either side. They were all locked. Which left the door on the far end of the corridor. Ourcq approached it without a sound, tried the knob with his left hand, realized that this door wasn't locked. He withdrew his hand, pulled a handkerchief from his trouser pocket and went back along the corridor unscrewing the three overhead bulbs. Then he felt his way back along the wall to the unlocked door. He drew his pistol from its holster, took the silencer from his jacket pocket and screwed it into the tip of the pistol.

Flattening himself against the wall, he again reached for the knob and softly eased open the door.

The area beyond, a large storage room stacked with round banquet tables of various sizes standing on their edges, along with hundreds of folded chairs, was totally dark except for the eerie red halo above the "Emergency Exit" sign at the far end. Ourcq, still flattened against the wall on the corridor side of the door, strained to catch the faintest sound in the storage room. Hearing nothing, he bent his body until he was doubled over in a crouch, then sprang over the threshold and straightened with his back flat against the wall inside the room. Barely breathing, he devoted another long minute to listening. It was Ourcq's theory that he had a fixed amount of time to spend when stalking a target; that half of it should be spent on his own safety, and the other half on the target's death. Having used up the portion for himself, Ourcq stepped off smartly from the wall and headed down the aisle formed by the stacked tables toward the emergency exit. He was halfway across the room when he heard a scraping sound ahead. He stopped in his tracks.

"I know you are fucking there," Ourcq called. "Come out where I can fucking see you and nothing will happen to you. I just want to ask you a few fucking questions."

In the dull glow of the "Emergency Exit" sign, Kaat moved into his field of vision farther along the makeshift aisle. "Why are you following me?" she asked.

Ourcq could see her outline, but not her features. He had to make sure it was the right woman. Keeping his pistol parallel to his leg so that she wouldn't notice it, he said, "I'm the fucking house detective. You asked at the fucking desk about one of our clients. The clerk said there was no one registered under that fucking name. Then you fucking described who you were looking for."

Kaat said, "Are you really incapable of saying a sentence without using the word 'fucking' in it?"

"I can fucking well say a sentence without the word 'fucking' in it if I fucking want to. But I don't fucking want to. Now, how about if you describe for me the fucking man you were looking for."

Kaat described Peter Raven to Ourcq.

"That is who I fucking thought you were looking for," he said. He took a step in Kaat's direction. "You were looking for him in the fucking Seventh Heaven, too, weren't you?"

"And you were one of the two men in the Dodge who shot my cat," Kaat said.

"I definitely did not shoot no fucking cat," Ourcq contradicted her. "Appleyard shot the fucking cat. Where is the fucking dwarf who was traveling with you?"

It was at that instant that Ourcq felt the icy burn of metal against the nape of his neck. "The dwarf is right behind you, if you please," the Potter said with quiet passion. "Far enough so that if you kick a foot back or try to catch me in the stomach with an elbow, you will come into contact with nothing but air. Near enough so that I can put a twenty-two-caliber bullet through your neck the instant I feel you move. Listen to me carefully. I am now going to count out loud to three. If you move before I reach three, or if I do not hear your gun fall to the floor, I will pull the trigger. I do not have a silencer. My Beretta makes a soft coughing sound. But you will not hear a thing. So. One. Two."

Ourcq's pistol clattered to the floor.

"Kick it away. Slowly. Good. Now undo your belt and let your trousers drop to your ankles. Good. Now turn very slowly to your right, facing the table, and reach up with your hands and grip the top edge of it, and lean your forehead against it. Very good. You have saved your life. For the moment." The Potter took a step backward. "You can turn on the lights now," he called to Kaat.

She found the switch, and the storage room was bathed in light. "Move your head so I can see your profile," the Potter instructed Ourcq.

Ourcq did as he was told.

"I have seen you before," the Potter announced.

Kaat came up behind the Potter. "In the Dodge," she suggested.

"I have seen him before the Dodge," the Potter said. "In Moscow." To Ourcq he said, "When were you in Moscow, if you please?"

Ourcq turned back to the table. "I have never been in Moscow in my fucking life," he said.

The Potter smiled faintly. "If you do not understand what I am now saying to you," he told Ourcq in Russian, "I am going to shoot you through your spinal column."

"I understand, I understand," Ourcq answered in Russian, which he spoke with a Canadian accent. In English he added, "We are both of us on the same fucking side!"

"You are sweepers," the Potter said.

"Fucking sweepers, yes," Ourcq agreed enthusiastically.

"Dispatched by a Soviet *rezident* to sweep the trail of an agent on a mission?"

"You know as much as I fucking do," Ourcq said. "Can I take my fucking hands down and pull up my fucking pants now?" And he added in a low voice, "In case you didn't notice, there's a fucking lady present."

"No," said the Potter.

"But I told you," cried Ourcq, his voice suddenly hoarse with emotion, "we are on the same fucking side."

"I think I know whose side you are on," the Potter said, "but I am not yet sure whose side I am on."

"What are you going to do with him?" Kaat asked.

"I am going to bombard him with questions. And I am going to shoot him if he does not answer them."

"All you can fucking talk about is shooting people," Ourcq complained.

"I did see you in Moscow, didn't I?" the Potter demanded.

"How should I fucking know if you saw me in Moscow? I was there three fucking years ago. There was a fucking medal ceremony. There was a fucking cocktail party with some fucking department bosses. There was a fucking debriefing on a job I had pulled off for my fucking *rezident*. There was even a fucking orgy in a fucking *dacha* on the fucking Black Sea."

"I saw you at the cocktail party," the Potter remembered. "You spread caviar on a slice of toast as if it were butter. I was a *novator* at the time, which is why I was invited. Everybody loved your accent when you spoke Russian. You were a big success. It comes back to me now—you had a Canadian father and a Russian mother."

"A Canadian mother and a Russian father," Ourcq corrected him.

"You didn't say 'fucking,' " Kaat noted. "Keep up the good work."

"Fuck off," Ourcq snapped in irritation.

"Watch how you talk, if you please," the Potter warned sharply.

Ourcq laughed under his breath. "You going to shoot me because you don't like the way I fucking talk?"

"I may," the Potter said.

"He might," Kaat chimed in, though she doubted he would.

Ourcq laughed out loud this time. "Imagine getting wiped away because you talk fucking dirty!"

"You are not a regular sweeper," the Potter suggested. "You are a hit man. A specialist in wetwork."

"Wet fucking work," Ourcq agreed. "But they needed sweepers fast, and we were fucking available."

"You were given an itinerary," the Potter said quietly.

Ourcq didn't say anything.

"Here's the thing," Kaat said from behind the Potter. "We know where he's going. How do you think we found him at Seventh Heaven? How do you think we found him here?"

Ourcq grunted. "You fucking missed him at Seventh Heaven. You fucking missed him here too." He turned to look over his shoulder at the Potter. "You are a fucking professional. You and I talk the same fucking language. You know where he's going, my fucking ass! If you knew where he was fucking going, you wouldn't need to ask me. I can give you any fucking answer under the sun. Why are we playing this fucking game anyhow?"

Ourcq turned back to the table and took a deep breath, and wondered if it would be his last.

The Potter grabbed Kaat's arm and pushed her in the general direction of the door with the "Emergency Exit" sign over it. She took a few steps, then hesitated. The Potter, who was wrapping a handkerchief around the muzzle of his Beretta, waved her on impatiently. She turned and walked briskly away.

"Where is the fucking lady going?" Ourcq inquired nervously.

"Do not turn around, if you please," the Potter instructed him.

"Jesus fucking Christ," muttered Ourcq. His knees started to tremble.

"How many people have you shot in your day?" the Potter asked him.

"My fucking share," Ourcq admitted. His voice was pitched high, off its usual key.

"Did you enjoy shooting them?"

Ourcq shrugged, and for an instant it looked as if he were physically shaking off the question. Then he decided to answer it; maybe it would give him more time. "I did not fucking enjoy it. I did not fucking *not* enjoy it. It was what I did for a fucking living. We have all of us got to fucking eat!" He pressed his forehead to the table and closed his eyes and said in a harsh voice, "Do me a fucking favor, get it fucking over with."

The Potter glanced at Kaat, who was watching from the door. They looked at each other for a long moment. Then in one flowing gesture he bent and pressed his pistol to the toe of Ourcq's right shoe and pulled the trigger. The Beretta coughed discreetly, just as the Potter had said it would. Moaning softly, Ourcq sank to the ground. "Is that fucking all?" he asked in a weak voice.

"Isn't it enough?" the Potter asked. He felt very tired.

"It will definitely give you a fucking head start," Ourcq muttered. He was looking at his foot as if it belonged to someone else.

"That is all I will need," the Potter said.

"Do not waste any fucking moment of it," Ourcq advised him, and grimacing from the pain, he started to unlace the scuffed black oxford from which blood was seeping.

23

*Khanda knew the building inside out. On one errand or an-
other, he had investigated every corner of it. At the very
beginning he had toyed with the idea of shooting from the roof.
He could keep out of sight beforehand behind the giant neon
Hertz sign that flashed the time and temperature, or the enormous rusted boiler, abandoned when the warehouse switched
from steam heat. But he had given up the idea because the
police accompanying the target would be scanning, as a matter
of habit, rooftops for the silhouette of a rifleman. Windows,
because there were literally hundreds of them along the route,
offered a much surer sniper's nest, he had decided.*

*Early on he had selected one, in the far corner of the sixth
floor, which gave him the best vantage point. He stood motion-
less before it now, watching as the motorcade going through a
dress rehearsal jogged right off Main Street and headed directly
toward the warehouse in which he worked. Just below the
warehouse the motorcade turned sharply left toward the railroad underpass and, eventually, the freeway that would take
the target to his luncheon rendezvous. Squinting through an
imaginary telescopic sight, Khanda went through the motions of
working the bolt of his rifle twice and firing off three shots at
the back of the Prince's head. It would be difficult to miss at
this range, since his four-power scope would make it appear as if
he were shooting at a target a mere twenty-two yards away.
Then, too, his rifle had less recoil than the average military
weapon, an advantage that increased its accuracy under rapid
fire conditions. It also had a tendency to fire a bit high and to
the right, a perfect defect when aiming at a target moving away
and slightly to the right; it meant that he wouldn't have to*

make allowances for the apparent upward drift of the target due to the height of his sniper's nest.

Having fired off three shots in his imagination, Khanda punched his stopwatch, then trotted across the filthy warehouse floor toward the enclosed stairway in the northwest corner of the building. Taking the steps two at a time, he descended to the second-floor lunchroom, where he inserted a coin in the vending machine and bought himself a Coke. It was a touch Khanda was particularly proud of; someone wandering down the steps casually sipping a Coke would appear particularly innocent to a policeman racing up looking for a sniper. Then he make his way, Coke in hand, down to the main door and out into the sun-drenched street.

He punched his stopwatch and looked at it. Even stopping for the Coke, it had taken him three minutes from the time he fired the rifle until the moment he emerged from the warehouse. It was extremely unlikely that the police would be able to seal off the building in that time span. Hell, it would take them that long just to figure out where the shots had come from!

Sipping from his Coke, squinting this time because of the sunlight, Khanda surveyed the traffic passing the warehouse. A thin smirk stretched across his lips. In four days he would know if his calculations were correct.

24

⚜

The Director, tall, thin, Midwestern in origin but very *nouveau* Georgetown in the way he dressed and carried himself, came around the desk and held out the box of chocolates toward Carroll. "The ones with the gold wrappers are filled with brandy," he told him. He flashed what had passed for an encouraging smile in the days when he had been an investment banker. "Two of them will ruin you for an afternoon. Three and you can testify before a Senate oversight committee and feel no pain whatsoever."

The Deputy Director, sitting on a couch made of leather as soft as kid gloves, chuckled appreciatively. G. Sprowls, leaning casually against a bookcase, looked on with his usual half-smile etched on his face. Carroll helped himself to a candy, undid the gold wrapper and popped it into his mouth.

"What did I tell you?" said the Director, settling back into his wicker swivel chair, a family heirloom that he had brought with him when he took the job.

Carroll swallowed. "Very good," he agreed. He arched his neck and wedged a finger under his starched collar. "You have done what you can to put me at ease. Now why don't we get on with it."

The Deputy Director leaned forward on the couch. "You are not going to be difficult, I hope."

Carroll concentrated on the wall above the Director's Toulouse-Lautrec, another family heirloom. "I'm not at all sure what I'm going to be," he admitted.

The Director tapped the eraser end of a pencil against his desk blotter. "If I understand you correctly," he told Carroll, "you take the position that I personally authorized an operation."

A muscle in Carroll's cheek twitched once as he nodded in agreement.

"Good. Fine," said the Director. "You are one of the old hands around the shop. I don't for an instant doubt that you and your colleague—what is his name again?"

"Francis," Carroll offered.

"Francis, exactly. I don't doubt that you and Francis are not motivated, like some people around here who shall remain nameless, by the current watchword, 'Don't do something, just stand there.'"

"We view the world situation as desperate," Carroll conceded. "We think it is—you yourself said it when you were pinning a medal on one of our neighbors recently—two minutes to midnight. If someone doesn't do something about it, and fairly quickly, time will run out on us."

"That is exactly how I see things," the Director, who had been well-briefed by G. Sprowls, insisted.

Carroll shrugged. "You spoke about the need for unleashing the Company."

"I have made no bones about where I stand," the Director readily agreed. "It is a matter of life or death, in my view."

"When you spoke at that reception for one of our British colleagues," Carroll continued, "you made a point of recalling Winston Churchill's preference, during the Second World War, for invading the Dardanelles before France."

"It would have changed the map of Europe," the Director pointed out. "It would have been the allied armies, and not the Red Army, that liberated the captive countries of Eastern Europe. We would have installed friendly democratic governments before they could have installed their dictatorial Communist regimes."

"Everyone understood what you were getting at between the lines," Carroll went on. "What we need in the Western world are leaders who are not soft on Communism."

"Leaders who are not afraid to bite the bullet," the Director offered.

"Who will stand up to the Communists," the Deputy Director added, "and not cut and run every time they confront them, whether at conference tables or invasion beaches."

"That's nicely put," the Director said approvingly. "I couldn't have phrased it better myself."

Everyone was staring at Carroll. Carroll was still focusing on a spot on the wall.

"So you see," the Director went on, "we are all of us in the same boat. If I authorized an operation, I won't back away from it now."

"Between us," the Deputy Director said, "what are you up to?"

"You can count on me to stand behind you," the Director vowed.

G. Sprowls straightened up at the bookcase. "You awakened the Soviet sleeper," he drawled, "and sent him off to kill someone whom you knew the Director wanted dead. That's it, isn't it?"

Again a muscle twitched in Carroll's cheek, only this time it wouldn't stop. He nodded imperceptibly.

"Who?" G. Sprowls asked quietly.

"Is it anyone we know?" the Deputy Director demanded. "The Russian ambassador, say, or that actor out in Hollywood who plays the Commie game by speaking out all the time against racism?"

"I have no doubt whatsoever that you have done the right thing," the Director observed. "But there may be loose ends to tie up. There may be ways we can enlarge the operation, or set in motion other auxiliary operations designed to take advantage of your"—he searched frantically for an appropriate word, and came up with—"initiative."

Carroll brought his fingertips up to his cheek to still the twitching. Then he quietly pronounced the name of the target of the operation that he and Francis had launched.

The Director stiffened in his wicker swivel chair as if he had received a heavy jolt of electricity. The Deputy Director's mouth gaped open and he collapsed weakly into the relative safety of the couch. Only G. Sprowls accepted the revelation with anything resembling equanimity. "Of course," he muttered to himself, "how could I have missed it!"

"You *what?*" the Director cried when he discovered how his vocal cords operated. "You had the audacity, the temerity, the *gall* to order the assassination of—" He couldn't bring himself to say the name of the target.

"I must be dreaming," the Deputy Director moaned from the couch. "I must be imagining things." He looked at G. Sprowls. "Tell me I am imagining things," he pleaded. "Tell me I will wake up at any moment and laugh at this whole business."

Carroll shifted his gaze from the wall to the window. "You authorized the operation," he reminded the Director. "You admitted as much a few minutes ago. There are witnesses . . . the walls have ears."

"My walls," the Director announced in an icy voice, "do not have ears. I authorized nothing of the kind. It never occurred to me that anyone would interpret my comments as an invitation to launch an operation. You and your friend are certifiably insane. Stark raving mad. My God, do you realize what has happened? If anybody in Congress or the press gets so much as a whiff of this, the Company will be ruined forever."

G. Sprowls came around behind the Director's desk and whispered for a moment in his ear. The Director appeared to calm down instantly. His eyes narrowed, and he began tapping the eraser end of his pencil thoughtfully against the blotter again. G. Sprowls looked at Carroll and asked in his slow drawl that suggested he knew the answer, "Who exactly knows about what you have done?"

"I know. Francis knows. Now you three know."

"If I can recapitulate," G. Sprowls said evenly. "You organized the defection from the Soviet Union of the Potter, who gave you the identity and awakening signal of a Soviet sleeper. You and Francis delivered the signal, activating the sleeper and dispatching him on a mission. Even as we speak, a Soviet agent—"

The Director saw what G. Sprowls was driving at. "Born and raised in Communist Russia, recruited and trained by the KGB and presumably—who could prove otherwise?—still under its operational control . . . ."

The color had flooded back into the Deputy Director's face, and he leaned forward and finished G. Sprowls's line of reasoning. "A Soviet agent is traveling across the country to commit a crime."

Carroll leapt out of his chair. "Don't you see the infinite possibilities, the absolute beauty of the operation? If our sleeper succeeds, we eliminate someone who has hurt the United States more than any single person in recent history; someone who has sucked up to the Communists and tied the hands of those of us who are willing and able to fight them. If the sleeper is caught in the act, his identity will eventually come out, and the whole Soviet intelligence apparatus—"

"The whole idea that you can conduct business as usual with the Russians!" the Director interjected.

"—will be discredited," Carroll plunged on. "If, by any chance, the sleeper is not caught, we will identify him and place the onus for the assassination on his masters in Moscow." Carroll sank back into his chair, drained. "It is like a diamond with many facets—it is the most perfect, the most beautiful operation that has ever existed in the annals of intelligence work," he continued in an undertone. "The worst that can happen is that the sleeper will fail and the Russians will be blamed for the assassination attempt. The best that can happen is that he will succeed—and the Russians will be blamed for the death."

The Director regarded Carroll, then lowered his eyes to his blotter, then abruptly swiveled his chair around so that he could stare out the window. "I have to admit," he said after a moment, "it does have a certain—" He didn't finish the phrase.

G. Sprowls and the Deputy Director exchanged knowing looks. "If the Soviets are blamed," the Deputy Director offered from the couch, "Congress and the public will begin to see the world as we see it; as it really is! The Company will be unleashed to take its place in the front line of battle. We won't have to go begging hat in hand up on the Hill every time we need a few hundred million dollars."

The Director slowly swiveled back toward the room. It was apparent that he had come to a decision. "As far as I am concerned, gentlemen," he announced in a businesslike tone, "this meeting never took place."

The Deputy Director's eyes widened in complicity. "What meeting," he asked innocently, "are you talking about?"

25

There were loose ends. (There were always loose ends, the Potter would tell his students at the sleeper school; it was one of the few things people in their line of work could count on.) G. Sprowls was authorized to tie them up, a matter, he confided to the Director, of erasing footprints so that nobody could see who had passed this way.

Oskar, who happened to be recruiting for his network in East Berlin at the time, received a coded message summoning him West for an urgent meeting. Using one of his many aliases, he crossed through Checkpoint Charlie, took a taxi to a business district, and continued on foot to his safe house in West Berlin. He buzzed twice, sensed someone looking at him through the peephole, then heard the locks on the door being opened. He wasn't so much alarmed as annoyed when he didn't recognize the man who held the door for him; the fewer people he was exposed to, the safer he felt. But he became upset when the second man, waiting for him in the living room, turned out to be a stranger also. "So," Oskar said in German, sensing that something out of the ordinary was happening. "You must have a very important message for me, yes?"

The man Oskar spoke to was leaning against the wall next to a phony fireplace. He was wearing an overcoat and carrying a bouquet of plastic roses. The other man, the one who had let him into the apartment, came into the living room behind him and closed the door. "We are deliverymen," the man next to the phony fireplace told Oskar. He spoke German with a distinct Bavarian accent.

Oskar didn't like the look of him. "So what is it you are delivering?" he asked.

"Your body," the Bavarian replied just as the other man stepped forward and plunged a long, thin kitchen knife up to its hilt into Oskar's back.

"Why?" Oskar managed to gasp, as if it would be easier to deal with death if he understood the motives of his killers; as if his own fate, as long as it was logical, would be acceptable.

The Bavarian only shrugged. "They only told us who, not why," he informed Oskar.

The man behind Oskar caught him under the armpits and lowered him gently, solicitously even, to the floor. Oskar attempted to turn his face and get his mouth off the dirty carpet. But he couldn't move. He could feel the strength ebbing from his body. Someone was feeling for his pulse. He tried to open his eyes, to work his lips, to tell them to be sure not to bury him until they were positive he was dead, yes? Because he had a lifelong horror of waking up in a sealed coffin. But he was too dizzy to function. The carpet under his face was suddenly spinning; a whirlpool was sucking him into its center. Why? he thought to himself as he plunged head first toward it. At the last instant of consciousness, an acceptable answer occurred to him: Why not!

Within an hour of Oskar's rendezvous in the safe house, two middle-level West German intelligence operatives—the senior of the two habitually pinned a black homburg to his head with the curved handle of an umbrella, the junior trudged around in galoshes at the slightest hint of rain—were driving along an *autobahn* toward Berlin in response to a verbal summons from an American contact. They chatted about pay scales, and the political situation in West Germany, and whether they would live to witness the reunification of the two halves of their country. Galoshes told Homburg he was curious to know what had become of the dwarflike Russian defector and his floozy of a wife whom they had been assigned to welcome to Vienna several months before. Homburg shook his head. Curiosity, he informed his younger colleague, was what killed the cat. Galoshes took the hint and didn't pursue the subject.

Rounding a curve thirty miles from their destination, the

Mercedes veered out of control. The steering pinion had snapped—at least that was what an in-house postmortem attributed the accident to. The car skidded off the highway, down an embankment into a ravine, where it burst into flame and exploded, killing the two men instantly.

The afternoon of Oskar's disappearance, Svetochka's body was discovered at the bottom of an elevator shaft in a downtown Vienna office building. There was a suicide note, written in her own hand, in the pocket of the used fur coat she had bought the previous week with the money she had wormed out of one of the Austrians in return for services rendered. "Excuse Svetochka," it read in English, "for the trouble she has caused. She is not wanting to stay here and she is not willing to go back, so she is going to put herself to sleep."

The Viennese detective who investigated the death was mildly curious how a woman could have pried open the doors to the elevator shaft. One of the uniformed policemen accompanying him managed to do it, but he was an amateur wrestler. The chief of detectives who read the preliminary report asked the detective to retype it leaving out his doubts about whether Svetochka had the strength to pry open the doors, or the ability to write a suicide note in English when she couldn't speak it. Quite obviously, the Viennese police were happy to accept the note, and the suicide of a recent immigrant from the Soviet Union, at face value. Why muddy the water? the superintendent in charge of homicides said when he closed the case.

G. Sprowls received reports of Oskar's disappearance and the deaths of the two Germans and Svetochka in the overnight pouch, shredded the only copies in existence, then dispatched Thursday's orders, in triplicate, through the interoffice routing system. The Sisters' former man Friday was cooling his heels in a basement cubbyhole, wading through piles of transcripts of obituaries from provincial Soviet newspapers and matching up the names with those of former members of the Politburo and Central Committee. The fact that he could discern no rhyme or reason in what he was doing didn't make the chore any easier, so that when the orders arrived sending him overseas, he barely glanced at the fine print to see where exactly he was off to. Anything, he decided, would be better than reading

Russian obituaries in a stuffy basement cubbyhole. It was only after he had countersigned the orders, and returned the pink copy to the originating desk, that he bothered to identify his new post. "You will proceed, on a priority-one voucher via a military-air-transport flight out of Edwards Air Force Base, to Bangkok," the orders read, "where you will report to the adjutant station chief, Bangkok, for further assignment to listening post Echo-Charlie-Hotel, situated on the Cambodian–South Vietnamese frontier, 1.7 kilometers from the Ho Chi Minh trail. On arrival you will relieve the acting post chief, and file a full KIA report on the circumstances surrounding the death of your precedessor, as well as carry out to the best of your abilities the mission of the listening post as set forth in the listening-post operating-procedure annex to these orders."

Thursday's case officer, an older woman with a cigarette dangling from her lips and ashes dropping on the papers that passed across her desk, supplied him with a voucher for *per diem* funds to cover his travel expenses until his arrival in Bangkok. She also asked him to fill out and sign a standard next-of-kin form, and identify his beneficiaries in the event anything happened to him in the field. Thursday protested that he had never given the matter of beneficiaries much thought. The case officer brushed ashes off the appropriate form with the back of her hand and suggested that the time had come to do so. You are not going to a tea party, she informed him in a voice that was anything but motherly. The last two people we sent out to Echo-Charlie-Hotel came back in pine boxes.

In pine boxes, Thursday repeated, and he astonished the case officer studying him through a haze of cigarette smoke by giggling uncontrollably.

G. Sprowls's damp half-smile evaporated when the case officer phoned him to confirm that Thursday was off and running. He produced an index card with the words "Loose Ends" typed at the top, and carefully erased Thursday's name. Four other names had already been erased. All of them had "died of measles," Company argot for killing someone and making the death look natural. Which left three names on the card. The Potter, Feliks Arkantevich Turov, was the next on the list. G. Sprowls had put out discreet feelers. It was only a matter of time before his sources would locate the Potter. Then he would erase his name from the card too, and concentrate on the last two loose ends.

G. Sprowls looked up suddenly from the index card. A chilling thought had appeared on the horizon of his consciousness. He had caught sight of it while it was still a vague menace, too distant to define. He watched it draw closer. And then a shudder threaded its way down his spinal column as he identified it. If Francis could lie to the black box about his name, he could also have been lying when he claimed that he had not had any contact with agents or representatives of another country!

26

The sign in the window of the Chinese health-food restaurant announced, in ridiculous lettering with Chinese curlicues, that it was under new management. "We should at least give it a try," Carroll insisted, and he led the way past the new owner, smiling uncertainly from his seat behind the cigarette counter, to their usual booth in the far corner.

They spent a long time studying the menu, made sure the waiter understood that they didn't want any monosodium glutamate sprinkled on their dishes, and then ordered, Carroll with undisguised enthusiasm, Francis with undisguised suspicion. Waiting for the food to come, they discussed the weather, the film Francis had seen the previous Tuesday, Carroll's sister's recent menopausal outburst when she discovered that he was throwing out socks instead of giving them to her to darn; in short, they discussed everything *but*. Until Carroll, midway through his plate of wild rice and steamed shrimp, slammed his chopsticks down on the table so loudly that the owner, watching them out of the corner of his eye for some sign that they were enjoying the food, looked over with an anguished expression on his face. Francis smiled innocently in his direction, and nodded encouragingly, and the owner, appeased, turned back to his abacus and toyed with it as if it were strung with worry beads.

"The way I see it," Carroll said quietly, staring off into space, "is that what we had before was a brilliant operation for which we could never get credit. Now our masters are bound to see our talents in a new light."

Francis gestured with the back of his hand. "Raises, promotions, don't interest me anymore. I am too old to appreciate that sort of thing."

"I'm not talking about raises or promotions," Carroll hissed. "I'm talking about the plots we can hatch now that we have credit in the bank. The next time we come up with a scheme, the doors in the Athenaeum will open to us of their own accord. Listen to me, Francis. Between us, you and I can stop the hemorrhage that is sucking the lifeblood out of this country. America can return to being America the beautiful."

Francis toyed with his Chinese cabbage, which he found overcooked and underspiced. "What made you tell them?" he wanted to know.

"Pure instinct," Carroll replied without a trace of modesty. Modesty, in his book, was for people who had something to be modest about. "I knew the Director would have to be on our side." He leaned toward Francis. "I remember when you first noticed there was a pattern to his off-the-cuff remarks. That thing he said about it being two minutes to midnight, for instance. Or about the need for unleashing the Company. And how what the Director was really saying with the business about Churchill and the Dardanelles was that we desperately needed leaders who were not soft on Communism." In an unusual gesture that Francis found almost touching, Carroll shifted his eyes and actually focused on him across the table. "I have to hand it to you, Francis. You were the one who ignited the fuse. Without you, there would have been no scheme in the first place."

"You were the one who came up with the idea of using a Soviet sleeper," Francis said graciously. He had never been one to hog credit, and he wasn't about to start now.

"But you thought of getting the Potter to give us a sleeper," Carroll reminded him. He shifted his gaze back to some undefined spot on the wall. "We are a perfect couple," he concluded. "We complement each other. Where you see forest, I see trees."

Francis nodded in agreement. "What we are," he said with a touch of pride, "is the sisters Death and Night."

Carroll leaned back in his seat and breathed in and out

with evident emotion. "That's us," he said quietly. "The sisters Death and Night."

"That is certainly us," Francis agreed with an innocent smile.

27

It was not the first time in his professional life that Francis was moved to reflect on the role that luck played in any operation. With good luck things could go right instead of wrong. With incredible luck they might go very right indeed. And a stroke of incredible luck, in the form of Carroll's "pure instinct" that the Director would go along with them, had just come Francis' way.

He looked up from his yellow legal pad and tried to recall the exact words Carroll had used to describe the meeting in the Athenaeum, then bent his head and continued writing. Not typing: he knew the day would come when handwriting experts would be called in to verify that Francis himself was the author of the notes in question. Carroll, he wrote, had delivered his report on the operation to the Director himself, in the presence of the Deputy Director and the Company's erstwhile utility infielder, G. Sprowls. Let them wriggle out of that when *they* were hooked up to the little black box, Francis thought. Carroll had reminded the Director that he had personally authorized the operation. "If I authorized an operation, I won't back away from it now," the Director had said. And the meeting had ended on a suitably conspiratorial note. "As far as I am concerned, gentlemen," the Director had announced, "this meeting never took place." "What meeting," the Deputy Director had asked innocently, "are you talking about?"

Francis felt a wave of exhilaration pass through his chest. For a moment he thought he might have trouble breathing, the sensation was so strong. The Athenaeum was locked into the conspiracy by a stroke of incredible luck. Now they would be trapped by the truth, as revealed by the scratching styluses of a lie-detector machine.

Francis dated the sheet of yellow paper, scribbled across the top, "Notes on conversation with Carroll in Chinese restaurant," then folded it in half and added it to the pile of office papers that he was supposed to have shredded. They were all stuffed into the false bottom of the kitchen garbage pail. The time was fast approaching, Francis realized, when he and his friends would have to organize his own death, along with a trail of evidence that led investigators to the treasure trove of incriminating notes in the bottom of the pail.

28

✤

For once, Francis enjoyed the Tuesday-night movie enormously. It was a musical comedy starring Judy Garland, for whom he had a lingering soft spot. She had a way of belting out songs that took his breath away; she conveyed the impression that she was ready to explode if she couldn't sing. When "The End" finally appeared on the screen, Francis was in love again, with the result that he almost forgot why he had come. Only when the people around him started to head for the exits did he remember to light up the cigarette. As usual, he used the last match in the book to do it, then casually dropped the empty matchbook under his seat and, still preoccupied with Judy Garland, headed up the aisle.

From his seat in the third row of the balcony, G. Sprowls observed the people on the main floor. A short man with wavy hair moved toward the aisle past the seat Francis had been in. Then a young couple. Then an older man with a young woman, probably his daughter, judging from the care they took to avoid touching. Then two middle-aged women, one with bleached blond hair piled in a knot on the back of her head, the second with short straight hair and an open handbag hanging from a strap over her shoulder. As the second woman came abreast of the seat Francis had used, the handbag slipped off her shoulder and fell to the floor, and several things in it spilled out. Laughing in embarrassment, the woman bent and stuffed the spilled items back into her handbag, and then hurried after her bleached-blond friend up the aisle.

As she passed underneath the balcony, G. Sprowls stood up and took a good look at the woman with the open handbag over her shoulder. All that remained for him to do now was attack the photo albums that the Company kept in the Identities Section, piled up on shelves as if some doting great-grandfather were keeping track of his progeny. Somewhere in one of those books G. Sprowls would come across the photo of the woman he had seen at the Judy Garland film. And then he would know what else Francis, his features frozen in an expression of pained innocence, had been lying about as the styluses scratched away in the black box behind his back.

29

To the Potter, it seemed as if America consisted of an endless string of small towns with curious names (Wishbone, Adam's Apple, Point Blank) and main streets inevitably named Main Street. Between towns there were billboards in the middle of nowhere advertising things he had no interest in: radio stations, beers, tractors, mobile homes, even advertising space on the billboard in question. Sometimes he and Kaat would pass a single home, hundreds of miles from open water, with a boat up on chocks in the yard. Once they spotted a run-down bar that advertised "bad whiskey," once a run-down church with a sign planted on the lawn that read, "Everybody *ought* to know Jesus." America, the Potter decided, was seeded with drive-in movies and trailer camps and baseball diamonds, and, most of all, discount stores; if you drove long enough and far enough, he commented to Kaat, you would get the impression that everything in the country was sold at a discount.

Kaat spent a great deal of time explaining things to the Potter: a sign that said "Soft Shoulders," for instance; or a Negro teenager overheard in the diner calling another Negro boy "Mother"; or an advertisement in front of a bank that said, "Throckmorton Savings and Loan Talks Turkey." The Potter remembered that Thursday had used the same expression in Vienna. How do you talk when you talk turkey? the Potter asked Kaat, and when she told him he broke into a smile for the first time since he had shot one of the sweepers in the foot. You should smile more, Kaat commented. The Potter asked her why, and she said the first thing that came into her head: that it made him look less arachnoid—another one of her

A words, which meant "cobwebby." Which made him smile again.

They drove past sheep ranches and cattle ranches, and the Potter wondered out loud what it was that made one man raise sheep and another cattle; he guessed it was surely a preference that revealed a lot about someone's character.

At one point the highway climbed along a ridge and they could see a valley stretching out below them with dozens of neat farmhouses and sparkling white silos and manmade ponds and fences that always seemed to be in good repair. Perhaps there was something to be said for letting the peasants own the land they worked, or at least (here the Potter quoted what Piotr Borisovich had once told him back in Russia) the crops they harvested. At the mention of Piotr Borisovich, Kaat grew melancholy and began chewing on a cuticle.

The Potter realized he had said the wrong thing, and tried to distract her by asking her questions about herself. Where was she born? What had become of her parents? Did she have brothers? Sisters? What had she wanted to be when she grew up? And when she grew up, what had she wanted to avoid being? She answered, reluctantly at first, in abrupt phrases meant to discourage further questions. But the Potter would not be put off. What started out as therapy turned into thirst, as if knowing more about her would eventually give him access to her genitals.

Kaat was not misled. She understood enough about men to realize that he was trying to seduce her the only way he knew. Still, she found the questions irresistible. Neither W.A. nor the Sleeper, nor the dozen or so men who had played walk-in roles in her life, had ever asked her very much about the life that they had wandered into; the Sleeper—unlike the Potter now—had never even asked her what her first name was: Veronica.

They pulled into a motel on Route 35 outside Wichita, rented a room from a fat woman doing needlepoint in atrocious color combinations, and waited for the Sleeper to phone Millie again. There was no news that night, or the next day. The Potter and Kaat whiled away the time between phone calls to Millie walking in the woods behind the motel, or driving to a diner two miles down the road to get a bite to eat, or roaming around the streets of Wichita. During one meal, Kaat dangled her grandmother's ring over a road map and came to the conclusion that they should head south, but the Potter was not convinced; they would stay where they were, he decided, until they had something definite to go on.

Kaat fell asleep, fully dressed, on her bed in late afternoon, and woke to find the shades drawn and the Potter sitting on the edge of her bed, the palm of one hand resting tentatively on her breast. His desire, his need to touch her, was etched into the lines of his face. For a moment neither of them uttered a word. Then Kaat brought her hand to rest on the back of his, and ran her fingertips over his knuckles.

Taking the gesture as a sign of encouragement, the Potter buried his face in her crotch. Kaat stiffened and muttered, "Don't."

The Potter took the hint. "I am sorry, if you please," he said, sitting upright abruptly.

She regarded him with her deep-set eyes. "Here's the thing," she whispered. "I would if I could, but for it to work for me I need to feel like a co-conspirator." She tossed her shoulder in exasperation. "With you I don't have the sensation of sharing conspiracies. You have yours. I have mine."

The Potter closed his eyes and breathed deeply. "In the end everyone has his own conspiracies."

"Maybe another time," Kaat suggested gently. "Maybe when all this is over . . ."

The Potter elevated his chin and stared off into space. "All this"—he had in mind much more than she thought—"will never be over."

When Kaat phoned Millie after dinner, she came on the line in tears. "What's the matter?" Kaat demanded.

Millie was too choked up to answer. Instead she fumbled with her tape recorder and held the telephone to the speaker so that Kaat could hear for herself.

"Let me talk to Kaat," the Sleeper ordered on the tape. He seemed to be pressed for time.

"Kaat's not here," Millie replied. "I'm here."

"When is she coming back?" the Sleeper demanded.

"Where are you?" Millie asked. "When are *you* coming back?"

"That's just it," the Sleeper told Millie. "I'm not coming back. I called to say good-bye to Kaat."

"And me?" Millie burst out angrily.

"And you too, naturally."

"You bastard," Millie flared. "Where are you?"

"Tell Kaat," the Sleeper said. There was a long silence on the tape.

"Tell Kaat what?" Millie asked.

"I thought," the real Millie managed to say now between her tears, "that he was going to say he loved you."

"It would be totally out of character for him," Kaat told Millie.

"Tell Kaat that I met someone who wants to buy all the mobiles I can make," the Sleeper said on the tape. "I'm going to get rich," he added.

"You're not a capitalist," Millie told him. "You're an artist."

"I'm going to make a killing," the Sleeper said in a voice that had a bitter edge to it. "I'm going—" Then: "Shit." Then the line went dead.

"What does it mean in English?" the Potter asked Kaat when she had hung up on Millie. " 'I'm going to make a killing'?"

"It means he's going to make a lot of money," Kaat explained.

The Potter got up and began pacing the tiny room. "There is something I never told you about Piotr Borisovich," he said. "He is not an espionage agent in the ordinary sense of the expression. During the war he was a sniper, a crack rifle shot. Now he is a specialist in what we call wetwork—he is a professional assassin."

Kaat's eyes glistened, and she looked quickly away before the Potter could spot the tears. If someone had asked her, she would have sworn that she could never love someone who was capable of killing. Yet she had loved the man whom the Potter called Piotr Borisovich. She had sensed the mystery in him all along; it occurred to her now that she might also have sensed that violence was at the heart of the mystery. "It doesn't surprise me," she remarked. "Deep down I always saw him as an acutiator—in medieval times that meant a sharpener of weapons." A terrible possibility struck her. "You don't think . . ."

"He said he was going to make a killing," the Potter reminded her.

"Oh," Kaat breathed. "Whom is he going to kill?"

"If we knew the whom," the Potter said, "we might know the where."

They checked out of the motel and drove into Wichita for lunch. Afterward they ordered coffee. Almost as if they were putting off the inevitable, each ordered a second cup. "We've come a long way from that coffee shop in Brooklyn Heights," Kaat noted.

The Potter took a wad of twenty-dollar bills from a pocket and pushed it across the table toward her. "For your fare home." When she started to protest, he said, "If you please."

Kaat pocketed the money. "Where will you go?" she asked.

The Potter shrugged. "There are not many countries left for me to defect to," he answered. He thought a moment and said, "I will go to Canada. They say the climate is very close to Russia's. I like it when it is very cold because it gives me an excuse to drink a great deal of vodka."

They asked directions to the bus station, and the Potter drove her there. Kaat discovered she had an hour and a quarter until her bus left, so they settled down on a wooden bench to wait. A clock on the wall over their heads marked off the minutes with a loud clicking sound that resembled a door closing or a lock opening. After a while the Potter went over to a newsstand. The newspapers were arranged in two tiers, in-state and out-of-state. The Potter bought half a dozen out-of-state newspapers, carried them back to the bench and started going through them. "What are you looking for?" Kaat asked.

"The whom, the where," the Potter said without looking up.

He was reading an inside page of his fourth newspaper when his eye fell on a boxed item in the lower-left-hand corner. Once again the skin on the back of the Potter's neck crawled; once again his body knew before he did. (He could hear the squirrellike taxi driver with the worker's cap pulled low over his eyes calling, "And what about you, comrade fur cap?" almost as if the start of the journey had taken place that morning.) He ripped out the boxed item and reread it.

"What is it?" Kaat asked in alarm.

"Look at this," he instructed her. He handed her the clipping. It reminded readers of the impending visit to the city in which the newspaper was published of the Prince of the Realm, and announced the route he would take on his way from the airport to a luncheon at which he would speak.

"I don't—" she started to say.

"This is the whom," the Potter whispered fiercely, "and the *where!*"

It dawned on Kaat what he was talking about. "How could you know such a thing?"

"I know," the Potter insisted.

"You're guessing," Kaat said.

"I am guessing, yes," the Potter conceded. "But it all fits. Someone went to an enormous amount of trouble to organize my defection; to get the identity of a sleeper; to activate him and send him on a mission. They are not going to order him to hold up a candy store. The target has to be worthy of all this trouble. And then there is the matter of why they wanted Piotr Borisovich to commit the crime for them. There are local people, criminals, who do this kind of thing. But they wanted a Russian so that the crime would be traced back to Moscow, which would make it, from their point of view, a perfect crime." When Kaat stared at him, still not convinced, he added lamely, "You told me we should go south."

That made an impression on her. She brought a nail to her mouth and started biting on it nervously. "What if you're wrong?" she demanded. "What if this has nothing to do with him?"

"If I am wrong," the Potter said, "you will have lost three days and visited another American city." He added, "Have faith, if you please."

"All I come equipped with," Kaat said, "is a longing for

faith." She got up and stalked off a few steps, stopped to think, then turned and came back to the Potter. "Let's say, for argument's sake, that you're right. How are you going to find Peter before he commits the crime?"

The Potter had an answer for that one too. "You forget that I trained Piotr Borisovich. What he knows, he learned from me. To find him, all I have to do is study the route through the city and calculate the best place from which to commit the crime. If Piotr Borisovich is half as good as I think he is, he will select the same place."

Kaat laughed under her breath. "All this is what we refer to in English as a long shot."

"It may be a long shot," the Potter said grimly, "but it is also our only shot."

30

If the Sleeper never saw the inside of another bus in his life, it would be too soon. The wrinkles in the countryside he had passed through the day before had been flattened out, like a shirt that had been ironed. The only thing to break the monotony was an occasional road sign indicating how far it was to the city. "This here ain't the real West," a man wearing blue jeans and tooled cowboy boots shouted across the aisle to the Sleeper. He leaned into the aisle, but he didn't lower his voice. "Hell, the real West don't start for another hundred or so miles. There the damn cities are so far apart you forget they exist by the time you get to one of them. Say, this your first time down to God's country?"

"First time," the Sleeper told him.

"Business or pleasure?"

"Both, I hope," the Sleeper said with a knowing smile.

In the back of the bus, a Negro woman scolded her eight-year-old boy for running in the aisle. "Thomas James, you get yourself right back here, hear?" she called. "Thomas James, you set yourself back down. What you got, ants in your pants? I don't want to hear another meow out of you, Thomas James."

"That there is the airo-port," the man across the aisle told the Sleeper in a booming voice, gesturing with his chin out the window. "Me, I'll take a bus over a plane any day of the week. Plain truth is that planes scare the pants off me. Afraid the damn things will come to a sudden stop—like against a mountain!" He howled at his own joke.

The bus driver (Safe-Reliable-Courteous, according to the plaque over his head) steered the Greyhound into Lemmon

Avenue. Up ahead, through the front window, the Sleeper could make out the downtown area. "How long you say you were planning to stay?" the cowboy asked.

"Two days at the outside," the Sleeper told him.

The cowboy snorted. "First time I came down here," he recounted, "I was going to stay two days also. Came on down from Minnesota to visit an old lady who said she was my aunt. Wound up staying seventeen years. Ain't that something? I just plain liked the climate, is what kept me. They got themselves six weeks of what they call winter down here, but I sure as hell don't call it winter."

The Sleeper smiled pleasantly. Small wrinkles fanned out from the corners of his eyes. "In two days," he reassured the cowboy, and himself, "I will have accomplished what I came to do, and I'll be on my way."

"That's what they all say," the cowboy remarked with a wink.

The Sleeper turned to stare out of the window. The Greyhound was passing a small park with a statue of Robert E. Lee in it. A Mustang with its top sawed off wheeled past the bus. A girl was driving, another sat next to her. Looking down at them from the bus, the Sleeper noticed that their skirts had edged up along their thighs. He remembered the way Kaat had of planting herself in a chair with her legs spread and her skirt hiked up above her knees and dipping between them in a way that outlined her thighs. The Sleeper had always appreciated the innocence, the openness of her posture. Why, he asked himself, do my thoughts keep drifting back to Kaat? Is it because, as the Potter had noted back in Moscow, sex turns me on to violence, and I am getting close to the time and the place where I need to turn on to violence? I was a fool to phone her last night, he berated himself. What would I have said to her if she had been there? That I longed for her in ways that I can't explain, even to myself? That if things go badly in the next two days, reporters will be breaking down her door to get from her insights into the man she had lived with; had shared, along with Millie, a bed with? That if I manage to make my killing, I can retire to the relative luxury of a *dacha* on the Black Sea, and that I might ask her, once the dust has settled, to come live with me? Knowing Kaat, she would laugh in my face. She would produce an appropriate A word to sum up what she thought of the idea.

The Sleeper shifted into the window seat and pressed his forehead against the glass. The Greyhound was cutting across Main Street now, and the Sleeper, peering down it, was struck by how closely it resembled a canyon. Near the end of it several new buildings protruded, like new shoots in a hedge, from the mass of older ones. The modern steel-and-glass monsters reminded him of the pair of Polaroid sunglasses he had once bought and then thrown away because Kaat categorically refused to talk to someone if she couldn't see his eyes. I miss Kaat, the Sleeper admitted to himself. I miss her sadness and her insolence and her independence. I miss her telling me to watch out for ides, or who I was in a previous incarnation. I miss making love with her. Most women, in the Sleeper's experience, treated their lovers as fathers or sons, either snuggling into their arms or talking baby talk to them. Kaat treated hers as comrades, as someone she could share conspiracies with. And she gave and took pleasure according to a meticulously measured formula that never varied very far from fifty-fifty. Which was, when all was said and done, the way the Sleeper liked it.

"End of the line," the bus driver called as he swung the Greyhound into its berth and braked to a stop. The doors opened with a rush of air.

"See you in seventeen years," the cowboy told the Sleeper as he headed down the aisle.

Carrying his viola-da-gamba case in one hand and his worn leather valise in the other, the Sleeper turned his back on the downtown canyon and made his way toward a run-down section of town and the shabby one-story rooming house specified in the original orders he had recovered from the dead-letter drop in Brooklyn. Perspiring from the long walk, he eventually passed the yellow-brick self-service laundry and the pharmacy with a parking lot next to it full of pickup trucks. He stopped to loosen his tie and pass his handkerchief under his collar, and glancing back over his shoulder, took a long look at the center of the city rising from the flat like a wart. Tomorrow, if things went well, he would look back at the wart for the last time. If things went badly, he would be trapped in it.

Ignoring the "No Vacancy" dangling under the "Rooms for Rent" sign on the front lawn of the rooming house—his room would have been reserved for him by letter—the Sleeper cut across the front lawn to the porch. A cat with its head cocked, as if it expected the Sleeper to say something, stared impassively at him from the top step. "I am not a cat person," the Sleeper told the cat, but he knew he didn't mean it; given half a chance, he could become a cat person. He pushed open the screen door with his foot. A wiry young man was going out as the Sleeper entered. He held the screen door open so the Sleeper could pass, and nodded impersonally when he thanked him. Inside, the Sleeper found a room reserved in the name he was traveling under. "You must be a musician," the woman who ran the rooming house said when she spotted his viola-da-gamba case. "Don't get many musicians out here. More's the pity, 'cause if there's one thing I admire, it's music played by musicians." She reached under the desk blotter and produced a letter. "This here came for you. It was marked hold, so I went and held it."

The Sleeper deposited his belongings in his room, locked the door from the inside and opened the letter the woman had given him. In it he found a street map of the downtown wart, along with an item, clipped from a local newspaper, giving readers the route that the target would take on his way from the airport to the luncheon the following day.

The Sleeper didn't have time to waste. "Going prowling so soon?" the woman who ran the rooming house asked in a singsong voice when she spotted him on his way out several minutes later. The Sleeper mumbled something about wanting to see the downtown area while there was still some light left in the sky, and the answer seemed to please her because she reeled off a list of the things in the city he shouldn't miss. He put several blocks between himself and the rooming house, then hailed a passing cab and instructed the driver to take him to the far end of the downtown wart. The Sleeper remembered the Potter's lessons well. There was no point in starting at the airport itself. Having just landed in a strange city, the people responsible for security would be at their sharpest there. On the roads leading from the airport to the wart, the motorcade would move at a brisk clip, and since there would be relatively few people lining the route it would be difficult for the Sleeper to judge from the cheers when the car containing the target was approaching. Even if he managed to get off a shot, the problem of escaping afterward would be compounded by the fact that there wouldn't be many onlookers.

You must start to look for a place to shoot from, the Sleeper could almost hear the Potter explaining in the patient voice he used when he was very sure of himself, where the crowds grow thick; where the cheers of the people lining the route announce the approach of the target; where the sound of a shot will send people scurrying in every direction, which means that you can run away from the scene along with everyone else without attracting attention. In the case at hand, the crowds would grow thick at the downtown wart, or more precisely at the point where the car containing the target turned into the Main Street canyon and proceeded through it at a leisurely pace so that the people lining the route could get a good look at him.

The Sleeper walked the route from one end to the other. He began at the city jail, where the motorcade was scheduled to enter the canyon, and wound up at the far end where the motorcade would jog right toward a warehouse and then left before turning up onto the freeway. Having gotten the general lay of the land, he flagged a taxi and returned to the city-jail end of the downtown canyon and started over the route a second time. There was a hotel situated at the corner where the motorcade would turn into Main Street, but hotels had house detectives who would be curious about a client carrying a viola-da-gamba case and asking for a room overlooking the route the Prince of the Realm would take. There was a mercantile bank building two blocks down the canyon from the hotel that attracted his attention. It wasn't so much the roof that interested the Sleeper (every policeman in town would be scanning roofs for the silhouette of a rifleman) as the upper-floor windows, which would give an excellent view of the canyon floor below. But when the Sleeper stuck his nose inside the lobby, he saw instantly that the mercantile bank building was not for him. Two uniformed policemen stationed behind a table were waving on the employees they recognized, and questioning everyone else. An hour before the motorcade passed, the Sleeper reasoned, it would be a risky business trying to talk his way past the guards.

There were several other buildings along the route that tempted the Sleeper, but in the end he dismissed them all: one because there seemed to be a series of factories on every floor, which meant the windows would be lined with workers; another because the lobby was plastered with "Wanted for Treason" posters carrying a photograph of the Prince of the Realm on them, and the local police would be sure to plant a handful of plainclothes detectives around the building the moment the motorcade passed; a third because a poster in the lobby announced that the pro-Prince contingent planned to rain confetti down on him from every window as he went by. The warehouse at the far end of the downtown canyon would have been an ideal choice, but the Sleeper decided it was so obvious—at one point the motorcade would jog directly toward it, and then move off obliquely away from it—that the building would certainly be crawling with police.

What you really want, the Potter had instructed him back in Moscow when they were scouting the route that the Indian Prime Minister would take from the airport to the Kremlin, is an open space. A window is an excellent place to shoot from if you have a great deal of time to prepare the assignment. You can select your building carefully, and even get a job in it so that it will seem natural for you to be there; natural also when you leave the building in the confusion that inevitably follows an assassination attempt. But for an assignment that you don't have weeks, or even months, to prepare, what you need is an open space, some place you can get to easily—and just as easily get away from afterward.

Several open spaces were scattered along the route that the Prince of the Realm would take. Two blocks down the canyon from the mercantile bank, there was a construction site with two cranes lying on their sides that might have provided excellent cover for a sniper. But workers wearing hard hats were installing the last segment of a chain-link fence that would make access to the construction site difficult. Farther along the canyon, on the right side, the Sleeper explored a small vest-pocket park sandwiched between two buildings. It had a patch of shrubbery in which a rifleman could hide as he waited for the motorcade to pass. But the park was set into a slight depression, and the Sleeper was afraid that the people lining the route would mask the target. Toward the end of the canyon, near the old courthouse building, there was a series of open plazas, but the areas were paved and didn't offer an obvious place to shoot from.

Which narrowed the choice of an assassination site down to the open space that the Sleeper had spotted the first time he had gone over the route of the motorcade. It had the advantage of being at the end of the downtown canyon, between the warehouse and the freeway, which meant that the people protecting the target would have passed the hundreds of windows on Main Street in a state of full alert, and with the freeway in sight just ahead would be breathing their first sighs of relief. It was a grassy area, elevated above street level, with a line of shrubs to obscure a rifleman, and a parking lot behind it to make access—and escape—relatively easy. There was one disadvantage: the target would be passing at practically right angles to the shooter, which would complicate the ballistic problem, but the Sleeper was confident of his ability to calculate lead angles.

He explored the site from every side; in the fading light he turned around it like a moth. There was an old man stationed in the parking lot behind the hedges, but he didn't appear to pay any attention to the Sleeper as he wandered through the area. From the street side the shrubs looked perfectly innocent, a small screen of decorative foliage that would be unlikely to draw more than a cursory glance from the people who were responsible for the safety of the Prince. At this point in their route they would be more interested in the windows of the warehouse behind them, and the overpass ahead.

"So," the woman who ran the rooming house asked when the Sleeper reappeared at the screen door, "what did you think of it?" She nodded toward the downtown wart. "The city, I mean? Some folks say it's pretty much like New York."

It dawned on the Sleeper that she seemed to be desperate for reassurance that she was not wasting her life in a backwater. "It would be difficult to tell them apart," he said, suddenly anxious to supply her with what she needed.

But the woman only turned away, shaking her head in disappointment, as if to say she knew a backwater when she saw one; as if to say she recognized an exaggeration when she heard one.

31

❧

The Sisters arrived on the last flight that night, Carroll struggling to control a twitching facial muscle, Francis nervously
fingering the knot of a taxicab-yellow silk bow tie and smiling
angelically, as if he were going to officiate at a baptism. G.
Sprowls, who had flown into the city the previous day, picked
them up in a rented car and drove them into town, depositing
them on the doorstep of a hotel overlooking Main Street, at the
city-jail end of the downtown canyon. "I still don't see why
we had to be here personally," Carroll complained as G. Sprowls
pulled up to the curb.

"It's a matter of loose ends," G. Sprowls replied.

"That's what you told us over the phone when you asked
us to come," Francis noted. "I wasn't sure what you meant by
loose ends then. I'm still not sure."

G. Sprowls focused his half-smile on Francis, and the two
men eyed each other for a moment. "There will be pieces to
pick up after an operation of this kind," G. Sprowls finally
drawled. "Depending on whether this sleeper of yours succeeds, depending on whether he is caught in the act or manages
to elude capture, there will be clues to draw attention to,
people to point in certain directions."

"That is the kind of thing you are supposed to excel at,"
Francis said. He tried to sound as if he were thinking out loud.
"Carroll and I, on the other hand, have not operated in the
field for years."

"If someone has to lend a hand, we thought"—G. Sprowls
managed to put a subtle emphasis on the word "we"—"that it
would be more discreet to call upon you two than to bring
someone else into the picture."

"It was the Director's idea to have us come down here, then?" Francis asked. In his mind's eye he was already composing a memorandum on the conversation to add to the pile in the false bottom of his garbage pail.

"Trust me," was all that G. Sprowls offered, and he said it in a way that left them few alternatives.

32

✤

There was no position that Ourcq could find to alleviate the pain that throbbed through his foot. "Maybe take another one of those painkillers," Appleyard, his eyes glued to the road ahead, suggested from the front seat.

"I took one of those fucking pills twenty fucking minutes ago," Ourcq snapped. He rearranged his leg on the pillow that he had swiped from the hotel, but it didn't seem to make any difference. Each time the Dodge went over a bump, he cried out in agony. "I am supposed to take one of them every four fucking hours, not every twenty fucking minutes."

"I was only trying to be helpful," Appleyard remarked, and he went back to imitating the sound of the windshield wipers.

For once, Ourcq didn't complain. The sound made him drowsy, and the drowsiness seemed to dull the pain in his foot. "How fucking far are we from—" He cried out as the front wheels of the car rippled over a washboard section of road.

"Maybe another hour," Appleyard called back over his shoulder. "Maybe forty-five minutes if I do not run into traffic when we get there."

Ourcq fumbled for another of the painkillers that the hotel doctor had given him. He had been fucking lucky in the end: fucking lucky that the bullet had passed cleanly through his foot, taking a toe along with it but not shattering any bones; fucking lucky, too, to have fallen on a doctor who, for a price, agreed not to report the shooting accident to the police. He had disinfected the wound, given him an injection against tetanus and another against pain, and pills to take when the injection wore off. He had even come up (again, for a

270

price) with an old pair of wooden crutches, which Appleyard had imitated the sound of as soon as Ourcq hobbled across the floor on them.

"You want me maybe to pull over for a while?" Appleyard called from the driver's seat. He got a certain amount of satisfaction from being healthier than Ourcq, and he rubbed it in by being overly solicitous.

Ourcq, for his part, was touched by his colleague's concern. "You fucking want to do something for me?" he whined.

"You maybe name it," Appleyard shot back.

Groaning, Ourcq shifted his body to get more weight off his bad foot. "Imitate the sound of the fucking sun setting," he demanded. "You said you could fucking do it, but you never fucking did it."

Appleyard shook his head stubbornly. "I got to be in the mood," he explained. "I got to be inspired. Maybe later. Maybe."

33

❧

Kaat was all for turning back when the Chrysler's high beams picked out the sign nailed to the stump of a dead tree at the end of the driveway. "Combes's Retreat, Whites Only," it read, and then in smaller print it specified: "No Animals, No Children Neither." But the Potter insisted on continuing. The rooming house at the bitter end of an unpaved road at the edge of the prairie, sixteen miles as the crow flies from the center of the city, was precisely what he was looking for. If the Prince of the Realm was really the target, if the Potter managed to figure out where the Sleeper would shoot from and find him, he would require an out-of-the-way place to take him to. They would need a breathing spell; time to put their heads together and come up with a permanent line of retreat. Between them they would have money, false papers, a clearer idea of what had happened; a clearer idea of where to go from here.

Assuming there was anywhere to go from here.

Assuming the Prince of the Realm was really the target.

Assuming the Potter managed to figure out where the Sleeper would shoot from.

"Mighty late to be sucking around for a place to spend the night," the owner of the rooming house said, squinting out suspiciously at the Potter and Kaat through the partially opened door. He was wearing a jacket without any shirt or undershirt beneath it. "Got half a mind to send you packing."

"We're whites," Kaat said with a straight face.

"There are whites, and there are whites," the owner muttered.

"Let's go," Kaat whispered, tugging on the Potter's arm. She regarded the house, large, Victorian, with bay windows and shingles and rusted drainpipes angling off in every direction, with apprehension.

"It is this way," the Potter told the rooming-house owner. "We are not married. What we need is a place to stay, if you please."

"It'll cost you," the owner, the Combes of Combes's Retreat, said. He scratched at a cheek that hadn't seen the cutting edge of a razor in days.

"Only name your price," the Potter said.

The rooming-house owner, a policeman who had been kicked off the city force several years before for shaking down illegal aliens, opened the door a bit more and studied his prospective clients closely. "Twenty a night," he finally announced.

"We will take it," the Potter said immediately.

"Plus five dollars a night for hot water."

"That will be fine," the Potter agreed.

"In advance," Combes insisted. He was annoyed with himself for not having asked for more.

The Potter counted out one hundred dollars in twenty-dollar bills and handed it to the owner through the open door. "This is for four nights, if you please," he explained.

"No refunds if you leave early," Combes warned.

"That is perfectly reasonable," the Potter said. "Can we come in now?"

The room they got was a large one with a bay window looking out over a copper-colored prairie that stretched off to where the horizon would have been if it wasn't too dark to see it. There was a tarnished brass bed with a mattress that sagged like a hammock in the middle, and threadbare carpets that smelled of cigarette ashes and mildew. Kaat went out to use the toilet at the end of the hallway, and came back with a look of sheer disgust on her face.

There was a washbasin in a corner of the room, but no hot water. Kaat wanted to complain; it was a matter of principle, she said. But the Potter told her not to bother. He would have paid three times as much for the room if the owner had had the sense to ask for it, he explained, and he sat her on the edge of the sagging bed and told her why.

273

"I never thought about what we would do after we found him," Kaat admitted. "That's very smart of you, actually."

"It is not a question of intelligence," the Potter said. "It is a question of experience. Generally speaking, people in my business live longer if they think about what to do *after*."

The Potter wedged a chair under the doorknob, placed his Beretta on a low table, loosened his tie and settled into the only seat in the room, an old easy chair that smelled as if it had once been in a fire. Biting nervously on a cuticle, Kaat asked why they didn't scout the downtown area immediately. The Potter said he preferred to wait for daylight because he would be able to see more, and because people strolling the streets would be less conspicuous. Kaat kicked off her shoes, propped the two old pillows up and leaned back against them. "You remember the other night?" she began. She left the rest of the thought hanging.

"The other night?"

"The other night, in the motel, when you wanted to make love to me," Kaat said. "You remember what I said about needing to share conspiracies?"

The Potter nodded tiredly. He wanted to sleep, not talk.

Kaat took a deep breath. "Here's the thing," she said. "I still think I need to share, but I'm not so sure about the conspiracies part. What I'm trying to say is, if you're still in the market to make love . . ." The sentence trailed off. Kaat smiled at the Potter across the room.

The Potter shifted in his chair, cleared a constricted throat. "You are an extremely nice human being," he told her. He spoke slowly, deliberately, anxious to express his own feelings without hurting hers. "Please understand, I did want to make love with you. I still do. But I am an old man, and I am getting older by the minute. I am tied up to the pier of old age. And the moment has passed. Which is not to say that it will not come again. Until it does, I thank you for bringing up the subject. I appreciate it. I appreciate you. Most affection between men and women these days is a matter of habit. But I am pleased to think that there is a real affection between us. Offered without being asked. Accepted without owing anything in return. Now go to sleep, my noiseless patient spider.

In the morning we will find Piotr Borisovich, and then we will, all three of us together, contemplate the elusive thing called the future." The Potter reached over and switched off the table lamp. "Okay?" he asked into the darkness.

"Okay," Kaat replied in a puzzled voice.

34

The owner of the motel waited until he was sure the dwarf and his lady friend would be asleep. Then, taking his six-battery flashlight down from its hook, he went out to take a closer look at the Chrysler. Somewhere out on the prairie behind the house, a coyote howled. Combes flicked on the flashlight and played it over the car. Eventually he came to the license plates. They were from New York State, yet the sticker on the rear bumper advertised the advantages of vacationing in Ohio. Combes knelt and ran his fingers over the rear license plate. He could feel a crease in it where the screw held it to the body of the car, almost as if it had been pried loose and then replaced.

Combes straightened up. Maybe it had been the sight of the dwarflike man with a beautiful young girl trailing up the steps after him. Maybe it had been the way he spoke English with a foreign accent. Maybe it had been the ease with which he peeled off twenty-dollar bills from a wad as thick as a fist. Whatever it was, the dwarf had gotten on Combes's nerves. It would give him a certain amount of visceral pleasure to tag him.

The owner returned to the rooming house and dialed the number of his old precinct downtown. "It's me, Combes," he said when the patrolman on duty answered. "Who's minding the store? Pass him to me, will you? . . . Mac, it's me, Combes. Listen up. I got me a car out here with New York plates and an Ohio bumper sticker. I thought maybe you could see if anything was on the wire. . . . Sure I can." Combes described the Chrysler and gave the license-plate number. "Sure thing,

Mac. I'll wait on your call." He hung up the phone and stared out of a window across the prairie. It would sure as hell tickle him to tag the foreigner. Yes, indeed. It would tickle the hell out of him.

35

⚜

Studying the canyon formed by the buildings on either side of
Main Street, the Potter sensed he had reached the end of the
line. The sun was still out of sight behind the canyon, but
shards of metallic light filtered through the narrow spaces
between the buildings, sending alternating slats of shadow and
light slanting across the gutter. Wielding canvas fire hoses that
snaked back along the curb to a large mobile water wagon, two
Chicanos in hip boots were hosing down the route the motorcade would take in a few hours. Up ahead, several men in
impeccable three-piece suits looked on as sanitation workers
pried up manhole covers and then lowered themselves through
the openings to search for explosives.

"What about the hotel across the street?" Kaat asked.

The Potter sized it up with a professional eye. "Hotels,"
he said, "are the natural habitat of a very special breed called
house detectives. The farther you stay from them, the better
off you are. No, I don't see Piotr Borisovich marching up to
the front desk, probably carrying some kind of package in
which a rifle is hidden, and asking for a room with a view of
the street through which the target will soon pass."

Around them scores of people, their heads angled against
a nonexistent wind, were hurrying to work. Did they really
think that getting there on time would change their lives? the
Potter wondered. He made a mental note to tell Kaat how, in
Moscow, people moved as if getting where they were going
wouldn't change anything. Maybe he had put his finger on the
real difference between the two countries, the two systems.
Maybe hurrying to where you were going didn't have anything

to do with an extra wet dream a week. He would have to talk to the Sleeper about it later, he decided.

The Potter strolled into the lobby of the mercantile bank building, and strolled out again two minutes later shaking his head. "Too much security," he muttered. "He would not pick this one." Making his way down Main Street, the Potter resembled nothing so much as a diviner searching for water, the only difference being he didn't have a forked stick. He examined several other buildings, always with the same result. One building he thought extremely promising until he discovered that it housed a factory on every floor.

Kaat asked him about the roofs. Even if he could get to them without attracting attention, the Potter explained, it was the last place a professional would shoot from, if only because every policeman was trained to scan rooftops for the silhouette of a sniper. Also, there was a good chance that the police would station snipers of their own on several of the highest roofs along Main Street to make sure the others were secure. If I were planning to pick off the target, the Potter reasoned, I would look for an open space. And if I would look for an open space, Piotr Borisovich would also look for an open space.

"What if you're wrong?" Kaat asked, biting on a hangnail.

The Potter looked down the canyon. The Sleeper was out there somewhere, he felt it in his bones. "I am not wrong," he told Kaat. "I cannot be wrong."

"What if?" Kaat persisted. But when she saw the expression on the Potter's face, she said, "I take back the 'what if.'"

Continuing down Main Street, the Potter investigated the construction site with several cranes lying on their sides, but saw the chain-link fence around the area and the uniformed guard checking work papers at the only door in the fence. The vest-pocket park sandwiched between two buildings on the right side of the street looked promising until the Potter discovered that it was in a slight depression, which meant that the people who would eventually line the route would mask the target from anyone in the park. At the far end of the downtown canyon there was an old sandstone courthouse, and a series of paved plazas around it, but for the life of him the Potter could not see where a rifleman could hide. Beyond the courthouse the motorcade would jog to the right and then left again, going directly toward and then passing under a rust-colored brick warehouse with a red-white-and-blue Hertz sign on the roof that told the time and the temperature.

"What's wrong with that building?" Kaat asked.

"Nothing," the Potter said, "which is what is wrong with it. It is probably the single best site for a rifleman along the entire route. The angle of fire, the distance to the target, are ideal. Unless the local police are fast asleep, they will post a man at every window."

"What are you staring at?" Kaat asked suddenly.

"I have found what I was looking for," the Potter announced in a low voice. "Look there, to the left of the warehouse building. Do you see it?"

"You mean the slope over there?" Kaat asked.

"Those bushes provide a perfect screen for a rifleman," the Potter said excitedly. "Come on, I want to get a closer look at it."

They crossed Main Street and skirted behind the warehouse, through the parking lot, to the top of the incline at the edge of the lot. The Potter studied the street below through the bushes. "This is it," he told Kaat. "The perfect place for a sniper. The only drawback is that the target will pass at almost right angles to the rifleman, but Piotr Borisovich is an excellent marksman and would not hesitate because of that. He would consider the parking lot at his back a great advantage for the escape, because he does not suspect that he is not meant to escape. He is meant to be caught."

Kaat looked at the Potter in awe. "How can you know all these things?"

"He will not come here until the last minute to avoid the possibility of running into anyone," the Potter continued in a low voice. He seemed to have forgotten that Kaat was next to him, and talked to himself. "In three hours and forty-five minutes, he will be standing where we are standing now. He will hear the cheers coming from Main Street, indicating the motorcade is approaching. The limousine will come into view, turn under the warehouse and pass directly under here. The guards accompanying the target will start to relax when they spot the freeway entrance ahead. Piotr Borisovich will aim for the jugular, as he did during the war." A distant look obscured the Potter's normally alert gaze. "Piotr Borisovich's father talked about myths just before he died. In one way or another, he said, all of us are acting out myths. Even Piotr Borisovich. Especially Piotr Borisovich," he said.

"What myths is Piotr Borisovich acting out?" Kaat wanted to know.

"What day are we today?" the Potter asked.

"Twenty-two November. Why?"

The Potter imagined he could hear the cheering of the crowds lining the canyon on Main Street, announcing the approach of the motorcade. "Have you ever noticed how autumn always makes people uneasy?" the Potter asked. "The days grow shorter and colder. Leaves fall from the trees and decay on the ground. The wind picks up and takes on a cutting edge. The clouds overhead appear to be lower and thicker and heavier than usual. The mountains on the horizon seem closer, more menacing. In ancient times the peasants began to worry that they had offended God. It was usually toward the end of autumn that they sacrificed their prince so that he could ascend to heaven and intercede with God, could make sure that spring would come again." The Potter took Kaat's elbow and drew her away from the line of bushes. "I remember something else Piotr Borisovich's father told me. He said he thought Piotr Borisovich was meant to be a prince, or kill a prince."

36

❦

Looking out from the window of his room on the fourth floor, Francis observed with a feeling of infinite detachment—he had imagined the moment so many times, he felt as if he were watching an old film—the security precautions along the route the Prince of the Realm would soon take. He could make out a burly policeman armed with binoculars and a walkie-talkie on the roof across the way. Below, workmen in overalls were removing wooden police barriers from an open truck and stacking them next to the curb; at noon they would be used to close off the cross streets to traffic.

The phone next to the bed rang. Francis picked up the receiver. "Do you see what I see?" a voice asked.

Francis almost convinced himself that he could *hear* a facial muscle twitching in excitement. "You mean the cop with binoculars across the street?" Francis asked.

"They were pulling up manhole covers and looking for bombs earlier," Carroll said. He sounded as if he were feverish. Slurring his words, he hissed into the phone, "Poor saps." When Francis didn't respond, he asked, "What are you going to do now?" As if knowing how Francis planned to while away the morning would help him do the same.

"I am going to select an appropriate necktie to wear," Francis replied. And when Carroll finally hung up, he did exactly that. Picking the bow tie was, in fact, Francis' major preoccupation of the morning. He took one with mauve polka dots from his canvas tie case and held it up to his neck so he could see it in the mirror. It wasn't quite what he was looking for. He tried a solid-colored one next, a particularly generously cut bow tie in a washed-out orange silk. He eventually settled on one of his favorites, a pale green bow tie with rust-colored pinstripes running horizontally through it. Francis pulled up his collar, and with several deft hand-over-hand gestures knotted the tie, then adjusted the collar and studied the effect in the mirror. If he could save only one of his ties, this one would definitely be it. He detested the idea of abandoning the others, but he recognized the necessity and, as was his habit, bowed to it. If everything went according to plan, if the Sleeper were caught in or after the act, Francis would immediately dial the phone number he had been given before he left Washington. And wearing only the clothes on his back, the pale green bow tie with rust-colored pinstripes around his neck, the shoes on his feet and the Cheshire cat's pained smile that hinted at nothing more morally compromising than the death of an occasional rodent, he would disappear, within the hour, from the face of the earth.

37

Carrying a long, thin package wrapped in brown paper, Khanda turned up for work at the warehouse a few minutes early that morning.

"What you got yourself there, a fishing rod?" one of the older hands who passed Khanda in the stairwell asked.

"It's curtain rods," Khanda explained briefly, "for my room."

"Too bad it ain't a high-powered rifle to put a hole through that son of a bitch who's supposed to be passing by today," the other man said.

"I got nothing against him," Khanda said.

"Well, I reckon that makes you the only one in the whole entire state who don't," the other said, and muttering under his breath about how the punishment ought to fit the crime, and the crime was high treason, he went on about his business.

Using the stairway instead of the elevator to avoid other workers, Khanda made his way to the sixth floor. Near the window he had picked out, he shoved aside some cartons and slid the curtain rods in behind them. It occurred to him, as he went downstairs to report to work, that this was his last day on the job; that if things went well, he might never have to work another day in his entire life.

38

❧

A teenager outside the window of the motel room was walking across the gravel driveway in thick motorcycle boots. Watching from behind the half-drawn shades, Appleyard softly imitated the sound until he thought he had it right. Then he took a deep breath and did it at full volume. It sounded as if someone were walking across gravel *inside* the room.

Ourcq limped out of the bathroom on his wooden crutches. "Maybe you should fucking phone again," he said.

Appleyard stopped making the sound of a boot crunching on gravel. "He specifically said he would call us when he knew something," he reminded Ourcq.

"What I wouldn't give to get my fucking paws on him," Ourcq said. He leaned the crutches against the wall and sat down heavily on the bed, careful to keep his weight off his bad foot.

"What would you give?" Appleyard asked, his eyebrows dancing in curiosity.

"I would give a fucking year of my life," Ourcq replied with obvious sincerity. "I would give my fucking right arm. It is just not right to shoot somebody in the fucking foot. It causes too much fucking pain."

Appleyard came to the conclusion that the wound had had a humanizing effect on his partner; for the first time in memory, he seemed to hate the person he might have to kill. "If he had not shot you in the foot," Appleyard pointed out, "he might have shot you in the head." He cocked his forefinger as if it were a pistol and produced a perfect imitation of a gun going off. "At least," he added, "where there is pain there is life."

"Now you are imitating the sound of a fucking intellectual," Ourcq said in disgust. "Do me a fucking favor, go back to doing somebody walking on fucking gravel."

39

✣

It was twenty minutes to noon when the Potter went to pick up the Chrysler at the garage on Elm Street. One block to the south, crowds were already forming along the route. According to the newspaper clipping, the motorcade would jog past the red-brick warehouse—and the bushes on the rise just after it—at about twelve-thirty. The Sleeper, the Potter calculated, would wait until the last minute before taking up position. The Potter planned to pull the Chrysler into the parking lot next to the rise at twelve-twenty-five, and drive off with the Sleeper before the motorcade emerged from the Main Street canyon.

Kaat went into the garage to give the stub to the man on duty. Five minutes later she came hurrying out to the street with a strange look on her face; the last time the Potter remembered seeing it was when she had turned to stare at the lifeless body of her cat on the back seat of the car.

"What is happening, if you please?" the Potter asked in alarm.

"Here's the thing," Kaat said. "The attendant called on his intercom, and the man who moves the cars called back to say that the Chrysler had a flat tire. They said that for ten dollars they would fix it, so I told them to go ahead and do it."

The Potter stepped out into the street to see the time atop the brick warehouse at the end of Elm Street. "Thirteen minutes to twelve," he said when he returned to the sidewalk. He made a quick calculation. "I am counting on the car to get the Sleeper to safety," he told Kaat. "Go back in and tell them you are in a hurry. Tell them you will give them twenty dollars if they will change the tire and get the Chrysler down quickly."

Kaat ducked back into the garage. The Potter paced up

and down the sidewalk in front of it. Every once in a while he would step into the gutter and glance nervously at the time atop the brick warehouse. At one minute after twelve, Kaat appeared at the entrance of the garage. "They say they're bringing it down any minute," she called. She hunched her shoulders in frustration and returned to the garage.

On the side street that led to Main Street, the police were starting to drag wooden barriers over to block cross traffic. The Potter looked at the clock on the roof of the warehouse again. He had just made up his mind to go on foot and let Kaat follow him in the Chrysler when she dashed out of the garage. "It's on the elevator," she called, and raced back in.

It was twelve-seventeen when Kaat gunned the Chrysler out of the garage into Elm Street. The Potter jumped into the passenger seat. Before the door had slammed shut, Kaat had thrown the car into gear and started north so that they could come around behind the warehouse to the parking lot where, according to the Potter, the Sleeper would just be taking up position behind the hedges.

40

Khanda felt as if time were trickling away in a kind of suspended slow motion. When he held his wristwatch to his ear to check if it was still working, the spaces between the seconds seemed to be abnormally long, as if the moment were so exquisite it had to be drawn out. He glanced back at the cartons he had dragged over to form a wall so that anyone who happened to mount to the sixth floor wouldn't catch sight of him sitting in front of the partly open window, the homemade sling of his Italian military rifle wrapped around his left arm. The act of entwining himself in the sling had created the final intimacy between the shooter and the rifle; from that moment on, there had been no turning back.

He had decided to stay well away from the window when the motorcade appeared out of Main Street and headed directly for the warehouse, to reduce the possibility that any of the security people accompanying the Prince might spot him up ahead. Only when the limousine turned under the warehouse and started toward the overpass and the freeway, when the security people had their backs to the warehouse, would he move into firing position. He had placed three cartons on the floor next to the window, one on top of the other, and he planned to brace the rifle on the top box when he shot.

Outside, the canyons of Main Street formed a giant echo chamber. Somewhere up this echo chamber, people were cheering. It sounded to Khanda like surf beating against a distant shore. He worked the bolt of the rifle, throwing the first round into the chamber. Then he brought his wristwatch to his ear again. The spaces between the ticks seemed even longer than before.

No matter. In a minute or two he would speed time up. He would accelerate it into chaos.

41

❧

Slipping through the open parking lot behind the line of hedges, his viola-da-gamba case tucked casually under one arm, the Sleeper sensed the wave of excitement approaching, like a groundswell, from Main Street. From his experiences in the war, he knew that he would soon reorder reality. When you looked at someone with the naked eye, you automatically put him into context; you related him to the world around. But when you observed someone through a scope fixed on top of a rifle, you *detached* him from the world around you; you isolated him; you created a very special relationship between the two of you, even if only one of you was aware of it.

The first vehicle in the motorcade emerged from the Main Street canyon. The Sleeper, alone at the edge of the parking lot, crouched and rested the viola-da-gamba case on the ground and undid the catches that held the lid. Cheers welled up from the crowd as the Prince's limousine came into view, then slowly jogged right toward the warehouse.

Moving with the deliberation of a sleepwalker, the Sleeper prepared the instrument that would detach the Prince from reality.

42

♣

The Potter and Kaat had been delayed by the traffic backed up on Houston Street. It was twelve-twenty-nine by the time Kaat maneuvered the Chrysler into the parking lot behind the warehouse. "Wait here, if you please," the Potter instructed Kaat with unaccustomed sharpness, and he leapt from the car and darted between the parked automobiles toward the row of hedges at the far end of the lot.

On the street below, the Prince's limousine jogged left underneath the slightly open window on the sixth floor of the warehouse and headed toward the freeway. The Prince lifted a hand and waved at the people lining the route, and the crowd cheered back.

Crouched amid the hedges, the Sleeper worked the bolt, throwing a round into the chamber. Then he raised the sniper scope to his eye and sighted on the jugular of the target coming into view.

Breathing heavily, the Potter came around the front of a pickup truck and saw the familiar figure crouching in the hedges ahead, the right knee on the ground, the left elbow braced on the raised left knee, the rifle extended in the classical firing position used by the Red Army. "Piotr Borisovich," the Potter gasped, and then he filled his lungs with air and opened his mouth and cried out the name of the son he had always wanted with all the force he could find in his body. "*Piotr Borisovich!*" But even to his own ear his voice seemed lost in the roar of the crowd saluting the passage of the Prince.

At the mouth of the Main Street canyon, on the steps of the old sandstone courthouse, G. Sprowls was about to turn to the Sisters and make an ironic comment about the best-laid plans of mice and men when the sharp crack of a rifle, a dry twig snapping in a forest, echoed over the heads of the crowd. On the roof of the warehouse, several hundred pigeons nesting in the abandoned boiler swarmed into the sky in panic.

A second twig snapped.

And then a third.

And the world was accelerated into chaos.

"It came from the warehouse," Carroll blurted out excitedly. His cheek muscles went on a rampage. "I knew in my bones he would pick the warehouse."

On the street, the crowd spilled away in every direction. Several people fell to the ground screaming. A policeman pointed toward an upper floor of the warehouse.

"The first shot came from the grassy knoll," G. Sprowls said matter-of-factly. "I spotted the smoke from the cartridge." As if to prove his point, a motorcycle policeman skidded his machine onto the sidewalk below the hedges, and drawing his pistol, charged up the incline.

"My God," Francis said, "that means that there must have been *two* people shooting!"

For once, there was not the faintest trace of pained innocence on his face.

43

The moment was electrically charged. No one seemed quite sure what role to play. There was a father and a son, a teacher and a pupil, a betrayer and a betrayed; even a savior and a saved.

The Sleeper stared out of the window of Combes's Retreat at the prairie. "So you told them what they wanted to know," he was saying.

It had never occurred to the Potter that he would have to justify himself to the Sleeper when he caught up with him. "Please put yourself in my shoes," he pleaded. "I had no choice. They would have loaded us on the next plane to Moscow. Aside from everything else, there was the body at the airport to answer for." He fingered an empty coffee cup, unconsciously measuring the thickness of its walls between his thumb and third finger. "I had Svetochka to think of," he added plaintively.

"And yourself," the Sleeper answered harshly. "Let us not forget yourself."

"Since when is it a crime to think of yourself?" the Potter retorted.

The Sleeper turned on his teacher. "It is a crime for a teacher to betray his student."

"And what do you call it when the student betrays his teacher?" the Potter demanded. "You who are so offended by betrayals—tell me that if you can."

"So you found out about me and Svetochka," the Sleeper said wearily. "Everyone was sleeping with her, Feliks."

"I knew that *everyone* was sleeping with her. I didn't know that *you* were."

293

The Sleeper drifted across the room, and then back to the bay window. "One thing has nothing to do with the other," he said finally. "Sleeping with Svetochka was an act without consequences—for me, for her, for you as long as you didn't know about it. But betraying me to an enemy service was pregnant with consequences." He turned his back on the Potter and breathed on the windowpane, fogging it. "If only I had known my father was dead . . ."

"I was trying to catch up with you to tell you," the Potter whispered. "He was dead, and you were free."

"Here's the thing," Kaat said. "It is frustrating enough to listen to the two of you argue. But to hear you argue in Russian is pure torture."

"Even if we spoke in English," the Potter told her, his eyes glued on the Sleeper, "there are things you wouldn't understand."

"He is not the hero he makes himself out to be," the Sleeper informed Kaat. "He betrayed me to get himself and his wife out of Russia."

"Then he crossed the Atlantic and trailed after you across America to try to save you," Kaat said. She looked from one to the other. "Don't you see, you're turning in circles." She stared the Sleeper in the eye. "Vicious circles! What's done is done. The important thing is to look ahead, not back."

The Potter shook his head sadly. "You have it wrong. Piotr Borisovich has it right," he told her. "In order to look ahead, we must first look back." And he quoted Akhmatova's line, " 'My future is in my past.' "

The Sleeper nodded grimly. "We must settle the business of the betrayal before we move on," he insisted. He turned to the Potter and switched into Russian. "You expect me to fall on my knees and thank you for saving me." The Potter started to interrupt, but the Sleeper cut him off with a snap of his hand. "Don't deny it—it is written on your face. None of this would have happened if you hadn't betrayed me in the first place. That's what I can't swallow, Feliks. In my mind's eye, I try to put myself in your shoes. I really do try. But I don't see myself betraying you to get myself out. I would have killed myself first."

"You say that now," the Potter murmured. He held both hands to his stomach as if he had cramps. "But you can't be sure whose back you will climb on until you are at the foot of the wall."

"I had faith in you," the Sleeper said. "You let me down."

"I let myself down," the Potter observed acidly. He tried to muster a smile, but it only distorted his face more. "That's something else we have in common now," he added bitterly.

"I may not understand a word you say," Kaat told the Sleeper, "but you are hurting him very much. He doesn't deserve that."

The Sleeper eyed the Potter, then nodded. "I am willing to concede that you did try to undo the damage."

The Potter moaned. "I did try," he agreed, "but I failed."

"Maybe not entirely," the Sleeper said. "You are absolutely sure that it was the Americans you betrayed me to?"

"I was contacted by someone who called himself Oskar. He was probably German, and everyone knows the Americans have the Germans in their pocket," the Potter recounted. "In Vienna, I was debriefed by someone who spoke Russian with an American accent. In any case, the lengths they went to to get me out, to get access to a sleeper, only make sense if you assume the Americans are behind the whole thing."

"I might understand," Kaat announced in an exasperated voice. "If you spoke English, I might pick up a word now and then that seemed familiar."

"Your theory," the Sleeper told the Potter, "is that the Americans awakened me and sent me on a mission so that I would be caught, and the Russians would be blamed."

"That is what I thought," the Potter agreed.

The Sleeper walked across the room and sat down at the small bridge table facing the Potter. "Do you still think it?" he asked.

"I am less sure than before."

"Because of the sweepers?"

The Potter looked up sharply. "So you spotted them?"

"I had a good teacher in such matters," the Sleeper said

grudgingly. "The technique they used—lingering twenty-four hours—was straight out of the KGB sweeper manual."

"We ran into them several times also," the Potter said. "The first time they killed her cat. The last time I shot one of them in the foot. That was in the storage room of a hotel." The Potter frowned. "I recognized the man I shot. I had seen him once before. In Moscow."

The Sleeper's eyes narrowed thoughtfully. Tiny wrinkles fanned out from the corners of his eyes. Someone who didn't know him would have thought he was amused. "If the Americans were controlling me, as you say, how is it that the Russians were sweeping me? How did they know my route?"

"That," the Potter said, "is what the Americans call the sixty-four-dollar question."

"Go on speaking Russian if it gives you pleasure," Kaat snapped in annoyance. "To me it's all the same."

"There's another thing," the Sleeper said. "When you arrived in Vienna, you gave the American who spoke Russian with an American accent the line of poetry from Walter Whitman. But how could the Americans know where I was? How could they know where to deliver the line of Whitman poetry?"

"I told them," the Potter admitted morosely.

"How did you know?"

"From the picture postcard you sent me."

"What picture postcard?"

Now the Potter was staring at the Sleeper. "The one showing the Walter Whitman plaque on the door of a house in Brooklyn Heights."

The Sleeper said quietly, "I never sent you a picture postcard. It was against regulations to contact people in the homeland while on a mission. You know that."

"When you have finished with the past," Kaat muttered from the bed, "be sure to let me know."

"You never *finish* with the past," the Potter told her. "You take it with you, like baggage."

"Who did send me on this mission?" the Sleeper asked the Potter. "Who am I working for?"

"Do you think it is important to find out?" the Potter asked.

"If we don't find out," the Sleeper said, "we risk going on without baggage."

"If you don't talk English," Kaat said suddenly, "I'll scream!"

The Potter smiled faintly at his last, his best sleeper. "I think I know what we can do to find out," he said.

Kaat screamed.

44

The building, lighted up like a Christmas tree, could have passed for an ocean liner in mid-Atlantic, a fact that several hands arriving late from various corners of the world would have commented on if they had had time. Which they didn't. The Prince of the Realm was dead. There was a suspect in the hands of the local police. There were rumors, fueled by vague reports of an entry wound in the throat, of a second shooter still at large, though cooler heads tended to discount this possibility. Sandwiches, beer, were ordered up, delivered by a downtown caterer with a security clearance. The bottoms of barrels were being scraped for leads, theories, coincidences, pieces out of place, people who had dropped from sight, others who were too conspicuously in sight. Anything and everything was being fed into the hopper.

Except telegrams that weren't addressed to anyone or signed by anyone.

"What you make of this?" the communications assistant, fresh from the Company's Farm and eager to be useful in a crisis, asked. The night watch, his head swimming from the message load, plucked it from the board. It had the look of a normal telegram; had in fact come in over the Western Union printer. " 'The hands of the sisters Death and Night incessantly wash again comma and ever again comma this soil'd repeat soil'd world stop,' " the night watch read out loud.

"Maybe it's a cipher," the communications assistant offered eagerly.

"Sounds more like the ravings of some crank," the night watch said. He was about to throw it into the burn basket when it occurred to him that the Company had in its employ two esoteric types known in the house as the sisters Death and Night. Could it be that the telegram was meant for them? "Listen up," the night watch instructed his communications assistant. "There are two guys up in Planning. Both have girls' first names. Carroll something, Francis something. The one who is named Francis always wears loud bow ties. Find out where they are and read this over the phone to them. Maybe they'll know what it's all about. Now, what else do you have on that message board of yours?"

45

At first Francis assumed he was imagining things. Only when he lifted a tentative finger to his cheek did he realize what was actually happening. He had seen it often enough on Carroll's face to know what a twitching muscle looked like. Now he knew what it felt like.

What it felt like was exaltation rising, like a bubble in a still pond, to the surface of his imagination.

Thank goodness some idiot in Washington had had the good sense to try the telegram out on him. Francis had phoned Carroll immediately to share the good news, but Carroll was off God knew where with G. Sprowls. So as not to waste any time (who could say how long the birds would remain in the nest?), Francis had contacted Western Union and, citing urgent government business, had gotten from the supervisor the phone number from which the telegram originated. Flashing his laminated credentials in the general direction of a nearsighted telephone-company official, Francis had gotten the address that went with the telephone number. At which point he had put in a call from a pay phone to the special number in Washington reserved for extraordinary circumstances. "The Potter has caught up with the Sleeper," he told the person on the other end who lifted the receiver without a word of greeting and simply listened.

There was a long, awkward silence on the line. Then a voice, pronouncing each word meticulously in an effort to suppress an accent, said, "How can you know this?"

Francis explained about the telegram that had arrived in Washington containing, word for word, the line from Whitman that constituted the awakening signal for the Sleeper;

explained the coincidence of him and Carroll being known, within the Company, as the sisters Death and Night; explained how because of this coincidence the telegram had been routed to him. "If the Potter and the Sleeper have put their heads together," Francis explained, "the Sleeper will know he was controlled by the Company and not his masters in Moscow. All we have to do now is arrange for them to be captured. The story they tell will eventually lead the authorities to Carroll and me. My disappearance, my written confession, the scribblings they will find hidden in my garbage pail will all confirm that the Sleeper was activated, and controlled, by the Company. Let the Director try to deny it when he is hooked up to a lie detector!" Once again exaltation manifested itself as a twitch of a cheek muscle.

The person on the other end of the line cleared his throat, almost as if he were embarrassed. "There is a complication," he said carefully.

It took a moment for the word to sink in, it was so unexpected. Francis repeated it to be sure he had heard correctly. "Complication?"

"The telegram that was sent to the Company was also sent to us at the embassy."

"To you?" Francis breathed into the phone. "Why would they send the awakening signal to *you*?"

"Several days ago, the Potter cornered one of our sweepers in a hotel," the voice on the phone recounted tonelessly. "Unfortunately for us, he recognized him."

"Recognized the sweeper?" Francis couldn't believe this was happening to him.

"He had seen him once before, in Moscow, some years ago, when the sweeper was given a medal," the voice said.

The phone started to buzz in Francis' ear. He force-fed his last handful of quarters down the slot. The line cleared. "Are you still there?" he shouted.

"So you see," the voice continued as if there had not been an interruption, "they will have posed the question: if the Sleeper was being controlled by the Americans, as the Potter said, why was he being swept by Russians who knew his itinerary?"

"How could you assign a sweeper whom the Potter could recognize?" Francis asked incredulously.

The person on the phone cleared his throat again. "Our resources in this hemisphere are limited," he said defensively. "When you told us you thought the Potter might be trying to catch up to the Sleeper and stop him from carrying out his assignment, we called in the Canadians, Ourcq and Appleyard. We have used their services for years. It did not occur to us to check to see if the Potter might know one of them. But then it did not occur to us that they would fail to eliminate him if, as you suspected, he was following the Sleeper."

Francis' mind was racing. "The telegram they sent to the Company, to you—it means they are not sure who is controlling the Sleeper. Of course, why didn't I see it! *They don't know!* So they fired off the awakening signal left and right, and are waiting to see which side *understands* it, which side responds to it. Then they will know who awakened the Sleeper. And knowing, they can try to save their skins. They can deal from strength."

"I can see," the voice on the phone said from what seemed an enormous distance, "that we have come to the same conclusion."

Francis transformed his face into a mask of pained innocence. "I will turn up at Combes's Retreat. Your telegram was routed to me, thank you very much for sending it, I will tell them. Yes indeed, I am your control. You want to know whom I work for? Surely you are joking! I work for the organization that arranged the Potter's defection, that awakened the Sleeper, that sent him across the country to terminate a Prince of the Realm we could no longer put up with. Why did we want a Russian sleeper? Because if you had been caught in the act, an eventuality that we had to plan for, the Russians would have been blamed. But you weren't caught in the act. You got away. The Prince of the Realm is no longer among the living, so we have accomplished what we set out to accomplish. You, in turn, seem to have figured out who was controlling you, else why would you have sent a telegram containing the awakening signal to the Company. We share a mutual interest now—you must both disappear. With the resources at my command, I can arrange this." Feeling his quarters were about to run out, knowing that he had used his last one, Francis began talking rapidly. "Only sit tight. Don't move. Give me twenty-four hours. I will organize everything—money, identities, travel plans. Of course they will agree. What choice will they have? After that it will only be a matter of an anonymous phone call to the local police. Detectives will capture a shooter who was controlled by the Company. I will disappear, leaving behind confirmation." Francis' cheek muscle twitched again. His voice soared half an octave. "It is still the perfect crime!"

"I quite agree with your analysis," the voice on the line said. "I authorize you to—"

The buzzing filled the receiver. Francis searched frantically to see if he had overlooked a quarter in one of his pockets. Reluctantly he placed the receiver back on its hook. I quite agree with your analysis, the voice on the line had said. I authorize you to . . . what? Fingering his pale green bow tie with rust-colored stripes running horizontally through it, Francis stepped out of the booth into the sunlight. He thought he knew what he was authorized to do.

He was authorized to put the finishing touch on the perfect crime.

46

✤

Propped up amid the pillows at the end of the bed, nibbling nervously on an already mutilated fingernail, Kaat recognized it for what it was: an acronical (occurring at sunset) anagnorisis (denouement of a plot).

The Sleeper took his eyes off Francis for the first time since he entered the room. "She collects words that begin with the letter A," he informed the Potter, who was sitting at the bridge table, his eyes half-closed, his Beretta out in plain view on the torn green felt.

"He knows that," Kaat said from the bed. "He also knows what my first name is, which is more than you know."

"I see," said the Sleeper, and he did: the complicity between the Potter and Kaat was thick enough to cut with a knife.

Francis, leaning against a fireplace that had been bricked over, produced a particularly innocent smile. "To move on," he continued, looking from the Sleeper to the Potter and then back to the Sleeper again, "all I need is twenty-four hours to put together the package. There will be an appropriate amount of money. There will be passports, driving licenses, Social Security cards for everyone, including the girl. There will be plane tickets to the country of your choice. Do you prefer the southern or northern hemisphere? Sun or snow? Are you urban-oriented, or do you feel more at home in a rural atmosphere? I know you Russians put great store by your *dachas*." Here Francis forced a dry laugh through his lips.

Kaat said, "That is an unusual bow tie you have on."

"Thank you," Francis said, taking Kaat's comment for a compliment. "I'm rather attached to it myself. If my apartment was on fire and I could save only one tie from my rather large collection, this is definitely the one I would pick."

The Potter said, "There is still the question of the sweepers to straighten out."

"If you were controlling me, as you say," the Sleeper asked Francis, "how is it that the Russians were sweeping my trail?"

With almost no effort Francis managed to project pained innocence. "You are referring to the Canadians who go by the names of Ourcq and Appleyard. It is true that they have been used on several occasions by our Russian friends; one of them, I don't remember which, was said to have been awarded a medal for services rendered. But they have nothing against accepting a free-lance contract now and then to augment their income. In this particular instance, we hired them to sweep your trail in order to keep the Potter from catching up with you. Obviously, if you had learned that he had betrayed you to the Americans, you would not have carried out the assignment we gave you. Using sweepers who employed Soviet techniques had an added advantage, from our point of view: if you spotted them, it would only reinforce your conviction that you had been awakened and sent on a mission by your legitimate control in Moscow. If you were caught in the act, we wanted the onus to fall on your masters in the Kremlin. You are both professionals. Surely you can understand our attitude even if you cannot sympathize with it."

"Personally," Kaat piped up from the bed, "I don't believe a word he says. He was a liar in his previous incarnations. He is a liar in his present incarnation. He will surely be a liar if he is lucky enough to have a future—"

Downstairs, the chimes that Combes's ex-wife had brought back from Memphis sounded.

The Potter reached for his Beretta. Francis fingered his bow tie. "Are we expecting anyone?" he asked into the silence.

The Sleeper shook his head.

"Maybe it is Combes," Kaat whispered, "returning from wherever he raced off to in such a hurry this morning."

"We would have heard his car," the Potter said.

"He wouldn't ring his own doorbell," the Sleeper said.

He put his ear to the door of the room. "Someone's coming into the house."

"Francis?" a voice called from the entrance of Combes's Retreat.

"My God, it's Carroll!" exclaimed Francis. "Carroll, we are up here," he called back. To the others he explained, "Carroll is my partner. We are a team. I more or less specialize in forests, he in trees."

Carroll could be heard mounting the staircase. The Potter nodded at the Sleeper, who shrugged and pulled open the door of the room. Looking pale as death, Carroll appeared on the threshold. He was clutching a tiny pistol in his right fist and aiming it at Francis' stomach.

"If you come in and tell us who you are," Kaat said with a nervous laugh, "I'll tell you who you *were*."

Carroll stared at a point on the wall over Francis' right shoulder. "How could you have done it?" he asked in a voice that trembled with hate. He arched his neck and dispatched a finger to patrol the no-man's land between his neck and his starched collar. "We were colleagues, you and I. We were comrades in arms. We were *sisters*!"

Francis' mask of pained innocence started to melt. "What are you talking about?" he breathed in a barely audible voice.

Carroll stepped into the room. "You are not going to deny it, I hope. We are well past that stage. G. Sprowls saw you drop the empty matchbook under your seat after the film. He identified the woman who recovered it." He advanced on Francis, who shrank back into the wall. "I am going to end your life," he announced. "I am going to begin your death."

From across the room the Potter asked calmly, "How did you find us?"

Carroll never shifted his gaze from the wall over Francis' shoulder. "My colleague G. Sprowls has been looking for you. He had lines out. One of them paid off. The local police got a report of a stolen Chrysler turning up at Combes's Retreat. There were descriptions of you, of the girl, and after the death of the Prince of the Realm, of the Sleeper." Carroll must have noticed the Potter's finger curling around the trigger of the Beretta, because he said very quietly, "My colleague is nearby.

306

He is not alone. I tell you this in case you are thinking of resorting to violence."

Kaat said, "I don't understand a thing he's saying, and he's speaking English."

The Potter stood up from the table, slipped his Beretta into his jacket pocket, walked over to the window and stared out at the sun dipping toward the edge of the prairie. It occurred to him that the Sleeper's father had been wrong—for him, there was to be no life before death. "I think I understand," he said, turning back to the room. "The Company of yours wanted to eliminate the Prince of the Realm, and put the blame for his assassination on the Russians in order to discredit those outside the intelligence and military communities who favor a détente with the Soviet Union. But one of the two principal planners was actually a Soviet agent working, in all probability, for Department 13, the assassination specialists of the Komitet Gosudarstvennoy Bezopasnosti. After the assassination, after the capture of the assassin, he would disappear. A confession would turn up in the mail of a senator known for his support of the Prince and his opposition to the intelligence community. If something happens to me, the confession would say, I have arranged for this letter to be mailed to you. Acting on precise verbal orders issued by my superiors, I and my partner organized the death of the Prince. We awakened a Soviet sleeper and used his services so that the blame would fall on Moscow. Something along these lines. There would probably be a cache of documents somewhere—transcripts of conversations, deciphered one-time pad messages, notes on my defection and debriefing—to support the story. There would be corroboration from the giggling idiot you sent to Vienna to debrief me; you probably sent him, as opposed to going yourself, just so there would be an outside witness to my defection."

Carroll raised his free hand to his cheek muscle. "You were supposed to shred the office notes, the messages, but you saved every scrap of paper," he told Francis. "G. Sprowls found them in the false bottom of your garbage pail."

Francis said weakly, "It was a perfect crime."

The Sleeper asked the Potter, "How did you figure it out?"

The Potter shrugged. "Once you told me you never sent the picture postcard with your address on it, everything became clear. The only people who knew *where* you were, who knew I had entered the Walter Whitman line that awakened you in your dossier in my own handwriting, were our Russian colleagues. So the plot originated with them. If an American had the good sense to get to you through me, he had to be working for the Russians too."

The Sleeper nodded thoughtfully. "You are still the *novator*," he noted.

The Potter turned to Francis. "Are the Cousins behind it? Is the blind man behind it?"

Francis managed to produce a sickly smile. "The blind man is my control," he said. "We met secretly in Mexico a year ago. He had heard people in high places rant against the Prince of the Realm after the humiliation they suffered at his hands during the missile crisis. He took this for an order. He and I devised a perfect crime. We would get rid of the Prince of the Realm in such a way that the blame would fall on the Company, on Carroll here. For this we needed the services of a Russian sleeper. To get the sleeper, we needed to force the defection of the man who trained him. Which is where you came in. We gave away the three sleepers you had inserted into the United States in order to ruin you professionally. Then we got you to defect and give us access to the agent you always referred to as your last and best sleeper."

The Sleeper looked across at the Potter. "Was I really your best?"

The Potter said, "My last and my best. Absolutely."

Francis' knees began to give way and he had to hang on to the bricked-over fireplace to keep from sagging to the floor. He felt drained of energy, of hope, of all possibility of exaltation. "For the blind man," he informed Carroll, "there was a bonus. Do you remember the German diplomat you brought in during the war? The one with the valise full of very useful papers?"

"What has that got to do with it?" Carroll demanded.

"There was a go-between in the affair, a Soviet agent working under deep cover in Germany," Francis told him.

"You were already a rabid anti-Communist at the time. So you betrayed the Soviet agent to the Gestapo. One less Commie to deal with later, you probably said. They tortured him for weeks. At one point the Germans poured lye in his eyes. He was blinded for life."

The Potter said, "The blind man who runs Department 13 was the Soviet agent betrayed by your partner here?"

"The blind man worked nineteen years to get his revenge," Francis said. "He came within a hairsbreadth of having it."

Outside, the sun was knifing into the horizon. From under the window of their room came the sound of someone walking on gravel—except there was no gravel under the window, there was just prairie. Everyone in the room stiffened.

"He may still get his revenge," Francis said. He stared vacantly at the tiny pistol in Carroll's hand. "Don't you see it, Carroll—to G. Sprowls we are all loose ends."

"You are *my* loose end," Carroll sneered. He lowered his gaze until he was looking directly into Francis' eyes. "I detest you as much as anyone can detest another human being."

Francis straightened with an effort and regarded his executioner. "I have loathed you from the moment I met you," he told Carroll. His lips seemed to curl insolently over the words he spoke. "If your life depended on it, you couldn't see the forest for the trees."

Carroll's tiny pistol jumped imperceptibly in his fist. Francis exhaled as if he had been punched in the chest. He looked down at the ragged hole that had suddenly appeared in the front of his tweed jacket. Blood oozed from it. He brought a hand up to cover the hole, almost as if it *embarrassed* him.

Carroll stepped up to Francis and pressed the pistol to a point over his heart and pulled the trigger again. When he removed the pistol, Francis sank to the ground.

Kaat, thoroughly frightened, leapt off the bed to join the Potter at the bay window. "Here's the thing," she whispered fiercely. "The Tibetans say that your last thoughts determine the quality of your reincarnation. Mine are of you. I hope to God we are reincarnated at the same time. I would like to spend an entire life with you sometime."

The Potter took the Beretta from his jacket pocket and pulled Kaat close to protect her from what was surely coming. He smiled at his last, best Sleeper as he spoke into Kaat's ear. "We will share conspiracies," he said. "It will be us against the world," he said. "For us, there will be life before death," he said. "If you please," he said.

47

"What did I do with the fucking lighter?" Ourcq muttered to himself.

Appleyard stopped imitating someone walking on gravel long enough to say, "Don't tell me you maybe can't find it."

Ourcq finally produced the lighter from a side pocket. "Stop imitating every fucking thing you hear and cover me," he ordered. Fitting a crutch under one armpit, gripping the homemade incendiary grenade filled with a flammable magnesium-like substance, he limped along the side of the house until he was directly under the bay window.

Appleyard fitted the silencer onto his pistol and bracing his arm with his other hand, aimed at the window. He caught a flicker of light—Ourcq would be igniting the fuse now, he knew. In a moment he would maybe arc the grenade up through the second-floor window. It would explode with a great whooshing sound, sucking up all the oxygen in a split second, suffocating every living thing in the room. The air would be sucked maybe out of their lungs even.

If ever there was an appropriate moment, this was maybe it. Filling his own lungs, drawing his lips back against his teeth, Appleyard began to imitate the sound of the sun setting.

In a car parked down the road, G. Sprowls heard a noise he couldn't identify, and then one he could—glass breaking, followed by a great sucking sound, as if all the air in the universe were being consumed. G. Sprowls frowned. He was not happy to be working with Russians, but it was unavoidable. The Director's instructions had been explicit. People in high places had communicated with each other; had decided that each side had too much on the other; that if they contin-

311

ued to play the game, there would only be losers. The only thing left to do was acknowledge the standoff and assign trusted people on both sides to tie up the loose ends. The suspect in police custody had been shot that morning by a local bar owner. All traces of a second shooter on a grassy knoll had been removed. The world would be invited to accept as fact that there had been one shooter, a demented loner acting on his own initiative. G. Sprowls had been given the phone number of the Canadians. Together they had just taken care of the other loose ends.

The idea flashed through G. Sprowls's head that someone might one day consider him a loose end. But he dismissed it as preposterous.

The Canadians were coming down the unpaved road toward the car now. The heavyset one was limping painfully along on two crutches, cursing with each step. The other one trailed after him, imitating the sound (so he claimed) of a noiseless patient spider spinning its web.

Ourcq thought he had finally tripped up Appleyard. "How come I can hear it if the fucking spider is fucking noiseless?"

"Concentration," Appleyard, unfazed, suggested, "is what it's a question of. You have got to listen with both ears so you can maybe hear what's there to be heard." And he repeated the sound that he said was produced by a noiseless patient spider.

Understanding
Shakespeare's *Julius Caesar*

The Greenwood Press "Literature in Context" Series

Understanding *To Kill a Mockingbird*: A Student Casebook to Issues,
Sources, and Historical Documents
Claudia Durst Johnson

Understanding *Adventures of Huckleberry Finn*: A Student Casebook to Issues, Sources, and
Historical Documents
Claudia Durst Johnson

Understanding *Macbeth*: A Student Casebook to Issues, Sources, and Historical Documents
Faith Nostbakken

Understanding *Of Mice and Men, The Red Pony*, and *The Pearl*: A Student Casebook to
Issues, Sources, and Historical Documents
Claudia Durst Johnson

Understanding Anne Frank's *The Diary of a Young Girl*: A Student Casebook to Issues,
Sources, and Historical Documents
Hedda Rosner Kopf

Understanding *Pride and Prejudice*: A Student Casebook to Issues, Sources, and Historical
Documents
Debra Teachman

Understanding *The Red Badge of Courage*: A Student Casebook to Issues, Sources, and
Historical Documents
Claudia Durst Johnson

Understanding Richard Wright's *Black Boy*: A Student Casebook to Issues, Sources, and
Historical Documents
Robert Felgar

Understanding *I Know Why the Caged Bird Sings*: A Student Casebook to Issues, Sources, and
Historical Documents
Joanne Megna-Wallace

Understanding *The Crucible*: A Student Casebook to Issues, Sources, and Historical
Documents
Claudia Durst Johnson and Vernon E. Johnson

Understanding *A Tale of Two Cities*: A Student Casebook to Issues, Sources, and Historical
Documents
George Newlin

UNDERSTANDING
SHAKESPEARE'S
Julius Caesar

A STUDENT CASEBOOK TO ISSUES, SOURCES, AND HISTORICAL DOCUMENTS

Thomas Derrick

The Greenwood Press
"Literature in Context" Series
Claudia Durst Johnson, Series Editor

GREENWOOD PRESS
Westport, Connecticut • London

Library of Congress Cataloging-in-Publication Data

Derrick, Thomas J.
    Understanding Shakespeare's Julius Caesar / a student casebook to
issues, sources, and historical documents / Thomas Derrick.
       p.   cm.—(Greenwood Press "Literature in context" series,
ISSN 1074–598X)
    Includes bibliographical references (p.   ) and index.
    ISBN 0–313–29638–3 (alk. paper)
    1. Shakespeare, William, 1564–1616.   Julius Caesar.
2. Shakespeare, William, 1564–1616.   Julius Caesar—Sources.
3. Shakespeare, William, 1564–1616—Stage history.   4. Caesar,
Julius—In literature.   5. Rome—In literature.   I. Title.
II. Series.
PR2808.D47   1998
822.3′3—dc20   96–25005

British Library Cataloguing in Publication Data is available.

Library of Congress Catalog Card Number: 96–25005
ISBN: 0–313–29638–3
ISSN: 1074–598X

First published in 1998

Greenwood Press, 88 Post Road West, Westport, CT 06881
An imprint of Greenwood Publishing Group, Inc.

Printed in the United States of America

The paper used in this book complies with the
Permanent Paper Standard issued by the National
Information Standards Organization (Z39.48–1984).

10 9 8 7 6 5 4 3 2 1

822.33
D438

Contents

Introduction

This book displays evidence that Julius Caesar is not dead. The general, statesman, and dictator survived his assassins in fame, even though he did not avoid a premature death. His symbolic vitality began soon after the Ides of March, 44 B.C., when Brutus and fellow Republicans (believers in the freedom of the Roman Republic which flourished from 509 B.C.) killed Caesar, under whose rule the Republic had effectively diminished into an autocratic state. Caesar symbolized the personal rule that undercut a more representative practice of government. His violent removal created opportunities for peace, realized only after a bloody civil war that eventually pitted Antony, Caesar's revenger, against his partner in that movement, Octavian. The survivor, Octavian, renamed himself Augustus Caesar, thus building a peaceful regime in the name of Julius Caesar. Historically, this was the first appearance of Caesar's ghost.

Shakespeare's play arose from a long tradition that glorified and scorned both Caesar and Brutus. The victim and his betrayer received almost equal attention because their friendship struck people's imaginations. What if my friend should become my enemy? Under what conditions does politics destroy loyalty and friendship? *Julius Caesar* was as pertinent to these human issues when it was first performed in 1599 as it will be in 1999, when the approaching second millennium (in the Christian calendar that Julius Caesar strongly influenced) will stimulate fears and hopes about the future. Shakespeare's Caesar play was almost certainly the one selected to open the new Globe Theater in London at a time when doubts about

the succession of Queen Elizabeth weighed on the minds of the
mixed audience that crossed the Thames River (therefore moving
beyond tight city control) to spend a couple of hours in the pursuit
of pleasure.

The documentation of the rich history of this play is arranged to
take you from the play itself into the cultural context and back
again. The journey must be incompletely mapped, because students
of Shakespeare's *Julius Caesar* must do much of the work themselves. This historical guidebook will point out some of the features
to look for when you do your own exploring. Each chapter con-
cludes with interpretive ideas to strengthen your understanding of
the play, and with suggested readings to take you farther along the
way for the current topics. Teachers and students are encouraged to
adapt these suggestions to suit their needs.

ORGANIZATION OF THIS CASEBOOK

The first chapter examines the events of the play and the language of Shakespeare's dramatic poetry. We start and end with the
language because our insights are ultimately based on personal judgments about the meanings that the words convey. Beyond the simple
level of noting the rough sequence of events and the straightforward
meanings of words lie intricate planes of meaning. Examples from
the text of *Julius Caesar* will suggest ways of approaching plot and
the uses of metaphor.

The second chapter focuses on the theater. Understanding the
public and private stages where the play was performed will deepen
our appreciation when we attend live performances today. If this
chapter does nothing else than stimulate playgoing, then it will have
achieved its purpose. Even if you cannot attend a performance, this
section will prepare you for doing your own dramatic reading.
Shakespeare's vitality—to evoke another ghost—is assured when
you read his dramatic poetry aloud.

The third chapter examines the traditions of European literary history that preceded and followed Shakespeare's handling of the
Caesar story, from roughly the thirteenth and fourteenth centuries,
up to the eighteenth century. This material seems remarkably
ancient, but it is not as old as the records of Roman historians, which
were also revived by scholars in Shakespeare's era. English

Renaissance interpretations are featured because they affected Shakespeare's thought more than did the classical sources. Elizabethan translations of the Greco-Roman historian Plutarch and the Augustan poet Ovid represent this kind of revival of Caesar's spirit. The trend is from an awed respect for Caesar toward an amused skepticism, that is, from an attitude respecting the legacy of Caesar to questioning whether the would-be Caesars live up to their idol.

The fourth chapter examines a special case of nineteenth-century Caesar lore, the assassination of Abraham Lincoln. The theatrical world of John Wilkes Booth's family presents a fascinating spectacle of drama mingled with society. What happened when Shakespearean acting converged with political murder? The Brutus legend is featured here to give a context for the shocking drama at Ford's Theater, where the Union's president was shot by the South's self-appointed avenger.

The fifth chapter traces Caesar's ghost in the middle of the twentieth century by means of issues that concern teaching. The terrifying conflicts of World War II and the international tensions of the Cold War prompted educators to try to explain where things went wrong in the hope of preventing future cataclysms. Studies of *Julius Caesar* aided the quest for the causes of totalitarianism and the promise of literacy to support democracy.

The sixth chapter offers commentary and excerpts from popular-culture versions of the play. The inclusion of a Victorian takeoff on Caesar, juxtaposed with a rap music version, reminds us that satirizing Caesar is nothing new. Comparisons between high and low art mirror one another. The first chapter reinforces the idea that mirrors symbolized comparison and introspection in the Renaissance, and so the last chapter reflects the first.

SOURCES

The documents originally printed in Renaissance English have been rendered into modern spelling to make them easier to read. Outdated words or verb forms not readily recognizable to the modern reader have been silently modernized or else explained in a gloss note. The punctuation has been left in its unregulated state, which, curiously, resembles trends in our own day. Avoiding the apostrophes in possessives and contractions, and running sentences together without periods join other grammatical faults that English teachers are notorious for correcting. Shakespeare's English and Renaissance printing practice give us a holiday from punctuation.

Quotations from Shakespeare's plays are from the *Riverside Shakespeare* (1974; 1997), whose editors were my teachers. Other editions of *Julius Caesar* will read substantially the same, as long as you make a few adjustments in the line numbers.

The use of parallel texts and the literal comparison of passages belongs to the work of I. A. Richards. Methods of teaching people to read by inviting them to look have frequently affected my thinking. The illustrations in this book have been selected to mirror the words.

Composing the facing-page layout of the Plutarch and the Basic English texts would not been possible without the loving assistance of Phoebe, the graphic artist in our household, and my Portia.

1

Interpreting
Julius Caesar

The many-headed multitude were drawn
By Brutus speech, that Caesar was ambitious,
When eloquent Mark Antony had shown
His virtues, who but Brutus then was vicious?
    Man's memory, when new, forgets the old,
    One tale is good, until another's told.
        John Weever, *The Mirror of Martyrs* (London, 1601), sig. A3v

Shakespeare's *Julius Caesar* is a play about a political killing. It is a tragedy of an assassin who is too honorable to succeed. It is a ghost story, seduction, study of marriage and fortune-telling. It is also a course in public speaking, social studies lesson, history of civil war and revenge and forgiveness, dramatic poem about regretted decisions, tribute to the power of mental images.

All these conceptions of the play are valid. On stages, in libraries, about town, in classrooms and homes, people for four hundred years have been periodically returning to admire *Julius Caesar*. And each reader or viewer sees the play slightly differently. How can the "same" play be interpreted in so many different ways?

This book will help you sort out your own perceptions of *Julius Caesar* by examining different moments in its history, that is to say, different versions of its telling. Documents that have survived by chance affect our perceptions just as much as historical records carefully preserved to uphold important social values. Learning about this play is self-educating, since we must personally come to terms with the events, the language, the settings. This book will not offer an official outlook on Shakespeare's *Julius Caesar*. Rather than dictate a view of the great dictator, it will lead you to materials and invite you to make sense of them. Many editions of this play and countless study guides offer plot summaries, and some minimal ones will be given here, but the purpose of this book goes beyond the memorization of "what happens in *Julius Caesar*" or what happened to Caius Julius Caesar. It affords students the opportunity to remake the story in their own image and to learn how they arrived at their perceptions, and why. Students should be able to answer the challenge, "I don't see *Julius Caesar* that way. Tell me how you saw it, what directions you looked in, what you noticed, why you portray things as you do."

A moderator can encourage us to compare the views of earlier critics and viewers to our own. Long after the teacher leaves or the student graduates, Shakespeare's plays remain for us to examine without prompting. Clarity of understanding grows with practice, and this book will give you plenty of material for exercise and amusement. Look hard. Enjoy the process of insight.

MIRROR IMAGES IN *JULIUS CAESAR*

Today, if we think about mirrors at all, we regard them as accurate reflectors. People gazing into a "mirror, mirror, on the wall" tend to see themselves truly, without considering the distortions of optics. We seldom imagine that a mirror can give magic insight—as in crystal ball—nor do we confuse the amusing distortion of carnival funhouse mirrors with the morning's ritual of checking our appearance before going out in public.

By contrasting this perception of mirror images with that of the the Renaissance viewer, we better understand Cassius' question-and-answer routine with Brutus. Cassius the schemer asks the noble Roman whether he can directly see his own face and receives the obvious reply that no eye can see itself or any other facial part except in a reflection from another object. Cassius then remarks that "it is very much lamented, Brutus, / That you have no such mirrors as will turn / Your hidden worthiness into your eye . . . I, your glass, / Will modestly discover to yourself / That of yourself which you yet know not of" (1.2.56-77). Both senses of mirroring work here. We have the physical reproduction of an image and the mental perception of a personality, which can best be perceived by an outsider.

Since the mirror, or "glass," as it was called in Shakespeare's time, was not very clear by modern standards, we miss part of the context of this powerful metaphor for imitation and insight. A typical reflecting glass made in Venice or the Netherlands and imported to England was not a common household item, nor was it especially faithful to the dazzled courtier's or noble lady's face. An alternative to looking into a pool of still water was a polished metal reflector, called a "steel glass." It rendered a dark, wavy image, and had the slight advantage, over watery reflections, of unbreakable stability. It did not give as clear an image as the modern mirror, but then again, no one expected anything better. True reflections were matters of inner spirit, not external features.

How many of us today consistently believe the accuracy of mirror images? "That's not the real me," we fool ourselves into thinking after partying the night away and glancing at a bleary mirror image, while at other times we believe the mirrored vision of splendor presented during a final checkout of tuxedo or gown on prom night. Like these imaginary mirror gazers, Brutus does not take Cassius' assessment of him at face value; unlike most of us, he thinks deeply about situations and tries to perceive the hidden distortions.

This speculation is a model for what this book seeks to accomplish. The play *Julius Caesar* mirrors modern reflections about authority figures like parents, teachers, principals, and bosses; about conflicting values such as duty/love, spirit/flesh, seriousness/fun; about the nature of drama and politics. It served Shakespeare's audiences in similar ways, although the cultural events are harder for us to recapture. This book will provide Caesar material from classical and English Renaissance sources of the time of its first performance in 1599. Further references from later times will remind us of the perpetual interest in Julius Caesar, Superstar.

This multi-generational drama should not be seen as veneration of a historical god. We come neither to bury Caesar in learned treatises nor, frivolously, to praise his ghosts in popular culture, though both he and his reputation are worthy of modern eulogies. Rather, we are participating in a process of imaginative exercise. Drawing on the past, we enrich our present dreams or add to our nightmares.

REFLECTION OF CULTURE

A quick glance at a current approach to history and literature will orient us. A momentous event like the assassination of a political leader involves more than the immediate grief, anger, revenge, and veneration of the slain hero. Its re-creation in literature belongs to a larger process of social adjustment that is sometimes called "cultural poetics." This term means that social controls are linked to literary practices in predictable ways.

Suppose an anthropologist from the future was studying Julius Caesar's fame. Everything from fast-food advertising to Fascist propaganda, sandwiched with Shakespeare's play and its predecessors and successors, would make up the field research. She would ask several kinds of questions.

- In general, how does/did this phenomenon either encourage or restrain people? That is, how did it inspire them or praise things? How did it disapprove or blame?

- How did it affect either behavior (physical actions) or thinking (values, beliefs)?

- What social institutions were reinforced by this work?

- How did this work change the lives of its original viewers, listeners, readers, participants?

- What qualities enabled the work to endure until now, or what factors caused its cultural death?

- What social institutions does the work now address, directly or indirectly?

- How do these social institutions affect me?

- To what extent does my personal situation affect my interpretation of this phenomenon of Julius Caesar?

All these questions must be asked without separating high literature from popular culture or by separating poems from plays from screen-plays. Whether Caesar figures in Shakespeare's drama or on a pizza box is equally important during the initial investigation. No matter if Caesar's image appears in a picture (portrait, city scene, advertisement or his character in a play (of whatever type—tragedy, comedy, satire). The scope of research is interdisciplinary when the whole culture is viewed. Judgments will finally be made that some parts of the picture are more important than others. Making these interpretive conclusions does not imply that the emphasized ideas are naturally, inevitably dominant. Rather, the literary anthropologist acknowledges that our social assumptions (ideology) form our perceptions.

It may turn out that our female anthropologist is especially concerned with Calpurnia or Portia, because of their womanhood, and that personal angle will not be excluded from the investigation. The critic is part of the interpretive process. A genteel Southerner, to take a social instead of a gendered example, may be attracted to the proudly defiant Caesar or repelled by his autocratic tendencies. Whatever image is mirrored in our minds when thinking about literature in culture, we should try to understand how our personalities affect that history. Contrasted with the "old-fashioned history" of undistorted truths, this cultural poetics is also known as "New Historicism."

Let us look at Shakespeare's *Julius Caesar* in relation to this way of seeing. Some social facets include politics, the nature of personal character, and the relations among family members.

BOSS CAESAR

Suppose that Julius Caesar's rise to fame resulted from his pursuit of a brilliant political career based on success as a military leader. The pre-Shakespearean plot would go something like this:

The infant is delivered by a uterine incision ("Caesarian section"). This son of a distinguished family is trained in the arts of Roman citizenship. He marries well, gets into trouble over his alliances, wins and loses a religious title, offends the ruling party even further, flees for his life. He joins the army and serves successfully, using that foreign experience to enhance his return to Roman politics when his Roman persecutor dies. He becomes an activist at home, speaking against corruption, wooing the people. A further military engagement abroad polishes his reputation, and a new rivalry at home sharpens his survival instincts. He is locked in a power struggle with the military commander and political chief he helped. Meanwhile, he manages public festivities and gets the Roman in the street to favor him, and he maneuvers tax breaks for the rich. He forms an uneasy triple alliance with his rival and a wealthy supporter.

Stalemate. It's off to foreign war again, on a four-year campaign against various barbarians—some as far north as Britain—and the loyalty of his armies increases. His other two partners engineer alliances against him and receive more and more support from the chief legislative body, the Senate. The victorious commander returns from the battlefield with his army and dares his surviving partner to oppose him.

"The die is cast." Caesar marches on Rome and sweeps away opposition. He pursues his rival to Greece, and to Egypt, his rival's son to Spain, fighting a civil war with boldness and good fortune.

Dictatorial control. He serves in the temporary office of dictator, the elected post of consul, and then a life-dictatorship. Having come full circle to the political conditions of his upbringing, he now inspires resentment among those he controls.

Conspiracy and assassination. Admirers of the Roman Republic gather against him, and they murder him in a public meeting of the Senate.

Recriminations. The conspirators enjoy brief approval, and then slip into disfavor as the boss' friends remember his gifts, his power, his glory. The killers are hunted down and slain.

TRAITOR/PATRIOT BRUTUS

This glimpse at the political life of Caesar would not be complete without a parallel look at his killer. Brutus' story features another privileged family with ties to the people, in this case to the founder of the Roman Republic. He grows to political maturity under the party of Caesar's rival, Pompey. Even though he takes the side opposite Caesar in the civil war, Brutus' integrity prompts the victor to pardon him, and to award him a governorship and an urban office. Somewhere in observing Caesar's rise, Brutus fears the consequences of an unchecked ruler. Other discontented politicians encourage his suspicions. He joins a conspiracy that strikes its dramatic blow before the statue of Pompey. The Senate pardons him, rewards him, then prosecutes him. Dogged by an army led by Caesar's loyalists, he commits suicide rather than surrender.

VIEWPOINTS

This political telling of the story emphasizes the contest between strong-willed men in office. One could examine the same incidents in another light, that of family dynamics. Caesar is the father figure to Brutus' rebellious teenager. The forgiving old man is experienced enough to know that sentiment is fatal in war, but he still ignores the potential danger. The son recognizes what he owes in trust, and yet he allows himself to be convinced that nostalgia for the state is more important than personal commitments, even at the risk of civil war.

We can tell and retell these events by adding or subtracting parts of the historians' versions. A political tale almost always reflects our own hopes and fears about society, just as family dynamics mirror the relationships of our fathers and mothers. It would not take much to look at the marriages of Caesar and Brutus and derive a feminine prehistory of Shakespeare's play. Portia was a strong woman with philosophical learning that met her husband Brutus' Stoic cast of mind. Cornelia married the upstart Caesar and aided his political career. After Cornelia's death, Pompeia won Caesar and then lost him in a scandalous divorce. Calpurnia took him up when he was at the height of success, but they could not conceive a child to succeed them.

All these Caesar histories tell us who the tellers are and what they care about. Shakespeare was just another dramatist looking for a lively conflict when he picked up bits from fifteen-hundred-years of legends about Caesar and crafted them into his own play. What follows our prehistory of Caesar and Brutus is an attempt to present the episodes of *Julius Caesar* in a straightforward but not completely unbiased account, for that would be impossible. In this process, we will not learn who Shakespeare was; but from scrutinizing the material available to him, we can glimpse his shadow stretching beyond our own projections.

EPISODES IN *JULIUS CAESAR*

The earliest printed source of Shakespeare's play divides it into acts, but gives no scene divisions or stage directions. Ever since 1623, editors have been tinkering with scene divisions and stage directions. Rather than using these aids to reading, it makes as much sense to examine the related parts of the play according to episode.

This highly personal approach to describing the contents makes every reader a potential editor, and that is a responsibility that encourages active thinking. The best plot summary is your own plot summary.

The following division of episodes emphasizes Caesar's potential for tyranny, and it correlates the physical setting with human emotions.

Public and Private Aspects of Caesar

- Two tribunes confront plebeians for their veneration of Caesar rather than Pompey.
- Caesar instructs Antony to touch Calpurnia in the fertility ritual; the soothsayer warns Caesar against the Ides of March.
- Cassius cajoles Brutus by telling stories of Caesar's physical weaknesses.
- Caesar returns with Antony from the festival race and deprecates Cassius.
- Casca informs Brutus of Antony's attempts to crown Caesar, which were interrupted by his epileptic seizure.
- Cassius (to himself) admits his plan to manipulate Brutus' feelings until he joins in a conspiracy against Caesar.

The Stormy Night and Threatening Dawn of the Conspiracy

- Casca explains to Cicero all the fateful sights accompanying the storm; Cassius secures Casca's and Cinna's help in striking Caesar down; they leave anonymous appeals on Brutus' windowsill.
- Brutus, alone, convinces himself that Caesar is too dangerous to ignore.
- The conspirators call on Brutus and they pledge to act that coming day; Brutus talks them out of killing Antony also.

Wives Almost Succeed in Thwarting the Assassination Plot

- Portia detects Brutus' agitation and pleads with him to share his worries; he agrees but is interrupted by Ligarius, another potential conspirator whom Brutus leads off in conference.
- Calpurnia pleads with Caesar to stay at home because of her dream and

the frightful signs in the storm; she kneels and receives his assent, but
Decius arrives to shame Caesar and entice him with the rumor that the
Senate may again offer to crown him; Brutus and the other conspirators
arrive to escort Caesar to the Capitol.

- Artemidorus reviews his letter warning Caesar against the conspirators;
Portia sends a servant to bring any news; she meets the soothsayer,
whose fears increase her worry.

The Bloody Assassination

- The conspirators converge on Caesar before the Senate meeting; in denying petitions he asserts his constancy, and they stab him.

- Brutus makes them all signify their responsibility by covering their hands
in blood; Brutus grants safe conduct to Antony, who shakes each bloody
hand and receives permission to speak at Caesar's funeral.

- When he is alone, Antony swears vengeance, and he passes word to
Octavius to stay away from Rome.

Speeches of Praise and Blame

- Brutus addresses the crowd and briefly explains how his love of freedom
exceeded his friendship for Caesar; he offers his own life if he ever
offends the city.

- Antony addresses the crowd and slowly builds the case for Caesar's patriotism, the public gifts in his will, the dishonorable motives of the assassins, the cruelty of their stabbing.

- The crowd riots, burning the abandoned houses of the conspirators and
murdering a poet with the same name as one of them.

The Harshness of the Revengers/The Discord of the Defenders

- Antony and Octavius fill out death warrants, deprecate the third member
of their alliance, and plan the attack.

- Brutus and Cassius quarrel about bribery, then make up; they scorn a
poet who scolds them for unfriendliness; Brutus reveals Portia's suicide
and receives Cassius' sympathy.

- They listen to news of the revenge killings in Rome, including a report of Portia's suicide, which Brutus seems to be hearing for the first time.

- Brutus argues for an offensive at Philippi; Cassius favors a defensive strategy; Cassius reluctantly accepts Brutus' plan, and they part as reconciled friends.

Personal Tributes During and After Battle

- Caesar's ghost appears to Brutus and makes an appointment to see him again at Philippi.

- The armies meet under truce and their commanders insult each other.

- Cassius takes his farewell of Brutus, commenting that natural signs foretell doom.

- Cassius thinks he sees his friend Titinius killed, and, perceiving defeat, he orders his servant to kill him.

- Titinius arrives with news that the conspirators' side is winning; a messenger seeks Brutus, while the grieving Titinius kills himself.

- In the second part of the battle, Antony's soldiers mistakenly think they capture Brutus; the real Brutus recognizes military defeat and commits suicide.

- Octavius and Antony discover Brutus' body and praise his nobility and virtue, promise a respectful funeral, and go off to celebrate victory

The seven divisions of this episodic summary could be expanded or contracted. When you look beyond the reading habits of an act by act arrangement and seek the continuous theatrical sequence, you observe comparisons. For example, the paired sides of the wives' episode let us examine marriages, just as the Octavius/Antony versus Cassius/Brutus sections bring friendships under scrutiny. You also notice inconsistencies. Something has happened to the 1623 Folio text at the point where two reports of Portia's death occur (4.3.155; 4.3.181), probably reflecting different acting versions that somehow were included in the same manuscript.

From another angle, we can see that a summary based on five acts finds a pattern of rising and falling action that is observable in other tragedies. This literary approach stresses the dramatic traditions Shakespeare worked within.

Act 1: Exposition of Caesar's glorious reputation and its detractors.

Act 2: Complications from Brutus' ideas about honor.

Act 3: Climax of the murder and Antony's turning the crowd against the assassins.

Act 4: Declining fortunes of the assassins, from the forces ranged against them and their own dissensions.

Act 5: The catastrophe for Cassius and Brutus; the triumph of Octavius and Antony.

Both literary and dramatic conceptions have something to tell us about *Julius Caesar*. The five act view stresses the apparently inevitable death of a hero, whether it is Caesar or Brutus. The analysis by dramatic episodes emphasizes contrasts in the characters and moods of the play. In all this thinking, it is easy to forget that our own preferences also influence pronouncements on the play's structure. Fatalists and hero worshippers are perhaps inclined toward the classical approach to tragedy. Those who believe in a measure of human freedom may indulge themselves with the contending to and fro of natural forces upon strong-willed people. The only avenue that active students of this play cannot choose is accepting others' opinions without thinking.

HERO OR PROTAGONIST?

Over the centuries critics have debated the character of *Julius Caesar*. But the play has one principal character. Typically, the case is made that Caesar is the hero, and Brutus and Cassius the villains. But another interpretation holds that Brutus is the protagonist and Caesar the occasion of Brutus' mental and physical struggles. We can explore both of these interpretations and imagine others.

A tragedy, according to Aristotle's *Poetics*, concerns a great person involved in a reversal of fortune that leads him to some important insight. Because Caesar is the acknowledged center of political and social attention in the play, and the most notorious sufferer of an unexpected death, Renaissance viewers familiar with his reputation would be apt to take the title literally: *The Tragedy of Julius Caesar*. He seems full of pride, the "sin" of Oedipus that was Aristotle's chief model for the tragic figure, proclaiming in a typical remark to Antony, while defaming Cassius' skepticism:

Seldom he smiles, and smiles in such a sort
As if he mock'd himself and scorn'd his spirit
That could be mov'd to smile at any thing.
Such men as he be never at heart's ease
Whiles they behold a greater than themselves,
And therefore are they very dangerous.
I rather tell thee what is to be fear'd
Than what I fear; for always I am Caesar.
                                                    1.1.205-12

Caesar's implication that he is the great one provoking Cassius' envy confirms his high opinion of himself, and if Shakespeare did not give us inside knowledge of Cassius' schemes, we might take Caesar's self-appraisals as the only truth.

From another perspective, Caesar is the potential hero. His human infirmities make him less than a god, and that fulfills the Aristotelian requirement that the tragic character be above ordinary men, but below the deities. Caesar, by Cassius' tainted report, almost drowned while swimming. He is subject to epileptic fits, "the falling sickness" in one sense. (The undisputed "hero" of *Othello* is marked by the same noble condition, just as Macduff also survived the trauma of a Caesarian-section birth—see *Macbeth* 5.8.15.) Cassius, in order to secure Brutus' aid, had reasons to exaggerate Caesar's frailties, yet Caesar himself closes the above conversation with Antony by directing him to move to the other side because he is deaf in his left ear.

The plot itself undercuts the heroic status of Caesar. He is killed off in the middle of the play, and only his ineffectual ghost returns toward the end of what is more notably Antony and Octavius' triumph. Brutus is scared by this vision, though the promise to "meet me at Philippi" (4.3.275-86) is far from a death threat or a revenging nightmare. Caesar has relatively little to say in this play compared to Brutus, and so his recognition or tragic insight must be inferred from passages like his "constant as the northern star" remarks (3.1.58-73). Even this succinct insight on constancy comes before his immediate knowledge of death, and thus makes him into a different sort of tragic hero than Romeo and Juliet, Othello, Macbeth, and Hamlet.

The idea of "hero" implies a perfection and a plot-dominating presence that is more appropriate to fairy tales, medieval romances, and comic book characters than Caesar in this play. However, the term "protagonist" gives us other implications and another character to consider as the leading one in *Julius Caesar*. The protagonist is a type of dramatic character who takes the lead, who is on the front lines of a conflict. He was originally the spokesman for the chorus in early Greek dramas. Suffering the most, the protagonist represents humanity instead of deity.

Brutus rises to this status by virtue of his much noted honor, which fouls up the efficiency of the grim assassins; by his speech of self-reflection (2.1.10-85); by his taking responsibility for the conspiracy; by his acknowledgment of death; and by the recognition he receives at the end of the play from Antony and Octavius. The "noblest Roman" succeeds despite his weaknesses. They consist of an incapacity to deal with political and social realities, such as the popular reaction against the murder. Brutus vetoed Antony's assassination, in what was just as disastrous an omission as overruling Cassius' military strategy of letting the opposing forces attack near Philippi. Brutus deluded himself into thinking everyone else was as honorable as he, or, to put it another way, he refused to allow himself to act contrary to his personal sense of dignity. This attitude leads to his fall, and, significantly, he does not care. "Countrymen, My heart doth joy that yet in all my life / I found no man but he was true to me" (5.5.333-35). By defining his own sense of value, he stands above the politicians and generals who measure their achievements by earthly success. Caesar may have attained divinity just because he stood colossally over the world. Brutus rules this play, one can argue, because it focuses continued attention on his struggles and rewards him for persevering.

The heroic Caesar and the struggling Brutus are two identifiable conceptions in Shakespeare's play. The lesser roles of Antony and Cassius deserve some attention as "antagonists." They occupy the position of opposing some dominant character—Antony versus Brutus, and Cassius versus Caesar. Shakespeare's Antony has a reputation for frivolity that does not quite correspond to his vengeful single-mindedness, and Cassius' supposed cynicism differs somewhat from his stage-villain's scheming. The antagonist stands against the protagonist, and Shakespeare's doubling of this kind of situation indicates the complications that also make it hard to choose between Caesar and Brutus.

ANTAGONISTS

Antony's talents suggest those of a playboy. His athleticism is hinted by his participation in the fertility race during Lupercalia (a festival celebrating the goat-god Faunus or Pan). Caesar favorably compares the pleasure-seeking Antony to the critical Cassius. "He loves no plays, / As thou dost, Antony; he hears no music" (1.2.203-4). Caesar, at least, prefers loungers with a few extra pounds showing around their waists:

> Let me have men about me that are fat,
> Sleek-headed men, and such as sleep a-nights.
> Yond Cassius has a lean and hungry look.
> He thinks too much; such men are dangerous.
> 1.2.192-95

Here, Antony may impress Caesar as not being the deep-thinking type, because Shakespeare was reserving the story of lover Antony for a future play about Cleopatra. Or he may have simply picked up another of Plutarch's details about Cassius that became dramatically intensified by a comparison of Caesar's friends and enemies.

Cassius' strengths of mind threaten anyone who wants confirmation of how great and powerful he is. Caesar's dislike is proportional to his vanity. "Dangerous" critics in our own time have inspired politicians to play dirty tricks against notorious reporters or simply against the press and the opposition generally. Caesar's charge against Cassius reveals part of his own anxiety, which continues in a related deprecation: "He reads much, / He is a great observer, and he looks / Quite through the deeds of men" (1.2.201-3). Such a mind is respected in Brutus. What is odd about Cassius?

Shakespeare presents Cassius working behind people's backs, in the kind of slandering that Elizabethans observed in their own society but that appeared reprehensible on stage. Richard III, Aaron the Moor in *Titus Andronicus*, Don John in *Much Ado About Nothing* preceded *Julius Caesar* in the role of stage villain or Machiavel that Christopher Marlowe's Barabas typified in *The Jew of Malta*.

Cassius' mirror routine in 1.2.66-78 is a thinly covered method of flattering Brutus and filling his mind with anti-Caesar ideas. When Cassius finishes this seduction, so much more easily practiced on Casca than on Brutus, he gloats to himself. His soliloquy (1.2.308-22) combines the triumph of winning Brutus' attention with the challenge of devising further plans to trick him into lending his good name to the conspiracy. When Casca describes Brutus' powerful righteousness, Cassius quickly assents:

Casca. O, he sits high in the all people's hearts;
And that which would appear offence in us,
His countenance, like richest alchemy,
Will change to virtue and to worthiness.
Cas. Him and his worth, and our great need of him,
You have right well conceited.

1.3.157-62

This strategy of manipulation is conducted without ethical second thoughts, and that is just what often characterizes the successful politician in any age. Cassius, like the real Machiavelli (not the stage villain), knows that you cannot mix morality and practicality if you want to win. Ruthlessness is the mark of those who rise in society.

Thus, we can speculate that Caesar dislikes Cassius because he is so much like himself. No one is said to have ordered the suppression or the murder of Flavius and Murellus for desecrating Caesar's statues ("put to silence"; 1.2.286). However, such retaliation occurs because the ruler desires it. Cassius and Antony are, respectively, antagonistic because the one stares hard at Caesar's faults and the other looks away.

LANGUAGE

So many of our impressions of the plot and characters in Shakespeare's drama rest on interpretations of the language. Determining the shades of meaning in Caesar's comments is not possible unless we pay close attention to the multiple senses of words. Dramatic poetry is an adequate term for the range of rhythms, rhymes, and metaphoric suggestions that Shakespeare commonly used for his staging of the Caesar story.

As soon as basic distinctions like prose and verse or rhythm/rhyme are made, the major task begins: interpreting the verbal meanings. The play opens with the prose of the workers, that is, unaccented, everyday speech grouped into paragraphs on the page and heard as uneven talk on the stage. Murellus first breaks into blank verse in line 32: "Wherefore rejoice? What conquest brings he home?" Regularly stressed, unrhymed poetic lines were called "blank verse." Most blank verse conforms to the five stresses and heartbeat unit of iambic pentameter.

/   /   /   /   /
Where fore re joice? What con quest brings he home?

The major stresses usually number five, though the syllables do not always add up to the ten expected in a regular set of five iambs. Neither does the iambic pattern of light-heavy always beat out the same rhythm, as the above marking indicates for "wherefore." Yet, most of the time, Shakespeare wrote dramatic poetry in a virtuoso display of variations on the blank verse norm. It is easy to hear end-rhymes, which occur infrequently in *Julius Caesar* and more often in comedies where the repeated sounds reinforce associated meanings (see *Romeo and Juliet* 1.2.219-24; 1.5.44-53) or indicate some magic incantation, like the speech of the *Midsummer Night's Dream* fairies or the *Macbeth* witches.

The difficulty arises when we undertake the challenge of interpreting the metaphors. In theory, any statement that changes or "twists" the basic sense of the words is a metaphor. "Brutus, as you know, was Caesar's angel" (3.2.181) is not Antony's literal statement about the mighty lord's winged supporter but a metaphoric claim that Brutus served Caesar in the capacity of loyal follower. In form, metaphors can be direct statements of "this is that," or they may be similies, indirect statements of the sort "this is *like* that." Antony, addressing Caesar's body in private, shows his mastery of the simile as well:

Over thy wounds now do I prophesy
(Which like dumb mouths do ope their ruby lips
To beg the voice and utterance of my tongue)
                    3.1.259-61

In practice, we must be alert to more subtleties than those occurring because of changes in the meanings of words (for example, "dumb" meant "silent" to Elizabethans not "stupid," a common meaning in modern English).

Examining the art of paraphrase, or parallel statement, is the best way to start appreciating Shakespeare's poetic language. Breaking down the parts of metaphoric comparisons can be the beginning of a lifelong pre-occupation, or may be merely a preliminary phase for students who are serious about understanding Shakespeare's words. You cannot rely forever on teachers' explanations or editorial notes.

Using a method borrowed from mathematics, we can compare statements in the form: [A] is to [B], as [C] is to [D], where these letters represent the subjects and verbs of a metaphoric sentence. The technique is as simple as pie (simile), and it is a piece of cake (metaphor). By looking at several metaphoric lines in the opening of the play, we also learn about the general tenor of the language, which varies from play to play. The context of the following example is Cassius' sly description to Brutus of the shouts made for Caesar at the Lupercalian ceremony.

> *Bru.* I do believe these applauses are
> For some new honors that are heap'd on Caesar.
> *Cas.* Why, man, he doth bestride the narrow world
> Like a Colossus, and we petty men
> Walk under his huge legs, and peep about
> To find ourselves dishonorable graves.
>   1.2.133-38

You can ask "who or what is being compared to what else?" in the specific form:

who (or what)	[in a similar	who (or what) else
does what?	way that]	does what?

Caesar		a huge statue
spans the relatively small earth		spreads its legs on either side of a narrow strip of land or water

You do not have to recognize that an actual statue of Apollo, the Colossus at the harbor of the island of Rhodes, was a world wonder to appreciate Cassius' simile, because his thought consists of a second simile that explains the sense of Caesar's magnitude. Caesar looms above the world with the effect that

unimportant people [seem to]
_____

walk beneath his towering legs and
look around, unsuccessfully, for a proper
place to die.

Cassius expresses a full measure of contempt for Caesar by comparing him to an enormous statue. Shakespeare's associative mind
spun out many metaphoric webs from these similes, as we can
detect in the sense of "petty" (small in height, insignificant) joining
with "underlings" in line 141. A neat analysis of one simile gives way
to greater complexity, once you look at the fuller setting.

Another simple case will illustrate the use of similes in the opening of *Julius Caesar*. We take our bearings on the play (a metaphor
from navigational compasses) by this method. Brutus is describing to
Casca the facial expression of Cicero when Caesar comes sweeping
back from the ceremony with all his followers:

> Cicero
> Looks with such ferret and such fiery eyes
> As we have seen him in the Capitol,
> Being cross'd in conference by some senators.
> 1.2.185-88

Cicero [regarding Caesar]	Cicero
looks with the fierce, red eyes of a ferret	stares angrily at his opponents in the Senate

It is not necessary to know about Cicero's reputation as a sharp
critic or about the red-tinged eyes of this member of the polecat
family to perceive the thrust of this simile. In compressed form,
Shakespeare implies just how much Cicero's agitation has been
raised by Caesar's performance. The simile makes the associations
explicit enough.

Metaphors work with deceiving directness. [A] equals [B]. No
"like" or "as" qualifies the comparison. We are left to decide just what
is being equated with what else. "For always I am Caesar" (1.2.212) is
not a literal statement of the physical fact that Caesar is himself, perpetually, and not any other person. This metaphor requires interpre-

tation of what senses "Caesar" can carry. It might mean "a great being who never changes" or "a model for others to imitate." (We might now leave aside but anticipate the associations that post-Shakespearean uses of "Caesar" have, such as the German imperial title, "Kaiser" or the Russian one, "Czar.") The immediate dramatic context of Caesar's defensive reactions against Cassius guides us here. The metaphor opens into many possible meanings, upon consideration. Sometimes a phrase is obviously metaphorical, such as Cassius' "We have the falling sickness" (1.2.256), said in extended reference to epilepsy. At other places in Shakespeare's verbal network, a metaphor shares literal and figurative senses.

CLOSE PARAPHRASES

Closely paraphrasing an ornate metaphor in deliberately simple terms is another method of analysis Cassius opens his soliloquy,

> Well, Brutus, thou art noble; yet I see
> Thy honorable mettle may be wrought
> From that it is dispos'd.
>
> 1.3.308-10

A loose paraphrase of the approximate sense might be "So, Brutus, your instinctive behavior can be changed." A close paraphrase of the metaphor's details might go thus: "It is possible to contort, to twist around, to give a new shape to, your tendency to place high value on nobility, similar to the way that iron may be hammered into a form that it naturally, or at first, does not have." The wordplay on the material "metal" and the mental "mettle" sounds the same on stage. Part of Shakespeare's game is lost on readers who cannot imagine how homonyms can be confused, and on playgoers who have no access to the written text.

Such moments pass quickly, and the exercise of paraphrasing stretches them out too long. A reasonable compromise is to analyze a few metaphors, always returning to the Shakespearean lines after you have mangled them for a while in your own simpler words. You are not trying to write better poetry, but to feel the several tensions implied in the original metaphor. When finally you relax this study, you can begin to appreciate the effects concentrated in a "simple" metaphor.

NEW HISTORY/OLD HISTORY

The questions about culture that arise from *Julius Caesar* have provoked diverse responses. The historical documents in this book attest to how many ways people have responded to the incidents in the plot and the shaded meanings in the language. This play is a thoughtful piece of human drama. Each of us brings personal angles of view to the events of the assassination, as well as different childhood experiences contending with parents, and especially relevant here, with fathers. Reading experience of other literature and historical incidents certainly affects how we respond to the mental and dramatically vivid representations of Caesar's fall and Brutus' conscience.

Our task as students of Shakespeare's *Julius Caesar* is to gather as much background as we can, and then to apply those perceptions to the mental foreground of the tragic action. To ourselves, we might admit that we are avoiding some ideas and exaggerating others. With others' ideas mixed in, we are apt to confuse our sources. Remembering Brutus' cautious optimism toward Cassius is instructive:

> What you have said
> I will consider; what you have to say
> I will with patience hear, and find a time
> Both meet to hear and answer such high things.
>   1.2.167-70

Living up to this ideal is worth the effort.

TOPICS FOR WRITTEN OR ORAL EXPLORATION

1. Perform the experiment of distorting a modern mirror by stretching a piece of plastic wrap over its surface. Or use a polished piece of metal, such as the back of a tray, to simulate a Renaissance mirror. Write a careful description of your features reflected in this "glass." Analyze how your perceptions are affected by your normal experience of looking at yourself in clear, modern mirrors.

2. Pair up with another person and record the physical features of the other person's face. You are mirrors to one another, as Cassius says he is to Brutus. Speculate on features of personality that you "see" in specific aspects of the other person's face. Try to eliminate qualities you already know, and concentrate on those mental insights that you imagine are related to physical aspects of the persons' face. At the end of this session, tell your observations to your partner and let him or her comment on their accuracy. Then each of you write a paragraph on the deceptions of this process of interpretation.

3. Before you read Shakespeare's play, list all the qualities you associate with Julius Caesar, the person. After finishing the play, compose a second list about Caesar, the character. Write an essay on how your perceptions changed after reading the play.

4. Think of a situation comparable to the "putting to silence" of Flavius and Murellus for defacing the statues of a powerful leader. How did these retributions in the comparable situation affect other people's subsequent behavior? Follow the same procedure for the event where Caesar puts aside the crown, that is, think of a moment when a powerful person publicly refuses some honor or increase of authority. How did this show of humility affect other people's attitudes or behavior toward the person who acted humbly? How do you judge the sincerity of such an act?

5. Consider the social values that the play appears to promote. Do those values contribute to the literary value or experience of the play?

6. Compare a "popular" governmental body, versus a "prestigious" one: the House of Representatives or House of Commons, versus the Senate or House of Lords, for example. (If you are more familiar with the institutions of state or local government, use them instead.) Which parts of *Julius Caesar* would appeal to each body, and why?

7. In what ways does a legislative or executive official affect your personal life? Examine your individual reaction to actions of your city mayor, or the governor of a state. You might consider the authority of the principal of your school. Examine the effect of your attitudes toward authority to incidents in *Julius Caesar* involving the individual's reac-

tion to authority, for example, Cassius in 1.2.135-60, Casca in 1.3.103-15, Brutus in 2.1.21-34.

8. Write your own plot summary of Shakespeare's play. Compare yours to others' summaries, noting any differences in emphasis. Try to explain why your version differs from those of others.

9. Divide the class into three groups: one group will discuss Caesar as the lead character, a second will discuss Brutus as the lead character,and the third will discuss the interpretation that both share the lead. Discuss your reasons within the group and present them in a meeting of the whole class. The moderator should point out the assumptions behind these "proofs" and correct any mistakes of "fact."

10. Caesar and Antony are like father and son; Brutus and Cassius seem like straightforward and crooked brothers. Describe the civil war in the play as the unfortunate extension of both of these "family" relationships.

11. Mark all the prose passages in the play and try to explain, from the context (who speaks, what is spoken about) why Shakespeare did not use blank verse on those occasions. Choose one passage and recast it into blank verse. Read this aloud and describe the difference, in general tone, from Shakespeare's chosen mode.

12. Hold a conversation in blank verse. To what degree is iambic pentameter a natural rhythm for you?

13. Express Cassius' metaphor as a double ratio: "This rudeness is a sauce to his good wit, / Which gives men stomach to digest his words / With better appetite" (1.2.300-302). After working out the details of what is being compared, comment on the effect of this metaphor within the context of Cassius' designs on Brutus.

14. Look at Cassius' metaphor of the "falling sickness" (1.2.254) and list as many senses of the metaphor as you can perceive. Compare Antony's "falling" metaphor in 3.2.190-02. Comment on why the imagery of falling down is appropriate to this play.

15. Casca does not understand Cassius' "falling sickness" metaphor, and he gives his own theater simile in reply (1.2.257-61). Compare his ability to express this theatrical comparison with that of Brutus, who, in 2.1.225-27, expresses himself in the same kind of comparison. Can you detect differences in the quality of thinking?

16. Write a close paraphrase of Brutus' similes in 2.1.61-69 ("Since Cassius first did whet me . . . an insurrection.") Use simple words and do not try to sound poetic. If some ideas have multiple senses, write them all down in series. Now, compare your paraphrase to the one given in Chapter 5 of this book in Basic English. Discuss the extent to which

your version says the same thing, and try to explain any differences. Finally, reread the original passage and write down what you now notice about the suggestiveness of the similes.

SUGGESTED READINGS

Aristotle's Poetics: A Translation and Commentary for Students of Literature. Translated by Leon Golden, Edited by O. B. Hardison. Tallahassee: University Presses of Florida, 1981.

Frye, Northrop. "My Father as He Slept: The Tragedy of Order." In *Fools of Time: Studies in Shakespearean Tragedy*. Toronto: University of Toronto Press, 1967. 3-39.

Greenblatt, Stephen. "Culture." In *Critical Terms for Literary Study*. Chicago: University of Chicago Press, 1995. 225-32.

———. *Shakespearean Negotiations: The Circulation of Social Energy in Renaissance England*. Berkeley: University of California Press, 1988.

———. "Towards a Poetics of Culture." Edited by H. Aram Veeser. *The New Historicism*. New York and London: Routledge, 1989. 1-14.

Levin, Richard. *New Readings vs. Old Plays: Recent Trends in the Reinterpretation of English Renaissance Drama*. Chicago: University of Chicago Press, 1979.

Montrose, Louis A. "Professing the Renaissance: The Poetics and Politics of Culture." In *The New Historicism*. 15-36.

———. "Renaissance Literary Studies and the Subject of History." *English Literary Renaissance* 16 (1986): 5-12.

2

Caesar on the Elizabethan Stage

A poetic understanding of the language in Shakespeare's *Julius Caesar* should be complemented by knowledge about the dramatic context. While the metaphors that describe characters' minds and the particular places of the action can be analyzed verbally, this perception of staged reality needs to be supplemented with a study of imagined space—the physical space in the theater, the actors' zones of movement, the audience's viewpoints. This chapter will present information about the theaters where Shakespeare worked, mainly the public ones in London, because that is where *Julius Caesar* was presumably honored, if (as there is no evidence to doubt) it was the Caesar play observed in 1599 when the Globe playhouse opened. But private theaters also existed for the exclusive pleasure of nobles and students. An example of a university play, *Caesar's Revenge*, gives us special insight into the strong desire to continue the story, not quite like modern money-making sequels of popular movies, but more in the spirit of completing gaps that an artist like Shakespeare chose to leave open or to complete later, with a focus on the character of Antony, and Caesar's companion/lover, Cleopatra. We can appreciate how college entertainments, though they might be exaggerated and flamboyant, teach us about Shakespeare's carefully controlled tragedy.

THEATRICAL SITES

The citizens of Shakespeare's London who attended plays were a mixed lot—apprentices, workmen, noble men and women, prostitutes, country visitors, other actors and playwrights, theater shareholders, city officials and disapproving churchmen on investigative missions. They had a taste for the exotic as well as for the violent, the slanderous, and the comic. Few would make the trip across the Thames or over St. George's fields without some hope for excitement, whether it was an afternoon of watching a bear or bull being attacked by dogs, a secret or public encounter with whores, some hours drinking strong ale or more time guzzling the less alcoholic "small beer." The hub for these diversions in 1599 was the theater district.

Several maps record this shoreline area, called Bankside or Southwark, located in the "liberty" (a district free of City of London laws) of the Clink (a prison), bounded on one end by London Bridge and less clearly on the other end by fields, ditches, and rutty roads converging on Paris (that is, "parish") Garden landing stage for boats plying passengers to and from the City of London. Anyone could see the spire of St. Paul's church from Bankside, but what a difference the river boundary made, for city ordinances against crowds and lewd activities could not be enforced outside the old city walls. Georg Braun's "Cities of the World" (1574), Ralph Agas' map of London (about 1590; printed 1633), John Norden's *Speculum Britanniae* (1593), Jodocus Hondius' map in John Speed's *Theatre of the Empire of Great Britain* (1611), J. C. Visscher's *View of London* (1616), and Wenceslas Hollar's *Long View* (1647) variously depict the Globe, the Rose, the Hope, the Swan, the Bear Garden, the Curtain. A close-up sketch of the Swan survives in a copy of Johannes De Witt's observations about London, circa 1596. One must not trust the accuracy of these maps too much, since scientific draftsmanship was not yet developed. Moreover, the original Globe burned down in a spectacular fire during a June 29, 1613 performance of Shakespeare's *Henry VIII* (see the stage direction to 1.4.49), and thus the original playhouse for most of Shakespeare's public productions is missing from the visual record, and the replacement Globe is shown (and mislabeled) in the Visscher and the Hollar drawings that happen to depict that part of the riverbank.

The theaters' names themselves echo Londoners' conceptions of dramatic life in the southern suburbs. Swans were symbols of poetry; "Hope" expresses eternal optimism; "Bear Garden" gives a pastoral feeling to a bloody pit. Shakespeare had bought into a theatrical company whose playhouse seems to have been grandly styled by the slogan *Totus mundus agit histrionem*, "the whole world plays the actor." Rosencrantz's allusion to Hercules bearing the world on his shoulder (*Hamlet* 2.2.362) corroborates the Globe's supposed motto. Jacques' meditation on "All the world's a stage" (*As You Like It* 2.7.139), responding to the Duke's comment that "This wide and universal theatre, / Presents more woeful pageants than the scene / Wherein we play in" (lines 137-39), increases the association between the Globe and an international outlook on dramatic representation.

James Burbage invested in the theater business of the Globe from the ground up. A penniless carpenter, he turned to acting and then hammering together a playhouse on the city side of the Thames. He acted on his own stage. His sons Richard and Cuthbert performed about the same time that Shakespeare presumably acted in the thundering history plays of the early 1590s, such as the two parts of Marlowe's *Tamburlaine the Great* (first printed together in 1590) and *The Massacre at Paris* (about 1594). In the latter play, a French Catholic leader, the Duke of Guise, struts out in front of his assassins, boasting,

> Yet Caesar shall go forth.
> Let mean conceits and baser men fear death.
> Tut, they are peasants; I am the Duke of Guise,
> And princes with their looks engender fear.
> > scene 20, lines 67-70

The emperor's fame easily crossed the Channel, and would put money in the purse of anyone clever enough to exploit the dramatic possibilities.

LONDON AND ROME

A principal model for playactors on a world stage was the Roman Empire and its capital. Not that anyone worked out the analogies geographically, but culturally, the commercial, governmental, and religious life of the Forums (the Julian, the Augustan, the Trajan, the original Roman Forum) corresponded to the old walled city of London. The Tiber functioned like the Thames, as a route to empire and a winding physical divider of parts of the capital. The Flavian amphitheater, which we now call the Colosseum, entertained the populace with as much violence as the animal-baiting arenas of Southwark. The gardens and theater of Pompey, in the Campus Martius, provided recreations like those of the rusticated playhouse district where Shakespeare's work was publicly acted.

It was in the portico adjoining one of the Roman Senate's meeting places, graced by a statue of Julius Caesar's former rival, Pompey the Great, that the dictator was slain in 44 B.C. This *Curia Pompeii* was later called just the *Curia*, and became confused with the site around the ancient Temple of Jupiter on the Capitoline Hill. This Capitol, long associated with governmental business, was not bloodied by Julius Caesar's body, though English writers as early as Chaucer and as late as Shakespeare placed the assassination there.

The murder or political demise of ponderous officials made an irresistible tradition for narrators. As Chaucer's Monk tells it, "This Julius to the Capitolie wente . . . " and was stabbed by "This false Brutus" (*The Monk's Tale* fragment 7, 2703). Polonius lectures Hamlet on his (the counsellor's) former acting career. "I did enact Julius Caesar. I was kill'd i' th'Capitol; Brutus kill'd me" (3.2.103). In Protestant England the association of Rome with Catholicism enabled religious propaganda against "princes," which was the Italian term for any magnate, whether a churchman or a warrior. Cardinal Wolsey was just such a towering figure who fell from grace. This Catholic cardinal held the highest political and diplomatic office in England, Lord Chancellor, but his personal wealth, power, and ambitions to be Pope brought him against the secular ambitions of Henry VIII. Shakespeare makes him describe himself in language applied to Julius Caesar and other Phaetons such as Richard II (see *Richard II* 3.3.178).

> I have touch'd the highest point of all my greatness,
> And, from that full meridian of my glory,
> I haste now to my setting. I shall fall
> Like a bright exhalation in the evening,
> And no man see me more.
>
> (*Henry VIII* 3.2.223-27)

Phaeton was the son of Apollo who rashly tried to rein in the horses of the sun chariot and nearly burnt up the world in his fall. Caesar's desires for glory brought down his own successes in later life, though the example has not stopped the wheel of Fortune from lifting and dropping his admirers ever since. The collapse of the Roman Empire struck Elizabethan historians as a bitter moment, but not a precedent that in any way affected their own imperial designs. It is worth speculating whether a keenly aware dramatist like Shakespeare was not able to glimpse the eventual decline of the British Empire, when he created history plays and tragedies whose imagery and narratives imitated sunrise and sunset.

EYEWITNESS AT THE GLOBE

Elizabethan playgoers were more apt to want comic entertainment than heavy doses of Roman or ancient British history. Julius Caesar, after all, conquered large parts of ancient Britain, but that was not a proper subject for a popular drama, though Shakespeare glanced at it in *Cymbeline*. What thrived was the festive spirit of an opening season in the newly rebuilt Globe. (London officials had made the Burbages so uncomfortable with their otherwise unrenewable lease on a theatrical enterprise just north of the walls, at Shoreditch, that Richard and Cuthbert tore the place down. Solid timber being so well joined and easily taken apart, they floated the structure's beams across the Thames and reconstructed it in 1598-99 as the Globe.) There, a Swiss visitor attended a Fall staging of a Caesar play and wrote in his diary about what is presumably Shakespeare's *Julius Caesar*.

FROM THOMAS PLATTER'S OBSERVATIONS OF LONDON (1599)

On September 21 [1599] after lunch, around 2 o'clock I crossed the river [Thames] with my companions and saw, in a building with a thatched roof, the tragedy of the first emperor Julius Caesar excellently performed by about 15 actors. At the end of the play, the actors, as is their custom, danced together absolutely gracefully and beautifully; two were attired in men's clothing and two in women's.

On another occasion, not far from our inn in the suburb of, if I remember correctly, Bishopsgate, and also after lunch, I attended a play which presented characters of various nationalities. An Englishman fought with each one of them over a maiden and defeated them all except for the German, who won the girl through his prowess at fighting. He sat down next to her and proceeded to get himself and his servant completely drunk; the servant hit his master over the head with his shoe and then both fell asleep. In the meantime, the Englishman entered the tent and made off with the German's prize; thus, he outwitted the German as well. At the end, they also danced very gracefully in the English and Irish manner. And so it is that everyday at 2 o'clock in the afternoon in the city of London, two and sometimes even three plays are performed at different sites; one tries to outdo the other and whichever is best has the largest audience. The sites are built in such a way that the actors perform on an elevated platform, and everyone has a good view of everything. However, there are different areas where the seats are comfortable and better and therefore cost more. Whoever stays below and stands pays only 1 English penny; if he wants to sit, he goes through a door and pays another penny; however, if he wishes to sit in the best location and on cushions, where he can not only see everything well, but also be seen, he must pay another English penny at another door. During the play food and drink are carried around among the spectators, in case they want to pay to refresh themselves, too.

The actors are dressed most exquisitely and gracefully, for it is the custom in England that when aristocratic lords or knights die, they bequeath some of their most beautiful clothes to their servants, who, because it is not appropriate for them to wear such clothes, offer them for sale to actors at a good price.

What a good time can be had every day at the plays is well known by anyone who has ever seen them acted or performed.

Gustav Binz, "Londoner Theater und Schauspiele Im Jahre 1599," *Anglia* 22 (1899): 458-59. Translated by Thomas G. Sauer.

Firsthand accounts always incorporate the particular whims of the witness, and Platter's passing over the details of the Caesar play may only mean that he was more impressed by the German characters than by the Roman ones. This document is still an important record of the comic mood that attended a serious play.

His notice of the merriment tells us that the play was not the only thing that attracted the crowd. Dances at the ends of plays, such as the jig, or the civilized rustic dance called a "Bergomask"(a masque for burghers) concluding *A Midsummer Night's Dream*, celebrated the comic spirit of love plots, but even Shakespeare's most serious tragedies contain songs that contrast or deepen the somber moods. Brutus asks his servant Lucius to sing a restful song; presumably a young boy performed the song to his own accompaniment on a stringed instrument such as the lute-like cittern (5.1.255-72). Stage directions like "music and a song" are easily overlooked by readers and sometimes cut by directors. The full effect of this Elizabethan performance, however, brought English folk music into a Roman setting without any disturbance of the historical accuracy, since there was not much attempt to inaugurate the new Globe Theater with anything but indigenous British culture. One artist has drawn and described what Platter may have seen during the gala event (Hodges, *Theatre* 79-93).

The cast of approximately fifteen actors that Platter watched would not cover, one-for-one, the thirty-five nominal roles in the play. Elizabethan companies doubled the acting parts, since the same boy could play Calpurnia and Portia, for instance, with different costumes. As long as the doubled characters did not appear on stage at the same time, the ten principal members of the Lord Chamberlain's men, plus their apprentices and possibly a few hired extras, could act *Julius Caesar* convincingly. For this period, of course, "realism" was achieved by Shakespeare's verbal art in describing places (or being vague about them), by suggestive sound effects such as the offstage "alarum" shouting noise of battle or the cannonball-down-the-chute crash of thunder and the black-powder flash of lightning (see editorial stage directions to 1.3.1, 5.2.1 and 5.4.1), by clusters of people representing plebeian crowds hearing Brutus' or Antony's orations, and so forth. (Hollywood Shakespeare relied on a nearly opposite strategy of visual effects.) Platter's comments on the ornate costumes of the actors imply that playgoing was a process of social display. The highly visible groundlings jostled with the noble lords, who competed with the actors in dress and claims to attention. In a large sense, the spectators at the Globe—the boisterous and drunken as well as the plumed and the refined—contributed to the dramatic immediacy of *Julius Caesar* by responding to the orations and fights. The audience was part of the show.

SEQUEL AT OXFORD UNIVERSITY: THE REVENGE OF

GREAT CAESAR'S GHOST

When the onlookers were not London citizens, but dedicated students of theology or medicine, the tone of a Caesar play shifted toward classical themes and references. About 1607, not satisfied with Shakespeare's dramatized ghost murmuring his appointment with Brutus at Philippi (4.3.282-86), an Oxford student wrote a blood-and-thunder play for the amusement of his fellows. It was published anonymously as *Caesar's Revenge,* though it included Caesar's victim Pompey as well. As a sequel to Shakespeare's 1599 play, and an improvement in the extravagant dramatic style that the new King James favored, this play elevates Caesar by giving him the privilege of personally terrifying his killer. Even better, he does not actually kill Brutus, but drives him to despairing suicide. The play also features the allegorical figure of Discord, who functions like the mock Revenge in *Titus Andronicus* (act 5, scene 2), an embodiment of an idea brought terrifyingly to life. Shakespeare wrote that blood-soaked play about 1593; his much more refined and classical *Julius Caesar* was finished in 1599. His masterpiece, *Hamlet,* was developing in his mind during this flourishing time for the Globe Theater, and in the Oxford revenge play we can perceive the elements of ghosts, stabbing, and turbulent minds that occupy the Danish prince. The opening excerpt presents a Caesar not unlike the relentless warrior Macbeth described in 1.2.16-23. The second excerpt features a ghost more offended than Hamlet's father's spirit, and true to the university atmosphere, more learned. Modern readers have to interpret long lists of gods, kings, places, and mighty deeds as the necessary sign that an educated audience wanted compliments. For example, if an allusion to the war goddess Bellona would have been missed by the Globe groundlings when it appeared in context (*Macbeth* 1.2.54), the Oxford students needed no explanation (*Revenge* act 4, line 9). The glee Discord expresses at Caesar's death (*Revenge* act 5, lines 90-103) exaggerates the triumph far beyond the mood of restrained celebration that Shakespeare gives to the death of Claudius in *Hamlet.* To observe the difference between art and indulgence is a valuable lesson for students of Shakespeare.

FROM *THE TRAGEDY OF CAESAR AND POMPEY;* OR *CAESAR'S REVENGE* (1607)

Sound alarm then flames of fire.
Enter Discord.

Hark how the *Roman* drums sound blood and death,
And *Mars* high mounted on his Thracian Steed:
Runs madding through *Pharsalias* purple fields.
The earth that's wont to be a Tomb for Men
It's now entomb'd with Carcasses of Man.   5
The Heaven appal'd to see such hideous sights,
For fear puts out her ever burning lights.
The Gods amaz'd (as once in *Titans* war,)
Do doubt and fear, which bodes this deadly jar.
The stars do tremble, and forsake their course,   10
The *Bear* doth hide her in forbidden Sea,
Fear makes *Bootes* swiften her slow pace,
Pale is *Orion*, *Atlas* gins to quake,
And his unwieldy burden to forsake.
Caesars keen *Falcon* through the Adverse ranks,   15
For his stern Master hews a passage out,
Through troops and trunks, and steel, and standing blood:
He whose proud Trophies whilhom *Asia* field,
And conquered *Pontus*, singed his lasting praise.
Great *Pompey*, Great while Fortune did him raise,   20
Now veils the glory of his vaunting plumes
And to the ground casts off his high hang'd looks.
You gentle Heavens, O execute your wrath
On vile mortality, that hath scorned your powers.
You night born Sisters to whose hairs are tied   25
In Adamantine Chain both Gods and Men
Wind on your web of mischief and of plagues,
And if, O stars you have an influence:
That may confound this high erected heap
Down pour it; Vomit out your worst of ills   30
Let *Rome*, grown proud, with her unconquered strength,
Perish and conquered Be with her own strength:
And win all powers to disjoin and break,
Consume, confound, dissolve, and dissipate
What Laws, Arms and Pride hath raised up.   35

Act 3, scene 1
       Enter Caesars Ghost.
 Ghost: Out of the horror of those shady vaults,
Where Centaurs, Harpies, pains and furies fell:
And Gods and Ghosts and ugly Gorgons dwell,
My restless soul comes here to tell his wrongs.
Hail to thy walls, thou pride of all the world,   5
Thou are the place where whilom in my life
My seat of mounting honour was erected,
And my proud throne that seem'd to check the heavens,
But now my pomp and I are laid more low,
With these associates of my overthrow,   10
Here ancient *Assur* and proud *Belus* lies,
Ninnus the first that sought a Monarchs name.
Atrides fierce with the *Aeacides*,
The *Greek Heroes*, and the *Trojan* flower,
Blood-thirsting *Cyrus* and the conquering youth: 15
That sought to fetch his pedigree from Heaven,
Stern *Romulus* and proud *Tarquinius*,
The mighty *Syrians* and the *Pontic* Kings,
Alcides and the stout, *Carthagian* Lord,
The fatal enemy to the *Roman* name.   20
Ambitious *Sylla* and fierce *Marius*,
And both the *Pompeys* by me done to death,
I am the last not least of the same crew,
Look on my deeds and say what *Caesar* was,
Thessalis, Egypt, Pontus, Africa,   25
Spain, Britain, Almany and France,
Saw many a blood trial of my worth.
But why do I my glory thus restrain,
When all the world was but a Chariot,
Wherein I rode Triumphing in my pride?   30
But what avails this tale of what I was?
Since in my chiefest height *Brutus* base hand,
With three and twenty wounds my heart did gore,
Give me my sword and shield I'll be reveng'd,
My mortal wounding spear and golden Crest.   35
I will dishorse my foemen in the field,
Alas poor *Caesar* thou a shadow art,
An airy substance wanting force and might,
Then will I go and cry upon the world,
Exclaim on *Antony* and *Octavian*,   40
Which seek through discord and dissentious broils,

T'imbrue their weapons in each others blood,
And leave to execute my just revenge...

                    . . .

Act 4
 Discord: *Brutus* thou hast what long desire hath sought,
Caesar Lies weltering in his purple Gore,
Thou art the author of *Romes* liberty,
Proud in my murdering hand and bloody knife.
Yet think *Octavius* and stern *Antony*   5
Cannot let pass this murder unrevenged,
Thessalia once again must see your blood,
And *Roman* drums must strike up new alarms,
Hark how *Bellona* shakes her angry lance:
And envy clothed in her crimson weed,   10
Methinks I see the fiery shields to clash,
Eagle gainst Eagle, *Rome* gainst *Rome* to fight,
Phillipi, *Caesar*, quittance must thy wrongs,
Whereas that hand shall stab that traitorous heart
That durst encourage it to work thy death,   15
Thus from thine ashes *Caesar* doth arise
As from *Medeas* hapless scattered teeth:
New flames of wars, and new outrageous broils,
Now smile *Aemathia* that even in thy top,
Romes victory and pride shall be entombed,   20
And those great conquerors of the vanquished earth,
Shall with their swords come there to dig their graves.

                    . . .

Act 5, scene 1
                    Enter Ghost.
 Gho.: *Brutus,* ingrateful *Brutus* seest thou me:
Anon In field again thou shalt me see,
 Bru.: Stay what so ere thou art, or fiend below,
Raised from the deep by enchanters bloody call,
Or fury sent from *Phlegetontic* flames,   5
Or from *Cocytus* for to end my life,
Be then *Megera* or *Tysiphone*,
Or of *Eumenides* ill boding crew.
Fly me not now, but end my wretched life,
Come grisly messenger of sad mishap,   10
Trample in blood of him that hates to live,
And end my life and sorrow all at once.
Gho.: Accursed traitor damned *Homicide*,
Knowest thou not me, to whom for forty honors:

Thou three and twenty Ghastly wounds didst give?   15
Now dare no more for to behold the Heavens,
For they today have destined thine end:
Nor lift thy eyes unto the rising sun,
That nere shall live for to behold it set,
Nor look not down unto the Hellish shades,   20
There stand the furies thirsting for thy blood,
Fly to the field but if thou thither go'st,
There *Anthonys* sword will pierce thy traitorous heart.
Brutus today my blood shall be revenged,
And for my wrong and undeserved death,   25
Thy life to thee a torture shall become,
And thou shalt oft amongst the dying groans,
Of slaughtered men that bite the bleeding earth
With that like baleful cheer might thee befall,
And seek for death that flies so wretched wight,   30
Until to shun the honour of the fight,
And dreadful vengeance of supernal ire,
Thine own right hand shall work my wish'd revenge,
And so Fall ill, hated of Heaven and Men.
   Bru.:   Stay *Caesar* stay, protract my grief no longer,   35
Rip up my bowels, glut thy thirsting throat,
With pleasing blood of *Caesars* guilty heart:
But see he's gone and yonder Murder stands:
See how he points his knife unto my heart.
Althea raveth, for her murdered Son,   40
And weeps the deed that she herself hath done:
And *Meleager* would thou livest again,
But death must expiate. *Altheas* come.
I, death the guerdon that my deeds deserve:
The drums do thunder forth dismay and fear,   45
And dismal triumphs sound my fatal knell,
Furies I come to meet you all in Hell,

                           . . .

        Enter Brutus the Ghost following him.
Bru.:   What dost thou still pursue me ugly fiend,
Is this it that thou thirsted for so much?
Come with thy tearing claws and rend it out,   65
Would thy appeaseless rage be slacked with blood,
This sword today hath crimson channels made,
But hears the blood that thou wouldst drink so fain,
Then take this piercer, broach this traitorous heart,
Or if thou thinkest death too small a pain,   70

Drag down his body to proud *Erebus*,
Through black *Cocytus* and infernal *Styx*,
Lethean waves and fires of *Phlegeton*,
Boil me or burn, tear my hateful flesh,
Devour, consume, pull, pinch, plague, pain this heart,   75
Hell craves her right, and here the furies stand,
And all the hell-hounds compass me around
Each seeking for a part of this same prey,
Alas this body is lean, thin, pale and wan,
Nor can it all your hungry mouths suffice,   80
O tis the soul that they stand gaping for,
And endless matter for to prey upon.
Renewed still as *Titius* pricked heart.
Then clap your hand, let Hell and Joy resound?
Here it comes flying through this airy round.   85
Gho: Hell take their hearts, that this ill deed have done
And vengeance follow till they be overcome:
Nor live t'applaud the justice of this deed.
Murder by her own guilty hand doth bleed.
                    Enter Discord
Dis.:   I, now my longing hopes have their desire,   90
The world is nothing but a massy heap:
Of bodies slain, The Sea a lake of blood,
The Furies that for slaughter only thirst,
Are with these Massacres and slaughters cloyed,
Tysipones pale, and *Megeras* thin face,   95
Is now puffed up, and swollen with quaffing blood,
Charon that used but an old rotten boat
Must not a navy rig for to transport,
The howling souls, unto the *Stygian* strand.
Hell and *Elysium* must be digged on one,   100
And both will be too little to contain,
Numberless numbers of afflicted ghosts,
That I myself have tumbling thither sent.
Gho.: Now nights pale daughter since thy bloody joys,
And my revengeful thirst fulfilled are,   105
Do thou applaud what justly heavens have wrought,
While murder on the murderers head is brought.
Dis.:   *Caesar* I pitied not thy Tragic end:
Nor tyrants daggers sticking in my heart,
Nor do I that that thy deaths with like repaid,   110
But that thy death so many deaths hath made:
Now cloyed with blood, I'll hie me down below,

And laugh to think I caused such endless woe.
Gho.: Since my revenge is full accomplished,
And my deaths causers by themselves are slain, 115
I will descend to mine eternal home,
Where everlastingly my quiet soul,
The sweet *Elysiums* pleasures shall enjoy
And walk those fragrant flowery fields at rest:
To which nor fair *Adonis* bower so rare, 120
Nor old *Alcinous* gardens may compare.
There that same gentle father of the spring,
Mild Zephirus doth *Odors* breathe divine:
Clothing the earth in painted bravery,
The which nor winters rage, nor Scorching heat, 125
There with the mighty champions of old time,
And great Heroes of the Golden age,
My dateless hours I'll spend in lasting joy.

These excerpts illustrate the learned man's taste in classical mythology, while still giving the regular citizens (especially butchers!) something to cheer. *Caesar's Revenge* is not high art or popular art. It is poetic justice, taken to dramatic extremes.

Shakespeare's play works by suggestion rather than by the blatant symbols Discord and Revenge. Antony's violence is suggested by his remark "Now let it work. Mischief, thou art afoot" (3.2.260), referring to the mob he has incited and turned loose on the conspirators. Shakespeare's restraint and classical reserve prevented him from introducing a character named Mischief. The mob's fury is forcefully implied by the murder of Cinna the poet, dragged down because he bore the same name as the conspirator Cinna. The ghost of Caesar is merely a suggestion of the tragic figure's dominating spirit. These cases of artistic control argue for Shakespeare's wisdom as a playwright. He knew how to entertain his own people, and visitors like Platter or the many foreign residents of London, with dramatic art suited to its subject. For *Julius Caesar*, this meant a play that appealed to the Globe's unruly, restless penny-patrons while at the same time inspiring the educated nobles in the galleries.

TOPICS FOR WRITTEN OR ORAL EXPLORATION

1. Describe one of the areas in your town or city where public entertainments occur, whether theatrical, athletic, or of some other kind. What unstated activities are associated with these places? How does their look change when the entertaining is in full swing? In what ways do people behave differently from normal when they inhabit this zone? In dress or attitude, do any of them make themselves conspicuous in order to be seen and admired? Having collected these impressions, write a dialogue like that among Brutus, Casca, and Cassius (1.2.215-75). Let the people present describe the mood to the absent person, using details from your impressions. Try to work in a twist of meaning like Cassius' "falling sickness" remark, where a straightforward sense of some word is contrasted with a special sense.

2. Gather your classmates into a noisy group that responds loudly and long to the speeches of Brutus and Antony, in Act 3, scene 2. (Better do this outside, where the crowd is so agitated that the people reading Brutus' and Antony's lines must shout to be heard.) For the body of Caesar, Antony can bring in a long coat and display its wounds, and the mob can carry it off at the end of the scene. Antony must decide on his tone of voice for "Now let it work . . . take what course thou wilt" (lines 259-60). Since the stage has been cleared, what emotions can he reveal now that he is not "performing" for the plebs?

3. While you are still excited from the orations scene, try to enact the bullying of Cinna the Poet, an innocent bystander in Act 3, scene 3. Did those who were watching laugh at the mistake? Discuss how this case of mistaken identity can be funny or horrifying, depending on the mood of the mob.

4. Have some students read aloud the parts of Discord, Caesar's Ghost, and Brutus from the Oxford play. Compared to this farce, how does Shakespeare's play seem restrained and classical?

5. What sort of education lies behind the allusions in both works? What do you have to know in order to understand the references in the Oxford play, compared to those in Shakespeare's tragedy? To explore this question, write a dialoague between Shakespeare and Edward Vere, Earl of Oxford. Suppose that Vere scorned Shakespeare's play because most people could understand its references; Shakespeare ridiculed Oxford for aiming too high over people's heads, with all those allusions to constellations, classical place names, and mythological references. After imagining this exchange, read some of the actual controversy about whether Vere wrote Shakespeare's plays. Reassess the authorship arguments in relation to the two Caesar plays.

SUGGESTED READINGS

Chambers, E. K. *The Elizabethan Stage*. 4 vols. Oxford: Oxford University Press, 1923.

Evans, G. Blakemore. *Elizabethan-Jacobean Drama: The Theatre in Its Time*. New York: New Amsterdam Books, 1988.

Gurr, Andrew. *Rebuilding Shakespeare's Globe*. New York: Routledge, 1989.

———. *The Shakespearean Stage, 1574-1642*. Cambridge: Cambridge University Press, 1980.

Hodges, C. Walter. *The Globe Restored: A Study of the Elizabethan Theatre*. New York: Norton, 1973.

———. *Shakespeare's Theatre*. New York: Coward-McCann, 1964.

"Looking for Shakespeare: Two Partisans Explain and Debate the Authorship Question." *The Atlantic Monthly* October 1991: 43-85.

Ripley, John. Julius Caesar *on Stage, in England and America, 1599-1973*. Cambridge: Cambridge University Press, 1980.

Schoenbaum, Samuel. *Shakespeare, the Globe, and the World*. New York: Oxford University Press and the Folger Shakespeare Library, 1979.

Shapiro, I. A. "The Bankside Theatres: Early Engravings." *Shakespeare Survey* 1 (1948): 25-37.

Wright, Louis B. *Shakespeare's Theatre and the Dramatic Tradition*. Washington, D.C.: Folger Shakespeare Library, 1958.

"Julius Caesar thanks to Venus is turned into a comet" from Ovid's *Metamorphoses* (Antwerp, 1606).

When BRUTUS knew, AUGUSTUS part prevailed,
And saw his friends, lie bleeding on the ground,
Such deadly grief, his noble heart assailed,
That with his sword, he did him self confound:
But first, his friends persuaded him to flee,
Who answered thus, my flight with hands shall be.

And bending then to blade, his bared breast,
He did pronounce, these words with courage great:
Oh Prowess vain, I see, thou doest on fortune wait.
Wherefore with pain, I now do prove it true,
That fortunes force, may valiant hearts subdue.

Geoffrey Whitney, *A Choice of Emblemes*
Leiden (1586)

3

Elizabethan Legacies

Two Julius Caesars emerge from the history of the Western world: the sainted conqueror who brought civilization to barbarians, and the ambitious tyrant who subjugated people for his own glory. In the first interpretation, Brutus is a damned traitor, and in the second Brutus becomes a patriot. In literary and historical interpretation both characters mirror one another. At the moment of their deaths, Caesar and Brutus are represented according to the writer's cultural values. If Caesar's talents for organization and mental toughness are appreciated, his passing from human defeat to divine fame is a celebration of honor; if his capacities for ruthlessness and self-regard predominate, then his death brings relief. So with Brutus' demise: he is either shown as a Judas who betrayed his divine friend, or as a staunch defender of the many against the threats of the mighty.

This chapter will present some of the interpretations that influenced Shakespeare. It will trace some of the legacies that Elizabethan historians passed on to later writers. Although this material is sometimes difficult in style, it is important to a thorough understanding of the literary legends about Caesar. It is worth the interpretive challenge. One reason Caesar concerns the twentieth-century world is the extraordinary attention paid to his achievements and his mind. If his life meant anything to the heirs of Roman civilization, and if there are ideas worth preserving for the future, we should study the documents that preceded and followed Shakespeare's famous re-creation.

Shakespeare's major source for his dramatic portrait of Julius Caesar was the biography by Plutarch (A.D. 46-120). The version

Shakespeare read was filtered by English translations of several classical and modern languages that it passed through. Caesar and
Brutus received mixed reviews from Plutarch, who gave a fairly balanced account of them in his *Lives of the Noble Greeks and
Romans*. Dante, the medieval Christian apologist, harshly condemned Brutus and Cassius, putting them in the same category with
Judas, who had betrayed his master. Thomas Elyot, a follower of the
vigorous Henry VIII before his momentous break from Catholic obe-
dience, looked at Caesar with considerable sadness at his lost potential. Elyot's *The Governour* (1531) admiringly presented Caesar's
flaws almost as a warning to Henry, whereas John Higgens' *The
Mirrour for Magistrates* (1587) delighted in an imagined Caesar's
confessions of his sins, for the benefit of Queen Elizabeth's commonwealth. The *Mirrour for Magistrates* also came just before a dangerous moment in monarchical history, the 1588 invasion by the
Spanish armada. Philip II, king of Spain, sent a fleet of ships to attack
London and drive Elizabeth off the throne. Strategic maneuvering by
the smaller English vessels, plus some bad weather for the Spanish,
led to the complete ruin of the Catholic crusade against the
Protestants. The *Mirrour* provided support for a regime that happened to need moral as well as military defences.

Together, the reputation of these works might have impressed on
young Shakespeare that Julius Caesar was not dead in popular and
learned minds. His presumed acquaintance with Ovid's
Metamorphoses, at Stratford grammar school, provides another angle
on Caesar, the reverential one. Whether or not he turned with relief
or simple pleasure to Arthur Golding's 1567 translation of the Caesar
passages, he probably found poetic justification for combining the
political Caesar with the divinity. The same translator provided
Shakespeare's contemporaries with an autobiographical account
known as Caesar's *Commentaries*. What the general wrote about the
British phase of the Gallic Wars confirms the unusual interest in the
authorship of Caesar.

Just how much more mileage was left in the Caesar story after
Shakespeare's version is evident in the Caesar-and-Brutus episode
tucked into Jonathan Swift's *Gulliver's Travels* (1726). This satirical
masterpiece came a century after the 1623 Folio of Shakespeare's
works provided the first printed text of *Julius Caesar*. The full
extent of Caesar's tarnished glory will appear in the chapter on
popular culture.

CAESAR THE CONQUEROR

Caesar's conquest of Britain, although not as successful as that of William the Conqueror, the illegitimate Frenchman whose invasion in 1066 established a Gallic presence in English culture, was looked upon as a kind of forerunner. When Renaissance artists and monarchs sought the sources of their civilization, they tended to locate them in glorious empires that swept into Britain, were resisted, and then later embraced. Through a cultural marriage of Rome and Britain, it seemed that a new and invincible family was begun. Wherever there is a British town containing "-chester" (Gloucester, Worcester, Chester, and Chesterfield), there was once a Roman camp ("castrum"). The Latin name for a fortified town evolved through Old and Middle English into its present form.

The patriarch of military adventurers was Julius Caesar. In fact, he did take some time off from his conquest of the Gauls to make two expeditions across the Channel, but these were short incursions. That did not stop the legend-makers from attributing great works to Caesar. Shakespeare glances at the story that the Tower of London, a dominant fortress protecting the city, was actually a Roman structure. There are sinister overtones in his *Richard III* to the conversation among the murderous Duke of Gloucester, the Duke of Buckingham, and the young prince who stands in Richard's way.

> Gloucester: Your highness shall repose you at the Tower;
>   Then where you please, and shall be thought most fit
>   For your best health and recreation.
> Prince: I do not like the Tower of any place.
>   Did Julius Caesar build that place, my lord?
> Buckingham: He did, my gracious lord, begin that place.
>   Which, since, succeeding ages have re-edified.
> Prince: Is it upon record, or else reported
>   Successively from age to age, he built it?
> Buckingham: Upon record, gracious lord.
> Prince: But say, my lord, it were not regist'red,
>   Methinks the truth should live from age to age,
>   As 'twere retail'd to all posterity,
>   Even to the general all-ending day.
> Gloucester [aside]: So wise so young, they say do
>   never live long.
>   *Richard III* 3.1.65-79

The admitted process of building upon Roman foundations coincides with the passing down ("registering" and "retailing") of historical monuments. The prince's insight that truth would succeed even without historians is Shakespeare's deliberate way of making the doomed boy seem innocently wise.

ELIZABETHAN ROMAN HISTORY

To justify a curious cultural legacy of Rome to ancient Britain, historians embellished a legendary founding of the British commonwealth. Brut the Trojan (yet another Brutus appearing in the story of Julius Caesar) supposedly fled Rome after accidentally killing his father, who was none other than Aeneas' great-grandfather. As Geoffrey of Monmouth told the tale in his twelfth-century *History of the British Kingdom* (*Historia Regum Britanniae*), and as the exiled Elizabethan courtier Edmund Spenser elaborated in *The Faerie Queene* (3.9.48-51), this Brut bestowed the prestige of the hero of Troy, the founder of Rome—father Aeneas—upon the capital of the British race, in New Troy, otherwise known as London. He had to slay a few giants, defeat some wild natives, and with valor overcome the shame of being so clumsy with the bow that his arrows glanced off his intended target and killed his father. The line of kings descending from him led directly to Arthur, and the weight of that ancestry carried this fantastic tale into the realm of acceptable myth.

The fact that Julius Caesar actually invaded Britain gave credibility to the generally accepted poetic history. Documentary evidence rested on an ancient book in Geoffrey of Monmouth's possession. Queen Elizabeth was quite willing to play this game, since her Tudor ancestors claimed to come from the Welsh house of Arthur. Elizabethan "historians" of Rome were thus in the company of balladeers, poets, and storytellers. In *The Mirrour for Magistrates*, for instance, Caesar boasts of his Trojan heritage (see lines 110-12). Shakespeare's Roman (and British) history plays fit easily into this tradition of dramatized fiction. *Cymbeline* is set in ancient Roman Britain; *Titus Andronicus* in Rome with fictional characters; *Coriolanus* in Rome with "real" characters like Junius Brutus, a tribune who took the people's side against "the lonely dragon" *Coriolanus* (act 2, scene 1). Shakespeare took many of these details, and much of the bold spirit, from the same source that he consulted for *Julius Caesar*—Plutarch.

Shakespeare's Use of Plutarch's Lives

Plutarch's biography of Julius Caesar was the most famous of the many records available to Shakespeare. This Greek historian and moralist relied on information only about a century old, whereas Shakespeare worked from the distance of fifteen hundred years and two languages. Whether or not Shakespeare had enough classical and modern languages to read the original or its French version, he took the easier path of Thomas North's translation (1579). English was growing into a literary language with its own merits, and Renaissance scholars considered it almost patriotic to import the work of classical authors and improve on contemporary renderings.

Modern standards of reliable documentation and unbiased reporting belonged neither to the Elizabethan nor to the Roman world. Telling a good story and glorifying ethical traits were priorities that led to the inclusion of many anecdotes, rumors, guesses, and bloody deeds done for personal or imperial glory. The purpose was to teach lessons in social power by looking at how the greatest achievers clawed or schemed their way to the top and then plunged.

Shakespeare did not have to take sides for or against Caesar, any more than Plutarch did. The English playwright could take exciting details and adapt them to a glorious stage character battling worthy opponents and winning a hero's reputation despite his misfortunate death. Yet, Shakespeare did have to be careful not to appear to stir audiences into mutiny or to justify political rebellion. He managed to look evenhandedly at Caesar's potentially good and bad aspects. Reading Thomas North's translation of Plutarch confirmed the former actor Shakespeare's observation that a strong rivalry packed in both learned and uneducated playgoers.

Plutarch's *Parallel Lives of the Noble Greeks and Romans* presented an unbeatable plan for dramatizing history. Match a notable Roman with a worthy Greek: the orators Cicero and Demosthenes; city founders Romulus and Theseus; anti-tyrants Brutus and Dion of Syracuse. The English edition of Plutarch also included individual biographies, sometimes forming implicit comparisons; for example, Alexandar the Great is followed by Julius Caesar and preceded by the latter's rival, Pompey. Antony's life is paired with that of the Greek conqueror Demetrius.

Following the tradition of biographical contrast, the excerpts from the lives of Caesar and Brutus are presented side by side. You can examine how a skillful playwright took bits and pieces of Plutarch's life stories and made them into a drama of betrayed friendship–or is it prevented tyranny? Renaissance books showed readers where to look for important information by putting gloss notes in the margins. These are preserved in the following excerpts, so you can get a taste of what Shakespeare would have seen as he turned page after page after page of North's translation. Because indented paragraphs were seldom used in this huge book, the 1579 edition had to be navigated by other markers besides the marginal glosses. Names and places were italicized to help readers pick them out from the big blocks of print dominating the pages. Representing this style of printing will suggest where Shakespeare was alerted to noteworthy events, and what achievements he omitted. (To avoid confusing modern readers too much, the irregular spelling of Elizabethan English has been modernized throughout this chapter. After all, Shakespeare read Plutarch in the then-current style, just as we do today.)

When comparing the lives of Caesar and Brutus, imagine that you are looking over Shakespeare's shoulder as he skims the massive volume, searching for raw material. To aid your speculations about why he included and excluded what he did, the following list of main events will provide a third viewpoint.

CHRONOLOGY OF JULIUS CAESAR'S CAREER

102 B.C.	Born into an old noble family noted for privilege and anti-popular politics.
87 B.C.	Appointed priest of Jove by his uncle, Caius Marius, an enemy of Sulla and a supporter of the popular party.
83 B.C.	Married Cornelia, the rich daughter of Marius' colleague, Cinna.
82 B.C.	Lost priesthood, dowry, and property when he refused to divorce Cornelia, as Sulla commanded.
81-78 B.C.	Fled Rome to join army in Asia.
77 B.C.	Death of Sulla allowed Caesar to return to Rome where he continued his uncle's political career in the popular party eventually controlled by Pompey.
70 B.C.	Fought in Spain and helped Pompey become consul.
68 B.C.	Returned to Roman politics, prosecuting senators for bribery; Cornelia's death.
65 B.C.	Served as director of public works (aedile), notoriously erect-

ing statues of Marius in the Capitol.

63 B.C.   Elected chief priest; reformed the calendar from ten to twelve months, thus correcting accumulated discrepancies that had placed January in the autumn.

60 B.C.   Divorced second wife, Pompeia, after her involvement in a scandal; married Calpurnia.

59 B.C.   Organized an alliance with Pompey, Crassus, and himself (army chief, money bag, political operator) later known as the First Triumvirate ("three men"); married his daughter Julia to Pompey.

58-54 B.C.   Commanded the army suppressing the Gauls and Britons; Julia died, and Crassus the next year.

52 B.C.   Pompey drawn toward an exclusive Senate faction while Caesar hailed as military hero of the people; Caesar returned with his army.

49 B.C.   Challenged by Pompey and the Senate, Caesar began civil war when he crossed the Rubicon and marched on Rome; Senate fled and Pompey's army pressed to flee to Greece; Caesar assumed the office of dictator and was then elected consul; pursued Pompey in Greece.

48 B.C.   Defeated Pompey's army at Battle of Pharsalia; pursued Pompey to Egypt, instigating his assassination; became Cleopatra's lover and political supporter.

47 B.C.   Quickly defeated the Persians ("I came, I saw, I conquered") and quelled a mutiny; returned to wipe out Pompey's followers in Egypt; in Rome, as dictator and tribune of the people, staged four triumphal celebrations.

46-45 B.C.   Took his army to Spain to finish off Pompey's sons.

44 B.C.   Elected Consul for fifth time; made Dictator for life; planned war against Parthians while his former rivals agitated against him; conspirators assassinated him on the Ides of March (15th day of the month in the Julian calendar).

CHRONOLOGY OF MARCUS BRUTUS' CAREER

85 B.C.?   Born to his Marcus Junius Brutus and Servilia.

46 B.C.   Caesar appointed him governor of a province in Gaul, after pardoning him for allying with Caesar's rival in the civil war, Pompey.

44 B.C.   Became praetor at Rome and joined the conspiracy that

killed Caesar; after the assassination, the Senate sent him to Asia to import grain, and then it granted him command of troops in Macedonia, where he was joined by fellow conspirator Cassius.

43 B.C.   Condemned by a Roman law pressed by one of Caesar's relatives, the consul Quintus Pedius.

42 B.C.   Defeated by the forces of Octavian (later called Augustus Caesar) and Antony at the second battle of Philippi, October 23, after which he killed himself.

DIFFERENCES BETWEEN ACCOUNTS:

PLUTARCH	SHAKESPEARE
• No mention of Calpurnia's sterility	• Asserted in 1.2.6-9
• Admires Caesar's feasts, calendar reform	• [Ignored in *Julius Caesar*]
• Praises conspirators' solidarity	• Attributes their resolve to Brutus (2.1.112-40)
• Calpurnia explains her bad dream	• Decius interprets it favorably (2.2.83-103)
• Assassination in Pompey's theater	• In Senate-house of the Capitol (2.2.59; 2.4.19)
• Senate pardons the assassins	• Antony immediately begins his revenge by asking private pardon, over Caesar's body (3.1.254-75)
• Conspirators flee after Cinna's murder	• Brutus and Cassius escape murder before the Cinna incident shows popular rage (3.2.26-71)
• Two battles at Philippi	• One battle, with Brutus winning briefly (5.3.51)
• Antony honors Brutus' body with expensive armor	• Antony praises him; Octavius orders the military honors

FROM THOMAS NORTH'S TRANSLATION OF PLUTARCH'S *LIFE OF CAESAR* AND *LIFE OF BRUTUS* (1579)

Plutarch's *Life of Julius Caesar*

Caesar joined with Cinna and Marius.

AT what time *Sylla* was made Lord of all, he would have had *Caesar* put away his wife Cornelia, the daughter of *Cinna* Dictator: but when he saw, he could neither with any promise nor threat bring him to it, he took her jointer [1] away from him. The cause of *Caesar*'s will unto *Sylla*, was by means of marriage: for Marius the elder, married his father's own sister, by whom he had *Marius* the younger, whereby *Caesar* and he were cousin germans.[2] *Sylla* being troubled in weighty matters, putting to death so many of his enemies, when he came to be conqueror, he had no reckoning of *Caesar*: but he was not contented to be hidden in safety, but came and made suit unto the people for the Priesthoodship that was void, when he had scant any hair on his face. Howbeit he was repulsed by *Sylla's* means, that secretly was against him. Who, when he was determined to have killed him, some of his friends told him, that it was to no purpose to put so young a boy as he to death. But *Sylla* told them again, that they did not consider that there were many *Marians* in that young boy [...]*Caesar* being now returned out of AFRICA, first of all made an oration to the people, wherein he greatly praised and commended this his last victory, declaring unto them, that he had conquered so many countries unto the Empire of ROME, that he could furnish the commonwealth yearly, with two hundred thousand bushels of wheat, and twenty hundred thousand weight of oil. Then he made three triumphs, the one for EGYPT, the other for the kingdom of PONTUS, and the third for AFRICA: not because he had overcome *Scipio* there, but king *Juba*. [...]After these three triumphs ended, he very liberally rewarded his soldiers: and to curry favor with the people, he made great feasts and common sports. For he feasted all the ROMANS at one time, at two and twenty thousand tables, and gave them the pleasure to see diverse sword players to fight at the sharp, and battles also by sea, for the remembrance of his daughter *Julia*, which was dead long afore. Then after all these sports, he made the people (as the manner was) to be mustered: and where there were at the last musters before, three hundred and twenty thousand citizens, at this

Caesars feasting of the Romans.

The muster taken of the Romans.

1 dowry, the wealth given from wife to husband at marriage
2 close relatives

Plutarch's *Life of Marcus Brutus*

Marcus Brutus came of that *Junius Brutus*, for whom
the ancient ROMANS made his statue of brass to be set up
in the Capitol, with the images of the kings, holding a
naked sword in his hand: because he had valiantly put
down the TARQUINS from their kingdom of ROME. But
that *Junius Brutus* being of a sour stern nature, not softened by reason, being like unto sword blades of too hard a
temper: was so subject to his choler and malice he bare
unto tyrants, that for their sakes he caused his own sons to
be executed. But this *Marcus Brutus* in contrary manner,
whose life we presently write, having framed his manners
of life by the rules of virtue and study of Philosophy, and
having employed his wit, which was gentle and constant,
in attempting great things: if there were any noble attempt
done in all this conspiracy, they refer it wholly unto
Brutus, and all cruel and violent acts unto *Cassius*, who
was *Brutus* familiar friend, but not so well given, and conditioned as he...Now there were diverse sorts of
Praetorships at ROME, and it was looked for, that Brutus
or *Cassius* would make suit for the chiefest Praetorship,
which they called the Praetorship of the city: because he
that had that office, was as a Judge to minister justice unto
the citizens. Therefore they strove one against the other,
though some say that there was some little grudge between
them for other matters before, and that this contention did
set them further out, though they were allied together. For
Cassius had married *Junia*, *Brutus* sister. Others say, that
this contention between them came by *Caesar* himself,
who secretly gave either of them both hope of his favor. So
their suit for the Praetorship was so followed and labored
of either party, that one of them put another in suit of law.
Brutus with his virtue and good name contended against
many noble exploits in arms, which *Cassius* had done
against the PARTHIANS. So *Caesar* after he had heard
both their objections, he told his friends with whom he
consulted about the matter: *Cassius* cause is juster, said he,
but *Brutus* must be first preferred. Thus *Brutus* had the
first Praetorship, and *Cassius* the second: who thanked not
Caesar so much for the Praetorship he had, as he was
angry with him for that he had lost. But *Brutus* in many
other things tasted of the benefit of *Caesars* favor in any
thing he requested. For if he had listed, he might have been

*The parentage of
Brutus.*

Brutus manners.

*Brutus and
Cassius contend
for the Praetorship
of the city.*

*Cassius married
Junia, Brutus sis-
ter.*

*The first cause of
Cassius malice
against Caesar.*

Plutarch's *Life of Julius Caesar*

Caesar consul the
fourth time.

Battle fought
between Caesar
and the young
Pompeys, by the
city of Munda.

Caesars victory of
the sons of
Pompey.

Caesars triumph of
Pompeys sons.

muster only there were but a hundred and fifty thousand. Such misery and destruction had this civil war brought unto the commonwealth of ROME, and had consumed such a number of ROMANS not speaking at all of the mischiefs and calamities it had brought unto all the rest of ITALY, and to the other provinces pertaining to ROME. After all these things were ended, he was chosen Consul the fourth time, and went into SPAIN to make war with the sons of Pompey: who were yet but very young, but had manhood and courage worthy to command such an army, insomuch as they put *Caesar* himself in great danger of his life. The greatest battle that was fought between them in all this war, was by the city of MUNDA. For then *Caesar* seeing his men sorely distressed, and having their hands full of enemies: he ran into the press among his men that fought, and cried out unto them: what, are ye not ashamed to be beaten and taken prisoners, yielding yourselves with your own hands to these young boys? And so, with all the force he could make, having with much ado put his enemies to flight: he slew above thirty thousand of them in the field, and lost of his own men a thousand of the best he had. After this battle he went into his tent, and told his friends, that he had often fought for victory, but this last time now, he had fought for the safety of his own life. He won this battle on the very feastday of the BACCHANA-LIANS, in the which men say, that *Pompey* the great went out of ROME, about four years before, to begin this civil war. For his sons, the younger escaped from the battle: but within few days after, *Diddius* brought the head of the elder. This was the last war that *Caesar* made. But the triumph he made into ROME for the same, did as much offend the ROMANS, and more, then any thing that he had ever done before: because he had not overcome Captains that were strangers, nor barbarous kings, but had destroyed the sons of the noblest man in ROME, whom Fortune had overthrown. And because he had plucked up his race by the roots, men did not think it meet for him to triumph so, for the calamities of his country, rejoicing at a thing for which he had but one excuse to allege in his defence, unto the gods and men: that he was compelled to do that he did. And the rather they thought it not meet, because he had never before sent letters nor messengers unto the commonwealth at ROME, for any victory that he had ever won in all the civil wars: but did always for shame refuse the glory

Plutarch's *Life of Marcus Brutus*

one of *Caesars* closest friends, and of greatest authority and credit about him. Howbeit *Cassius* friends did dissuade him from it (for *Cassius* and he were not reconciled together since their first contention and strife for the Praetorship) and prayed him to beware of *Caesars* sweet enticements, and to flee his tyrannical favors: the which they said *Caesar* gave him, not to honor his virtue, but to weaken his constant mind, framing it to the bent of his bow. Now *Caesar* on the other side did not trust him overmuch, nor was not without tales brought unto him against him: howbeit he feared his great mind, authority and friends. Yet on the other side also, he trusted his good nature, and fair conditions. For, intelligence being brought one day, that *Antononius* and *Dolobella* did conspire against him: he answered, that these fat long haired men made him not afraid, but the lean and whitely faced fellows, meaning that, by *Brutus* and *Cassius*. At an other time also when one accused *Brutus* unto him, and bade him beware of him: What, said he again, clapping his hand on his breast: think ye that *Brutus* will not tarry till this body die? Meaning that none but *Brutus* after him was meet to have such power as he had. And surely, in my opinion, I am persuaded that *Brutus* might indeed have come to have been the chiefest man of ROME, if he could have contented himself for a time to have been next unto *Caesar*, and to have suffered his glory and authority, which he had gotten by his great victories, to consume with time. But *Cassius* being a choleric man, and hating *Caesar* privately, more then he did the tyranny openly: he incensed Brutus against him. It is also reported, that *Brutus* could evil away with[3] the tyranny, and that *Cassius* hated the tyranny: making many complaints for the injuries he had done him, and amongst others, for that he had taken away his Lions from him. *Cassius* had provided them for his sports, when he should be Aedilis, and they were found in the city of MEGARA, when it was won by *Calenus*, and *Caesar* kept them. The rumor went, that these Lions did marvelous great hurt to the MAGARIANS. For when the city was taken, they brake their cages where they were tied up, and turned them loose, thinking they would have done great mischief to the enemies, and have kept them from setting upon them: but the Lions contrary to expectations,

Caesar suspected Brutus.

Caesars saying of Brutus.

Cassius incenseth Brutus against Caesar.

Cassius Lions at Megara.

3 despise? That is, Brutus disliked the tyranny and Cassius hated the tyrant.

Plutarch's *Life of Julius Caesar*

of it. This notwithstanding, the ROMANS inclining to *Caesar's* prosperity, and taking the bit in the mouth, supposing that to be ruled by one man alone, it would be a good mean for them to take breath a little, after so many troubles and miseries as they had abided in these civil wars: they chose him perpetual Dictator. This was a plain tyranny: for to this absolute power of Dictator, they added this, never to be afraid to be deposed. *Cicero* propounded before the Senate, that they should give him such honors, as were meet for a man: howbeit others afterwards added to, honors beyond all reason. For, men striving who should most honor him, they made him hateful and troublesome to themselves that most favored him, by reason of the unmeasurable greatness and honors which they gave him. Thereupon, it is reported, that even they that most hated him, were no less favorers and furtherers of his honors, then they that most flattered him: because they might have greater occasions to rise, and that it might appear they had just cause and color to attempt that they did against him. And now for himself, after he had ended his civil wars, he did so honorably behave himself, that there was no fault to be found in him: and therefore me thinks, amongst other honors they gave him, he rightly deserved this, that they should build him a temple of clemency to thank him for his courtesy he had used unto them in his victory. For he pardoned many of them that had borne arms against him, and furthermore, did prefer some of them to honor and office in the commonwealth: as amongst others, *Cassius* and *Brutus*, both the which were made Praetors. And where Pompey's images had been thrown down, he caused them to be set up again: whereupon Cicero said then, that *Caesar* setting up *Pompeys* images again he made his own to stand the surer. And when some of his friends did counsell him to have a guard for the safety of his person, and some also did offer them selves to serve him: he would never consent to it, but said, it was better to die once, then always to be afraid of death. But to win him self the love and good will of the people, as the honorablest guard and best safety he could have: he made common feasts again, and general distributions of corn. Furthermore, to gratify the soldiers also, he replenished many cities again with inhabitants, which before had been destroyed, and placed them there that had no place to repair unto: of the which the noblest and chiefest cities were these two,

Caesar Dictator perpetual.

The temple of clemency, dedicated unto Caesar, for his courtesy.

Cassius and Brutus Praetors.

Caesars saying of death.

Good will of subjects, the best guard and safety for Princes.

Plutarch's *Life of Marcus Brutus*

turned upon themselves that fled unarmed, and did so cru-
elly tear some in pieces, that it pitied their enemies to see
them. And this was the cause, as some do report, that
Cassius conspire against *Caesar*. But this holdeth no
water. For *Cassius* even from his cradle could not abide
any manner of tyrants, as it appeared when he was but a
boy, and went unto the same school that *Faustus*, the son
of *Sylla* did. And *Faustus* bragging among other boys,
highly boasted of his fathers kingdom: *Cassius* rose up on
his feet, and gave him two good whirts on the ear. *Faustus*
governors would have put this matter in suit against
Cassius: But Pompey would not suffer them, but caused
the two boys to be brought before him, and asked them
how the matter came to pass. Then *Cassius*, as it is written
of him, said unto the other: go to *Faustus*, speak again and
thou darest, before this noble man here, the same words
that made me angry with thee, that my fists may walk once
again about thine ears. Such was *Cassius* hot stirring
nature. But for *Brutus*, his friends and countrymen, both
by diverse procurements, and sundry rumors of the city,
and by many bills also, did openly call and procure him to
do that he did. For, under the image of his ancestor *Junius
Brutus*, that drove the kings out of ROME, they wrote: O,
that it pleased the gods thou wert alive, *Brutus*: and again,
that thou wert here among us now. His tribunal (or chair)
where he gave audience during the time he was Praetor,
was full of such bills: *Brutus*, thou art asleep, and art not
Brutus indeed. And of all this, *Caesars* flatterers were the
cause: who beside many other exceeding and unspeakable
honors they daily devised for him, in the night time they
did put Diadems upon the heads of his images, supposing
thereby to allure the common people to call him king,
instead of Dictator. Howbeit it turned to the contrary, as
we have written more at large in *Julius Caesars* life. Now
when *Cassius* felt his friends, and did stir them up against
Caesar: they all agreed and promised to take part with him,
so *Brutus* were the chief of the conspiracy. For they told
him, that so high an enterprise and attempt as that, did not
so much require men of manhood, and courage to draw
their swords: as it stood them upon to have a man of such
estimation as *Brutus*, to make every man boldly think, that
by his only presence the fact were holy, and just. If he took
not this course, then that they should go to it with fainter
hearts, and when they had done it, they should be more

*Cassius an enemy
of tyrants.*

*How Brutus was
incensed against
Caesar.*

Plutarch's *Life of Julius Caesar*

CARTHAGE, and CORINTH, and it chanced so, that like as aforetime they had been both taken and destroyed together, even so were they both set afoot again, and replenished with people, at one self time. And as for great personages, he won them also, promising some of them, to make them Praetors and Consuls in time to come, and unto others, honors and preferments, but to all men generally good hope, seeking all the ways he could to make every man contented with his reign. Insomuch as one of the Consuls called Maximus, chancing to die a day before his

Caninius Rebilius Consul for one day.

Consulship ended, he declared *Caninius Rebilius* Consul only for the day that remained. So, divers going to his house (as the manner was) to salute him, and to congratulate him of his calling and preferment, being newly chosen officer: *Cicero* pleasantly said, come, let us make haste, and be gone thither, before his Consulship come out. Furthermore, *Caesar* being born to attempt all great enterprises, and having an ambitious desire besides to covet great honors: the prosperous good success he had of his former conquests bred no desire in him quietly to enjoy the fruits of his labors, but rather gave him hope of things to come, still kindling more and more in him, thoughts of greater enterprises, and desire of new glory, as if that which he had present, were stale and nothing worth. This humor of his was no other but an emulation with himself as with an other man, and a certain contention to overcome the things he prepared to attempt. For he was determined, and made preparation also, to make war with the PERSIANS. Then when he had overcome them, to pass through HYRCANIA (compassing the sea Caspium, and mount Caucasus) into the realm of PONTUS, and so to invade SCYTHIA: and overrunning all the countries, and people adjoining unto high GERMANY, and GERMANY itself, at length to return by GAUL into ITALY, and so to enlarge the ROMAN Empire round, that it might be every way compassed in with the great sea Oceanum. But whilst he was preparing this voyage, he attempted to cut the bar of the strait of PELOPONNESUS, in the place where the city of CORINTH standeth. Then he was minded to bring

Anienes. Tiber. flu.⁴

the rivers of Anienes and Tiber, straight from ROME, unto the city of CIRCEES, with a deep channel and high banks cast up on either side, and so to fall into the sea at TER-

---

4 "flumen" is the Latin word for "river"

Plutarch's *Life of Marcus Brutus*

fearful: because every man would think that *Brutus* would not have refused to have made one with them, if the cause had been good and honest. Therefore *Cassius* considering this matter himself, did first of all speak to *Brutus*, since they grew strange together for the suit they had for the Praetorship. So when he was reconciled to him again, and that they had embraced one another: *Cassius* asked him if he were determined to be in the Senate house, the first day of the month of March, because he heard say that *Caesars* friends should move the council that day, that *Caesar* should be called king by the Senate. *Brutus* answered him, he would not be there. But if we be sent for said *Cassius*: how then? For my self then said *Brutus,* I mean not to hold my peace, but to withstand it, and rather die than lose my liberty. *Cassius* being bold, and taking hold of this word: why, quoth he, what ROMAN is he alive that will suffer thee to die for the liberty? What, knowest thou not that thou art *Brutus*? Thinkest thou that they be cobblers, tapsters, or such like base mechanical people, that write these bills and scrolls which are found daily in my Praetors chair, and not the noblest men and best citizens that do it? No, be thou well assured, that of other Praetors they look for gifts, common distributions amongst the people, and for common plays, and to see sensors fight at the sharp, to shew the people pastime: but at thy hands, they specially require (as due debt unto them) the taking away of the tyranny, being fully bent to suffer any extremity for thy sake, so that thou wilt show thyself to be the man thou art taken for, and that they hope thou art. Thereupon he kissed *Brutus*, and embraced him: and so each taking leave of [the] other, they went both to speak with their friends about it. Now amongst *Pompeys* friends, there was one called **Caius Ligarius*, who had been accused unto *Caesar* for taking part with *Pompey*, and *Caesar* discharged him. But *Ligarius* thanked not *Caesar* so much for his discharge, as he was offended with him for that he was brought in danger by his tyrannical power. And therefore in his heart he was alway his mortal enemy, and was besides very familiar with *Brutus*, who went to see him being sick in his bed, and said unto him: O *Ligarius*, in what a time art thou sick? *Ligarius* rising upon his bed, and taking him by the right hand, said unto him: *Brutus*, said he, if thou hast any enterprise in hand worthy of thyself, I am whole. After that time they began to feel all their acquaintance whom they

Cassius praiseth Brutus first, to help him to put down the tyrant.

* In an other place they call him Quintus. Brutus maketh Ligarius one of the conspiracy.

Plutarch's *Life of Julius Caesar*

RACINA, for the better safety and commodity of the merchants that came to ROME to traffic there. Furthermore, he determined to drain and sieve all the water of the marshes betwixt the cities of NOMENTUM and SETIUM, to make it firm land, for the benefit of many thousands of people: and on the sea coast next unto ROME, to cast great high banks, and to cleanse all the haven about OSTIA, of rocks and stones hidden under the water, and to take away all other impediments that made the harbor dangerous for ships, and to make new havens and arsenals meet to harbor such ships, as did continually traffic thither. All these things were purposed to be done, but took no effect. But, the ordinance of the calendar, and reformation of the year, to take away all confusion of time, being exactly calculated by the Mathematicians, and brought to perfection, was a great commodity unto all men. For the ROMANS using then the ancient computation of the year, had not only such uncertainty and alteration of the month and times, that sacrifices and yearly feasts came by little and little to seasons contrary for the purpose they were ordained: but also in the revolution of the sun (which is called Annus Solaris) no other nations agreed with them in account: and of the ROMANS themselves, only the priests understood it. And therefore when they listed, they suddenly (no man being able to control them) did thrust in a month, above the ordinary number, which they called in old time, *Mercedonius. Some say, that *Numa Pompilius* was the first, that devised this way, to put a month between: but it was a weak remedy, and did little help the correction of the errors that were made in the account of the year, to frame them to perfection. But *Caesar* committing this matter unto the Philosophers, and best expert Mathematicians at that time, did set forth an excellent and perfect calendar, more exactly calculated, then any other that was before: the which the ROMANS do use until this present day, and do nothing err as others, in the difference of time. But his enemies notwithstanding that envied his greatness, did not stick to find fault withall. As *Cicero* the Orator, when one said, tomorrow the star Lyra will rise: yea, said he, at the commandment of *Caesar*, as if men were compelled so to say and think, by *Caesars* edict. But the chiefest cause that made him mortal hated, was the covetous desire he had to

Caesar reformed the inequality of the year.

* *Mercedonius,[5] mensis intercularis.*

5 "Mercedonius, an inter-calendar month"

Plutarch's *Life of Marcus Brutus*

trusted, and laid their heads together consulting upon it, and did not only pick out their friends, but all those also whom they thought stout enough to attempt any desperate matter, and that were not afraid to lose their lives. For this cause they durst not acquaint *Cicero* with their conspiracy, although he was a man whom they loved dearly, and trusted best: for they were afraid that he being a coward by nature, and age having also increased his fear, he would quite turn and alter all their purpose, and quench the heat of their enterprise, the which specially required hot earnest execution, seeking by persuasion to bring all things to such safety, as there should be no peril. *Brutus* also did let other of his friends alone, as *Statilius* EPICURIAN, and *Faonius*, that made profession to follow *Marcus Cato*. Because that having cast out words afar off, disputing together in Philosophy to feel their minds: *Faonius* answered, that civil war was worse than tyrannical government usurped against the law. And *Statilius* told him also, that it were an unwise part of him, to put his life in danger, for a sight of ignorant fools and asses. *Labeo* was present at this talk, and maintained the contrary against them both. But *Brutus* held his peace, as though it had been a doubtful matter, and a hard thing to have decided. But afterwards, being out of their company, he made *Labeo* privy to his intent: who very readily offered himself to make one. And they thought good also to bring in another *Brutus* to join with him, surnamed *Albinus*: who was no man of his hands himself, but because he was able to bring good force of a great number of slaves, and sensors at the sharp, whom he kept to show the people pastime with their fighting, besides also that *Caesar* had some trust in him. *Cassius* and *Labeo* told *Brutus Albinus* of at the first, but he made them no answer. But when he had spoken with *Brutus* himself alone, and that *Brutus* had told him he was the chief ringleader of all this conspiracy: then he willingly promised him the best aid he could. Furthermore, the only name and great calling of *Brutus*, did bring on the most of them to give consent to this conspiracy. Who having never taken oaths together, nor taken or given any caution or assurance, nor binding themselves one to another by any religious oaths: they all kept the matter so secret to themselves, and could so cunningly handle it, that notwithstanding the gods did reveal it by manifest signs and tokens from above, and by predictions of sacrifices: yet all this

They do hide the conspiracy against Caesar, from Cicero.

Civil war worse than tyrannical government.

The wonderful faith and secrecy of the Conspirators of Caesars death.

Plutarch's *Life of Julius Caesar*

be king: which first gave the people just cause, and next his secret enemies, honest color to bear him ill will. This notwithstanding, they that procured him this honor and dignity, gave it out among the people, that it was written in the Sibylline prophecies, how the ROMANS might overcome the PARTHIANS, if they made war with them, and were led by a king, but otherwise that they were unconquerable. And furthermore they were so bold besides, that *Caesar* returning to ROME from the city of ALBA, when they came to salute him, they called him king. But the people being offended, and *Caesar* also angry, he said he was not called king, but *Caesar*. Then every man keeping silence, he went his way heavy and sorrowful. When they had decreed diverse honors for him in the Senate, the Consuls and Praetors accompanied with the whole assembly of the Senate, went unto him in the market place, where he was set by the pulpit for orations, to tell him what honors they had decreed for him in his absence. But he sitting still in his majesty, disdaining to rise up unto them when they came in, as if they had been private men, answered them: that his honors had more need to be cut of, then enlarged. This did not only offend the Senate, but the common people also, to see that he should so lightly esteem of the Magistrates of the commonwealth: insomuch as every man that might lawfully go his way, departed thence very sorrowfully. Thereupon also *Caesar* rising, departed home to his house, and tearing open his doublet collar, making his neck bare, he cried out aloud to his friends, that his throat was ready to offer to any man that would come and cut it. Notwithstanding, it is reported, that afterwards to excuse this folly, he imputed it to his disease, saying, that their wits are not perfect which have his disease of the falling evil, when standing of their feet they speak to the common people, but are soon troubled with a trembling of their body, and a sudden dimness and giddiness. But that was not true. For he would have risen up to the Senate, but *Cornelius Balbus* one of his friends (but rather a flatterer) would not let him, saying: what, do you not remember that you are *Caesar*, and will you not let them reverence you, and do their duties? Besides these occasions and offenses, there followed also his shame and reproach, abusing the Tribunes of the people in this sort. At that time, the feast of Lupercal was celebrated, the which in old time men say was the feast of shepherds or

Why Caesar was hated.

The Feast Lupercalia.

Plutarch's *Life of Marcus Brutus*

would not be believed. Now *Brutus*, who knew very well that for his sake all the noblest, valiantest, and more courageous men of ROME did venture their lives, weighing with himself the greatness of the danger: when he was out of his house he did so frame and fashion his countenance and looks, that no man could discern he had any thing to trouble his mind. But when night came that he was in his own house, then he was clean changed. For, either care did wake him against his will when he would have slept, or else oftentimes of himself he fell into such deep thoughts of this enterprise, casting in his mind all the dangers that might happen: that his wife lying by him, found that there was some marvelous great matter that troubled his mind, not being wont to be in that taking, and that he could not well determine with himself. His wife *Porcia* (as we have told you before) was the daughter of *Cato*, whom *Brutus* married being his cousin, not a maiden, but a young widow after the death of her first husband *Bibulus*, by whom she had also a young son called *Bibulus*, who afterwards wrote a book of the acts and jests of *Brutus*, extant at this present day. This young Lady being excellently well seen in Philosophy, loving her husband well, and being of a noble courage, as she was also wise: because she would not ask her husband what he ailed before she had made some proof of herself, she took a little razor such as barbers occupy to pare mens nails, and causing all her maids to go out of her chamber, gave herself a great gash withal in her thigh, that she was straight all of a gore blood, and incontinently after, a vehement fever took her, by reason of the pain of her wound. Then perceiving her husband was marvelously out of quiet, and that he could take no rest: even in her greatest pain of all, she spake in this sort unto him. I being, O *Brutus*, (said she) the daughter of *Cato*, was married unto thee, not to be thy bedfellow and companion in bed and at board only, like a harlot: but to be partaker also with thee, of thy good and evil fortune. Now for thy self, I can find no cause of fault in thee touching our match: but for my part, how may I show my duty towards thee, and how much I would do for thy sake, if I can not constantly bear a secret mischance or grief with thee, which requireth secrecy and fidelity? I confess, that a woman's wit commonly is too weak to keep a secret safely: but yet, *Brutus*, good education, and the company of virtuous men, have some power to reform the defect of nature. And for myself, I

Porcia, Catos daughter, wife unto Brutus.

Bibulus book of Brutus acts. Porcia studied in Philosophy. The courage of Porcia.

Great difference betwixt a wife and a harlot. Porcias words unto her husband Brutus.

Plutarch's *Life of Julius Caesar*

herdsmen, and is much like unto the feast of the
LYCAEIANS in ARCADIA. But howsoever it is, that day
there are diverse noble mens sons, young men, (and some
of them Magistrates themselves that govern then) which
run naked through the city, striking in sport them they
meet in their way, with leather thongs, here and all on, to
make them give place. And many noble women, and gen-
tlewomen also, go of purpose to stand in their way, and do
put forth their hands to be stricken, as scholars hold them
out to their schoolmaster, to be stricken with the ferula:
persuading themselves that being with child, they shall
have good delivery, and also being barren, that it will make
them to conceive with child. *Caesar* sat to behold that
sport upon the pulpit for orations, in a chair of gold, appar-
elled in triumphing manner. *Antonius*, who was Consul at
that time, was one of them that ran this holy course. So
when he came into the market place, the people made a
lane for him to run at liberty, and he came to *Caesar*, and
presented him a Diadem wreathed about with laurel.
Whereupon there rose a certain cry of rejoicing, not very
great, done only by a few, appointed for the purpose. But
when *Caesar* refused the Diadem, then all the people
together made an outcry of joy. Then *Antonius* offering it
him again, there was a second shout of joy, but yet of a
few. But when *Caesar* refused it again the second time,
then all the whole people shouted. *Caesar* having made
this proof, found that the people did not like of it, and
thereupon rose out of his chair, and commanded the crown
to be carried unto *Jupiter* in the Capitol. After that, there
were set up images of *Caesar* in the city with Diadems
upon their heads, like kings. Those, the two Tribunes,
Flavius and *Marullus*, went and pulled down: and furthermore, meeting with them that first saluted *Caesar* as king,
they committed them to prison. The people followed them
rejoicing at it, and called them *Brutes*: because of *Brutus*,
who had in old time driven the kings out of ROME, and
that brought the kingdom of one person, unto the government of the Senate and people. *Caesar* was so offended
withall, that he deprived *Marullus* and *Flavius* of their
Tribuneships, and accusing them, he spake also against the
people, and called them *Bruti*, and *Cumani*, to wit, beasts,
and fools. Hereupon the people went straight unto *Marcus
Brutus*, who from his father came of the first *Brutus*, and
by his mother, of the house of the *Servilians*, a noble house

*Antonius being
Consul, was one of
the Lupercalians.*

*Antonius present-
ed the Diadem to
Caesar.*

Plutarch's *Life of Marcus Brutus*

have this benefit moreover: that I am the daughter of *Cato*, and wife of *Brutus*. This notwithstanding, I did not trust to any of these things before: until that now I have found by experience, that no pain nor grief whatsoever can overcome me. With those words she showed him her wound on her thigh, and told him what she had done to prove herself. *Brutus* was amazed to hear what she said unto him, and lifting up his hands to heaven, he besought the gods to give him the grace he might bring his enterprise to so good pass, that he might be found a husband, worthy of so noble a wife as *Porcia*: so he then did comfort her the best he could. Now a day being appointed for the meeting of the Senate, at what time they hoped *Caesar* would not fail to come: the conspirators determined then to put their enterprise in execution, because they might meet safely at that time without suspicion, and the rather, for that all the noblest and chiefest men of the city would be there. Who when they should see such a great matter executed, would every man then set to their hands, for the defence of their liberty. Furthermore, they thought also that the appointment of the place where council should be kept, was chosen of purpose by divine providence, and made all for them. For it was one of the porches about the Theater, in the which there was a certain place full of seats for men to sit in, where also was set up the image of *Pompey*, which the city had made and consecrated in honor of him: when he did beautify that part of the city with the Theater he built, with diverse porches about it. In this place was the assembly of the Senate appointed to be, just on the fifteenth day of the month of March, which the ROMANS call, Idus Martias: so that it seemed some god of purpose had brought *Caesar* thither to be slain, for revenge of *Pompeys* death. So when the day was come, *Brutus* went out of his house with a dagger by his side under his long gown, that nobody saw nor knew, but his wife only. The other conspirators were all assembled at *Cassius* house, to bring his son into the marketplace, who on that day did put on the mans gown, called Toga Virilis: and from thence they came all in a troupe together unto *Pompeys* porch, looking that *Caesar* would straight come thither. But here is to be noted, the wonderful assured constancy of these conspirators, in so dangerous and weighty an enterprise as they had undertaken. For many of them being Praetors, by reason of their office, whose duty is to minister justice to

The wonderful constancy of the conspirators, in killing of Caesar.

Plutarch's *Life of Julius Caesar*

Caesar saved Marcus Brutus life, after the battle of Pharsalia.

Brutus conspireth against Caesar.

Cassius stirreth up Brutus against Caesar.

Predictions, and foreshows of Caesars death.

as any was in ROME, and was also nephew and son in law of *Marcus Cato*. Notwithstanding, the great honors and favor *Caesar* showed unto him, kept him back that of himself alone, he did not conspire nor consent to depose him of his kingdom. For *Caesar* did not only save his life, after the battle of Pharsalia when *Pompey* fled, and did at his request also save many more of his friends besides: but furthermore, he put a marvelous confidence in him. For he had already preferred him to the Praetorship for that year, and furthermore was appointed to be Consul, the fourth year after that, having through *Caesars* friendship, obtained it before *Cassius*, who likewise made suit for the same: and *Caesar* also, as it is reported, said in this contention, indeed *Cassius* hath alleged best reason, but yet shall he not be chosen before *Brutus*. Some one day accusing *Brutus* while he practiced this conspiracy, *Caesar* would not hear of it, but clapping his hand on his body, told them, *Brutus* will look for this skin: meaning thereby, that *Brutus* for his virtue, deserved to rule after him, but yet, that for ambitions sake, he would not show himself unthankful nor dishonorable. Now they that desired change, and wished *Brutus* only their Prince and Governor above all other: they durst not come to him themselves to tell him what they would have him do, but in the night did cast sundry papers into the Praetors seat where he gave audience, and most of them to this effect. Thou sleepest *Brutus*, and art not *Brutus* indeed. *Cassius* finding *Brutus* ambition stirred up the more by these seditious bills, did prick him forward, and egg him on the more, for a private quarrel he had conceived against *Caesar*: the circumstance whereof, we have set down more at large in *Brutus* life. *Caesar* also had *Cassius* in great jealousy, and suspected him much: whereupon he said on a time to his friends, what will *Cassius* think you? I like not his pale looks. Another time *Caesars* friends complained unto him of *Antonius*, and *Dollabella,* that they pretended some mischief towards him: he answered them again, as for those fat men and smooth combed heads, quoth he, I never reckon of them: but these pale visaged and carrion lean people, I fear them most, meaning *Brutus* and *Cassius*. Certainly, destiny may easier be foreseen, then avoided: considering the strange and wonderful signs that were said to be seen before *Caesars* death. For, touching the fires in the element, and spirits running up and down in the night, and

Plutarch's *Life of Marcus Brutus*

everybody: they did not only with great quietness and courtesy hear them that spake unto them, or that pleaded matters before them, and gave them attentive care, as if they had had no other matter in their heads: but moreover, they gave just sentence, and carefully dispatched the causes before them. So there was one among them, who being condemned in a certain sum of money, refused to pay it, and cried out that he did not appeal unto *Caesar*. Then *Brutus* casting his eyes upon the conspirators, said, *Caesar* shall not let me to see the law executed. Notwithstanding this, by chance there fell out many misfortunes unto them, which was enough to have marred the enterprise. The first and chiefest was, *Caesars* long tarrying, who came very late into the Senate: for because the signs of the sacrifices appeared unlucky, his wife *Calpurnia* kept him at home, and the Soothsayers bade him beware he went not abroad. The second cause was, when one came unto *Casca* being a conspirator, and taking him by the hand, said unto him: O *Casca*, thou keptest it close from me, but *Brutus* hath told me all. *Casca* being amazed at it, he went on with his tale, and said: why, how now, how cometh it to pass thou art thus rich, that thou dost sue to be Aedilis? Thus *Casca* being deceived by the others doubtful words, he told them it was a thousand to one, he blabbed not out all the conspiracy. Another Senator called *Popilius Laena*, after he had saluted *Brutus* and *Cassius* more friendly then he was wont to do: he rounded softly in their ears, and told them, I pray the gods you may go through with that you have taken in hand, he presently departed from them, and left them both afraid that their conspiracy would out. Now in the meantime, there came one of *Brutus* men post haste unto him, and told him his wife was dying. For *Porcia* being very careful and pensive for that which was to come, and being too weak to [do] away with so great and inward grief of mind: she could hardly keep within, but was frighted with every little noise and cry she heard, as those that are taken and possessed with the fury of the Bacchantes, asking every man that came from the market place, what *Brutus* did, and still sent messenger after messenger, to know what news. At length, *Caesars* coming being prolonged as you have heard, *Porcias* weakness was not able to hold out any longer, and thereupon she suddenly swounded, that she had no leisure to go to her chamber, but was taken in the middest of her house, where her

Sundry misfortunes to have broken off the enterprise.

The weakness of Porcia, notwithstanding her former courage.

Plutarch's *Life of Julius Caesar*

Caesars day of his death prognosticated by a Soothsayer.

also these solitary birds to be seen at noon days sitting in the great market place: are not all these signs perhaps worth the noting, in such a wonderful chance as happened. But *Strabo* the Philosopher writeth, that diverse men were seen going up and down in fire: and furthermore, that there was a slave of the soldiers, that did cast a marvelous burning fire out of his hand, insomuch as they that saw it, thought it had been burnt, but when the fire was out, it was found he had no hurt. *Caesar* [him]self also doing sacrifice unto the gods, found that one of the beasts which was sacrificed had no heart: and that was a strange thing in nature, how a beast could live without a heart. Furthermore, there was a certain Soothsayer had given *Caesar* warning long time affore, to take heed of the day of the Ides of March, (which is the fifteenth of the month) for on that day he should be in great danger. That day being come, *Caesar*

The dream of Calpurnia, Caesars wife.

before going unto the Senate house, and speaking merrily to the Soothsayer, told him, the Ides of March be come: so they be, softly answered the Soothsayer, but yet are they not past. And the very day before, *Caesar* supping with *Marcus Lepidus*, sealed certain letters as he was wont to do at the board: so talk falling out amongst them, reasoning what death was best: he preventing their opinions, cried out aloud, death unlooked for. Then going to bed the same night as his manner was, and lying with his wife *Calpurnia*, all the windows and doors of his chamber flying open, the noise awoke him, and made him afraid when he saw such light: but more, when he heard his wife *Calpurnia*, being fast asleep, weep and sigh, and put forth many stumbling lamentable speeches. For she dreamed that *Caesar* was slain, and that she had him in her arms. Others also do deny that she had any such dream, as

Decius Brutus Albinus persuasion to Caesar.

amongst other, *Titus Livius* writeth, that it was in this sort. The Senate having set upon the top of *Caesars* house, for an ornament and setting forth of the same, a certain pinnacle: *Calpurnia* dreamed that she saw it broken down, and that she thought she lamented and wept for it. Insomuch that *Caesar* rising in the morning, she prayed him if it were possible, not to go out of the doors that day, but to adjourn the session of the Senate, until another day. And if that he made no reckoning of her dream, yet that he would search further of the Soothsayers by their sacrifices, to know what should happen [to] him that day. Thereby it seemed that *Caesar* likewise did fear and suspect somewhat, because

Plutarch's *Life of Marcus Brutus*

speech and senses failed her. Howbeit she soon came to herself again, and so was laid in her bed, and tended by her women. When *Brutus* heard these news, it grieved him, as it is to be presupposed: yet he left not of the care of his country and commonwealth, neither went home to his house for any news he heard. How, it was reported that *Caesar* was coming in his litter: for he determined not to stay in the Senate all that day (because he was afraid of the unlucky signs of the sacrifices) but to adjourn matters of importance unto the next session and counsel holden, faining himself not to be well at ease. When *Caesar* came out of his litter: *Popilius Lena*, that had talked before with *Brutus* and *Cassius*, and had prayed the gods they might bring this enterprise to pass: went unto *Caesar*, and kept him a long time with a talk. *Caesar* gave good ear unto him. Wherefore the conspirators (if so they should be called) not hearing what he said to *Caesar*, but conjecturing by that he had told a little before, that his talk was none other but the very discovery of their conspiracy: they were afraid every man of them, and one looking in anothers face, it was easy to see that they all were of a mind, that it was no tarrying for them till they were apprehended, but rather that they should all kill themselves with their own hands. And when *Cassius* and certain other clapped their hands on their swords under their gowns to draw them: *Brutus* marking the countenance and gesture of *Laena*, and considering that he did use himself rather like an humble and earnest suitor, then like an accuser: he said nothing to his companion (because there were many amongst them that were not of the conspiracy) but with a pleasant countenance encouraged *Cassius*. And immediately after, *Laena* went from *Caesar* and kissed his hand: which showed plainly that it was for some matter concerning himself, that he had held him so long in talk. Now all the Senators being entered first into this place or chapter house where the council should be kept: all the other conspirators straight stood about *Caesars* chair, as if they had had some thing to have said to him. And some say, that *Cassius* casting his eyes upon *Pompeys* image, made his prayer unto it, as if it had been alive. *Tribonius* on the other side, drew *Antonius* at one side, as he came into the house where the Senate sat, and held him with a long talk without. When *Caesar* was come into the house, all the Senate rose to honor him at his coming in. So when he was set, the con-

Brutus with his countenance encouraged his fearful consorts.

* *In Caesars life it is said, it was Decius Brutus Albinus, that kept Antonius with a talk without.*

Plutarch's *Life of Julius Caesar*

his wife *Calpurnia* until that time, was never given to any fear or suspicion: and then, for that he saw her so troubled in mind with this dream she had. But much more afterwards, when the Soothsayers having sacrificed many beasts one after another, told him that none did like them: then he determined to send *Antonius* to adjourn the session of the Senate. But in the meantime came *Decius Brutus*, surnamed *Albinus*, in whom *Caesar* put such confidence, that in his last will and testament he had appointed him to be his next heir, and yet was of the conspiracy with *Cassius* and *Brutus*: he fearing that if *Caesar* did adjourn the session that day, the conspiracy would out, laughed the Soothsayers to scorn, and reproved *Caesar*, saying: that he gave the Senate occasion to mislike with him, and that they might think he mocked them, considering that by his commandment they were assembled, and that they were ready willingly to grant him all things, and to proclaim him king of all the provinces of the Empire of ROME out of ITALY, and that he should wear his Diadem in all other places, both by sea and land. And furthermore, that if any man should tell them from him, they should depart for that present time, and return again when *Calpurnia* should have better dreams: what would his enemies and ill willers say, and how could they like of his friends words? And who could persuade them otherwise, but that they would think his dominion a slavery unto them, and tyrannical in himself? And yet if it be so, that you utterly mislike of this day, it is better that you go yourself in person, and saluting the Senate, to dismiss them till another time. Therewithal he took *Caesar* by the hand, and brought him out of his house. *Caesar* was not gone far from his house, but a bondman, a stranger, did what he could to speak with him: and when he saw he was put back by the great press and multitude of people that followed him, he went straight unto his house, and put himself into *Calpurnias* hands to be kept, till *Caesar* came back again, telling her that he had great matters to impart unto him. And one *Artemidorus* also born in the Isle of GNIDOS, a Doctor of Rhetoric in the Greek tongue, who by means of his profession was familiar with certain of *Brutus* confederates, and therefore knew the most part of all their practices against *Caesar*: came and brought him a little bill written with his own hand, of all that he meant to tell him. He marking how *Caesar* received all the supplications that were offered

Decius Brutus brought Caesar into the Senate house.

The tokens of the conspiracy against Caesar.

The place where Caesar was slain.

Antonius, Caesars faithful friend.

Plutarch's *Life of Marcus Brutus*

spirators flocked about him, and amongst them they presented one *Tullius Cimber*, who made humble suit for the calling home again of his brother that was banished. They all made as though they were intercessors for him, and took him by the hands, and kissed his head and breast. *Caesar* at the first, simply refused their kindness and entreaties: but afterwards, perceiving they still pressed on him, he violently thrust them from him. Then *Cimber* that stood behind him, drew his dagger first, and strake *Caesar* upon the shoulder, but gave him no great wound. *Caesar* feeling himself hurt, took him straight by the hand he held his dagger in, and cried out in Latin: O traitor, *Casca*, what doest thou? *Casca* on the other side cried in Greek, and called his brother to help him. So diverse running on a heap together to fly upon *Caesar*, he looking about him to have fled, saw *Brutus* with a sword drawn in his hand ready to strike at him: then he let *Cascas* hand go, and casting his gown over his face, suffered every man to strike him that would. Then the conspirators thronging one upon another because every man was desirous to have a cut at him, so many swords and daggers lighting upon one body, one of them hurt another, and among them *Brutus* caught a blow on his hand, because he would make one in murdering of him, and all the rest also were every man of them bloodied. *Caesar* being slain in this manner, *Brutus* standing in the midst of the house, would have spoken, and stayed the other Senators that were not of the conspiracy, to have told them why they had done this fact. But they as men both afraid and amazed, fled upon anothers neck in haste to get out at the door, and no man followed them. For it was set down, and agreed between them, that they should kill no man but *Caesar* only, and should entreat all the rest to look to defend their liberty. All the conspirators, but *Brutus* determining upon this matter, thought it good also to kill *Antonius*, because he was a wicked man, and that in nature favored tyranny: besides also, for that he was in great estimation with soldiers, having been conversant of long time amongst them: and specially, having a mind bent to great enterprises, he was also of great authority at that time, being Consul with *Caesar*. But *Brutus* would not agree to it. First, for that he said it was not honest: secondly, because he told them there was hope of change in him. For he did not mistrust, but that *Antonius* being a noble minded and courageous man (when he should know that

In Caesars life he is called Metellus Cimber.

The murder of Caesar.

Casca the first that wounded Caesar.

Why Antonius was not slain with Caesar.

Plutarch's *Life of Julius Caesar*

him, and that he gave them straight to his men that were about him, pressed nearer to him, and said: *Caesar*, read this memorial to yourself, and that quickly, for they be matters of great weight and touch you nearly. *Caesar* took it of him, but could never read it, though he many times attempted it, for the number of people that did salute him: but holding it still in his hand, keeping it to himself, went on withall into the Senate house. Howbeit other are of opinion, that it was some man else that gave him that memorial, and not *Artemidorus*, who did what he could all the way as he went to give it *Caesar*, but he was always

Casca, the first that strake at Caesar.

repulsed by the people. For these things, they may seem to come by chance: but the place where the murder was prepared, and where the Senate were assembled, and where also there stood up an image of *Pompey* dedicated by himself amongst other ornaments which he gave unto the Theater: all these were manifest proofs that it was the ordinance of some god, that made this treason to be executed, specially in that very place. It is also reported, that *Cassius* (though otherwise he did favor the doctrine of *Epicurus*) beholding the image of *Pompey*, before they entered into the action of their traitorous enterprise: he did softly call upon it, to aid him. But the instant danger of the present time, taking away his former reason, did suddenly put him into a furious passion, and made him like a man half besides himself. Now *Antonius*, that was a faithful friend to *Caesar*, and a valiant man besides of his hands, him, *Decius Brutus Albinus* entertained out of the Senate house, having begun a long tale of set purpose. So *Caesar* coming into the house, all the Senate stood up on their feet to do him honor. Then part of *Brutus* company and confederates stood round about *Caesars* chair, and part of them also came towards him, as though they made suit with *Metellus Cimber*, to call home his brother again from banishment: and thus prosecuting still their suit, they followed *Caesar*,

Caesar slain and had 23 wounds upon him.

till he was set in his chair. Who, denying their petitions, and being offended with them one after another, because the more they were denied, the more they pressed upon him, and were the earnester with him: *Metellus* at length, taking his gown with both his hands, pulled it over his neck, which was the sign given the confederates to set upon him. Then *Casca* behind him strake him in the neck with his sword, howbeit the wound was not great nor mortal, because it seemed, the fear of such a devilish attempt

Plutarch's *Life of Marcus Brutus*

Caesar was dead) would willingly help his country recover her liberty, having them an example unto him, to follow their courage and virtue. So *Brutus* by this means saved *Antonius* life, who at that present time disguised himself, and stole away. But *Brutus* and his consorts, having their swords bloody in their hands, went straight to the Capitol, persuading the ROMANS as they went, to take their liberty again. Now, at the first time when the murder was newly done, there were sudden outcries of people that ran up and down the city, the which indeed did the more increase the fear and tumult. But when they saw they slew no man, neither did spoil or make havoc of any thing: then certain of the Senators, and many of the people emboldening themselves, went to the Capitol unto them. There a great number of men being assembled together one after another: *Brutus* made an oration unto them to win the favor of the people, and to justify that they had done. All those that were by, said they had done well, and cried unto them that they should boldly come down from the Capitol. Whereupon, *Brutus* and his companions came boldly down into the market place. The rest followed in a troop, but *Brutus* went foremost, very honorably compassed in round about with the noblest men of the city, which brought him from the Capitol, through the market place, to the pulpit for orations. When the people saw him in the pulpit, although they were a multitude of rakehells of all sorts, and had a good will to make some stir: yet being ashamed to do it for the reverence they bear unto *Brutus*, they kept silence, to hear what he would say. When *Brutus* began to speak, they gave him quiet audience: howbeit immediately after, they showed that they were not all contented with the murder. For when another called *Cinna* would have spoken, and began to accuse *Caesar*: they fell into a great uproar among them, and marvelously reviled him. Insomuch that the conspirators returned again into the Capitol. There *Brutus* being afraid to be besieged, sent back again the noble men that came with him, thinking it no reason, that they which were no partakers of the murder, should be partakers of the danger. Then the next morning the Senate being assembled, and holden within the temple of the goddess *Tellus*, to wete[6] the earth: and *Antonius, Plancus*, and *Cicero*, having made a motion to

Brutus with his consorts went unto the Capitol.

6 that is to say

Plutarch's *Life of Julius Caesar*

did amaze him, and take his strength from him, that he killed him not at the first blow. But *Caesar* turning straight unto him, caught hold of his sword, and held it hard: and they both cried out, *Caesar* in Latin: O vile traitor *Casca*, what doest thou? And *Casca* in Greek to his brother, brother, help me. At the beginning of this stir, they that were present, not knowing of the conspiracy were so amazed

The murderers of Caesar go to the Capitol.

with the horrible sight they saw: that they had no power to fly, neither to help him, not so much, as once to make any outcry. They on the other side that had conspired his death, compassed him in on every side with their swords drawn in their hands, that *Caesar* turned him nowhere, but he was stricken at by some, and still had naked swords in his face, and was hacked and mangled among them, as a wild beast taken of hunters. For it was agreed among them, that every man should give him a wound, because all their parts should be in this murder: and then Brutus himself gave him a wound about his privities. Men report also, that *Caesar* did still defend himself against the rest, running every way with his body: but when he saw *Brutus* with his sword drawn in his hand, then he pulled his gown over his head, and made no more resistance, and was driven either casually, or purposefully, by the council of the conspirators, against the base whereupon *Pompeys* image stood, which ran all of a gore blood, till he was slain. Thus it seemed, that the image took just revenge of *Pompeys* enemy, being thrown down on the ground at his feet, and yielding up his ghost there, for the number of wounds he had upon him. For it is reported, that he had three and twenty wounds

Caesars funerals.

upon his body: and diverse of the conspirators did hurt themselves, striking one body with so many blows. When *Caesar* was slain, the Senate (though *Brutus* stood in the midst amongst them as though he would have said somewhat touching this fact) presently ran out of the house, and flying, filled all the city with marvelous fear and tumult. Insomuch as some did shut their doors, others forsook their shops and warehouses, and others ran to the place to see what the matter was: and others also that had seen it, ran home to their houses again. But *Antonius* and *Lepidus*, which were two of *Caesars* chiefest friends, secretly con-

Cinnas dream of Caesar.

veying themselves away, fled into other mens houses, and forsook their own. *Brutus* and his confederates on the other side, being yet hot with this murder they had committed, having their swords drawn in their hands, came all

Plutarch's *Life of Marcus Brutus*

the Senate in that assembly, that they should take an order
to pardon and forget all that was past, and to establish
friendship and peace again: it was decreed, that they
should not only be pardoned, but also that the Consuls
should refer it to the Senate what honors should be
appointed unto them. This being agreed upon, the Senate
brake up, and *Antonius* the Consul, to put them in heart
that were in the Capitol, sent them his son for a pledge.
Upon this assurance, *Brutus* and his companions came
down from the Capitol, where every man saluted and
embraced each other, among the which, *Antonius* himself
did bid *Cassius* to supper to him: and *Lepidus* also bade
Brutus, and so one bade another, as they had friendship
and acquaintance together. The next day following, the
Senate being called again to council, did first of all command *Antonius*, for that he had wisely stayed and quenched
the beginning of a civil war: then they also gave *Brutus*
and his consorts great praises, and lastly they appointed
several governments of provinces. For unto *Brutus*, they
appointed CRETA: AFRIC, unto *Cassius*: ASIA, unto
Trebonius: BITHYNIA, unto *Cimber*: and unto the other
Decius Brutus Albinus, GAUL on this side the Alps. When
this was done, they came to talk of *Caesars* will and testament, and of his funerals and tomb. Then *Antonius* thinking good his testament should be read openly, and also that
his body should be honorably buried, and not in hugger
mugger, lest the people might thereby take occasion to be
worse offended if they did otherwise: *Cassius* stoutly
spake against it. But *Brutus* went with the motion, and
agreed unto it: wherein it seemeth he committed a second
fault. For the first fault he did was, when he would not
consent to his fellow conspirators, that *Antonius* should be
slain: And therefore he was justly accused, that thereby he
had saved and strengthened a strong and grievous enemy
of their conspiracy. The second fault was, when he agreed
that *Caesars* funerals should be as *Antonius* would have
them: the which indeed marred all. For first of all, when
Caesars testament was openly read among them, whereby
it appeared that he bequeathed unto every Citizen of
ROME, 75. Drachmas a man, and that he left his gardens
and arbors unto the people, which he had on this side of the
river of Tiber, in the place where now the temple of
Fortune is built: the people then loved him, and were marvelous sorry for him. Afterwards when *Caesars* body was

*Honors decreed
for the murderers
of Caesar.*

*Caesars will, and
funerals.*

*Brutus committed
two great faults
after Caesars
death.*

Plutarch's *Life of Julius Caesar*

The murder of Cinna.

Caesar 56 year old at his death.

Cassius being overthrown at the battle of Philippes, slew himself with the self same sword wherewith he strake Caesar. Wonders seen in the element 7 after Caesars death. A great comet.

Brutus vision.

in a troupe together out of the Senate, and went into the market place, not as men that made countenance to flee, but otherwise boldly holding up their heads like men of courage, and called to the people to defend their liberty, and stayed to speak with every great personage whom they met in their way. Of them, some followed this troupe, and went amongst them, as if they had been of the conspiracy, and falsely challenged part of the honor with them: among them was *Caius Octavius* and *Lentulus Spinther*. But both of them were afterwards put to death, for their vain covetousness of honor, by *Antonius* and *Octavius Caesar* the younger: and yet had no part of that honor for the which they were put to death, neither did any man believe that they were any of the confederates, or of counsel with them. For they that did put them to death, took revenge rather of the will they had to offend, then of any fact they had committed. The next morning, *Brutus* and his confederates came into the market place to speak unto the people, who gave them such audience, that it seemed they neither greatly reproved, nor allowed the fact: for by their great silence they showed, that they were sorry for *Caesars* death, and also that they did reverence *Brutus*. Now the Senate granted general pardon for all that was past, and to pacify every man, ordained besides, that *Caesars* funerals should be honored as a god, and established all things that he had done: and gave certain provinces also, and convenient honors unto *Brutus* and his confederates, whereby every man thought all things were brought to good peace and quietness again. But when they opened *Caesars* testament, and found a liberal legacy of money, bequeathed unto every citizen of ROME, and that they saw his body (which was brought into the market place) all bemangled with gashes of swords: then there was no order to keep the multitude and common people quiet, but they plucked up forms, tables, and stools, and laid them all about the body, and setting them afire, burnt the corpse. Then when the fire was well kindled, they took the firebrands, and went unto their houses that had slain *Caesar*, to set them afire. Other also ran up and down the city to see if they could meet any of them, to cut them in pieces: howbeit they could meet never a man of them, because they had locked themselves up safely in their houses. There was one of *Caesars* friends called *Cinna*, that had a marvelous strange and terrible dream the night before. He dreamed that *Caesar* bade

Plutarch's *Life of Marcus Brutus*

brought into the market place, *Antonius* making his funeral oration in praise of the dead, according to the ancient custom of ROME, and perceiving that his words moved the common people to compassion: he framed his eloquence to make their hearts yearn the more, and taking *Caesars* gown all bloody in his hand, he laid it open to the sight of them all, showing what a number of cuts and holes it had upon it. Therewithal the people fell presently into such a rage and mutiny, that there was no more order kept amongst the common people. For some of them cried out, kill the murderers: others plucked up forms, tables, stalls about the market place, as they had done before at the funerals of *Claudius*, and having laid them all on a heap together, they set them on fire, and thereupon did put the body of *Caesar*, and burnt it in the middest of the most holy places. And furthermore, when the fire was thoroughly kindled, some here, some there, took burning fire brands, and ran with them to the murderers houses that had killed him, to set them afire. Howbeit the conspirators foreseeing the danger before, had wisely provided for themselves, and fled. But there was a Poet called *Cinna*, who had been no partaker of the conspiracy, but was alway[s] one of *Caesars* chiefest friends: he dreamed the night before, that *Caesar* bade him to supper with him, and that he refusing to go, *Caesar* was very importunate with him, and compelled him, so that at length he led him by the hand into a great dark place, where being marvelously afraid, he was driven to follow him in spite of his heart. This dream put him all night into a fever, and yet notwithstanding, the next morning when he heard that they carried *Caesars* body to burial, being ashamed not to accompany his funerals: he went out of his house, and thrust himself into the press of the common people that were in great uproar. And because some one called him by his name, *Cinna*: the people thinking he had been that *Cinna*, who in an oration he made had spoken very evil of *Caesar*, they falling upon him in their rage, slew him outright in the market place. This made *Brutus* and his companions more afraid, then any other thing, next unto the change of *Antonius*. Wherefore they got them out of ROME, and kept at the first place in the city of ANTIUM, hoping to return again to ROME, when the fury of the people were a little assuaged. The which they hoped would be quickly, considering that they had to deal with a fickle and uncon-

Antonius funeral oration for Caesar.

The strange dream of Cinna the Poet.

The murder of Cinna the Poet mistaken for another of that name.

Brutus and his consorts do flee from Rome.

Plutarch's *Life of Julius Caesar*

him to supper, and that he refused, and would not go: then that *Caesar* took him by the hand, and led him against his will. Now *Cinna* hearing at that time, that they burnt *Caesars* body in the market place, notwithstanding that he feared his dream, and had an ague on him besides: he went into the market place to honor his funerals. When he came thither, one of the mean sort asked what his name was? He was straight called by his name. The first man told it to another, and that other unto another, so that it ran straight through them all, that he was one of them that murdered *Caesar*: (for indeed one of the traitors to *Caesar*, was also called *Cinna* himself) wherefore taking him for *Cinna* the *Cinnas dream of* murderer, they fell upon him with such fury, that they *Caesar.* presently dispatched him in the market place. This stir and fury made *Brutus* and *Cassius* more afraid, then of all that was past, and therefore within few days after, they departed out of ROME: and touching their doings afterwards, and what calamity they suffered till their deaths, we have written it at large, in the life of *Brutus*. *Caesar* died at six and fifty years of age: and *Pompey* also lived not passing four years more than he. So he reaped no other fruit of all his reign and dominion, which he had so vehemently desired all his life, and pursued with such extreme danger: but a vain name only, and a superficial glory, that procured *The murder of* him the envy and hatred of his country. But his great pros- *Cinna.* perity and good fortune favored him all his life time, did continue afterwards in the revenge of his death, pursuing the murderers both by sea and land, till they had not left a man more to be executed, of all them that were actors or counsellors in the conspiracy of his death. Furthermore, of all the chances that happen unto men upon the earth, that *Caesar 56 year old* which came to *Cassius* above all other, is most to be won- *at his death.* dered at. For he being overcome in battle at the journey of Philippes, slew himself with the same sword, with the which he strake *Caesar*. Again, of signs in the element,[7] the great comet which seven nights together was seen very bright after *Caesars* death, the eight[h] night after was never seen more. Also the brightness of the sun was darkened, the which all that year through rose very pale, and shined not out, whereby it gave but small heat: therefore the air being very cloudy and dark, by the weakness of the heat that could not come forth, did cause the earth to bring

7 the heavens

Plutarch's *Life of Marcus Brutus*

stant multitude, easy to be carried, and that the Senate
stood for them: who notwithstanding made no inquiry of
them that had torn poor *Cinna* the Poet in pieces, but
caused them to be sought for and apprehended, that went
with fire brands to set fire of the conspirators houses...

[Antony pursues Brutus into Greece.] Furthermore,
Brutus thought that there was no great number of men slain
in battle, and to know the truth of it, there was one called
Statilius, that promised to go through his enemies (for otherwise it was impossible to go see their camp) and from
thence if all were well, that he would lift up a torch light in
the air, and then return again with speed to him. The torch
light was lift up as he had promised, for *Statilius* went
thither. Now *Brutus* seeing *Statilius* tarry long after that,
and that he came not again, he said: if *Statilius* be alive, he
will come again. But his evil fortune was such, that as he
came back, he lighted in his enemies hands, and was
slain. Now, the night being spent, *Brutus* as he sat bowed
towards *Clitus* one of his men, and told him somewhat in
his ear, the other answered him not, but fell aweeping.
Thereupon he proved *Dardanus*, and said somewhat also
to him: at length he came to *Volumnius* himself, and speaking to him in Greek, prayed him for the studies sake which
had brought them acquainted together, that he would help
him to put his hands to his sword, to thrust it in him to kill
him. *Volumnius* denied his request, and so did many others: and amongst the rest, one of them said, there was no
tarrying for them there, but that they must needs fly. Then
Brutus rising up, we must fly indeed said he, but it must be
with our hands, not with our feet. Then taking every man
by the hand, he said these words unto them with a cheerful
countenance. It rejoiceth my heart that not one of my
friends hath failed me at my need, and I do not complain of
my fortune, but only for my countrys sake: for, as for me, I
think myself happier than they that have overcome, considering that I leave a perpetual fame of our courage and manhood, the which our enemies the conquerors shall never
attain unto by force nor money, neither can let their posterity to say, that they being naughty and unjust men, have
slain good men, to usurp tyrannical power not pertaining to
them. Having said so, he prayed every man to shift for
themselves, and then he went a little aside with two or
three only, among the which *Strato* was one, with whom
he came first acquainted by the study of Rhetoric. He came

*The death of
Statilius.*

*Brutus saying of
flying with his
hands, and not
with feet.*

Plutarch's *Life of Julius Caesar*

forth but raw and unripe fruit, which rotted before it could ripe. But above all, the ghost that appeared unto *Brutus* showed plainly, that the gods were offended with the murder of *Caesar*. The vision was thus. *Brutus* being ready to pass over his army from the city of ABYDOS, to the other coast lying directly against it, slept every night (as his manner was) in his tent, and being yet awake, thinking of his affairs: (for by report he was as careful a Captain, and lived with as little sleep, as ever man did) he thought he heard a noise at his tent door, and looking towards the light of the lamp that waxed very dim, he saw a horrible vision of a man, of a wonderful greatness, and dreadful look, which at the first made him marvelously afraid. But when he saw that it did him no hurt, but stood by his bed side, and said nothing: at length he asked him what he was. The image answered him: I am thy ill angel, *Brutus*, and thou shalt see me by the city of PHILIPPES. Then *Brutus* replied again, and said: well, I shall see thee then. Therewithal, the spirit presently vanished from him. After that time *Brutus* being in battle near unto the city of PHILLIPES, against *Antonius* and *Octavius Caesar*, at the first battle he won the victory, and overthrowing all them that withstood him, he drove them into young *Caesars* camp, which he took. The second battle being at hand, this spirit appeared again unto him, but spake never a word. Thereupon *Brutus* knowing he should die, did put himself to all hazard in battle, but yet fighting could not be slain. So seeing his men put to flight and over thrown, he ran unto a little rock not far off, and there setting his swords point to his breast, fell upon it, and slew himself, but yet as it is reported, with the help of his friend, that dispatched him.

The end of Caesars life.

Plutarch's *Life of Marcus Brutus*

as near to him as he could, and taking his sword by the hilts with both his hands, and falling down upon the point of it, ran himself through. Others say, that not he, but *Strato* (at his request) held the sword in his hand, and turned his head aside, and that *Brutus* fell down upon it: and so ran himself through, and died presently. *Messala,* that had been *Brutus* great friend, became afterwards *Octavius Caesars* friend. So, shortly after, *Caesar* being at good leisure, he brought *Strato, Brutus* friend unto him, and weeping said: *Caesar*, behold, here is he that did the last service to my *Brutus*. *Caesar* welcomed him at that time, and afterwards he did him as faithful service in all his affairs, as any GRAECIAN else he had about him, until the battle of ACTIUM. It is reported also, that this *Messala* himself answered *Caesar* one day, when he gave him great praise before his face, that he had fought valiantly, and with great affection for him, at the battle of ACTIUM: (notwithstanding that he had been his cruel enemy before, at the battle of PHILIPPES, for *Brutus* sake) I ever loved, said he, to take the best and justest part. Now, *Antonius* having found *Brutus* body, he caused it to be wrapped up in one of the richest coat armors he had. Afterwards also, *Antonius* understanding that this coat armor was stolen, he put the thief to death that had stolen it, and sent the ashes of his body unto *Servilia* his mother. And for *Porcia*, *Brutus* wife: *Nicolaus* the Philosopher, and *Valerius Maximus* do write, that she determining to kill herself (her parents and friends carefully looking to her to keep her from it) took hot burning coals, and cast them into her mouth, and kept her mouth so close, that she choked herself. There was a letter of *Brutus* found written to his friends, complaining of their negligence, that his wife being sick, they would not help her, but suffered her to kill herself, choosing to die, rather then to languish in pain. Thus it appeareth, that *Nicolaus* knew not well that time, since the letter (at the least if it were *Brutus* letter) doth plainly declare the disease and love of this lady, and also the manner of her death.

Brutus slew himself. Strato, Brutus familiar and friend.

Strato received into Caesars friendship.

Messala Corvinus, Brutus friend.

Brutus funerals.

Porcia, Brutus wife, killed herself with burning coals.

MILITARY CAESAR

Julius Caesar's military reputation preceded his political fame. Shakespeare assumes his learned audience's familiarity with the author of the so-called Commentaries on the Roman campaign in Gaul. A typical patron was the country minister William Harrison, author of a geographical and social history entitled *The Description of England* (1587), who cites Caesar as an authority. Caesar wrote about himself in the third person, boastfully perhaps in the eyes of modern readers, but Elizabethan heirs of Roman traditions excused this self-congratulation in a great general. Shakespeare's audience of relatively uneducated workers, the groundlings, still had plenty to crow about concerning Caesar's exploits. His legions subdued the French, a fact that exalted him in the stout hearts of Englishmen who had cheered the warrior king in Shakespeare's *Henry V*.

The significance of Caesar's *Gallic Wars* surfaces when Antony reminisces to the crowd about the first time the now fallen Caesar donned his battle cloak, in a campaign against a Belgian tribe (3.2.17-73). This part of the war against various Franco-Germanic people came just before Caesar launched his troops against British tribes. Shakespeare diverts attention from Caesar's triumph over English "barbarians" by targeting the French. However, the invasion across the Channel, its supply, and the military strategies forced by fierce, chariot-driving fighters all point to another reason for being acquainted with these commentaries. They celebrate the young Caesar's decisiveness, boldness, and good fortune. When Shakespeare causes the old Caesar to declare that he will not attend the Senate simply because he wills it (2.2.71), and then shows him being flattered into changing his mind by Decius Brutus, the readers of *The Gallic Wars* would shake their heads. As in the case of other commanders turned into politicians—Othello, for instance—Caesar's military career hinders his civic effectiveness. The difference between what he could do in the field and what he is constrained to do in the Capitol highlights his tragic vulnerablility.

In the following passage, preceded by the original title of the translation, notice Caesar's confident assessment of the geographical conditions of Britain. He constantly weighs military advantages against the problems of the terrain. His keen perception of social customs such as blue-dyed bodies ultimately describes the frightfulness of these fighters, whom he admires as if they were wild animals.

FROM ARTHUR GOLDING'S TRANSLATION OF CAESAR'S *GALLIC WARS*
(1565)

THE EIGHT BOOKES OF CAIUS JULIUS CAESAR CONTAINING HIS MAR-
TIAL EXPLOITS IN THE REALM OF GALLIA AND THE COUNTRIES BOR-
DERING UPON THE SAME

The inner part of Britain is inhabited of such as by witness of their aun-
cient records were born and bred in the Isle: and the sea coast by such as
have passed thither out of Belgicke to fetch booties and to make war: All
the which well near, are called by the same names that the Cities are
where they were born and from whence they first came, remaining there
still when the war was done, and tilling the ground. The country is marvelously well replenished with people, and there be very many buildings
almost like in fashion to the buildings of Gallia. There is great store of cattle. The coin that they use, is either brass, or else rings of iron filed at a certain weight in stead of money. In the inner parts of the Realm groweth tin:
and in the sea coast groweth iron: but hereof is small store. The brass that
they occupy is brought in from the sea. There is timber of all kinds as in
Gallia saving Beech and Fir. They think it a heinous matter to taste of a
hare, and a hen, and a goose. Nevertheless they cherish them for their
minds sake and for their pleasure. The air is more temperate in those
places than in France, and the cold lesser. The island is in fashion three-
cornered, whereof one side is toward France. The one corner of this side
which is in Kent where for the most part ships arrive out of France, is
toward the East: and the other nethermore is toward the South. This side
containeth about five hundred miles. Another side lieth towards Spain and
the sun going down: on the which side is Ireland less then Britain (as is
supposed) by the one half. But the cut between them is a like distance as is
the cut between France and Britain. In the middest of this course is an
Island called Man. Also there are reported to be many more less Isles about
Britain: of the which Isles, some have written that in the winter season
when the days are shortest, the nights are a full month longer together. We
could learn nothing by inquiry: but we saw it tried by hourglasses of water,
that the nights were shorter there, then in the firm land. The length of this
side is (according to the opinion of the inhabiters) seven hundred miles.
The third side is northward: and against it lieth no land: but the point of
that side butteth most toward Germany. This they esteem to be eight hundred miles long. And so the circuit of the whole Island is two thousand
miles. Of all the inhabitants of this Isle the civilest are the Kentishfolk, the
which country marcheth altogether upon the sea, and differeth not greatly
from the manner of France. Those that dwell more into the heart of the
Realm, for the most part sew no corn: but live by milk and flesh, and clothe

themselves in leather. All the Britons do dye themselves with wood, which setteth a bluish color upon them: and it maketh them more terrible to behold in battle. They wear their hair long, and shave all parts of their bodies saving the head and the upper lip. They have ten or twelve wives apiece, common among themselves, specially brothers with brothers, and Parents with their children. But the issue that cometh of them, is accounted his that first married the mother when she was a maid.

The horsemen and wagoners of our enemies gave a hot skirmish to our men by the way: but yet in such wise, that our men were every way too good for them, and drove them into the woods and hills: howbeit by following them overgreedily we lost divers of our company. But they after taking breath a while, when our men thought of no such thing, as they were busy in fortifying their Camp, suddenly burst out of the woods, and giving a charge upon them that were set toward before our camp, fought eagerly with them: insomuch that Caesar was fain to send two Cohorts, and those the chief of two Legions, to the rescue: the which being placed but a little way one from another. When our men began to be discouraged at the strange kind of fight, [they] brake through the midst of our enemies by fine force, and recovered them thence safe. The same day was Quintus Laberius Durus the Tribune slain: and yet by sending many Cohorts to the rescue: our enemies were put to the worse. In all this kind of conflict forasmuch as it was fought in the sight of all men and in the open face of our camp, it was perceived that our men by reason of the weight of their armor, for that they could neither pursue them when they gave back, nor durst depart from their antesigns [standards, flags carried before the troops], were not meet enough to encounter with such a kind of enemy: and that the men of arms could not fight, but in great peril, because our enemies would many a time and often lose ground for the nonce, and when they had edged our men a little from the main battle, would leap out of their chariots and fight afoot, which was an unequal match. And they kept such an order in their fighting on horseback, that whither our men fled or chased, they were always in like danger. For they never fought in great companies together, but scattering a great way of one from another, and had stales [secondary fighters] lying in divers place one to serve anothers turn, and fresh and lusty men always in the rooms of such as were weary.

The next day the enemies stood aloof in the hills far from our camp: and showed themselves here a few and there a few, and began to assail our horsemen more faintly than they had done the day before. But about midday, when Caesar had sent forth a Lieutenant of his called Caius Trebonius with three Legions, and all his men of arms for forage, suddenly they came flying upon the foragers on all sides, in such sort that they would not [go] from our Legions and our Antesigns. Howbeit our men laid so sore to their charge that they put them to the foil, and never left pursuing them, until such time as our horsemen taking courage upon the aid when they saw the footmen at hand behind them, drove their enemies headlong, and slew a great number of them, giving them no respite either to gather themselves together, or to stay any where, or to leap out of their Chariots. Immediately upon this discomfiture, such as were assembled from all quarters to aid in this war, departed: neither did our enemies at any time after that, encounter with us with their whole power. Caesar having knowledge of their intent, marched with his army to the Thames, into the Seniory of Cassibelan. This river can be passed but only in one place afoot and that very hardly. When he came thither, he saw a great power of his enemies in battle array on the other side of the river. Now was the bank sticked full of stakes sharpened at the fore end, and likewise other stakes of the same making were driven in the channel and hidden with the water. Caesar having understanding hereof by his prisoners and runaways, sent in his horsemen before, and commanded his footmen to follow immediately after them. But our soldiers went with such speed and force having no more than their heads above the water, that the enemy being not able to withstand the violence of our footmen and men of arms, forsook the banks and took them to flight. Cassibelan (as is above mentioned) dispairing of his good success by fighting in plain battle, sent away all his greater powers, and keeping still a four thousand waggoners watched which way we went, and drew somewhat aside out of the way, hiding himself in cumbersome and woody places: and where so ever he knew our men should march, he drove both cattle and people from thence into the woods. And when our horsemen ravaged any thing freely abroad into the fields for forage or to harry the country, he sent his waggoners by all ways and paths out of the woods upon our men of arms and encountered with them to their great prejudice: through the fear whereof he kept them short from ranging at their pleasure. So the matter was brought to this pass, that Caesar would not suffer his horsemen to stray any farness from his main battle of footmen, and adventured no further to annoy his enemies in wasting their fields, and burning their houses, than he was able to compass by the travail of his footmen as they were able to foray.

In the meanwhile, the Trinobantes, which is the strongest City well near of all those countries, (out of the which City a young gentleman called Mandubrace upon confidence of Caesars help coming unto him into the main land of Gallia, had escaped death by flight which he should have suffered at Cassibelans hand, as his father Imanuence had done, who had reigned in that City), sent Ambassadors to Caesar, promising to yield unto him and to do as he should command them: and they desired him to defend Mandubrace from the tyranny of Cassibelan, and to send him into the City, to take the government and sovereignty thereof upon him. Caesar assessed them at forty hostages, and besides that, to find grain for his army: and he sent Mandubrace unto them. They executed his commandment out of hand, and sent him both his full number of hostages, and also grain for his army. When Caesar had defended the Trinobantes, and saved them harmless from his soldiers, the Cenimagues, Segontians, Avcalits, Bibrokes, and Cassians sending Ambassadors to Caesar yielded them selves unto him. By them he learned that not far from the same place was Cassibelans town fortified with woods and marisgrounds [marshes]: into the which was gathered a great number of men and cattle. Now the Britons call it a Town, when they have fortified a cumbersome wood with a ditch and a Rampire [rampart]: and thither they they report to eschew the invasions of their enemies. To this place marched Caesar with his Legions, he found it excellently well fortified both by nature and by mans device. Nevertheless he intended to give assault unto it in two places at once. Our enemies after they had tarried a while, being not able to endure the force of our men, fled out at another part of the town. A great number of cattle was found there, and many being taken in the chase, were slain.

While these things were a doing in these quarters, Cassibelan sent messengers into Kent, (which we showed before to lie upon the sea, in the which country were four kings, Cingetorix, Carvill, Tarimagull, and Segonar) commanding them to raise all the power they could make, and suddenly to set upon and assault our camp by the sea side. As soon as they came to our camp our men breaking out upon them slew a great sort of them, and taking Cingetorix their noble captain, prisoner, conveyed themselves back again in safety. When Cassibelan heard of this battle, for as much as he had taken so many losses, and had had his country wasted, but chiefly moved with the rebellion of the Cities, sent Ambassadors by Comius of Arras to Caesar to entreat with him of submission. Caesar in as much as he had determined to pass the winter in the firm land because of the sudden commotions in Gallia, and for that there remained not much of the summer, the which he perceived, might easily be trifled out by his enemies: commanded to send him hostages, and assessed the Realm of Britain, at a yearly tribute to be paid to the people of Rome: giving slight charge and commandment to Cassibelan, that he did no displeasure to Mandubrace nor to the Trinobants. As soon as he had received the hostages, he conveyed his army again to the sea, where he found his ships repaired. When he had set them afloat again, for as much as he had a great number of prisoners and many of his ships were perished by tempest, he determined to ferry over his army at two convoys. And so it chanced that of so great a fleet, at so many voyages, neither this year nor the year before there was not any one ship missing that carried over our soldiers: but of those that should have been sent back again empty from the mainland when they had set the soldiers of the first convoy ashore, and of those that

Labienus caused afterward to be made, which were to the number of three-score, very few could attain the place, and all the rest were cast back. The which when Caesar had awhile tarried for in vain, lest through the season of the year he might be disappointed of sailing, because the Equinoctial was at hand, he was fain to pack up his soldiers in less room closer together. And so taking the opportunity of a very calm weather that ensued, he launched forth in the beginning of the second watch, and by the break of the day came safe to land with all his whole fleet.

Book 5, chapters 13-23 [in modern editions]; Folio 115-22, in the *Short Title Catalog* microfilm (STC 4335, reel 488).

POLITICAL CAESAR

Much advice to sixteenth- and seventeenth-century English princes referred to the mighty path that Caesar cut through the world of politics, which at the time meant not the electoral process of modern democratic states, but the control exercised by the monarchy over ambitious noblemen, restless merchant-adventurers, devout and powerful churchmen, an explosive though economically depressed yeomanry of farmers and displaced workers, and other domestic forces that struggled with Henry, Elizabeth, and James during Shakespeare's cultural memory.

GOVERNOR CAESAR

Shakespeare could have gleaned some knowledge of Julius Caesar from the books written during Henry VIII's reign. Thomas Elyot (1490-1546) was educated in the traditions of classical languages and literatures that today are called humanism. His study of Latin and Italian works that taught how to cultivate rulers—among them Cicero's and Quintilian's treatises on public speaking, Castiglione's study of the ideal courtier—interested the internationally acclaimed scholar Erasmus and his English friend, Thomas More. Whereas the Lord Chancellor More defied King Henry (1491-1547) over the question of the Pope's versus the English King's authority, Elyot befriended the Henry, who was nearly his exact contemporary. Elyot's *The Governour*, a manual on statecraft, or how to govern according to the experience of ancient rulers like Julius Caesar, won him an ambassadorship to the German court of the Holy Roman Emperor, Charles V, while Thomas More, for his painful conscience, went to the executioner's block.

Sir Thomas Elyot interested the dramatist Shakespeare not at all, though the latter was probably familiar with a book as popular as *The Governour*. Sir Thomas More attracted Shakespeare enough for him to contribute to an unpublished play dating from about the time he wrote *Julius Caesar*. Elyot's influence on Shakespeare was slight, but nevertheless intriguing, since Elyot compiled the first Latin-English dictionary (1538), which was expanded by another humanist, Thomas Cooper, into the *Thesaurus* (1565). This was the sort of reference Shakespeare would have relied on when his grammar-school Latin faltered.

Elyot propped up Caesar's reputation and denigrated Brutus'. Elyot's references to Caesar consolidated the humanists' praise and blame. Shakespeare knew that earlier generations of scholars deeply admired Caesar's military and political decisiveness, eloquent writing, and princely charm. They also were dismayed at his stubborn pride, leading to personal carelessness. A prudent monarch should not throw his life away, yet Caesar ignored warnings. Elyot also drew the curious lesson that assassins, even in striking divinely-approved blows, are never honored. Shakespeare's closing eulogies of Brutus, by his sworn enemies Antony and Octavius, are therefore opposed to the Elyot tradition.

FROM SIR THOMAS ELYOT'S *THE GOVERNOUR* (1531)

[Book 2, chapter 5] Of Affability, and the Utility Thereof in Every Estate

But I had almost forgotten Julius Caesar, who being not able to sustain the burden of Fortune, and envying his own felicity, abandoned his natural disposition, and as it were being drunken with overmuch wealth, sought new ways how to be advanced above the estate of mortal princes: wherefore little and little he withdrew from men his accustomed gentleness, becoming more sturdy in language, and strange in countenance than ever before had been his usage. And to declare more plainly his intent, he made an edict or decree, that no man should please to come to him uncalled: and that they should have good await, that they spake not in such familiar fashion to him, as they before had been accustomed: whereby he so did alienate from him the hearts of his most wise and assured adherents, that from that time forward, his life was to them tedious: and abhorring him as a monster or common enemy, they being knit in a confederacy, slew him sitting in the Senate: of which conspiracy was chief captain Marcus Brutus, whom of all other he best loved, for his great wisdom and prowess. And it is of some writers, that he was begotten of Caesar: for as much as Caesar in his youth loved Servilia, the mother of Brutus: and as men supposed, used her more familiarly than honesty required. Thus Caesar by omitting his old affability, did incend his next friends and companions to slay him.

But now take heed what damage ensued to him by his decree, wherein he commanded, that no man should be so hardy to approach or speak to him. One which knew of the conspiracy again him, and by all likelihood did participate therein, being moved either with love or pity, or otherwise his conscience remording again the destruction of so noble a prince, considering that by Caesars decree he was prohibited to have to him any familiar access, so that he might not plainly detect the conspiracy, he thereto vehemently moved, wrote in a bill all the form thereof: with the means how it might be espied, and since he might find none other opportunity, he delivered the bill to Caesar the same day that his death was prepared, as he went toward the place, where the Senate was holden. But he being radicate in pride, and neglecting to look on that bill, not esteeming the person that delivered it, which perchance was but of a mean behavior: continued his way to the Senate: where he incontinently was slain by the said Brutus, and many mo[re] of the Senate for that purpose appointed.

Who beholding the cause of the death of this most noble Caesar, unto whom in eloquence, doctrine, martial prowess, and gentleness, no prince may be compared, and the acceleration or haste to his confusion caused by his own edict or decree, will not commend affability, and extol liberty of speech? Whereby only love is in the hearts of people perfectly kindled, all fear excluded, and consequently realms, dominions, and all other authorities consolidate and perpetually established. The sufferance of noblemen to

be spoken unto, is not only to them an incomparable surety, but also a confounder of repentance, enemy to prudence, whereof is engendered this word Had I wist [known], which hath been ever of all wise men reproved.
. . .

[Book 3, chapter 6] Of faith or fidelity, called in Latin Fides, which is the foundation of justice.

In what hatred and perpetual reproach ought they to be, that corrupted with pestilential avarice or ambition, betrayed their masters, or any other that trusteth them? O what monstrous persons have we read and heard of. Which for the inordinate and devilish appetite to reign, have most tyrannously slain the children, not only their sovereign lords, but also of their own natural brethren, committed unto their governance? Of whom purposely I leave at this time to write: to the intent that the most cursed remembrance of them shall not consume the time that the well disposed reader might occupy the examples of virtue.

This thing I would were remembered: that by the just providence of god, disloyalty or treason seldom escapeth great vengeance: All be it be pretended for a necessary purpose. Example we have of Brutus and Cassius, two noble Romans: and men of excellent virtues. Which pretending an honorable zeal to the liberty and commonweal of their city, slew Julius Caesar (who trusted them most of all other) for that he usurped to have the perpetual dominion of the empire, supposing thereby to have brought the senate and people to their pristinate liberty. But it did not so succeed to their purpose. But by the death of so noble a prince happened confusion and civil battles: And both Brutus and Cassius after long wars, vanquished by Octavian, nephew and heir unto Caesar, at the last falling into extreme desperation, slew themselves. A worthy and convenient vengeance for the murder of so noble and valiant a prince.

CAESAR'S CONFESSION

Compared to Elyot's balanced view of Caesar's faults and virtues, the character invented for *The Mirrour for Magistrates* is a deluded politician. He could not see where his fortunes led him—toward ruin. This formula of a talented but unstable leader's demise was taken from the fourteenth-century Italian humanist Giovanni Boccaccio's "On the Falls of Illustrious Men" and adapted to every principal ruler of the English Renaissance: Henry, Mary, Elizabeth, and James. Each version selectively looked back on previous bad examples, and effectively summarized the behavior that princes should try to avoid.

The 1587 version of the *Mirrour,* by John Higgens, includes Caesar's autobiography. Because the author employed the same poetic meter and "rhyme royal" of previous *Mirrours,* the effect sounds a little strange, even to modern readers of Shakespeare's blank verse. We must remember that the 1587 *Mirrour* was composed as poetry, rather than as verse for the just-developing popular stage. Shakespeare tried his hand at this refined and supposedly noble stanza, which Chaucer had mastered in his *Troilus and Criseyde* (about 1375), and practiced skills that would guide his *Caesar* characters. The *ababbcc* rhyming pattern and something of the elevated style of rhyme royal are evident in this stanza from *The Rape of Lucrece* (1594). Brutus, the tyrant-removing ancestor of Caesar's killer, is swearing vengeance against Lucrece's murderer:

Now by the Capitol that we adore,	*a*
And by this chaste blood so unjustly stained,	*b*
By heaven's fair sun that breeds the fat earth's store,	*a*
By all our country rights in Rome maintained,	*b*
And by chaste Lucrece' soul that late complained	*b*
Her wrongs to us, and by this bloody knife,	*c*
We will revenge the death of this true wife.	*c*

(lines 1835-41)

Despite Shakespeare's skill in rhyme royal, he chose unrhymed blank verse for *Julius Caesar,* because that was the accepted pattern for the public stage. And yet he learned from poetic propagandists like Higgens that the fall of princes by the hand of Fortune was a powerful theme. Antony's comment that a smiling Fortune will give the revengers anything affirmed the principle of luck (3.2.266), and Brutus' famous advice to Cassius about seizing opportunity (4.3.217-24) confirmed the likelihood of noble failure.

The full title of Higgens' work indicates that, while these verbal portraits were meant to instruct educated people and delight the few poets among them, they were composed for somber enjoyment, not the loud responses of theater audiences. Shakespeare, having proved that he could write and publish poems, reversed this situation by letting Caesar and Brutus speak as dramatic characters.

FROM JOHN HIGGENS' *MIRROUR FOR MAGISTRATES* (1587)

THE MIRROUR FOR MAGISTRATES, WHEREIN MAY BE SEEN, BY EXAMPLES PASSED IN THIS REALM, WITH HOW GRIEVOUS PRINCES AND MAGISTRATES AND HOW FRAIL AND UNSTABLE WORLDLY PROSPERITY IS FOUND, WHERE FORTUNE SEEMETH MOST HIGHLY TO FAVOUR

. . . I Caius Julius Caesar Consul had to name,   25
That worthy *Roman* born, renowned with noble deeds:
What need I here recite the lineage whence I came,
Or else my great exploits perdy tis more then needs:
But only this to tell, of purpose now proceeds:
Why I a *Roman* Prince, no *Britain,* here   30
Amongst these *Britain* Princes now appear,
As if amongst the rest a *Britain* Prince I were.

And yet because thou maist perceive the story all
Of all my life, and so deem better of the end:
I will again the same to mind yet briefly call,   35
To tell thee how thou mayest me praise or discommend.
Which when hou hast, perdy, as I recite it, pend,
Thou shalt confess that I deserved well,
Amongst them here my tragedy to tell,
By conquest since I won this Isle before I fell.   40

What need I first recite my pedigree well known:
No noble author writes that can forget the same:
My praise I know in print through all the world is blown,
There's no man scarce that writes, but he recites my fame.
My worthy father *Lucius Caesar* had to name,   45
Aurelia eke my mother also hight,
Of *Caius Cotta* daughter born by right,

As fair and wise a dame as ever saw the light.

How I was trained up in youth what need I tell:
Since that my noble Aunt (that *Julia* hight) me taught, 50
Who could with moral doctrine good instruct me well,
And saw the frame in me that natures skill had wrought,
By her instructions aye I wit and favour sought.
I was accounted comely of my grace,
I had by natures gift a Princely face, 55
And wisdom high to weigh and deem of every case.

Of stature high and tall, of colour fair and white,
Of body space and lean, yet comely made to see:
What need I more of these impertinent recite,
Since *Plutarch* hath at large described it all to thee, 60
And eke thy self that thinkest thou seest and hearest me
Mayest well suppose the rest, or take the view
Thou mayest by talk of these which erst me knew,
And by my statures tell of my proportion true.

In journey swift I was, and prompt and quick of wit, 65
My eloquence was like of all that heard me plead,
I had the grace to use my terms, and place them fit,
My rolling Rhetoric stood my Clients oft in stead:
No fine conveyance past the compass of my head.
I won the spurs, I had the laud and praise, 70
I passed them all that pleaded in those days,
I had of warlike knowledge, Kaisar, all the keys.

At seventeen years of age, a *Flamin* was I chose,
An office great in *Rome* of priesthood Princely high,
I married eke *Cossutia* whereof much mischief rose, 75
Because I was divorc'ed from her so speedily.
Divorcement breeds dispite, defame is got thereby.
For such as fancies fond by change fulfill,
Although they think it cannot come to ill,
The wrong they show them doth cry to God for
vengeance still. 80

Of these the stories tell, what need I more recite,
Or of the wars I waged *Consul* with the Gauls?
The worthiest writers had desire of me to write,
They plac'st my life amongst the worthies and their falls.

So fame methinks likewise amidst the *Britains* calls　　　　　　85
For *Caesar* with his sword, that bare with them the sway,
And for the cause that brought him into such decay,
Which by his noble acts did bear their freedom first away.

When I in *France* had brought the *Gauls* to bend,
And made them subject all obeisant unto me:　　　　　　　90
Methought I had unto the world his end
By west subdued the Nations whilehom free.
There of my wars I wrote an history
By nights, at leisure times so from my Country far,
I did describe the places and the sequels of my war　　　　95
The Commentaries called of *Caesars* acts that are.

At length I did perceive there was an Island yet
By west of *France*, which in the *Ocean* see did lie:
And that there was likewise no cause or time to let,
But that I might with them the chance of Fortune try.　　　100
I sent to them for hostage of assurance, I,
And willed them tribute pay unto the *Roman* stout,
Or else I would both put their lives and goods in doubt,
And also reave away the best of all their rout.

But they a people scarce and reckless of my powers,　　　105
Abused those which brought th'ambassage that I sent:
Now since (quoth they) the land and region here is ours,
We will not *Caesar* to thy rightless hests assent.
By doom of friendly Gods first this Isle we hent,
Of *Priams* blood we are, from *Greece* we *Trojans* came.　　110
As *Brutus* brought us thence, and gave this land his name,
So for our freedom we will freely fight to keep the same.

This land reported was full fertile for the soil,
The wealthy warlike sort of *Britains* stout within
Were rathe able well to give, then take the soil,　　　　115
To those which came by wars, their freedom for to win.
Myself made first assault, with them I did begin,
Of all the *Romans* first I waged with them war:
Ant this I can report, they valiant people are,
They scare no foes, they reck no fame, of people near or far.　　120

. . .[Caesar describes his subjugation of the Britons and of Pompey.]
This they envied that sued aloft to climb,

As *Cassius*, which the *Praetorship* did crave,   330
And Brutus eke his friend which bare the crime
Of my dispatch, for they did first deprave
My life, mine acts, and sought my blood to have,
Full secretly amongst themselves conspired, decreed
To be attempters of that cruel bloody deed,   335
When *Caesar* in the *Senate* house from noble heart should bleed.

But I forewarned was by *Capis* tomb,
His *Epitaph* my death did long before foreshow:
Cornelius Balbus saw mine horses headless run
Without a guide, forsaking food for woe.   340
Spurina warned me that sooth of things did know,
A wren in beak with Laurel green that flew
From woods to *Pompeys* Court, whom birds there slew,
Foreshowed my doleful death, as after all men knew.

The night before my slaughter, I did dream   345
I carried was, and flew the clouds above:
And sometimes hand in hand with Jove supreme
I walked methought, which might suspicions move.
My wife *Calphurnia*, *Caesars* only love,
Did dream she saw her crest of house to fall,   350
Her husband thrust through breast a sword withal,
Eke that same night her chamber doors themselves flew open all.

These things did make me doubt that morning much,
And I accrazed was and thought at home to stay:
But who is he can void of destiny's such,   355
Where so great number seeks him to betray.
The traitor *Brutus* did me not delay,
Nor yet to frustrate there so great assembly sat:
On which to hear the public please I got,
Mistrusting nought mine end and fatal fate.   360

There met me by the way a *Roman* good,
Presenting me a scroll of every name:
And all their whole devise that sought my blood,
That presently would execute the same.
But I suppose that for some suit he came,   365
I heedless bear this scroll in my left hand,
And others more, till leisure, left unscanned,
Which in my pocket afterwards they found.

Spurina as I came at sacrifices was,
Near to the place where I was after slain: 370
Of whose divinings I did little pass,
Though he to warn me oft before was fain.
My haughty heart these warnings all disdain.
(Quoth I) the Ides of March be come, yet harm is none.
(Quoth he) the Ides of March be come, yet they're not gone.   375
And reckless so to Court I went, and took my throne.

As soon as I was set, the traitors all arose,
And one approached near, as to demand something:
To whom as I laid ear, at once my foes
Me compassed round, their weapons hid they bring.   380
Then I too late perceived the fatal sting.
O this (quoth I) is violence: then *Cassius* pierced my breast:
He stabbed me in, and so with daggers did the rest.

You princes all, and noble men beware of pride,
And careful will to war for Kingdoms sake: 385
By me, that set myself aloft the world to guide,
Beware what bloodshed you do undertake.
Ere three and twenty wounds had made my heart to quake,
What thousands fell for *Pompeys* pride and mine:
Of *Pompeys* life that cut the vital line,   390
Myself have told what fate I found in fine.

Full many noble men, to rule alone, I slew,
And some themselves for grief of heart did slay:
For they nay would mine Empire stay to view.   395
Some I did force to yield, some fled away
As loath to see their Countries quite decay.
The world in *Afric*, *Asia*, distant far,
And *Europe* knew my bloodsheds great in war,
Recounted yet through all the world that are.   400

But since my whole pretence was glory vain,
To have renown and rule above the rest,
Without remorse of many thousands slain,
Which, for their own defence, their wars addressed:
I deem therefore my stony heart and breast   405
Received so many wounds for just revenge, they stood
By justice right of Jove, the sacred sentence good,
That whoso slays, he pays the price, is blood for blood.

POETIC JUSTICE FOR CAESAR

Against such detracting views of Caesar's fame stood the counter-tradition glorifying him and condemning Brutus.[1] Dante took great delight in organizing his vision of Hell around the physical body of Satan, buried upside down in the earth and surrounded by so many circles of moral losers. At the end of the *Inferno* (early fourteenth century) he places Brutus, with the other arch-traitors Cassius and Judas Iscariot, inside the mouth of Satan, where they are eternally chewed. About the best that can be said about the two Roman traitors is that they face outside, while Judas' head is munched within. The tour-guide, Virgil, describes them scornfully:

> Of the other two, who have their heads thrust forward,
>   the one who dangles down from the black face
>   is Brutus: note how he writhes without a word.
>
> And there, with the huge sinewy arms, is the soul
>   of Cassius—But the night is coming on
>   and we must go, for we have seen the whole.
>   *The Inferno*, Canto 34, ll 64-69

CAESAR AMONG THE NINE WORTHIES

English Christian poets, more forgiving than Dante was to pagan heroes like Ulysses, honored Caesar. Neatly divided into trios of pagans, Jews, and modern Christians, the list of Nine Worthies, formulated by such printers as William Caxton in his preface to *Le Morte d'Arthur* (1485), excused the unfortunate fact that Caesar was born before the Christian era. He stood beside Hector of Troy and Alexander the Great; flanking them were the Old Testament heroes Joseph, King David, and Judas Maccabeus; the envied Christians were Arthur, Charlemagne, and Godfrey of Bouillon.

Caesar fared even better in the poetic tribute to Augustus written by an exiled poet who realized that his hopes for return might be improved by a little flattery. Ovid's *Metamorphoses* turned out to be a lot more than that. Publius Ovidius Naso (43 B.C.-18 A.D.) grew up in the glory of Caesar's successor, Augustus. Banished for some unknown offense, he invested his time writing a mammoth poetic study of change, in life-forms, in spirit. It was a treasure house of mythology, and for that reason Elizabethan translators such as Arthur Golding and schoolboys like Shakespeare turned to its resources.

Shakespeare the mature playwright who gave Octavius those magnanimous lines praising the dead Brutus (*Julius Caesar* 5.5.76-81), must have been aware of the Ovidian elevation of Augustus, both from his inheritance of Caesar's glory and the Christian memory that Jesus was born during Augustus' reign.

Ovid made Augustus into Caesar's son, not his nephew, and in the course of praising the emperor he tells the glorious story of how Julius was received into Jove's heaven. The narrative proceeds from the case of the Greek god of healing, Aesculapius, and thus implies Caesar's superiority as a native Roman.

FROM ARTHUR GOLDING'S TRANSLATION OF OVID'S
METAMORPHOSES (1567)

But Caesar hath obtained

His Godhead in his native soil and City where he reigned.   835
Whom peerless both in peace and war, not more his wars up knit
With triumph, nor his great exploits achieved so speedily,
Have turned to a blazing star, than did his progeny.
For of the acts of Caesar, none is greater than that he
Left such a son behind him as Augustus is, to be   840
His heir. For are they things hard: to overcome thy Realm
of Britain standing in the sea, or up the sevenfold stream
Of Nile that beareth Paper-reed victorious ships to row,
Or to rebellious Numidie to give an overthrow,
Or Juba, king of Moors, and Pons (which proudly did it bear   845
Upon the name of Mythridate) to force by sword and spear
To yield them subjects unto Rome, or by his just desert
To merit many triumphs, and of sum to have his part,
Than such an heir to leave behind, in whom the Gods do show
Exceeding favor unto men for that they do bestow
So great a prince upon the world?. . .   850

[Jove declares Augustus' destiny]
And therefore from the murdered corpse of Julius Caesar take
His [Augustus'] soul with speed, and of the same a burning crescent 945
    make,
That from our heavenly palace he may evermore look down
Upon our royal Capitol and Court within Rome town.
 He scarcely ended had these words, but Venus out of hand
    Amid the Senate house of Rome invisible did stand,
And from her Caesars body took his new expulsed spright   950
The which she not permitting to resolve to air quite,
Did place it in the sky among the stars that glister bright
And as she bare it, she did feel it gather heavenly might,
And for to waxen fiery. She no sooner let it fly,
But that a good shining star it up aloft did stay   955
And drew a great way after it bright beams like burning hair.
(Book 15, lines 834-50, 944-56)

The woodcut in the 1606 edition (at the head of this chapter) depicts this metamorphosis of the slain leader. Venus and Cupid are conducting Caesar into Olympus. The anguished look on his face is almost enough to make any assassin regret the deed.

FROM GOLDEN AGE TO LEAD

Sequels to *Julius Caesar* existed long before nineteenth- and twentieth-century parodies. One noteworthy example came from the satirical mind of Jonathan Swift. His *Gulliver's Travels* is a biting commentary on eighteenth-century society, while indulging in apparently amusing travel stories told by ship's surgeon Lemuel Gulliver. In the seventh chapter of the third book, we learn of adventures to the flying island of Laputa ("whore" in Spanish) where the wise men are notoriously stupid when it comes to common sense. Visiting the academy in the capital city, Gulliver is allowed to use the governor's magic to conjure any of the ancient spirits from the history of the world. He chooses the Roman Senate, and calls up a modern legislature for comparison. The contrast between noble statehood and greedy politicians is utterly disappointing. His visit with Julius Caesar and Brutus, however, shows a surprisingly happy reconciliation.

Brutus' striking heroism lacks the usual satiric undercutting, for Gulliver is genuinely pleased to join him and other worthies in the doubled triumvirate made famous by Octavius Caesar's alliance with Antony and Lepidus (see act 4, scene 1). It is Caesar's forgiveness of Brutus that distinguishes this fantasy. They are old pals, now that the centuries have healed their personal grievances.

FROM JONATHAN SWIFT'S "A VOYAGE TO LAPUTA," *GULLIVER'S TRAVELS* (1727)

I saw *Caesar* and *Pompey* at the head of their Troops just ready to engage. I saw the former in his last great Triumph. I desired that the Senate of *Rome* might appear before me in one large Chamber, and an Assembly of somewhat a latter age, in Counterview in another. The first seemed to be an Assembly of Heroes and Demi-gods; the other a knot of Peddlers, Pick-pockets, High-way-men and Bullies.

The Governor at my request gave the sign for *Caesar* and *Brutus* to advance towards us. I was struck with a profound Veneration at the sight of *Brutus*, and could easily discover the most consummate Virtue, the greatest Intrepidity, and firmness of Mind, the truest Love of his Country, and general Benevolence for Mankind in every Lineament of his Countenance. I observed with much pleasure, that these two persons were in good Intelligence with each other, and *Caesar* freely confessed to me, that the greatest Actions of his own Life were not equal by many degrees to the Glory of taking it away. I had the Honour to have much Conversation with *Brutus*; and was told that his Ancestors *Junius, Socrates, Epaminondas, Cato* the Younger, Sir *Thomas More* and himself, were perpetually together: a *Sextumvirate* to which all the Ages of the World cannot add a Seventh.

Jonathan Swift, *Travels into Several Remote Nations, by Lemuel Gulliver* (London, 1727), 2:101-3.

The revival of classical culture in eighteenth-century English literature created a second renaissance of Brutus' and Caesar's reputations. The many shifts of viewpoint occurring over such a long period ought to remind us of the continuous desire to reconcile a society's contemporary values with the ancient legends of Rome.

NOTE

1. Sidney Alexander instructively describes the negative and positive views of Brutus, and the remarkable shift from the one to the other in the conflicted politics of Florence. *Lions and Foxes: Men and Ideas of the Italian Renaissance*. New York: Macmillan, 1974. 122-25.

TOPICS FOR WRITTEN OR ORAL EXPLORATION

1. Look at the beginning and end of Plutarch's biographies of Caesar and Brutus. What advantages do you see in the strategy of opening with the story of young Caesar's escape from political murder, compared to beginning with the account of Brutus' parentage? What does Plutarch achieve by concluding Caesar's story with Brutus' suicide, as opposed to ending Brutus' story with Portia's swallowing hot coals?

2. Plutarch casts Cicero as an opponent of tyranny in the life of Caesar; Cassius is given this role in the life of Brutus. Find these references in Plutarch and then compare them with what Shakespeare does with Cicero (in act 1, scene 3) and with Cassius' talk to Casca (after Cicero leaves). Cassius rigs the "public" petitions to Brutus (1.3.142-45), whereas Plutarch implies that they were spontaneous (find this spot in the life of Brutus). Consider all these differences in order to describe how Shakespeare's treatment makes Cassius seem like a seducer of Brutus' good intentions.

3. Find and list Plutarch's anecdotes about Caesar's boasting and his accomplishments. Then mark the ones reflected in Shakespeare's play. Look especially at what Caesar actually says in the play (1.2.1-24, 190-214; 2.2.1-129; 3.1.1-77). Seen by itself, do Caesar's words uphold the charge of tyranny and excessive ambition? For each passage of Caesar's talk in Shakespeare's play, find a previous remark or report about Caesar that colors your interpretation of his political and human characteristics.

4. Compare Plutarch's account of Portia's wound (in the life of Brutus) with that of Calpurnia's dream (in Caesar's life). Then examine Shakespeare's paired scenes from two very different marriages (2.1.234-309; 2.2.8-107). Based only on these domestic exchanges, discuss your relative impressions of the two leaders. To what extent does Shakespeare accept Plutarch's views of these marriages? What does the play gain dramatically by placing these husband/wife conversations side by side?

5. Compare the assassination in Plutarch's life of Brutus with that in the life of Caesar. Caesar's words (not "et tu Brute") and the act of cloaking himself are similar in both accounts. What difference do the following elements make: Pompey's statue, the comparison of Caesar to a beast finished off by hunters, the assassins accidentally wounding each other. Why do you think Shakespeare gives Caesar his "constant as the northern star" remarks (3.1.58-73) just before the attack? What is implied by Caesar's last words, including the fact that Shakespeare puts them in Latin?

6. Plutarch describes, in both lives, a relatively mild response of the people, at first, to the assassination, and an official pardon by the Senate. Look at Shakespeare's dramatic strategy of giving Antony a primary role in the revenge, starting with his soliloquy before Caesar's corpse (3.1.254-275). List all the ways that Shakespeare's Antony creates the hatred of the assassins. In which of Plutarch's versions, does Antony play this role? What narrative advantage is there in emphasizing Antony's part in the one life, but not the other?

7. Compile a list of Caesar's qualities based on his account of the expedition to Britain. Which of these traits appear in *Julius Caesar*? Which are absent from Shakespeare's character. Use your insights to write an imaginary commentary by the ghostly Caesar on his "last campaign," that is, the events presented in Shakespeare's play. Your commentary might be compared in tone and substance with the confessions of Caesar in the *Mirrour for Magistrates*.

8. Read the poem attached to the emblem of Brutus' suicide. Find references to Fortune in Plutarch's lives, and then discuss the effects of introducing an unbeatable Fate into the story, as opposed to the actual ghost of Caesar in Shakespeare's play or Brutus' reference to Fortune (4.3.217-24).

9. What does Plutarch gain by not telling the story of Caesar's ghost in the life of Brutus? The appearance of the victors in Shakespeare's play is notably different from the conclusions of Plutarch's lives. Antony's and Octavius' final praise creates what impressions of Brutus for you?

10. From Elyot's *Governour*, extract lessons for modern politicians, not merely to avoid being assassinated, but to escape damage to their reputations. Do the same for friends of holders of high office. What limits does Elyot imply for the behavior of modern counterparts of Brutus and Cassius? Categorize the reasons for this behavior as moral or practical. Imagine a situation where the two value systems conflict, and compose an imagined letter (or visitation) from the ghost of Brutus or Cassius offering advice on how to resolve the conflict between ethical and pragmatic reasons for acting.

11. Rewrite Caesar's confessions in *The Mirrour for Magistrates*, as if it were a speech by a fallen politician at his last press conference.

12. Comment on the use of rhyme royal in Higgens' version of *The Mirrour*. Where does he force his story in order to make a rhyme, where does the rhyme make an idea easier to notice or remember? Now, look for Shakespeare's use of rhymed pairs (couplets) in *Julius Caesar* (there are not many, but they occur in strategic places for the structure of the drama). Find this device in other Shakespeare plays, as well as places where rhymed couplets occur throughout passages whose ideas have a particular nobility or comic spirit.

13. Compare the picture from the 1606 *Metamorphoses* with Ovid's translated text. Notice how the eagle and the two assassins' daggers form a triangle around laurel-crowned Caesar. His upturned face and the "comet's tail" issuing from his mouth lead the eye to the second visual element, the cloud-covered Venus making the catch, and winged Cupid offering the assist. By analogy, what is the thematic "focus" of Ovid's lines?

SUGGESTED READINGS

Bullough, Geoffrey. *Volume V: The Roman Plays. Narrative and Dramatic Sources of Shakespeare*. New York: Columbia University Press,1964.

Cantor, Paul. *Shakespeare's Rome: Republic and Empire*. Ithaca: Cornell University Press, 1976.

Dudley, Donald R. *The Romans: 850 B.C.–A.D. 337*. New York: Barnes and Noble, 1970.

Green, Robert. *Julius Caesar*. New York: Franklin Watts, 1996.

Harrison, William. *The Description of England*. Edited by Georges Edelen. Washington and New York: Folger Shakespeare Library and Dover Publications, 1994.

Meier, Christian, and David McLintock, trans. *Caesar*. New York: Basic Books, 1982.

Miola, Robert S. *Shakespeare's Rome*. Cambridge: Cambridge University Press, 1983.

Nims, John F. *Ovid's Metamorphoses: The Arthur Golding Translation*. New York: Macmillan, 1965.

"Sir Thomas More, the Additions Ascribed to Shakespeare." In *The Riverside Shakespeare*. Edited by G. Blakemore Evans. Boston: Houghton Mifflin, 1974. 1683-1700.

Walworth, Nancy Zinsser. "The Soothsayer," "Heir to Caesar," "Son of a God." In *Augustus Caesar*. New York: Chelsea, 1989. 13-41.

The Booth brothers as they acted in *Julius Caesar, November 25, 1864*: (left to right) John Wilkes as Marc Antony, Edwin as Brutus, Junius as Cassius. Courtesy of Brown University Library.

4

Julius Caesar and the Lincoln Assassination

Politically inspired assassinations have been all too frequent in the late nineteenth and twentieth centuries for anyone to dismiss the relevance of the act that Shakespeare re-created on stage. Lincoln (1865), McKinley (1901), the archduke Ferdinand (1914), Mussolini's rival, Matteotti (1924), Louisiana governor Huey Long (1935), John and Robert Kennedy (1963, 1968), Martin Luther King (1968), Yitzhak Rabin (1994), plus the attempts to kill Alabama governor George Wallace (1972), President Ronald Reagan (1981), and threats against Queen Elizabeth II, like those feared by Elizabeth I—all these violent attacks, and hundreds more upon other officials, mark our era by the same desperate bloodletting and assassination plots that we may carelessly ascribe only to Renaissance Italy and England.

The political assassin seeks to "save" the state by eliminating a threat to popular sovereignty. He often yearns for a simpler government and imagines that if only the symbol of oppression were eliminated, the people would return to their natural prominence and all the ideals of a sentimentalized past would flourish. Finally, the self-sacrificing Booths and Brutuses convince themselves that people will applaud the killing and admire the martyred killer. Such fantasies usually underestimate the power of presidents like Lincoln and emperors like Caesar to represent stability. When the victim has treated his own people decently, and only threatened absolute control in theory or against approved enemies, then in practice the assassin is usually crushed by popular disapproval.

ENGLISH MONARCHY

Compared to modern constitutional governments, Elizabethan authorities protected the privileges of the monarch at all costs. English history as recorded in *The Mirrour for Magistrates* showed a succession of fallen princes, and each new king or queen took extraordinary precautions to avoid the mistakes of his or her predecessor. Then, as now, changing social and political conditions thwarted attempts to manage the present in relation to the past. Henry VIII struggled with popular restlessness over his break with Roman Catholicism; his nine-year old son Edward VI (reigned 1547-53) was too young to escape the control of his guardians; Queen Mary (reigned 1553-58) reopened the wounds of the Protestant revolution by persecuting those considered heretics to the Catholic Church. Her half sister Elizabeth (reigned 1558-1603) re-consolidated Protestant power, but she allowed greater tolerance toward Catholicism. She was mature enough to direct her own affairs and sufficiently prudent to back off from religious persecution. Being relatively tolerant of Catholic customs and extreme Protestant desires for reform, she avoided the perils that had ruined Edward and Mary in their own quite different cultural situations.

Elizabeth was still her authoritative father Henry's daughter in matters of loyalty. Treason was not tolerated. The "putting to silence" of Flavius and Murellus in *Julius Caesar* for showing disrespect to Caesar's statues (1.2.285) was the kind of political trouble that Elizabeth's detractors risked for civil disobedience. (Henry David Thoreau would have suffered worse than a night in jail had he protested against injustice three hundred years earlier, in Elizabethan England.) The queen insisted on loyalty, because she knew that Catholic Europe, especially Spain and France, conspired against her, and still she played a clever game of independence by not marrying into an alliance. Her virginity bought time for her to deal with protracted domestic problems from an economic slump. Thirty years into her reign, when the Spanish Armada of 1588 failed to overthrow her, the military threat subsided, only to open the undecided question of succession. The old maid of the 1590s worried people who remembered the bloody fights over Henry VIII's successor.

Elizabeth's shrewd maneuvering about marriage was less believable when she dallied with younger courtiers. The Earl of Essex was one of her favorites. His military adventures against the Spanish and the Irish displayed a bold but dangerous independence that eventually led him to consider seizing the monarchy with his army. The obsession with conspiracy in *Julius Caesar* came at just this period of Essex's crisis, around 1599. History plays evoked politics more directly than did the stories of the fall of princes in the *Mirrour for Magistrates*. Both the Crown and the City of London authorities considered it a little dangerous to portray the killing of any monarch before an audience of unruly citizens, hence the uneasiness associated particularly with the deposition scene of *Richard II* (4.1.154-318). The rebellious followers of the Earl of Essex staged this play at the Globe on February 7, 1601, the afternoon before their attempt to solve the problem of Elizabeth's succession by raising troops against the factions supporting the enfeebled queen. Essex was convicted of high treason and decapitated. No one dared eulogize him as the noblest Englishman of them all, the way Antony praised the defeated Brutus. The lessons suggested by Cassius' conspiracy and Brutus' noble-minded, fatal participation were publicly displayed in the form of severed heads on London Bridge. Julius Caesar may not have built the Tower of London, but his merciless spirit still occupied it.

THE AMERICAN PRESIDENCY

A similar atmosphere of shock and vengeance surrounded the actor John Wilkes Booth's killing of Abraham Lincoln, at Ford's Theater, Washington, D.C., April 14, 1865. The strong political motives of the Confederate partisan were immediately evident to the shocked audience when Booth leapt onto the stage from the presidential box where he had fired a pistol bullet into the back of Lincoln's head, shouting "Sic semper tyrannis. The South is avenged."

The story of Booth's plots against Lincoln is not complete without consideration of the strange role that Shakespeare's *Julius Caesar* played. Although the thoughts of desperate assassins are not as easily traceable as Brutus' meditations, the case of John Wilkes Booth provides enough evidence to link the drama to the presidential killing in more than the coincidental ways that conspiracy theorists love: counting the letters in the victims' names, working out anagrams, noting dates like the death of John Wilkes Booth 301 years to the day after Shakespeare's christening at Stratford, and so forth.

In this chapter you will find the advertisement for the benefit performance of *Julius Caesar* starring all three of the Booth brothers.

The review of that one-night event in the fall of 1864 is accompanied by newspaper accounts, two days later (November 27) of a series of arsons in New York city that John Wilkes Booth certainly witnessed. Whether he saw them as preludes to his own murder of Lincoln cannot be known, but the diary he left from the time he limped off the Ford's Theater stage until he was trapped and shot by Federal troops casts a chilling Shakespearean light on the most notorious presidential assassination in American history. Parts from a "Brutus play" set in pre-Republican Rome complete a family portrait of Shakespeareans obsessed with dramatic feeling.

THE BOOTH FAMILY

John Wilkes Booth was the son of a renowned and more than slightly eccentric English actor, Junius Brutus Booth (1796-1852). Classically ornate names were a family tradition. Booth Senior was named after the Lucius Junius Brutus who was the agitator against the Tarquin kings and the ancestor (and role model) for Caesar's fatal friend. "Junius" had also been the penname of a parliamentary critic (1769-1772) of King George III, and another one, John Wilkes (1727-1797), had similarly attacked the king in print. Father Booth had made his reputation as a forceful actor of Lucius Brutus among many other roles in Britain (including the part of Cassius in an 1820 production of Shakespeare's *Julius Caesar*) the year before he abandoned his first wife, eloped with a florist's daughter, and left his native England eventually to reestablish himself on a Maryland farm, Tudor Hall. There, he set up housekeeping with Mary Ann Holmes, who bore three sons: Junius Brutus, Jr. (born 1822), Edwin (1833), and John Wilkes (1838), and a daughter, Asia (1835), plus two other daughters and a son who all died in infancy.

Despite these family tragedies, and being given to fits of strange behavior and alcoholic delusions, the Booths' father was still a masterful actor. He taught his sons the business of the stage, both economic and inspirational. The family suffered the ups and downs of their provider's touring career, and they were raised on his rehearsing in the then-popular style of acting, which emphasized bold gestures, booming voice, and strong facial expressions.

A sign of the elder Booth's trans-Atlantic fame was an oil painting of him in Roman toga, from his enactment of Brutus in John Howard Payne's *Brutus*, one copy hanging in the Garrick Club of London and another now in New York.[1]

John Wilkes Booth respected his father's acting and revered Southern values. The Maryland homestead lay close enough to Virginia to attract the young actor's Confederate sympathies, despite his family's apparent support for the Union. Booth briefly served in the Virginia militia that helped Colonel. Robert E. Lee capture the Abolitionist John Brown's raiders at Harper's Ferry (1859). At the outbreak of the Civil War, Booth kept to the stage, rather than enlist as a Rebel. His deep resentment of Lincoln grew as the War continued to destroy Booth's adopted South and challenge its fierce independence. Booth conceived of Lincoln as a counterpart to the Roman king that the classical Junius Brutus heroically opposed. The image of the elder Booth playing a stage Brutus somehow inspired the handsome younger Booth to become a real conspirator. He must have taken some of his cues from the plot of the drama where his father was the star actor.

In the excerpts from this play that follow, the pattern of defiance against inhuman tyranny is strongly established. The protagonist wages a secret war against the evil King Tarquin, who had murdered Brutus' eldest son and keeps close watch on his younger one, Lucius. Junius pretends to be mad, in the Hamlet tradition, to disguise his revenge. In a bloody showdown, the father exposes and kills Tarquin but wrestles with the fact that his Titus has fallen in love with a Tarquin princess. This son nobly refuses to give up his love, and the play ends with the tearful father Brutus ordering his execution.

The American author explains in his preface that he borrowed from the seven Brutus plays then current around 1813. Payne's *Brutus* premiered in London on December 3, 1818 and in New York on the Ides of March (the fifteenth), 1819. The Brutus legend was theatrically very alive, and the Booth name closely associated with it.

The play opens with an actor's introduction of the same sort that begins Shakespeare's *Romeo and Juliet, Henry V,* and *Pericles.* This prologue sets the tone less by the pun on the principal actor's name than the grand idea of the Roman Republic, though the generally flowery language of this play exaggerates the pathos of the story of popular revenge. The leader of forces against the tyrant destroys part of his family in order to preserve honor. Brutus' grand gestures at the beginning of the drama end it in a scene of pitiful regret.

FROM JOHN HOWARD PAYNE'S *BRUTUS; OR THE FALL OF TARQUIN* (1819)

Prologue: . . . Here, yet, no chargers wheel,
No foreign slaves on ropes or scaffolds reel,
No gallie amazons, half naked, climb
From pit to gallery—the low sublime!
In Shakespeare's halls, shall dogs and bears engage:
Where brutes are actors, be a booth the stage!
And we shall triumph yet. . . .

To night we take our lessons from the tomb:
Tis thy sad cenotaph, colossal Rome!
How is thy helmet cleft, thy banner low,
Ashes and dust are all thy glory now!
While o'er thy wreck, a host of monks and slaves,
Totter "to seek dishonorable graves."

The story is of Brutus, in that name
Tower'd to the sun her eagle's wing of flame!
When sank her liberty, that name of power,
Pour'd hallow'd splendours round its dying hour.
The lesson lived for man—that heavenward blaze
Fixed on the pile the world's eternal gaze.

[pp. 5-6]

The play opens with a set of noblemen commenting on colossal infamy, somewhat like the anti-tyrannical commentary of Shakespeare's Flavius and Murellus.

Act 1, scene 1, a street in Rome

Valerius: Words are too feeble to express the horror
With which my soul revolts against this Tarquin.
By poison he obtain'd his brother's wife,
Then, by a baser murder, grasp'd the crown.

[p. 7]

Son Lucius muses, Hamlet-like:

. . . a thousand opportunities
I've had to strike the blow,—and my own life

I had not valued as a ruth [sic]. But still—
There's something nobler to be done—my soul!
Enjoy the strong conception. Oh! 'tis glorious
To free a groaning country—
To see revenge
Spring like a lion from its den, and tear
These hunters of mankind! grant but the time,
Grant but the moment, gods!

[p. 10]

Act III opens in storm that would do credit to *King Lear*.

Brutus: . . . Launch forth thy thunders, capitolian Jove!
Put fire into the languid souls of men,
Let loose thy ministers of wrath amongst them
And crush the vile oppressor!

[p. 25]

Lightning strikes the statue of Tarquin, and Brutus acknowledges this sign from heaven, even as he laments his impotence. He secures the help of Valerius, and the Romans finally revolt against their corrupt ruler soon after Brutus delivers an Antony-like funeral oration for Lucretia, who committed suicide rather than suffer her family's disgrace.

III.iv the funeral

Brutus: Thus, thus, my friends, fast as our breaking hearts
Permitted utterance, we have told our story:
And now, to say one word of imposture,—
The mark necessity has made me wear.
When the ferocious malice of your king,—
King do I call him?—When the monster, Tarquin,
Slew, as you most of you may well remember,
My father Marcus and my elder brother,
Envying at once their virtues and their wealth,
How could I hope a shelter from his power,
But in the false face I have worn so long?
1st Roman: Most Wonderful!
2nd Roman: Silence! he speaks again.
Brutus: Would you know why I summon'd you together?
Ask ye what brings me here? behold this dagger,

Clotted with gore! behold that frozen corse!
See where the lost Lucretia sleeps in death!
She was the mark and model of the time,
The mould in which each female faced was form'd,
The very shrine and sacristy of virtue!
Fairer than ever was a form created
By youthful fancy when the blood strays wild
And never resting thought is all on fire!
The worthiest of the worthy! not the nymph
Who met old Numa in his hallow'd walks
And whisper'd in his ear her strains divine
Can I conceive beyond her;—the young choir
Of vestal virgins bent to her. Tis wonderful
Amid the darnel, hemlock, and base weeds
Which now spring rife from the luxurious compost
Spread o'er the realm, how this sweet lily rose,—
How from the shade of those ill neighboring plants
Her father shelter'd her, that not a leaf
Was blighted, but array'd in purest grace,
She bloom'd unsullied beauty. Such perfections
Might have call'd back the torpid breast of age
To long forgotten rapture; such a mind
Might have abash'd the boldest libertine,
And turn'd desire to reverential love
And holiest affection! oh, my countrymen!
You all can witness when that she went forth
It was a holiday in Rome; old age
Forgot its crutch, labour its task, all ran
And mothers turning to their daughters, cried,
"There, there's Lucretia!" now, look ye where she lies!
The beauteous flower, that innocent sweet rose
Turn up by ruthless violence—gone! Gone!
All: Sextus shall die!
Brutus: But then—the king—his father—
1st Roman: What shall be done with him?
2nd Roman: Speak Brutus!
3rd Roman: Tell us!
Brutus: Say, would ye seek instructions? would ye ask
What ye should do! Ask ye yon conscious walls
Which saw his poison'd brother, saw the incest
Committed there, and they will cry, Revenge!
Ask yon deserted street, where Tullia drove
O'er her dead father's corse, twill cry, revenge!

Ask yonder senate house, whose stones are purple
With human blood, and it will cry, revenge!
Go to the tomb, where lies his murder'd wife,
And the poor queen, who lov'd him as her son,
Their unappeased ghosts will shriek, revenge!
The temples of the gods, the all viewing heavens,
The gods themselves, shall justify the cry
And swell the general sound, revenge, revenge, revenge!
All: Revenge! revenge!
Brutus: And we will be reveng'd, my countrymen;
Brutus shall lead you on; Brutus, a name
Which will, when you're reveng'd, be dearer to him
Than all the noblest titles earth can boast.
1st Roman: Live, Brutus!
2nd   Valiant Brutus!
3rd   Down with Tarquin!
2nd   We'll have no Tarquins!
1st   We will have a Brutus!
3rd   Let's to the capitol, and shout for Brutus.
Brutus: I, your king!
Brutus your king!—No, fellow citizens!
If mad ambition in this guilty frame
Had strung one kingly fibre,—yea, but one—
By all the gods, this dagger which I hold
Should rip it out, though it entwin'd my heart.
Valerius: Then I am with thee, noble, noble Brutus!
Brutus, the new restor'd! Brutus, by Sybil,
By Pythian prophetess foretold, shall lead us.
Brutus: Now take the body up. Bear it before us
To Tarquin's palace; there we'll light our torches,
And, in the blazing conflagration, rear
A pile for these chaste relics, that shall send
Her soul amongst the stars. Oh! Brutus leads you.
                    Exeunt; the mob shouting
                         [pp. 32-34]

Almost re-enacting the mobs of the French Revolution whose actions the British of the Napoleonic era well remembered, the rioters break into the palace and seize but spare the Tarquin queen, Tullia (womanhood is still sacred). Brutus confronts his son Titus and says he must choose between Rome and his love for Tarquinia.

In act 5 Titus and Tarquinia are captured. Tarquinia pleads to the father, but he is barely moved to mercy. "My honour he had stabb'd— I pardon that, / He hath done more—he hath betray'd his country. / That is a crime which every honest heart / That beats for freedom, every Roman feels, / And the full stream of justice must have sway" [p. 47].

The play reaches its depth of pathos as he signals for his son's execution, much agitated. The final stage direction reads:

He rises and waves his hand, convuls'd with agitation, then drops on his seat and shrouds his face with his toga. Three sounds of the trumpet are heard instantly. All the characters assume attitudes of deep misery, Brutus starts up wildly, descends to the front in extreme agitation, looks out on the side by which Titus departed for an instant then, with an hysterical burst, exclaims. Justice is satisfy'd and Rome is free! *Brutus falls. The characters group around him.*
END OF THE TRAGEDY
[p. 54]

Early American Imprints, 2nd series Shaw-Shoemaker Bibliography, 1801-1819. Year 1819. No. 49029.

THE BROTHER ACT

Edwin inherited more of his father's acting talent than his brothers did. He attracted the attention of the theater public, including that of President Lincoln, who loved plays and greatly admired Shakespeare. Junius Jr. was more inclined to the managerial role and John Wilkes, to a lesser degree than Edwin, became an actor. He had also performed before Lincoln, though few people knew his bitterness toward the symbol of the Union and the foe of the Confederacy.

Actors made their living touring the major cities and smaller towns. Shakespeare was brought to the frontiers by the lesser talents and promoted with the sort of hoopla that Mark Twain satirizes in the King's and the Duke's performances in Chapter 21 of *Huckleberry Finn*. However, actors earned the most prestige by performing in gala events in New York. In a typically extravagent benefit on Thanksgiving Day, 1864, all three of the Booth brothers lent their talents to raise money for a statue of Shakespeare that still gazes down on the strollers of Central Park.[2]

The announcement of this benefit was full of promotional enthusiasm, referring to the brothers, in Latin, as "the distinguished sons of a distinguished father." Edwin's greater fame was recognized in the special billing he received for arranging this charity, and in the featured stardom of his upcoming role in *Hamlet*, which he was to repeat for an astonishing one hundred nights straight.

The Winter Garden Theater was an eminent opera house located in back of the 600 block of Broadway, behind the enormous Lafarge Hotel. A theatrical evening was convenient for any of the 1,200 possible lodgers and any of the high-society patrons of drama who would be on display in the exclusive boxes and the dress circle. Although the costs seem tiny compared to modern Broadway standards, ticket prices were doubled for this benefit. The announcement touted the celebration in anticipation of a packed house.

FROM "WINTER GARDEN, SPECIAL ANNOUNCEMENT" (Nov. 25, 1864)

Mr. Stuart has pleasure in announcing that owing to the generous zeal and untiring devotion of

MR. EDWIN BOOTH,

a performance will be given at this theatre on

FRIDAY EVENING. Nov. 25,

(Mr. J.S. Clarke having kindly ceded this evening for the occasion) for the benefit of the fund to raise a statue to Shakspeare in the Central Park, being the second benefit for this object at the Winter Garden. The evening will be made memorable by the appearance in the same piece of the three sons of the great Booth.

JUNIUS BRUTUS,

EDWIN

AND

JOHN WILKES,

–Filii patri digno digniores.

who have come forward with cheerful alacrity to do honor to the immortal bard, from whose works the genius of their father caught its inspiration, and of many of whose greatest creations he was the best and noblest illustrator the stage has ever seen.

The play selected for the occasion is the tragedy of

JULIUS CAESAR.

JUNIUS BRUTUS BOOTH

Appearing as

CASSIUS.

EDWIN BOOTH

as

BRUTUS.

and

JOHN WILKES BOOTH

as

MARC ANTONY.

Julius Caesar (first appearance)..	Mr. K. Varrey
Casca (first appearance).................................	Mr. Charles Kemble Mason
Octavius Caesar...	Mr. C. Walcott, Jr.
Trebonius..	Mr. C.R. Chester
Decius...	Mr. J. W. Burgess
Metellus..	Mr. T. S. Cline
Lucius..	Miss Fanny Prestige
First Plebeian..	Mr. E. Everle
Second Plebeian..	Mr. V.S. Fawcutt

Portia...Mrs. F. S. Chanfrau
Culphurnia..Mrs. C. Walcot, Jr.

The piece will be presented under the stage direction of Mr. J. G. Hanley. The proceeds will be handed to the Treasurer of the Shakespeare Statue Fund. The doors will be open at 7 1/4 and the performance will commence at 8 o'clock.

The prices of admission to the Dress Circle and Parquette will be $1.50. To the Family Circle, which has been handsomely fitted up, $1. A few extra orchestra chairs have been added, which will be disposed of at the Box Office this morning, $5 each. Mr. Stuart trusts that those who have paid or may pay a large price for seats, will remember that in addition to the value they receive in intellectual enjoyment, they are contributing to a great national work, and not to the personal advantage of any individual.

EXTRA ANNOUNCEMENT
SATURDAY , Nov. 26,
OPENING NIGHT

of the engagement of

EDWIN BOOTH.

Mr. Stuart begs to announce that on Saturday evening, 26th, Mr. Edwin Booth will make his first regular appearance this season in the play of

HAMLET

The piece will be placed on the stage under the immediate direction of Mr. Booth, by Mr. J.G. Hamly, Stage Manager, in a style, it is hoped, combining spendor of production with strict historical correctness. The play has been in active preparation for the last three months, and no expense or effort has been spared . . .

New York Times, Nov. 25, 1864.

CRYING FIRE IN A CROWDED THEATER

There is no evidence that John Wilkes Booth participated in the Confederate plot to strike at New York City, the Union's most prominent city. He could hardly have ignored the implications of this attempted terrorism, however. At the time of the Booth brothers' enactment of *Julius Caesar*, General Sherman was marching through Georgia. The campaign to burn cities and destroy Confederate cropland was front-page news in the New York papers until the events of the Thanksgiving weekend brought the Civil War closer to home.

FROM "ATTEMPT TO BURN THE CITY" (Nov. 27, 1864)

Discovery of a Vast Rebel Conspiracy
Twelve Hotels Fired by Turpentine and Phosphorus.
SINGULAR ATTEMPTS ON THE SHIPPING.
Prompt Frustration of the Scheme.
GREAT PANIC AT BARNUM'S MUSEUM
Excitement at Nible's and the Winter Garden . . .

The details published in yesterday's HERALD respecting what turns out to be a vast and fiendish plot to burn down our great Empire City gave rise to the most profound excitement among all classes of our citizens. There was no panic, no evidence of ridiculous fright or the wild apprehension that might naturally be expected to result from the discovery of a conspiracy, which, if successful, would have been accompanied by such unspeakable horrors. Our people took the affair very collectedly, taking all things into consideration; but they did not the less on that account realize the fact that they had escaped, as by a miracle, from a dreadful calamity, which might have left half the city in ashes and consigned thousands of innocent persons—men, women, and children—to a most horrible death. Viewing it in this light, our citizens may be said to have repeated the Thanksgiving festival yesterday, for in every quarter were to be heard the words of congratulation and gratitude to God for his unmistakable interposition in our behalf. . . It is well to remember also that we have long been threatened with the conflagration of our principal Northern cities by the Southern chivalry. Piracy on the seas and robberies on the land are their favorite methods of procedure. Bank robberies and conflagrations are the latest in order.

The whole war on their side has been marked with savage cruelty. The massacre of the wounded at Bull run, the poisoning of wells and of food, the infamous treatment of our prisoners, the assassination of non-combatants and the malignant spirit which has displayed itself toward the loyal people of the North are no doubt remembered by the recording angel and will be brought against them in Heaven's chancery. The desperate effort on Friday may be justly attributed to the fiendish principles of this same chivalry. The essence of war is violence, we admit, yet even that is subject to certain restrictions common to all civilized nations. It is one thing in battle or on a march to be violent; but to burn down hotels, where war does not exist, is quite another affair. The wretches who would have destroyed all our principal hotels but one by fire, and caused the death of their harmless occupants, deserve no pity, and should they be detected, and we have not doubt they will be, should be hung up in as brief a space as possible and as soon as the law will permit.

New York Herald, Nov. 27, 1864, p. 1.

A follow-up assessment laid further blame on the enemy:

THE ATTEMPTED INCENDIARISM IN THE CITY—FAILURE OF THE SCHEME (Nov. 27, 1864)

The desperate, but happily unsuccessful, attempt to spread conflagration throughout this city, on Friday night, is another evidence of the straits to which the rebels are driven; and it is an evidence also that failure attends every effort they make to gain advantage in the infamous cause in which they are engaged. We think there can be no doubt, from all the facts now in the hands of the police authorities, that the design to burn down the principal hotels, twelve of which were set on fire on that night, was the result of an organized play on the part of a band of paroled rebel prisoners, and some of the recently released occupants of Fort Lafayette, aided by other emissaries, male and female, from the South.

Some time ago the Richmond papers counselled this very idea. They boasted that, although they had not armies to send to overrun the North, and retaliate for the devastation which, in the ordinary circumstances of war, our forces were compelled to inflict upon Southern soil, that, nevertheless, a scheme might be arranged whereby the torch of the incendiary could carry destruction into our Northern cities, and burn down simultaneously New York, Boston and Philadelphia. They commenced this infernal business here on Friday night, by dispensing bottles filled with phosphorus and probably with sulphuric acid on the beds in the St. Nicholas Hotel; the Lafarge House, the St. James, Metropolitan, Lovejoy's, Belmont, Tammany, United States, and the Gramercy Park hotels. Early on Saturday morning similar attempts were made in the Astor House, Fifth Avenue Hotel, and New England Hotel. The intention, no doubt, was to create a general conflagration over the city. But the attempt failed miserably. In no single instance did the miscreants succeed. The failure was as complete as the efforts of the rebels to subdue our armies in the West, in Virginia and on the Atlantic coast—as complete as the failure of their designs on the Canada borders. It was the last attempt to succeed somewhere, and it has been defeated.

New York Herald, Nov. 27, 1864, p. 4.

Little of Marc Antony's irony besides the slighting references to chivalry was needed to scorn the Southern cause. How could John Wilkes Booth, having played Antony's part, not have read these accounts without seething in anger? The dogs of war that his role called him to release (3.1.273) were at his command, and we can imagine the hate-filled vengeance that Antony expresses alive in him against Lincoln.

Before Booth delivered the funeral oration that Thanksgiving night, *Julius Caesar* was interrupted by one of the worst fears of audiences in highly flammable wooden theaters. The arson attack had spread to the Lafarge House, which adjoined the Winter Garden.

The reviewer of the play had more to report on than the incendiary rhetoric of Shakespeare performed by the Booths.

FROM "WINTER GARDEN—THE SHAKSPERE BENEFIT" (Nov. 26, 1864)

The audience was fairly carried by storm from the first entrance of the three brothers side by side in their respective parts. Brutus was individualized with great force and distinctness—Cassius was brought out equally well—and if there was less of real personality given to Marc Antony, the fault was rather in the part than in the actor. The scene between Brutus and the conspirators, in the second act—the scene of Caesar's death—and the scene of the quarrel between Brutus and Cassius, were perfect pieces of dramatic art.

An unpleasant circumstance occurred early in the evening. Just at the commencement of the second act a fire engine was run to the theatre, in consequence of the alarm of fire at the Lafarge House, adjoining, and the firemen entered the house, dragging their pipes and hose, and shouting fire. It may be imagined how disastrous such an alarm might have proved. But the intelligence of the audience and the presence of mind of inspector Leonard who shouted that it was a drunken man, saved all. Though the whole audience was on its feet in an instant it was quieted in a short time, and the play went on.

Tonight Mr. Edwin Booth will appear in Hamlet, for the performance of which great preparations have been made. Every scene is new and has been made under the special direction of Mr. Booth . . .

New York Herald, Nov. 26, 1864, p. 5.

Another account makes the fire metaphor unconsciously literal, in judging that John Wilkes' performance was equal to that of his brothers'. Rather than playing merely competently or with less than Edwin's and Junius' feeling, John as Antony "played with a phosphorescent passion and fire which recalled to old theatregoers the characteristics of the elder Booth."[3]

The sensational reporting about the arsonists' use of "Greek fire" affected the reporter's language in ways probably less acute than those that presumably impressed John Wilkes himself. His inner conflict from entertaining the enemy may have been lessened by the fact that he was supporting his elder brother's career. His sister Asia certainly idolized him in her account of that evening when she and her mother soaked up the public acclaim: "The eldest [Junius Brutus], powerfully built and handsome as an antique Roman; Edwin with his magnetic fire and graceful dignity, and John Wilkes in the perfection of youthful beauty, stood side by side, again and again, before the curtain to receive the lavish applause of the audience mingles with waving handerchiefs and every mark of enthusiasm."[4]

Nonetheless, the Southern loyalist in John Wilkes almost certainly took offense at self-congratulatory reviews like the following:

FROM "PUBLIC AMUSEMENTS—NEW YORK DESTINED TO BE THE ART
CAPITAL OF THE WORLD" (Nov. 27, 1864)

The public amusements of this city for last night were of a very noteworthy character for their number, variety and excellence. Not that last night was so much richer in this respect than our nights usually are. It was rather a fair representative of the excellence and high standard of our public entertainments, and the occasion was noteworthy in so far as it affords a fair occasion to point out how much New York is ahead of other cities in this respect. First on the list stands a representation of one of Shakspere's plays. No playgoer has seen Shakspere presented with attraction more likely to draw and charm the true lover of the drama since the days when Shakspere himself appeared in his own plays. Three parts in the tragedy of Julius Caesar were personated by actors of the first merit—a thing that can hardly be seen in any city but ours. Only English cities could hope to rival us in this; and England does not now possess three tragedians, or even one, comparable to any one of the Booths. Moreover, if there were three men of such ability on the British stage, audiences would hope in vain to see them all together in one play.

New York Herald, Nov. 27, 1864, p.1.

Booth Senior had made himself famous as an adopted American actor who rivaled British tragedians. Edwin continued this tradition as Brutus and as Hamlet. The youngest son seized the opportunity to kill Lincoln, and came to be reviled not as a noble Roman, but as a Judas.

DESPERATE PLOTS

John Wilkes Booth's participation in Southern intrigue grew while Edwin was revenging the murder of Claudius nightly at the Winter Garden and the Union forces punished the Southern secessionists. The end of the Civil War approached with Sherman's successful invasion of Georgia. His capture of Atlanta had given Lincoln a needed boost in the fall 1864 election. The President had to overcome opposition for re-nomination in June, while General Grant was pushing General Lee's Army of Northern Virginia slowly back on its defenses. The Thanksgiving festivities for New York's seemingly miraculous escape from secret agents' fires yielded to Yankee Christmas celebrations of Sherman's capture of Savannah. By reaching the sea, he cut the Confederacy in half, while Grant beseiged Petersburg, the stronghold protecting Richmond.

Confederate sympathizers concocted several plots designed to defend the faltering Southern cause by enacting some stupendous surprise. Booth and other partisans, acting on their own initiative, had lain in wait to kidnap the President and instigate what they hoped would be a popular revolt against his "tyranny" or at least to hold him hostage against an almost certain military defeat. Their ambush failed because Lincoln canceled his expected public appearance that March 20th.

"The Night They Drove Old Dixie Down" came on April 3 when the Confederate capital, Richmond, had to be evacuated. The "Danville Train" carried Jefferson Davis and his cabinet to a safer haven near Danville, Virginia. The Union Army soon commanded the field, and General Lee surrendered at Appomattox less than a week later.

On Good Friday—for Christians the commemoration of Jesus Christ's crucifixion, for Booth the Ides of a tyrannous Julius Caesar's stabbing—Lincoln kept his intended date to see the actress Laura Keen perform in the farcical comedy *Our American Cousin* at Ford's Theater. He occupied a flag-draped presidential box from which he would take a public bow.

That night, Booth and at least three other plotters aimed to wipe out the principal Union officeholders. One was to kill Vice President Andrew Johnson; two sought the life of the Secretary of State, William Seward. John Wilkes Booth cast himself in the starring role of Brutus. Taking a drink before entering a theater where he was a recognized and accepted actor, he reportedly boasted to one of his friends in the saloon, who teased him about not living up to his father's dramatic achievements, that "when I leave the stage, I will be the most talked-about man in America."[5]

Because he was a familiar face at Ford's Theater, and because in that era presidential security did not insulate the chief executive, Booth had been able that afternoon to scout the approach to the gallery leading to Lincoln's box. He apparently drilled a peephole and hid a rod to block shut the door from the inside. He gave a sealed envelope to another actor friend, with instructions to release it to the *National Intelligencer* newspaper. He arranged for a horse to await him in the alley. On the fatal evening, he evaded the sentry and was able to enter unnoticed. There sat Mr. and Mrs. Lincoln and their guests, a young couple, Major Rathbone and his fiancée, Clara Harris, who had been invited because General and Mrs. Grant were unable to attend. (What Booth would have attempted with a symbolic "Mark Antony" next to a "Julius Caesar" can only be imagined.)

He left no time for "Et tu, Brute." One shot from his derringer pierced Lincoln's head. He stabbed and wounded Major Rathbone, who rose to the President's aid. Leaping to the stage some ten feet below, he was heard to shout the Virginia commonwealth motto with his Confederate coda. "Sic semper tyrannis. The South is avenged." Then, pursued by at least one person from the audience, he limped to his horse and away.

FLIGHT TOWARD PHILIPPI

Booth's escape and capture little resembled Brutus' flight from the Romans stirred up by Shakespeare's Antony, but the martyrdom of Lincoln, just as Shakespeare had dramatized public sympathy after Caesar's death, quickly raised popular horror. The manhunt led to the arrests of the Booth family—mother and two remaining sons. Bloodhounds yelped through the woods of Maryland and Virginia. Informants were asked to come forward.

During this frantic period, John Wilkes Booth took shelter in the Maryland backwoods, waiting a chance to cross the Potomac River and reach relative safety in Virginia. During this time he amended a memorandum book and calendar where some version of the letter he wrote to the press was written. (His friend had ignored his instructions and read the manifesto. He destroyed it for fear of being charged with complicity.)

BOOTH'S DIARY

This record of an escaped assassin reveals the mental life of a deranged Shakespearean, self-consciously imitating Brutus, flattering himself with the courage of Macbeth and the justification of Hamlet. It survived, apparently intact, with Booth's other equipment, and was carefully transcribed as a result of a Congressional investigation of the assassination.

The terms Booth uses—Country, the Government, God, Instrument—with his special meanings for them, provide a lesson in the same school of self-justification that Shakespeare's Brutus teaches.

This son of English immigrants had completely adopted America as his mother country. Devotion to his real mother blends with a patriotic identification of the America before the Civil War and excluded the people who served its institutions. To separate the country from the government is a classic means of rationalizing illegal acts. "Not that I lov'd Caesar less, but that I lov'd Rome more," said Brutus in his defense of killing the "king" while loving the city-state.

Booth invokes God as his only judge. His concept of a divine principle of justice that overrules human opinion reveals his self-importance. He is not an ordinary murderer but a divine agent, in the pattern of Hamlet's thinking that he has been chosen to wipe out a usurper. "I'll blessing beg of you [his mother]. For this same lord [Polonius], I do repent; but heaven pleas'd it so / To punish me with this [the mistaken murder of Polonius?], and this with me, / That I must be their scourge and minister" (3.4.172-75). Unlike Hamlet, Booth does not repent his killing of Lincoln, whom he cannot bring himself to name. Instead his victim is "him." Thinking about the human sufferer as an *object* of one's hate, not a person, is another classic strategy of assassins.

In the first section of the diary, up to the point where he breaks off the rationalization, Booth is proud and uncomplaining. He had read the savage attacks on him in newspapers, which is the evidence for his back-dating the first entry to April 13 and 14, and he is offended that anyone would think him cowardly or dishonorable. The Brutus instinct prompts him to reply that he exceeded his failed fellow assassins (who only wounded the Secretary of State and never approached the Vice President) by so boldly passing through Lincoln's supporters and by denouncing the "tyrant" after shooting him. Though he imagines himself to have acted like Macbeth wading through enemy soldiers to confront and kill Macdonwald (*Macbeth* 1.2.16-23), he ignores the fact that he walked through an audience watching a play, approached a man in an enclosed boxseat from behind, and shot him in the head.

In the second entry, evidently written when a week's fatigue had worn him down, he is more self-pitying, though still defiantly self-righteous. How can they treat me so? he seems to say. Where are the "people" who ought to admire a noble-minded Brutus and a brave William Tell, the legendary Swiss archer and anti-tyrant? Booth confuses his ideal countrymen with the degenerates he takes all Unionists to be, as we can see in his imagined return to the capital where he would face all his accusers and prove to them that his motives were pure. What he intended by his benedictions for the whole world is as uncertain as these other speculations about his Shakespearean meaning. It is not easy to explain rationally how Booth can conceive of himself as magnanimous ("great souled") while at the same time holding that his act was not a "wrong" and that he never hated anyone. Having given up on human reason, he falls back on the ultimate moral authority of God.

Booth's rambling expressions make some sense if he thought he was a tragic hero. Scorned by the world, possibly guilty of greater sins than his flaws allow him to realize, but nonetheless a bold fighter willing to accept death for his actions, Booth wraps himself in the cloak of manliness that was Macbeth's. His quotation of the opening lines of act 5 scene 7 leaves out the bear-baiting image: "They have tied me to a stake; I cannot fly / But bear-like I must fight the course." Brute and Brutus. In the back of his mind must have lain the many Shakespearean roles he, his brothers, and his father played in so many provincial and urban theaters. Secluded in his own mental drama, Booth was finally angered that no one applauded.

John Wilkes Booth did, notoriously, what we all do, innocently, when we apply Shakespeare's theatrical situations to our lives. *Julius Caesar* is a play especially applicable to political intrigue, war, and assassination, but also to loyalty, honor, and individual responsibility. In what context we choose to take these ideas is no fault of Shakespeare's, but our own.

FROM "BOOTH'S DIARY" (April 1864)

April 13th 14 Friday the Ides

Until to day nothing was ever thought of sacrificing to our country's wrongs. For six months we had worked to capture. But our cause being almost lost, something decisive & great must be done. But its failure was owing to others, who did not strike for their country with a heart. I struck boldly and not as the papers say. I walked with a firm step through a thousand of his friends, was stopped, but pushed on. A Col- was at his side. I shouted Sic semper before I fired. In jumping broke my leg. I passed all his pickets, rode sixty miles that night, with the bone of my leg tearing the flesh at every jump. I can never repent it, though we hated to kill: Our country owed all her troubles to him, and God simply made me the instrument of his punishment. The country is not what it was. This forced union is not what I have loved. I care not what becomes of me. I have no desire to out-live my country. this night (before the deed) I wrote a long article and left it for one of the Editors of the National Inteligencer, in which I fully set forth our reasons for our proceedings. He or the Govmt

Friday 21—

After being hunted like a dog through swamps, woods, and last night being chased by gun boats till I was forced to return wet cold and starving, with every mans hand against me, I am here in despair. And why; For doing what Brutus was honored for, what made Tell a Hero. And yet I for striking down a greater tyrant than they ever knew am looked upon as a common cutthroat. My action was purer than either of theirs. One, hoped to be great himself. The other had not only his countrys but his own wrongs to avenge. I hoped for no gain. I knew no private wrong. A country groaned beneath this tyranny and prayed for this end. Yet now behold the cold hand they extend to me. God cannot pardon me if I have done wrong. Yet I cannot see any wrong except in serving a degenerate people. the little, the very little I left behind to clear my name, the Govmt will not allow to be printed. So ends all. For my country I have given up all that makes life sweet and Holy, brought misery upon my family, and am sure there is no pardon in the Heaven for me since man condemns me so. I have only heard of what has been done (except what I did myself) and it fills me with horror. God try and forgive me, and bless my mother. To night I will once more try the river with the intent to cross, though I have a greater desire and almost a mind to return to Washington and in a measure clear my name which I feel I can do. I do not repent the blow I struck. I may before my God but not to man.

I think I have done well, though I am abandoned, with the curse of Cain upon me. When if the world knew my heart, that one blow would have made me great, though I did desire no greatness.

To night I try to escape these blood hounds once more. Who can read his fate. God's will be done.

I have too great a soul to die like a criminal. Oh may he, may he spare me that and let me die bravely.

I bless the entire world. Have never hated or wronged anyone. This last was not a wrong, unless God deems it so. And its with him, to damn or bless me. And for this brave boy with me who often prays (yes before and since) with a true and sincere heart, was it crime in him, if so why can he pray the same   I do not wish to shed a drop of blood, but "I must fight the course" Tis all thats left me.

William Hanchett, "Booth's Diary," *Journal of the Illinois State Historical Society* 72.1 (1979): 40-42.

NOTES

1. Stephen M. Archer, *Junius Brutus Booth, Theatrical Prometheus.* (Carbondale: Southern Illinois University Press, 1992), illustration following p. 198.

2. "Shakespeare and the Lincoln Assassination," *The Shakespeare Newsletter* 42.2, no. 213 (1992), illustration p. 21.

3. Gordon Samples, Lust for Fame: *The Stage Career of John Wilkes Booth* (Jefferson, N.C.: McFarland, 1982), 165.

4. Asia Booth Clarke, *The Elder and the Younger Booth* (Boston: Osgood, 1882), 159.

5. John Andrews, "Was the Bard Behind It?" *Atlantic Magazine*, October 1990, 27.

TOPICS FOR WRITTEN OR ORAL EXPLORATION

1. Collect information about famous assassins and conspiracy theories, such as the speculations about Lee Harvey Oswald and the Kennedy assassination. Without trying to prove the truth of these speculations or to fill in missing parts of the historical record, list the character traits and motivations of the accused, based on the accounts you have read. What human desires emerge to explain the tragedy? That is, what needs seem to be fulfilled by trying to explain the killing? To what extent do these accounts cast the assassin in this role? How are his words (if they are recorded) used against him?

2. Compose a wanted poster that describes Brutus and Cassius based on information from *Julius Caesar*.

3. Write a dialogue between John Wilkes Booth and Shakespeare's Brutus. Imagine what parallels the assassin would claim between his deed and Brutus'. Compose Brutus' interrogation of Booth's view of Lincoln, compared to that of Caesar. Would Brutus be more flattered or appalled by Booth's thinking?

4. Examine Brutus' soliloquy in *Julius Caesar* (2.1.10-34). Which justifications for assassination would John Wilkes Booth have found most compelling? Which imagery would have stirred him?

5. Compare the call of the plebeians to make Payne's Brutus a king with Shakespeare's version of the crowd's royal desires for Brutus (3.2.51-53). What do these scenes imply about the common people's (a) consistency (b) judgment? Does the context of Shakespeare's scene differ in important ways from Payne's scene? Is Payne's version closer to Antony's funeral oration than *Julius Caesar* 3.2.1-61 (Brutus' apology)?

6. What characters in Shakespeare's play are omitted from the players' list for the Booths' performance? Examine a standard text and try to determine what scenes were cut. How would such cuts affect the meaning of the play? Lucius was evidently played by an unmarried woman or girl. Discuss whether "Miss Fanny Prestige" was a real or a stage name; if it was the latter, discuss why it may or may not have been a joke in the 1860s theatrical world.

7. In the second paragraph of the November 27 *Herald* account of the arsons, the writer concedes that Union forces devasted Southern cities countryside. Pay close and serious attention to the difference between "the ordinary circumstances of war" and terrorism. Look again at the newspaper's distinction between what Sherman's army was doing in Georgia and what the arsonists attempted in New York City. Is this difference easy to apply to contemporary acts of violence?

8. Write down adjectives to describe your feelings of the North versus

the South in the American Civil War/War Between the States. (The choice of name is itself significant.) Listen to the lyrics of "The Night They Drove Old Dixie Down," performed by Joan Baez or The Band. How does this song affect your view of violent revenge if you assume a "rebel stand?"

9. Lincoln's reputation rose after his assassination, similarly to the way that John F. Kennedy became a fallen hero. With Antony's help, Caesar also rose in the plebeians' eyes. What elements of hero-worship are different about Shakespeare's Caesar? Describe the Roman ideal of a royal leader, based on Caesar's words and actions (including his ghostly words) in the play, and compare that standard with the democratic ideals represented about Lincoln, for example, in Walt Whitman's poem, "O Captain! My Captain!"

SUGGESTED READINGS

Bryan, George S. *The Great American Myth*. New York: Carrick and Evans, 1940.

Clarke, Asia Booth. *The Unlocked Book: A Memoir of John Wilkes Booth*. 1938; Reprint. New York: Arno, 1977.

———. *The Elder and the Younger Booth*. Boston: Osgood, 1882.

Clarke, James W. *American Assassins: The Darker Side of Politics*. Princeton: Princeton University Press, 1982.

Furtwangler, Albert. *Assassin on Stage: Brutus, Hamlet, and the Death of Lincoln*. Urbana: University of Illinois Press, 1991.

Hanchett, William. *The Lincoln Murder Conspiracies*. Urbana: University of Illinois Press, 1983.

Kimmel, Stanley. *The Mad Booths of Maryland*. New York: Dover, 1969.

5

Teaching *Julius Caesar*

JULIUS CAESAR GOES TO SCHOOL

Shakespeare's foremost Roman play has often been taught because of its supposed "safety." Compared to the bloodbath of *Titus Andronicus* and the austerity of *Coriolanus*, *Caesar* offers both the thrill of violence and the appeal to honor, both presented heroically. *Antony and Cleopatra* is a possible rival, though its sensuality resembles the sexual frankness of *Romeo and Juliet*, and thus it is not often considered suitable for adolescents.

When we ask why *Julius Caesar* is recommendable on its own merits as an early experience in Shakespeare's drama, teachers can review the answers from recent cultural history and proceed to justify these former values according to current needs and social conditions.

MCGUFFEY'S *CAESAR*

Classics teacher William Holmes McGuffey (1800-1873) included two passages from *Julius Caesar* in the last edition of his popular readers for American schoolchildren. The selections from Shakespeare fit right into a strong program for moral improvement, presenting, for example, Michael Cassio's lament about his lost reputation (*Othello* 2.3.262-65) under the heading "The Folly of Intoxication." McGuffey selected "The Quarrel of Brutus and Cassius" (*Julius Caesar* 4.3.1-123) without directly commenting on the lessons: anger between friends is regrettable, that between friendly assassins a divine punishment. There is no mistaking the high esteem in which he holds Caesar when you read the notes to the selection from Antony's funeral oration (3.2.73-230):

> Gaius Julius Caesar (b. 102, d. 44 B.C..) was the most remarkable genius of the ancient world. . . . Under his rule Rome was probably at her best, and his murder at once produced a state of anarchy.
>
> The conspirators against Caesar—among whom were Brutus, Cassius, and Casca—professed to be moved by honest zeal for the good of Rome; but their own ambition was no doubt the true motive, except with Brutus.[1]

The begrudging acknowledgment of Brutus' superior morality came at the expense of making no comment on Antony's zeal in whipping up the crowd. In fact, some of the plebeians' lines are silently omitted (108-17, 161-68, 200-202), partly to emphasize Antony's independence from an approving audience, and partly to tailor the oration for reading aloud.

McGuffey's books, besides their moral instruction, were also intended to teach elocution, the art of public speaking. Antony's speech was divided into verse paragraphs so that its pronouncing and pacing could be more easily managed by students who, although they lived in an era of debating, declamations, and Sunday sermons, needed training in oral delivery. McGuffey's Antony expresses himself in the following units:

> FRIENDS, Romans, countrymen, lend me your ears (l. 73)
> He was my friend, faithful and just to me (l. 85)
> You all did see, that on the Lupercal (l. 95)
> But yesterday the word of Caesar might (l. 118)
> But here's a parchment with the seal of Caesar (l. 128)
> If you have tears, prepare to shed them now (l. 169)
> This was the most unkindest cut of all (l. 183)
> Oh, what a fall was there, my countrymen! (l. 190)
> I come not, friends, to steal away your hearts (l. 216)

By memorizing and reciting from such passionate speech, students drank Shakespeare's language and imbibed the implicit lessons about respect for elders, contempt for traitors, and disbelief that statesmen were capable of deception.

BOWDLERIZED *CAESAR*

McGuffey did not have to censor *Julius Caesar* in the same way that Thomas Bowdler (1754-1825) cleaned up *Romeo and Juliet* or *Hamlet*. *The Family Shakespeare* (1818), succeeding an anonymously expurgated edition in 1808, proudly scoured out the indelicate parts. Along with his sister Harriet, Dr. Bowdler, a former physician who retired on his inheritance, took up the cause of saving Shakespeare's drama from moral embarrassment. They removed or changed the parts that could not be read aloud in the family circle, that is, in the middle-class homes of parents and married couples. The Bowdlers' efforts resemble modern efforts to use ratings systems to insure that movies or evening television programs will not upset the most sensitive viewers.

Any attempt to sanitize *Julius Caesar* usually fails because Shakespeare's very language is drenched in sensuous suggestion. At least in the medium of the imagery, the play is full of references to blood and sacrifice, storms and fire. "Ah gentle friends," argues Brutus to the conspirators, "Let's kill him boldly, but not wrathfully; / Let's carve him as a dish fit for the gods, / Not hew him as a carcass fit for hounds" (2.1.171-74). Even the most bored sophomore on earth can be challenged to explain the difference between conducting political murder according to noble or brutal motives. That the effect is the same corpse on the marble floor is precisely the challenge created by the language of this play: what is said versus what is done.

ET TU, CAESARE?

The elimination of Caesar as an authority figure suggests the latent desires of many schoolchildren day-dreaming about how much they wish they could get rid of the teacher who assigned this daunting play. This resentment, if it exists, is misdirected. Statewide, or school-appointed committees usually put *Julius Caesar* on the curriculum. Shakespeare's plot for the fall of Caesar is full of conventional teaching advantages: grand Roman spectacle; "Friends-Romans-Countrymen" familiarity for speeches and memorable lines; even the ambiguous choice of "hero"—Brutus or Caesar—contributes to a basic familiarity that assists the creative teacher and satisfies the traditional one.

Working within someone else's guidelines for how Shakespeare is intended to benefit students, the effective teacher is in a position similar to that of his or her students. The word is coming down from on high, just as the textbook itself is usually not a matter of choice. Lessons can be made from detective work on the editions themselves. Furthermore, the editors who arrange and comment upon the events of the Caesar story can be investigated. Their biases and prejudices usually come out, and it is worthwhile to familiarize students new to Shakespeare with the issues of the plot. By shifting attention to the "father knows best" attitudes of the editor of the assigned *Julius Caesar*, a skillful teacher can become a temporary ally of the class, until such time when he or she wishes to reassert authority and become a potential dictator. Of course, as in ancient Rome, the role of dictator is useful for controlling a crisis and inspiring confidence, but in classrooms modeled after democracies, the Caesar stance is likely to produce student resentment at worst, and in better circumstances, to foster conspiratorial mockery.

TEXTUAL HISTORY OF *JULIUS CAESAR*

A primary lesson for *Julius Caesar* involves a comparison of the edited text and its ultimate printed source, the First Folio (1623). The printing history of Shakespeare's plays is an academic specialty that seems scientific, though it amounts to skillful deduction aided by much time spent on picky details. (Sherlock Holmes would have been an excellent textual editor of Shakespeare, had he not been drawn to the pursuit of criminals and bees.) Much of the textual scholar's time is devoted to understanding the different versions of the First Folio, that large format, double-columned, supposedly definitive, posthumously gathered collection of Shakespeare's plays. Without it, we would not have eighteen of the now famous plays, including *Julius Caesar*.

The genealogy of the play-script assigned in school reveals many interventions between the original printing and the edited, annotated, cleaned-up version. Typesetters made many of these changes; the early ones did not care about spelling, but rather were motivated by the workmanlike desire to make the lines fit on the page. Editors introduced other changes, or "emendations" as they were called, in order to correct what may have been Shakespeare's or other printers' mistakes. The job of producing the First Folio was so big that errors discovered by proofreaders were corrected on the spot, but the mistaken pages were not removed. Thus, not all copies of F1, its technical name, are the same. Moralists, too, influenced editors to remove offensive references, and translators, in far more sweeping ways, changed the words into other languages. Arguably, the Early Modern English that Shakespeare thought and wrote *is* different from contemporary English—but not as completely incomprehensible as students first suppose.

The unfamiliar vocabulary and the cunning metaphor of Shakespeare take second place, when you look at the 1623 collection, to the startling impression of the words themselves. The letterforms and typefaces, capitalization and punctuation, abbreviations and spelling seem antique, the way that an American colonial chair is recognizable but old-fashioned and probably not very comfortable. Contemplate the following passage, the first version from one of the 1623 printings of *Julius Caesar*, the second from the 1972 Riverside edition. Cassius is conspiring with Decius Brutus about how to trick Caesar into ignoring the signs of bad luck and come up to the Capitol building where the Senate sits with a crown at its disposal.

> Clocke ſtrikes.
> *Bru*.   Peace, count the Clocke.
> *Caſ*.   The Clocke hath ſtricken three.
> *Treb*.   'Tis time to part.
> *Caſ*.   But it is doubtfull yet,
> Whether *Cæſar* will come forth to day, or no:
> For he is Superſtious growne of late,
> Quite from the maine Opinion he held once,
> Of Fantaſe, of Dreames, and Ceremonies :
> It may be, theſe apparant Prodigies,
> The vnaccuſtom'd Terror of this night,
> And the perſwaſion of his Augurers,
> May hold him from the Capitoll to day.
>   *Decius*.   Neuer feare that : If he be ſo reſolu'd,
> I can ore-ſway him : For he loues to heare,
> That Vnicornes may be betray'd with Trees,
> And Beares with Glaſſes, Elephants with Holes,

Lyons with Toyles, and men with Flatterers.

                     Clock strikes.
Bru. Peace, count the clock.
Cas.   The clock hath stricken three.
Treb. 'Tis time to part.
Cas.   But it is doubtful yet
Whether Caesar will come forth to-day or no;
For he is superstitious grown of late,   195
Quite from the main opinion he held once
Of fantasy, of dreams, and ceremonies.
It may be these apparent prodigies,
The unaccustom'd terror of this night,
And the persuasion of his augurers   200
May hold him from the Capitol to-day.
Dec. Never fear that. If he be so resolv'd,
I can o'ersway him; for he loves to hear
That unicorns may be betray'd with trees
And bears with glasses, elephants with holes,   205
Lions with toils, and men with flatterers;
                  2.1.192-206

To read the Elizabethan printing, one must learn that the upside-down umbrella handle-shaped letter is an "s," that "u" is substituted for "v" without changing pronunciation, that "y" is sometimes put in place of "i," that principal nouns are not always capitalized, that the distinctive spelling of proper names like "Capitol" is intended—even though extra consonants appear—and that colons, commas, and periods are the only punctuation marks. Modern editions, unless they are set up to preserve the old spelling and punctuation, generally adopt the typographical and spelling conventions of current textbooks.

One must also compensate for cultural inconsistencies and learn new terms. Never mind the cultural fact that Romans had no bell-clocks, that the unicorn is a fabulous beast easily tricked to ram its non-existent horn into a tree trunk if you get out of the way soon enough, that "glass" stands for "mirror" and real bears are not fooled by them either, nor elephants with elephant pits too deep for safe digging, that "toils" means "nets," and, sure enough, lions can be captured in them, but not as easily as people who will listen to false praise.

Tracking the editor's presentation of the words on the printed page leads to other discoveries about the history of the play. Teachers who present facsimiles of the First Folio can easily get students to notice that the iambic pentameter lines are preserved in modern editions, by the convention of offsetting them in the manner of lines 192 and 193 above. Observing the modern line count reveals that they make up two lines instead of the four in the Folio printing. In many such ways, the rules accepted by the modern editor can point to silent changes that sometimes add up to differences in tone and signification.

Deeper than the surface features of the printed text are the basic assumptions of the editor about what Caesar and Brutus stand for, and how the assassination should be interpreted. Introductions sometimes convey these biases; at other times, teachers must sift through the explanatory notes. Relatively basic glosses about antique words and myths get mixed with human tendencies to shape the motives of the characters and to skew the meanings of events. Teachers do this, students also. It takes some honest evaluation to sort out what we add to *Julius Caesar* because we want to see some particular thing there from what we are only understanding by an act of historical recovery.

A profile of the editor's unstated assumptions can be almost as engaging as the mind of Brutus, though less eloquently stated and dramatically vivid. In the following excerpt from a comparative study of several editions of Shakespeare, a Shakespeare editor comments on the special case of *Julius Caesar*.

FROM ANN THOMPSON'S "DOES IT MATTER WHICH EDITION YOU USE?" (1991)

THE CASE OF *JULIUS CAESAR*

On stage, *Julius Caesar* has been a politically contentious play. During the Restoration and the eighteenth century it was interpreted as an attack on tyranny and a rousing celebration of republicanism: Caesar was the villain and Brutus the noble defender of the liberties of Rome. This tradition continued into later times, with the representation of Caesar as a totally unsympathetic dictator reinforced by overt allusions to Fascism in productions from the 1930s to the 1950s. In more recent times, however, an increasing cynicism about politics and politicians in general has led to less partisan productions which still see Caesar as an unacceptable tyrant but fail to glorify Brutus as a credible alternative, stressing instead the apparent futility of both revolution and counter-revolution.

A parallel tendency in literary criticism up to 1950 is perceived by T. S. Dorsch who, in his Arden edition of the play (1955), consciously sets out to reverse the traditional view of Caesar as a tyrant and Brutus as a hero. He argues that if Shakespeare had "really wished to denigrate Caesar" he could have found plenty of material in his sources (p. xxviii), defends Caesar against the charge of arrogance by remarking that "we have good-humouredly accepted arrogance of this kind in recent English leaders who have served us conspicuously" (p. xxxi), and against the charge of suscepti-bility to flattery on the grounds that this weakness is "not uncommon in great men" (p. xxxiii). He stresses constantly throughout his Introduction that Caesar was "the one undoubted genius of his age" (p. xxxix), "a great national leader" (p. xlv), "the greatest man of his age" (p. l), minimizes his faults ("Caesar's shortcomings give him concrete reality as a fallible human being like ourselves," p. xxxviii), and asks rhetorically "Can it be doubted that Shakespeare wishes us to admire his Caesar?" (p. xxxviii). The murder is referred to as Brutus' "treachery" (p. xxxvi), and "his crime" (p. xliv), and as "this almost incredible piece of criminal folly" (p. xxxix). Consistently minimizing the play's politics and presenting its conflicts on personal terms, Dorsch naturally denigrates Brutus as "pompous, opinionat-ed and self-righteous," and, worst of all, an "ineffectual idealist" (p. xxxix).

Subsequent editors of *Julius Caesar* have been less partisan in their approach to the play, often stressing Shakespeare's apparent ambivalence both towards the characters and towards their politics rather than taking sides, but one of the most recent, Arthur Humphreys (in the Oxford edi-tion of 1984), while conceding that "Whatever the political rights and wrongs of the situation, it is for most readers the republican cause that moves the heart" (p. 36), nevertheless calls the murder of Caesar "sacri-lege" (p. 35) and comments that "Caesar's authority and popularity are in fact Rome's safeguards, and the generosity his will reveals does more for the common good than does his republican idealism" (p. 36). This funda-mentally pro-Caesar attitude also creeps into his commentary, as for exam-ple on the first mention of Decius Brutus at 1.3.148 when he comments quite gratuitously that, as one especially favoured by Caesar (a fact not of course mentioned by Shakespeare), "his participation in the conspiracy is gross treachery, and carried through most unscrupulously" (p. 127).

Bias of this kind in the commentary or notes is perhaps more of a prob-lem, because less easy to identify and challenge, than bias in an introduc-tion where, as quite explicitly in the case of Dorsch in the Arden *Julius Caesar*, the editor is engaging in critical debate. Bias in the notes, however, can masquerade as neutral glossary (the editor simply explaining what the words mean) or scholarly reference to sources. An example of this occurs towards the end of 1.2 of *Julius Caesar* when Casca reports to Brutus and Cassius that "Marullus and Flavius, for pulling scarfs off Caesar's images, are put to silence." What exactly does this mean? The parallel-text translation in the *Shakespeare Made Easy* edition (Alan Durand, 1984) reads "For pulling the decorations off Caesar's statues, Marullus and Flavius have been executed." This is arguably how most people in an audience would understand "put to silence" since the interpretation is supported both by the general context of anxiety about Caesar's potentially tyrannical ambitions and by the linguistic fact that "put to" formulations are often sinister, as in "put to the sword," "put to torment," or "put to execution." Editors steer readers away from this interpretation. In the Signet edition (edited by William and Barbara Rosen, 1963), the note on "put to silence" reads "silenced (by being stripped of their tribuneships, and perhaps exiled or executed)." The Bantam edition (edited by David Bevington *et al.*, 1988) has "dismissed from office (so reported by Plutarch)," while the Penguin (edited by Norman Saunders, 1967) actually quotes the passage from Plutarch to support this reading. Finally, Arthur Humphreys in the Oxford edition (1984) acknowledges the sinister implication, saying "This looks like a euphemism for 'put to death,' but reference to Plutarch makes it less odious—'deprived of their Tribuneships.'" What seems to have happened here is that Shakespeare has been in effect rewritten by editors anxious to apologize for Caesar. (In their haste to excuse him from the "odious" charge of executing the tribunes, they seem to overlook the fact that to dismiss elected representatives from their offices might also constitute an act of tyranny.)

SO DOES IT MATTER WHICH EDITION YOU USE?

It will probably be apparent that I would answer this question in the affirmative: yes, it does. I have not had space to deal with considerations such as cost and durability which are obviously important, nor with issues such as whether the notes are at the foot of the page of text, on the facing page or at the back of the book. These choices will be a matter of personal preference, or they may be determined by the kind of use envisaged for the edition. I have, though, tried to indicate the most significant *kinds* of difference between available editions in two crucial areas: the choice and handling of the text itself and the question of editorial input into the introduction and commentary.

As far as the text is concerned, it is unlikely that all readers will acquire the expertise to become textual scholars, but we can all be aware of the general nature of the debates that are going on. This is an area in which it is very important that an edition should be as up to date as possible. (Publishers are sometimes rather coy about this: the publicity for the 1988 Bantam Shakespeare, for example, relies on the modernity claim—"the only absolutely current and complete mass-market Shakespeare series available (Competing editions are at least twenty years old)"—and you have to read the small print in the copyright acknowledgements to discover that the copyright for the text goes back to at least 1951.) It is also important that the textual information should be as accessible as possible. The material *is* complicated, but it ought to be possible for an editor to describe what procedures have been followed and why, in language that an interested but non-specialist reader can understand.

While there are some aspects of textual editing that genuinely are quite like a dispassionate science, where truths can be established (and disputed), the introduction and commentary to an edition, though they may acquire authority from the generally formidable expertise of an editor who has spent a long time working intensively on the play, remain subjective and open to bias. There is nothing wrong with this so long as it is openly acknowledged and understood by both editor and readers: attempts by editors who aim for "balance" are likely to result in dullness as well as dishonesty. But by all means let us have the republican *Julius Caesar* as well as the fascist *Julius Caesar*, the feminist *Taming of the Shrew* as well as the archly apologetic male chauvinist *Taming of the Shrew*: there is room in the market for variety and it would be refreshing for editors not to have to pretend to be above the critical fray. Meanwhile, it is up to buyers and users of editions to be alert to the ways in which editors can influence what text they read and how they read it. Teachers in particular might consider ways in which students can be made aware of these issues—perhaps by comparing a passage of an edited text with a facsimile of the original to see how many changes have been made and why; or by comparing passages from the Folio and Quarto texts of plays like *King Lear* or *Othello* where substantial differences exist; or by comparing the commentaries provided by different editors on particular passages as I have done with the *Julius Caesar* passages here. In my experience students who are bored by standard "lit. crit." approaches to Shakespeare often enjoy doing the sort of detective work involved in such exercises, when resources (including time) allow.

Shakespeare in the Changing Curriculum (New York: Routledge, 1991), 74-86.

WHAT IS BURIED IN THIS PLOT?

The history of teaching *Julius Caesar* is often a study in rigorous concern with the plot. The pedagogical argument is that students must learn the sequence of events, then add an appreciation of the characters, and finally master the language. Since it is confusing to conceive of these activities as simultaneous, students frequently are set the task of memorizing the sequence of events. Usually, school texts and study guides provide plot summaries to aid this process of learning how Shakespeare deployed his story. A counterargument is that first priority should be the realization of the dramatic situations, a baptism in the Shakespearean waters of language. Once immersed and converted to the human elements, then students can recognize how the placement of incidents and episodes fits within the artificial acts and scenes established by the First Folio and, if they survive, the one-play editions called "quartos." An appreciation for Renaissance artifice itself may be the result.

These tensions between form and verbal medium will never be resolved. However, exclusive stress on plot or language hampers the ability to understand the relationship between "what" and "how." And a one-sided approach may weaken the quality of the inevitable question, "Why?" *Julius Caesar* presents ample opportunity to inquire into these teaching issues.

The following lecture by Maynard Mack, Sr., a respected English professor and Shakespeare editor, to a group of New England public and privateschool teachers, addresses the dilemmas of literary education during the period of the Cold War. In the middle of the 1950s unresolved tensions from the World War II erupted in anti-communist fervor. Senator Joseph McCarthy, Republican from Wisconsin, investigated the patriotism of many prominent government officials and private citizens, especially people in entertainment and the arts, including the Screen Actors Guild president, Ronald Reagan, who testified about alleged communist activity in Hollywood. McCarthy's public accusations caused sensational fear that reminded Mack of the tyrannical power latent in Shakespeare's Julius Caesar character. His anecdote about supposedly slow students mimicking the senator's mannerisms while reciting parts from *Julius Caesar* illustrates the potential value of teaching the dramatic situation before drilling students through the plot. Mack's analysis of *why* incidents occur reinforces his point that learning about this play should not stop at *what* happens in *Julius Caesar*. (He later published these ideas in a remarkable teaching edition of the play, co-edited by another of the contributors to the Yale Conferences on the Teaching of English, Robert Boynton.) Finally, Mack's references to the "marmoreal Caesar" recall those marble statues of Mussolini imitating Roman imperialism, monuments that inspired (or horrified) Orson Welles and John Houseman and thus prompted the 1937 Mercury Theatre production. It seems that war, threats of war, and war's aftermath encourage the revival of *Julius Caesar*.

FROM MAYNARD MACK'S "TEACHING DRAMA: *JULIUS CAESAR*" (1960)

I want to preface my remarks on *Julius Caesar* this morning with one expression of wonderment. Wonderment that there is not more use made of plays—plays of all shapes, sizes, and periods, including Shakespeare's—in our schools. I know that usage in this matter varies somewhat from system to system, state to state, public to independent school, but in general I believe it is fair to say that if drama appears at all in our scholastic English programs outside of the college preparatory course, it runs a poor third or fourth to novels, short stories, poems, and discursive prose. This is an odd state of affairs, I think, not only because drama is far the easiest of all the literary forms to make exciting in the classroom, but because, all things considered, it is also the most effective introduction to the pleasures of reading literature and the skills involved in enjoying it.

The reasons for its outstanding usefulness are not far to seek. The appeal of drama is elemental and instinctive: the infant in his playpen is director, dialoguist, and actor by the time he can talk; his dramatic sense is highly selective before he has a narrative sense at all. Moreover, there is a vast latent experience of drama in children of almost any age, waiting only for the teacher to evoke and build on it. The pupil may never have had acquaintance with poetry or novels outside of school requirements, but he is sure to have met with drama in abundance. He sees it constantly on the motion picture screen and the television tube, and, what is much more important, he is reasonably certain to have participated at first hand, through the normal stresses and strains of growing up, in most of the basic dramatic situations. It will be a rare child who reaches adolescence without experiencing, in his own way and degree, what it is to be tempted and fall, like Macbeth; deceived by appearances or false friendship, like Othello; perplexed and disillusioned, like Hamlet. It will be a still rarer one who gets past adolescence without seeing one or more of his friends walk into disaster by the very steps taken to evade it, as with Oedipus; or become trapped in the unforeseen consequences of a "noble" act, as with Brutus.

For the adolescent, to be sure, such experiences will not ordinarily take place under the kind of pressures that passion builds in the adult world; for him, the escape hatches are usually still open, and he is unlikely, on the whole, to assassinate his guests, marry his mother, or run upon his own switch blade. Nevertheless, the latent connections are there, and it has been my observation that when the public experience of a great play is brought into the right kind of relation with the private experience of the individual student, there comes a flash of illumination into the classroom that nearly crumbles the plaster, as the student contemplates his own image in the play and the play's image in himself. At this moment, what we like to call education, the "leading out" of the intelligence and human spirit, takes place. No one will have to tell that student that reading is a key to understanding, that knowledge gives self-knowledge, that literature has much to say to him about life. He knows.

There is a third advantage, too, in extensive use of drama in the classroom, and this is the unparalleled degree of student participation that it enables and invites, even from pupils of the most modest aptitudes. The practice of assigning parts and informally putting on the scenes of a play takes literature off the page for those who are not verbally oriented, lifts it out of the abstractness of the reading process into the kinetic and sensory world of voice, gesture, movement, stance. The exciting problem of how to interpret a scene—all the more exciting with Shakespeare and the older dramatists since their plays come to us blissfully bare of author's comment—promotes speculation, argument, debate, leading to more and more exacting consultations of the text, and to projects suited to all levels of ability. Those with verbal facility can be given historical or dictionary projects. Those with talent for drawing, for seeing things spatially, can be assigned the job of deciding how to project ideas of a scene in visual terms, as if on an actual stage. Even those with no apparent talent at all can be set to working out the movements and groupings of persons that they feel will best dramatize the content of a passionate speech. One of the most effective demonstrations of this kind was described to me not long ago by a friend who witnessed it while visiting a high school in his vicinity in 1953. A trio of boys, whose I.Q.s, according to the teacher, amounted to about 200 among them, were struggling to bring before their classmates the succession of bodily motions and gestures with which they imagined Antony would have accomplished the phases of his oration to the Roman populace. The effort was crude enough by the standards of the Old Vic, but the assignment had clearly brought to life for those boys the meaning of the situation in Shakespeare's play and also its timelessness. For the postures on which they were quite unmistakably, although apparently quite unconsciously, modeling their interpretation were those of a well-known senator from Wisconsin, whom they had seen all that fall talking on television to the populace of the United States.

As this story suggests, I am one of those who believe that Shakespeare can be taught to almost any sort of audience. I am perfectly aware, of course, of the language problem that Shakespeare presents for today's students, particularly for the nonverbalizers to whom I have already referred; and I am perfectly willing to admit that there are classes to whom it would be preposterous to offer his plays. I would only argue that to any group to whom literature in any form may be offered with any prospect of success, Shakespeare may be offered with equal and usually with greater success. After all, it was not mainly the verbalizers and the "brighties" of Elizabethan London who showed up with their penny at the Globe to stand for two and a half hours in the pit. It was the odoriferous and stupid, the groundlings, capable, as Shakespeare himself said, of little but "inexplicable dumb shows and noise." Yet he had something to say to these people: he *held* them. In the hands of a patient teacher, who will make the most of student participation, he still does—as no other reading but the comics will. And when he does not, I suggest it is almost invariably for one of two reasons. On the one hand, the teacher is a bardolater and holds the play aloft for distant veneration as if it were a thing too refined for human nature's daily food. I had a teacher like this myself. Whenever we came to any of the great speeches in the plays, he would lean back in his chair, close his eyes, and murmur, in a voice you could pour on a waffle, "ah, the magic of it, the magic!" That same magic took me a whole year to get over and almost sent me into chemical engineering.

Then there is the other alternative: the teacher is not actually interested in the play except as a scratching post for the student's memory. In *this* teacher's class, the interminable question is "What next? What after that? What then?" as though the play were a timetable to a destination that could never be reached. I get a good many of that teacher's pupils in my classes here. They know exactly what follows what in the first act of *Macbeth*, say, but nobody has ever asked them any questions beginning with "Why?" Why does the play *open* with the witch scene? Why is the number of witches *three*? Is there any significance in the fact that there are also three banquets, three murders, three apparitions, and even three murderers at Banquo's death? And what does the second witch mean by saying "When the battle's lost *and* won"? What battle? And how can it be won and lost at the same time?

Questions like these, I feel, suggest the approach that most of us who are neither bardolaters nor mnemonicists will wish to take to Shakespeare, and if we are taking it with *Julius Caesar*, I think the place we may want to begin is with I.ii; for here, as in the first witch scene in *Macbeth*, most of the play to come is already implicit. We have just learned from scene i of Caesar's return in triumph from warring on Pompey's sons, we have seen the warm though fickle adulation of the crowd and the apprehension of the tribunes; now we are to see the great man himself. The procession enters to triumphal music; with hubbub of a great press of people; with young men stripped for the ceremonial races, among them Antony; with statesmen in their togas: Decius, Cicero, Brutus, Cassius, Casca; with the two wives Calpurnia and Portia; and, in the lead, for not even Calpurnia is permitted at his side, the great man. As he starts to speak, an expectant hush settles over the gathering: what does the great man have on his mind?

CAES.	Calpurnia.
CASCA	Peace, ho! Caesar speaks.
CAES.	Calpurnia
CAL.	Here, my lord.
CAES.	Stand you directly in Antonius' way
	When he does run his course. Antonius.
ANT.	Caesar, my lord?
CAES.	Forget not, in your speed, Antonius,
	To touch Calpurnia; for our elders say,
	The barren, touched in this holy chase,
	Shake off their sterile curse.
ANT.	I shall remember:
	When Caesar says, "Do this," it is perform'd.

What the great man had on his mind, it appears, was to remind his wife, in this public place, that she is sterile; that there is an old tradition about how sterility can be removed; and that while of course he is much too sophisticated to accept such a superstition himself—it is "our elders" who say it—still, Calpurnia had jolly well better get out there and get tagged, or else!

Then the procession takes up again. The hubbub is resumed, but once more the expectant silence settles as a voice is heard.

SOOTH.	Caesar!
CAES.	Ha! Who calls?
CASCA	Bid every noise be still; peace yet again!
CAES.	Who is it in the press that calls on me?
	I hear a tongue shriller than all the music
	Cry "Caesar!" Speak. Caesar is turn'd to hear.
SOOTH.	Beware the ides of March.
CAES.	What man is that?
BRU.	A soothsayer bids you beware the ides of March.

CAES.	Set him before me; let me see his face.
CAS.	Fellow, come from the throng; look upon Caesar.
CAES.	What say'st thou to me now? Speak once again.
SOOTH.	Beware the ides of March.
CAES.	He is a dreamer. Let us leave him. Pass.

It is easy to see from even these small instances, I think, how a first rate dramatic imagination works. There is no hint of any procession in Plutarch, Shakespeare's source. "Caesar," says Plutarch, "*sat* to behold." There is no mention of Calpurnia in Plutarch's account of the Lupercalian race, and there is no mention anywhere of her sterility. Shakespeare, in nine lines, has given us an unforgettable picture of a man who would like to be emperor pathetically concerned that he lacks an heir, and determined, even at the cost of making his wife a public spectacle, to establish that this is owing to no lack of virility in him. The first episode thus dramatizes instantaneously the oncoming theme of the play: that a man's will is not enough; that there are other matters to be reckoned with, like the infertility of one's wife, or one's own affliction of the falling sickness which spoils everything one hoped for just at the instant when one had it almost in one's hand. Brutus will be obliged to learn this lesson too.

In the second episode the theme develops. We see again the uneasy rationalism that everybody in this play affects; we hear it reverberate in the faint contempt—almost a challenge—of Brutus' words as he turns to Caesar: "A soothsayer bids you beware the ides of March." Yet underneath, in the soothsayer's presence and his sober warning, Shakespeare allows us to catch a hint of something else, something far more primitive and mysterious, from which rationalism in this play keeps trying vainly to cut itself away: "He is a dreamer. Let us leave him. Pass." Only we in the audience are in a position to see that the dreamer has foretold the path down which all these reasoners will go to that fatal encounter at the Capitol.

Meantime, in these same two episodes, we have learned something about the character of Caesar. In the first, it was the Caesar of human frailties who spoke to us, the husband with his hopeful superstition. In the second, it was the marble superman of state, impassive, impervious, speaking of himself in the third person: "Speak! Caesar is turn'd to hear." He even has the soothsayer brought before his face to repeat the message, as if he thought that somehow, in awe of the marble presence, the message would falter and dissolve: how can a superman need to beware of the ides of March?

We hardly have time to do more than glimpse here a man of divided selves, when he is gone. But in his absence, the words of Cassius confirm our glimpse. Cassius' description of him exhibits the same duality that we had noticed earlier. On the one hand, an extremely ordinary man whose

stamina in the swimming match was soon exhausted, who, when he had a
fever once in Spain, shook and groaned like a sick girl, who even now, as
we soon learn, is falling down with epilepsy in the market place. On the
other hand, a being who has somehow become a god, "who bears the
palm alone," who "bestrides the narrow world like a colossus." When the
procession returns, no longer festive now, but angry, tense, there is the
same effect once more. Our one Caesar shows a normal man's suspicion of
his enemies, voices some shrewd human observations about Cassius, says
to Antony, "Come on my right hand, for this ear is deaf." Our other Caesar
says, as if he were suddenly reminded of something he had forgotten, "I
rather tell thee what is to be fear'd / Than what I fear, for always I am
Caesar."

Whenever Caesar appears hereafter, we shall find this singular division
in him, and nowhere more so than in the scene in which he receives the
conspirators at his house. Some aspects of his scene seem calculated for
nothing else than to fix upon our minds the superman conception, the Big
Brother of Orwell's *1984*, the great resonant name echoing down the halls
of time. Thus at the beginning of the scene:

> the things that threatened me
> Ne'er look'd but on my back; when they shall see
> The face of Caesar, they are vanished.

And again later:

> danger knows full well
> That Caesar is more dangerous than he:
> We are two lions litter'd in one day,
> And I the elder and more terrible.

And again still later: "Shall Caesar send a lie?" And again: "The cause is in
my will: I will not come." Other aspects, including his concern about
Calpurnia's dream, his vacillation about going to the senate house, his anxiety about the portents of the night, plainly mark out his human weaknesses. Finally, as is the habit in this Rome, he puts the irrational from him that
his wife's intuitions and her dream embody: he accepts the rationalization
of the irrational that Decius skillfully manufactures, and, as earlier at the
Lupercalia, hides from himself his own vivid sense of forces that lie beyond
the will's control by attributing it to her:

> How foolish do your fears seem now, Calpurnia!
> I am ashamed I did yield to them.
>   Give me my robe, for I will go.

So far in our consideration of the implications of I.ii, we have been look-ing only at Caesar, the title personage of the play, and its historical center. It is time now to turn to Brutus, the play's tragic center, whom we also find to be a divided man—"poor Brutus," to use his own phrase, with "himself at war." The war, we realize as the scene progresses, is a conflict between a quiet essentially domestic and loving nature, and a powerful integrity expressing itself in a sense of honorable duty to the commonweal. This duality in Brutus seems to be what Cassius is probing at in his long disquisi-tion about the mirror. The Brutus looking into the glass that Cassius figura-tively holds up to him, the Brutus of this moment, now, in Rome, is a grave studious private man, of a wonderfully gentle temper, as we shall see again and again later on, very slow to passion, as Cassius' ill-concealed disap-pointment in having failed to kindle him to immediate response reveals, a man whose sensitive nature recoils at the hint of violence lurking in some of Cassius' speeches, just as he has already recoiled at going on with Caesar to the market place, to witness the mass hysteria of clapping hands, sweaty nightcaps, and stinking breath. This is the present self that looks into Cassius' mirror.

The image that looks back out, that Cassius wants him to see, the poten-tial Brutus, is the man of public spirit, worried already by the question of Caesar's intentions, the lineal descendant of an earlier Brutus who drove a would-be monarch from the city, a man whose body is visibly stiffening in our sight at each huzza from the Forum, and whose anxiety, though he makes no reply to Cassius' inflammatory language, keeps bursting to the surface: "What means this shouting? I do fear the people / Choose Caesar for their king." The problem at the tragic center of the play, we begin to sense, is to be the tug of private versus public, the individual versus a world he never made, any citizen anywhere versus the selective service greetings that history is always mailing out to each of us. And this problem is to be traversed by that other tug this scene presents, of the irrational ver-sus the rational, the destiny we think we can control versus the destiny that sweeps all before it.

Through I.ii, Brutus' public self, the self that responds to these selective service greetings, is no more than a reflection in a mirror, a mere anxiety in his own brain, about which he refuses to confide, even to Cassius. In II.i, we see the public self making further headway. First, there is Brutus' argu-ment with himself about the threat of Caesar, and in his conclusion that Caesar must be killed we note how far his private self—he is, after all, one of Caesar's closest friends—has been invaded by the self of public spirit. From here on, the course of the invasion accelerates. The letter comes, tossed from the public world into the private world, into Brutus' garden, and addressing, as Cassius had, that public image reflected in the mirror: "Brutus, thou sleep'st: awake and see thyself." Then follows the well-known brief soliloquy (which Shakespeare was to expand into the whole play of *Macbeth*), showing us that Brutus' mind has moved on now from the phase of decision to the inquietudes that follow decision:

> Between the acting of a dreadful thing
> And the first motion, all the interim is
> Like a phantasma, or a hideous dream.

What is important to observe is that these lines stress once again the gulf that separates motive from action, that which is interior in man and controllable by his will from that which, once acted, become independent of him and moves with a life of its own. This gulf is a no man's land, a phantasma, a hideous dream.

Finally, there arrives in such a form that no audience can miss it the actual visible invasion itself, as this peaceful garden quiet is broken in by knocking, like the knocking of fate in Beethoven's fifth symphony, and by men with faces hidden in their cloaks. Following this, a lovely interlude with Portia serves to emphasize how much the private self, the private world has been shattered. We have something close to discord here—as much of a discord as these very gentle people are capable of—and though there is a reconciliation at the end and Brutus' promise to confide in her soon, this division in the family is an omen. So is that knock of the latecomer, Caius Ligarius, which reminds us once again of the intrusions of the public life. And when Ligarius throws off his sick man's kerchief on learning that there is an honorable exploit afoot, we may see in it an epitome of the whole scene, a graphic visual renunciation, like Brutus', of the private good to the public; and we may see this also in Brutus' own exit a few lines later, not into the inner house where Portia waits for him, but out into the thunder and lightning of the public life of Rome. It is perhaps significant that at our final view of Portia, two scenes later, she too stands outside the privacy of the house, her mind wholly occupied with thoughts of what is happening at the Capitol, and trying to put on a public self for Brutus' sake: "Run, Lucius, and commend me to my Lord / Say I am merry. . . ."

Meantime, up there by the Capitol, the tragic center and historical center meet. The suspense is very great as Caesar, seeing the Soothsayer in the throng, reminds him that the ides of March are come, and receives in answer, "Ay, Caesar, but not gone." More suspense as Artemidorus presses forward with the paper that we know contains a full discovery of the plot. Decius, apprehensive, steps quickly into the breach with another paper, a petition from Trebonius. More suspense still as Popilius sidles past Cassius with the whisper, "I wish your enterprise today may thrive," and then moves on to Caesar's side, where he engages him in animated talk. But they detect no telltale change in Caesar's countenance; Trebonius steps into his assignment and takes Antony aside; Metellus Cimber throws himself at Caesar's feet; Brutus gives the signal to "press near and second him," and Caesar's "Are we all ready?" draws every eye to Caesar's chair. One by one they all kneel before this demigod—an effective tableau which gives coloring of priest-like ritual to what they are about to do. Caesar is to bleed, but, as Brutus has said, they will sublimate the act into a sacrifice:

> Let's kill him boldly but not wrathfully;
> Let's carve him as a dish fit for the gods,
> Not hew him as a carcass fit for hounds.

Everything in the scene must underscore this ceremonial attitude, in order to bring out the almost fatuous cleavage between the spirit of this enterprise and its bloody purpose.

The Caesar that we are permitted to see while all this ceremony is preparing is almost entirely the superman, for obvious reasons. To give a color of justice to Brutus' act and so to preserve our sense of his nobility even if we happen to think the assassination a mistake, as an Elizabethan audience emphatically would, Caesar has to appear in a mood of superhumanity at least as fatuous as the conspirators' mood of sacrifice. Hence Shakespeare makes him first of all insult Metellus Cimber: "If thou dost bend and pray and fawn for him, / I spurn thee like a cur;" then comment with intolerable pomposity, and, in fact, blasphemy, on his own iron resolution, for he affects to be immovable even by prayer and hence superior to the very gods. Finally, Shakespeare puts into his mouth one of those supreme arrogances that will remind us of the destroying *hubris* which makes men mad in order to ruin them. "Hence!" Caesar cries, Wilt thou lift up Olympus?" It is at just this point, when the colossus Caesar drunk with self-love is before us, that Casca strikes. Then they all strike, with a last blow that brings out for the final time the other, human side of this double Caesar: "Et tu, Brute?"

And now this little group of men has altered history. The representative of the evil direction it was taking toward autocratic power lies dead before them. The direction to which it must be restored becomes emphatic in Cassius' cry of "Liberty, freedom, and enfranchisement." Solemnly, and again like priests who have just sacrificed a victim, they kneel together and bathe their hands and swords in Caesar's blood. Brutus exclaims:

> Then walk we forth, even to the market place;
> And waving our red weapon o'er our heads,
> Let's all cry, "Peace, freedom, and liberty!"

If the conjunction of those red hands and weapons with this slogan is not enough to bring an audience up with a start, the next passage will be, for now the conspirators explicitly invoke the judgment of history on their deed. On the stages of theatres the world over, so they anticipate, this lofty scene will be re-enacted, and

> So oft as that shall be.
> So often shall the knot of us be call'd
> The men that gave their country liberty.

We, the audience, recalling what actually did result in Rome—the civil wars, the long line of despotic emperors—cannot miss the irony of their prediction, an irony that insists on our recognizing that this effort to control history is going to fail. Why does it fail?

One reason why is shown us in the next few moments. The leader of this assault on history is, like many another reformer, a man of high idealism, who devoutly believes the rest of the world is like himself. It was just to kill Caesar—so he persuades himself—because he was a great threat to freedom. It would not have been just to kill Antony, and he vetoed the idea. Even now, when the consequence of that decision has come back to face him in the shape of Antony's servant, kneeling before him, he sees no reason to reconsider it. There are good grounds for what they have done, he says; Antony will hear them, and be satisfied. With Antony, who shortly arrives in person, he takes this line again:

> Our reasons are so full of good regard
> That were you, Antony, the son of Caesar
> You should be satisfied.

With equal confidence in the rationality of man, he puts by Cassius' fears of what Antony will do if allowed to address the people: "By your pardon; I will myself into the pulpit first / And show the reason of our Caesar's death." Here is a man so much a friend of Caesar's that he is still speaking of him as our "Caesar," so capable of rising to what he takes to be his duty that he has taken on the leadership of those who intend to kill him, so trusting of common decency that he expects the populace will respond to reason, and Antony to the obligation laid on him by their permitting him to speak. At such a man, one hardly knows whether to laugh or cry.

The same mixture of feelings is likely to be stirring in us as Brutus speaks to the people in III.ii. As everybody knows, this is a speech in what used to be called the great liberal tradition, the tradition that assumed, as our American founding fathers did, that men in the mass are reasonable. It has therefore been made a prose oration, spare and terse in diction, tightly patterned in syntax so that it requires close attention, and founded, with respect to its argument, on three elements: the abstract sentiment of duty to the state (because he endangered Rome, Caesar had to be slain); the abstract sentiment of political justice (because he was ambitious, Caesar deserved his fall); and the moral authority of the man Brutus. As long as that moral authority is concretely before them in Brutus' presence, the populace is impressed. But since they are not trained minds, and only trained minds respond accurately to abstractions, they do not understand the content of his argument at all, as one of them indicates by shouting, "Let him be Caesar!" What moves them is the obvious sincerity and the known integrity of the speaker; and when he finishes, they are ready to carry him off on their shoulders on that account alone, leaving Antony a vacant Forum. The fair-mindedness of Brutus is thrilling but painful to behold as he calms this triumphal surge in his favor, urges them to stay and hear Antony, and then, in a moment very impressive dramatically as well as symbolically, walks off the stage, alone. We see then, if we have not seen before, the first answer to the question why the attack on history failed. It was blinded, as it so often has been, by the very idealism that impelled it.

When Antony takes the rostrum, we begin to get a second answer. It has been said by somebody that in a school of demagogues this speech should be the whole curriculum. Antony himself describes its method when he observes in the preceding scene, apropos of the effect of Caesar's dead body on the messenger from Octavius, "Passion, I see, is catching." This is a statement that cannot be made about reason, as many a school teacher learns to his cost. I have not time at my disposal to do anything like justice to Antony's speech, but I should like to make the following summary points.

First, Brutus formulates from the outset positive propositions about Caesar and his own motives, on no other authority than his own. Because of his known integrity, Brutus can do this. Antony takes the safer alternative of concealing propositions in questions, by which the audience's mind is then guided to conclusions which seem its own:

> He hath brought many captives to Rome,
> Whose ransoms did the general coffers fill:
> Did this in Caesar seem ambitious?

> * * *

> You all did see that on the Lupercal
> I thrice presented him a kingly crown,
> Which he did thrice refuse: was this ambition?

How well Shakespeare knew his crowds can be seen in the replies to Antony. Brutus, appealing to their reason, was greeted with wild outbursts of uncomprehending emotion: "Let him be Caesar!" Antony appeals only to their emotions and their pockets, but now they say, "Methinks there is much reason in his sayings," and chew upon it seriously.

Second, Antony stirs up impulses and then thwarts them. He appeals to their curiosity and their greed in the matter of the will, but then he doesn't come clean on it. In the same manner, he stirs up their rage against the conspirators, yet always pretends to hold them back: "I fear I wrong the honorable men / Whose daggers have stabb'd Caesar; I do fear it." Third, and this is largely the technical means by which he accomplishes the stirring up, his speech is baited with irony. The passage just quoted is a typical specimen. So is the famous refrain, "For Brutus is an honorable man." Now the rhetorical value of irony is that it stimulates the mind to formulate the contrary, that is, the intended meaning. It stimulates what the psychologists of propaganda nowadays call the assertive factor. "Are you the one man in seven who shaves daily?" "Did your husband forget to kiss you this morning?" The advertiser's technique is not, of course, ironical, but it illustrates the effect.

Finally, Antony rests his case, not, like Brutus, on abstractions centering in the state and political justice, but on emotions centering in the individual listener. The first great crescendo of the speech, which culminates in the passage on Caesar's wounds, appeals first to pity and then to indignation. The second one, culminating in the reading of Caesar's will, appeals first to curiosity and greed and then to gratitude. The management of the will is particularly cunning: it is an item more concrete than any words could be, an actual tantalizing document that can be flashed before the eye, after the manner of the senator mentioned in my preamble. It is described, at first vaguely, as being of such a sort that they would honor Caesar for it. Then, closer home, as something which would show "how Caesar lov'd you." Then, with an undisguised appeal to self-interest, as a testament that will make them his "heirs." The emotions aroused by this news enable Antony to make a final test of his ironical refrain about the "honorable men," and finding the results all that he had hoped, he can come down now among the crowd as one of them, and appeal directly to their feelings by appealing to his own: "If you have tears to shed, prepare to shed them now."

The success of this direct appeal to passion can be seen at its close. Where formerly we had a populace, now we have a mob. Since it is a mob, its mind can be sealed against any later seepage of rationality back into it by the insinuation that reasoning is always false anyway—simply a surface covering up of private grudges, like the "reason" they have heard from Brutus; whereas from Antony himself, the plain blunt friend of Caesar, they are getting the plain blunt truth and (a favorite trick of politicians) only what they already know to be the truth.

But also, since it is a mob and therefore eventually will cool off, it must be called back one final time to hear the will. Antony no longer needs this as an incentive to riot; the mingled rage and pity he has aroused will take care of that. But when the hangover comes, and you are remembering how that fellow looked swaying a little on the rope's end, with his eyes bugging out and the veins knotted at his temples, then it is good to have something really reasonable to cling to, like seventy-five drachmas (or even thirty pieces of silver) and some orchards along the river.

At about this point, it becomes impossible not to see that a second reason for the failure of the attack on history is what it left out of account—what all these Romans from the beginning, except Antony, have been trying to leave out of account; the phenomenon of feeling, the nonrational factor in men, in the world, in history itself—of which this blind infuriated mob is one kind of exemplification. Too secure in his own fancied suppression of the subrational, Brutus has failed altogether to reckon with its power. Thus he could seriously say to Antony in the passage I quoted earlier: Antony, even if you were "the son of Caesar / You should be satisfied," as if the feeling of a son for a murdered father could ever be "satisfied" by reasons. And thus, too, he could walk off the stage alone, urging the crowd to hear Antony, the very figure of "embodied reason," unaware that only the irrational is catching.

Meantime, the scene of the mob tearing Cinna the Poet to pieces simply for having the same name as one of the conspirators (III.iii) gives us our first taste of the chaos invoked by Antony when he stood alone over Caesar's corpse. And as we consider that prediction and this mob, we are bound to realize that there is a third reason why the attack on history failed. As we have seen already, history is only partly responsive to noble motives, only partly responsible to rationality. How we see—what Shakespeare hinted in the beginning with those two episodes of Calpurnia and the soothsayer—that it is only partly responsive to human influence of any sort. With all their reasons, the conspirators and Caesar only carried out what the soothsayer foreknew. There is, in short, a determination in history, whether we call it natural or providential, which at least *helps* to shape our ends, "rough hew them how we will." One of the names of that factor in this play is Caesarism. Brutus put the point, all unconsciously, in that scene when the conspirators were gathered at his house. He said:

> We all stand up against the spirit of Caesar:
> And in the spirit of men there is no blood:
> O that we then could come by Caesar's spirit,
> And not dismember Caesar! But, alas,
> Caesar must bleed for it.

Then Caesar did bleed for it; but his spirit, as Brutus own remark should have told him, proved to be invulnerable. It was only set free by his assassination, and now, as Antony says, "ranging for revenge,...Shall in these confines with a monarch's voice / Cry 'Havoc' and let slip the dogs of war."

The rest of the play, I think, is self-explanatory. It is clear all through Acts IV and V that Brutus and Cassius are defeated before they begin to fight. Antony knows it and says so at V.i. Cassius knows it too. Cassius, an Epicurean in philosophy, and therefore one who has never heretofore believed in omens, now mistrusts his former rationalism: he suspects there may be something after all in those ravens, crows, and kites that wheel overhead. Brutus too mistrusts *his* rationalism. As a Stoic, his philosophy requires him to repudiate suicide, but he admits to Cassius that if the need comes he will repudiate philosophy instead. This, like Cassius' statement, is an unconscious admission of the force of unreason in human affairs, an unreason that makes its presence felt again and again during the great battle. Cassius, for instance, fails to realize that Octavius Is "overthrown by noble Brutus' power," becomes the victim of a mistaken report of Titinius' death, runs on his sword crying, "Caesar, you art reveng'd," and is greeted, dead, by Brutus, in words that make still clearer their defeat by history: "O Julius Caesar, thou art mighty yet!/ Thy spirit walks abroad, and turns our swords/ In our own proper entrails." In the same vein, when it is Brutus' turn to die, we learn that the ghost of Caesar has reappeared, and he thrusts the sword home, saying, "Caesar, now be still."

To come then to a brief summary. Though I shouldn't care to be dogmatic about it, it seems clear to me that Shakespeare's primary theme in *Julius Caesar* has to do with the always ambiguous impact between man and history. During the first half of the play, what we are chiefly conscious of is the human will as a force in history—men making choices, controlling events. Our typical scenes are I.ii, where a man is trying to make up his mind; or II.i, where a man first reaches a decision and then, with his fellows, lays plans to implement it; or II.ii, where we have Decius Brutus persuading Caesar to decide to go to the senate house; or III.i and ii, where up through the assassination, and even up through Antony's speech, men are still, so to speak, impinging on history, moulding it to their conscious will.

But then comes a change. Though we still have men in action trying to mould their world (or else we would have no play at all), one senses a real shift in the direction of the impact. We begin to feel the insufficiency of noble aims, for history is also consequences, the insufficiency of reason and rational expectation, for the ultimate consequences of an act in history are unpredictable, and usually, by all human standards, illogical as well; and finally, the insufficiency of the human will itself, for there is always something to be reckoned with that is nonhuman and inscrutable—Nemesis, Moira, Fortuna, the Parcae, Providence, Determinism: men have had many names for it, but it is always there. Accordingly, in the second half of the play, our typical scenes are those like III.iii, where Antony has raised something that is no longer under his control; or like IV.i, where we see men acting as if, under the control of expediency or necessity or call it what you will, they no longer had wills of their own but prick down the names of nephews and brothers indiscriminately for slaughter; or like IV.iii and all the scenes thereafter, where we are constantly made to feel that Cassius and Brutus are in the hands of something bigger than they know.

In this light, we can see readily enough why it is that Shakespeare gave Julius Caesar that double character. The human Caesar who has human ailments and is a human friend is the Caesar that can be killed. The marmoreal Caesar, the everlasting Big Brother—the Napoleon, Mussolini, Hitler, Franco, Peron, Stalin, Kruschev [sic], to mention only a handful of his more recent incarnations—that Caesar is the one who must repeatedly be killed but never dies, because he is in you, and you, and you, and me. Every classroom is a Rome, and there is no reason for any pupil, when he studies *Julius Caesar* to imagine that this is ancient history.

Essays on the Teaching of English, Reports of the Yale Conferences. Edward J. Gordon and Edward S. Noyes, eds. (New York: Appleton-Century-Crofts, 1960), 320-36.

WHERE IS THIS LANGUAGE GOING?

The history of Shakespeare education ought to be a chronicle of ever-increasing appreciation of the works, and yet many students think it is a "tale told by an idiot, full of sound and fury, signifying nothing." The foreignness of Elizabethan English is often blamed for this attitude. Shakespeare's language is too hard for beginners to reconcile with their own dialects. So strong is the desire to avoid the metaphoric nature of Julius Caesar's or Brutus's speech that paraphrases are sometimes taught by themselves, such as Charles and Mary Lamb's *Tales from Shakespeare* (1807). The complexity of the ideas expressed in metaphor can be reduced to insignificance, unless by some parallel means the student is led from the paraphrase back to the original.

Fascination with the links between prose paraphrase and poetic metaphor, as well as the larger challenge of the interrelatedness of language and thought, animated two British academics, I. A. Richards and C. K. Ogden. Their collaboration at Cambridge University led to a seminal book, *The Meaning of Meaning* (1923), that, in turn, underlay a method in the history of literacy called Basic English. This simplified vocabulary and grammatical system was used to train non-native speakers in the shortest amount of time, to aid the war effort in World War II. The planned invasion of Britain by Germany in 1940 coincided with efforts to educate Allied refugees and compatriots at home and abroad. Although this project had a lower priority than breaking German code or building Spitfires, it was with the support of Prime Minister Churchill and President Roosevelt that Richards, Ogden and other collaborators developed Basic English. Their teaching system became a tool for employing Shakespeare, *Julius Caesar* in particular, as a linguistic experiment.

SHAKESPEARE AS A SECOND LANGUAGE

One of their colleagues in the project, A. P. Rossiter, wrote a paraphrase of *Julius Caesar* (1941). It was intended to demonstrate that Basic English could span the gap between beginning-level instruction and intermediate or advanced levels. Furthermore, the paraphrase was set up in parallel with the commonly available Globe edition (1864) so that readers could understand immediately how expansively Shakespeare's words were working with reference to the deliberately limited senses of Basic English. Stressing that the two versions were comparable but not equivalent, Rossiter sought to avoid an old charge against Basic, that it debased the "real" language. He even extended his efforts to revitalize Renaissance English by creating a Basic version of Thomas North's Plutarch.

These and other paraphrases of classic works of literature in English aimed to provide sophisticated reading for students of English as a Second Language (ESL) to move up to, before getting entangled in ornate literary language. It was, then, a sign of respect for these students, an acknowledgment that they deserved help along the whole spectrum of difficulty. Now, Basic English is disregarded by ESL specialists in favor of fully developed, relatively unmediated English. During the war years and after, the proponents of Basic held high hopes for decreasing world illiteracy, making a simplified English into a global medium of exchange, somewhat like Latin in Renaissance Europe. Rossiter noted these ideals in his *Julius Caesar*.

> Basic (British—American—Scientific—International—Commercial) English is . . . something more than a list of 850 words. It is a *system* for saying things simply and clearly and, at the same time getting free from the unnecessarily complex rules of the old "Grammar." Only 18 of the words are "verb" forms,

which not only makes what is normally the hardest part of the learner's work—the complex structure and changing forms of the "verb"—unnecessary, but gives him a range far greater than would be possible with so small a list under any other conditions. By putting together the names of simple operations, such as *get; give, come, go, put, take,* the words for directions, like *in, over, through,* 2,000 or 3,000 complex ideas—like *insert,* which becomes *put in*—are made part of his store. In this way the 850 words may be made to do the work of 20,000.[2]

Compare the language in the above passage, which is written in Basic English, to that in his preface to regular English readers:

The aim throughout is the restoring to life of words numbed by time and literary remoteness; and since the effect of the Basic paraphrase will often seem diametrically opposed to this end, it is perhaps worth stating here and in plain terms, that this paraphrase *is never meant to be poetry* or the murder of poetry; but is simply and *only* a piece of *linguistic apparatus* whose purpose is to take you back to Shakespeare's lines with a clearer intellectual understanding of what his words subsume. All critical opinion is secondary to this essential comprehension without which *reading-in* supplants *reading.* (It may be tentatively suggested, that the passages which show up worst in Basic may, in consideration, be seen to contain little but empty rhetoric of the sort to which most Elizabethans were addicted.)[3]

The differences in diction in the two samples presented above indicate the kind of comparison that the Basic *Julius Caesar* displays on its parallel pages. "Big words" have many suggestions that are only gotten from long reading experience, and so the use of a few more words in a Basic statement (like this sentence) is a small price for the added knowledge it gives about language.

A primary effect of this system is to show how the "same" word in Shakespeare has multiple senses. Notice especially the careful distinctions made in the notes, to distinguish shades of meaning in Shakespeare's natural language.

An explanation, in Basic, of the conventions for notation and layout precedes two examples of highly metaphoric passages from the play. The first is Brutus' soliloquy where he meditates on his reasons for joining the conspiracy, and the second is Marc Antony's highly rhetorical speech at Caesar's funeral. (British 'single quotes' have been changed to "double quotation marks" and some of the abbreviations such as *elizn.* have been expanded.)

FROM A. P. ROSSITER'S *JULIUS CAESAR, A BASIC ENGLISH EXPANSION* (1941)

SPECIAL SIGNS, SHORT FORMS, WORDS USED

The division of the play into five *Acts* and of those Acts into *Scenes* is the same as in all later copies. *Act* and *Scene* are given in Roman numbers (i.iv) but *Lines* in Arabic:—ii.iii.36 is "act two, scene three, line thirty-six." ll. is used for "lines." ll. 32-40 is "lines 32 to 40."

In the Basic on the right-hand pages *italic* (sloping) *print* is used for words not in the common Basic list (the senses are given in foot-notes, or in the Word-list at the end.)

Words in *brackets* (. . . . .) sometimes give a fuller expansion of the thought. Separate words in sloping print in brackets come from the play and are generally a sign that the Basic is only a rough guide. Brackets are used for stage-directions, as in (*He goes out*).

In the Word-lists the words taken from the Basic list (100) for reading verse first printed in *Stories from the Bible* are in a different print from those here used specially for Shakespeare. The Word-list is to be used for getting to the places where these words are first used, or where their senses are made clear: and specially in the *General Notes*. ii.i.36n. is "see the note on ii.i.36."

In the Notes the sign † is put against all words which are (a) no longer in common use in normal English, or (b) no longer used in the sense which is given in that note. Such words are for reading, not for writing or talking.

Pr. Eng. is used for "present-day English."

elizn. is used for "Elizabethan" : or "the English of from about 1550 to 1660 (the limits being widely different with different words, some being used till 1800 or later)."

etc. is used for "and so on," "and the rest," "and others (of the same sort)."

F. is used for "the 1623 Folio copy of Shakespeare's plays."

S.D. is "stage direction."

Names of other Shakespeare plays are given in italics, without his name.

Plutarch is *Julius Caesar, from the Histories of Julius Caesar and Brutus in North's Plutarch*, put into Basic by A. P. Rossiter (Kegan Paul, 1933). This is a selection of the materials used in the play, and where the word "Plutarch" is not in italics, the point of that note is not limited to the Basic selection.

In the Copy (the play itself) stars are put opposite the lines where words have been changed to make better sense, or (one star) where the right reading is in serious doubt.

Words in *italic* are not in the F [1].

The Stage-directions are generally those of Shakespeare's time, and are made clearer (when necessary) in the Basic. The names of places, such as "Rome, a Street" etc. which later writers have commonly put at the head of the scenes are not given here.

Stage-directions in brackets are additions.

Act-divisions are in the Folio: *scene*-divisions are not.

Line-numbering keeps to that of the Globe Shakespeare, because it is the most widely used by writers for noting lines. *In the prose* this will make the numbering seem not to be quite regular. *In the verse,* where lines are broken, the number is opposite the *first* part of the line.

---

[1] But small changes where there is no doubt, are not noted: for example: *hit* (for *his*) at ii.i.267, and *teethes,* at v.i.41; *Antonio* for *Antonius,* etc.

Teaching *Julius Caesar*

JULIUS CAESAR **IN SHAKESPEARE'S (EDITED) ENGLISH**

AND

JULIUS CAESAR **IN BASIC ENGLISH**

FROM A. P. ROSSITER'S *JULIUS CAESAR, A BASIC ENGLISH EXPANSION*
(1941)

JULIUS CAESAR IN SHAKESPEARE'S (EDITED) ENGLISH

Act II. Scene I

Enter Brutus in his orchard

BRUTUS: What Lucius, ho?
    I cannot, by the progress of the stars,
    Give guess how near to day—Lucius, I say!
    I would it were my fault to sleep so soundly.
5   When Lucius, when? awake, I say: what Lucius?

Enter Lucius

LUCIUS: Call'd you, my Lord?
BRUTUS:
    Get me a taper in my study, Lucius:
    When it is lighted, come and call me here.
LUCIUS: I will, my Lord.

Exit

10   BRUTUS   It must be by his death: and for my part,
    I know no personal cause, to spurn at him,
    But for the general. He would be crown'd:
    How that might change his nature, there's the question.
    It is the bright day that brings forth the adder,
15   And that craves wary walking: crown him that,
    And then I grant we put a sting in him,
    That at his will he may do danger with.

S.D. One of the very small number of stage-directions in the Folio naming a place. Possibly a tree (or trees) was put upon the stage for the *Orchard* (fruit garden).

2-3 Said to give an idea of the dark night, the Elizabethan stage being in daylight all the time.

progress: motion forward (across the sky).

5 † *When?* : Used as a sign of being tired of waiting.

11 *no personal cause. . . general*: no reason from my private feelings, only the general (public) good.

† *spurn at*: to be turned unkindly away from (his offered love).

13 *his nature*: his natural tendencies, as seen in behaviour. Brutus has little knowledge of men, and it seems probable to him that giving a *crown* to Caesar may "make another man of him."

14 *adder*: the only English poison-snake. *brings forth*: makes come out (1) from sleeping in the dark; or (2) from the egg (as in l. 32).

15 *walking*: "taking steps" (doing things), in addition to the simple physical sense of "moving about." *Crowne him that*," is the Folio reading, generally changed to "crown him—that—," though it makes good sense.

JULIUS CAESAR IN BASIC ENGLISH

Act II. Scene I

Brutus (comes in) in his Garden

BRUTUS: Lucius! come here! (*To himself*) I am not able
to get any idea of how near to day it is, by the
motion of the stars...Lucius, I say! (*To himself
again*) Better for me if I had this fault [1] of sleeping
so deeply. (*Loudly, almost angrily*) Come on Lucius!
How long are you going to be? Awake! Lucius!

(*Lucius comes in*)

LUCIUS: Yes, my lord? [2]

BRUTUS: Get me a light in my library, Lucius. When it
is burning, come and give me word here.

LUCIUS: I will, my lord.

(He goes out)

BRUTUS: It will have to be by his death...and for my
part, I have no (knowledge of any) private cause for
turning against him...only the public interest. He
has a desire to be crowned. How that might make a
change in him—there is the question!

   It is the bright daylight which makes the poison-
snake come out; [3] and that makes it necessary to go
about with care, watching our steps. Make him

---

1 *Fault*: see *Word List* and iv.iii.89.
2 This is what a servant might say in Present-day English. See iv.iii.245.
3 (1) from sleeping in the dark, or (2) from the egg

JULIUS CAESAR IN SHAKESPEARE'S (EDITED) ENGLISH

Th'abuse of greatness, is, when it disjoins
Remorse from power: and to speak truth of Caesar,
20 I have not known, when his affections swayed
More than his reason. But 'tis a common proof,
That lowliness is young ambition's ladder,
Whereto the climber upward turns his face:
But when he once attains the upmost round,
25 He then unto the ladder turns his back,
Looks in the clouds, scorning the base degrees
By which he did ascend: so Caesar may;
Then lest he may, prevent. And since the quarrel

18 *Th'abuse of greatness* : (1) the wrong use of great position; (2) the special wrong tendency of the great (man).

19 *Remorse* : in Present-day English, the self-hating feeling caused by the memory of wrong acts past: in Elizabethan, *pity* or regret (as in Pr. Eng., *remorseless*—without feeling for the pain of others). Here the word seems to be representative of "the sense of right and wrong" or "right reason," and is the same as *reason* in l. 21.

20 † *swayed* : had (more) power or authority.

21 *proof* : example or argument from fact making it clear that something is true. "It is commonly seen that..."

23 *turns his face* : as if to a person in authority (in addition to the simple sense of "facing the steps"). Queen Elizabeth once gave Essex a blow for turning his back on her. The *climber* has a respect for the *ladder* as long as it is of use to him.

25 The *ladder* is now *lowliness* again. He gives his back to a seemingly low opinion of himself, and to those (lower) persons who have given him help, "looking down" on them and on his earlier behaviour as not good enough for him.

26 † *degrees* : (1) steps ; (2) the different groups or levels in society; so that *base* has two suggestions (1) at the base, or low; and (2) of low birth, poorer quality.

28 † *prevent* : (1) go in front of (especially, to keep from doing something unsafe, unwise, etc.); (2) in Present-day English, keep from doing, not let (do).

quarrel : what we have against him in our minds. Brutus makes it quite clear that his argument against Caesar is a very feeble one. Unable to say anything against Caesar as he is, he has to make up a Caesar who may be a public danger; and then put the true Caesar to death on account of this fiction of his mind.

JULIUS CAESAR IN BASIC ENGLISH

King? then certainly we give him a power (of
putting men to death), which, at his desire, he
may make bad use of. The special danger of great
position is when it keeps the sense of right and wrong
separate from the use made of power. And, to say
what is true about Caesar, I have never seen (him) when
his feelings had more weight (with him) than his
reason. But it is a common experience that respect
for others is used by those with high designs as steps
are: to which the man who is attempting to go up
keeps his face turned. . . .[1] But when he has got to the
top step, then his back is turned on them, his eyes
are in the clouds, and he takes a low view of the
base degrees [2] by which he came up. Caesar may
do that . . . so, to keep him from it, (let us) do
something first. And because our argument against
him

1 *keeps his face turned*: as if to a person in authority, in addition to the simple picture-sense of "facing the steps." The suggestion that persons are "degrees" and have places at different levels of society is working all through these lines. In l. 25 the man is turning his back on others as a sign of no longer respecting them: in l. 26 he is "looking down on" them.

2 *degrees* has the two suggestions given in the earlier note; so that *base* has the senses of (1) at the base, and (2) lower down in society, and so (3) common, of low birth (as in I.i., *their basest metal*).

JULIUS CAESAR IN SHAKESPEARE'S (EDITED) ENGLISH

Will bear no colour, for the thing he is,
30 Fashion it thus: that what he is, augmented,
Would run to these, and these extremities;
And therefore think him as a serpent's egg,
Which hatch'd, would as his kind grow mischievous;
And kill him in the shell.

Act III Scene II
78 ANTONY: Friends, Romans, countrymen, lend me your ears:
I come to bury Caesar, not to praise him:
80 The evil that men do, lives after them,
The good is oft interred with their bones;
So let it be with Caesar. The noble Brutus
Hath told you Caesar was ambitious:
If it were so, it was a grievous fault,
85 And grievously hath Caesar answer'd it.
Here, under leave of Brutus, and the rest
(For Brutus is an honourable man,
So are they all; all honourable men)
Come I to speak in Caesar's funeral.

29 † *bear* : take, give support to: will not take on "any colour of reason."
30 *fashion* : make into a form: used of turning an argument the best way. *augmented*: made greater by addition (of power).
31 † *extremities* : limits (in a bad sense): dangers
33 † *mischievous* : a danger (stronger than in Present-day English)

78-102 Antony is very uncertain at first. His hearers are against him, more or less, though most of them have not been able to see what Brutus was talking about. (He has, in fact, said nothing to the point). For this reason Antony makes attempts in first one direction and then another, taking care to get the feeling of his hearers, and making half-statements on a number of points, all with the tendency to give the suggestion that Brutus is a very high-minded man, but somehow in error.

84-5 *a grievous fault...and grievously*, etc.: a serious error or wrong in him; and he has been made to give an anser for it in a serious way. *Answering* is put in the position of having to give an answer for; that is, being made responsible.

JULIUS CAESAR IN BASIC ENGLISH

will not seem to take on any (colour of) reason
because of what Caesar is, (we will have to) put it
this way: that what he is, (if) made greater, would
take him to such and such limits [1] . . . and for that
reason he may be looked on as a snake's egg, which,
when the snake comes out, becomes naturally
(like all of its sort) a danger; and so put an end to
him in the earlier stage.

ANTONY: Friends, Romans, Countrymen...give ear to me for a time....I
have come to give back Caesar's body to the earth, not to say how great
he was. The *evil* (wrong) which men do goes on living after them; the
good is frequently put in the earth with their bones. Let it be so with
Caesar....The *noble* Brutus has said that Caesar was *ambitious* † (had a
great desire for power and place). If that was so, it was a very serious
fault in him, and Caesar has been made sadly responsible for it....Here,
with the authority of Brutus and the others (for Brutus is an *honourable*
man—so are they all: all *honourable*†† men) I have come to say something in Caesar's *funeral*...

1 *limits* : in a bad sense; and so dangers to the common good."

2 *flint* : See note on I.ii.177, p. 41

3 *thou art* : an old form of the 2nd person: = you are. *thy* : your. Old forms of language are
commonly used in this way, to make what is said to seem more serious : as in *prayers* etc., in
church, which are put into something like elizabethan.

† The word *ambitious* (full of *ambition*, with a tendency to *ambition*) has a wide range
of changing senses, and the Common Romans have no clear idea of it. By taking different
examples, Antony makes it clear that in this, that, and the other, it is not possible to say that
Caesar was *ambitious*. The effect is to give them the idea that Caesar was in no sense an
ambitious man (which is quite untrue), and from this it only a step to the view that Brutus
was not only in error, but a bad man. The possible senses of the word have been given at the
different places; but to most of Antony's hearers, the only sense is "what Brutus says he was;"
and for that reason the word *ambitious* has been kept.

††*Honourable* : is another word with a range of uncertain and changing senses. By l. 154
it has been twisted round to something near its opposite. The feeling that the small-minded
Commons have about anyone greater than themselves (*envy*) makes them ready to see the
"*honourable*" act of the "*noble*" Brutus as a crime.

On the face of it, to be *honourable* is to be a man able to be *honoured* (respected); which
may take in almost anything which comes into the mind in connection with such men:—Of
good birth: high-minded: full of self-respect: keeping his word at all times, even to his private
loss: working only for the general good, not for private credit; and, at the other end of the
scale, simply: of a great family (good or bad): in high position: important. The suggestions
have got as far as this by line 130. It might be said that Antony's one purpose is to make the
right adjustment (for *his* purposes) of the feelings experienced in connection with these two
words; and in so doing, he is not "*honourable*" in any sense of the word but the lowest and
least.

JULIUS CAESAR IN SHAKESPEARE'S (EDITED) ENGLISH

90   He was my friend, faithful, and just to me,
     But Brutus says, he was ambitious,
     And Brutus is an honourable man.
     He hath brought many captives home to Rome,
     Whose ransoms did the general coffers fill:
95   Did this in Caesar seem ambitious?
     When that the poor have cried, Caesar hath wept:
     Ambition should be made of sterner stuff,
     Yet Brutus says, he was ambitious:
     And Brutus is an honorable man.
100 You all did see, that on the Lupercal,
     I thrice presented him a kingly crown,
     Which he did thrice refuse. Was this ambition?
     Yet Brutus says, he was ambitious:
     And sure he is an honourable man.
105 I speak not to disprove what Brutus spoke,
     But here I am, to speak what I do know.
     You all did love him once, not without cause,
     What cause withholds you then, to mourn for him?

90 *just* : the same at all times, like a good judge.

Antony is answering the suggestion that *ambition* would make a man put himself higher than all others.

93 Answering the suggestion that if Caesar was *ambitious*, he would be ready to take everything for himself.

93-4 *captives...ransoms* : prisoners of war, whose payments for being made free again went into the public chests, not into Caesar's pocket.

96 *cried...wept* : When the poor have made an outcry (against their hard conditions), Caesar has been moved to *tears* by his feeling for them (*pity*). The idea of *tears* comes into *cried* and *wept*.

97 *Ambition* would make him have no respect for the feelings of others. *Should* has the sense of "it would be natural for *ambition* to be made of harder (more unfeeling) material than to do this."

stern : hard of mind; unmoved by feelings.

105 Naturally: this is quite untrue. Antony is uncertain how they are taking his arguments, and so first goes back on them (saying he is not doing what he is doing), and then gets to work on their feelings.

JULIUS CAESAR IN BASIC ENGLISH

. . .He was my friend, true and straight with me; but Brutus says he was *ambitious* (desiring to be greater than all others), and Brutus is an *honourable* man. . . . He has come back to Rome with numbers of prisoners, whose payments (for being made free again) went into the public chest: Did this seem *ambitious* (as if desiring all for himself) in Caesar? . . .When the poor have been crying out, Caesar was *crying* for them: *ambition* [1] would be made of harder substance; but Brutus says he was *ambitious*, and Brutus is an *honourable* [2] man. All of you saw that, on the day of Lupercal, three times I made him the offer of a King's *crown*, which three times he put away from him. Was this *ambition* (desire of high place)? But Brutus says he was *ambitious*; and certainly he is an *honourable* man. I am not talking with the idea of making what Brutus said seem false, I am only here to say what is in my knowledge....You all had a love for him at one time, and not without good reason—what reason keeps you back, then, from *sorrowing* for him? Why, the power of

1 ambition : here, the quality of being all for himself (and having no feeling for others).
2 Honourable : here, a man who will not say what seems false to him. Antony is ready to make his attack, and has got as far as the suggestion that Brutus was in error. He keeps this up till l. 105, and then seems to have no idea that it is unsafe, and goes back on it.

JULIUS CAESAR IN SHAKESPEARE'S (EDITED) ENGLISH

O judgement! Thou art fled to brutish beasts,
110 And men have lost their reason. Bear with me,
My heart is in the coffin there with Caesar,
And I must pause, till it come back to me.
FIRST PLEBEIAN:
Methinks there is much reason in his sayings.
SECOND PLEBEIAN:
If you consider rightly of the matter,
115 Caesar has had great wrong.
THIRD PLEBEIAN:
        Has he masters?
I fear there will a worse come in his place.
FOURTH PLEBEIAN:
Mark'd ye his words? He would not take the crown,
Therefore 'tis certain, he was not ambitious.
FIRST PLEBEIAN:
If it be found so, some will dear aby it.
SECOND PLEBEIAN:
120 Poor soul, his eyes are red as fire with weeping
THIRD PLEBEIAN:
There's not a nobler man in Rome than Antony.
FOURTH PLEBEIAN:
Now mark him, he begins again to speak.

109-10 Without the feeling put into them, these lines give something like Antony's probable opinion of his hearers, as he sees them in front of him, unable to see his argument. His stop at l. 110 is simply for the purpose of "getting the feeling of the meeting"; and when he goes on (123) it is in quite a different key.

109 *judgement* : the power of judging things rightly, and seeing them as they are. Almost the same thing as reason." *Brutish* (low, unfeeling) is used to make the effect greater: not only to *beasts* (animals, as separate from, and lower in every way than man) but to the lowest of the low.

110 † *bear with me* : put up with me, do not be angry, give some thought at least to the feelings which are moving me.

111 *coffin* : the boxes in which the Elizabethans took dead bodies to their *funeral* were frequently open at the top (as in *Hamlet* e.g.). Antony is making time for thought, and turning their attention to dead Caesar, while moving them with the signs of his deep feelings.

119 † *dear aby it* : some will have to take the outcome at a high price to themselves (dear).

JULIUS CAESAR IN BASIC ENGLISH

seeing things clearly has gone away to the poor low animals, and men have had a general loss of reason. Do not be angry with me, give me time...my heart is shut up there with dead Caesar, and I will have to be quiet, waiting till it comes back to me...

1ST: It seems to me that there is much reason in what he says.

2ND: If you give enough attention to the question, Caesar has had a great wrong done him.

3RD: Has he, friends? I am fearing that a worse one will come in his place.

4TH: Did you take good note of his words? He would not take the *crown*; and so it's quite certain he was not *ambitious*.

1ST: If it is seen to be so, some will make a dear payment for it.

2ND: Poor man, his eyes are red as fire with crying.

3RD: There's not a *nobler* man in Rome than Antony.

4TH: Give attention to him, he is starting (to say something) again.

JULIUS CAESAR IN SHAKESPEARE'S (EDITED) ENGLISH

ANTONY

123   But yesterday, the word of Caesar might
       Have stood against the World: now lies he there,
125   And none so poor to do him reverence.
       O masters! if I were dispos'd to stir
       Your hearts and minds to mutiny and rage,
       I should do Brutus wrong, and Cassius wrong:
       Who (you all know) are honourable men.
130   I will not do them wrong: I rather choose
       To wrong the dead, to wrong myself and you,
       Than I will wrong such honourable men.
       But here's a parchment, with the seal of Caesar,
       I found it in his closet, 'tis his will:
135   Let but the commons hear this testament:
       (Which pardon me I do not mean to read),
       And they would go and kiss dead Caesar's wounds,

123-5 Working on the strong feelings caused by thoughts of great men in their fall. "Who is there so poor and low as to have any respect for a dead body?" and at the same time pointing out the simple fact that "he is lower than you are now."

126 The same line of attack as in ll. 105 etc.: saying the opposite of what he is doing, while putting the right suggestion before them.

127 †*mutiny* : used in a more general sense than now: an attempt against ruling authority, not only (as today) against authority in armed forces. Antony puts the idea into their minds with very great care. Here, he says, such an idea would be quite wrong. At l. 215 he comes back to it, and by ll. 234-5 the Commons are ready to take up arms against authority in an *insurrection* (See note on II.i.69) as it would be named. *rage* : angry hate.

130 A development of his earlier observations (79-81) that when dead, men get no credit for their good works. The general feeling is, quite naturally, that this is so, but is all wrong: every man is greater and better to himself than in his public self, as seen by others. Antony is working on this strong sense of unrewarded men, and the feeling that if it was not for all the "honourable" men (the great), everyone would have a chance. The connection might be put clearly as a statement to this effect:—"Wrong is done to the dead, and to me, and to you; but we have to keep quiet about it, and do no wrong to the men who get the name for being *honourable*."

135 *testament* : a statement or account making it clear that something is true. The common form of words is "*The last will and testament*" (of the person making it).

JULIUS CAESAR IN BASIC ENGLISH

ANTONY: Only yesterday the word of Caesar might have kept its place
(authority) against the united earth: now, he is resting there, and there
is not anyone low enough to be bent down before him...Good sirs, if I
had any desire to get your hearts and minds moved to violent outbursts
and angry hate I would be doing Brutus a wrong, and Cassius a wrong;
those who (you are all conscious of it) are *honourable* [1] men...I will
not do them wrong: it seems better to me to do wrong to the dead, to
myself, and you, than to do wrong to such *honourable* [1] men. But here
is a paper (writing) with Caesar's stamp (in wax) on it. I came across it
in his private room, it is his *Will*.[2] If only it came to the ears of the
Commons what was in this statement (which—you will give me your
pardon [3] for this—I have no purpose of reading out to you)—then they
would go and give kisses to dead Caesar's wounds, and put bits of cloth

---

1 The sense of *honourable* here is little more than "men of high birth and in great position." Antony is playing on the feeling that "we had better say nothing about our wrongs
before these important men," and in this way putting himself before the Commons as an
equal. See opposite and ll. 220-223, where he is quite certain of his effect.

2 *Will* : a writing giving an account of what is to be done with one's property after one is
dead. Antony is fully conscious that the best way of getting the support of the Commons is to
give them something.

3 *pardon* : "you will not be angry with me (for reading it)."

JULIUS CAESAR IN SHAKESPEARE'S (EDITED) ENGLISH

And dip their napkins in his sacred blood;
Yea, beg a hair of him for memory,
140   And dying, mention it within their wills,
Bequeathing it as a rich legacy
Unto their issue.
FOURTH PLEBEIAN
We'll hear the will, read it Mark Antony.
ALL
The will, the will; we will hear Caesar's will.
ANTONY
145   Have patience gentle friends, I must not read it.
It is not meet you know how Caesar lov'd you:
You are not wood, you are not stones, but men:
And being men, hearing the will of Caesar,
It will inflame you, it will make you mad;
150   'Tis good you know not that you are his heirs,
For if you should, O what would come of it?
FOURTH PLEBEIAN
Read the will, we'll hear it Antony:
You shall read us the will, Caesar's will.
ANTONY
Will you be patient? Will you stay awhile?
155   I have o'ershot myself to tell you of it,
I fear I wrong the honourable men,
Whose daggers have stabb'd Caesar: I do fear it.
FOURTH PLEBEIAN
They were traitors: honourable men!

141 *legacy* : property given by *will*.
155 *o'ershot myself* : gone farther than I had any idea of going: like an archer whose arrow goes over his mark; and so, "gone farther than is right."
158 *traitors* : see *General Notes (a)*.

JULIUS CAESAR IN BASIC ENGLISH

into his *holy*[1] blood—yes, they would go down on their knees to him, requesting him to let them take a hair to keep in his memory, and when their death came, they would give it by their *wills* to their offspring, as a property of the highest value.

4TH   We are going to see what the *will* says. Let us have a reading of it, Mark Antony.

ALL   The *will*! The *will!* We will have Caesar's *will!*

ANTONY   Be quiet, *gentle* friends, reading it would be wrong. It is not good for you to have any idea of how great a love Caesar had for you. You are not wood, you are not stones, but men; and being men, hearing the *will* of Caesar, it will make you on fire, it will send you off your heads. It is good that you have no idea that you are those to whom he has given all—for if you were conscious of that, O what might come of it?

4TH Give us the *will*, we are going to have a hearing of it, Antony. You have got to let us have the *will*, Caesar's *will*.

ANTONY   Will you keep waiting quietly a little? Will you put it off for a little time? I have gone farther than is right, to give you any idea of it. My fear is that I have done wrong to those *honourable* men whose knives were put into Caesar. That is what I am in fear of.

4Th   They were *traitors* ! *Honourable* men!

---

1 *holy* : as respected and valued as if he were a *god*.

JULIUS CAESAR IN SHAKESPEARE'S (EDITED) ENGLISH

ALL
  The will, the testament.
SECOND PLEBEIAN
160   They were villains, murderers: the will,
  read the will.
ANTONY
  You will compel me to read the will:
  Then make a ring about the corpse of Caesar,
  And let me show you him that made the will.
  Shall I descend? And will you give me leave?
165   SEVERAL PLEBEIANS Come down.
SECOND PLEBEIAN Descend.
THIRD PLEBEIAN You shall have leave.
FOURTH PLEBEIAN A ring, stand round.
FIRST PLEBEIAN   Stand from the hearse, stand from the body.
170   SECOND PLEBEIAN   Room for Antony, most noble Antony.
ANTONY
  Nay press not so upon me, stand far off.
ALL   Stand back: room, bear back.
ANTONY
  If you have tears, prepare to shed them now.
  You all do know this mantle, I remember
175   The first time ever Caesar put it on:

---

160 †*villain*: the word is simply a sign of strong feeling against the person or persons it is used about, and the only statement-value is that he or they are bad." It still kept some of the earlier suggestions—"of low birth," "not of good family"—but was used so widely and loosely that nine times out of ten the word "dog" would say as much—and as little. In a narrower use it has the sense of "one who has done a great crime," or one living by designs against others" (or looking as if able to do so!).

169 *hearse*: a carriage for a dead body, but here one without wheels, lifted by two men—a sort of stretcher (See *Richard III*, I.i).

172 †*bear*: (here) give a push, or make use of force in some given direction.

174 *mantle*: a general name for a bit of loose clothing. The Elizabethan actor probably had a loose coat without arms, made of a half-circle of cloth put round the top part of the body (*a cloak*). The Roman *Toga* was made of a straight bit of cloth and came farther down the body.

JULIUS CAESAR IN BASIC ENGLISH

ALL   The *will*! The statement!

2ND   They were bad men, *murderers* [1]! The *will*, let us have the *will*!

ANTONY   You are forcing me, then, to give you a reading of the *will*. Make a ring about Caesar's body, then, and let me come and let you see him who made the *will*. May I come down? And will you give me word that I may?

A NUMBER OF COMMONS   Come down.

2ND   Come down.

3RD   You have our word for it.

4TH   A ring, make a ring round (him).

1ST   Back from the carriage, get away from the body.

2ND   Make room for Antony, most *noble* Antony.

ANTONY   No, don't come pushing in on me like that, keep farther off.

ALL   Get back, room, push back!

ANTONY   If you have *tears*, now be ready to let them come. You all have seen this coat: I have a memory of the first time Caesar ever put it

JULIUS CAESAR IN SHAKESPEARE'S (EDITED) ENGLISH

'Twas on a summer's evening in his tent,
That day he overcame the Nervii.
Look, in this place ran Cassius' dagger through:
See what a rent the envious Casca made:
180   Through this, the well-beloved Brutus stabbed,
And as he pluck'd his cursed steel away,
Mark how the blood of Caesar follow'd it,
As rushing out of doors, to be resolv'd
If Brutus so unkindly knock'd, or no:
185   For Brutus, as you know, was Caesar' angel.
Judge O you gods, how dearly Caesar lov'd him:
This was the most unkindest cut of all.
For when the noble Caesar saw him stab,
Ingratitude, more strong than traitors' arms,
190   Quite vanquish'd him: then burst his mighty heart,
And in his mantle muffling up his face,
Even at the base of Pompey's statue
(Which all the while ran blood) great Caesar fell,
O what a fall was there, my countrymen!
195   Then I, and you, and all of us fell down,
Whilst bloody treason flourish'd over us.

177 *Nervii* : a nation of Gaul (France and Belgium, etc.) against which Caesar had one of his hardest fights.

178-80 It is probably unnecessary to say that Antony had not seen this. He makes it up (and very well) to put the Commons against the chief Conspirators one by one and by name.

188-94 This is straight from North. See *Plutarch*, p. 61.

190 Antony sees no danger now in the suggestion that Brutus was in the wrong: they have such a strong desire to be given a reading of the *will,* and are so certain that a distribution of Caesar's property is to be made among them, that they are ready to take whatever he has to say.

195 *Then I and you...* : Antony is now able to say that Caesar was the representative of the interests of everyone—that, in fact, Brutus and his supporters were attacking the nation when they put Caesar to death: and the commons are given the feeling that they will only make themselves safe by putting down the conspirators.

196 *treason* : (See *General Notes* (a)). *flourished:—flourishing* is (1) waving (something) about in the air: and (2) (of plants, etc.) in strong growth, getting stronger and greater. The mind-*image* of the tree (*treason*) is united with that of the Conspirators waving their arms. (There is no play on words here: in Elizabethan English *trea-* had the sound of *tray*).

JULIUS CAESAR IN BASIC ENGLISH

on. It was on a summer *evening*,[1] in his *tent*,[2] on the day when he overcame the Nervii.[3] Look! This is where Cassius' knife went through: see what a hole that bitter Casca made: through this the well-loved Brutus sent his knife; and when he took his *cursed* steel away, see how the blood of Caesar came after it—as if it was running out of doors to see for certain if it was Brutus who gave such unnatural blows or not. For Brutus, as is common knowledge to all of you, was an *angel*[4] in Caesar's eyes. Be judges, O you *gods*, how dearly he was loved by Caesar! This was the most unkind and unnatural cut of all. For when the *noble* Caesar saw him give that blow, the sense that he had been given bad for good (was) stronger than the arms of traitors, (and) quite overcame him. Then it was that his great heart was broken: and covering up his face in his coat, there at the base of Pompey's *image*—which was running with blood all this time—there great Caesar went down in his fall. O, what a fall that was, my countrymen! Then it was that I, and you, and all of us went down, while red-handed *treason* was waving its strong arms over us.

1 *evening*: nightfall.

2 *tent*: structure of canvas (or skin) stretched over wood supports, and kept up by cords fixed to pins hammered into the earth; used as a house, specially for military purposes.

3 See opposite (l. 177n).

4 *Angel* : a good *spirit*, the servant of *God*, and specially one watching over and taking care of someone; here, everything good: one of whom Caesar would never have the smallest doubt.

JULIUS CAESAR IN SHAKESPEARE'S (EDITED) ENGLISH

O now you weep, and I perceive you feel
The dint of pity: these are gracious drops.
Kind souls, what weep you, when you but behold
200   Our Caesar's vesture wounded? Look you here
Here is himself, marr'd as you see with traitors.
FIRST PLEBEIAN   O piteous spectacle!
SECOND PLEBEIAN   O noble Caesar!
THIRD PLEBEIAN   O woeful day!
205   FOURTH PLEBEIAN   O traitors, villains!
FIRST PLEBEIAN   O most bloody sight!
SECOND PLEBEIAN   We will be reveng'd:
Revenge, about, seek, burn, fire, kill, slay, let not
a traitor live.
210   ANTONY Stay countrymen.
FIRST PLEBEIAN   Peace there, hear the noble Antony.
SECOND PLEBEIAN   We'll hear him, we'll follow him, we'll die for
him.
ANTONY
Good friends, sweet friends, let me not stir you up
215   To such a sudden flood of mutiny:
They that have done this deed, are honourable.
What private griefs they have, alas I know not,
That made them do it: they are wise, and honourable,

197 *O now you weep. . . pity.* Having given them the feeling that they see all they are most desiring in Caesar, and that, with him, they have had a cruel wrong done to them, Antony takes the cover from Caesar's wounded body: and their feelings of *pity* and angry hate overcome the last of their powers of reasoning.

207 *We will be revenged:* (We will have *revenge*): we will give punishment for the wrongs done us.

209 *kill, slay:* put to death. The words have the same sense. †Slay is not commonly used in Present-day English.

215 †*flood of mutiny:* the comparison of an angry outburst against ruling authority with waters lifted higher than their normal level is frequent in Shakespeare. The suggestion is that there is something unnatural about it.

217 *What private griefs . . . :* The suggestion that Brutus and his friends might have sent Caesar to death on account of some private wrong makes them seem anything but *honourable* men, in all but the lowest sense—"men of high family": and Antony (by taking no note of other possible arguments) seems to make clear that this is their only possible reason for their act.

JULIUS CAESAR IN BASIC ENGLISH

O now you are *weeping*, and I see that you are feeling the force (blows) of *pity*: these are drops which do you credit. Kind hearts, what are you *weeping* for when you see no more than our Caesar's wounded dress? See here! (*Uncovering the body*) here is himself, marked *evilly* as you see by *traitors*.

1ST   O sad thing to see!

2ND   O *noble* Caesar!

3RD   O black day!

4TH   O *traitors, villains* [1]!

1ST   O most cruel thing to see!

2ND   We will have *revenge*! *Revenge*[2]! About! See where they are! To the flames! Get fire! Put them to death! Put an end to them! Let not one of the *traitors* be living!

ANTONY   One minute, countrymen....

1ST   Quiet there! See what the *noble* Antony has to say.

2ND   We'll give ear to him, we'll go with him, we'll go to the death with him!

ANTONY   Good friends, sweet friends, do not let yourselves be worked up by me to such a sudden lifting up of angry force against authority. Those who have done this act are *honourable*. What private wrongs they have to make them do this, *alas*, I've no idea. They are wise and *honourable*,[3] and will (no doubt) give you an answer with reasons....

1 *villains* : See note on l. 160.

2 *revenge* : See III.i.270. "We will have blood for blood!"

3 *honourable* : it is hard to say what sense of the word is here; but Antony is certain by now that their hate will be moved by it. They are important men with ideas and reasons which do not make sense to simple straightforward men such as you and I." The word *reasons* is a sharp blow at Brutus.

JULIUS CAESAR IN SHAKESPEARE'S (EDITED) ENGLISH

And will no doubt with reasons answer you.
220   I come not (friends) to steal away your hearts,
I am no orator, as Brutus is:
But (as you know me all) a plain blunt man
That love my friend, and that they know full well,
That gave me public leave to speak of him:
225   *For I have neither writ nor words, nor worth,
Action, nor utterance, nor the power of speech,
To stir men's blood. I only speak right on:
I tell you that, which you yourselves do know,
Show you sweet Caesar's wounds, poor poor dumb mouths
230   And bid them speak for me: but were I Brutus
And Brutus Antony, there were an Antony
Would ruffle up your spirits, and put a tongue
In every wound of Caesar, that should move
The stones of Rome, to rise and mutiny.

221 *I am no orator*....While seeming to have respect for Brutus, Antony is putting a doubt into the minds of the commons. "What Brutus says is *only* talk: I am not able to do anything but give you a true account, and make you my judges." The opposite is true—Antony, not Brutus, is able to get the townsmen on his side by "talking them round."

222 *Blunt* : (1) not sharp; (2) not "sharp" of mind enough to make up a probable-sounding story; and so, (as here) "the sort of man who says straight out what is in his mind." Antony's picture of himself as a simple man talking to simple men is touching—as a work of art.

225 *writ* : the Folio reading, which may be an error for *wit*, the Elizabethan sense of which would be "power of mind." If *writ* is right, it would be "something put in writing ready for my present purpose."

226 *Action* : the motions of the arms, body, etc., made by one talking in public. *utterance* : control of the way in which words are said.

232 *ruffle* : to put up from the skin, like hair brushed the wrong way, and specially like the neck-feathers of fighting-birds when angry.

234 *mutiny* : see note on III.ii.127. Antony has said the word again at the right time, and the Commons have now taken it up as a war-cry.

JULIUS CAESAR IN BASIC ENGLISH

I have not come (my friends) to take away your hearts (from them) secretly—I am not a great public talker, such as Brutus is, but (this is no news to you all) a simple rough sort of man, who had a deep love for my friend—and *that* they were fully conscious of when they gave me public authority to say something about him. For I have nothing put in writing,† no words, no value myself, no art of moving signs or change of voice, no power of talking well to get men's feelings moved. I do more than go on talking, simply as my feelings give me direction—I am saying what is common knowledge to you all—have let you see sweet Caesar's wounds, poor, poor dead mouths, and given them the word to do my talking for me. But if I was Brutus, and Brutus (was) Antony— why, then there would be an Antony who would get your *spirits* (feel- ings) rubbed up like angry feathers, and put a tongue in every wound of Caesar's which would make the very stones of Rome get up and take up arms (against such a rule).

JULIUS CAESAR IN SHAKESPEARE'S (EDITED) ENGLISH

ALL   We'll mutiny.

FIRST PLEBEIAN   We'll burn the house of Brutus.

THIRD PLEBEIAN Away then, come, seek the conspirators.

ANTONY

    Yet hear me countrymen, yet hear me speak.

ALL

    Peace ho, hear Antony, most noble Antony.

ANTONY

240   Why friends, you go to do you know not what:

    Wherein has Caesar thus deserv'd your loves?

    Alas you know not, I must tell you then:

    You have forgot the will I told you of.

ALL

    Most true, the will, let's stay and hear the will.

ANTONY

245   Here is the will, and under Caesar's seal:

    To every Roman citizen he gives,

    To every several man, seventy five drachmas.

240-3 To make their desire for the destruction of the conspirators even stronger, he keeps them back a little longer, by putting them in mind of the *will* (which, at first, he said it would be wrong for them to have any knowledge of).

247 †*several* : separate, every one man. *drachma*: A Greek measure, used for silver money. 100 drachmas made a mina, and 60 minae made a talent. The last was about 1,200 (U.S.) dollars; so that the drachma would be about 20 cents, and the Romans had been given 15 dollars, or £3 English.

JULIUS CAESAR IN BASIC ENGLISH

ALL   We'll take up arms!

1ST   We'll put fire to the house of Brutus.

3RD   Away, then, come, after the *conspirators*!

ANTONY   Give me a little longer hearing, countrymen, still give me a hearing!

ALL   Quiet! Give Antony a hearing, most *noble* Antony.

ANTONY   Why, friends, you are going to do something you have no idea of. What has Caesar done to be given your love like this? *Alas*, you have no idea: I will have to let you see what it is. You have let the *will* I said something about go from your memories.

ALL   Very true! The *will*! Let us keep on and see what the *will* says.

ANTONY   Here is the *will*, and with Caesar's stamp in wax on it:—To every Roman townsman he gives, to every one of them, seventy-five *drachmas*.[1]

JULIUS CAESAR IN SHAKESPEARE'S (EDITED) ENGLISH

SECOND PLEBEIAN
  Most noble Caesar, we'll revenge his death.
THIRD PLEBEIAN
  O royal Caesar.
ANTONY
250   Hear me with patience.
ALL Peace ho.
ANTONY
  Moreover, he hath left you all his walks,
  His private arbours, and new-planted orchards,
  On this side Tiber, he hath left them you;
255 And to your heirs for ever: common pleasures
  To walk abroad, and recreate yourselves.
  Here was a Caesar: when comes such another?
FIRST PLEBEIAN
  Never, never: come, away, away!
  We'll burn his body in the holy place,
260 And with the brands fire the traitors' houses.
  Take up the body.
SECOND PLEBEIAN Go fetch fire.
THIRD PLEBEIAN Pluck down benches.
FOURTH PLEBEIAN Pluck down forms, windows, anything.
                         Exeunt with the body
ANTONY
  Now let it work: Mischief thou art afoot,
  Take thou what course thou wilt.

---

260 †*brands* : burning sticks.

265 *mischief* : trouble or *evil* caused to another, as much for the pleasure of causing it as for any possible good effect. (The Elizabethan sense is generally stronger than the present one).

JULIUS CAESAR IN BASIC ENGLISH

2ND   Most *noble* Caesar, we'll have *revenge* for his death!

3RD O King-like Caesar!

ANTONY   Give me a little longer hearing in quiet.

ALL   Quiet!!

ANTONY   What is more, he has given you (by his *will*) all his walks, his private garden-houses, and new-planted fruit-gardens on this side of the Tiber: he has given them to you, and to your offspring forever: public pleasure-places for walking about and taking rest and amusement in. Here was a Caesar; when will we see such another?

1ST   Never, never! Come! Away, away! We'll have his body burned in the *holy* place, and with the flaming sticks put fire to the *traitors'* houses. Take up the body!

2ND   Go and get fire!

3RD   Take down the seats!

4TH   Take down the seats, windows, anything!

(*They go out with the body*)

ANTONY Now let it have effect. Trouble, you are about: take what way you will.

NOTES

1. *McGuffey's Sixth Eclectic Reader* (New York: American Book Co., 1896), 286.

2. A. P. Rossiter, *Julius Caesar by Shakespeare: A Basic English Expansion* (Cambridge: Basic English Publishing, 1941) 10.

3. Ibid., 6.

TOPICS FOR WRITTEN OR ORAL EXPLORATION

1. Make your own paragraph markings in Antony's funeral oration. Arrange the first lines in this new order and explain how the emphasis changes from these "topic sentences." Recite this enhanced speech, giving vocal stress to the highlighted openings. Perform your version alongside that of another rendering, and ask a jury of your peers to describe the differences.

2. Carefully read the comments about the characters and motives in your edition of *Julius Caesar*, or look in the notes for signs of editorial attitude toward Caesar and the events of the play. Create a profile of these personal values, one list of the editor's comments and one of your own attitudes. Then choose a scene and write your own notes, so that anyone reading them would be able to figure out your biases. Discuss the extent to which the published editor has directly stated his or her biases.

3. Choose a passage of the Basic English version and compare it to the edited Elizabethan English until you are familiar with the style of the simplified English, especially the verbs. Now, select a passage of Shakespeare's English that is not expanded into Basic, and try to paraphrase it. This is not as easy as it seems, because you must understand what the original means. Remember that your paraphrase is not supposed to sound poetic; you should not substitute word-for-word equivalents. After struggling in this activitiy, return to Shakespeare's English and see if it doesn't make a new kind of sense to you.

4. Find a piece of puffy, ornate writing, for example, in memos or political speeches. Translate it into a simplified English like Basic. Have you said the "same" thing? Was the original merely inflated rhetoric? Was there some emphasis given by its style, a feeling that is lost in your simplified version?

SUGGESTED READINGS

Burke, Kenneth. "Antony in Behalf of the Play." *The Philosophy of Literary Form.* Berkeley: University of California Press, 1973. 329-43.

Charney, Maurice. *Shakespeare's Roman Plays: The Function of Imagery in the Drama.* Cambridge, Mass.: Harvard University Press, 1961.

Hinman, Charlton. *The First Folio of Shakespeare.* New York: Norton, 1968.

Johannessen, Larry R. "Digging into *Julius Caesar* through Character Analysis." In *Teaching Shakespeare Today.* Edited by James E.

Davis, and Ronald E. Salomone. Urbana, Illinois: National Council of Teachers of English, 1993. 207-17.

Mack, Maynard, and Robert W. Boynton, eds. *The Tragedy of Julius Caesar*. Portsmouth, N.H.: Heinemann, 1981.

Perrin, Noel. *Dr. Bowdler's Legacy: A History of Expurgated Books in England and America*. New York: Athenaeum, 1969.

Richards, I. A. "Paraphrasing in Basic."In *So Much Nearer: Essays Towards a World English*. New York: Harcourt, Brace and World, 1968. Rpt. *Richards on Rhetoric: I. A. Richards, Selected Essays (1929-1974)*. Edited by Ann E. Berthoff. New York: Oxford University Press, 1991. 256-63.

Scott, Mark W., ed. "Julius Caesar." In *Shakespeare for Students*. Detroit: Gale, 1992. 164-234.

Thompson, Ann et al. *Which Shakespeare? A User's Guide to Editions*. Bristol, Pennsylvania: Taylor and Francis, 1991.

Wilders, John. "Dramatic Structure and Effect in *Julius Caesar*." In *Teaching with Shakespeare*. Newark: University of Delaware Press, 1976. 142-51.

Production still from John Houseman's *William Shakespeare's Julius Caesar* (1953). Above, James Mason as Brutus; middle, Marlon Brando as Antony; below, Louis Calhern as Caesar. Courtesy Turner Entertainment Co.

6

Julius Caesar: Popular Culture and High Art

JULIUS CAESAR, SUPERMAN

Shakespeare's "noblest" Roman play has inspired many imitations that silently remind us of the cultural legacy of the Roman Empire in Europe, and especially in Great Britain as well as its former colonies. In the United States, the high status of Julius Caesar has been associated with a mixture of high and low celebrity. In passages and references that follow we can see evidence of Caesar's influence on New England private schooling, Italian-American food, high-tech video games, white Southern aristocratic pride, and Black awareness of poetic language. If we interpret them as indirect statements of social value, we can begin to see remarkable tendencies. It was not just the convenience of a mostly male cast that made *Julius Caesar* a frequent choice for a Shakespeare play at exclusive prep schools in Britain and the Northeast. The play represented nostalgia for empire and upper-class rule. These yearnings also affected Southerners, for the study of Caesar's commentaries on the Gallic War belonged to a strong tradition of classical studies in major universities of the South. "Veni, vidi, vici" (I came, I saw, I conquered) became a password for middle-school and high-school students of Latin, and members of the Junior Classical League could not ignore Caesar if they hoped to score well in the school competitions. Many English teachers preferred this Shakespeare play because it did not reek of sex, the great fear about teaching *Romeo and Juliet.*

CAESAR AND FOOD

The Caesar salad was an indirect product of the popularity of the emperor's name. Sometime in the 1940s, in Tijuana, Mexico, a restaurateur invaded the market with a combination of romaine lettuce, olive oil and garlic dressing, croutons, and the distinctive Roman ingredient: a raw egg. (Roman banquets traditionally began with eggs and ended with apples.) This Caesar's garlic war was so successful that almost any American restaurant with high pretensions serves this salad, fifty years later.

The pizza business quickly realized that it could trade on the association between the Italian Caesar and the Italian-American snack food. In the Midwest, one large chain, picking up Shakespeare's phrasing of Marc Antony's tribute to Brutus (5.5.68), calls itself Noble Romans. The couple who founded the Little Caesar's stores chose their name and logo because the businessman's wife admired Julius Caesar's strength and courage; she hoped her relatively unsuccessful husband would conquer the growing market in 1959 for bread and tomato sauce served fresh, hot, and fast. Veni, vidi, vici.

CAESAR AND ENTERTAINMENT

Caesar in Las Vegas

The peculiar appeal of Roman debauchery to American popular taste is nowhere better expressed than in Caesars Palace, one of many casinos glittering in the Nevada desert. Although Caius Julius Caesar was not a legendary playboy like Marcus Antonius, the dictator's fondness for producing lavish public entertainments encouraged his association with glitzy shows, gambling, and sex. One of his early elections as aedile, a director of public works and entertainments, taught him the value of spoiling people with opulence. The developers of Caesars Palace played up the Roman orgy theme by blurring distinctions among the Caesars and decorating the casino like a banquet hall for the debauched Nero. Supposedly, the apostrophe never appeared after Caesar's name because this palace belonged to all Caesars, and these customers were all to be treated like emperors. So, statues of Augustus Caesar flank those of Apollo, Venus, Bacchus, and the Rape of the Sabine Women. The glory that was Rome is symbolized in the American imagination by Caesar.

Video Caesar

The Latin word for "I see" is appropriately applied to the video game, which literally means a visual entertainment, as opposed to a reading or a thinking game. The video game market has developed rapidly in the decades following the 1981 introduction of the IBM Personal Computer. Now it has incorporated Caesar. His city and empire-building reputation is the theme behind *Caesar II*, a simulation of third century B.C. life in the provinces of the Roman Republic. Players position houses, hospitals, libraries, theaters, arenas, baths, barracks, forts, quarries, and roads. Within these structures placed on the chosen site of the "city level," players regulate taxes, contend with slave revolts, and enhance land value. The game rewards ambition and adventure at the "province level" where legions of soldiers guard the hoarded wealth, groups of imperial officers demand tribute money, and barbarians attack the game player for attempting to civilize them by force. (The values are heavily weighted toward Roman virtues of courage, aggression, and domination, and the native culture is generally degraded to the status of "enemy.")

The goal of this game is for the provincial governor to become emperor. Through promotions for increasing prosperity and culture, and for successfully defeating internal rebellion and external enemies, the winning player achieves imperial status. This game uses "Caesar" as a general title for emperor (as indeed it became after the rise of Julius Caesar's successors) and plays on the civil war rivalry between Caesar and Pompey by naming an aggressive general Pompous Maximus. (Shakespeare made similar jests at Pompey the Great, in *Measure for Measure*, act 3, scene 2, and *Love's Labour's Lost,* act 5, scene 2.)

The significant achievement of the Caesar game is that the cultural memory of Roman conquest symbolized by Julius Caesar is retained so strongly in a modern, technological era. The Roman model for technical advances like plumbing, engineering, and architecture still inspires ambitious adolescents who play simulation games, and the Roman record of military domination supplies more than enough of the lust for combat that video games usually fulfill with futuristic combat against monstrous aliens. "O tempora. O mores," the Roman critic Cicero would be apt to say: "Oh, the times [how they change]. Oh, the values [how they stay the same]."

Caesar at the Movies and on the Stage

Lines from Shakespeare's *Julius Caesar* echo in movie scripts, poems, other plays, and songs. Artists explore its verbal imagery, because it is recognized by both educated and uneducated people. Filmmakers and playwrights exploit the potential irony in comparing lesser situations with the remembered greatness or terribleness of "the great dictator." Charlie Chaplin's film of that title (1940) ridiculed Hitler (the blundering "Adenoid Hynkel") and Mussolini (a braggart "Benzino Napaloni"). Orson Welles staged Shakespeare's play during the rise of Mussolini's self-professed revival of the Roman Empire.

The Mussolini Connection

Benito Mussolini, a former schoolteacher, had left the classroom for social battles in the streets of Milan and Rome. His rallying of Italian veterans of World War I against a declining economic and social situation made "Il Duce" at first a rival and then an ally of "Der Führer." Both titles meant "the leader," and both dictators swept their people toward a war that was supposed to glorify and rejuvenate their nations. The Roman symbol of the "fasces," a bundle of rods bound to an axe-head, represented the united strength of the Fascist Party and decorated monumental buildings in Italy. Mussolini staged his speeches in front of these architectural settings. He seemed unstoppable.

The 1937 production of *Julius Caesar* at New York's Mercury Theatre cast the formidable actor/director Orson Welles as Brutus confronting a proud, imperious, ruthless Caesar who was dressed in the black-shirted uniform of Mussolini. The director, John Houseman, proclaimed these parallels in the Communist Party newspaper that launched the Mercury Theatre's first production. *Julius Caesar* was "the most contemporary of Elizabethan plays," and this modern-dress staging exploited "the social implications inherent in the history of Caesar [and] the atmosphere of personal greed, fear and hysteria that surround a dictatorial regime."[1] Welles cut Shakespeare's text to stress Caesar's bloody ambitions, and ultimately to justify his assassination on moral grounds; many Americans were praying for the deaths of Hitler and Mussolini.

Shakespeare's drama was boldly staged to evoke the popular image of the strutting step and glaring face of Mussolini. Caesar met his match in the heroic, trench-coated Brutus. The agitation of the playgoing audience was sustained by such confrontations highlighted against a backdrop of fear. Some people felt that the United States should remain isolated from international conflicts then raging in the Spanish Civil War. Others, including writers Ernest Hemingway and George Orwell, fought in and supported the International Brigade helping the Spanish Republic against German and Italian troops whom Hitler and Mussolini had sent to assist the right-wing General Franco. At home the influential automaker Henry Ford was a strong Isolationist; members of President Roosevelt's cabinet favored intervention. Many anxious Americans were caught in the middle. According to Welles' editor:

> In the 1930s, the sight of fascist salutes and martial throngs, and the sound of demagogic ranting and angry mobs, had become a commonplace for anyone who listened to the radio or saw the newsreels or read such popular magazines as *Time* and *Newsweek*. Whatever else was not within their personal experience—such as stealth or conspiracy or gangsterism—had, in all probability, become familiar to the general public through their exposure to the movies. These were the sights and sounds that Welles employed as theatrical devices in *Julius Caesar*. For his audience, the production, which Welles subtitled, "The Death of a Dictator," had the same immediacy as banner headlines that day after day proclaimed new and increasingly gruesome horrors being committed just across the Atlantic Ocean.[2]

A mob killing an innocent bystander is represented in the scene where Cinna the poet is murdered because his name resembles that of Cinna the conspirator, and Welles, somewhat contrary to the political sympathies of his Communist Party backers, emphasized this reminder of the uncontrollable passions of revolutionaries.

Turning *Julius Caesar* into political propaganda was a successful strategy for actor/directors with Welles' and Houseman's sophistication, as long as the audience was distracted by war. A year before the Mercury Theatre *Julius Caesar*, Welles had mounted his "Voodoo Macbeth" boldly transported to nineteenth-century French colonial Haiti.

After the Allies had defeated Germany, Italy, and Japan, American popular taste in drama turned increasingly to the movies more than the stage, and Welles, chasing this audience, disgraced himself among critics by taking the offer of a low-budget studio to make a film version of *Macbeth* (1948). It was set in primitive Scotland but inspired by his witch-doctor Caribbean staging. An unsynchronized voice track tortured the eyes and ears of the observers. (Welles redeemed his Shakespeare film reputation in 1964, with a remarkable adaptation of the Falstaff character in the Henry IV plays, *Chimes at Midnight*.) However much his *Macbeth* attempt failed to make Shakespeare into a box-office sensation, the idea occurred to a few American businessmen in the 1950s that if a major Hollywood studio did Shakespeare "right"—and that meant casting a star—then, with the proper play, money would be made and high culture advanced. The fulfillment of this dream came in the person of Marlon Brando, and, naturally, the play *Julius Caesar*.

Caesar in Hollywood

In 1952, Orson Welles' former partner John Houseman undertook a film version of Shakespeare's *Julius Caesar* for the powerful corporation Metro-Goldwyn-Mayer. MGM hired the eminent British Shakespearean actor John Gielgud to play Cassius, and the well-trained Hollywood actors Louis Calhern and James Mason for the roles of Caesar and Brutus. Houseman's instinct for seeking quality talent and sensual appeal led him to propose Marlon Brando for Marc Antony. The MGM officials could not believe it. No one thought that Brando, known for his shouting, sloppy-speaking Stanley Kowalski in *Streetcar Named Desire* (on Broadway, 1947; as a movie, 1951) and the Mexican revolutionary Emiliano Zapata (*Viva Zapata!*, 1952) could do justice to Shakespeare, but Houseman, who had seen him act, knew better. And he sensed that Gielgud, who had never worked with Shakespeare on film, might teach and learn.

Here is an excerpt from the veteran British actor's promotional praise for the American masterminds:

> I find that Mr. Houseman and Mr. Mankiewicz have used the technique of the screen to the utmost advantage in the use of close-ups, of detail to illustrate key moments in film terms. . . . Shakespeare himself would surely have been pleased to be able to transport his audience in a few seconds from the hot sunlight of the stadium—where Caesar passes Brutus, Cassius and Casca,

on his return from the games with Antony—to the night scene, with its flapping shutters and windsoaked cobblestones, where Cicero hurries by torchlight through the rain, and Cassius and Casca whisper of the meeting to plan Caesar's murder. A moment later, the camera slides again to the silent garden, where Brutus paces to and fro, in troubled indecision, amid the shattered branches and the litter of the storm.[3]

Houseman recalls one of the many moments when Brando proved his worth beyond sex appeal. Marc Antony's funeral oration required depth of sincerity mounting to passionate scorn.

> The big surprise was Brando. Even those of us who recognized him as one of the most exciting young actors of his time were astonished at the quality of his preparation for his long and immensely difficult speech. I knew he had been working on it: as rehearsals progressed it was fascinating to follow his growing awareness of the nature of classical acting. He came to me one day in a state of excitement to report an astonishing discovery he had just made. As a pupil of Stella Adler and a member of the Actors Studio, he was familiar with the uses of affective emotion and the importance of "subtext"—the need to enrich and strengthen a role through subjective exploration beneath and between the author's lines. Now suddenly he had discovered that with a dramatist of Shakespeare's genius and in a speech as brilliantly and elaborately written as Antony's oration, it was not necessary nor even possible to play between the lines, and that having, in his own mind, created the character and personality of Antony, he must let Shakespeare's words carry the full flood of his own emotion from the beginning to the end of the scene.[4]

Although the final scene had to be edited by piecing together the best takes, Brando's performance was stunning.

Interpreting Shakespeare's Globe Theatre text for the cinema required the film-makers, screen writers, and actors to adapt Shakespeare's script written for a relatively bare stage to the huge sets of the movie studio. The visual grandeur of the Hollywood-Rome was suddenly made intimate by close-ups of faces, and the momentum of Shakespeare's language could not easily be interrupted, or mistakes corrected, without reshooting the whole speech.

Houseman addresses these challenges in an article about the play, published after critics had all hailed *Julius Caesar*. He reminds us of the common problems arising from adapting Shakespeare to a new medium.

FROM JOHN HOUSEMAN'S "FILMING *JULIUS CAESAR*" (1953)

Platform-stage or proscenium-arch, radio, TV, or motion picture—no matter what medium you employ, the problems of effectively presenting an established masterpiece to contemporary audiences remain essentially the same. Time, by itself, has little to do with the case. A three-century-old classic, artfully reincarnated, may establish a more vital and immediate communication with today's public than a modern play revived within its author's lifetime. Shakespeare seems closer to us than O'Neill.

There are two things the producers of a revival must achieve, over and above the normal requirements of an effective dramatic presentation: first, they must cut away the traditional fustian which, visually no less than verbally, tends to collect around the body of a famous work; second, they must, without distorting it, adapt the text and intention of the original dramatist to the technical resources and psychological climate of their own time. The success of a revival depends largely upon the degree to which the work in question proves itself adaptable to these changing conditions.

For Shakespeare the present time is particularly propitious. Seemingly indestructible though his texts may be, the truth is that for hundreds of years his plays were performed under theatrical conditions totally alien and generally hostile to his own. It is only in the last fifty odd years, with the theatrical use of the electric lighting and under the indirect influence of the other newer electronic media, that we have succeeded in recapturing some of the swift, fluid wonder of the Elizabethan stage.

Of all Shakespeare's plays, *Julius Caesar* benefits from one further, specific circumstance—the automatic empathy it evokes in modern audiences, to whom gang war among the great is a habitual subject of melodrama, and to whom the tragic conflict between personal ambition and democratic integrity is painfully and dramatically familiar.

When Mercury Theatre put on its modern-clothes, bare-stage *Caesar* in 1937 (a production which used movie technique), the late John Anderson wrote:

> *Julius Caesar* has about it the immediate ring of today's headlines, and the majestic voice of the drama's greatest mouthpiece. One man brooding against Caesar's ambition finds anoth-

er man to share his thought. The two become four, then six and eight, until they stand around a single man to strike him down to save their liberties. Then one man emerges to stand alone against them and the mob rises and they answer for what they did singly. . . . Shakespeare's language presents no incongruity. It is simply released to work its supreme magic in terms of theatre, as if this method had renewed vouchers of immortality, as if, in fact, a great poet had risen in our midst only yesterday, a poet who understands the *movies*, as profoundly as he does the human heart.

For audiences whose daily news diet was being poisoned by the unchecked growth of Fascist and Nazi power, Orson Welles prepared a script that was as sharp and violent as his production. Since it was clearly impossible to bring the pomp of the Roman state, the city mob's massive violence or, above all, the changing tide of battle onto his small stage, they were handled impressionistically. Out of the darkness, into the crude electric glare of innumerable projectors, dark uniformed figures appeared in conflict and vanished with stylised and shocking suddenness. Like all the best of Welles's work, it was magically and brilliantly theatrical.

Now, fifteen years later, I find myself, in a different association, faced with an even greater challenge—that of helping to transfer *Julius Caesar* to the screen.

In preparing this project we started with two assets: the psychological climate for such a drama remains propitious; and, in this new medium, we had no fustian to strip away, no accreted tradition of Shakespearean movie-acting to inhibit us.

This left us free to attack our main artistic problem—that of translating Shakespeare's bloody and turbulent melodrama into a medium where both mass effects and personal conflict can be more closely observed and more fully developed than under the constant and unchanging focus of a playhouse stage. Yet, while exploiting the camera's brooding mobility, we had to be careful never to substitute effect for tension; not to sacrifice—as some Shakespearean movies have—the dramatic unity of the work as a whole.

For these reasons we were particularly fortunate in having as our director and collaborator a man well known for his experience and skill in the writing and staging of intelligent talking pictures. As our work progressed it was Joe Mankiewicz, the movie maker, who proved to be the conservative among us. He it was who held us most severely to a direct and smooth transition from playscript to screen-play; he who insisted, and then went on to demonstrate, that the diverse and special resources of the movie medium should be used not to supercharge or distort but to render Shakespeare's political thriller faithfully and imaginatively for the screen.

When we had finished, we found, to our surprise, that we had adhered more closely not only to Shakespeare's text but also to Shakespeare's stage directions than would have been possible or desirable on a modern stage.

From the start we set ourselves one basic rule: that at no point must the words or the action of the drama be swamped by "production"—either by spectacular mass or by irrelevant detail. For this reason, in spite of the studio's offer of Technicolor, we chose to film *Julius Caesar* in the familiar and concentrated dramatic tones of black and white.

Our costumes, while authentic in style, are simple and functional. Formal or informal, civilian or military, we tried to give the impression at all times that our actors were men wearing clothes, not characters wearing costumes.

Our sets are architectural: some small, some massive, but all, we trust, dramatically effectual. Our main stage, the Roman forum with the "pulpit" and the long, steep flight of steps leading up to the pillared porch of the Capitol where Caesar is murdered, has the line and scope of great stage design. For years we have all been admiring Gordon Craig's magnificent theatrical conceptions while regretfully realising that their proportions could never be satisfactorily contained within the restricted frame of our modern proscenium arches. In the motion picture *Julius Caesar*, however, we have to a great extent been able to satisfy our hunger for heroic setting. And through the magic power of lens and microphone, registering every syllable and every facial expression, no matter how whispered the voice or how intimate the secret thought, the actors and their conflicts are never dwarfed by their surroundings. Rather, they gain from the set's great size and their own changing and controlled dramatic relation to it.

In sharp contrast to the official magnificence of the Capitol is the sweaty congestion of our Roman slums. Here, as in the later military scenes, it was action, not spectacle, we were after, dramatic reality rather than archaeological realism. (Not that we weren't pleased the afternoon Vittorio de Sica came onto our set and, walking up our dark and crooked street, asked if we had not copied it from an existing alley in present-day provincial Ferrara rather than from ancient Rome.)

While never deliberately exploiting the historic parallels, there were certain emotional patterns arising from political events of the immediate past that we were prepared to evoke—Hitler, Mussolini and Ciano at the Brenner Pass; the assemblage at Munich; Stalin and Ribbentrop signing the Pact; and similar smiling conference-table friendships that soon ripened into violence and death. Also Hitler at Nurenberg and Compiègne, and later in the Berlin rubble; Mussolini on his balcony with that same docile mob massed below which later watched him hanging by his feet, dead. These sights are as much a part of our contemporary consciousness—in the *black and white* of news-reel and TV screens—as, to Elizabethan audiences, were the personal and political conflicts and tragedies of Essex, Bacon, Leicester and the Cecils.

There was another challenge of which we were aware, but of which, no matter how carefully we planned, little could be learned until we got into production: the proper visual and acoustical treatment of Shakespearean dialogue on the screen.

In one respect we were fortunate: the action of *Julius Caesar* is swift, concentrated, intense. Thus, we were spared some of the grievous problems that beset the film-maker who undertakes a *Hamlet*, a *Macbeth* or a *Lear*. The cinematic treatment of the soliloquies in *Julius Caesar* presented no hazard, for there are none. The words of Cassius as he watches Brutus' retreating figure and plans his next move to enmesh him, and of Brutus in his orchard at dawn awaiting the coming of the conspirators and reluctantly conceding the necessity of Caesar's murder, were not treated as soliloquies (with sound-track riding over a frozen close-up or the camera wandering across irrelevant scenery), but as highly charged dramatic speech.

The basic problem, of course, was how to transfer the dramatic action of a great playwright whose essential instrument of communication is the spoken word, to a medium in which the auditory is habitually subordinate to the visual. Beyond that, there was the problem of fixing in a permanent print, for projection before diverse audiences separated by time and place, words intended to be spoken directly by living actors to living audiences whose daily mood the actors could gauge and whose measure they could take at each performance.

No matter how carefully and cautiously we rehearsed, with camera and sound crew present, a new hazard faced us when we came to shooting. The layman is probably not aware of the extent to which Hollywood studios have come to rely on voice tracks corrected and put together long after the actual shooting is over. Does a boom squeak or a dolly-track rumble, an arc-light hum or the natural-gas flame in a fireplace hiss? Does distant traffic or a plane overhead or the whir of a ventilator on the next stage throw a faint but pervasive rumble under your most intimate scene? Does an actor fluff a line in a long speech, or mar an otherwise thrilling reading with some slight verbal error? Rather than delay or retake the scene, it is cheaper and far more convenient—though not always preferable—to amend the voice track in the sound department by an ingenious system known as "looping," whereby the actor, standing cold before a microphone in a dark room, matches a new voice track, phrase by phrase, to his original image.

For the classic dialogue of *Julius Caesar* it soon became apparent that no such corrective measure could be counted on. The dramatic curves are too long, the tension too high, the speeches too carefully phrased and plotted for them to be splintered, later, into arbitrary fragments. Technically, the proper dramatic delivery of iambic pentameter requires of an actor, in his breathing and in his thinking, a rhythm and a flow that cannot be checked or suspended at the whim of a sound engineer. The necessity to secure a perfect and final voice-track *on the set during shooting,* added several days to our schedule. Precious hours were consumed while rails were adjusted, uneven stage floors leveled, and microphones manoeuvred into the ideal, rather than the possible position. These precautions paid off. In the picture as released, there are not a dozen lines of "looped" dialogue. Every speech is clear and firm, we trust, with the finality of its original delivery.

For all our planning and precaution it was inevitable, in making such a picture, that new problems—visual and aural—should have been encountered right through to the last phases of editing and preparing the film for release.

We soon found that a Shakespearean scene, no matter how conventionally shot, is not subject to the normal laws of film cutting. With the intuitive skill of a sensitive editor watching new film running through his moviola, Jack Dunning soon discovered that a Shakespearean scene had certain general rules of its own, differing from those of the other movies.

The reaction-shot, for instance, which has long been the basis of dramatic cutting in both silent and talking pictures, becomes a tricky thing to use in editing Shakespearean dialogue. Silent reactions, even when carefully planned by the director to fall in predetermined places during a long speech, were rarely used by the editor, who developed a strong reluctance—born not of veneration for classics but of sound cutting instinct—to interrupt the line and cadence of a speech in the mouth of one character, by cutting away to the reaction of another. It struck him as arbitrary and false. And he was right. The film, as he worked on it, developed its own proper cutting-rhythm and form. The result was no less sharp of dramatic than other cutting—only different.

Special problems arose for Robert Shirley, our chief mixer, when he came to make the final composite sound track for *Julius Caesar*—perspective, volume, voice-coloration, the balance of voice and sound and music, to mention only a few. Time after time, the conventions of realistic voice-recording and mixing, as generally practised in dramatic pictures, had to give way to a more sustained and lyric treatment. The Forum scene, with its acoustical and dramatic problem of a single human voice fighting and riding the roar of a great mob, while constantly changing not only its volume but also its relation and perspective to the crowd below it, took days of trial and error and tentative combinations of tracks at various levels, before it finally jelled.

No aspect of our production has raised as many questioning eyebrows as our casting. The choice of Marlon Brando as Marc Antony led some skeptics to quip that "Friends, Romans, Countrymen" might become "Kowalski Variations on a Speech by Shakespeare." A few feet of film will silence, once for all, any remaining doubts as to the quality of Brando's diction. Beyond that, there is no question in my mind that in natural equipment, temperament and application he is one of the very great actors of our time.

For the rest of the cast, Joseph Mankiewicz, Dore Schary and I feel we have fulfilled our original hope—to obtain the best available classic talent on either side of the Atlantic.

The Cassius of the Stratford Festival, that undisputed master of English dramatic verse, John Gielgud, is our Cassius. For our hero, the noble Brutus, we had never thought of but one man. James Mason, after years of motion picture stardom, is repeating in our picture a part he played at the Gate Theatre in Dublin sixteen years ago. Louis Calhern is, we think, a more human and disturbing Caesar than many of the pompous and hollow dictators of past productions. Douglas Watson, who two seasons ago played Romeo on Broadway, is the young Octavius Caesar. Greer Garson, our Calpurnia, and Deborah Kerr, Brutus' wife Portia, are both actresses trained in the classic tradition.

With such a mixture of talent and temperament we were warned to expect trouble. There was none. Whatever the cause—the pleasure of speaking noble and well-rehearsed lines on a movie set, Joe Mankiewicz's expert and sensitive direction or the pure excitement of the drama itself—the agreeable truth is that we could not have had a happier or more absorbed company. When an actor was not on call, the chances were that one might find him on the set or out on a broiling location, intently watching the performance of his colleagues. When Marlon Brando finished Antony's speech in the forum, nine hundred extras burst into applause—and John Gielgud was leading them.

Sight and Sound ns 23:1 (July-September 1953): 24-27.

ALLUSION

The game of literary allusion is played by simple rules. The author either directly presents references to a famous work or indirectly plants them. The reader's or listener's part is to notice or detect the allusion. Then, personal satisfaction begins. You might congratulate yourself for recognizing what less-educated people had missed; you might suppose yourself to belong to the author's select circle of "ideal readers;" you might not understand what the allusion meant, and thus return to the original work. Careful writers allude in such a way that even if someone does not make the connection, the words make sense anyway.

Shakespeare was a master at this game, for it was part of his artistic culture to flatter his contemporary listeners, readers, and patrons. The traditions of Latin and Greek literature had presumably been beaten into him in grammar school, and that education provided rich material for blatant or subtle allusion. The Bible was another obvious source, and also, more risky, the politics of court and city. His own plays and those of his rival playwrights supplied another field of reference that the most dedicated playgoers might be pleased to notice.

Star Trek

This situation—well-trained onlookers, crafty author—is apparent in popular culture as well as high culture. The screenplay of *Star Trek VI, The Undiscovered Country* explicitly alludes to Shakespeare's *Hamlet*: ". . . death, / The undiscover'd country, from whose bourn / No traveller returns" (3.1.77-79).[5] The title comes from a moment when the scornful General Chang quotes Shakespeare right and left at a formal dinner with the Star Fleet officers, and mocks them by claiming that no one understands Shakespeare until he has read him in the original Klingon language.

Two of the most clever allusions come from *Julius Caesar*. General Chang, made up to look like a one-eyed Genghis Khan, spins in his battleship commander's chair and howls vengefully, "cry havoc and let slip the dogs of war." This evocation of Marc Antony's private thoughts before the body of Caesar (3.1.273) invites us to see the treacherous villain in the role of a pitiless revenger. Examining the context of Shakespeare's lines shows a brutal side of Antony inspired by the anger of his murdered master.

And Caesar's spirit, ranging for revenge,
With Ate by his side come hot from hell,
Shall in these confines with a monarch's voice
Cry "Havoc!" and let slip the dogs of war
3.1.270-73

The screenwriters understood that their source was a battle cry but shifted the blame onto a "bad guy" and omitted the context of the victim's anger plus the assistance of Ate, classical goddess of revenge. Some viewers might not recognize this classical allusion and yet the image of releasing war-dogs is terrifyingly understandable to modern people.

The second case involves an allusion only slightly less familiar than "Et tu, Brute?" It is Caesar's comparison of his steadiness to the unchanging appearance of the North Star, uttered when he denies Casca's request to pardon a friend.

> I could be well mov'd, if I were as you;
> If I could pray to move, prayers would move me;
> But I am as constant as the northern star,
> Of whose true-fix'd and resting quality
> There is no fellow in the firmament.
>   3.1.58-60

Navigators and hikers have long known that they can find north without a compass, if they can locate at night the star at the handle end of the Little Dipper (part of the Little Bear, or Ursa Minor). That is, you do not have to know your Shakespeare to catch this allusion. However, it makes you feel good to put yourself in Shakespeare's company when, in the Star Trek movie, the President, costumed like a futuristic Uncle Sam, addresses the United Federation of Planets (a representation of the United Nations General Assembly) with these same words. "I am constant as the northern star" is heard as a voice-over, while the movie audience is shown an assassin sighting the President down a rifle barrel. A parallel to Caesar's case is implied. A leader's supreme moment of confidence precedes his violent death. In an entertaining movie that is full of Shakespeare fragments, such an inference is likely to be drawn, and, if no one notices, the comparison is not confusing.

Lyrical Caesar

Sometimes allusions are not so obvious. Poets frequently allude for their own amusement. The example of the Shakespearean northern star appears in the lyrics of a poetic songwriter, Joni Mitchell. Her "A Case of You" begins with a near quotation from Caesar's comment on constancy.[6]

The singer makes a joke out of the midnight hiker's dilemma of finding north without a compass and plays around with the idea of constancy in love versus perpetual uncertainty, but does she allude to Julius Caesar? Yes. An almost direct quote of line 360, adding an "as" to make the simile clearer, substituting "a" for "the" [northern star], cannot be a coincidence. In fact, the final authoritative printed version of the recorded lyrics was corrected to match Shakespeare's definite "*the* northern star." This change indicates Mitchell's own awareness of the source, without settling the question of whether listeners were expected to hear a deliberate echo from Shakespeare. Only a very attentive listener would notice this allusion in the first place, since the song's context has nothing to do with Rome or leadership. Even if it were recognized as Shakespearean, the allusion would not necessarily recall *Julius Caesar*, because this, like so many other of Shakespeare's poetic images, has passed into popular phrasing and the public domain of copyright.

To care about sources and influences is an academic habit. Many people do not worry whether the exclamation of surprise uttered in the television Superman episodes, "Great Caesar's ghost!" came from the appearance of the "evil spirit" in Brutus' tent (4.3.275-86), and yet they would be right to perceive an allusion to the Caesar legend that Shakespeare also made popular.

T. S. Eliot and *Julius Caesar*

To speculate about the source of a famous poet's allusion is a more serious business than to second-guess references in popular music, only because Western European culture elevates pure poetry above popular song. ("Pure entertainment" is thought to ignore the instruction attributed to poetry according to the classical model of teaching first, and delighting second.) The poems of T. S. Eliot (1888-1965), one of the foremost Modernists, are frequently allusive, and since he studied and listened to Shakespeare with great care, it is tempting to wonder what influence a bit of Shakespeare's *Caesar* had on the title of Eliot's poem "The Hollow Men" (1925).

Brutus speaks scornfully of Cassius, whom he suspects to be wavering in devotion to personal honor, by commenting on how Brutus' servant was received with stiff formality by Cassius' forces on the eve of the decisive battle against Antony and Octavius.

> When love begins to sicken and decay
> It useth an enforced ceremony.
> There are no tricks in plain and simple faith;
> But hollow men, like horses hot at hand,
> Make gallant show and promise of their mettle;
>
> 4.2.20-24

Although the horse simile is mixed with the hollowness metaphor, these lines describe how the overt behavior of secretly disgusted lovers is full of formal protests of true affection, while, inside, there is emptiness, contempt, and despair. When they proclaim true love most, they are least sincere. Similarly, Eliot, opening his poem, imitates the voices of people who have lost religious faith.

> We are the hollow men
> We are the stuffed men
> Leaning together
> Headpiece filled with straw. Alas!

The second epigraph of this poem is "A penny for the Old Guy," which is an allusion to the thwarted English assassin, Guy Fawkes. (The first epigraph refers to the deranged protagonist of Joseph Conrad's *Heart of Darkness*.) Children used to go door-to-door and present a hollow Fawkes doll to collect money for fireworks that were shot off on November 5, the day in 1605 when Catholic conspirators planned to blow up the Protestant king as he opened Parliament. Unlike Caesar, he paid attention to a note warning him of danger, and the English have ever since celebrated this escape from the "Gunpowder Plot."

Allusions work in a poet's mind much more complexly than they do when someone mockingly refers to a threatening situation by saying "Beware the Ides of March." Eliot absorbed Shakespeare along with English folk traditions, poems like William Morris' "The Hollow Land" and Rudyard Kipling's tale, "The Broken Men," and thus some commentators, encouraged by Eliot himself, attribute this poem's title to a non-Shakespearean mixture. We can as easily speculate that Brutus' lines contributed the whole title of Eliot's poem, because *Julius Caesar* deals directly with assassination and the disillusionment of the conspirators.[7]

JULIUS CAESAR AND BLACK VOICES

Although this very Roman play was welcomed by Anglo-Saxon Protestants belonging to a racially white social majority, *Julius Caesar* contains ideas rising above religion and race. We have Shakespeare to thank for inspiring the Harlem-born novelist and poet James Baldwin. He felt particularly close to the conspirators at the moment of their triumph—and, in hindsight, on the edge of their downfall. The symbolic act of dipping their hands in Caesar's blood and dreaming of being celebrated as liberators (3.1.111-14) jolted Baldwin out of his hatred of Shakespeare. The second inspiration came from his awareness of Shakespeare's acceptance of erotic passion.[8] Baldwin may have been thinking of the symbolic eroticism of homosexual love that is conceivably latent in Brutus' attraction to Caesar or Cassius, but more likely of the frank, heterosexual imagery notorious in *Romeo and Juliet* or *Hamlet*.[9]

Baldwin speaks directly to minority students about the worth of *Julius Caesar*'s revolutionary theme and Shakespeare's poetic language in finding a voice to protest, to express. His comparison of the experience of an African American writer immersed in France duplicates the feelings of minorities forced to converse in a "foreign" language. Students often find themselves in a similar straitjacket, when they resist high-brow literature, the unfamiliar and frightening poetry of Shakespeare. Any agitated onlooker of *Julius Caesar* is thus half-cheering the stabbers of the father/authority, and anxious to make fun of those who take him seriously. Baldwin describes how this play allowed him to pass from this phase into a more mature appreciation of Shakespeare's artistic dissent.

FROM JAMES BALDWIN'S "WHY I STOPPED HATING SHAKESPEARE"
(1964)

Every writer in the English language, I should imagine, has at some point hated Shakespeare, has turned away from that monstrous achievement with a kind of sick envy. In my most anti-English days I condemned him as a chauvinist ("this England," indeed!) and because I felt it so bitterly anomalous that a black man should be forced to deal with the English language at all—should be forced to assault the English language in order to be able to speak—I condemned him as one of the authors and architects of my oppression.

Again, in the way that some Jews bitterly and mistakenly resent Shylock, I was dubious about Othello (what did he see in Desdemona?) and bitter about Caliban. His great vast gallery of people, whose reality was as contradictory as it was unanswerable, unspeakably oppressed me. I was resenting, of course, the assault on my simplicity; and, in another way, I was a victim of that loveless education which causes so many schoolboys to detest Shakespeare. But I feared him, too, feared him because in his hands, the English language became the mightiest of instruments. No one would ever write that way again. No one would ever be able to match, much less surpass, him.

Well, I was young and missed the point entirely, was unable to go behind the words and, as it were, the diction, to what the poet was saying. I still remember my shock when I finally *heard* these lines from the murder scene in "Julius Caesar." The assassins are washing their hands in Caesar's blood. Cassius says:—

Stoop then, and wash.—How many ages hence
Shall this our lofty scene be acted over,
In states unborn and accents yet unknown!
[3.1.111-13]

What I suddenly heard, for the first time, was manifold. It was the voice of lonely, dedicated, deluded Cassius, whose life had never been real for me before—I suddenly seemed to know what this moment meant to him. But beneath and beyond that voice I also heard a note yet more rigorous and impersonal—and contemporary: that "lofty scene," in all its blood and necessary folly, its blind and necessary pain, was thrown into a perspective which has never left my mind. Just so, indeed, is the heedless State overthrown by men, who, in order to overthrow it, have had to achieve a desperate single-mindedness. And this single-mindedness, which we think of (why?) as ennobling, also operates, and much more surely, to distort and diminish a man—to distort and diminish us all, even, or perhaps especially, those whose needs and whose energy made the overthrow of the State inevitable, necessary and just.

And the terrible thing about this play, for me—it is not necessarily my favourite play, whatever that means, but it *is* the play which I first, so to speak, discovered—is the tension it relentlessly sustains between individual ambition, self-conscious, deluded, idealistic or corrupt, and the blind, mindless passion which drives the individual no less than it drives the mob. "I am Cinna the poet, I am Cinna the poet . . . I am not Cinna the conspirator"—that cry rings in my ears. And the mob's response: "Tear him for his bad verses." And yet—though one howled with Cinna and felt his terrible rise, at the hands of his countrymen, to death, it was impossible to hate the mob. Or, worse than impossible, useless: for here we were, at once howling and being torn to pieces, the only receptacles of evil and the only receptacles of nobility to be found in all the universe. But the play does not even suggest that we have the perception to know evil from good or that such a distinction can ever be clear: "The evil that men do lives after them: The good is oft interred with their bones . . . "[3.2.74-76]

Once one has begun to suspect this much about the world—once one has begun to suspect, that is, that one is not, and never will be, innocent, for the reason that one is—some of the self-protective veils between oneself and reality begin to fall away. It is probably of some significance though we cannot pursue it here, that my first real apprehension of Shakespeare came when I was living in France, and thinking and speaking in French. The necessity of mastering a foreign language forced me into a new relationship to my own. (It was also in France, therefore, that I began to read the Bible again.)

My quarrel with the English language has been that the language reflected none of my experience. But now I began to see the matter in quite another way. If the language was not my own, it might be the fault of the language, but it might also be my fault. Perhaps the language was not my own because I had never attempted to use it, had only learned to imitate it. If this were so, then it might be made to bear the burden of my experience if I could find the stamina to challenge it, and me, to such a test.

In support of this possibility, I had two mighty witnesses: my black ancestors, who evolved the sorrow songs, the blues and jazz, and created an entirely new idiom in an overwhelmingly hostile place; and Shakespeare, who was the last bawdy writer in the English language. What I began to see—especially since, as I say, I was living and speaking in French—is that it is experience which shapes a language; and it is language which controls experience. The structure of the French language told me something of the French experience, and also something of the French expectations—which were certainly not the American expectations, since the French daily and hourly said things which the Americans could not say at all. (Not even in French.) Similarly, the language with which I had grown up had certainly not been the King's English. An immense experience had forged this language, it had been (and remains) one of the tools of a people's survival, and it revealed expectations which no white American could easily entertain. The authority of this language was in its candour, its irony, its density and its beat: this was the authority of the language which produced me, and it was also the authority of Shakespeare.

Again, I was listening very hard to jazz and hoping, one day, to translate it into language, and Shakespeare's bawdiness became very important to me since bawdiness was one of the elements of jazz and revealed a tremendous, loving and realistic respect for the body, and that ineffable force which the body contains, which Americans mostly lost, which I had experienced only among Negroes, and of which I had then been taught to be ashamed.

My relationship, then, to the language of Shakespeare revealed itself as nothing less than my relationship to myself and my past. Under this light, this revelation, both myself and my past began slowly to open, perhaps the way a flower opens at morning, but, more probably, the way an atrophied muscle begins to function, or frozen fingers to thaw.

The greatest poet in the English language found his poetry where poetry is to be found: in the lives of the people. He could have done this only through love—by knowing, which is not the same thing as understanding, that whatever was happening to anyone was happening to him. It is said that his time was easier than ours, but I doubt it—no time can be easy if one is living through it. I think it is simply that he walked his streets and saw them, and tried not to lie about what he saw, his public streets and his private streets, which are always so mysteriously and inexorably connected; but he trusted that connection. And, though I, and many of us, have bitterly bewailed (and will again) the lot of an American writer—to be part of a people who have ears to hear and hear not, who have eyes to see and see not—I am sure that Shakespeare did the same. Only he saw, as I think we must, that the people who produce the poet are not responsible to him: he is responsible to them.

That is why he is called a poet. And his responsibility, which is also his joy and his strength and his life, is to defeat all labels and complicate all battles by insisting on the human riddle, to bear witness, as long as breath is in him, to that mighty, unnameable, transfiguring force which lives in the soul of man, and to aspire to do his work so well that when the breath has left him, the people—*all people!* —who search in the rubble for a sign or a witness will be able to find him there.

London Observer, April 19, 1964, 21.

PARODY

In popular culture, the direct opposite of complicated art is deliberate simplicity, and parody is the means of simplifying and thus accommodated. The impatience of youth with fuddy-duddy old age often is expressed by parodies of Shakespeare, his plays, and his protagonists. The playwright's image from the First Folio is caricatured on tee-shirts or in the illustrations of literary supplements in cultured newspapers.

CAESAR GOES MAD

Mad magazine often spoofed Shakespeare's plays.[10] In one of its more blatant reductions, Caesar's story is cleverly turned into a primary-school reader. The "See Dick and Jane. See Spot run. Run, Spot, Run" formula applied to the emperor's tragedy appeals to adolescent humor, which avoids the grossness of the murder by pretending that it is innocent. The cartoon figure waves to a crowd of grim conspirators, one of them grinding a knife, and this combination of picture and words creates a corrosive irony that is meant to dissuade any politician from taking himself too seriously.

FROM *MAD* MAGAZINE'S "JULIUS CAESAR, LESSON 1" (1965)

See the mighty Caesar.
See Julius, the conquering General!
See Caesar, the Invincible Emperor!
See, see, see!
Better look quick, though.
This may be your last chance.
Tomorrow, Caesar will dead as a mackerel.
Some of the Senators will stab him in the Forum.

Also in the Duodenum, Esophagus, and Belly.
Stab, stab, stab.
Tough bananas, Julius.
That's what you get for going into politics!

The Mad Sampler (New York: Signet, 1965), 166.

A second example of *Mad* parody is a mock mini-musical, "Call Me Julius." The caricatured Brutus, Caesar, and Antony are drawn from the likenesses of James Mason, Louis Calhern, and Marlon Brando, who starred in the 1953 film version of the play. The entire cartoon piece is only six panels. The fourth shows the maniacal conspirators plunging daggers into a startled Caesar and singing to the tune of the Broadway musical hit "Hello Dolly":

FROM *MAD* MAGAZINE'S "CALL ME JULIUS" (1971)

Goodbye, Julie!
It's goodbye, Julie!
'Cause our knives are in your back
    where they belong!

You bugged us all, Julie!
With your Gaul, Julie!
Your ambition kept us wishin'
    for this parting song!

So farewell, Julie!
It's been swell, Julie!
But we hadda take a stab at
    jabbin' you!
Yeah!

We hope your will's made up!
And you have your bills paid up!
Julie, as a big shot,
    you are through!

Polyunsaturated Mad (New York: Paperback Library, 1971), n.p.

This sort of macabre humor is not at all ghoulish, since the cartoon and the show tune lend an air of fantasy wish-fulfillment. The writer takes revenge on his eighth grade Latin teacher for assigning Caesar's Gallic Wars ("Omnia Gallia in tres partes divisa est" All Gaul is divided into three parts). The pun on the place name and the liver excretion is positively Shakespearean. (See *As You Like It* 3.2.47; *Two Gentlemen of Verona* 5.4.1-6). And, like the primer, the cultural lesson is that proud politicians and big shots have foolishly imagined that they are invincible.

Mad ran a series of Shakespeare parodies called "The Bard of Birdland." This title relies on the urban jazz and beatnik culture idol, Charlie "Bird" Parker (1920-1955), who was one of the most influential saxophonists in the New York scene. Taking off from the superficial jargon of Beat poets, whose *Mad* image put the magazine's trademark face of Alfred E. Newman in a beret, goatee, and sunglasses, the update claims to bring Shakespeare's language from old-fashioned (= "square") heights down to the pavement level of young kids (= "the hip"). The cover of this anthologized version shows Alfred E. Newman as a classical statue—toga, laurel wreath, incised motto ("WHAT—ME WORRY?")—with a pigeon standing on his head. Either the classical ideal is being portrayed as a monument to dead images like the ignored sculpture of big-city architecture where pigeons roost, or it is an omen that the bird is about to splatter on him. Alfred E. Newman is thus compared to Caius Julius Caesar who disregarded the soothsayer's warning that he had, indeed, something to worry about. A conventional and accurate text of Marc Antony's opening of the funeral oration (3.2.72-107) is presented parallel to the "easy-to-understand" version:

FROM *MAD* MAGAZINE'S "THE BARD IN BIRDLAND" (1961)

Friends, Romans, hipsters,
Let me clue you in;
I come to put down Caesar, not to groove him.
The square kicks some cats are on stay with them;
The hip bits, like, go down under;
So let it lay with Caesar. The cool Brutus
Gave you the message Caesar had big eyes;
It that's the sound, someone's copping a plea,
And, like, old Caesar really set them straight.
Here, copacetic with Brutus and the studs,—
For Brutus is a real cool cat;
So are they all, all cool cats,—
Come I to make this gig at Caesar's lay down.
He was my boy, the most and real gone to me;
But, like, Brutus pegs him as having big eyes;
And old Brutus is a real cool cat.
He copped a lot of swinging heads for home,
Which put us way out with that loot;
Does this give Caesar big eyes?
When the square cats bawled, Caesar flipped;
Big eyes should be made of more solid megillah;
Yet Brutus pegs him as having big eyes;
And Brutus is a real cool cat.
You all dug that bit at the Lupercal scene
Three times I bugged him with the King's lid,

And three times he hung me up; was this big eyes?
Yet Brutus pegs him with big eyes;
And, sure, he is a real cool cat.
I don't want to double-O what Brutus gummed,
But, like, I only dig what comes on straight.
You all got a charge out of him once,
So how come you don't cry the blues for him?
Man! You are real nowhere.
You don't make it anymore. Don't cut out on me;
My guts are in the pad there with Caesar,
And I gotta stop swinging till they round-trip.

The Ides of Mad (New York: Signet/New American Library, 1961), 131-32.

Reduced Shakespeare

The "What, me worry?" gesture of *Mad* magazine's Alfred E. Newman, and the irreverent spirit of satire can be seen in the act of the Reduced Shakespeare Company. This three-person show makes fun of high culture by boiling down all of Shakespeare's plays into a two-hour entertainment, which is also printed as a script.[11] The pace is so quick and the abridgments so absurd that the audience laughs at the pretentiousness of Shakespeare worship. When performed on a stage that is normally the acting space for serious drama, this farce gains extra irony from the situation. Such clowning coincides with many of Shakespeare's own jibes at the court or at city life versus country life (for example, see *As You Like It*, act 3, scene 2). This kind of satire is usually delightful to city dwellers looking down their noses on country bumpkins, rather than the other way round, when a popular road-show snickers at urban culture. The Reduced Shakespeare's review works so well in either the city or the country because people in late twentieth-century culture are aware of both worlds, through exposure to televison and mass media coverage of events downtown and out of town. Caesar is a figure recognized from Broadway to the Baja.

The Reduced Shakespeare perform the murder scene in *Julius Caesar.* Photo Copyright by Peter Cunningham.

RAPPING ON CAESAR

From the same New York City satirists who contributed to *Mad* magazine's ridicule came a rap parody of *Julius Caesar*. Black voices are often not heard in high-cultured satire, but not because the black urban scene is irrelevant to Shakespeare. James Baldwin reminds us of the connection. His point about Shakespeare's powerful language is amplified—to the level of distortion—by the pumping rhythm, forced rhymes, and artless clichés that one *Mad* magazine writer, Frank Jacobs, customarily designed for print. When his *Julius Caesar* parody is produced as rap music, however, the poetic takes over from the visual. The lines fall into four stresses, the same meter that Shakespeare used for the witches in *Macbeth* and much of the fairy talk in *A Midsummer Night's Dream*. Whereas Shakespeare made fun of indulgent rhyming, in Bottom's bellowing in *Midsummer Night's Dream* or the sonnet-mad lovers in *Love's Labour's Lost*, the rap style takes this nursery-rhyme simplicity as a poetic norm. Metaphors for murder, such as "waxing" or "sleeping with the fishes," derive from the lethal realities of big-city street life, reminding us of Mafia bosses as well as drug dealers. Although the narrator dominates this version of the story, the personal dialogue is suggested by the same technique of shared lines that allowed Shakespeare to keep his verses rolling when one character took over from another. This device appears in his script at moments like this one just before the killing:

CAESAR   What, Brutus?
CASCA   Pardon, Caesar! Caesar, pardon!
           As low as to thy foot doth Cassius fall,
           To beg enfranchisement for Publius Cimber.
                                              3.1.55-57

Twice the rap version uses this method of maintaining the beat.

All the disturbing rage and macho potential is filtered through the comparably bloody plot and imagery of the Caesar story, but lightened in its tone. The story is all about Caesar displaying his cool, ignoring the doubts of his wife and the fortune teller; Brutus grooving on Rome and defying the ghost; Antony pulling off a slick double-cross, but admiring his victim. Unhistorically, Rome is said to be a democracy, when in fact the Roman Republic during Caesar's time was dominated by the emperor. That interpretation only makes the rap version fit the current American perception the Revolutionary War when a democratically elected government fought against a repressive monarchy, or from the continued defense of individual freedom against fascism. Yet, everybody who enjoys parody knows that historical or literary accuracy is not the point. You have a good time stretching the original work into contorted shapes.

The rap text verifies James Baldwin's insights that Shakespeare's language can be reawakened after you struggle with it, and that the verbal art of black urban America—just like jazz and the blues—is born from a recognition of human sensuality.

FROM FRANK JACOBS' "THE JULIUS CAESAR RAP" (1992)

NARRATOR
　　If you're hot for Shakespeare, then you know that he
　　Was a dude turned on by history;
　　He'd pick up his pen and write a play
　　About the big-shot bosses of yesterday;
　　He was hooked on wild, real-life events
　　Full of murders pulled off by high-class gents;
　　So if that's your pref, then you'll get your fill
　　With "Julius Caesar," by Will the Thrill.
　　In Rome, way back in 44 B.C.
　　Ruled Caesar—"Big Julie" to you and me;
　　He was Number One Boss, everyone was taught,
　　And he was set for life, least that what he thought.
　　Let's join him now as he splits his home
　　And is struttin' his stuff on the streets of Rome;
　　He's gettin' it on with the local crowd
　　When he hears an old gent comin' on real loud;
　　It's the Soothsayer man, who predicts events,
　　And he warns Big Julie what the future presents.
SOOTHSAYER
　　Big Julie, I've looked in my crystal ball,
　　And I don't like the hang of it—not at all;
　　On the Ides of March, you'd better lay low—
　　That's March fifteenth, in case you didn't know.
CAESAR
　　I get your drift; you're clang'in loud and clear,
　　But the Ides of March ain't nothin' to fear;

I'm Caesar, the greatest you'll ever see;
Don't front me, old man—you're borin' me.
NARRATOR
Lookin' on this scene are a couple of gents,
And the rap they're makin' is quite intense;
The first dude is Brutus, a big-wheel ace;
The other is Cassius, who's in his face.
CASSIUS
Listen up now, Brutus. It's all over town
Big Julie's got plans to wear a crown;
He'd like to be king, and you've got to agree
That could really bum out our democracy.
BRUTUS
I hear you, Cassius, and I do agree
That Big Julie could zap our liberty;
But I ain't so sure it's reached the point
We should wax the dude who runs this joint.
NARRATOR
Out on the street, Big Julie's aware
That there's somethin' sneaky happenin' there;
He's feelin' stressed out, as we can see,
As he raps with his buddy, Marc Antony.
CAESAR
I'm tellin' ya, Marc, that I'm startin' to think
That Cassius has the makin's of a first-class fink;
Whatever he's up to, it's got me shook—
I can tell from his lean and hungry look;
I'd much prefer toadies who are fat, you see,
'Cause finks like Cassius—they worry me.
NARRATOR
When Brutus gets home, he's all in a sweat,
'Cause he still ain't certain Big Julie's a threat;
Hey, sure, Big Julie comes off ambitious,
But that don't mean he should sleep with the fishes;
He paces the floor all through the night,
Then at last decides to do what's right,
And when Cassius comes in with his killer crew,
Brutus tells 'em all—
BRUTUS
                  I'm in with you;
Big Julie's got to go, I do agree,
So he'll take the hit and we'll keep Rome free.

CASSIUS

> Way to go there, Brutus, you won't regret it;
> 'Fore the day is done, Big Julie will get it;
> And when we're through and he's history,
> We'll also wax Marc Antony.

BRUTUS

> Not so fast there, Cassius, one hit's enough;
> Marc's only a wuss, so forget that stuff;
> Big Julie's our target, and with him rubbed out,
> Marc'll cool it for good—I have no doubt.

NARRATOR

> While the killers make plans to take over Rome
> Big Julie's takin' five in his fancy home;
> He's gettin' a pitch from his stressed-out wife;
> Calpurnia's her name, and she fears for his life.

CALPURNIA

> I had a dream last night, Big Julie, honey
> Which bummed me out crazy, and that ain't funny;
> You were layin' there dead in a real bad way
> On the Ides of March, which is today.

CAESAR

> Calpurnia, baby, don't fret about Caesar,
> I'm the town's top dude, not some small-time geezer.

CALPURNIA

> I know you're boss, and I groove your style,
> But cool it, honey, stay home for a while.

CAESAR

> I hear ya, baby, but while I've still got clout,
> I gotta show my face—I can't wimp out.

NARRATOR

> Big Julie heads out, and who does he meet
> But the Soothsayer man, spoutin' on the street.

CAESAR

> Soothsayer man, don't give me no line;
> It's the Ides of March, and I'm doin' just fine.

SOOTHSAYER

> Maybe so, Big Julie, but knock on wood,
> The day ain't over, and it don't look good.

NARRATOR

> In the Senate House, where the killers wait,
> Big Julie shows up to meet his fate;
> They rap for a spell—then, in a flash,
> They stab big Julie with an awful gash;
> The last one to knife him is Brutus, his friend,

And before Big Julie meets his bloody end,
He looks at his one-time pal and sighs;
CAESAR
You, too, Brutus?
NARRATOR
                    Then he falls and dies.
For folks of Rome, it's a funky time—
Big Julie's been waxed, which seems a crime;
Soon Brutus comes out to do his bit—
To tell the crowd why Big Julie was hit.
BRUTUS
Folks, whatever you've heard, I'm tellin' you straight
We had to wax Big Julie—we couldn't wait;
He was gonna be king, and once he was crowned,
You'd wind up slaves if he stuck around;
So we did our thing and stuck HIM instead,
So don't get steamed just 'cause he's dead;
If ya wonder what I did it for—
I dug big Julie, but I groove Rome more.
NARRATOR
The crowd gives Brutus a thumbs-up sign;
He's a home-boy hero, who did just fine;
The vibes feel good, they all agree,
But they've yet to hear from Marc Antony.
Though he's promised Brutus he'll keep his cool,
Young Marc's a sharpie and he ain't no fool;
He's out to make points and to make himself boss
While he zaps poor Brutus with a double-cross;
He's as smooth as they come, lookin' fine and proud,
As he takes the stage and plays to the crowd.
MARC ANTONY
Hey, friends and Romans, they've knifed Big Julie
So clean out your ears while I tell you truly,
He was Rome's big boss—the town's top gun,
And for years in the charts was Number One;
But Brutus and his gang said, "We'll wax the schmuck,"
So they make their point and Big Julie got stuck;
Now I truly believe they're wonderful guys,
Even though some folks think otherwise;
Sure, they stabbed Big Julie again and again,
But we know those creeps are honor'ble men;
Hey, I'm not suggestin' that you rub 'em out too,
Even though that thought's occurred to you;
But in case you do, and the rats all die,

If you need a new boss, then I'm your guy.
NARRATOR
    Marc's wacko rap really steams their guts,
    And as soon as he's through, the crowd goes nuts;
    They yell and stomp and demonstrate,
    'Cause now it's Marc they groove and Brutus they hate.
    Now, Brutus knows he was double-crossed,
    But he won't give up, no matter what the cost;
    With Cassius he vows to settle the score—
    They'll take on Marc in an all-out war.
    Many miles from Rome, Brutus sets up camp
    To lead his army and wind up champ;
    Just before the big battle, while his army sleeps,
    Brutus sees a ghost, which gives him the creeps;
    It's the ghost of Big Julie, or so it would seem,
    And it freaks out Brutus like a wacked-out dream.
BRUTUS
    Lay it on me, ghost—tell me why you're here.
CAESAR
    To let you know, Brutus, that the end is near.
    We'll meet again soon at Philippi—
    Now I've got to split, so, for now, goodbye.
NARRATOR
    When Brutus arrives at Philippi,
    He finds that it ain't no piece of pie;
    He spots poor Cassius, dead as can be,
    His army chopped up by Marc Antony;
    Brutus leads his troops in one last thrust,
    But his army's wiped out and his hopes go bust;
    He's lost the war and his Number One chum,
    And now for him, at last, the end has come;
    Big Julie's ghost meant for him to die,
    And he kills himself there at Philippi.
    Marc Antony, he's won the war—
    He's wasted Brutus and settled the score;
    But though he's won a famous victory,
    He sends Brutus off with a eulogy:
MARC ANTONY
    Brutus was an ace who hung in tough—
    A first-class gent who showed his stuff;
    This was a dude who stood real tall—
    The noblest Roman of them all.

Frank Jacobs, lyricist, *Teacher's Discovery,* audio cassette ([Auburn Hills, Mich.], 1992)

VICTORIAN TRAVESTY

A British satire of Julius Caesar entertained English observers of the American Civil War. Shakespeare's most famous plays allowed amateur playwrights to score political points against ridiculous members of Parliament, and the second-rate actors could lampoon the foremost tragedians. Produced in a spirit similar to that of our contemporary comedy troupes like Monty Python or the Reduced Shakespeare Company, the anonymous script was published, probably at Brighton about 1861, to continue the enjoyment of its brief life in the burlesque theater.[12]

Artistically, the work pays homage to Shakespeare's comic spirit. The writer kept Shakespeare's five-stressed line, but chained it into couplets with the sort of outrageous rhymes that Gilbert and Sullivan made popular. Shakespeare's fondness for puns is celebrated in almost every speech, with music-hall songs liberally included. Even the Confederate song "Dixie" found its way into the piece. Many of the laughs at foreigners were directed more noticeably against the French. In characterization, Caesar is recast as a greedy politician out to please the people with "bread and circuses" (free lunch and sports spectacles). Antony becomes an opportunist and a vengeful demagogue, traits not too far removed from Shakespeare's character.

FROM *JULIUS CAESAR, TRAVESTIE* (c. 1861)

CHARACTERS

JULIUS CAESAR, not at all the modern style of Emperor. In fact, rather mild. So much so, that it is only when he is dead, that the people cry" Vive l'empereur." Equally wonderful to relate, though named July-us, and considering himself August, he ends his year in March.

MARK ANTONY, a young swell, whose toga is the perfection of toga-ry. He never ceases to lament the de-cease of de Caesar, taking good care, however, not to disarrange his own propertie. In fine, though decked in finery, a capital fellow, who lives close to the Capitol.

BRUTUS, a polished Brute, with very oily manners, who, like that novel character, eventually gam-mons his own bac-on, and after having tried his little game on, for some time, makes an April fool of himself, by falling his own back on.

CASSIUS, a very blunt ruffian, though sporting a sharp and Kean dagger.

CASCA, to our mind a gem in the cask-et, but not at all given to the purest water.

LUCIUS, a sleepy Pickwickian sort of fat boy given to jam, and hard to satis-fy in that particular.

CINNA, no great sinner than the rest, though very eager to join in the striking situation.

DECIUS, a precocious youth, who likes the play but doesn't like work.

FLAVIUS, a sooth-sayer, though not a soothing-prophet.

PORTIA, a shrew-d woman, though a shrew with a d-evil of a temper.

CALPHURNIA, though Caesar's better half, an equally mild half and half character, which may account in some measure for his being drawn and quartered.

SCENE IV, The Capitol
A flourish of Trumpets, The Senate sitting.

DECIUS   My lords, great Caesar comes—he bid me say
  He'll be here sharp, nor loiter on the way
[Enter Caesar, Soothsayer, Cinna, Cassius, Casca, Brutus]
SOOTHSAYER   Caesar, all hail!
CAESAR   The ides of March are come.   5
SOOTHSAYER
  True, but not gone; you'd best have stay'd at home.
CASSIUS
  I feign would urge on you a little suit.
SOOTHSAYER
  I feign would have *my* jaw first coute qui coute.
  Delay not Caesar—listen to my word.
CAESAR (pompously)
  Profit I crave not from prophet so absurd.   10
                       [Soothsayer exit]
CASSIUS
  Caesar, I kiss thy hand, but would not flatter—
CAESAR
  Quite right, tis useless. Cease thy stupid chatter.
CASCA (kneeling)
  Pardon me, Caesar, I've the same petition.
CAESAR
  Oh! That accounts for your abject position.
CASCA
  I'd ask, what Cassius would have, when a stopper   15
  You put to his petition.

CAESAR (with uplifted hands)

What a whopper!

BRUTUS

I beg you don't include in your new act,
Our little favour'd boroughs closely pack'd.
I wish to shield you from the rising storm,
The folks are quite indifferent to Reform.   20
From many hands it's suffer'd such distortion,
Worse than the first un was the last abortion.

CAESAR

Amongst the twinkling stars that paint the sky,
One spark does all the rest by far outvie,
Amongst the painted swells that here do shine,   25
I'm the chief spark, and right supreme is mine.
Which means, from my opinions I won't rat,
Not e'en if in the fire fall the fat.

CASSIUS

Those words are past—but stay, will you retract?

CASCA

Consent to quash this most uncall'd for act.   30

CAESAR

He dares to threaten me, great Caesar, drat him.

BRUTUS

You'll yield.

CAESAR (with great energy)

No, never, never.

BRUTUS

Then up Guards and at him.

(Cassius stabs Caesar in the back, Caesar catches
hold of his arm. Casca, Cinna, and Decius fall on him,
and at last Brutus stabs him.)

CAESAR

You too, ungrateful Brute, then fall without a tear,
Last of the Cardigans—I mean the Caesars here.   35

(Caesar falls near a pedestal inscribed,
"To the memory of the mighty Pompey.")

BRUTUS

Liberty, equality, fraternity—but mind sobriety. (To Casca.)

CASCA

Liberty, equality, fraternity—and lulleliety.

CHORUS—"Dixey's land."—Buckley.

BRUTUS

I never could to Caesar cotton.

CASSIUS
  His name will quickly be forgotten.
CHORUS
  In the land, in the land, in the land, in the land.   40
BRUTUS
  With him it's now all dicky.
CHORUS
  Oh! In this free land we'll take our stand,
    With him it's all now dicky
  In the land, in the land
    With him it's all now dicky   45
  In the land, in the land
    With him it's all now dicky.
                        [General dance and exeunt.]
SCENE V
The Forum—Caesar's Tomb
Enter Ballet of Flower Girls, who, during the dance, hang
immortelles on Caesar's Tomb, and exeunt.
                                        [Enter Antony.]
ANTONY
  Shrunk to this little measure are thy glories,
  Victim of quarrels 'twixt the Whigs and Tories.
  If it were not, that I can ne'er decide,   50
  I really should incline towards suicide.
  Once mighty Caesar since thou liest so low,
  A solo in thy praise I'll sing before I go.
SONG
Air—"Unfortunate Miss Bailey."
  Those horrid ruffians have assassinated Julius Caesar
  Just like a bull they baited him,   55
    And worried him, poor old dear, sar.
  They have, I fear, no conscience left,
    Which can their souls e'er worry,
  And now the people will expect,
    For vengeance I shall hurry.   60
  Oh! poor Caesar, unfortunate old Caesar,
  Unfortunate, unfortunate, unfortunate old Caesar.

  'Tis true, I deem'd him rather mild;
    My thoughts I never could disguise.
  They ne'er had prov'd such arrant knaves,   65
    Had Caesar not been so unwise.
  But yet I wish that Caesar's ghost

Each night would visit their bedside,
And put them in a precious funk,
    Their drivelling terrors to deride.   70
Oh! poor Caesar, &c., &c.

                                          [Exit.]

[Enter Brutus, Citizens]
BRUTUS
  Gents most intelli-gent I know will tell,
  Feelingly, if I can, why Caesar fe-ell,
  Brief shall my words be—you shall soon decide,
  Antony's brief is for the other side.   75
  I feel as if engag'd at the old Bailey,
  Forgive my Manners, Bucks I'm Dizzy Really,
  Him you'll ne'er Seymour turn a Somerset,
            [see-more]   [summersault]
  In his New-castle over-Baring sit,
  Unhonour'd, like great Napier, he'll take his nap-here.   80
  O'er us again to peer it he'll ne'er appear.
  'Appier you now will be—so just decide,
  It's unjust-ifiable, lawful, Caesarcide,
  If Caesar's side move the Lord Chancellor
  And gain a verdict, by some chance, sell or   85
  Dodge of that sort, I'll to the country go,
  "Blow it," they'll say "he fairly struck that blow,"
  I can't wait longer, for I bear the weight
  Of the whole nation on this luckless pate.
  So though much griev'd to lose your company,   90
  I'll now make room for that loose Antony.

                                          [Exit.]

1ST CITIZEN
  His words are fair—but we, that is the nation,
  Will not decide, till we've heard Mark's oration.
[Citizens shout silence for Mark Antony.]
                                     [Enter Mark Antony.]

ANTONY
  Friends, Rummuns, countrymen, lend me your ears,
  I know a trick or two, though not advanc'd in years.   95
  I come to bury Caesar, not to praise him,
  Whate'er I'd do, you know, I couldn't raise him.
  Though living in an educated age,
  "De Mortuis" etcetera's not the rage.
  Our friend, the noble Brutus, hath us told,   100
  Caesar was precious greedy, fond of gold.

Well! If the honest truth explain I must,
No doubt that's why he made him bite the dust.
Caesar much plunder gain'd, 't must be confess'd,
But to the people always gave the best.   105
No end of cakes and ale—nor pouch'd the stuff,
Little he car'd, if you had but enough.
Can you forget his "panem et Circenses,"
(Aside.) —I'll pain'em, work upon those good sirs' senses.

1ST CITIZEN

Methinks in what he says there is much reason.   110

ANTONY

(Aside)—Not bad for me, in town too out of season.

2ND CITIZEN

Caesar by secret voting ne'er did bring,
Dummy electors up to make him King.

3RD CITIZEN

Or Emperour either. Now that he is dead,
I vote for polling Antony instead.   115

ANTONY

Oh! I'm no pol-itician. How could I,
Presume so far, I'm but Mark Antony.
We ne'er shall look upon his like again,
Yet Cassius, Brutus, all are honest men;
But here's a parchment sign'd with Caesar's name,   120
Not that I mean to read it, all the same.
Could be the Commons now this parchment read,
At Caesar's wounds their very hearts would bleed;
Each one'd from Caesar seize a lock of hair,
A legacy much priz'd to leave his heir.   125

CITIZENS

The will, the will, read it.

ANTONY

                        'Twere better not.
You heard how overboil'd that precious pot.
How the first favourite who had winter'd well,
Fell a fell victim to those ringmen's sell.

CITIZENS

The will, the will, the will, that will we hear.   130

ANTONY

Well if you will, give me a pull of beer.   (Drinks)
If of his bier and will I must descant,
A constant pull of bitter I shall want.

CITIZENS
　Room for Mark Antony, here, all give way,
ANTONY
　(Aside.)—I know at last must come this long expected day.　135
　All who have wipes, I beg them first produce,
　For all will blubber like the very jeuce.
　Just as the juice from high genteely drops
　Liquid, as school-boy's suction—lollipops.
　　　　　　　　　　(Takes cloak, and shows it all in holes.)
　See what a rent that envious tenant paid,　　　　　　140
　When Cassius such a rent in this cloak made.
　Through this the well beloved Brutus struck,
　And as his steel thereout he tried to pluck.
　Great Caesar's pluck pre-eminent in death,
　Though he could scarce gasp out from want of breath.　145
　From want of breath he died, as you all knows,
　As much as from each treacherous monster's blows.
　Bid him exclaim, you most ungrateful dog,
　You Brute you've kill'd me, as you'd stick a hog.
　　　　　　　　　　　　　(Shame, shame.)
　When Caesar fell we all of us fell down,　　　　　　150
　And chopp'd in two the stake that held the crown.
CITIZENS
　Revenge, seek, burn, each foetid traitor slay,
　Not one base traitor shall survive to-day.
ANTONY
　You know not yet how Caesar earn'd your loves,
　He's left you more than a pair of mourning gloves,　155
　Seventy-five drachmas to each several cit.
　　　　　　(Dramas)
　(To audience.)—Quite tragical is't not? excuse my wit.
　But more, he's left you every private walk,
　Where he was wont to stroll and have a talk.
　There can you now each Sunday, if you please,　　　160
　Perambulate and flirt quite at your ease.
　This was a man, when shall we see his like.
CITIZENS
　Never. Pursue, revenge, bring firebrands, strike.
1ST CITIZEN
　To Brutus', Cassius', Casca's, slay them all;
　Show no respect, be they big swells or small.　　　165
ANTONY
　(Aside.)—It's all serene, I now must doff the swell,

And see if I can act the don as well.
CHORUS—Air—"To the West, to the West."
ANTONY
From the east to the west, not a soul let off free,
Strike, slay, kill them all, of whatever degree;   170
From the east to the west, be they big or small fry
No matter, let every base murderer die.
First go to the dwellings of those who have most,
And vengeance exact for great Caesar's ghost:
Be they old, be they young, scotch them all in their nest,   175
Use your pitiless swords from the east to the west.
CHORUS
From the east to the west, not a soul shall go free,
We'll strike, kill them all, of whatever degree:
From the east to the west, be they big or small fry,
No matter, each coward assassin shall die.   180

Julius Caesar, Travestie. A Burlesque, in one act. By an amateur.[Brighton, probably 1861].

The ending of this five-act reduction to one act with five scenes is superbly farcical, in the manner of the Pyramus and Thisby play in act 5 of *A Midsummer Night's Dream*. Brutus and Caesar come back to life; they all forgive each other, with festive spirit.

ANTONY
Confound it! my oration in the *Times*
Will seem so premature—
CASCA
                    Oh! Blow your rhymes.
Burlesques don't countenance such bloody deeds.
CASSIUS
We'll all live yet to grace the Lord Mayor's feeds.
ANTONY
I trust the house we have not made weary,
Attending to a tale that's somewhat dreary.
BRUTUS
We did our best, and more we could not do,
We hope to gain some slight applause from you.
Should you indulgence show to this attempt,
The author's maiden essay to invent,
On us, on him, smile kindly and approve
He'll own the labour's been a toil of love.

Shakespeare's Puck said almost the same thing in the epilogue to *A Midsummer Night's Dream*. The curtain falling on this travesty of *Julius Caesar* did not end a still-living tradition of comic self-awareness: human folly masking as human tragedy.

NOTES

1. Richard France, ed., *Orson Welles on Shakespeare: The W.P.A. and Mercury Theatre Playscripts* (New York: Greenwood Press, 1990), 18.

2. Ibid. 103.

3. John Gielgud, Introduction to *Julius Caesar and the Life of William Shakespeare* (London: Gawthorn Press, n.d.).

4. John Houseman, *Front and Center* (New York: Simon and Schuster, 1979), 397.

5. *Star Trek VI, The Undiscovered Country*, dir. Nicholas Meyer, screenwriters, Nicholas Meyer and Denny Martin Flinn, Paramount Pictures, 1991.

6. Joni Mitchell, *Blue* (Reprise/ MS 2038, 1971).

7. See George Williamson, *A Reader's Guide to T. S. Eliot* (New York: Noonday Press, 1953), 154-55.

8. The classic collection of sexual references is Eric Partridge's *Shakespeare's Bawdy* (New York: Dutton, 1948).

9. G. Wilson Knight, "The Eroticism of Julius Caesar," in *The Imperial Theme* (London: Oxford University Press, 1931), 63-95. For his special sense of the erotic, see the first chapter, "The Torch of Life," 32-62.

10. See, for example, "The Balcony Scene from Romeo and Juliet," *Fighting Mad* (Signet/NAL, 1961), 178-81.

11. Jess Borgeson, Adam Long, and Daniel Singer, *The Complete Works of William Shakespeare (abridged)* (New York: Applause Books, 1994). The Julius Caesar section is on pp. 46-47, including beyond the script a funny interpolation of modernized Latin. See also the review by Ben Brantley, "All of Shakespeare (Sonnets, Too) at Warp Speed," New York Times, February 27, 1995: B3.

12. Stanley Wells, Preface to *Nineteenth-Century Shakespeare Burlesques* (Wilmington, Del.: Michael Glazier, 1978), 4:vii-ix.

TOPICS FOR WRITTEN OR ORAL EXPLORATION

1. Imagine that you belong to a committee charged with choosing a Shakespeare play for a public performance. What arguments would you use in behalf of *Julius Caesar*? Specifically, what values would you argue that the play invites the public to think about?

2. Watch the MGM movie of *Julius Caesar* (1953). Divide the class into four groups who will carefully monitor the movements of the actors of Caesar, Brutus, Cassius, and Antony. Each group should pay attention to: (1) the actor's gestures, (2) the way the film makers kept the visual focus on the actor during speeches (note the "reaction shots" that Houseman describes), and (3) the effect on the character's presence of background music and the physical background of the set. Let each group report their observations and conclude by answering the question, "What adjectives best describe the effect that our character had *on the movie?*" Start a general discussion of how this film version differs from Shakespeare's play script. Your goal is to discover what you now realize about the written play.

3. With the aid of a concordance to the works of Shakespeare, track down all the Shakespeare allusions in *Star Trek VI, The Undiscovered Country*. How well do the allusions fit the context of the movie? In what ways are they changed from the context of the Shakespearean passage or play?

4. List all the metaphors in the *Mad* magazine parody of Antony's famous speech according to their cultural origins. For instance, "megillah" is a Yiddish word meaning "big fuss" or "big mess," and its presence signals that New York City was influenced by Eastern European Jewish culture. If you cannot identify such specialized terms as "copacetic" by looking them up in a dictionary of slang, try to figure out how they work in context. Examine your lists and comment on the appropriateness of updating Antony's appeals to a diverse Roman people compared to the parodied Antony's acknowledgment of different voices in urban New York.

5. Listen to the "Julius Caesar" rap and a commercial rap piece with a dominant character. To what degree is the Marc Antony voice an authentic imitation of the rapper? Write and perform your own rap version of *Julius Caesar*, retelling parts of Shakespeare's play omitted in the rap version quoted here. What ideas from the play are you stressing in this selection? Whom are you trying to reach?

6. Perform the *Julius Caesar, Travestie*, making up a tune for the first song and using "Dixie" for the second. (You may want to subsitute the names of local politicians or school officials in places where British references are made.) Now switch the tone to tragic, and write some

lyrics for an appropriate song that Lucius could sing in 4.3.266. How does music affect the mood of a comic farce compared to a serious tragedy?

7. Compare Shakespeare's nothern star imagery (3.1.60-65) with that of the *Travestie* (scene 4, lines 23-28). How important is consistency when you judge the value of dramatic poetry? To explore this question, list the qualities that stars, sparks, and fire share. Although the proverbial idea of the fat falling into the fire means "the trouble is now really beginning," this nineteenth-century cliché is consistent with most of the other imagery in the *Travestie* passage, because burning fat flames up with spectacular heat and light. One exception is "painted swell," which refers to a conceited person, a "swell-" [swollen-] head stuffed or covered with too many ideas (see lines 165-66). How important is rhyme when you evaluate dramatic poetry? Judge the effect of the emphasis in the *Travestie* passage given to rhymed pairs, by describing how this feature changes Caesar's tone compared to the grave seriousness in Shakespeare's version of this speech. Sum up the analysis by separately listing adjectives that describe each passage. Would your choices be the same if both passages were by an unknown author?

8. In the *Travestie* (lines 175-76) Antony's inflammatory speech to the commoners contains an argument similar to one Brutus made in his private thoughts on getting rid of tyrants (2.1.32-34). State this argument in neutral terms, that is, with minimal metaphor. Now look up the source of the *Travestie* author's allusion: *Macbeth* 3.2.13 (some editions read "scotch" instead of "scorch"—both mean "to slash or score with a knife"). Despite the humorous exaggeration of this burlesque, discuss whether the allusion to the murderer Macbeth suggests the serious point that Antony's revenge is potentially tyrannical.

SUGGESTED READINGS

Asplund, Uno. "The Great Dictator." In *Chaplin's Films*. New York: A S. Barnes, 1976. 162-69.

Caesar II, Game Manual. Bellevue, Wash.: Sierra On-Line, 1995.

"Julius Caesar. "In *Shakespeare in Performance*. London: Salamander Books, 1995. 100-105.

Seldes, George. *Sawdust Caesar: The Untold Story of Mussolini and Fascism*. New York: Harper, 1935.

Stern, Jane and Michael Stern. "Las Vegas." In *The Encyclopedia of Bad Taste*. New York: Harper Collins, 1990.

Index

About the Author

THOMAS DERRICK is Associate Professor of English at Indiana State University, where he has taught compostion, literary criticism, and English Renaissance literature for a dozen years. He has edited *Studies in Medieval and Renaissance Literature* and is author of *Thomas Wilson's Arte of Rhetorique* (1982). He is the recipient of his university's highest teaching award and codirected a grant from the National Endowment for the Humanities on democratic education.